CHRONICLES OF THE ANCIENT SEA KINGS

BY

KYLE CLAYTON

1

LINE CROSSING

The ship lurched, vomiting Foster onto the icy deck. He slipped and slid to his feet like a loud orange penguin, only his goatee visible in the face hole of his immersion suit. The deck of the *Qarapara* sank hard to stern as they hit the trough, then bobbed up. Freezing seas spilled off to all sides. Somehow, the Old Man kept her into the waves. The gale slashed the tops from the thirty-foot swell and stung his cheeks with icy spray. It was loud enough to drown out the sound of the engine, so that only the rumble underfoot told him they still had power. Storm clouds cast a twilight gray at mid-morning on the little 90-footer as she gasped against the blows that buffeted her out of the southwest. He couldn't even keep his eyes open in that direction to anticipate the rise of the bow. Foster clung to the rail, and as the next wave lifted them, he watched a baby blue chunk of ice duck below the surface to starboard. It made him shudder.

As far as he could see, its cousins, neighbors, kin, jostled with the odd white pad of young ice that bloomed on colder nights—a reminder of the hospitality the Southern Ocean held for swimmers. Hand over hand, he waddled through slush to where three-and-a-half more orange blobs huddled just aft of midship. Parks clung to a line that ran overboard, his immersion suit hanging from his waist. A yellow slicker topped off the 6'4 frame. His dirty-blonde shag spilled a wet brown over his glasses, fogged on one side and streaked on the other.

"The fuck you doin'? Put that thing on!"

"It's hard, dude." Foster couldn't blame him there. Trying to stand, much less work in one of these suits was a cruel prank. "Besides, we're goin' in the boats."

"Ideally." Foster helped yank him out of the slicker and zip the thick neoprene up to his chin.

"You're choking me," Parks hacked.

"Shut up." Foster paused to take in the 12-man inflatable life raft his friend held flush against the hull—a little black hexagon with an orange dome covering all but the opening to board. He'd never seen one in person. They lived in a pair of white barrels on the top deck rail until now. Their ice-hardened, refitted Norwegian rescue vessel foundered when a wave set them down on top of a small berg. Now, they would try their luck with a quarter-inch of rubber.

"Goddamn," he muttered.

"Looks like a wigwam," Parks remarked. Another jolt snapped them out of their admiration. The sea sloshed angrily back and forth between the cabin and the stern as it searched for a way out.

"Old Man wants me and Carabiner to go with the fuckin' nincompoops." He nodded at the woman and her twelve-year-old daughter who clung to the gunwale beside Parks. The mother had both hands on the rail with the girl secured to her body between them. It was hard to tell—everything was wet— but it seemed like they were crying. Bosun Carabiner hung on a few feet closer to the temporary swamp of the aft deck, struggling to decide between being useless and trying to look busy.

"That sucks, dude," Parks yelled over the wind.

"No, it doesn't, cause *you're* goin'."

"No way."

"Yes way, motherfucker. I outrank you."

"I'm pretty sure Captain outranks you."

"I'm the rankin' man on deck. You need to load up all this shit in that raft," he waved his hands over the emergency supplies piled up beside them, "so I can launch you the second that retard gets done takin' a shit, or whatever he's doin' down there. Then I'm gonna launch the port raft, bring the line around this side, rope 'em together, and the rest of the crew comes in that one."

"Carabiner's the ranking man on deck." They looked over at him. Another wave rolled under them, and he fell to his butt. His head darted around in search of the culprit, then he scrambled up and stiffened as though it never happened. Parks turned back to Foster.

"Fuck it, he can go with them. I'm going with you. We enlisted men gotta stick together."

"We can't leave them alone with Carabiner. It's unethical. He'll eat the man and rape the women if he has to spend more'n a couple hours on that fuckin' thing. Besides," Foster took the line from Parks' hands. "We can move rafts later when it's calm. We gotta share the supplies, anyway."

"Excuse me," the dark-haired lady shouted around Parks. "We are right here, and I'd appreciate it if you could watch what you say in front of my daughter."

"Carabiner!" Foster waved. "Get over here!"

"Ma'am," Parks turned to the woman. "We're all gonna die, so you'll excuse me if I take the opportunity to be honest about my feelings. I hate you and your husband. Ex-husband. Mostly him, but you for bringing me here. If Carabiner doesn't get you, the ocean will, so it really doesn't matter. Little girl, you're fine. I haven't had that many interactions with you, you seem nice. But your parents or ex-parents or whatever are fucking assholes, so you're probably gonna be that way, too. Hope you don't die, but let's face it."

"Carabiner!" Foster repeated.

"You're not going to send us with the man you just said is a rapist," she challenged Parks.

"He's not really a rapist." Foster said.

"*Allegations.*" Parks added. "New Navy."

"Allegations of what?"

"Nothing that anyone ever bothered to prove, not before he resigned his commission, anyway. You'll be in great hands, lady." Parks smiled.

Carabiner waited for the next trough. He held the rail in his right and refused to let go as he wrapped his left around the woman to the rail on the other side, and did an awkward shuffle behind her, then repeated the maneuver around Parks.

"*Bosun* Carabiner, Foster." He looked like an even bigger dork than usual, squashed baby face peeking out of an orange hood. "Or Lieutenant, if you prefer."

"I prefer to throw your ass overboard. We're not in the fuckin' Navy, and the only thing you're bosun of," he pointed to the pitiful raft, "is *that*. Captain wants you to go with the passengers. Keep 'em calm."

"It's a twelve-man. I say we stick together."

"Two rafts is twice the emergency kit, and backup if one gets popped."

"Second-in-command needs to be near the captain to carry out his orders."

"Those are his fuckin' orders." Foster didn't blame him for not wanting to be adrift at sea with those three. Neither did he. Neither did Parks. "I think he realized you're the only one besides him with the leadership skills to command a raft of civilians in an Antarctic storm." Foster held his breath. Carabiner frowned in consideration, then nodded at what he must have thought was impeccable logic.

"Where's the guy?"

"He's at the bottom of the ocean if he don't hurry. You're up first!" Foster swung the ladder they used to board the Zodiac over the side and held it firm. Carabiner's eyes widened at the notion of backing down that little thing on a heaving ship into a raft that tossed like a dead leaf. It would be a good test. They'd get to see what they were in for, and if Carabiner vanished into the boil, it might actually lighten the mood. He could feel the cold terror radiating off the poor bastard. It was near impossible to stand. How he was going to swing a leg over and gain purchase on a ladder slapped by the sea was beyond Foster's reckoning.

"Gimme a life preserver. In case I slip." Foster did him one better. He unhooked the rope from the life preserver and clipped it to the D-ring on Carabiner's suit. "Hold on to that thing!" Carabiner ordered Parks. The big man tied off the raft line to the rail and used the slack to haul it right beneath the ladder. Carabiner looked back at the damage, the water seeping up over the aft deck at nearly every wave now.

"Go!" Foster shouted.

"Parks, you board first. I'll hold that."

"Parks is goin' on the other raft," Foster said. He caught a gleam of gratitude in his friend's eye. "This is your command, Lieutenant. Go, or we'll throw you in."

"I thought I heard you say—"

"You heard wrong. Come on, these people are dependin' on you. We got you, brother! We all gotta do it, too."

His face paled by another shade, and despite a burning distaste that he was eager to resume as soon as they were safe and sound, in that moment, Foster felt for the man. Carabiner let out a series of quick huffs to psych himself up. He looked like a sad little boy being forced onto stage at school.

"Go!" The little girl shouted impatiently. It was all the shame he needed. Carabiner pressed himself to the gunwale and snaked his right leg over and felt for a rung. Foster and Parks each hooked an armpit as he shimmied over into place and squared up. His usual affectedness took over. His movements were a mixture of rigid calculation and overcorrection. Down a couple of steps, then he shook the hands free and hugged the ladder close like a cat who could neither climb up nor down. The raft tossed side to side, never more than a few feet on the taut line. The ship raced down the backside of a wave and Carabiner rode it out. In the narrow stability of the bottom, he toed into the raft, and the second he was sure his feet were planted, thrust himself backward, thwacking his head on the soft top of the opening. It was an inglorious performance, but one that was graded only pass or fail. His head poked back out.

"I made it!" Foster saw Parks roll his eyes. "Send down the passengers!"

"We're gonna send down the supplies," Foster took a small delight in ignoring every one of his orders. "The weight'll make the raft more stable."

"How should we split them up?" Parks asked.

"Load it all. We can split it up later when we're launched."

One-by-one they handed down canisters of water, an emergency handheld transceiver, a heftier first aid kit, whatever boxes of food Parks had managed to bring up.

"What's he doing?" Foster followed Parks' gaze to the upper deck, where Hapgood, the engineer, climbed as far as he dared up he mast ladder. He hadn't even begun to don his immersion suit. His arms wrapped through the rungs that led up to the comm array: one held a radio, the other a small antenna.

"Fuck," Foster said. "Is the comm down?"

"What's down?" The lady asked. "Are you saying the radio is down?"

"I don't know, he should be using the inboard. Why would he be up there with that rinky-dink shit if he could just call from the cabin?" He remembered the jolt when she sat down on the berg. The *Qarapara* had spun like a bus hit broadside across the tail. Steel rung, followed by a cascade of terrible noises above and below—he imagined bolts shearing, pipe bursting, frame buckling, though he'd long since learned that ships complained, and it was likely nothing the re-inforced hull couldn't shrug off. Except she stayed fast. The ice dug in beneath her like a reef, and when the prop turned to push her off, the sound was so terrible that the Old Man killed the engine. The next two waves took her abeam. Everyone was below and battened down, but they were thrown into the nearest immovable object as water crashed over the upper deck. The first drug her across the berg with a shriek that convinced him the ship was alive, and dying. The next knocked them free, with a shudder and a quick stop to the inhuman wail. They were gashed, bleeding in instead of out. The engine fired back up, but it was clear the prop blades were fucked. They barely had steering.

Apparently, the antenna had been a silent casualty.

"So we're going overboard and no one even knows to come looking for us." Her voice was remarkably even. A few weeks on board had initiated her to the routine of small disasters that the crew had come to take for granted.

"See that?" He pointed to a little orange gadget attached to the rail. "EPIRB. It'll automatically send a distress call with our coordinates when the ship goes down. They're comin' either way."

She locked onto his eyes as if to measure how much he believed what he was saying. "My daughter goes down next."

"You go down next. Then we hand her to you while Carabiner stabilizes the raft."

She nodded, then leaned over and said something to her girl. Foster hooked her in. With none of the pomp of the Bosun, she moved her daughter under Parks' arms and found the ladder. The *Qarapara* faltered in her fight to take the waves head-on, and they climbed the next one at a slight angle to port. The top scraped down the starboard side and spilled over. "Hang on!" They tightened their grip on her as the water smashed through them. One of her feet lost the rung, and scrambled to reclaim it. As soon as it passed, she hurried down to where Carabiner could catch her belt.

Parks passed off control of the line to Foster. He scooped his broad arms under the girl's, and raised her feet over the gunwale while leaning into it with his knees for balance. The water level was much closer to the deck now, and it was an easy handoff to get her into the raft.

The door to the deck burst open. A man in his forties with mostly black hair and salt and pepper whiskers stumbled out wearing a wool shirt and the same technical pants he had on every minute of every day since they boarded. Three PVC orange cylinders twisted to get free of his arms.

"You idiot!" The woman screamed up as he made the rail. "Where's your suit?"

"No time," he called. The first of the tubes shot past her into the opening of the raft. He tossed the others after it.

"Good idea. Bring your orange dildos as flotation devices," Parks chided him. "Immersion suit's only good for maybe six hours in the water, anyway—versus a minute without it."

The glare that met Parks was as cold as the gale. "Thank you for the safety briefing."

"You like it? I've been trying out this honesty thing. You know, ever since I realized we're all dead. It's pretty sweet. Wish I'd thought of it before. Now get in the raft, and try not to fall face-first on a dick in the process." The man bit back his response. Foster offered him the life preserver—the only thing he could hook a line to. He waved it off with a sheepish smile.

"What's a minute, anyway?" He clambered down the ladder to join his family in the raft.

Foster leaned over and shouted. "Parks is gonna give you some rope so you don't bang on the ship. Once we launch the other raft, we'll tie-in. If she goes down before we can do that, I'd advise cuttin' that line."

"Wait. Carabiner!" Parks added. The Bosun hung his slick orange dome out the hole. "You're a twat. I've always thought you were a twat. Your name sounds made up—like an idiot who works part-time for REI. I hope you die first." To the family, "If you run out of food, or if it doesn't taste good, eat Carabiner. Eat, or be eaten!" He let the rope out hand over hand until the raft drifted as far starboard as it could before it caught the tension and curled behind. Parks tied it off. They watched for a second as the little bath toy heaved and spun, like bait for some leviathan.

"Nice work, brother," Foster clapped his arm. "Let's get the other one rigged up. Old Man and Gardner'll be up top any minute."

"You know something else? I've always wanted to tell you this."

Foster's grin disappeared. "Parks, think long and fuckin' hard about your next words, because I intend to live to tarnish your memory."

"It can wait."

A shudder caught their attention. The rope on the rail hung slack. They looked back in time to see the little orange raft disappear as the crest of the next wave moved between them. "Fuck!" Foster slammed the metal rail while they sank down the back of the swirling water. "They got all our shit!" The swell reached the place they should have bobbed back into sight and carried past without a glimpse of color beyond the haunted blues and grays and the frothing white.

"*Fuck!* We're fucked!" He repeated. They instinctively found Hapgood, still fiddling with buttons and waving the antenna like a blind man feeling for a doorway. "Goddammit. I'm gonna launch the other one. Grab that ladder and meet me to port." Foster took off into the cabin. Parks lifted the ladder free, and paused at the wavering rope. He didn't know why he began to reel it. Maybe they would need some extra line. Foster reappeared up top and wasted no time making for the white barrel that held the other raft. Hapgood stood over him on the ladder in his work wear, but they didn't acknowledge one another. Each had a mission. The EPIRB would still go out, he tried to reassure himself. It didn't matter what happened with the radio, or that the other raft took the only spare outside of Hapgood's. There would be a basic ration of food and water in the onboard kit, too. It felt like he was talking to a child who was too old to fall for it.

The coil around his arm grew, and at last the end slapped up onto the deck. Parks rubbed the inside of his glasses with his clumsy glove and squinted at a straight, clean cut. "Son of a bitch," he muttered. For a moment, he lost track of where he was, and wondered whether it was Carabiner or the old dude he would have to murder if they made it out of this alive. There was a sudden quiet. The gale blew as hard as ever, roared so he could hardly hear his thoughts. It was more like a stillness. His feet tingled, and he realized the deck had ceased its rumble. The big diesel had bowed out. They would take the waves head-on only as long as it took for the whims of the sea to turn them. Launching a raft off the side in this weather was dangerous. If their port came forward, boarding it into the sets was suicidal. He felt the inertia of the ship swish and suck, a whale with fluid in its lungs. Despite all the noise, there was a strange peace. No more motors or gadgets. It was unadulterated fury, but he sensed it was a fury that paid them no mind. A passing chance that it found them at all. Low over the mast, he sighted an albatross twisting in the wind. It was obscene that a creature could live here, let alone make it look so effortless. The bird seemed to study them. If it was considering a brief stop to rest its wings, it thought otherwise and beat higher to float by.

Parks took off his glasses and gave them a rub. He was about to start to port when he saw it. A shadow rose out of the northwest, across the grain of the southwest swell. The rogue wave loomed twice the height of the ones that snuck over her bow as she rode lower in the wet fingers of the ice-scarred ocean. It bore down abeam. He jerked his neck around. Hapgood was huddled over his radio, a brave step higher up the ladder on the mast. Foster struggled with the barrel in his cumbersome suit. They hadn't seen it. Parks thought to yell a warning. It would have been the honest thing to do, but it wouldn't have mattered. For some reason he put his glasses back on. In that moment, he wanted to live.

The cliff of water slammed into the ship, and there was cold and darkness.

The first thing he was aware of was the pressure in his ears. A ringing so faint it wasn't a sound at all. Nor did it rise, or fall, but drew through him like a string pulled taut, resonating at a single pitch. He was weightless. The tight outline of his face felt like a mask of thin ice that would shatter if he pressed it. His parts came back to him, one-by-one. The still chest. Arms suspended. Legs adrift. He became aware of the absence of chaos. The deafening wind, the driving spray, and the pitch of the horizon—it was gone. The people were gone. His lids clenched tight, and his eyeballs froze behind them. An instinct begged him to flail. He wanted to touch something, to hear, to see, but he refused it. The only thing that moved was the plodding thump of his heart. It was a frigid womb, and he was a helpless babe.

Parks wasn't sure how long he'd been underwater, or which way was up, but he was certain he was alive. The burning in his lungs told him so. One, ten, one, he remembered. One minute to get your breathing under control, to stop hyperventilating. Did that count if you were in an immersion suit, or couldn't breathe at all? He'd remember the rest later, if he had time. How his breath stopped when he was out of his senses, or how he could get one in the first place, was lost to him. He had no idea if he was six feet under or sixty, but it was far enough that the waters were calm, absent the swells and thunder and sleet of the surface. Maybe thirty seconds, he thought, before he would have to exhale and swallow whatever was in front of his lips. He considered turning to give a few kicks, but the suit would have been too clumsy. Wasted energy wastes oxygen. The floaties would have to do the work. The dark clouds flashed in his memory. The pale green spot on the surface with a ship rolling beneath it. Parks could see all of it, like an albatross in flight. It was not a place for any man to be—blowing east or going nowhere. In the distance, hidden behind the foaming crests and the fog, over a field of sharp ice, the arm of the peninsula, frozen stiff. Glaciated mountains that toed up the sea. Nowhere to get warm, nowhere to rest, just elements pitched in permanent battle. No place to be.

He went limp. A gentle tug, at first as though pulled by a thread, then gaining velocity. Parks floated toward the surface. Twenty seconds. His face was down, and he didn't care to peek for light in Antarctic waters. There was a finish line, and he wouldn't know it until he crossed it. At any moment Foster's hand would drag him by the collar to the other life raft, that miraculously launched at the moment the wave hit the ship, he told himself. Salt stung his sinuses. His face and neck tingled, running down to his fingertips. Pressure built in his throat. His chest heaved one, twice, and he choked back the reflex. Surfing in Santa Cruz, winter swell and thick wet suits. Ten seconds. Blocking tight end, the same play from goalline at practice, over and over. His dad. His granddad. Five seconds. The bunk on the *Harry S. Truman*. Hairy Ass Truman. The prostitute in Dubai who wouldn't fuck him because she said her shift ended in fifteen minutes. The face of the lady looking back at him when he let out their raft. The face of the wife of Neptune, the fat warrant officer dressed as the wife of Neptune the first time he crossed the equator. His face was ready to explode. Foster, showing him his new Shellback tattoo. Firehose. Water dumped over his head. Water rushed around his neck, swirled into his nostrils. *I am a Son of Neptune!*

Air burst from his lungs in a fit of bubbles as he shot through the surface. He gasped, and swallowed a splash of seawater. A violent cough, and the next wave sent him under. Heaved him up again headfirst down the trailing side. Water smashed his face. Spun him, pulled him under, spit him back. He sipped what air he could between coughs. Sleet stung his face. Salt fingers clawed at his eyes. He could see only a few feet, a flash of white ice, a blur of sky. There was no boat and no raft. Just the unforgiving ocean and a distant rumble from the clouds. A maelstrom of violent elements ripped at one another for claim of his life, and he preferred it infinitely to the peace he felt below. Parks folded his arms across his chest, lay his head back on the rectangular headrest stitched into his neck, and gave up the fight.

Briny drool dribbled down his chin. He shortened his coughs and his breaths, unable to see when and where he could expect the next surge over his face, terrified of being caught amid a long drink of air when it happened. Soon came the telltale rise. He struggled to keep his head up, but his feet dropped and it swamped him. His stamina to hold his breath was gone. It was all he could do to prevent himself coughing underwater as he cut through the width of the thick crest and emerged on the backside. There would be a brief dip at the bottom, he realized. It took longer than he expected. His huge frame rotated rudderless like the ship that birthed him. They came over his head, his feet, abeam his body. His hands trembled, though he wasn't cold, yet. Shock, probably.

One, ten, one, he remembered. Ten minutes of meaningful movement. He wouldn't waste it. Maybe the insulation would afford him more. Lying on his back felt incredibly vulnerable, but that's what the suit wanted. The next time he felt the surface rise beneath him, he took a gulp and let his head go under, holding his torpedo shape. It was a pleasant surprise when he shot out the other side with lungs to spare. His fingers trembled over the strobe light attached to his suit, but he couldn't get it to fire. There was a whistle. He laughed and coughed at the futility of it. Save you breath, bro, he told himself.

It was relentless, the way one followed another. Trillions of gallons on an afternoon stroll around the planet. The small effort of taking a breath for a backward duck dive felt like a marathon before him. Worse. Marathons end. Now that his air settled into a rhythm punctured on occasion by a soggy cough, the cold announced itself. His nose and his cheeks felt on the verge of icing over, unshielded from the water and raked by the wind. The suit was not meant to be warm. The difference between the sharp sting on his face and the rest of his body was tremendous. It might allow him to bob like a buoy for a few hours. That was it. Already, the unshakable clammy chill permeated the rest of him. He wiggled his toes and fingers as lazily as he could to coax a little blood to make the trip. A shiver raced up and out the top of his head, and when it left him, his teeth clacked. A thick layer stood between him and death like a heavy door, and each wave battered new splinters and teased the hinges from the wall.

Now, he thought. A moment later, the water swelled again, and he bit off a breath before cutting under the top. From the way his body sank at the bottom, Parks suddenly became aware of the direction the waves were heading. East, always east here. East of him was the peninsula. West is where the winds were born. It was a modest summer rain that fell on him. Most of what felt like a downpour was spray blown by an air current that ran free through the southern latitudes, not a continent to slow it down. It was wetter than the icy melt from the clouds, and it came nearly horizontal. The second he surfaced, it howled over him, all the way to the bottom. Then the roar of the wind went slack, and the spray ran above him like a misty cloud, only a lighter sleet dappled his face. It was the shadow of the next wave, and another ride up and under. The storm had a rhythm, a melody to it. As soon as he sussed it out, it felt altogether calmer. He was sure nothing had changed. The only thing he knew was the steady bass of the swell. He still took a faceful here and there. But the surprises were smaller now, and within a certain allowance.

He'd gone from man overboard to flotsam, part of the storm—however temporary his part might be. He was no longer a person, but a piece of a wave. Moving at the will and to the heights and depths that the wave wanted. Man is separate from the ocean, Parks thought. He was not.

One, ten, one. An hour in the water before deadly hypothermia—that was calm water, without a suit. Here? Hell if he knew. Six hours, give or take, he recited the safety data he could remember from one of the more recent among the thousands of dry briefings he'd blinked through in his time. People with a higher body fat percentage could last longer. Parks was never more grateful for his midship lard. Why hadn't he just done as Foster said and gone in the raft? Those timelines were for raw survival, in the technical sense. He'd lose consciousness long before he died.

He was an orange needle in a frozen haystack, *if* the emergency beacon deployed. During the late December tourist season, there would be enough boats scattered up and down the peninsula, but he was off the beaten track, thanks to their charters. A six hour steam wouldn't get you far, especially in this weather.

Most of the traffic—tourist and scientific, alike—was on the other side of the peninsula, thanks to a major calving event at the Larsen C. That was the hot ticket. Any ships that were interested in conducting actual science or avoiding storms, which was all ships, were lightyears from being able to attempt a rescue within the survival window of a man in an immersion suit, suitably immersed. The only thing he knew of in the area—his only snowball in Hell—was Carabiner's raft. It had no power, and even if he floated within ten feet of it, he wasn't sure he had it in him to swim over. Nor was he sure it was right side up.

"Goddammit, Foster," he shivered through clacking teeth. "Had to send the 'Biner." Foster would be looking for him if the raft was in his command. He couldn't steer it, but at least he'd look. What was the last thing he told the Bosun? Parks couldn't even remember. Twat, or die, or something like that. Hopefully, Lieutenant Shrivel Dick's ego wouldn't be too bruised to toss him a line. Then he could throw everyone except maybe the kid overboard, and survive for a few days until the rescue bird could pin him down. Just the notion of a helicopter warmed him, and he fumbled again for his strobe light. No luck. A thick glove mashed the whistle to his lips and he tried to blow. It fell out of his mouth in a sputter, his lips too cold and cracked to lock down. *I am a Son of Neptune,* he reminded himself through a shiver. Only Pollywogs are allowed to drown.

Hypothermia was fair game, though. He crossed his feet and clenched his thighs to warm his man parts. Fuck Foster for getting him the job.

Antarctica with three tourists sounded like easy money. Especially since they booked all twelve berths on the ship. To say the guy was a bit of a personality was an understatement, but that was Carabiner's problem. The man-bitch. A glorified butler whose job it was to tend to their every need and keep them from annoying the *real* crew. Carabiner was at least good at schmoozing with rich people. It might have been his only virtue.

The hardest part of the journey for Parks came at the tiller of the Zodiac, listening to the nutty professor argue with his lady friend about the risks and merits of dancing through ice. Low ice, they told him. It was some some sort of record minimum. Carabiner would pretend to be interested to the point that he rarely got a moment's peace. The magic of his first season working the southern continent faded sometime around the twelfth of what felt like 4,000 runs so they could chart the positions, do their survey thingy, then off to the next, endlessly down the peninsula. Parks couldn't tell if it was supposed to be a shitty family vacation or a scientific research excursion, and it seemed like a pathetic excuse for either. The daughter had enough after the third trip. Even the captain stopped going with them in the zodiac once he was happy with Parks' motoring. Then it was up to him to beat back their requests to make unscheduled—and uncharted—landings. Even Carabiner would goad him to comply, knowing full well he'd be eviscerated and fired, just to make himself look like a cool guy. Then he'd whisper a condescending congratulations, a 'proud of you' for not doing what they both knew was suicide, as if it was some test of character Parks had passed.

Sea ice minimum, my ass, he thought. That just meant it was broken into tumbling mines, lilypads that split apart and reconverged, crystal sheets, filthy snowballs. He blinked as a light-blue boulder appeared not thirty feet to his right. Things that would shred him with a brush. It was unbelievable how fast the weather could turn, here. He barely got the zodiac back to the ship in chop that sent them airborne, the motor screaming for a taste of the sea. Within half an hour of getting stowed, the radar screen was a swirling nightmare as they beat hard to open sea to avoid being driven into the ice. The little bit of coastal froth dissipated around them, when they bottomed out on a massive straggler that seemed to surge up from the deep like a hungry monster, content to wound its prey and swim off to wait. The way it unfolded had a terrifying momentum to it. The initial calm, joking as they poked around for damage. It wasn't much of a surprise to take on water. They thought the pumps would be fine. If anything, it meant an early return to Puntas Arenas, non-refundable, of course. Then it was the prop. Then it was the sea—the uninvited guest—shouldering its way in faster than they could belch it out. A small electrical fire near the engine—he put it out immediately, but the air choked them away. Hapgood and Foster, arguing about something. The family, upset. He took them to the galley and offered to feed them, though he didn't know why he was being nice. He couldn't cook in this weather, so he served energy bars and cold leftover ravioli. The captain called him by name over the loudspeaker, and when he found the rest of the crew waiting for him, the bottom fell out of his stomach.

The order came that he hadn't heard in eight years of Naval service: prepare to abandon ship. He recited the litany: it was a joke, they wanted to see his expression; it was a precaution, in case things turned for the worse; it would take hours to sink, they would float right over to the rescue ship. Everything he imagined collapsed piece by piece. It was the life rafts, a miserable compromise. Now he lay on his back, dumped without ceremony and left to freeze or be fucked by a leopard seal. It would have been better to go over in a comfortable shirt. Faster, at least. This was the misery of a thousand deaths, vying to be the one to take him. All those mouths sunk into his flesh in a tug-of-war for supremacy.

A smaller wave came across the main swell and dunked him for longer than he was accustomed to. Parks moaned in exasperation when he bobbed up. He was far from religious, but he was equally far from proud.

"Lord," he called over the ocean. "I know we haven't exactly been homeys—" A wave gave him a mouthful of water. He coughed violently, tried to speak a few times, and coughed again. "Fuck. OK, that's fair. Maybe I deserve that." Another cough. "But right now, your boy needs a little help. A little helicopter, or a cruise ship full of sorority girls. Hell, I'll even take Carabiner, pardon my language—you know I swear. Anything—anything at all. A mermaid. I don't mean that in a sexual way, a rescue mermaid is fine." He tried to recall the three or four times he'd been inside a church while having a sleepover with a childhood friend. "These thy blessings I bestow upon me— I ask you to bestow upon me—and Lord, grant me a sign if you are down with my prayer. But preferably, we can skip the sign and just get a boat. I'll be here, nowhere to go. Just chillin'. Just waiting for your magnificent blessings. Oh Lord. I pray. Amen," he shivered.

The storm seemed unimpressed. Ahead, dark clouds piled up like a stone fortress that reached down to the sea. New ice patched up around him, thin crisp plates he wouldn't have trusted to hold him. Was he heading toward land, or was it taking advantage of a day without sun to rear up before it disappeared with the weather? A distant thunder rolled across what he hoped was coast. His dirty-blond whiskers froze in between dunks. Frost blossomed or collected from the freezing rain on his chest until he rose again to duck dive. How long had he been in the water? It seemed like it could have been hours. It could as easily have been ten minutes. For a moment, he felt himself doze and had to shake himself like a midnight driver. It was exhausting, doing little more than taking a gulp of air and slipping under, then again, then again. Parks' fingers and toes would turn purple if an air conditioner was on. They were probably milk-white prunes by now. The warm current of blood from his heart beat back the cold undertow in his veins. Without his glasses, everything reduced to a watercolor painting. The sting in his eyes didn't help. He watched the tiny ripples in between the waves run past him and lap against his body. The bigger disturbances, a few inches high, splashing over his less-buoyant parts. Until another wave scooped him up. They were all going somewhere, riding the gale. He felt the direction of the dark water. Saw it leap up as it clapped together, then hollow out on the fall. The tiniest flake of snow in the flurry, and the wake of a gust across the surface. Then the entire thing. More than a wave, or a summer storm, he felt the ocean itself, moving him between the wrinkles of its great skin. He belonged to the Old Man—the *real* Old Man—like the ice, the fish, the fucking leopard seals. The entire time he puttered around in the zodiac, or helped Gardner over a sizzling pan in the galley, it was no different. A little floating cabin convinced him it was something other than a floe, or a skua. All around him, water as far as he could dream.

The memory of the line crossing flashed again. The carrier was like a city. A filthy slum of a city. A dress-up game they played to convince him he was not at sea. A wave washed over him, and when he returned, a chill so cold that for a moment he felt warm. This was the *real* line. The gray wall between him and the monster. The thin layer of orange: a wet suit and a whistle. Only now had he crossed over to the ocean. All who love land were held at its pleasure, and taken at its will. Only the creatures of water were safe here. They were born in water, they *were* water, and didn't ask it any favors. It was father, mother, and home, and they were grateful for as much. His lips moved.

"I am a s-s-s-son of-f-f N-neptunnne." He stuttered.

He relaxed the last muscles he had any control over. His eyes were heavy now. It was darker, and not from lack of Sun. Parks blinked hard. He was no longer under the impression that he was alive. No boat was coming. As the portliest crew member he was likely the last to go. Whatever the others had suffered, he imagined it was quicker. The water glided over him. He hardly noticed. It was a habit now. Lightning flashed above and he turned away from the brilliant glare. In the nanosecond before it faded, he saw to his left a blemish on the unbroken gray. Disappearing behind a crest, a glint of very bright orange. Parks stirred. The raft? He scanned but it was gone. A minute later, another glimpse. Too small to be the raft. It looked like...an arm. A man in an immersion suit. His brief hopes relaxed again. If Foster still had a pulse, he would be even more useless than Parks, with his stupid low body fat percentage. Maybe he could wrangle up the strength to carabiner their suits together. (*Carabiner*, he scoffed. What a stupid fucking name). At least their bodies were more likely to be recovered. The next dip of the waves brought it closer—much closer, as though it leaped over the surface. At once he could see it wasn't Foster. A trick of perspective. It seemed like a man in the distance. Now riding the same trough as him, mere feet away, was a cylinder.

An orange waterproof cylinder of PVC. The reason they had come on this stupid trip to begin with, the one and only thing the nutty professor cared to take into the life raft. Guess that tells me what happened to the raft, he thought. Parks couldn't swim, but he locked his eyes and willed it closer. Each wave rocked it back and forth, and a little more forth. *Come on, you bastard.* Hope beyond logic told him that maybe it didn't contain what he knew it did. Maybe there was food, or a flare, or a knife to cut his own throat. Closer still. He tried to grab it and realized his fingers were frozen stiff. His forearms slapped it around like a ping pong ball until it came to rest on his great belly, and he hugged it close. On the top was a bar where you could attach a lanyard, or get purchase to unscrew it. He clenched it with his teeth and twisted his forearms with his all his might. It popped loose.

Parks reached in four gloved fingers now only willing to function as one, and drug the roll from the container. Nearly two feet wide and weathered a shade short of brown, the map was tied with a strand of red silk. He was surprised that he didn't just abandon it to the water, but all that effort compelled him to bite the silk bow and unfurl on his chest the 15th century map of some Italian dude whose name he couldn't remember. Names were not for Parks. What he did recall was the nutty professor spewing to Carabiner's feigned interest about how unique it was in its prominent attention to the southern continent, which it showed stretching for the tip of South America and in great detail compared to others of the period, especially given that no European had visited that continent when the map was drawn. He claimed the southern landmass was Antarctica, not sighted until the 19th century, and reconciling the land features of the old charts with the actual coastline had been the reason for the voyage in the first place. "In my book," Parks recalled hearing forty or fifty times. "I talk about all of this in my book." He insisted on loaning Carabiner a copy he happened to pack.

Parks didn't give a shit. He was mostly impressed that a very old map that made the landmasses look like penises swollen with gonorrhea could bring him to the south of the earth to die. He let it lie across his body, lapped with seawater. The ornate compass drew his attention, south pointed up his chest, and something told him that at this moment, that was incorrect. He folded it in half and turned it so that the needle showed the pole to his right, somewhere off-map where the longitudinal lines tried to converge. The chips and dents of the coast were drawn with great attention to detail, the curves of ink smaller and more numerous than the blurry Mediterranean that cartographer called home.

Confidence, the word rang in his head. That's what it was—a confident outline, though to Parks inaccurate compared to the modern day charts he'd used over the past few weeks. The discrepancies were close enough to explain away if it depicted a different ice pattern—or a lack of it—but how a 15th century Italian could possibly know the shape of an ice-free coast of a continent no one had ever seen was beyond him.

Studying the features brought a calm, took the edge off the cold. North toward the Drake Passage, a spear-toothed monster of a fish sunk its fangs into a sailing ship. Little peaks poked up here and there, and bisecting the continent, an unmistakable range. On the southwest side of the map, something that looked like the Antarctic Peninsula jutted out, and beyond it the detail of the eastern shore of South America became hazy, as if someone got tired and just drew a curve. Mapmakers were as much educated guessers as cartographers in those days, and education lacking, just plain guessers. The precision picked up a notch partway over Brazil leading into the Caribbean, and strangely, the western side of the continent looked better than the eastern one.

And here I am. His eyes fell on a spot just offshore, west of the peninsula. Like an orange turd in the punch bowl. Dying somewhere man was never meant to set foot. A land for nutty professors and penguins. That dude would have a conniption fit if he saw the way Parks was manhandling his Precious, soaked with saltwater. It took warmed to imagine. He squinted at the wet leather. The glare off the water blurred his already suspect vision.

It took a moment to dawn on him in his early-hypothermic daze. The rain had stopped. The wind petered out to a strong breeze, gusting at less than half the previous force. Parks realized he had not taken a breath to dip under a wave in some time. A hand raised to shield his eyes from the low sun. The sea was no longer trying to brain him like a fish on the deck. The swell still rolled beneath him, but he lofted over it for the most part with barely a sputter. The only clouds he saw congregated in a line dead ahead. As quickly as it descended on them, the storm was gone. The air was dry, and he licked his broken lips. It struck him that it would be easy to put a small zipper pocket on the suit with an emergency chapstick. No extra weight at all, but a lifesaver. If he ever made it back, he would invent that.

A pang of guilt struck him, and he shook the map, brushed it clean of water, and stuffed it back in the tube as best he could. Parks clipped it onto his suit so it wouldn't wander off. Without the freezing spray whipping his face, it felt almost warm. Almost. He shivered. His visibility was as good as the roller that just passed. Well overhead, a troop of birds flew in the same direction. As soon as they passed, they circled back and went around him a few times. Bastards. Probably hoping for a bloated corpse. Parks raised a middle finger. After a few more rounds, they resumed course. He lifted his head off the pad and blinked away another splash of water. The gray blur slowly separated itself into a darker one and a lighter one, sea and sky. Then it emerged between them, a thick black strip across the horizon. Hidden by his own disbelief, it now loomed much closer than he could have expected, or even prayed.

Land.

He didn't dare swim, even if he would have had the strength. But it didn't feel like he'd need to. Obscured by dark skies and the lash of the storm, he'd been drifting back toward the peninsula this entire time. It wasn't clear how far out the ship made it before they foundered, but it was probably driven back for the hour or so it took to abandon ship—if that's what you could call what they did. They were probably much closer than they suspected. Only for lack of major ice had he thought otherwise, and the low year combined with a pounding surge could have driven the floes elsewhere.

No sign of the raft, or the color orange in general. While his prospects of survival marooned on the Antarctic coast were almost as dismal as the zero-chance he had in the water, the promise of a temporary stay of execution felt almost as good as the idea of rescue. How long had he been in the water? A month, at least. Call it an hour. Parks knew that visibility from sea level was short, and he was as level as they got. The jagged white peaks shot straight up out of the ocean, and when he bobbed he could see their dark foundation. His muscles twitched uncontrollably. It was tantalizingly close, but how long would it take to drift the rest of the way? The suit might have had it covered. He may well have been alive-enough for a PJ to pluck him up in a basket and revive him. Whether or not he could work himself onto something solid was in doubt.

He heard the breaks before he saw them. Water crashing on something. A beach, a cliff face, a thick floe. His angle did him no favors. Now and then a distant glimpse of the shore that sunk before he could size it up. With every pulse, he imagined himself light, carried along with an extra mental heave, followed by the brief panic as he swirled back for a second. The water felt thin and nimble now, in contrast to the heavy thump. Still cold. Still ungodly cold. A quick spot check revealed no ice cubes in his immediate drink. Maybe he stumbled into a "warm" current. His ears studied the sound echoing back to him. It reminded him of the anticipation he felt approaching the beach back home with a surfboard under his arm, the growing crash and hiss of waves he couldn't yet see. They were patient travelers. It took every ounce of control to resign himself to his drift. His body would touch solid ground again, one way or another.

It was the coldest Parks had ever been in his life. He'd surfed winters in Oregon, and camped in freezing temperatures. He didn't know it was possible to be so cold. The little nucleus of warm blood in his core fought back an invasion on all sides. The warm blood stung everywhere it forced back the chill. His toes were a lost cause. A roll of his ankles told him his feet were not far behind, but he fought to keep them above the water, if nothing else to make himself more streamlined, so he could milk every last inch out of a wave. Yet he wasn't getting any colder. This was terminal misery, or it was the worst the ocean had to offer. Without all the incessant dunking, he no longer felt every little blow sap his strength. It was near-gone, but it had ceased going. He felt like he could crawl forever.

At last, a lift, and he locked eyes on the white breaks. Willed the current to pull him like the tractor beam to the Death Star. Parks would take a Death Star over death. Minute by painstaking minute, he rode on. His neck had long tired of craning to see the distance. It would come, or it wouldn't. The crash of the surf alone marked his progress. He considered praying again, but decided this was about all he could ask for. Better not fuck it up. Blast after blast, he drew near. Something uncanny hit the pit of his stomach. A fart rumbled into the torpedo tube of his large intestine. It wasn't right, in some way he just couldn't pinpoint. Years on the water on everything from shortboards to Nimitz-class carriers had taught him that his intestines had a keener awareness of nautical danger than his brain did, and that gastric distress was not something to ignore, for a variety of reasons. Features began to reveal themselves. The mountains of the peninsula seemed to gather round and snicker at this thing that dared approach the giants. Jagged black rock stood against the waves as they slammed and shot skyward. This was not a sandy beach where he could hope to wade to safety. The sound told of a brutal crack against a near-vertical surface. It hit him: of course there nowhere to waddle up. Antarctica isn't Rio de Janiero. It's *ice*. They spent weeks toodling around icebergs and reefs, and he could count the number of places you could safely land a motorboat within a 600-mile stretch on his frozen dick. It was a blue wall of razor blades, surrounded by a minefield of the same. It was as if he were being slowly shoved off a cliff. Land was not salvation. It was a curtain of peaks drawing closed between him and the daylight.

He lifted his head. The world that he imagined waited for him melted in a disturbing blur. This was something else entirely. The ice clung to the heights. As far to either side as the eye could see, the current swept him into black rock, not a floe between them. He must have been on a northeasterly drift. This was not where he hauled ass back to the ship that morning. It was unclear if it was even the mainland, or some island just off it. He scanned the shore for a welcoming spot. Sheer bluffs stretched unbroken to either direction. The waters in front of them were studded with crowns of rock that cut the surf on the way in. It pounded against the wall and reverberated back. Where the incoming waves met the ones retreating, the sea foamed and leaped. Suddenly, he felt a tug. A rock ahead began drifting to his right. He found himself in a longshore current, pulling him parallel to land and north. A quick glance that way. As unwelcoming as they seemed, the small bluffs before him rose sharply into cliff and jagged peaks that cropped up like sentinels as they proceeded. It was a bad spot, and every second made it worse.

Nausea made the seawater in his stomach gurgle. If he let himself drift in the hope of finding somewhere better, he might freeze along the way. But to commit here was insanity. There was nothing. There would only be one good chance. No swimming back to the current if he didn't like it. If he went on, though, he may not have the chance to leave it at all. Just ahead, there was a line in the water as clear as a dirt trail. It went from gray-blue to a lighter color, flecked with white air bubbles from the backwash that spun off as soon as they hit the boundary. That was it. If he could make it that far, he was shore-bound. The panic of indecision ripped him like the ice ripped their hull. He thought of the prop, twisted and unable to steer. Felt the engine rumble to a halt beneath his feet. *Rudder*, the word flashed through his head. I have to go while I can steer.

Warmed by the faint sun, Parks yanked his body until his head pointed to land. At first, they refused to turn over, but after a few flurries, his thighs separated and churned. It was more of a stir than a kick. He could hear the waves yawning up behind him and foaming like angry soda around the rocks. If he made progress, he couldn't tell. Another wave rolled through the current and washed up his nose. He blew hard to expel it. It was too much energy. Parks let his paddle slow. Barely moving. It was all he could sustain. The next wave treated him just as badly. His feet were useless flippers that dragged with each kick. Once more, he was swamped. When he surfaced, there was a stillness. To his right, he could see the glimmer of the current now and then as it moved on without him. He turned his body around so that his feet once again faced land, and gave his burning legs a rest. One good minute. That was all he paddled, and he felt like he just swam two miles. His breath ragged, he surveyed what the effort had earned him.

The top of the bluff was about ten feet above the waterline. If he was facing east like he thought, the surf swung in out of the southwest, crashed into the rock, and bounced out again heading northwest. It whipped up a whirlpool of confused sea between the northbound current and the shore. Some of the waves roared in and slammed the wall with such force that they climbed up and over the edge. Others were obliterated by the previous ones echoing back to lap against the sharp bluffs like an animal licking its wounds, still with several times the power needed to break every bone in his body. His heart sped up, and he felt the hollow toll of hypothermia. He was used to sitting on a board for a few chilly hours waiting for the right set, but that was surfing, not beaching yourself like a whale. It wasn't enough to just study the incoming sets. He had to account for the way they broke on the shore, and which, if any, gave him hope of finding something smooth to hit. And there wasn't time. He could still feel the northward tug pulling along the rising wall, from dire to hopeless.

Most of the waves rolled all the way to the bluff, telling of deep water, but to his left, they curled up just beforehand and closed out with a white surge. There had to be a reef giving them oomph. Nothing cleared the top, but all of it was strong enough to smash him. The most violent section was his only hope of a leg up. It would be over soonest if it failed. It felt like that's where the suction of the water was taking him. He watched several die in the wash, before a particularly large one reared up and thundered to impact. Something caught his eye. Seconds after the main thrust, water ran off the top back into the ocean in a brief waterfall. Almost invisible in the bluffline was a small cove—more of a scoop carved out of the face. It turned north around a corner of rock. As he drifted, he saw how they hit the back of the cavity, swirled, and ran sideways up a mercifully smooth slab two feet lower than the rest of the bluff. The larger breaks would top out before turning and spilling into the churn.

Most of them were too weak to clear it.

He'd need the right one to make it up top instead of slamming face first into a wall. Parks turned sideways and gave a few good kicks to complement his trajectory and line himself up with the cove. His legs cramped right away. *That may have been it.* But it got him just shy of where they broke. How shallow was that reef, now? He went limp and let his feet droop to slow down his approach and rest his legs. He would need one more good paddle, and his arms were done.

With a slow egg beater, he flipped around to face the incoming sea. It had to be soon, or he'd be swept north of the narrow opening. The first set bobbed past, much too small. Parks was no longer sure if he was lined up, but as the second set approached, he knew he would find his wave or drown. A few gentle strokes of his legs moved him into position to strike, then he let them hang again in time to brake himself while the first wave passed. It bumped him closer. The second nearly took him, leaving him in the path of the third—the smallest yet—right where they reared up. As it coiled to strike him, he took a deep breath and drove his knees under, his head following as it arrived. A near miss. The fourth was bigger. Here we go, he told himself. Last best shot. He wasn't convinced it would be enough to vault him up and over the ramp, but what choice did he have? He lay back with his head to the rock and raised his feet in preparation. There would be no arm paddling today, even if the suit wasn't too clumsy to allow it. Something hot ran through his body. He'd felt it before—when a head-high winter wave closed out on him, freshman year of high school on the first good day of the season, and held him under long enough that he didn't surf again until summer. Right as he should have kicked, fear flooded over him and he duck dived again. He shook his eyes clear and saw one more. This had to be it. The last chance, and looming. He kicked with all he had left.

It lifted him and shot his 230-pound body like a bar of soap in a bathtub. Within seconds it closed on him and raced ahead. He shut his eyes and took a last breath as foam swallowed him up. His inability to ride it out worked in his favor. It smashed into the rock ahead and turned hard right into the cove. Parks couldn't see any of this, but he felt the sudden change of direction, the rise, his ass scraping smooth rock. He quickly flopped over on his belly to catch something. His shin banged hard into the sharp lip of the rock. He got high enough to see a mossy stone, but there was nothing to grab. Some of the water spilled back, but the rest yanked him down the ramp the way he came up. He panicked and flailed for anything. His fingertips clawed the slick rock and dragged without friction. He felt his feet go over. Water ran around him, and he slid to a stop just before his knees crossed the edge of the ramp. And like that, the sea was gone. Another six inches and his center of gravity would have flopped him back into the chop. He squirmed on his elbows to the level bluff like a kid crawling to safety under the bed. Parks rolled a few times to make sure nothing wet would touch him on even the highest break. His body convulsed, not from cold, but with the rattle of terror shaking itself loose. His strength, his will, everything left him. He lay like an offering on the cool hard rock and squinted into the hazy sun. Its glow fell, a miracle on his pruny face. Parks was too exhausted to be grateful. One more good shiver ran the length of his spine. His eyes closed like two heavy doors on a dreamless sleep.

When he finally blinked awake, he was only sure that it was the same day, in that it was always the same day in Antarctica, six months out of the year. Parks had no idea how much time had elapsed. The chills shot through him like currents of electricity. Rather than the bone-biting tremors that threatened to stop his heart in the water, it was the chill of cold leaving the body. Still uncomfortable, near numb in the extremities, coming up to something like the temperature at which a grown man can keep his internal organs functioning. His blurry eyes settled on his chest, covered in a thick mat of coarse hair. He'd always had a bit of a rug, but he didn't realize it had gotten that bad. His brain chugged like an old engine searching for the spark of ignition. Something was missing here. It dawned on him that he passed out in a full immersion suit, not a lock protruding. Why was he bare chested?

Parks sprung up on his elbows and realized he was covered in something other than the family down. A thick fur hide blanketed him from neck to shin. On his chest under a round rock the map sat drying. He flung everything off in a panic and tripped to his feet, butt-ass naked. As soon as the breeze hit him, the shivers kicked up. Cold as he was, the fur had worked up a decent sweat. He spun around every which way in his ready stance, as though looking for a pass rusher to pick up. There was no one. The waves still battered the place he flopped ashore. But the bright orange immersion suit and the tube that held the map were nowhere to be found.

A feeling of vulnerability swept him. He hurried for the blanket, expecting the freezing chill to set in at any moment. Parks wrapped it around his shoulders, fur-side in, and rattled with a deep cold that bubbled up from his marrow. It was his first look at his salvation. Inland, mountains raced to a dizzying height above the thin stretch of sloped around the coast. He got the sense he was not so much at the foot, as at the knee of the mountain, before it dove sharply again beneath the waves for another few thousand feet. The heights were covered in snow, and in the distance, a dirty glacier probed over the saddle and considered a descent. Rockfall boulders dotted the strip, painted by lichens in hues of green, orange, gray. There was no sign of life except a stray bird calling somewhere out of sight. The sun warmed the rock beneath his bare feet so that it was only as cool as a bathroom floor in the morning. His teeth chattered. His thighs hugged his junk, and he clung to the backs of his elbows beneath the hide. The wind made him cringe in anticipation of misery. At least this stretch was free of ice as far as he could see—admittedly, a pathetic range. Yet the freezing bite he expected never came. After a minute, he lowered the fur to the ground to face the weather. It was chilly, beyond a doubt. Most of the discomfort seemed to well up from within, though. The air was mild, a crisp Fall day in Northern California. His drift must have taken him up the peninsula. It was not so pleasant in any of the places they had visited.

The feeling of unease returned, and he snapped the fur back around his body. Someone had *undressed* him. Pulled him from his suit, from his undies, and left him with nothing but a throw rug and a misshapen map of *Terra Australis*, southern continent of rumor. He felt violated. Who the hell would do that? Maybe Foster made it ashore. He didn't see how the little dude could have survived, blubberless and unaware. Besides, where would he get furs?

Cannibals. No. Cannibals would have eaten him. No one lives here but a thousand dorks in research stations. Why wouldn't they have just taken him inside if they found him? A prank, then. Had to be Foster. Maybe he just wanted to let Parks dry out and warm up, and he left a map in case he wanted to walk around a bit while he went for help. No snow meant no footprints from his assailant-slash-rescuer. Where had he gone? Parks looked out at the empty sea and took a wild guess—inland. No boat would spot him if he left the bluffs, but what boat did he expect?

He shifted his weight and nearly collapsed in agony. The adrenaline of the landing left him. He realized his shin was gashed to the bone. Dry blood caked the opening. Every little bit of pressure on his left leg was excruciating. Might even be fractured, he thought. Parks was a big man to bear all his weight on a single frozen leg, barefoot on the rock. He looked once more out to sea. It lapped the rock face and seemed to study him like some monster who tossed him in his jaws and dropped him in what it thought was a gentle game. It was hard to believe he was out there, what? An hour ago? A day? Already he lost the time. That creature who sprawled the globe had returned him, more or less, to dry land. Where there was nothing to eat or drink, and no sign of humanity except a thief who saw his junk.

"Thanks, bro," he nodded to the water. "Hope I don't see you for a bit." Parks hobbled on.

The inland path was blocked. The mountains were a vicious barrier hatched with long spurs and dark ravines that slashed their way up to the snow line. It wouldn't have helped even if he could cross it. Most of the land around here was just that: a mountain with the sea on all sides. There were two ways he could go, and both followed the coast. For no reason he could explain, Parks unrolled the floppy wet map and rotated the peninsula to match where he assumed he was facing. It was exaggerated in size compared to the rest of the continent, but otherwise right where he expected it. On the other side, he thought he could make out the Transantarctic Mountains leading away from the Weddell Sea, dividing the land into east and west. If he followed the direction of his drift, he would continue north—the farther, the better. That's where he would mostly likely run into rescue. Traffic got exponentially heavier as you worked up the peninsula. It was missing virtually every island he knew of, though. He scrunched his nose up the peaks, and wondered if he was even on the mainland. It could easily have been one of the millions of shitty little islands just off the coast.

Parks wadded the map under his arm in disgust. Why bother? It wasn't supposed to be accurate. It was a placeholder for 15th century navigators who had never set foot in America, let alone here. An era when every rumor and daydream earned a place on the charts used by superstitious sailors who did as much to invent the details as survey them.

Water, the word entered his head. He didn't realize how thirsty he'd become. Was there fresh water here? Ice, for sure, but it looked high up, far off. He had little energy to find it and no means to melt it. What do penguins drink? Birds drink water. Can they just drink salt water? A few seabirds he didn't happen to know fluttered across a hundred feet up. No sign of wildlife otherwise. Something here drinks water, he insisted. And something has fur. And someone who can unzip a clingy suit from a big wet ass and drag him out of it is somewhere nearby, and if penguins don't drink water, he does. Where you at, Bobcat? That sounded like something Foster would say in a time like this. If it was Foster who left him butt naked in furs without explanation he was going to kill him. Then he was going to give him a big ol' hug, then kill him again.

His leg tightened in pain that went all the way to the crease on top of his foot. Parks tried to hop and instantly had to put the injured foot down. The calf seized up and sent him to his back with a cramp. He pulled his leg up as straight as it would go and clawed for the bottom of the foot, which he bent back toward his heart for a solid minute, writhing in agony, begging for it to forgive him. From all fours, he worked his way back up without using his left at all. One ginger step after another, his weight began to trust the foot, to reorganize itself. It was all uphill, this direction. The rest of his body felt on the verge of the same cramp that worked itself loose as he went. Though he was winded the moment he started, there was no way he could head downhill. At least this way he could lean into it.

All the while he lumbered, he scanned the ocean for a sign of a ship, of useful debris. He scanned the mountains to the other side for anything he might drink. He should probably sit and wait for another miracle, but no part of him wanted to be where he was anymore. Now the waves boomed into the cliffs, risen from the bluff, as he wove around the toes of rock that jutted toward the water. Each time he thought he was heading for a wall that would pen him in, and each time it gave way to a gradual slope that allowed him to pass around, or at least over with no more than a mild trudge. The coast wouldn't be passable forever. Sooner or later, he would have to sit and hope he was spotted without the aid of loud colors. As he crossed the next one, he startled and stopped dead.

A quarter-mile off, a thin plume of black smoke wafted up over a rise. Something on fire. What even burns here? He clutched his fur tight. A weak heart did its best to race. Was this rescue? Or someone who meant him harm? Whoever found him hadn't exactly left him better off. They could be content with a petty theft for the time, but how would they react if he demanded his suit back?

Fuck it. There was no other way. Now he wondered if the raft had somehow landed. The map was in the water. That pointed to capsizing. But they might have an emergency fire kit, and that would explain the utter disregard for him if Carabiner was alive. Cannibals or Foster, he prayed. Cannibals, or Foster.

It took ages to cover the distance. He made sure his flat feet didn't slap the ground anymore than they had to. At last Parks reached the rise. He looked around, and settled on a smooth fist-sized rock. Weapon in hand, he crouched up to the top and knelt on his good knee and the two hands. It just made his knee hurt, and the position was exhausting to hold. He slipped to his belly and squirmed the rest of the way. Every time the ground brushed his shin he cringed and choked down a moan of pain.

Parks crested. He could see the orange flames lick around the man crouched with his back to him, wrapped in fur. It was a man, and he was alone. The shape was alien to him. The position reminded him of the Hadji squat so popular among men of a terroristic disposition. No sign of the suit anywhere. He rose to his feet. His off-arm pinched the map to his ribs and secured the ends of the fur at his collarbone, while he white-knuckled the rock. Should he call out before getting too close? His gut wouldn't allow it. He tiptoed down the slope. Maybe he could just bash the guy and figure out who it was later. Then he would at least have a bit of food. Am I the cannibal? He brushed the thought aside. Thirty feet away. Terror gripped his throat. Even if he wanted to speak, it wasn't cooperating. Once again, he saw the rogue wave coming at him broadside, and remembered his silence before the blow.

His limp dragged. Pebbles clicked underfoot. The man rose. His pelt dropped in anticipation of a fight, and he stood naked. Parks let his own fall so that he could swing his broad arms if needed. He raised the stone.

Foster turned. A smile crept over the corner of his mouth.

"Hey, brother," he said. "Come get warm."

2

AKMANUAK

Parks tried to blink away the apparition, but nothing could wipe the grin off its face. He was too dry for tears. A lump welled up in his throat. The image of Orange Foster hunched over the barrel before the wave hit was burned into his memory. Now five yards separated him from an impossibility. It was as if the misery of the sea balled up into a few short flashes a lifetime ago, the rest lost to the storm. For a second, he wondered if it was just an angel come to greet him. Too ugly for an angel. This was one better.

"I'd hug you if you weren't butt-ass naked," Parks said.

"I was hopin' that would be your disposition."

"Ah, screw it." He let the rock fall and lumbered forward. Foster scooped up his fur and held it around his waist as the big man brought his pale body in for a crushing embrace. They laughed until they were out of breath and their arms gave out.

"I knew you'd make it, you magnificent fucking redneck! I mean, I was a little worried about this skin and bone situation," he punched Foster's stomach. Foster squirmed away. "But you mountain folk are hard to kill." Parks grabbed his own pelt and wrapped it around his shoulders, then huddled over a small fire pouring thick black smoke out of a stoneware bowl.

"Well me, I had no good reason to expect your ass to do anything other than drown. But somehow, I had a feelin' you'd turn up."

"Insulation." He pressed his palms to the heat. "What the fuck did you put in this, dude? I feel like I'm getting the black lung."

Foster squatted beside him. "I think it's coal."

"The hell'd you find that?"

"I was gonna ask you. I thought this was your doin'."

The heat off the red embers singed his knees, but Parks didn't care. Warmth was something he never thought he'd feel again, even if it only reached a tenth of his body. He followed the inky plume up and inland. There was no wood for thousands of miles as far as he knew, and this made for a much nicer signal fire. Then again, there was no coal, either.

"You know? Much as I wish I had grabbed a big bowl of Kingsford and a lighter before we got tossed over, I'm as baffled as you are."

"So you didn't take my suit?"

"I thought you took mine."

Foster wrinkled his brow. "I saw the smoke soon as I landed," he nodded the direction. "Thought somebody had made it in with some gear, but this is all I found. So I took off my suit and left it in case they came back, and went for a look-see to dry my balls. When I got back, my suit and the little orange tube were gone. He pointed to a wet brown map laid flat on the other side of the fire.

"Don't ask me, dude. I PTFO'd soon as I beached my ass and woke up under a pile of fur." Parks picked his own map from the ground and tossed it where Foster could see it. "Well, at least we won't get lost."

"Weird."

"Are there people here?"

"I don't know where here is," Foster admitted.

"Neither do I. I meant Antarctica."

"Does this look like fuckin' Antarctica to you?" He waved his hand around.

"Yeah, kind of. Minus most of the ice."

"Minus the ice? You can't just 'minus' millions of tons of glaciers and snow pack."

"I don't know. It's supposed to be a low year."

"I ain't talkin' about last year. I'm talkin' about earlier this mornin'. It ain't like it melts while you were takin' a nap."

"Maybe we got washed to some part of the peninsula that's a little warmer than where we were."

"Yeah, I'll say."

They paused to shift their bodies against the glaring heat to avoid being overcooked in any one spot. Both men stared into the flame. The whole thing was a whirlwind of disbelief to Parks. Had he ever been on the ship at all? Even that moment hardly felt real. Like he was watching himself watch a fire crackle and spark as coals collapsed into another. Ash fell out of a few holes bored in the bottom for airflow. The vessel was rough, with the veins and and ridges of stone left unpolished. No machine had hollowed it out, that was for sure. It had an "arts & crafts" feel to it—he could just see an old lady with her pants pulled up too far sitting behind a folding table at a swap meet with a few of these on display.

"Maybe there's Eskimos," Parks ventured.

"Eskimos live in the Arctic."

"Reverse-Eskimos. I don't know. Little native fuckers who take your state-of-the-art survival equipment and leave you a bearskin rug and a bucket of coal, like Santa's southern cousin."

"I might be wrong, but I could've sworn there's no native population on Antarctica."

"There is in South America. Maybe they come over in the summer to hunt? That's something your people would do."

"My people?"

"You know. Appalachians."

"Bro. You act like I'm from some indigenous tribe."

"Fine. Appalachian-American, then."

"Anyway, I take your point. If that's the case, at least they ain't tryin' to kill us. Maybe that means we can get picked up. Eskimos these days got all the modern conveniences: four-wheelers, sat phones, you name it."

"I'll settle for a seal burger," Parks spat a dry wad of saliva. "And a drink of water."

Foster looked up at the white-capped mountains. "That snow'll melt. What's that, about 2,000 feet up?"

"Fuuuck," Parks moaned. "You fetch the first load, I'll get the second."

"Fetch in what?"

"Well. This is good for now." He slumped in exhaustion. It felt like a rip-off to go through all that, claw his way onto land with his last good effort, then find himself naked, starving, and faced with a barefoot Alpine ascent to suck on ice. This was not safety. It was just a new thing to survive.

"Did you see anyone else in the water?" Foster asked. Parks shook his head. "Me neither." The talk fell flat. Cold rock drew heat out the skin that touched it, and part of him felt this was his toll. For being here, still able to suffer. Parks was not particularly close to anyone else, but he liked most of the crew. He disliked long silences. It felt like ice piling up in a heavy lattice, and all he wanted to do was swipe it to pieces.

"If we ever drink a cold one in Puntas Arenas again, remind me to pour a few out." It felt like a mandatory condolence issued at a wake. Something to say, and a duty fulfilled. As it was, he felt absolutely terrible, and no worse. There was no one he would rather see than the one beside the fire. And Puntas Arenas felt like a long dream—a freshman's fantasy of graduation, with an unfathomable course of events between that he didn't care to actually live through so much as arrive beyond. Foster must have read his thoughts.

"We will. Drink a cold one." A hand gripped Parks' shoulder too hard. "Mark my words. If we ain't dead yet, this place done missed its chance." He rose to his feet and hunched over the flame. "My gooch is freezin'."

It was all the permission Parks needed to make the same complaint, and he joined his friend.

"What are you going to do when you get back? First thing. Go." He had every intention of changing the subject from the thought of his shipmates succumbing to the frozen breath of sea that nearly filled his own lungs.

"Put on a goddamn sweater, crank up the heat, and never set foot on a boat for any reason as long as I live."

"Smear my whole face with chapstick and eat six double-doubles, animal-style. And the boat thing."

Foster grinned, and gazed off to the north.

"OK, new question," Parks added. "What are you going to do…before you *die?*"

"Hell, I don't know if I ever knew that."

"That's all I could think of while I floating out there. When I first saw land, and I was just drifting forever, like I would never get there. I got a solid thirty or forty all lined up."

"Parks."

"A good half of them are inventions. It's like once I knew I was a goner, all my creativity just came pouring out."

"Shut up, man."

"And God help whatever beauty next lays her big doe eyes on this fine specimen of death-defying—"

"Shut the fuck up!" Parks startled. "Look." Foster nodded in the distance.

Their eyes met at a figure a few hundred yards away and moving slowly toward them from the northeast. A man. His bare arms hung from a vest of leather that flapped like a sail around his gaunt torso. An oversized pair of trousers stopped short of odd footwear. He looked to Parks as if he just completed some weight loss challenge, or caught a sale at Big & Tall. Blurred and distant as he was, everything about him felt alien, from his dress right down to the way he moved with an inevitable stride and a sense of place, of purpose—far from their clumsy wandering. The man didn't seem to notice them. If he did, he didn't care.

"I'll bet *that* fool knows a thing or two about where we are, and where our shit went," Foster blustered.

"Hey!" Parks screamed and waved an arm. "Hey! Over here! Rescue! Rescue!"

Foster joined in. "Hey, brother!" He cackled with joy. "Help a fella out!"

They clamored and swung their hands overhead. Parks threw off the skin so he could use both arms to get the man's attention. "Sir! God bless you!

Over here! We are in need of rescue!" His tone sounded like he was addressing an imbecile who barely spoke English. Their voices echoed over the bare rock, and the man stopped. He faced them.

"Whoo! He seen us!" Foster, too, let his rag fall away. He pumped his fist and bounced up and down. Parks' waving began to look more like a bad dance move he used in the club. His shin suddenly felt good enough to slide his feet and flap like a penguin in celebration.

"Hey! You're a lifesaver!" Foster added to Parks: "I don't think he can understand us."

"Doesn't matter. He sees us. It's the universal sign of help." He did something like raise the roof, his manhood flapping with every movement.

Their rescuer hesitated. In a breeze, a lock of white hair lifted and fell onto his shoulders that slumped with age. His palms turned upward and raised above his head, though it didn't feel like a wave. His head cocked back and he faced the clouds. It was hard to make out, but Parks felt his lips were moving. It was strange enough that their celebration came to a temporary halt. Then his hands returned to his side, and he seemed to study them.

"Is he comin'?"

"I think he's coming. Great thanks to you, Grandfather!" Parks raised his voice.

Foster shrugged, and they resumed their waving.

Now the man reached to his side and in a flash, drew a long knife from his belt. He started their direction in a kind of urgent hobble, what might have been a best attempt at a run, arms pumping back and forth.

Foster gripped Parks' forearm. "Bro. He's got a knife."

"Is that a big-ass filet knife?"

"Looks more like a filet sword to me."

The elation spilled out of them, replaced by a paralyzed confusion. "Uh, hmmm. OK. Not sure what to think of this development."

"It looks like…is he—*charging* us?" Foster's voice broke.

"I would call it a slow charge, yeah."

"Did we piss him off?"

"I'm sure it's just a cultural misunderstanding. This could be the highest form of greeting for an honored guest of his people."

"Charging with a knife?"

"Easily. The ways of the natives peoples of the world are still mysterious to the white man." Parks offered as the gray-red tint of skin contrasted with the darker vest. "What to us is an act of aggression, to him could be an expression—it could be some kind of…ceremony, or ritual, to demonstrate kinship, and manly virtues—"

"I think we need to run."

"Nonsense. Look how slow he's going. We have plenty of time to clear this up."

"If he speaks fuckin' English."

Parks considered it. Gestures aside, turning tail from their best and only chance of encountering fellow humans felt like a bad idea. But he couldn't deny the unease that welled up and gurgled in his intestines, making him pucker.

"Screw it, let's just kick his ass and take the knife."

"How the hell you figure we're gonna do that?"

"Come on Foster, it's two-on-one. This dude's AARP card just fell out of his pocket. He's got pudding on his chin. Use your hillbilly knife disarmament techniques."

"Hillbillies don't knife fight, fucker. We punch you or we shoot you. There is no in-between."

"Fine. You distract him, draw his blade, I'll knock him out."

"*You* distract him, I'll knock him out."

"No good. You're more nimble than I am. And I've got the haymaker. Just draw his blade your way, I'll come in at the last possible second."

The man drew close. Only a football field away now. Legs still churning their direction in stiff, tiny steps.

"I think we might be underestimatin' the danger here, son. It don't take a world class knife fighter to slice you with a good blade. And there's no first aid shit here. What are we gonna do if he nicks an artery? Or if we even just need stitches? Hell, if we win, but by virtue of some luck or slowness on our parts, he gets in the smallest cut, it'll get infected way before we ever reach help. You could lose an arm, *if* you live. And that's assumin' this guy don't just kill us outright."

Parks suddenly felt vulnerable in his nudity. He glanced around for the rock he had earlier, but in his haste there was no time. He considered wrapping the skin around his body, or maybe throwing it over the guy's head then bear hugging him down. Was that a legit fighting technique? His mind did an emergency inventory of every martial arts movie he'd ever seen.

"Fine, we'll both take him at the same time. From either side. One knife, two assailants, game over."

"I still think you're underestimatin' what a sharp knife can do to an un-armed man, even in weak-ass hands. Besides, if this dude no bullshit lives on the harshest continent on Earth and wears sleeveless leather shirts when it's goddamn *freezin'*," he shuddered, "I reckon he knows how to cut shit."

Fifty yards. Parks remained wordless. Foster saw his nose wrinkle as a doubtful look fell over his face. He remembered that Parks always wore glasses. Suddenly, he wondered if they were even looking at the same thing. He shook his head and kicked his pelt out of what he assumed was now the Kumite grounds, and settled into a fighting stance. The man's face crystallized. It was calm. He wasn't breathing heavy. There wasn't even a sign of anger. And he was much older than they originally imagined. Weathered smooth, well-aged, but quite ancient. Something told Foster he kept that edge sharp. At most, he was five-foot-five, a buck-thirty-five if his clothes were soaked in freezing water. The white locks danced over his shoulders, and dark eyes fixed on their chests as if they were the only things in the world. A thin strip glinted at the end of the black patina protruding from his hand. His steps were short and quiet, but in that moment, he felt like a mastodon bearing down on them.

Foster braced for action. Out of the corner of his eye, he saw Parks turn and bolt. He looked back in time to see the blade arc towards him. Their eyes met. His body squirted out of the way and sprinted after his friend.

Their bare feet slapped cool rock and a sea breeze chilled their naked flesh as they jogged across the uneven terrain. To the right, steep cliffs and the water that had spat them out. To the left, sharp elevations, ridges and washes folded like skin wrinkled from a long bath. Foster could hear Parks' breath heave unevenly. They must have been at it a half hour by now. His heart still kicked with adrenaline, but his legs were stiff and swollen. The ground was littered with cracks and loose rock that could puncture a sole. There was no zoning out. Every step had to be chosen. Every line calculated for the elevation gain, though at least most of it seemed downhill. The sailors had to slow to a walk to get over the last rise. He commanded his legs to pump it out for the short distance. They promptly shut down without ever trying, and only the slope on the other side recharged their pace. Parks was doing it all with an extra sixty pounds.

"That's gotta be far enough," the big man said as he plodded to a halt and leaned on his knees. Foster glanced back to see the native top the same rise.

"Two hundred yards. Come on. Walk it out, you'll tighten up." They had the routine down now, Parks only needed coaxing. He lifted his chest and hobbled after as the old man gained.

"My shin is killing me."

Foster noticed the gash for the first time. He cringed. "Damn, brother. How'd you do that?"

"Smashed it," he gasped, "tryin to flop up on the bluff," another gasp, "like a fucking seal."

"You came in on the bluffs? I thought that looked like suicide."

"No choice," he hocked a dry loogie and spat on the ground. "Freezing. Cliffs. Do or die."

"Hundred-fifty."

Each breath came deeper and slower as Parks regathered himself. It took little effort to pull away from the crazy bastard, but as soon as they slowed he closed.

"How did you," Parks took one more deep breath. "Land?"

"Shit, I just let the current take me past the point. About a quarter-mile down, where it wraps around the end there, I walked up on a pebble beach."

"Are you fucking serious?"

"Well, maybe not pebble. Rocks. But it was better than chargin' the bluff."

"Yeah, but how could you know there was a place to make land?"

"I didn't. Just figured I'd take a small chance over none at all. Guess I could've done it your way and split a vagina on my shin."

"We gotta think of something else."

"There *ain't* nothin' else. Come on, you got this."

"Maybe you got this. I just spent hours wondering if I was going to freeze or drown. I got one good leg, no clothes, my balls are getting thumped between my thighs every time I take a step, I haven't run since Obama's first term, and I'm thirsty enough to drink your piss."

"I wouldn't call it hours."

"Hours."

"The fuck were you doin' out there?"

"Shivering my dick off and swallowing waves. What were you doing?"

"Hundred yards," Foster glanced back. "I ain't sayin' it was pleasant. But hell, the storm only lasted another fifteen minutes. I know cause that's when I found the tube, and I remember thinkin' how I was glad I didn't go on that raft. Then another hour or so to drift up on shore."

"The fuck it did, I was getting pounded for ages. Were you seriously only in the water a little over an hour?"

"Cold can fuck with your sense of time."

"Yeah, *your* sense, you skinny bastard."

"Yours. Come on, man, we gotta hump it."

Parks looked back. The bloodthirsty Reverse-Eskimo was closing at just over fifty yards away. The knife swung back and forth like a second-hand as he trotted, slow as ever, but no slower.

"How much longer do we have to do this?"

"Til he quits chasin' or we get cut. I'm too tired to fight now."

"Fuuuuck." Parks groaned.

"Sooner we put another two-hundred between us, sooner we get another rest."

They took a starting stance and watched. As soon as he eclipsed the imaginary midfield line, they took off again.

The men moved like a caterpillar across the coast of the peninsula, inching together and pulling apart. Each time it was harder to gain distance. The sailors weren't fast. They had young legs on an old man, but it was clear as time wore on who had the endurance. Foster and Parks picked their way gingerly on feet that weren't used to unshod travel, much less for an hour and a half straight. At least I'm warm now, thought Foster. It was a strange run. Too much to think about. Thirty minutes in he thought Parks was going to go down for good—mainly because he felt the same about himself, and figured he could outlast his friend if nothing else. That in itself haunted him. If it happened, would he keep going? So many people already lost that day. There was little he could do to help. He wondered if his pride would allow the sacrifice, if he'd turn and die together.

Or would it haunt him in Puntas Arenas, pouring out beer, that he alone made it home? The decision never came. Their second wind—or by now, third, maybe fourth—filled their lungs and slackened their pace, but he felt no worse since then. Not physically. There were even moments he forgot they were being chased, or who ran by his side. Sometimes the sheer forbidding majesty of the place hung over him like a shimmering dome, or the pounding sea heightened his senses and filled him with gratitude for any pain that reminded him he was alive. There were constant negotiations with the terrain itself. No more uphill, please. Stay open, stay open, no cliffs. So far, it cooperated. As did Parks. He could feel the misery radiating off of him, and knew who had the harder trip. Probably the weaker heart. But he kept turning over like a champ. Their procedure was dialed. Every two-hundred yard cushion earned a brief walk. The lead took between 130 and 136 seconds to unravel, then it was back at it from a fifty yard head start.

It was his hope that the constant disappointment of closing and being left behind would destroy the old man's spirits. Or that the run would break his body. Every time he looked back, his stomach got queasy. Foster thought about what kind of grandpa chases people for an hour and a half straight for a chance to kill them with a knife. That was no ordinary violence. He must have known what would happen when he started, and found it worthwhile. What began as ridiculous soon became frightening, and now it felt intensely personal. What could they have done to earn such a relentless hatred? It made him feel small and helpless, begging his mama not to whoop him, if only he could have a chance to explain. It vacillated with a rage of his own: fight me fair, hand-to-hand and man-to-man, motherfucker. His face would grow hot, it would become too much, and he would imagine himself pleading with all reason and respect. He would accept his death, then notice the golden sun bouncing off the water, the mountains strong and permanent stretching into the haze. And wonder how long he could last, if Parks would leave him, if he would leave Parks. Then it started over again.

It had been some time since he checked. Foster risked an exhausting glance over his shoulder. A nervous pang shot through him. The man was nearly the requisite two-hundred back, but something was wrong.

"He's veerin'."

"Veering?" Parks didn't waste the energy to look. "Is he giving up?"

"I don't think so. Veerin' inland. On a line. Fifty yards left." Parks may have been processing the information, or just trying to save breath. He didn't respond. "I think he's got a plan." Foster looked to his right at the cliffs, stretched out as far as the next ridge, at least. It looked like a clear shot if they hugged the cliff line, but their view was broken every several hundred yards by little knuckles in the land, and what lay beyond was anyone's guess.

"This fucker knows this place. If that cliff line cuts inland, it'll funnel us right to him." Foster craned to see farther but the land held its cards close. "He knows he can't catch us. He's cuttin' us off."

"The hell do we do?" Parks' limp became more pronounced as their desperation swelled.

"It's just pain," Foster noticed the compensation. "Try not to limp. It can't get any worse, you just gotta forget the pain."

"It can if it's broken."

"No one runs a half marathon on a broken leg. It's a bone bruise. Stay with me, brother."

"I can't think about shit. I'm a fucking dead man running. You need to come up with something."

Foster knew he was right. "See that ridge?" Parks didn't reply. "We're gonna take a look-see. Soon as we top it, we'll know more about what kinda mess we got."

"You and your 'look-sees.' That's your plan?"

"My plan is we make a plan on the other side of that."

"That's a shitty plan."

"I'm all ears."

His silence told Foster he'd consented, or ran out of energy to fight it. They shuffled up the shallow ridge like the dozens before it. This was the first time Parks leaned over and put his hands on the ground to stabilize himself on the incline. They used the momentum of the downslope to gain a little speed, and right away Foster saw it. The coastline ducked in at a sharp angle a quarter mile ahead. He was looking straight at horizon and sea. The cliffs shot toward the mountain, making a jagged inlet that led right up to the foot of the small peak they'd been circling for miles. It was a climb to get around—the kind you take slow, in switchbacks, even when you're fresh. There was no jogging it. Their Reverse-Eskimo friend crested behind them and inland. Three years of being a 150-pound kickoff and punt return man who didn't like getting smashed by the private school recruits with D-I offers told Foster that even had he wanted to attempt the climb, the native had all the angles. Parks would never have the sprint to make it past him. It just was a few moves to checkmate.

"Slow down." Foster shortened his step and Parks was glad to match. He saw the same thing Foster did.

"What now?" Their feet moved barely faster than a walk as the man gained on them.

"Think he got us on this one."

"Alright. My turn to plan. We stop here. We get some rocks. We throw them. David and Goliath, dude."

Foster shook his head. "Way I see it, we're runnin', but nowhere particular. We know we got miles of clear terrain behind us. Let him think he's closin', so he thinks he got the angle ahead. Meanwhile he loses the angle behind us. Then we just turn around."

"Turn around and run exactly where we've been running this whole time?"

"Yup."

"Then what? Run two hours, then turn around and run two hours, so we can turn around and run two hours?"

"We gotta hope he gets tired first."

"He didn't. I'm done."

"Two-hundred at a time. You got it, brother. We turn, we get two-hundred, we rest. Don't think of the miles. He might be sufferin' more on the inside than you are on the outside."

Parks glanced back. "My guess is he's not."

"Well I don't see any rocks bigger'n a pebble or smaller'n a boulder." There was no answer. "So what's the call? You in?"

"Can't."

"You want to stop and throw imaginary rocks."

"Have to."

"Think about what your sayin'. You know how that ends."

"Worth a shot."

"No. It ain't *even* a shot. That's suicide. I don't mean it like, that's somethin' crazy that'll probably get us killed. I mean: if you stop now, you knowingly, and willingly, are committin' suicide, same as if you swallowed a barrel and put one through the back of your head." Only raspy breath came in reply. "Parks. No."

"Can't. Not possible."

A panic flooded the pit of Foster's stomach. His friend was tying him to a immovable weight and forcing the decision he never wanted to make.

"Bitch, I don't care what you can and can't do. How do you think I'm gonna survive without you?" It was a flattering lie, and he prayed it went over. Neither of them was any good to the other at this point. Not in the material sense. Had Parks gone down with the ship, Foster would have been crushed, and he would have bore the brunt of it when he got home. To see him in the flesh, to struggle beside him, and to lose him after all would break him.

Parks made no rebuttal. He was probably too exhausted to consider it. The gap was only a hundred yards now, and fifty to their left.

"Fine, you forced my hand," Foster continued. "*D-BAP.*"

"Don't care."

"It ain't optional. I call D-BAP." Parks just shook his head. "You swore an oath. Before the image of Charles Bronson. 'Or may my balls climb into my throat, may I gargle them until I choke. May my cockskin hollow inside out, may the wardroom fill my birth canal,'" Foster recited. He was sure he heard a snicker among the panting. "Yeah? You remember that? Remember what smart guy came up with the whole thing?" They were fast running out of real-estate. The old man tracked them with a sidelong stare. "You think I wanted to do it when you called it on me in Thailand, with those Marines? They damn near stomped me to death!"

"We had you."

"Had me? You and Zemaitis were as good as a couple of tampons. But fuck it! I don't care. Point is, you're not supposed to *like* it. That's why it's there. You just gotta do it. Just this one thing. No more things after that." He could tell he sunk a hook. Now he just had to be careful not to reel too fast. There was no more time to ask, or to argue. It was up to him to move, and Parks to follow. The man was less than fifty yards back now and inland. If they followed the coast they would stagger right into his arms. "On my count."

At three, Foster planted and turned a hard 180 as if he were back running wind sprints, and loser runs again. He heard the thunder and scrape behind him as Parks did the same. Foster slowed a step, grabbed Parks arm as he approached, and flung him past before taking off himself. The man was clearly expecting the possibility. He turned too, and angled hard for an intersection.

"Sprint!" He called ahead. They managed something like a spirited jog. Within a few strides he reached his partner and leaned his left palm into his back as he ran and pushed. The distance between the parties evaporated. The old man's shuffle seemed to hasten after them. Foster steered them for the cliffs like a sideline. His heels pounded rock and sent jolts into his brain. The dark, determined eyes fixed on him. He knew better than to get caught admiring the coverage. Look where you want to go. Foster leaned hard and stared at a point over his friend's shoulder. He could hear the foot-slaps, see the brown blur out of the corner of his eye growing near. The blade flashed into his periphery. He was sure he could smell wet leather and saltwater. His legs crossed as he tight-roped the edge.

They bent through the hole between their pursuer and the cliffs. He fell back into pursuit barely ten yards away, all of them heading in the opposite direction.

There were times now when Foster left the peninsula entirely. As if he dozed into a light dream where he was just out for a naked run with a friend. Then he'd snap to, slow for Parks to catch up, and feel a rising feeling in his chest like he'd shown up to class without the assignment. It wasn't even terror anymore. You could only fear for your life so long. It was more of a frustration that no matter what he did, it was never good enough. There was no trick or triumph of strength that could save him. Only the same old ground to cover, with nothing getting easier. Especially not for Parks.

It was shorter, in the way that the second time you travel a route, it disappears quicker than the first. Memory alone was enough to tie places together and shave time between them. Certain landmarks stood out in reverse. A boulder; the backside of a spur; a smooth gouge where meltwater probably surged seaward in Spring. This way had the same humps as before, but it was ever-so-slightly uphill on average. Their pace dropped off. Luckily, the old man's must have, too.

Foster wondered again what might possess a fellow with probably all the meaningful years of his life behind him, generations of grandkids, great-grandkids, memories of seasons kind and cruel, women had, lost, honors won, opportunities that seemed so important missed and turned trivial in hindsight, someone whose mobility could barely propel him beyond a speedy walk—what would possess this man to chase two naked sailors across the southernmost continent for what must have been hours at this point? Unyielding hatred? Pride? Did he even know? Whatever it was, Foster thought, the options for escape were dwindling. If begging for mercy was ever feasible, he doubted the bastard would care to do anything but bathe in their blood at this point. It had seemed a foregone conclusion that they would run a little ways, a little faster than the geriatric, and he would give up, and they would return to the campsite if you could call it that, and go on about the business of finding a more hospitable rescuer. What they hadn't accounted for was the sheer murderous insanity of the man. And now Parks was tired. He was beyond that. Of the three marathoners, it was clear he would be the first to stop.

Truth be told, it was only the company that kept him going. Foster would have quit long ago, except the big man didn't, and his competitive nature couldn't fathom stopping if there was someone else still in the running. The notion of losing a contest of endurance to Parks was twice as shameful. The sound of heavy panting faded behind him. Foster looked back. Parks had already started walking. The man was as persistent as a shadow, not quite the 200 yards back they'd agreed on, but his friend was beyond the technicalities. When he saw Foster stop to wait for him, he just bent over.

"Done." Was all he could say.

"Not done. Breathe. Come on, you can outlast this old turd."

Parks shook his head and took a knee. Foster surveyed their surroundings. The ground was remarkably clean of any head-bashing-sized rocks, and had been for miles. Not a weapon in sight, and now down one fighter. He stood up tall even though his body screamed for him to fold over, too. A trick he'd learned from his Filipino boxing coach. Pretend you're not tired. Your opponent and your body will believe you. He could only hope that their pursuer was also pretending against unspeakable pain.

Parks yakked sea water on the ground, then dry-heaved.

"Hey. Foster," He managed between spews.

"Yeah, bud."

"I'll pray for you."

"OK." Foster would have preferred he stood up and took a few swings. He resumed vomiting instead, though nothing came out. Now that he was still, Foster's legs swelled with blood. For some reason, he looked out at the sea. He'd grown up atop a mountain in state forest lands a few hours' drive from the Atlantic. His first time even seeing an ocean came with the Navy. He'd looked a lot like Parks looked now when he first hit the water. This was his seventh continent. He was going to count it when he got home even though he was never supposed to make shore. No one could deny it now.

He returned his gaze to his opponent, running quiet as a church mouse. At a hundred yards, the man collapsed cold.

There wasn't so much as a twitch. The dude went down like a sniper took him and they were still waiting to hear the shot.

"The fuck." Parks looked over from his knees. Foster took a few steps that direction and squinted after the thin form.

"I don't know, man," he studied the unmoving figure. The exhaustion he'd been suppressing the entire time rushed over him, and suddenly his pulse sped and he drank deeply of the air as if a wave caught up to them—so much that he became lightheaded, and had to crouch with his hand on Parks' back to stabilize. Silver confetti glinted across his vision for half a minute until his breathing settled. Neither man was in a hurry to spring up. When Foster finally did stand, his quad spasmed. Whether or not they would need to run again, their bodies had decided this interruption meant they were done. The weakness and the thirst were unbelievable, and he wondered if they had been there the entire time beneath his awareness. They studied the motionless figure behind them.

"Fuck it, let's go," Parks crawled to his feet, though he couldn't yet stand upright.

"Go where?"

"Wherever we just were. That way." He pointed the way they'd been running.

Foster hesitated. "I think we should get the knife."

"Bro," Parks panted. "He's faking it. Just waiting for you to dangle your balls over his chin so he can castrate you."

"I'm aware."

"So let's go."

"I'll ask again: go where?"

"The fire. The spot with the maps and the fire."

"Then what?"

"I don't know, put our clothes back on and find some goddamn water," he spat. "Some rescue boats or—I don't fucking know."

"Our clothes? Those fur blanket things someone left us when they stole our shit?"

"Yeah. Those. And we find the guy who did that, and ask him for help. Cause if he wanted to kill us, he'd have done it. And this guy does. He wants to kill us. So we find the other guy."

"If we can't find him right away, we could use that knife. And whatever else he's got. Maybe he's got water."

"You think Eskimo Joe has a fucking Nalgene bottle?"

"Eskimos gotta drink, too."

"He's going to cut our throats and drink our blood."

Foster was relieved to hear the verbosity return to his friend. Silence from Parks was never a welcome omen. Now, he seemed to be the eager one. The end of the threat had renewed him as much as it brought home the fact that Foster was *done*, done. He knew they ought to put distance while they could. He just wasn't sure that any place here was better than the next. Somehow, the sight of another human—even a crazed enemy—brought him comfort.

"Wait here." Foster started slowly.

"Goddammit." Parks trudged after him.

The approach reminded him of bow hunting. The same tethered optimism as following the blood trail the time his arrow was a little off, wondering if the shot was good enough for a kill. They settled fifty yards out. Foster crouched on his tip toes. Parks stood over him. He remembered seeing the deer reclining through the brush, head up and alert as if nothing had happened— just taking a breather. Foster had known better. He kept his distance so as not to scare him into another sprint he couldn't follow, and soon the labored breathing and the jerking head confirmed he had put one through a lung. It seemed like a miserable way to go, drowning in its own blood, but he couldn't risk trying to put it out of his misery. It took almost two hours to die.

He sat to get comfortable. They waited wordless for several minutes. Once or twice, he thought he saw a chest rise, but it was still too far off. Could have been a shift of the light through a passing cloud.

"If he's playin' possum, he's good," Foster whispered. He wasn't sure why—hunting habits, probably. The man knew they were there.

"He just chased us for the past four days. You don't think he's willing to lie down with his eyes closed for a few minutes?"

The fear and hatred of the long run evaporated, and he felt respect for a fallen quarry. Again, it must have been out of habit. They hadn't conquered anything. Outlasted, maybe. Yet he couldn't help but be impressed. This creature had set out to kill them, and done a damn fine job. It was almost enough. A hard way to go, he thought.

Stark as this place was, it was peaceful when there were no seas to toss you or men to cut you. A breeze picked up out of the southwest and made him shiver, but now the chill felt welcome in contrast to the heat they put off earlier. It wouldn't be long before the pendulum swung back the other way, though. Parks was right, they should return to the fire and to the warmth of those hides. Something told him it would be a longer wait for their salvation than they hoped, though. A few dying coals and a loose wrap hardly seemed enough.

Foster rose and stalked forward. "Hey!" Parks called after him.

"I'm checkin' it out," he answered before the question came. Details he didn't have time for earlier began to take form. Thin boots of sewn leather, worn dark on the soles. A different kind than the pants he wore, with baggy legs that reminded him of jean he owned in the '90's. The vest was just as large. He wondered if the man had taken these things from a bigger person he killed. The closer he got, though, the more purposefully chosen they felt. All of it was of a thinner cut than the hairy skins they found. Those were thick to the point of stifling. Not exactly Summer fashion, and though it routinely dipped below freezing, this was the Southern Summer. He stopped fifteen yards out. There were things tied to a belt hidden somewhere beneath the overhanging vest tail. It wasn't clear what, other than the tip of a long sheath. The wind carried the slap of waves ahead, and soon he heard the high whistle of air. Not the slow, subtle breath of a man trying to act dead, but short, uneven gasps.

"He's alive, Foster called back to Parks.

"Told you."

He tossed his head to indicate that Parks join him.

"Hell, no. Let's fuck off." Foster crept to within five yards. "Goddammit," Parks muttered as he lumbered over. "This is classic possum. Classic possum. I recognize all the signs. Lying down…all the signs. Look!" Parks pointed. "His eyes are open. They're squinty—he's some sort of Indian or maybe some Asian in there—but you can tell. See? He's fucking looking at us."

Foster moved to the man's feet. He was indeed watching them. His light reddish-gray skin was stretched tight and dried on his face like leather, with surprisingly few wrinkles. What lines were present ran long and deep like the channels the melt carved in the mountains above them. The shoulder-length white hair had a single streak of black on the right side, the same black as the thick brows that arched over a pair of opaque eyes set close together. His nose came to a prominent peak before flattening downward, and he wore a thin, patchy stubble threatening to grow at a polar pace. Beside the hair he didn't look that old, but he gave off the sense of being much older than he seemed. His right hand gripped the knife tightly over his chest, and his left was clenched and twisted across his stomach. His breathing was shit, but his face betrayed not a glimmer of pain. Their eyes locked, and neither man blinked.

"Sir, do you speak English?" Parks said in a tone reserved for people who've lost their hearing aids. "Spekken ze English? Words that I am saying. Do you know them? We come in peace. Please do not kill us if you are just playing possum, as the people of my friend here call your deadly charade." Foster held eye contact. If he understood, he gave no indication. Parks continued. "We are tired of running. You look tired yourself. Do not be ashamed that you have fallen first. We are men of the United States Navy, the finest they have to offer. Many have been dropped by our endurance. Many men, and many ladies, for what we lack in positive attributes, we make up for in persistence."

"Sir," Foster cut in. "I doubt you understand a word of what I'm saying, but I hope you can see in my body language and my voice that I'm bein' real with you. I don't aim to hurt you. But I'm going to bend down, and take your knife." As soon as he said it Foster wished he'd been watching to see if the grip tightened.

He moved to the man's right side, the side of the weapon, and crouched as slow as he could. "If he tries anything, be ready to jump on him." Foster told Parks. It would be tough: not so fast as to give the sense of an attack, but not so meek as to give the man time to get off a slash. He slid down to a knee and clamped his hand over the man's where it held the handle of the foot-long blade. His grip was firm, not imposing, and he felt no resistance under his palm. The wrist was sinewy, bony, but strong—clenched tight around the bone handle. A greened metal ring lie at the bottom of the sweeping blade, and a similar one capped the pommel. Foster started to reach with his left to pry the blade free. He paused. Letting go of his hold he moved two fingers inside the wrist and held.

"I think he's having a heart attack."

"I'm not about to CPR this motherfucker."

"No need."

"I mean, I'll do the beats, but you have to do the breaths. I fucking hate the breaths."

"No need, brother. He's got a pulse. It's shit, but it's there."

He watched as Foster eased the blade from the man's grip. "I'm gonna set it here," he placed it on the ground behind him in clear view. Parks ventured around the left. The man was alert-enough that his eyes followed. It struck him that his own breathing was just as short and jagged as the dude dying at his feet. They had jogged their last marathon together. He was a bike ride short of his first triathlon. The heart of his old enemy clung to sputtering life, while his own tried to pound out of his chest. Looking on the face of the one who had tried to kill him didn't fill him with the hatred or the fear he expected. Nor did he feel sympathy, or even triumph. The closest word for what trickled through his veins was "tired." He felt a current of exhaustion running through the three of them like an electric circuit. Predator and prey, naked and furred, foreigner and native, living, dead, brought together by their absolute lack of energy to continue doing anything greater than draw a little air.

He moved around to the white head and lowered himself to his butt cross-legged with a bruising thud. Parks slipped his hands under the man's shoulder and scooted forward, elevating him on his lap. His breathing immediately lost its ragged edge, and with it so did Parks'.

"Sorry if my dick is on your head. No homo."

Foster pulled up the vest tail and untied a drawstring where it held a small pouch shut. He pulled out a smooth, flat rock, a tangle of thin leather binding, and a pair of bone needles. After looking them over, he stuffed them back and closed it again. Then he untied a bladder-like container of dark, greasy leather that squished to the touch. It had a neck that looked like a cross-section of a limb bone with the marrow removed, the hollow plugged with another tapered bone coated in more leather. Foster yanked it and sniffed. He recoiled.

"Water?" Parks asked.

"Maybe. Smells like piss."

He moved it toward the lips of the man, who closed his eyes and turned a fraction of an inch, the best he could do to refuse. Foster handed it to Parks. He, too, pulled back at the smell. His thirst won the argument though, and he drew a sip. Parks swallowed like it was a rock and made an awful face.

"Tastes like taint sweat soaked in rotten leather." He held it out to Foster, who took a greedy gulp and twisted his lips in disgust. Parks' belly had already forgotten the offense and was pleading for more when Foster plugged it. "That may have to last us." He rose and picked up the knife, then wrapped the excess strap from the water bladder around his grip for carrying.

"Where you going?"

"I'm gettin' chilly. We should go grab our shit."

"What about him?"

"You think we should put him out of his misery?"

"I don't know if I can cut an old dude's throat."

"I could if he was fightin' me." Foster looked at the helpless figure in Parks' lap.

"So what should we do with him?" Neither of them wanted to be the first to make the suggestion. Parks scooped under his armpits and pulled the man a little higher. He closed his eyes, and his breathing evened out. For a moment, Parks thought these breaths would be his last, but they rolled on, one after another.

"He doesn't look like he can walk," Foster remarked.

Parks nodded. "We'll wait here."

Foster returned at what should have been sundown with two maps and two furs. By then, the man sat upright, leaning back-to-back against Parks for support. The latter rambled on about something indistinct, as he had probably done since they parted. The man nursed the last of the water bladder.

"What the fuck!" Foster shrugged the knife in annoyance. Parks looked over his shoulder. "Hey! Not chill, dude. I told you that was for all of us!" All Foster could do was roll his eyes.

"Fur me." Parks clapped. He caught the toss and spread it over his chest, greedy for warmth. The sun dipped toward the horizon and seemed to consider it without committing. A mild wind worked its way under Foster's own fur and raised a chill up his thighs. His feet were long since numb from the cold stone. It was lucky they wouldn't have to face a night for months. He estimated it was in the 40's—mercifully warm for the peninsula, and miserable by any other count.

"I could use a fire," Parks confirmed.

"Went out." And that was it. Nothing else to burn, nothing to light it with. It was more of a tease than something useful. False advertisement to get them in the door. At least the sun was on the right side of the mountains, and would be for the coldest hours. It was a pale consolation.

Foster let the maps flutter to the ground. Useless souvenirs. The old man took note of them, then raised his eyes. His breathing was almost completely normal again. Neither turned as Foster addressed Parks.

"How's he behavin'?"

"Angel. Hasn't tried to kill me once. Not much of a talker, though. Ain't that right, Joe?" Joe was silent.

"I'm sure that hasn't stopped you from carryin' the conversation."

"He knows a lot about me. We're pals, now, right?" Parks nudged him with his elbow. "Bygones, officially gone."

"Joe, is it?"

"That's right. Eskimo Joe. Technically he's a Reverse-Eskimo. But he's not one to fuss about technicalities."

Foster's eyes fell on the empty bladder. "I could go for some of that taint water right about now." He swirled together just enough saliva to met his mouth. Joe stared. "Water," Foster indicated his throat. "Very thirsty. All of us are gonna need water real soon."

Joe planted his hands on the ground and tried to struggle to his feet. Parks felt the movement. "Whoa there, little guy." Without the support of a broad back, Joe slid to his side. The two sailors grabbed his armpits and helped him to a half-stand, still leaning on his thighs.

"Hang on, bud. Take your time. I think you just had a heart attack." Foster said. They hovered beside him. Joe bent his knee and half fell, half sat back down, this time supporting his own posture. He rolled to all fours and struggled to get a leg up. Foster extended a hand. Joe gritted his teeth, pressed his palms into the top of his thigh, and forced his way up without help. He tottered for a second and blinked hard. Parks spread his arms, ready to catch a fall, but he kept his feet out of sheer stubbornness.

"Next heart attack in three...two...one..." Parks quipped.

"Permission denied. He needs to be alive so he can find us some water. Maybe some less-crazy help."

"It's not like there's any hospitals we can bring him to. If we try to make him walk, he's gonna get about as far as David Carradine in *Kill Bill 2*."

Foster shook his head. "I don't know. My Uncle Wayne had a heart attack on his lease tryin' to get a deer back to his four-wheeler. He didn't even know what it was til my aunt finally made him go to the doctor three days later. He'd dragged it and dressed it and went back to work on Monday. You can do some shit on a heart attack."

"And he lived?"

Foster nodded. "Six more years of the same livin' he always did."

"Nice. Steady diet of Bud Light, Reds, and bitches." Parks said in a hammed up drawl. "What finally got him?"

"Heart attack."

Joe stepped and lost his balance. His right leg went behind the left and he staggered, but caught himself before they could intervene. They froze in their stances, waiting to catch him whichever way he tumbled. Instead, he leaned forward to gather momentum and pushed past Parks in the direction they originally fled. They looked at one another.

"Is he takin' us somewhere?"

"Fuck it." Parks gathered the maps and handed one to Foster. They headed after him, but right away he spun.

"*Napate!*" He shooed them with both arms. "*Napate! Napate!*" Joe turned again on his way.

"I didn't have the subtitles on for that one, but I think he wants us to fuck off," Parks guessed.

"Well we wanted him to fuck off, and he ran us halfway to the South Pole. I guarantee he's headed for water, food, shelter, or all of the above. I'd like to see him shake my ass now." They trotted after him. Joe could manage no more than a strolling pace. They only needed to move their feet to keep up. He turned again and repeated his command.

"Bitch, if you think you can get rid of us now, you're senile," Foster said.

"We're riding your coattails straight to the chopper, baby," Parks added. Joe took a few more steps, and when he saw they would not relent, turned to rejoin them.

"What's he doin' now? Isn't the water that way?"

"I think Magoo's confused. We just ran out of real estate that way and didn't see shit."

"Maybe we ought to take him back to the fire spot. At least we know there's someone—"

Joe reached with a right cross that landed square on Foster's orbital. The bony fist packed a shocking wallop. He staggered back a few steps and raised the knife. Joe's fists came up and he stalked forward.

"Motherfucker!" Foster swished the blade side-to-side as a warning, but the old man moved without hesitation. "I'll kill your ass!" Joe walked him down, and Foster took a few steps back to shake his head and blink his eye clear. Joe let out a cry from deep in his belly and waved his hands overhead, then clenched his fists as he tracked Foster's movements. There was no way Foster was going to run again. Despite his threats, he also had no desire to cut down someone who just stumbled out of hospice care, even if his face did hurt like a son of a bitch.

Parks swooped in from behind and threaded his arms under Joe's, and behind his head to lock him down in a full nelson. He squirmed and kicked. His legs flailed off the ground and slid for footing. Parks sat down, dragging the little man with him until he tired of fighting the hundred pound weight advantage. Foster stood between their legs and leveled the point of the blade at Joe's throat.

The old man lifted his chin to expose the flesh.

"Yo, chill! I got him. I got him."

"Look, you ornery bastard. We've had a shit day. I get that you're too old to give a rat's ass if you live or die, but we ain't. Just this mornin', we woke up warm and toasty in our bunks, with payin' jobs. Now everyone on our boat is dead, we're freezin' our balls off, tired as hell, thirsty as hell, and all we wanna do go is go the fuck home. I'm tired of bein' chased and swung at and robbed. We could've left you to die. I'd kill you now if I didn't think you'd like it. But here you are. And here we are. We just want to leave. You can have this place. Show us some water, some way of contactin' the outside world, and we're outta your hair forever. Do you understand a goddamn word of what I'm sayin'?"

A blank stare was his reply. Foster tossed his head in disgust. Parks raised the old man to his feet.

I give up," Foster said. "I don't know what to do with him."

"I say we catch and release. Something tells me he's not here alone."

"No shit. He's wearin' a cutoff shirt. Got nothin' but a knife and a sewin' kit. He's got to have handlers. A tent. Somethin'."

"Exactly. We let him go, and follow him."

"He'll see us."

"So? We can follow ten feet back. What's he gonna do? Lie down and starve to death?" Foster thought it over, then nodded. Parks' big arms gently unsnaked and he stepped back to see what their opponent would do. Joe bent, and rested his hands on his knees to gather his strength.

"Goddamn, he hits hard," Foster rubbed his eye. "Fuck. Is this still the same day?"

"You OK, buddy?" Parks leaned down to address Joe, who lowered himself to his knees. He fumbled with a knot, untied the leather belt around his waist, and threaded the purse and water bladder free. Joe lay the strip across the tops of his wrist and held out his hands.

"What's he doin'?"

"Is he telling us to tie him up?"

"Are you sayin' you surrender? You're done with your tricks?"

"I'm too tired to take prisoners," Parks said.

"Me too. Just search him. Make sure he don't have a shiv in there somewhere."

Parks felt about the man's torso, and stopped. He raised the vest to reveal a loose gridwork of beads separated by knots in different combinations, like a thin set of ribs atop the skin. It hung from a loop around his neck and another around his waist, with the back left exposed. Parks squeezed the vest while Foster admired the handiwork. They were simple designs, no writing, in a number of shapes that repeated at irregular intervals throughout the rows. None of it was colorful or ornate. It seemed like a grade school craft project. Yet there was a kind of plain beauty to it, a symmetry that Foster couldn't see, but stood apparent nonetheless.

Parks slid the vest back on and squeezed up and down his legs. "I'm not checkin' his sack or his asshole," he announced. The search concluded at the boots—more like socks than anything else. He tied the belt back around the man's loose waist with care, then stood. Foster came around to the other side, and each by an arm, they hoisted him to his feet.

"Upsy-daisy," Parks said. They backed off, and he wobbled. Again, they wrapped their arms around him. Foster held the knife in his left hand, with a map under his arm and a pelt draped over his shoulders like a scarf where it did little for warmth. Parks had to reach over the top to hang on, his neck too high for the man's arm.

"Alright. Walk," Foster said. They moved as a unit back in the direction Joe originally headed. He let his feet drag behind them. "Goddammit!" They stopped. Joe planted them again, and twisted to steer them in the opposite direction, back toward the fire where he found them.

"I thought you were goin' this way." Joe ignored him, though at least his feet cooperated.

It should have been midnight. Foster was sure of it. The horizon seemed to shrug off all the sun's advances—to cast doubt on whether the day would ever end. Here, time at once stretched out and stool still. Eons passed in an hour and his rhythms, his need to tire, to sleep, to eat and shit and move, were called into question by that one loitering star. Wherever they were, he knew it was Antarctica. His ears hurt from the cold. They'd been at it for hours, with as much time spent resting as walking. The rests were the worst. The imperfect cover of the pelt had to come off of their cores and onto the ground—the air was preferable to the rock. It leeched heat from them with every step, and to sit on it was intolerable. Light as it was, he felt they should have stopped for the night, and every time they stopped, he assumed they had. But eventually, Joe would work to his feet again. He never seemed bothered by the temperature. Maybe he was still trying to run them to death, having exhausted the rest of his arsenal. It was clear that he couldn't move far without support, though.

Foster felt the now-familiar tug of a group turn, never quite sure if it was initiated by Joe, the sheer mass of Parks stumbling off course, or some unconscious group-step. There were no trails here—but it always felt like they walked a line that was well-traveled, and begged for traffic. Joe's thick fur boots looked luxurious to his blistered soles. He was no stranger to going shoeless in the woods of his youth, but working on ships had cured him of the habit and softened his feet.

"Are we walking back to Chile?" Parks asked.

"Feels that way," Foster said. "I think we need to figure out what we're gonna do if it turns out to be an ambush."

"My plan is to get killed."

"I'm bein' for real, here. We have to consider that he might not be leadin' us to water, or help, or anything we want."

"Oh, I considered it. I also considered the fact that I'm not entirely sure if I'm holding him up, or the other way around. If you're asking me to run, or stab more than one or two Eskimos from a stationary position, I'm gonna choose a quick death. I've had enough of the slow kind."

"You might get your wish. This guy's no quitter. If he can't kill us himself, he's liable to bring us to someone who can."

"Good."

"Don't make me call D-BAP."

"You can't call it twice in a forty-eight hour period, fucker. You know the by-laws. I can be as big a pussy as I want."

"Well maybe you got to the end of your rope, but I ain't there yet. I didn't survive a shipwreck in freezin' waters and the longest attempted murder in human history to die so easy."

"That's where I was a few hours ago. Not all of us wiggled up on the shore." He held out his shin, black and blue and caked with blood. "Now? I could go either way."

Foster rolled his eyes. "Maybe you can be the knife decoy this time and I'll be the one who hauls ass."

"Are you going to bring that up every fifteen minutes for the rest of my short life? We decided to run after a spirited debate. Not my fault if you were slow to act."

"Decided. Way I remember, that debate was still in process, and I was the only one arguin' for retreat."

"Cold can fuck with your memory."

Foster shook his head. "If you wanna spend your final moments revisin' history, go right ahead. Me? I'ma scrap if I still have the chance of a snowball's pube in Hell's barbershop."

Joe stopped them in their tracks.

"You need to sit, pal?" Parks offered. The old man's eyes fell on a ridge in front of them. Foster squinted to follow his gaze, and saw nothing remarkable. Then Joe swung his head to the sea. The sailors were surprised at how far they'd come. Their path turned inland when the coast route was blocked, and they lost sight of the water until now. It appeared again, a pale gray line on the horizon, miles back and hundreds of feet below. It was impossible to reconcile what lay behind, still and shimmering in the low sun, with the dark, roiling body that battered them within an inch of their lives. Their guide once more switched his gaze to the ridge, then back to the water.

"Choose, Fucker." Joe spoke.

Parks and Foster turned whiter than when the cold waters spat them out. The sparse stubble on Joe's upper lip curled in a smile. He began with a chuckle. It gathered momentum into a deep belly laugh, and ended in a coughing fit. They took him by his elbows to steady him.

"You have been deceived by Tunguk." He interrupted himself with a round of hacks. "No one is my father. My uncles are Wakanat and Hawe, Junnlauk and Gunnlauk, Uppinikuanatuk and Akawake."

"Easy, Joe." Parks patted his back.

"I am called Tunguk, Brother." He found his balance and his voice.

"Son of a bitch." Foster shook his head and grinned.

"Dude, you were spying on us the whole time!" Parks practically applauded him. "I'm trying to think what I said. Hope I didn't offend your mom or talk about murdering you. In my culture it's a great dishonor to tell people what was said about them behind their back, so just keep in mind anything I may have mentioned while he was gone," he thumbed Foster, "is between us."

"Now you must choose. Over the hill are my people. That way," he pointed the direction they'd come from, "you have seen."

Parks clapped him on the back. "I'm going for the native hospitality."

"This man just tried to disembowel you, and then pretended he couldn't speak English so he could spy on us. You think those people are gonna welcome you with open arms?"

Parks shrugged. "I feel like we bonded."

"It is true," Tunguk said. "We have *akmanuak*. In your tongue, it is rope that binds as one."

"Enjoy that." Foster started to turn.

"Hear me, Fucker," Tunguk stopped him. "You and Brother have carried me to my people, delayed my death. I have a bond, as you say, to delay your deaths as many days and nights as it can be."

"It's Foster," he touched his chest, "and Parks," he pointed. "Not Fucker and Brother."

"For the Mattaka, a name is what others call you."

"Yeah, well for my people, you call a man Fucker one-too-many times, you get tuned up. Anyway, we'll pass on the whatever-you-said. Aka…ban…"

"It is decided. You have the soft feet of a foreigner. You will die without my help. If you return to the coast, I am too weak to follow."

"Great. So we hang with your boys," Parks said.

Tunguk was silent. Foster considered him. "And what are the chances that your people won't just kill us?"

"There are no chances. If we go, we will see."

"Aren't you some kind of elder?" Parks asked.

"I am the oldest."

"Maybe you can put in a good word for us."

Tunguk looked out over the coast.

"You want us to go, don't you?" Foster said. "Release you from your responsibility."

"Akmanuak is released but by death."

"But you can't help us there. If we go wait for a rescue ship, there's nothin' you can do."

A weak smile passed over Tunguk's face. "Ah. Will a ship come for you?"

"Eventually."

"Then it is best."

"You just said we would die without you," Parks frowned.

"If a ship does not come, you will die. It is better than to return with me. I am bound to tell you the truth, Brother."

Foster looked at Parks, faltering, pale and huddled in the skin. An egg-sized lump swelled on his leg under the gash, while dried blood crept down like a moraine. He told himself his friend couldn't make it any farther. That he must be cold, tired, miserable. If they couldn't hike up to the snow line for water, they would die before anyone got to the rescue beacon. Rescue might take weeks to happen upon them. Parks wouldn't last. He'd quit if he had to. And as soon as he thought it, he knew he was looking at his friend and seeing himself.

He nodded in the direction of the ridge. "But you'll protect us."

Tunguk seemed to think it over. "There are many things under the sun. Many strong clans. Some who steal, who take women, hate foreigners. Young men who meet the shore as when the sea returns, who cause much suffering and destruction. Beasts who kill you, take your boat. Great powers who take your life because they do not see you when they stretch out for sleep. Even the spirits do battle. These are the perils of the day. The night is worse."

"Leopard seals have also been known take a swimmer by the leg and drag them to an icy grave." Parks chimed in. "Saw that in a documentary once. Just sayin'."

"I am old," Tunguk ignored him. "What I can offer, is yours."

Truth was, Foster thought he'd won. They'd outrun the old man, disarmed him, and done a good deed by helping him out. The idea that the tables had turned made his asshole pucker. Now they had no more than the good word and the protection of their only enemy on the continent. Parks, for once, was silent. As if he knew one wrong word would break the thin possibility of Foster agreeing to Tunguk's offer, and knew equally well that all of his words were wrong.

"Do yall have water?" It was a throwaway concession. The moment it was out, he knew he said it to give himself plausible deniability as having negotiated, having taken a role in determining his fate.

"Aye."

Foster shook his head at himself as he joined them. Tunguk extended his hand. Foster put his out to shake it, but Tunguk pulled back.

"The knife." He said. "I will hold it when we approach."

Foster glanced up at the ridge. All that crap about whatever-it-was-called—was that even a thing? This dude was tricks on top of tricks. He glanced up at the ridge and wondered if there were even people over there. His eye still throbbed from the punch.

All the fight left his body when he placed the handle in Tunguk's palm. It was an act of surrender. Tunguk sheathed it, and let out a long sigh that made Foster wonder if the old man didn't feel the same way. He took a wobbly step. They moved to help, but he waved them off. With deliberation, one foot followed the other. The curved posture rose, though it seemed like a pain to hold it. Tunguk took another step, a pause, and another.

They struggled to control their speed down the hill into the little valley between a pair of long spurs running from the nearest peak. The wind that hounded them up had died, leaving it a solid ten degrees warmer. Parks' heart sunk as the details emerged. Carcasses of what looked like dogs but were probably seals hung on bone racks in the open air. He counted six things that would qualify as structures—round-top huts covered in sewn hide. There wasn't even a fire going. It was less a village than a hobo camp. Something you'd see in a hall of the natural history museum. Their arrival did nothing to interest the people below. Most of the ones ignoring them were women, and most of those were a bit old for his taste. All of them were dressed in a similar manner to Joe, who did his damnedest to hide his recent near-death experience. It was doubtful if any of them succeeded.

By the time they moseyed in, two men in their fifties or sixties had made their way to the edge of the huts. Joe turned to the sailors, and they understood he meant for them to hang back while he spoke. Their torsos were cold, but both of them wore their pelts around the waist like a bath towel. Maybe half-naked white dudes made regular appearances here, for all the fuss it caused. Parks craned his ear to see if he could gauge their fate by the tones. Their language was all native babble.

A pair of eyes studied them from a flap lifted at the bottom of one hut, where a number of children were shooed as soon as they arrived. It was hard to tell how many people lived here. It seemed like there were more ants when they were up high than he could see now. The few left minded their beeswax, mostly arts and crafts, a few loiterers. The only young woman in sight stood at the entrance to the hut where the kids were sent. A black tattoo marked her chin, and her top hung open, exposing her left breast while she unapologetically fed an infant in plain sight—like some sort of Californian, he thought. She glared hard at them, to the point it that gave him the creeps. Still, Parks got the sense she was more so guarding an exit than keeping anyone out.

A pair of older women emerged from a different hut and wordlessly set leather bladders full of water and bowls of dried meat at their feet. Foster seemed miffed that they left without acknowledging his profuse Southern gratitude. Parks was already on to solving the puzzle of dining while holding up your pants. He finished his water and was on to the meat before his friend could even start. It took him little time to catch up, though, and soon they were just as thirsty and hungry as before. The women made another pass while Tunguk did more listening than speaking. Parks slowed on the second pass, turned his attention back to the talk. With his stomach quieting, he had a vague recollection that his life may depend on what the old man said about them. He strained for anything sensible. An English word, or something that could mean yes or no. You could always tell the "yes" and "no," he learned from his Navy days. Even if you've never heard the language.

"Saber tits?" He blurted.

"What?" Foster said with his mouth full.

"Did that guy just say 'saber tits?'"

Foster snorted. "I doubt it."

"I swear that's what I heard."

"I reckon he said somethin' in his language, and that's what your brain wanted to hear."

"Why would I want to hear that? That sounds terrifying."

"I don't know, brother. I just got a feelin' if he were gonna suddenly say a random English phrase, that wouldn't be it."

"Hm." Parks wracked his imagination for the possibilities. Foster finished his second bowl and nudged his ribs, then nodded at the only two young men they'd seen, sitting thirty yards away.

"I don't get the sense we're bein' held."

"Looks a bit Down-y," Parks caught his gaze. He referred to the larger of the men, in his early twenties, who laughed to himself and fidgeted.

"Bet he's strong as fuck," Foster said. The two Reverse-Eskimos sat with the soles of their feet pressed together. Each took a grip on the same straight bone held in between them, then pulled with all his might to unseat the other. Every contest ended in the big man laughing and the other dragged across the ground until he tired of it, slapped the idiot about the ears, and settled in beside him.

"I know what you're thinking," Parks said. "We wouldn't last long."

"I'm just markin' my exits, brother. With any luck, we won't have to worry. You don't usually feed somebody first if you plan to jump their asses."

Parks allowed himself to sink into his belly, bulging with water and meat, and more than a little sick. It was still cold, but he no longer minded as much. He blinked hard and nodded himself back to his senses. A post-meal nap would be nice. He could sleep til day after tomorrow, he figured. Might not even make it to one of those tents. His attention drifted to the woman breastfeeding. A tuft of black hair poked out of the swaddle and blocked the best part of his view.

"Man, it's the simple things. Never thought I'd be full again. Much less see a naked lady." He sighed in satisfaction.

Foster considered her. "Not the best-lookin' I've seen at port, but can't say she's the worst, either. Though I'd hardly call her naked."

"I'm not even turned on," Parks' speech slowed as his eyelids dipped. "Just appreciative."

"Doubt any of these folks are more than second-cousin."

"You'd be the expert on that." Parks held his raptured gaze. "As for myself, I'm gonna stare at that one titty til I'm dragged from this mortal coil."

A pair of old women emerged from another hut with fur bundles in their arms. They gave Eskimo Joe's conversation a respectable berth as they approached the sailors.

"Dress," one said as she lay the bundles at their feet. It was the first word anyone had graced them with. At least they seemed to speak a little broken English.

"I'd prefer a male outfit if you have it," Parks joked. Not enough English to have a sense of humor, apparently. They ignored his remark. The second lay two pairs of boots, glistening with fresh oil. There was no tongue or split, only a loose top that tapered down and separate strands of leather that were probably meant to cinch them on. Everything was stitched with immaculate care, though it all somehow looked janky as hell to him.

The women stood waiting for something.

"Oh hey, you don't happen to have any Neosporin, do you?" He lifted the skirt to show his wound. "Neosporin? Antibacterial cream? No?"

The talkative one beckoned for their lap blankets.

"Oh, you'd like that, huh?" Parks grinned. Old ladies could never resist his racy charm. He was determined to endear them to a few grandmotherly spirits before the menfolk could get involved. But either they still didn't understand, or lacked the sophistication necessary to appreciate his wit. Foster handed his over. "Time for the main event," Parks tried once more. They managed to take the pelts and depart unimpressed.

"If they haven't already decided to kill us, there's no need to talk 'em into it," Foster scolded.

Four more old men joined the two who were already interrogating Eskimo Joe. Parks felt he was pretty decent at body language, but every one of them looked like they could have been discussing the results of last week's bingo game for all they gave him to work with. He shook out the pile of clothes and discovered nothing short of a wardrobe. His self-conscious haste to cover his junk was stymied by his confusion as to what he was supposed to do with everything. There was a vest like Joe's, which for some reason he threw on first, leaning forward in a useless effort for modesty. Between football and the Navy, being naked in front of crowds never bothered Parks to any degree—until now. He tossed aside a furry parka and two pair of fur pants, one of which looked hopelessly small, and shimmied into a simple trouser of the same material as the vest. There was already a belt threaded through loops, and he tied off the waist, though it fit pretty snugly. His huge thighs filled out nearly all the material, and the cuffs ended so high they might as well have been capris. Something told him they didn't have his size handy.

"Are these undies?" Foster turned over the smaller fair of fur pants, and suddenly they made sense to Parks, but he was already committed. They were more to his friend's size, and he slipped in quickly, followed by the same trousers Parks wore, though he chose the shirt over the vest. Neither put on the third pair of bottoms, a fur layer, but both snuggled into the hooded fur coat with gratitude. It hung baggy for Foster, while Parks'—likely the same size—fit perfect around the body, except for the sleeves that failed to reach his wrists. It took some finessing to work into the boots, which were much firmer than they appeared, yet lacked a rigid sole. None of the people they could see wore more than the vest layer.

"You look like a goober," Parks prodded Foster.

"Me? Bro, look at you. You look like a big gay bear who shaved his calves and forearms."

The old men broke the huddle and headed their direction. One of the younger men, who looked to be in his late fifties, took the lead.

"I am Ingut. Iake is my father. Kamapunankaman and Upisuk and Akawake are my uncles."

"Pleased to meet you, sir. Parks is the name. My old man is Marion, Jr. My uncles are Gary and Frank."

"Sir. Foster. My mom is Dawn. I got too many uncles to name."

Parks thought he saw the first ray of a smile out of Joe before it disappeared into his imagination.

"Tunguk says you are known to the Kapadak as Brother and Fucker. Please accept to be our guests. Our wives give you food and drink, and clothing for warmth. Is there anything we have not provided?"

"Do you do alterations?" Parks held up his arms.

"No sir," Foster interrupted. "Your people have been very kind."

The man nodded politely. "Tunguk tells a story. There are two more." Parks and Foster looked at one another.

"You wanna go first?"

"Doesn't matter to me," Parks said. "I can go."

"I'll go," Foster thought better of it. "Sir, first of all, many thanks to you and your beautiful wives for the hospitality. We owe you big time. You literally saved our lives."

"It is Tunguk who saves you," the man quickly clarified.

"Tunguk, then. But you as well."

"It is Tunguk, alone." He seemed almost worried, now.

"OK. OK," Foster eased his tone. "Tunguk, then. If you say." The old dude nodded for him to continue. "Anyway, we were workin' a private charter—I'll spare you the details. Our ship went down a little ways from here. We made it ashore, had a little miscommunication with Tunguk, but we got it sorted and it's all good now. We just want to go home. If you by any chance have a radio, or a sat phone we can use, or if you know where we can find someone who does, we would very much appreciate it, and we'll be out of your way in no time."

The man turned to Parks.

"What he said."

"You do not wish your own story?" He seemed alarmed at the idea.

"Nah. My tummy hurts." Ping Pong. His name melted in Parks' mind into something more memorable. Ping Pong studied him with suspicion.

"You carried these," he motioned to another old man, who handed him the maps they'd taken off Parks and Foster. "When a ship sinks, a man looks for the things he values most."

"Yeah, we just found those." Parks waved his hand. "You want 'em? We don't give a fuck."

"Those were some other dude's," Foster added. "I feel like this guy's got a better idea of where we are than some old ass maps." He nodded to Joe. "If we can just bother you for a little more water, maybe he can take us where we can get rescued?"

"The pelts. How did you come to these?"

"That wasn't you?" Foster frowned.

"Someone stole our real clothes. Orange immersion suits—kind of looks like a romper you might wear if you went hunting? No? Maybe someone you know?"

The elders stared blankly. Ping Pong shrugged it off. "Tunguk says you have akmanuak."

Parks nodded. "Oh, yeah. Total and complete akmanujad."

"We're real fortunate to have been able to help your kin," Foster added.

Ping Pong scoffed. "It is a misfortune to tie akmanuak. Tunguk is no kin." He reached forward and placed his left hand on Joe's right shoulder. Parks felt a ripple of something fan out from his gut. Their ally's face tensed, and it felt as though he was trying to say something when his eye fell to the corner and caught the sailors.

"Brother." Ping Pong addressed him head-on, his arm seeming to bar Joe from the exchange. "Where is your captain?"

Parks shrugged. "Bottom of the sea."

"And your crew?"

"Same."

He nodded. "You are strong to make shore. The water is cold."

"But the rescue ships are already on the way." Foster's jaw tightened. Parks sensed an urgency in his speech. "We need to get back soon."

"We have weighed your stories, and heard the one that is not told. Sons of Hadalis bring ill to the Mattaka."

"I don't know nothin' about no Sons of Hadalis," Foster grew somber. "We're American citizens. Veterans of the United States Navy, representin' a private interest, under Chilean registration. I realize you have no reason to believe me, but we didn't even know yall were here. We don't care what you're doin'. And we didn't come to harm you."

"I believe your story." Ping Pong took his hand from Joe's shoulder. "Many elders spoke against you. I was among them. They wished to see you killed." The bottom dropped out of Parks' heart. "But Tunguk favored you with fine words. He asks to delay your death. He is old. That is all he can do. Let it be known among the Mattaka that Tunguk honors his bond. You will have our tukit. Water and meat. Our hospitality."

"Jesus." Parks clutched his chest in relief.

"When the hunters return after sleep, you will be killed."

3

SONG OF THE HUNGRY DOG

Saltwater stung the eyes and rolled down the cheeks of the big man—who was not a sailor, who was not a Son of Hadalis, who was not a survivor. A breathy laugh burst loose on the back of a sigh. It was relief he felt, so unexpected it brought a brave smile to his face. There were few ways left to him to take his sentence. A foundered ship told him that morning, and a wave soon after. A storm, a sea cliff, and old man with a knife repeated the verdict. It wasn't that he disbelieved this one. In fact, it was the opposite. His fill of miracles were done, and knowing brought him a softness that embraced all around him. There was no way a day like this would let him live. What kind of fool could have thought so? And what kind of hero, engineered in a secret government lab, could have done any better? He would be allowed to sleep. Sleep sounded so precious, and it brought a kind of victory. For all his efforts, he would see morning. The tension of clinging to life streamed out of his eyes. He felt no shame, and even a bit of pride. Here was a helicopter mechanic, a Son of Neptune, the last man lost from the *Qarapara*.

There was pity on Foster's face. He hated that, and laughed again in attempt to show that he was fine—it was an admirable thing he felt. But that only seemed to deepen his friend's concern. For his part, Foster didn't seem to be taking it with the same kind of grace. Pursed lips, cold glare, a slight flush—Parks had seen that look before as many times as an officer demanded something idiotic of him, and Foster ran short of responses that didn't end in court martial.

"Hospitality, huh? That's what you call it?" Ping Pong waited for him to answer his own question. "Two strangers survive a shipwreck by the skin of their teeth, show up at your door cold and starvin', askin' nothin' but a rest and a little water before they move on, and your notion of hospitality is a one-night stay of execution? What the fuck did we ever do to you? We could've let this man die," he motioned to Joe. "Sounds like it would've been better for us."

Ping Pong nodded. "Aye. Do you refuse our hospitality, then?"

"Nah, dog, we'll take it," Parks cut in.

Foster considered it. "What, so you'll kill us now instead? No. But if you're actin' like you're doin' us some kind of favor—"

"It is Tunguk we favor. You are enemies of the people."

"*Enemies?* We never harmed nobody."

"You harm the land by your coming. You see her in her home, and speak of her to others. It is a man of shame who kills with his eyes and his mouth."

"The fuck is he on about?" Foster asked Parks.

"This man believes you are spies," Joe answered.

"Tunguk," Foster tested the name. "You gotta tell him."

"I, too, believe you are spies."

"Spies for who? We're civilians. And I guarantee you, the Navy don't give a fuck about yall. We didn't even know there were people here. Parks! Tell him we ain't snitches."

The whole thing felt desperate and useless. "Nah. He doesn't care."

Foster stung from the rebuff. He brooded for second, and Parks thought he was about to swing, or take off without him. Then the next look came—the one when he would realize the officer was wrong in every conceivable way, and he was powerless to do anything about. A pang of guilt stabbed him. Foster was a proud dude. He might have stood up for himself if anyone stood with him. It was too much trouble to go back that route, just as he began to feel the bittersweet peace of acceptance. But his friend looked like a sad dog, or a child who had been turned away to sulk without consolation.

"Spies, Navy, traders, whalers. No matter. It is trouble for Mattaka." Ping Pong looked Joe over. The slump had returned to his spine, and he faced his toes as he fought through a spell of shallow breath. "Do not run," Ping Pong continued. "There is no place on the island for you."

The old men went their ways. Even Joe went off, disappearing into the farthest hut without a word of apology or condolence. The little camp returned to its quiet order. The wives, to their huts. The young men to their laughter and their roughhousing. The carcasses once again caught Parks eye, and he wondered briefly if they would end up curing next to them. The light feeling of being awake at a time when you know you should long since have slept came over him, giving him the sense of stealing time in a secret world. The wee hours of the morning here were hardly distinguishable from the day. Now it occurred to him that even the few spare people who hadn't taken to the tents might have been odd for this time. Did their sleep change with the light? Or were they keeping an eye peeled? Not a soul made a pretense of guarding them. They could slink off at any time. That confidence told him Ping Pong was right: there was no place on the island for them. Foster must have been taking the same survey. They looked at one another, and neither spoke.

Parks extended his hand.

"I don't know how to feel about that," Foster left it hanging.

"I've been trying 'ambivalent.' Working so far."

"I'll shake it later if I have to." Foster walked to the center, near the racks where seal skin stretched and raw meat cured. There were three of the little dwellings to each side, and a lane between that lead to either of the low ridges that hemmed in the camp. Parks gathered both their spare articles of clothing and followed.

"There's gotta be somethin'." Foster scanned the area.

"That's probably what this guy said," Parks nodded at the cut-up seal.

"Some kind of a weapon. What'd they get *him* with? Maybe there's a rifle."

Parks took in the racks: triangular structures of large bones forming two A-frames, with smaller bone lashed between at intervals. "*2001: A Space Odyssey.* That's how I'm picturing your last stand."

"Mine? You don't think it's yours, too?"

Parks shrugged.

"Anyway, I've never seen it."

"The monkeys? The classic bludgeoning scene? Come on, dude!"

"What's that got to do with space?"

"Uh, it was our starting point, obviously. We were savage animals until we touched the big black rock, and learned how to use tools to crack skulls. It was the birth of Man. Bigger than the first steps on the Moon."

Foster perked up. "You might have a point there."

"I clearly have a point. I can't believe you're going to die with a basic ignorance of classic American cinema that causes you to miss opportunities staring you in the face," he waved his palm at the rack. "I'm not sure I'm down to join you, but I might see how it's going and jump in if you get up a quick lead."

"To hell with weapons, what do they *not* have?"

Parks looked around. "Everything? Fire, power tools, patience and kindness, food safety, personal hygiene…"

"Modern-ass brains. These people think it's the Stone Age."

"What're you going to do, build a wheel and roll away?"

"I don't know, but we're lookin' at a culture that's almost entirely resistant to adoptin' science and technology, to the point that they'll live a hunter-gatherer lifestyle on the last continent that we don't fuck with just to get some peace and quiet. There's gotta be some part of that we can exploit."

"Boats." A grin spread over Parks face. "That dude said it was an island."

Foster lit up to match. He clapped his friend on the arm. "I never thought I'd live long enough for you to be right about somethin'!" He laughed. "Of course they gotta have boats. They didn't swim here." They spun around in search but saw nothing.

"They said the hunters are coming back. That's probably where the boats are."

"And the weapons. I haven't seen much other than women and old people."

"True, but even if we do manage to hit everyone in the face with a drumstick, we still have hunters to worry about. And if we do take their boats, what are the chances they're seaworthy for the Drake's Passage? That's the only place any better than here."

"One thing at a time, brother."

"I don't want to bash some grandmas if all it gets me is shot or drowned. You gotta think this through."

"Man, the only time you ever think past the first step of anything is when you don't want to do it."

"OK. So who do you want to kill first? The breastfeeding mother, or the retard?" Foster visibly recoiled from the blow of what he hadn't considered.

"Well, what are our options?"

Parks' face fell again into resignation. "We could die. I told you back there, either these people save us, or they don't. After all the shit we've been through, I'm not sure we're even meant to survive."

"Meant by who?"

Parks had no answer. Beneath Foster's anger he could sense a helpless frustration. The two young Reverse-Eskimos now sat against the outside wall of one of the dwellings, exchanging a tired word now and then. The baby was still, held in a low, soothing song. No one else remained outside. The word "hunters" rung—he saw a band of rough men who looked more like California Indians straight off the Res, dressed in Real Tree and carrying AR-15s, shotguns, compound bows. Probably good dudes to drink with. They bounced across the water, leaning out of Zodiacs. A small armada weaving its way home.

And there was Foster, clinging to the last shred of fight left in him. Parks was too tired to care if he lived or died. It was satisfying enough to think of his great plans. Lists and lists of all he would do with ease and nobility. None of it actually needed to happen. He knew the possibility, and that made it feel lived. Nor did he care if he sat stoic and took his bullet, or got mowed down murdering the weaker members of some tribe he'd never heard of. All moral victories would expire with him, and there would be no rewards or consequences. But he wasn't sure Foster felt the same. He looked like a desperate ember, flaring this way and that for a scrap of something and a breath of air to keep the fire glowing.

His hand wrapped firm around one of the bone shafts in the rack, and he looked at his friend. "Say the word."

"What?"

Parks glanced back to the bone. "Say the word." Something primal coursed through his arm and flushed his cheeks. He didn't think he could make it, and didn't want to. The fear left him, and he grew. He could no longer find the high ground from which to pity himself. When that seeped away, he was eight feet tall, and he would smash every helpless child on his way out if that meant they could go together, grinning and cussing and long-remembered.

It felt like Foster took a step back in spirit. His fire dipped and stuttered. He took another slow look around, then brushed past Parks.

"I gotta talk to Tunguk."

Parks withdrew his hand. He almost felt ashamed, as if he had crossed a line. It quickly turned to annoyance with Foster, because he couldn't just either accept it or fight it. Parks was willing to do either. He was willing to do anything—he just didn't know what.

"Suit yourself."

"Where are you goin'?" Foster saw him veer off.

"If this is my last night alive, I'm gonna see if I can't bang this face tat chick." He went a little farther, then called a little too loud: "Let me know if you come up with an escape plan." The three natives who were still awake stared at them.

Foster cringed. He looked to the sky like a prayer, half-hoping to see a chopper beating down the coast. It was probably too early for that. So it was an island. Even if they had made the peninsula, the prospects would have been the same. Millions of square miles of rock and ice, separated from humanity by the most violent ocean in the world. Nothing more than a lichen grew. The interior was white-capped. The water, freezing. All things were hard, the hardness of rock and ice. Even the clothes, the shelters, and the fibers that bound them were made of animal skin and sinew. Nothing here lived unless it could kill another thing that wanted to live. So those things that survived were as hard as the country that bred them. *Give me the Blue Ridges and a .22*, he thought. *I could live to be as old as Tunguk.*

He wasn't even sure what the were up against. Six little houses didn't feel like a lot, but they had arrived too late to see how many people would be up and about. The hunters were gone. There was no way of telling if they were single-family apartments, or stacked twelve-deep. What he'd seen of the tribe wasn't much, yet he had to wonder if they showed him exactly what they wanted him to see. Maybe the heavy-hitters waited just out of sight. Maybe there was another camp like it just over the way, and another after that, ready to pitch in at a moment's notice. When your life's threatened, he thought, the only things that make sense are to run, or to fight. Yet here he was with is hands drawn up into his sleeves, gripping them shut from the inside for warmth. Did he even want to live? He was sure of it. The threat wasn't quite immediate-enough to stir him. It was quiet—immaculate weather for this place. The whole continent felt haunted to him. Not by ghosts of men, but by things much larger, difficult to feel or explain. It felt haunted for these people, too. After they threw his body in the sea, they would wait for the Sun to disappear and bring freezing, months-long dark-ness and an avalanche of wind that scoured everything that stuck up off the plain. Or a hellish ferry back to Tierra del Fuego. The thought of being in that ocean again made him quiver with despair. Foster never thought he'd see a human life again. Even if the only ones around wanted him dead, it still felt better than being alone with the elements. What held him where he stood was the same thing that held the natives plastered to a rock waiting for a hunting party to return with fresh meat to dry in the open air and eat raw. What else were they going to do?

He threw back the flap and ducked into the last tent—the one where Tunguk disappeared. When it fell closed behind him, all that remained was a shaft of light on the floor. A long oval stretched from a circular ventilation hole in the center of the roof. A metallic scrape greeted his ears. Something dragged back and forth at a steady rhythm. His eyes struggled to adjust as he took a seat on the ground. A shape moved across from him, a dim outline of a shadow on a dark wall.

Foster sure as hell blamed the man—it wasn't their fault their ship went down, or their choice where they washed up. But he felt no animosity toward him. Not even for the others. Of course they couldn't trust foreigners who showed up out of the blue. These people had little more than a fingertip grip on their day-to-day lives. Even back where he was from, there were places that a stranger wasn't likely to walk back out of if he turned down the wrong drive in the mountains. He was certain he would still be alive first thing in the morning. None of these folks had much more purchase than that. Least of all, the old man in the dark with the tired heart.

His eyes guessed at the shape of the long knife turning side to side. It had a soothing effect. Something about the sound of metal brought him home to a place where all he heard was the burble of water, the clack of smooth rocks, feet slapping the ground. Each stroke sung the gritty harmony of a dark stone and a bevel.

"How can you see what you're doin'? I can't see shit."

"Those who cannot do without seeing do not spend night on Ajatse."

Tunguk didn't offer any more, and Foster let the silence stand. He had adjusted enough now to see they were alone in a round hut, a few unidentifiable items scattered along the perimeter. It could probably sleep eight people comfortably, though he had the feeling they crammed a few more than that come winter.

Light flooded in from the flap, blinding him again. He could tell by the size of the intruder it was Parks.

"Not even a handy?"

"It's all about putting in the numbers," Parks replied. "Who's that, Joe?"

"It is good you came, Brother. You and Fucker must stay now."

"Look, I know we didn't meet on the best terms, but you can call me Foster. That's Parks. If anything, I should be Brother and he should be Fucker. I'm the one came back to get you when you went down."

"You must be careful how you name yourself to Mattaka. We cannot change unless all who call you do so."

"No one calls us that but you."

"These are your words. Ingut and the elders know you this way."

"Because you told 'em!" Foster said in exasperation.

"I think Fucker has a nice ring to it." Parks probably had a shit-eating grin if his face were visible.

"It is good. Some men do not have a name. They are called Wanderer. You are fortunate to be Brother and Fucker. If you are still called this when the hunters return, you will be rid of it, then." He chuckled.

"So is that it, then?" Foster felt his blood grow hot with frustration. The scrape of the knife held the rhythm of the second hand as the oval of light drifted almost imperceptibly over the floor. "You're done helpin' us?"

"I do what I can."

"Well no offense, but so far what you *can* do, ain't really cuttin' it. But you know these people and this situation better than we do. If that's all you got, fine. Tell us what *we* can do."

"Wait."

"Wait." He snorted. "For what? For the hunters to get back and kill us?"

The blade appeared in the little spot of light. Tunguk angled it so that it glinted toward him, and passed it through the length on both sides. He resumed work with the stone.

"Scale of one to ten. How much is this gonna hurt?" Parks asked.

"Yeah, maybe you can at least give us an idea of how this is gonna go down." Foster realized the old man may not recognize his figures of speech. "What's gonna happen to us?"

"We will see."

"You don't know *nothin'*? There's not one goddamn thing you can tell us, to maybe give us some idea of what to expect, so we can at least be ready for it?"

"I know one thing." The scraping stopped. They hardly breathed while they waited for him to continue. "When the men return, you will be taken to Urkuk." Foster paused, expecting more to follow. After a moment, the blade moved again across the stone.

"Oar cook? Where is that?"

"In your tongue, he is the fire who stands behind the shadow. Where souls go to get warm before they enter the next world. Where you must complete the tasks you have not finished."

"Is it a guy, or a place?" Parks saved Foster the trouble of revealing his confusion.

"It can be many things," Tunguk said. "He is the deceiver, who wears masks and calls men to their death. For those who are not deceived, who see his face, he has any secrets to teach."

"In other words, they're gonna kill us," Foster restated.

"No. They will first honor you, bring you to a table with food and drink, and women, where you will have your fill."

"And then they kill us?"

"How long would you say we have at this table, to do our thing, with the food and the women and all?" Parks broke in.

"You have again been deceived by Tunguk." He let out a modest laugh. Foster wrinkled his nose in disgust.

"Glad to see you still have your sense of humor," Parks said.

"We have a saying. When a man loses his sense of humor, he is a corpse, though he walks."

"What a clever sayin'." Foster said dryly. "Good thing we have you to cheer us up in our final hours."

"You must sleep now." Tunguk said.

"Can't say as I'm tired."

"So there's no drinking with women is what I'm understanding?" Parks clarified.

"You need rest after your journey," Tunguk drew ever-lighter strokes with his whetstone. "There is a long way yet to go."

An unease grew in Foster's breast. The rough sound of the stone washed itself smoother with every pass, until the thinnest of notes rung pure like a bow drawn across a string with a feather touch. He wanted to make eye contact, but even a foot away the man beside him was a dim specter. His hand reached out and squeezed the tremendous knee.

"Hey, Parks?" His voice rose high and soft.

"Yeah, Fucker?"

"You thinkin' what I'm thinkin'?"

"Nope."

"Tunguk. Whose job is it to kill us?" He felt the leg tense under his hand.

"The people of the clan."

"Anyone in particular?"

"Joe? Hey, buddy? You wouldn't be planning to cut our throats while we sleep, would you?"

"I am forbidden."

"Then why are you spending so much time on that elephant circumciser?"

"I do not know these words.

"The knife. Why are you sharpening a knife?"

He ran it through the light shaft again, then lay the blade across his thumbnail with the utmost care. Little more than gravity carried it down, peeling off a thin sliver of nail. Tunguk flicked it off the bevel.

"Akmanuak."

"I gotta be honest, brother, I don't understand shit about your culture. All I know is I ain't about to fall asleep with you sittin' over me like that. And if this is my last night, I might just go for a little walk." Foster started to get up.

"It is too late."

"Why is that?"

"They wait outside the tukit."

"So?"

"You are expected."

Foster's eyes fell on the door flap. There was no way to tell if anyone stood on the other side waiting for him, or if Tunguk was up to another one of his tricks.

"They expect me to walk out?"

"There will be many waiting. They know we have akmanuak."

"Which means…?"

"That Joe's got our back." Parks interjected. "Right Joe?"

"I must do all I can to delay your death. Ingut knows. There will be men at arms."

"I'm totally fuckin' lost. So you're back on our side?"

"Aye."

"But we're not leavin'?"

"No. We must sleep. The men will return soon. Then, there will be no escape. While we sleep, those outside must be alert. They will grow tired. Then we go." Foster heard the blade slide into the leather sheath. The vague shape of Tunguk curled into a ball on his side. Parks clapped Foster's thigh and rustled with anticipation. He felt it, too. It was less than a hope. Just enough to allow denial of what was bound to await them. That was all he needed.

"Won't your people be mad at you?" Foster's tone was almost apologetic.

It was some time before the old man answered. "They know it is my curse."

"One man's curse is another two men's blessing," Parks said.

"You have so far seen one side." Tunguk's voice now sounded thin and frail. "Sleep."

It must have been one of his jokes. Foster didn't yet understand the local humor, but sleeping for a few hours before a fight for survival was not a serious proposition. He lay on his side in the fetal position. The contours of the rock managed to find every stiff, sore corner of muscle, every protruding knob of bone. He'd slithered into every layer of clothing they gave him, and still he shook, though he was so warm he could feel sweat pooling. The walls of the hut flapped lazily between a frame of huge bones that arched over them, tensioned together with leather rope. His night vision caught up once he learned to turn away from the small light skating around the room. There were piles of fur, sacks, rope, odd objects littering the sides—everything except a weapon.

Any bit of rest would have paid dividends. Never in his life had he thought it was possible to be so tired. A couple of hours ago, he was ready to die in a berserker rage. They would have to pry him from this world while he gnashed at their ankles with his dying breath. Now, he wasn't sure if he could roll over. Whatever adrenaline-fueled delusions he held curled up to expire. In the confines of the dark walls that smelled of damp leather, the possibilities were suddenly much narrower. He was no stranger to the chaos of a good brawl, where fists flew at any of many targets and he might even get lost in the melee. This was not that. All eyes and weapons would be upon him. If he could batter a hole in the defense, it would be a mad sprint, with someone faster than Tunguk in pursuit. He hoped to God the old man had a plan, but for the moment, he was snoring a whistle. Foster wondered if he had some kind of alarm to tell him the right moment to go, or if they were supposed to wake him up.

"Fucker," A whisper came. "Hey Fucker, you asleep?"

"No."

"Me neither. I'm trying to visualize success."

"OK." The memory of Parks booking it as the knife slashed their way stung him. He recalled the tears that streamed down his friend's face when they were told of their deaths.

"You know, like when you shoot a free throw? There's studies that prove if you imagine yourself making the free throw over and over again, your statistical odds go up."

"If I were you, I'd imagine it's a half-court shot."

"Not literally a free throw. I'm imagining hordes of natives swarming us, and we're just cutting them down like Uma Thurman."

"Yeah?"

"Absolutely. You have a Roman sword and a shield, and I have a trident. You know what that is right?"

"Like in the Little Mermaid."

"Exactly. A fucking trident. And you're just blocking fools my way, and I'm forking them and raising them up and flinging the body at a big pile of charging bad guys, knocking them all down."

"I was thinkin' about somethin' similar, but—I don't wanna call it a dream, cause I'm awake. But in my head, I couldn't see a way out, and they just overrun us."

"Cut that shit out, bro. You gotta visualize success."

Foster never walked into a fight thinking he didn't have a shot. He'd damn sure been corrected a few times, but this was the first time it felt like a meaningless gesture.

"What kind of weapon do you have?" Parks pressed.

"I'll leave the success shit to you. Somebody's gotta take care of the reality."

"Nope. You're in this. What kind of weapon do you see yourself holding?"

Foster groaned.

"Come on. Arm yourself."

This wasn't a fight he cared to waste energy on. "Fine. AK-47."

"Be realistic. Did you see any AKs lying around?"

"About as many as I saw tridents."

"You have a Roman short sword and a shield."

"OK."

"Joe has his big knife. OK, go."

"What am I doin'?"

"You're describing what you see happening in a low voice so we don't wake up Joe. Old people need their sleep."

"Alright. I see—also hordes of natives." Foster began.

"Good."

"The hunters came back early and there's hundreds of 'em."

"Fuck yeah there are. What weapons do they have?"

"Regular ones. Like what they actually had outside."

"Boring, but OK."

"Even the women are armed."

"A whole company of *saber tits*. Now we're talking. What are they wearing?"

"The men have on—"

"The women, faggot."

"Regular clothes. Fur skins that cover everything except their faces. And they're all fat and ugly."

"We'll agree to imagine that differently. What are they doing?"

"Attacking us. They fight just like the men."

"And how do we respond?"

At once he could see it. The game evaporated and the black walls of the hut came alive for him. An axle of light spun from the hole in the center of the hut, and suddenly he was outside, surrounded by warriors. Tunguk on his left. Parks on his right. He could see the hillside crawling with them. Foster regretted making them ugly. They were perhaps even more terrifying, barking at him like huskies. Goading them to advance. The Reverse-Eskimos took turns darting in, swept back by Parks' long trident. Foster held his shield tight and sword cocked, ready to swipe. A great tension built between the sides like a line stretched tighter and tighter until it snapped. The vacuum filled with a rush.

"Here they come. It's hard for them to get inside your reach. One or two manages it. They're tryin' to get you but you ignore 'em cause you know I got it. I cut 'em down. Tunguk cuts 'em down, too. He's slow, but he ain't afraid of shit."

"Bodies pile up."

"They're pilin' up. But we're gettin' tired."

"Only stronger. We only grow stronger."

"No. It ain't realistic. We're tired. They know it. One of 'em…cuts a big vagina gash across your other shin. I'm wounded in the arm. Tunguk is covered in blood but we can't tell whose. They just keep comin' in waves.

Wave after wave, like the ocean. You stick one and swing him over to me, and I roll him over my shield to Tunguk. He stabs him. We're doin' ninja shit. Arrows and spears are flyin' like quail when a dog spooks 'em. I keep havin' to catch 'em on my shield. I'm thinkin', why am I the only one with a shield? And off in the distance, I see…a whole army. Not Indians. People dressed all in black, some of 'em on horses. Armor and weapons. And they're pourin' down our way. Every second I think the last ones had to have just topped the hill, but they're pourin' and foamin' like a Guinness. And we have to run. The natives are runnin', too. Not after us, just away."

"Let's undo the running. No more running."

"We run and run. Everyone disappears, but we realize the place we ran to is the same as the one we left. It doesn't matter if they catch us or not, cause nowhere we go is any better a predicament. And we're always tryin' to find this or that, but mostly water. We just want water."

"Timeout. OK, yours sucks. Mine'll have to carry us. In mine, we're fighting, but instead of the ugly—"

"We go now."

They startled at Tunguk's voice. He sat tall. Foster looked at the oblong light on the floor. It squashed back on itself and moved noticeably toward the center, though still far off. That was a place it would have to dream of. The sun would never be straight overhead here. It was long light, long shadows all the year round.

Tunguk rose to a crouch—the roof was no more than four feet high—and crossed to their side. He wobbled and toppled. Foster caught his arm and held off the brunt of the impact.

"Whoa, brother. Don't stand up so fast." The old man took a moment to collect himself. "You sure you're good?"

"We go now."

"How do you know?"

"I cannot know. I guess."

"So what's the plan," Park scooted close. "They're probably guarding the front door. Is there some sort of emergency exit?"

"This is the door," he indicated.

"And so what's the plan? Walk out the front? And then what?"

"We cannot know until we see."

"Yeah, but we can have some goals and contingencies," Foster said. "You know: they do that, we do this. Some hot routes and audibles, and shit." Tunguk was silent but for his light, wheezy breath. "What, you just wanna wing it?"

"Let's talk weapons. You got any knives or tridents?"

"I have my knife."

"Any more we can borrow?"

"No."

"Firearms? Rocks? Bones to club with?" Parks probed. "We'll take anything."

"There is nothing to take." He grasped the flap. "Stay in my shadow."

The light outside was blinding. Parks and Foster scrambled after him as their eyes adjusted. How could Tunguk see anything? Foster remembered that he didn't need to. His heart raced like he just ran up a hill, and the second he was out he realized he was too stiff to stand up straight. His left hand pressed into Tunguk's shoulder. The shapes in front of them settled into vague form. Two men, the idiot and his friend. The smaller one held a short spear of knapped stone and the other, a club. Tunguk stopped. Foster's eyes darted frantically, but he saw no one else.

The teen with the spear stepped forward. "Tunguk." He rattled off a few sentences in their native tongue. Foster caught "Brother," then "Fucker." There was half a smile on his face, and whatever he said sounded like a well-rehearsed proclamation. It was friendly. Respectful. But there was a tension to it. The spear dangled point-down at his side. A half-beat, then another short phrase that rose with inflection.

Tunguk paused long enough that he might have considered whatever question the boy posed.

"An*ka*." The second syllable bore the weight of his soft, even voice. Foster felt every bit of the resignation without having a notion of what they exchanged. The sun fell on their backs, and the cool air set off a shiver from the sweat under three layers of clothing. He felt like a child, overdressed on his first day of school, following the grown-ups lead and hoping things would work out for the best. The boy glanced at his friend, then back at Tunguk. The two held one another's eyes for long enough that Foster noticed Parks' attention flag. The boy grinned. Tunguk worked up a wry smile.

In an instant, the spear lifted. Before the weapon reached waist-high, Tunguk's hand flashed from his belt. The boy's guts spilled onto the rock as he wailed and scrambled to catch them. The big one raised his arm in an arc. Tunguk caught his elbow, ran the knife along the armpit so deep it nearly took the limb off, then swung behind to cut his throat. Three movements in under two seconds, and the youngest warriors lay dying at their feet. Foster was too shaken to even muter a profanity.

"Good thing we did my idea and ran," Parks' eyes bulged.

From the hut ahead, the young woman with the face tattoo emerged. She raised a small recurve bow, just yards away. Tunguk spun behind Parks and took his collar in one hand, using him as a human shield.

"Ah! What the fuck!" Parks tried to wriggle free, then raised his arms in surrender. Foster knew he'd he shot dead if he tried to cross the distance to the archer. His pride wouldn't let him duck behind, but he hung close and back.

An arrow zipped between Parks' forearm and ear, barely over Foster's head. Parks jerked in panic, while Tunguk fought to corral him in front. The old man's foot hooked Foster' calf and signaled him to bunch in. He didn't want them to break and run. Foster's stomach was ready to blow. The boy squirmed on the ground between them in loud agony. The woman already had another arrow nocked. Any second, he expected it to rip through his eye socket. Instead, she leveled it at Parks' chest and held.

"Dude, what the fuck did you say to her?"

"I was a fucking gentleman, I swear." Parks protested.

Foster checked his sides. The left was the shorter route up the ridge, but it was by far steeper, and there stood five men in a line at the top with spears at the ready—the elders. He looked back the way they came in, past the other huts.

"We're clear right." The lane was empty for a retreat.

Tunguk took note of both routes. "This way," he insisted. He drug them in a side-shuffle left. Foster slipped in the seeping entrails. Parks leaned to help him to his feet, and an arrow flew inches above his stooped back. Tunguk threw himself on the ground to avoid it. They all came up together to greet a third arrow peeking around the bow shaft.

"In my shadow," Tunguk said to Parks. Foster now realized that Tunguk's shadow was, in the literal sense, directly between him and the archer. The big man probably could have ripped free, but he was more afraid of the knife behind him. They inched away from the huts, toward the hill lined with old men. The woman matched their movements, her arrow never straying from its aim at center mass. She held the string at half-draw. Foster frowned.

"Why ain't she shootin'?"

"Dude, shut the fuck up."

"You are guests," Tunguk said. "Until the hunters return. Or you leave camp."

She paced this way and that, zigging and zagging for an angle around Parks. It dawned on Foster. "But you're not." Tunguk didn't need to confirm.

"Uh, aren't we leaving camp?" Parks said nervously.

"Between the heights, you will live." The elders and their spears waited on the border. Confusion and the imminent fear of death fell from the sailors.

They looked at one another. The archer seemed determined to keep leverage on them, to steer them away from the old men and back within the huts. Foster closed in and added to Tunguk's shield. The wall of fur now moved toward her. She shuffled faster. Only a few yards separated them. The string drew to her cheek. Parks hesitated, then tracked her backpedal. He broke free of the cluster, juked this way and that while Foster covered Tunguk. Then he lunged forward and grasped the arrow in one hand and the bow in the other. She threw down her quiver and drew a rocker knife with a bone handle fixed symmetrically to the spine of the U-blade. Parks tossed the bow and caught her wrist. His meaty hand pried the weapon from her grip.

"Do not hurt her," Tunguk called. Foster wasn't sure if it was out of chivalry, or the act would forfeit their hospitality. The cries of the eviscerated man made him suspect the latter. Parks released his grip.

"It is not allowed to steal a knife," Tunguk added.

"Serious?" He opened a palm toward the two young men splayed across the ground. Tunguk did not respond. Parks chucked the knife high and far over the huts. She backed off, then sounded a shrill word in her language. Behind her on the low hillside, seven more women topped the ridge with bows and headed down toward the camp. Natives emerged from each of the four far huts—another elder with a spear, and four older women with knives. He recognized the two who gave them the clothing. Had they gone Foster's way, they would now be surrounded, taking arrows from above and points from behind.

Tunguk said something to them in his language, then turned and headed for the five elders on the hill. The archers from the opposite side hurried to catch up into range, and the three men quickened their step. The ones from the village did their best to pace them, but did not approach. The first woman, now unarmed, let them scurry past her. She'd lost interest in the pursuit, and Foster didn't blame her. She was lucky not to lie with the other two who met them.

The ragged sound of the old man's breath turned his attention ahead. As soon as they met the grade, they slipped under his arms to support him and slowed to a walk. That would be a fine thing, if one-third of their outmatched forces died of a heart attack strolling into battle. In essence, it was a charge. They slipped and meandered left to right to reduce the grade, worn to useless, but if they didn't break that line when they reached the top, it was done. It felt like a pathetic game of red rover. The natives from the camp formed a second wall at the bottom to cut off their retreat and await the arrival of the arrows. Though he couldn't stand up straight, Tunguk seemed non-fucked over the whole affair. Nor did the elders look particularly threatened by the advance of a single geriatric and two unarmed fools from distant shores. Foster heard the sharp chip of rock behind him as the first speculative shot fell. They cut the curves and aimed straight up. He hoped Parks' imagination was up to something special, because he couldn't see an inkling of a chance. The spears lifted and pointed downward in a line.

Tunguk stopped them ten paces short.

"There was been bloodshed. Will there be more?" He spoke in English. Another arrow nipped just short of their heels. Ingut held up a hand, and the volleys stopped.

"No man doubts you, Tunguk. What more can you do for these men?"

Tunguk freed his arms from their support. The black blade hung at his side. "I think too little."

"I think you are right." Ingut looked at the red spatter on the old man's vest. "But you are still a whaler. You would take one of these brothers from us."

"I would take two."

"You should not have let these men help you. They are not worth the two already dead."

"Then we agree. I propose to try the bone."

Ingut chuckled. "I think you will name the big one to try."

"Aye."

"If you had not killed Wedrakut, he would throw Brother like a woman."

Parks whispered behind, "Did he just call me a bitch?"

"Sounded that way," Foster answered.

"Fuck it. Gimme a bone!" He challenged the elders. "I don't even know what's going on, but I'll throw down."

"A man is often lost, and another must take his place," Tunguk said. Ingut conferred with the others in their own language. Foster felt a distant prayer of a chance return. They couldn't win, and the other side didn't care to pay the price of victory. He snuck long, deep breaths through his nose. If nothing else, he was getting a blow after the climb in case they had to book it, after all.

"We do not accept. We are old men, Tunguk. We cannot pull the milk calf."

"Milk calf?" Parks frowned.

"I think that's you, brother. Milk calf bitch."

"I think it's a figure of speech. Like, 'pull out the win.'"

"When a whale gives birth," one of the other men spoke for the first time, "her calf drink of her until it is of great size, until it can eat of its own will."

"Isn't it against the rules of hospitality to insult your guests' figures?" Parks protested.

Tunguk ignored him. "You will not give battle. What, then?" The men leaned together in low tones. One of them kept a watchful eye on the trio. Finally, they broke.

"We will try songs. Gjardukut will sing for the clan," Ingut said. He gave no indication of who that was. Had to be ones of these bastards, though. Foster scanned the faces before them. "Will Brother sing? Or will Fucker?"

"We will speak." Tunguk pulled them close, but kept his own eye out. "We will not fight," his voice lowered. "These men wish to try songs. If you sing best, you will go free. If not, it is as before. The women will judge."

"Songs, like what? Like fucking American Idol?"

"You got this, brother," Foster said.

"No fucking way. I might fight like a milk calf, but I sing like one, too."

"It is not the songs of ships and taverns, as with your people. The voice is no matter. Our songs tell of where we come from, the stories of our ancestors, the shape of the land. Where the whales go. The invasions. They are too long for this purpose. Gjardukut will sing only a small portion. It will take no more than two of your days."

"Two fuckin' days?" Foster protested.

"Then you will be allowed to sing the songs of your people. It may not take more than two days, for this purpose."

Foster and Parks just looked at one another. "Can we tag team it?" Parks asked.

"I do not know this word."

"Wrestling-style. You know. The Hart Foundation. British Bulldogs. Tag in, tag out. I do a little Tom Petty, maybe Jack Johnson for the ladies, he comes in with the soundtrack from O Brother Where Art Thou?"

"No wrestling. You sing. Only one."

Parks looked doe-eyed at his friend. Foster headed him off. "Bitch, I don't even think I know all the words of one song, start to finish. You're the one can't cook a meal or launch a boat or put away his socks without beltin' some Miley Cyrus or *some* bullshit."

Parks nodded. "Then it falls to me. What exactly are the judges going to be looking for?"

Tunguk separated himself and stepped forward. "We agree to songs. Brother will sing." One of the five stepped forward. Gjardukut, the one who schooled him on milk calves. He lay his spear between himself and Parks.

"Am I supposed to pick it up?"

"No. You place an item that stands for your stories' power, to accept the contest."

"I don't have shit. I even left those fur undies back there cause they squash my nuts."

Foster reached into his belt where the two maps were pinched. He drew the top one and handed it to Parks, who held it up between himself and his opponent. He slapped it to the ground.

"I accept your gauntlet, and throw down mine. Hope the ladies don't fall asleep during you two day song. I'll be making a playlist the likes of which your people have never seen. The panties of every port of this round globe have peeled to just a brief selection of what I have to offer." He turned to Tunguk. "We get to sleep and potty, right?"

"When the sun sets," Tunguk replied. All of the men laughed except the foreigners. One of the elders added something in their tongue, and another round of laughter swept through them. Foster saw Parks swallow a lump, and knew they were good and fucked. Tunguk melted into the group and joked with Ingut as the whole mass moseyed downhill. Parks and Gjardukut collected their belongings and fell in behind. It was surreal beyond comprehension. Whatever locked their lives against one another in mortal combat evaporated—at least as far as the Reverse-Eskimos were concerned. An outsider coming on the scene would never know these men stood ready to slaughter each other one minute prior. That there were already two dead below. Everyone acted like it was a schoolyard shoving match they decided to settle on the basketball court. Hell, he could barely believe his own story as he told it and lived it. Part of him was ecstatic to avoid the head-on collision and certain death at the end of a spear. But he didn't see how Parks singing what verses he could remember of some Red Hot Chili Peppers song was going to persuade native judges that they should live. The whole thing sounded rigged from the get-go.

The old men fired back and forth, barbs for laughs, and though Foster hadn't the slightest notion what they said, they were clearly talking shit. For the first time, he noticed a familiar sensation. It made him think of wading ashore, of seeing the old man collapse, and the dark hut before they stormed out. There was relief to it, but it was nothing like safety, as he'd mistaken it so far. More like a pivot. Something mighty thundering past him with inches to spare, and the moments before it turned for another try.

"Brother," Tunguk switched to English. "Will you sing the song you sang to me before?"

"Did I sing you a song?"

"Aye, you know the one."

"I may have been a bit delirious and hypothermic at the time. I honestly don't recall that."

"He will do well. He has forgotten his songs already." Ingut said. His companions cackled.

"He remembers. The song we sang. Fucker, you sang too. All of us knew the words."

"Not ringin' a bell." Foster said. He walked just behind Tunguk and Ingut.

"We can sing it now for them."

"You know what Joe, I think I'll save my voice for the finals."

Tunguk stopped and turned. "It is best sung now." The others stopped in front of him. "It was about the young man who was chased by hungry dog." They gave him a perplexed look. "And he ran and ran. But the dog bit always at his heel." Parks squinted. "No matter how it chased he did not stop running."

"That might be one of yours. My people's songs are more like… *Tha block is hot, tha block is hot.*"

Tunguk snatched Ingut by the collar. He turned his hips and slung the man downhill into another. "Run, idiot." Then took off up the hill.

Parks' wide eyes met Gjardukut's. The old warrior tried to raise his spear but Parks caught it both hands. They tugged for control. Gjardukut pointed his butt downhill, sat down, and launched Parks over his head with his feet. He sprung to his feet and cocked his arm. Foster stepped in and grabbed the spear with his right hand. Gjarukut turned. But Foster had seen the singer's tricks. He let go and hurled a mighty left hook that dropped Gjardukut to his knees. Immediately, Foster clutched his fist and doubled over as knives of pain shot up his arm to his neck. Parks scrambled up the hill on all fours until he found his feet. He grabbed Foster and they hobbled after Tunguk. They could hear shouting behind them, the scrape of feet. A few stray arrows whizzed by them before they crested the top and threw themselves down the other side, part-slide, part-roll, a few steps thrown in for good measure.

Breathless, they caught Tunguk at the bottom of the far side just as the first figures popped up on top of the hill.

"We really have to work on our communication," Parks panted.

Tunguk did not run, and they did not chase. He and the clan stared at one another for a minute. Then he extended his arm, palm facing them, thirty degrees up from his leg in a low wave. Someone—probably Ingut—returned the salute, and their pursuers disappeared back to the encampment.

"Oh, thank God!" Parks exclaimed. "I don't have to sing."

"I thought they were gonna chase our asses all day like you did," Foster gasped.

"It is no concern to them."

"No concern?" Foster winced. "They were just about to execute us before you killed two of their dudes and then lied about a singin' contest so we could jump their asses and run. You chased us half a day for wavin' at you. If I were them, I'd be unfuckably pissed."

"All things want to live. It was an honest trick."

"Alrighty, well, could've used a little of that attitude from you earlier."

"Quiet, Fucker. Joe just saved our miserable white lives," Parks panted.

"Much appreciated, brother. I just don't get the ways of your people. Least not you."

Tunguk spent a long time looking up at the empty ridge. Finally, he turned to Parks. "It was well-tried, Brother. A fine battle."

"Thanks, dude. You didn't look so bad yourself."

"Was it as you saw it?"

"You mean in my imagination?" Tunguk awaited his answer. "Not even close. But a win's a win."

"I found many surprises, as well."

"You—imagine victory, too?" Tunguk just smiled. "Does it work?"

"Perhaps the next one will be the first time I am right." He looked again to the ridge line. "It is hard. All men see a different battle." His gaze turned to Foster. "Some dream only of misfortune."

"Misfortune?" Foster drew back defensively. "I'm what you call a goddamn realist. Are yall seriously gonna give me grief over thinkin' maybe we didn't have a great shot against almost twenty crazy Eskimo bastards with weapons? Hell, what did *he* do?" He waved toward Parks. "I'm the only one of us landed a fuckin' punch."

Tunguk looked at Foster, his throbbing fist clutched to his ribs and the good one cupped over it. He extended a palm. Foster hesitated, then placed his hand in Tunguk's. With the other, Tunguk rapped his knuckles.

"Ow! Motherfucker!" Foster yanked back.

"Broken."

"No shit, I could've told you that without you breakin' it some more."

"We are one good man, but hungry as three. The day is half done, and my shares are gone. If we will live to see dawn, we hunt."

Foster was bewildered by his sense of time. He was pretty sure "dawn" had just passed in a fight for their lives. "Can we hunt for a doctor, or a ship? Maybe an airstrip capable of landing a small plane?" He suggested.

"Our people will reward you with whatever you want," Parks offered. "Money, food, triple bypass, whatever you need. Screw hanging around here til Winter. We'll bring you to Chile and you can party on our dime where the sun shines. Booze, girls, whatever. You still fuck?"

"Your people have nothing more I want. If you need water, I will show you streams. If you need food, we hunt seal. This satisfies our bond." Tunguk started off along the foot of the spur.

"Hey Joe, can we take a blow?" Parks leaned on his knees and settled to his butt.

Foster stood over him. "What's the matter? You can't imagine walkin' a little farther?"

"You heard the man. Never turns out how you imagined it."

Foster extended his good hand. Parks grumbled as he took it and hauled himself back to his feet. He never quite stood upright, but managed to limp off after their caretaker. Foster peeked once more at the ridge, border of the home of Tunguk of Antarctica. A few hundred yards away, and it might as well have been as far as North Carolina for the old man, now. The image of his mama's house popped into his head. Porch light glowed yellow at dusk, and he could feel the chill of late Fall as the leaves made their way to red, then to the ground that flanked a wet gravel driveway high in the mountains. He wasn't sure if anyone was home. Somehow, the place felt empty, as though a knock may go unanswered. The muddy rock crunched underfoot as he stalked up, and the limbs swished a warning of a cold gust seconds before it came. It brought that lonesome holiday feeling, everything winding down, the longing for a warm place to sit while family milled in and out of the kitchen. Would they even remember him?

He shook his head—it was ridiculous. A single day. That's how long they'd been lost, so far. Why was it Fall? The sting of Tunguk's insult came back to him. Did he really think it would take that long to get home? He knew some folks of recent acquaintance who wouldn't make it at all. It didn't matter. Foster shivered as he watched the sunlight fail over the Blue Ridges. He would stand there again.

Parks and Tunguk shrank ahead. He bundled tight in his parka and hurried after them across the gray rock.

4

A Great Naval Battle Rages

Parks lay the paddle on the bottom of the kayak. Blood streamed down his nose into the stubble and dripped onto his sleeveless shirt. He rotated to stern, where a taut leather braid ran overboard from a bone that braced the gunwales. The rope disappeared into the ocean. He looped his forearm once under the line to anchor it, and began to reel. Hand over hand, he tugged patiently against the weight at the other end. It offered no fight. A little wake perked up as something glided just below the top of the waterline. Parks slowed his pulls so as to let it float instead of sucking under. One more good tug, and the whole line drifted into view. A native man, one arm missing, lay on his back. His hand gripped the other end of the rope where it disappeared into a bloody hole in his right stomach. Other than the tension in his fingers there were no signs of life. Parks leaned over for a closer look. The man coughed, and water dribbled down his chin.

"We meet again, my sea amigo."

It wasn't long before Foster peeled off his parka, too. Air billowed under the loose tail of his long-sleeve and in through the wide cuffs. The sweat gave him a chill. The balmy Antarctic Summer soared above freezing, especially on the sun-drenched slopes where the light climbed over the range behind them. The shadowed valleys made him shiver where the cold wind flowed down from the heights like melting water, but he was soon thankful for the baggy layers when the sweat dried and didn't return. Parts of him were a little too cold, and other parts—the ones beneath his furry underwear that he didn't have time to shed—were hot. In the balance, it was the most comfortable he'd been out in the elements since Santiago.

The comfort was purely thermal. His body felt like a rodeo clown waking up after a bad day at the office. His invincible twenties were years-past. There were few things left that a cup of coffee and a few hours of daylight could still cure. The last 24 hours were probably never among them. He opened and closed his hand to the point of pain, neither fist nor flat palm. The joints of his last two knuckles swelled with fluid and ached from the cold. As it were, he could still grip something lightly, and he preferred that to the stiffness he knew would set in with a vengeance if he stopped moving it.

They should have had to force Tunguk along, hold him up, something. The man was hours removed from a coronary. Yet it was Foster and Parks who begged the rests, and who fell asleep in whatever awful position they could find on the bare rock, until the old man roused them never more than ten or fifteen minutes later. The way Parks limped behind annoyed Foster. *He* was the one with the real injury. And his orbital was without a doubt swollen from the ancient knuckles that held fast when they clocked him the day before. Mostly, he longed to talk. It didn't feel right with Tunguk present. He still remembered the trick, every word falling right into the ears of an enemy. In spite of his efforts since, Foster trusted the man as far as he could throw him. There were too many things bedeviling him—he needed to unload, to debrief, and surely Parks did, too. It was a need that for now fell in limping behind sleep, water, food, bare survival.

Twice he stumbled when he nearly fell asleep walking. When he blinked, the whole place had the heavy feel of a dream. Forbidding mountains. The shrieks of sea birds. Sharp terrain of an alien planet. The strange man who led them on. Shake as he might, it stayed put. It reminded him of the sensation of waking in someone else's bed. That brief moment of panic before it dawns on you where you are, and the room takes shape in your mind even though you can't see a damn thing. Except there was nothing to orient to. He didn't know a single detail of where he was beyond a short horizon. Often on a long deployment he felt disoriented—no idea where they were and only a rough heading. Lost to the rest of a world, in an intimately familiar environment. That was different. It was the rest of the world Foster knew well. They were somewhere on the peninsula, and he knew right where that stood. But this place was nowhere he could name, and the names were far out of reach. Even in a strange city like Santiago, he felt settled. There was a word to call it. People, and buildings, and streets. If he got the notion, he could hail a cab for the airport, stuff into a metal tube, and wake up in Charlotte. He knew where one was in relation to the other. He didn't speak Spanish, but he knew the ring of it, and he could order off a menu. Those people dressed like his. Their buildings had corners of wood and brick. The streets crossed one another under neat signs, the way they did in all corners of the world.

Here? This place was utterly resistant to any kind of sense. There were no land forms to recognize. Not even a trail, or a line of footprints. They meandered after Tunguk along whatever path the slopes and washes swept them into. Foster had been lost plenty of times in plenty of places. Now he wondered what that word even meant, because if that sufficed for a downtown wandering, this was something else. Lost meant there was always a chance to stumble on found, and follow some road or river back to the familiar, one thing and then another until they clustered in his recognition and gave him a place to be. Even in the thick of it, it was never entirely without relation to something he knew, be it sassafras trees or a crowd of drinkers winding home.

This violent young rock bore no resemblance to his old Appalachians. The bird calls were strange. No inch of this country was subject to the rules of Man, least of all the people. Everything belonged here, and here alone. The borders were porous and warped like the ones on the crappy maps they ended up with. His heart skipped and his hand squeezed on the parchment that draped from his belt, a little to hard for his knuckles' liking. He didn't pull it free, instead staring at his sewn boots flicking out from his stiff trousers. The thin sheet was cool to the touch and nearly dry. There, at least, was one thing this place hadn't taken. He recalled the odd shape of the New World it depicted, a wishful prospect with no western edge at the time it was drawn. Foster tried to imagine a modern map of the east coast overlaid, but in his exhaustion he couldn't find the picture. Thousands of miles lay between. He'd been many thousands before, though.

They topped a ridge that lined the valley and a biting gust reeled up the coast. For the first time, the water came into view. Foster flushed with the consolation of something he knew. It may have been an ocean, but that body stretched all the way to the Eastern seaboard. This was the start. Tunguk planned only to keep them alive. They would have to do the rest themselves. And whatever contact they made with their own world would happen in sight of the coast. It should have made him more joyful. They weren't exactly home-free, but the highway loomed ahead. Yet as they descended to the vast waters, calm and shining, a deep current of unease welled within him. Though he walked North and to the sea, it felt as though something flowed beneath his feet and pulled him farther away with every step. The feeling of the carrier flooded back to him. Foster had a growing sense of where he was. It was everything else that was lost.Behind him, the sound of the clumsy shuffle of shoe leather over loose rock reminded him there was another thing he managed to keep. Right now, he wanted nothing more than to talk to Parks.

The sight of the coast quickened his hobble. Parks thought if he dragged enough ass, the other asses would slow on his behalf, but by now Joe had a fair lead on Foster, and Foster was a good ways off himself, though he made frequent welfare checks over his shoulder with the odd hurry-up gesture that for some reason he thought would heal the pain in Parks' shin, grant a twelve-hour sleep, and breathe energy back into his lumbering body. In fact, it was the sea that did it. There was a similar relief the day before, when he first saw land after hours of being surrounded by the shapeshifting waves. Now it was the water that drew him eagerly down the last slope despite the jarring impact and the pain in his knees. Not that anything particular awaited him—though it might mean another catnap. The sound of the waves on the bluffs washed up and ebbed away in turn. It was his favorite place in the world: where one ended and another began. A younger man once made the mistake of thinking he loved the ocean. Soon he was surrounded by it, crammed below deck among gray walls and uniforms. He fled inland when he got out. Three months working in the desert taught him that endless land was no kinder. What he loved was the beach. Places where things collide, one gives way to the other, then back again. Coast Guard would have been a better call. Maybe it wasn't too late for that if he ever made it home, but this was his consolation prize. Between a storm and an enemy, drowning and the point of an arrow. Parks raced to catch up.

At last, he reached the others at a flat, rocky shelf a couple of feet above the waves. Eskimo Joe studied the water. A light wind teased ripples from the surface but refused to commit to a full blow. There was no trace of the fury that barreled through the previous day. In his vast two weeks of experience, it was the most beautiful weather he had ever seen on the Antarctic Peninsula. This was new coast to him. The ground here was littered with smooth rocks that showed where the waves broke over the shelf from time to time. South and left, the coast extended a good quarter mile farther out to sea, then broke off and lost elevation as it trended inland to the place they stood before continuing on the same line. The headland bent the meager swell, leaving calm water to lap at their feet. This would have been a much nicer place to come ashore, he thought. In a storm, he might have just washed over the lip and set his feet down. Maybe that's what Foster's bitch-ass did.

Parks kicked a rock out of the way and lay his clothing on the ground as a butt pad. He lowered himself with a groan.

"Siesta?" He rolled up his pant leg over the knee and picked a few scraps of debris out of his wet scab. It was black and blue all around, and a pinkish white caked with dry blood. A quick press around the perimeter ached all the way to the bone.

No one responded. Foster kept his eye on Joe, who watched the water like he was waiting on a blind date. Probably couldn't wait to get rid of them. The Parks family optical genes weren't suited to ship spotting, so he was more than happy to rest his peepers while someone else kept a lookout. It made him nervous to have everyone standing over him, though. What if they ditched him? Or a wave came over and swept him out to sea? The last time he fell asleep on the shore, he woke up with a lot less than he arrived with. A shudder ran up his spine at the thought that someone undressed him—and he still wasn't sure who.

"Tunguk," Foster tried. "*Tunguk.*"

"Why do you insist on calling him that?" Parks yawned.

"That's his name."

"Clearly he prefers Eskimo Joe. Every time you say that, it sounds like you're trying to not vomit in your own mouth."

"I'm tryin' to show a little respect to the man who tried to disembowel us that one time he thought we were disrespectful. You remember that?"

"Maybe he was just alarmed by our dicks flapping in the wind. I'm sure he doesn't mind an honest nickname. He calls us Brother and Fucker."

"That's cause he heard us call each other that. I heard him call himself Tunguk."

"And he heard you call yourself Foster, but he went with my version."

"Maybe I should start callin' you Runs-with-Two-Vaginas," he pointed to Parks' wound.

"Tide is coming." Joe said.

"Is that why we're here?" Parks asked.

"Aye."

"To admire the coming of the tide." Parks exchanged a look with Foster. "And what's with all the '*ayes*'? At ease, sailor."

"It is the word of your people."

"We told you, we're not in the Navy anymore. If you're talking about my *people*, people, we have many ways to agree. You can say yes. Yep, yeah, yup, yea…you can say uh-huh, or mm-hm, or…"

"Sure," Foster added.

"Totes. You betcha," he imitated a Midwestern accent. "Forsooth. Aye is for pirates and pier queers."

Eskimo Joe let his eyes off the water to make Parks' gaze. At first, Parks feared he was annoyed, but the old man glanced up and nodded in consideration. "In Mattakatan, it is *ah*."

"We're never gonna remember that."

The old man turned to the sea again. His white hair lofted off his shoulder and settled while the gaunt frame stood like a gnarled promontory at watch. For the first time, Parks took note of the long hands that hung near his face. They were cracked and gray around the palms. Skin bunched over veins and the knuckles were a brown shade darker than the rest. Small lines of discoloration crisscrossed deeper scars, ages healed. The bony joints appeared knotted and frail. It was these that set down two men just that morning, and these alone that held their fate.

"What happens with the tide?"

"We hunt."

"Hunt what?" Parks ran his fingertips through the hair on the coat that separated him from the rock. "Is this seal?"

"Yes."

"We supposed to strangle 'em with our bare hands?" Leave it to Foster to fuss over the details, he thought.

"It is good if you can. Otherwise, we need a boat. Spears, harpoons, clubs. Arrows for bird."

The men were silent while the processed the remark. "This is where the huntin' party lands," Foster said.

"They land up the coast, on a beach. But they will be tired. With the tide, and with help, they can land here. Closer to camp."

Parks tensed as their purpose dawned on him. He rose to his feet and strained at the horizon. "The deadliest game," he intoned.

"We gonna bushwhack a whole huntin' party with one knife?" Foster complained.

"The first boat will be giuk. Too small. We will help, and take the second. Whale boat. The others will see, they will not land."

Concern darkened Foster's face. "I feel bad makin' you rob and kill your kinsmen for us."

"They are my people. I have my father's brothers for kin."

Parks tried to imagine how old an uncle of Eskimo Joe would have to be.

"This is fucking drama right here, buddy," he remarked. "Brother against brother for recent enemy, uncle against nephew, women with bows, Sabertits. Foster, we're going to option the shit out of this when we get home. A millennial tale of survival, lust, murder, betrayal. Friendship. Get some ghostwriter for the book version. Fuck, maybe Stephen King can do it."

"I'd prefer…I don't know, what's the name of somebody who writes happy endin's?"

"Fuck if I know."

"Let's survive first."

"Deal. We can call it…*Brother Fucker.*"

A black blip rounded the point into view. Parks' veins filled with acid. His catnap would have to wait. It was little more than a shadow on the water, but no animal glided along the top like that. He was certain it was a boat. Parks' dream of a hardened steel research vessel foundered as the shape settled into a small thing near, instead of a large thing far. Joe had barely seen a dozen distant paddle strokes when he said, "Something has happened."

It stopped moving for a second, then flailed again and reduced profile to bear for the shelf. Whoever it was had spotted them. It was only one—Parks was reasonably sure. A thin black line protruding over the hull.

"What do you need us to do?" Foster asked impatiently.

"We will see."

"Only one guy," Foster remarked.

Joe turned to Parks. "Now is the time to see your victory." His stomach churned.

Lines and colors faded in as the vessel flew toward them. It was narrow and tapered at both ends, no bigger than a two-man kayak. The hunter swung the paddle with a furious ease, a strange twisting stroke that propelled him across the water like a skate on ice. He neared, and they noticed his left arm was missing just below the shoulder. The shaft of the paddle by the grip was tucked under that armpit, and with the other hand he rotated the blade to orient to either way as he swung his torso back and forth, one stroke per side.

Parks tapped Foster behind Joe's back. He raised an index finger and mouthed, "He's got one arm," with a wink and a thumbs up.

The kayak drifted to a halt. Its occupant took in the two gringos who awaited him. Joe extended his right arm out from his side, his open palm at waist height. The man lay his paddle across the boat and returned the gesture. He approached and Joe said something in their native tongue. The man answered breathlessly. Somewhere in the barrage of sound, Parks felt like he and Foster were mentioned. The kayak floated twenty yards off the shelf. All he had to do was pick up on one bad twitch, a feeling that something wasn't right, and this man would turn back to his friends and warn them of the trio. There would be no weapons, no boat, no hunt, no food. Some part of him hoped that his fingers curled the wrong way, or he was a little too friendly, and the one-armed man would flip a bitch and save them the fight. As much as he wanted to live, the thought of killing and robbing strangers didn't sit well, ethically, and least-of-all on the practical side. He'd punched a few people in his day—not half as many as Foster—but Parks was less than eager to kill with his bare hands, or even have to hold a struggling opponent while Eskimo Joe did the deed. How many more were coming? How long would he have to play chummy with this fellow in order to entice the rest to dock? These were not children or old men. The others likely had more arms. Even the swift blade of Joe would have trouble going it alone. Foster was down a fist. What good would he be? Parks could feel his face flush with anticipation, every capillary tingling throughout his big limbs. Was he turning red? Would the man see? And if he did, would a white man suddenly flushed like a drunk Asian be enough to arouse suspicion? The conversation seemed settled, but the kayak made no move for shore.

Eskimo Joe turned to him. "You will paddle for this man."

"Pardon?"

"Some men have trapped the hunting party at a rock. We will go to them."

Parks wasn't sure if this was part of the ruse. A change of plans, a way to get after them. Or had the one-armed man smelled a turd and worked up his own scheme?

"In *that?*" He pointed to the kayak.

"He has paddled hard to reach us. Now he needs rest for the fight. You say you are a sailor. You will paddle for him."

"Yeah, I mean, sailor, fairly accurate. More of a helicopter mechanic, carrier group kinda guy. This is a summer camp type of situation. I'm not really seeing the transfer of skills."

"Are you not goin' in the boat with us?" Foster asked.

"Fucker will run with me. We will come by another way."

"Uh…OK. OK. And what is the things that I…need to be doing, or keeping in mind, if you're picking up on my outline?"

"I do not know this word."

"Outline. It's like, the outline in the pants, if we were wearing normal pants, you could kinda see my outline," he indicated where a pant leg would be. "Trace it with your eye, you know? See what I'm all about without me having to just whip it right out for you?" Parks leaned in to risk a whisper. "When do I clock this fool?"

"Go with this man," Joe said in a normal tone. "Do as he says."

Parks made eye contact with the hunter. He had a tense patience about him. Not a muscle moved, but there was urgency beneath his stare. Parks gave a nod. He raised his right hand. "How." There was no return of acknowledgment. "I am to go…with you." Parks shouted in a tone that made it clear he wasn't sure if the man even spoke English. No response. "If you can pull up to the curb here, I get in canoe…with you. We make great friends. As I am friends with your friend here."

"Tide is low," Tunguk explained. "You swim."

"Swim? Aw, hell no. I have recent trauma from this particular body of water. It's colder than Eskimo balls in an igloo." Everyone stared at him. "Hypothermia. My body would go into shock the second I hit the water, and I'd get instant hypothermia. The human body remembers the things that happen to it, you know. If you get diarrhea, you're body is just itching for it. You so much as *smell* some street vendor cooking carne asada, your butthole starts bubbling. It's like a virus that lives in your memory." Parks scanned the faces, Foster, Joe, his prey. No one offered any consolation. "It would have taken hours to kill me yesterday, but now that I've experienced it, I'll be dead before I swim halfway there."

Foster extended his hand. Parks bristled, then pulled the map from his belt and slapped it into the waiting palm. He peeled off the long sleeve shirt, piled it with his coat and underpants, and deposited the bundle with his friend. "Take care of my chonies. As if they were your own." He walked to the edge of the shelf. The pristine water sparkled like ice crystals. Twenty yards. That's all he had to travel this time. No walls of swell or unseen land. Still, he didn't see why the dude couldn't come a little closer. Parks gave one last protesting glance to his friends, then cannonballed in.

The familiar chill took his breath away. His face burned and he exhaled too fast as he fought for the surface. The few seconds it took felt as near to death as the geologic time for which the first wave held him under a day prior. He broke into air with his brain singing one-ten-one. One-ten-one. What was that rule again? Fuck it, he thought. He was too cold for a full stroke. A doggy paddle was the most valiant effort he could muster. The hunter didn't bother to approach the rock, just turned broadside for him.

He could see the man was younger—much younger. Early twenties with a greasy wet curtain of black hair that clung to a face of meager stubble. A slender arm extended the paddle and pulled him the last few feet. Parks latched onto the edge of the kayak. The lightness shocked him as it dipped his way and dunked him. One of his hands slipped free off what felt like slimy leather and slapped back on. The entire rig wobbled violently. A hand gripped his collar. The young man leaned back to steady him, but as soon as Parks tried to slip his chest over, the kayak rocked his way and capsized. A knee landed on his back as the young man tumbled over. Another dunk, and Parks came up gasping.

With an annoyed sense of calm, the man righted the ship and rolled in with little effort. Parks snagged the paddle as it floated by, a big bone, he noticed, with bony fingers extending from the end in a fan that supported a thin layer of what was probably more seal skin. He stretched out the grip and the man pulled, leaning back harder this time. Parks got his chest up and kicked like mad until he was able to flop a leg over the side. For a second, he thought she would sway over again, but a with quick tumble, he fell into place. The wobble settled. Under his back, an irregular frame shifted with each small adjustment. It seemed as though the whole thing would collapse if he moved. He grabbed the rails, and a hand pressed into his back to ease him into a seated position. In front of him, a leather strip hung between a pair of bones that spanned the beam—a little butt hammock. With the utmost care, Parks shifted himself into the seat and found another hard bone to place his feet on.

The hunter sat on a similar piece and reeled in a leather line by yanking and tucking under his armpit over and over. A bundle of spears and harpoons appeared. Parks glanced around and saw a fair assortment of debris floating by. He managed to snag what felt like a raincoat with the end of the paddle and bring it aboard, but another large sack was already too far. To his right, he spotted a bow and quiver. Arrows bled out, sinking as soon as they left the pouch. He moved to paddle for the sack and a few other odds that floated, but the hunter pointed insistently back the way he came. Parks indicated the gear. Another jab from the hunter, and Parks sank the paddle in to turn seaward. The sight of this man's crap abandoned to the waves, slowly giving in on a long trip to the bottom brought more regret than it should have. He pulled again, and felt the entire bench and the frame beneath him shift with his weight. The vessel was nothing but lashed bone, covered with animal skin, sewn with leather thread and sinew. When his hands passed by his face to switch the paddle over the stench made him recoil. Whatever grease coasted the thing now coated him as well and made the paddle slip. It felt like anything but the most delicate stroke would tear the frame apart and rip the paddle from his hand. He was already embarrassed about his first impression. Reverse-Eskimos were hard-ass dudes and his flailing hadn't won him any respect. Part of him hoped Joe would kill this guy just so one less person would think him a fool.

The hunter looked back as if to see what was wrong. Parks risked a harder stroke. The shaft flexed in the middle—it was two lengths of bone bound together—and rotated at the end where the small bones fanned out. When he moved it to the other side, it repeated the motions in the opposite direction. After a few awkward strokes, he felt the shape of it, the way he needed to turn it to bite the water. The bones of the entire kayak shifted one way and the other as he picked up speed. Each pull made him braver. It groaned under the new weight but picked up speed until it moved at something like a brisk walk. The delicate face of the vessel fell away. Every joint moved around him, but not like something that was on the verge of falling apart. They rode on the back of some sea beast that twisted with the force and flow, yielding where it needed and swimming with its own momentum, its own cadence of breath. The first time he dug in at full strength, it practically jumped with exhilaration. The hunter seemed to calm and face forward again, satisfied at last with the pace.

Over his left shoulder, Foster and Eskimo Joe disappeared up the shelf toward the bluffs without so much as a wave of encouragement. Once again, he found himself alone. Almost. Joe's habit of not telling anyone the plan, or even having one to begin with, wore on Parks. Was he working with this guy now, or was he supposed to bash him from behind and toss him into the ocean? He shivered in his tank top, and the low sun offered no pity. Now his eye turned to the pile of weapons between them: two fixed spears and a pair of toggling harpoons. The latter were jointed in the middle, with a loose head that fitted onto the far piece. A hole in the base of the point held one end of a line that ran down to an eyelet and a peg on the lower piece of the haft, then into a pile of rope that he assumed was neatly coiled before he upset the whole operation. The design didn't entirely make sense to him, but he assumed that somehow, the sharp end would come free in a seal—a whale, even—while the other remained anchored to the kayak so the prey couldn't escape. It would take some work to sort out all the tangled lines and untie the bundle. Not something he could do without the hunter noticing. If it came to a fight, it would have to be old-fashioned fisticuffs. Popeye and Bluto for supremacy of the waves. Maybe he could lie down and wobble the man overboard.

Until then, his arms burned with the inertia of the sea. Ol' Tripod wasn't much for conversation, but it didn't take long to realize that a half-glance back meant 'go faster.' Parks had a good 90 or 100 pounds on his adversary. That was estimating the way a man estimates size on the assumption of four limbs present and accounted for. How much did an arm weigh? At any rate, the load-to-stroke power ratio had not increased proportionally. At least there were no dead animals in here to weigh it down. Some hunter this guy was.

The strokes soon warmed his gooseflesh. It took some getting-the-hang-of to stop splashing icy water on his shipmate's back at every switch, but Parks rounded the point in rhythm. There, the going slowed. Luck had arranged an intermittent onshore breeze and relatively calm seas, but he felt the grind of the weak swell against them out of the southwest as they steered a near-southerly course. No amount of exertion ever brought warmth to his fingers and toes. He leaned in, hoping to earn this man's trust with effort. Parks couldn't see anything they might be paddling to. Beyond the headland it was all high bluffs, and the bluffs were bare. No sign of Foster keeping pace. He hated to think what they would do if the weather kicked up. The hunter pointed him wide to sea, and soon he picked out the light, foamy water that rustled over a hidden rock. They were alone. Wherever they might be bound, and however things went down, they were stuck with each other for the moment.

"So. How long you been into sea kayaking?" Parks waited. "I've done some fishing out of one. No harpooning. Did you make these yourself?" He nudged the bundle of weapon with his toe. "Sorry I dumped all your shit. I'm not used to falling out of boats. Done it twice now in twenty-four hours." The man held firm ahead. "Did Joe tell you my name? Cause if not, I wanna change it. I understand your people work on the dibs system. My culture uses it as well." Small talk didn't seem to grease his pan. Parks knew he should probably shut up before he gave something away he didn't even know he was supposed to keep.

"What happened to your arm?" He examined the stump. "I gashed my shin yesterday. But who needs a shin? Do you speak English?" He was wary of Joe's trick. Clearly, there were some within the tribe who knew it. "I'm afraid my Antarctic Eskimo is rusty. No? That's cool. Do you mind if I sing a song? I find long periods of silence awkward, especially when one party isn't making any effort." He let a few more strokes through the water in case the man was searching for an answer.

"I was in a singing contest once. My opponent was heavily favored, of course, but I imagine that was more a consequence of the ignorance of the judges, and the rigged nature of the competition itself, than any real evaluation of my talents. Unfortunately, I never got the chance to take the stage. It was canceled, you see. There was a big brawl. In the hotel lobby. I barely escaped with my life." Shut up, Parks, he told himself. "Ever since, I've found that there was always a song in my heart. It changes day-to-day, or minute-to-minute, but it's there.

"Had a whole playlist in my head, you know. I was singing for my survival. Metaphoricallly. To avoid the metaphorical death of embarrassment, and shame upon my family. If you've never prepared yourself for a performance of that magnitude, you wouldn't realize that you can't just walk away. You can't build up this massive weapons cache of heart and soul and fight for survival and just expect it to dissolve once the show is called off. It builds up, and it needs be fired. Like a nut that you were expecting to unload, and suddenly the audience is gone. If you let that shit stew, you'll have long-lasting psychological consequences. Possibly even testicular cancer. That's the situation with my heart, and all the songs I have saved up. Blue heart, they call it."

Parks could have sworn he felt something shift. As though the man's stillness was now the response, calculated to avoid engaging. But an imperceptible dip of relaxing shoulders, a slower breath, made it feel like he'd earned an ear.

He made a show of clearing his throat. "The seaweed is always greener, in somebody else's lake." A rich baritone welled up and occasionally found its note. "You dream about going up there, but that is a big mistake. Just look at the world around you. Right here on the ocean floor. Such wonderful things surround you. What more is you lookin' for?" He let the tension build in a pause. "Ohhhh….ohhhh….Under the sea. Under the sea. Darling it's better down where it's wetter, take it from me. Know what I'm sayin'?" He winked. "Up on the shore they work all day. Out in the sun they slave away, while we devotin', full time to floatin', under the sea."

"Perhaps you can fight." The man stopped Parks cold.

"He speaks! Lord, hallelujah! You understand my words?"

"Of course." The hunter still didn't turn.

"Was it my lovely voice that brought it out of you?"

"Your slow paddling. You are a singer as much as a sailor. But no man survives here who can do nothing. Perhaps you can fight."

"I've been known to toss a table."

"Then we will die well."

That didn't sound appetizing, but Parks felt it best not to press for what he meant. This man seemed to have certain disadvantages if it came down to the two of them, but then so had Eskimo Joe at first glance. *No man survives here who can do nothing*, he thought as he studied the scar where the skin folded around the bone. Whoever stitched it had done a fine job. It healed neater than he would have expected from the kind of facilities he'd seen earlier. Maybe it was a Western doctor. Some sort of bleeding heart mission, so he could brag about his third world generosity to his golfing buddies.

Parks was tired. But as he tired, he settled into the paddle more. Took the easy way, used his weight and momentum more than his muscle. If anything, he got faster. The hunter said nothing else to him. The sun peered over the backside of the island and the ripples coming off the bow bristled in its light. In his Navy, Parks rarely went topside to see water. Now he felt it press into the bottom of the skin boat, splash on his thighs as he switched the paddle over. His adult life had been spent at sea, but he hadn't been this near to it since his high school days, feet dangling from a surfboard in the line-up. It occurred to him that every part of his ship, from the paddle to the hull, was hide and bone. A manmade animal swimming off the southern coast. A skin-thin layer between him and the death he'd barely escaped, was it a year ago? Time swelled and contracted here. The *Qarapara* was at least a lifetime past. Mercifully, this part of the coast wasn't just unbroken glacier. The ice held at the high inland peaks. From the bluffs, he noticed a stream spilling thirty feet into the ocean. A meltwater fall, cool and fresh and delicious. Did people here even bother to hydrate? He'd barely been offered a few pints since he landed.

His rib cramped as cold air forced its way down his lungs. It felt like the oceanic version of jogging endlessly behind Foster, unsure of where they were headed or what to do if they ever got there. He thought he might recognize some section of the coast, get some sense of place. But even the black peaks looked different from this angle. Their pace slowed as he settled into his work. The hunter could bitch, but this was going to be it if he had to keep it up for any length of time. That must have come across, because the dude didn't say another word. Just pointed now and again to keep him out of some hidden current or off a reef. There was no speed that could have pleased the man, anyway. He glared ahead like some dog who had seen another and could barely keep from jumping out the truck for a fight. His was a stillness that hummed with anticipation. At least he was too fixated on what lie ahead to ferret out the plot against him—whatever it was. Parks scanned the bluffs. Around every point, he prayed to see two men waving above, or waiting to meet them in a boat. A much bigger boat. All he needed was the signal. That felt true, but something in him second-guessed whether he could murder a cripple he just met over a kayak. It might be as simple as knocking him in the water and pad-dling away. Leaving him to tread until the cold sapped him. He could see that one arm reach up through the surface before it disappeared for good. Then it swept over him: there were the others. Captain, Gardner, everyone. Floating swollen and blue, sinking and rising and sinking to where the light no longer penetrated. Beneath them, dozens more—hundreds more nameless corpses, dancing to the rhythm of the swell. How close had he come to their company? Even now, it felt like their fingers reached blindly upward, hoping to curl around a pant leg. Water, all around him and no place to land. If he wasn't careful, he may meet them yet. The kayak undulated over the top of a grave. It didn't scare him. He felt solemn.

The muscles of the hunter's back rose and fell. A breeze fluttered through his hair. This was a living thing, literally in the same boat as himself. He wondered if when the man woke up, he knew he might slip beneath the frigid waters for good today. Parks certainly never considered it until now. Nor did the crew the day before, even up the point that they launched the rafts. The panic of being held under was indescribable. What would it have felt like if he had taken a gulp? He drank deeply of the crisp air to banish the thought. Every lungful was a miracle. As long as he sat on these waters, he couldn't forget it. There would always be more to join the company of those who marched to the bottom. Maybe even today. It would bring him no joy to drown this motherfucker—less if it were him.

The paddle dug deep and the little boat slipped over the surface. In the survival suit, he was debris. The will of the ocean alone propelled him. The carrier was the opposite—the ocean didn't seem to exist. Different degrees of insulation. Parks relished the small control he had with the kayak. He had some steerage, and a little space between him and the waves. It felt honest, at least. You got back what you put out. A zodiac would have been nice, though. At least this was better company than the kind he was used to chauffeuring. The boat may have been quiet, but his mind was not. He should have taken the time to imagine himself sinking a spear in this guy, strangling him bare-handed, kicking him overboard. Something about it didn't right sit with him. Like masturbating with an unsuspecting woman nearby. It was one thing to engage in the act, and another to hunch over and sweat out a daydream. He settled for everything else. Over the course of the next two hours, he stumbled upon a research vessel, then an illegal fishing boat, or a Navy icebreaker. They were rescued, or captured a ship by force. Storms across the passage. Lifeboats launched. They didn't listen to his warnings in time, and he only managed to get Foster and Joe out. There was a run North to embarrass Shackleton, a reception of utter disbelief, tears of joy, and the other kind. A beautiful Chilean reporter interviewed him, grizzled and drenched as he disembarked in Puntas Arenas. They were only sitting down to a beer when the kayak rounded a point and the hunter's posture shifted.

In the distance, he could make out a big skerry a couple hundred yards off the cliff wall under the bluffs. All of it was a blurry mess and a guess without his contacts. A blind bastard who spends long enough on a board with salt water in his eyes was never at a complete loss, though. Deciphering shapes became an art. The bright rim around the skerry was the waves crashing into it, glowing white then coiling into the shadow of the coast. A dark cylinder loomed seaward. No doubt the boat of the hunting party. The question remained whether he'd come as a rescuer, or a pirate.

A flash of movement in the shadow caught his attention. The air pressure dropped and his ears felt like a plane taking off. Parks snorted and clicked to clear them. Something came into relative focus. Between the skerry and the cliff, a small boat turned broadside to them. Twenty-footer, *maybe*, and as soon as he saw it, he noticed a second, still pointed his direction. They were wider, but had the same coloration as the kayak. Little man-shapes poked up, making no attempt to move beyond keeping their boats off the skerry on one hand and the cliff on the other. They sat in the lee of the breaks, shielded from the wave momentum that bent all things coastward.

Parks turned back to the larger shape on the sea side as he gained on the position. It was three times the size of the other boats. A single mast rose from the mid-deck. No sail, or it was unrigged and stowed. Long oars dipped into the water on either side. They, too, made no moves other than corrections to keep them from the rock. This one was the earthy black color of wet timber. In an instant, the scene cleared in his mind. The two smaller vessels were the hunting party, trapped at the rock. The wooden sailboat waited like a dog at a tree for the slower animal to make a run for it so he could overtake it with a few long strides. It was too big to risk squeezing between the rock and the hard place, and the little boats could easily circle away like a merry-go-round, but they couldn't leave for open water. That's what Eskimo Joe meant when he said some men had them trapped.

"Who the fuck is that?" Parks nodded toward the large boat. He realized the man couldn't have seen his indication, but he apparently got the meaning.

"Your people."

"I don't have people. Eskimo Joe and Foster. That's it for this continent."

The man extended his right hand in what Parks now realized was the customary greeting. The hunting boats returned it.

"What do my people who are not my people want with your people?"

"Meat. They take the hunt. Too lazy to feed themselves."

"Seems like a lot of trouble to avoid going to the grocery store."

"More trouble to hunt seal and whale. They hunt each other."

"The deadliest game."

"Aye. A man needs weapons to hunt. Food. Women. They take from my people."

The going suddenly took on a grit. Something about the rock was causing the water downstream to speed up and hinder their advance. His arms burned against the added resistance. An extra paddler would have been nice for his sore lower back, throbbing with his pulse. As they drew near, Parks could began to count oars. There were two short quarter decks fore and aft,. Everyone crammed between them on benches, two to a row with maybe ten pairs of rowers. Now he saw there were only two hunters and a pile of carcasses in either boat. Six on twenty? No. Twenty-one. The rowers faced a man who sat in the center just in front of the aft deck. Parks' stomach curdled with the question of exactly what the fuck he was supposed to be doing here. Surely not a fight.

He squinted up and down for Joe and Foster. The kayak jerked and the nose tried to spin. Parks snapped back and pulled with all he had left. They moved as much laterally as forward. The hunter pointed, and he zagged hard to sea until he was clear of the worst of it, only a slight drift still apparent.

"So now would be a good time to fill me in," Parks kept the nose slightly to starboard to maintain a straight course. "I'm sensing some hostility between these dudes and your kemosabes. Um. I'm guessing you brought me here to mediate. Because I can't think of any other reason why one extra guy would make fuck-all difference. Also, what the hell is that boat?"

"It is darraig."

"What?"

"Light ship. Very fast."

"What kind of ordnance are dealing with?"

The man looked confused.

"Firepower. Weapons. We talking AK's, machetes, what?"

"Steel."

Parks suddenly broke free of whatever local current flared out from the channel. The slog seaward earned them up a much-needed zip with only a gentle swell over deep water to press them. As his eyes smoothed the edges of the boats and the water, he saw the hunters paddled steadily just to stay in one place. The breaks approached shore at a 45-degree angle. They sat in a wave shadow, while white eddies foamed around both sides of the skerry and the sea beside the cliffs rebounded through the lane. Too far one way, and they were committed to the current and the open water. Too little, and they'd be sucked onto the jagged rock.

A flash of foam caught his eye, like a splash in the channel, or a break over a subsurface rock. The channel was careening death unless you knew every ripple by heart. He could see why the larger ship kept its distance on the far side of the skerry. The only safe paddle for the kayak was toward the big single mast. The one hunting boat that had given him its profile turned forward again. Both pointed up the coast from where he'd come, like sprinters on the blocks.

"Stop." His companion commanded. Parks lifted the paddle. "They have chosen."

Parks squinted. He was still a ways off. Close enough to see the paddles surge through the water as the hunting boats jumped from the protection of the channel. They were making a run for it. The seaward vessel got momentum and pulled a few lengths ahead of its sister. Well back of the skerry, the wooden longboat saw them emerge and took an angle to cut them off. Its long oars sliced the waves at a terrifying clip even without the aid of a wind. From the first strokes, Parks could see the little boats had no hope.

"Go."

"Go where?"

"There!" He pointed at the pursuer.

"Straight at them?"

"*Go!*"

Parks churned frantically. He wasn't sure what charging the ship head-on was supposed to accomplish. His short stay with these people had told him they weren't much for explaining things in any kind of particulars. He guessed that reading currents, calculating nautical speeds, angles, and anything else that didn't involve poking a seal with something sharp wasn't in their wheelhouse. The longboat—he wasn't sure why he chose that word but it felt right—had surely seen them and made no attempt to alter course. They'd be content to plow over the kayak like a lump of driftwood. The man in the bow spun and deftly untied the lashing that bound the weapons. He pulled a spear and a toggle harpoon to his end, and pushed the other pair aft.

"I am called Klimut, son of Arkut. My uncles are Hawe and Akawake. What is the name of the man I die with?"

"Who, me?"

"Aye."

"You can die by yourself, buddy. I'm Parks. Son of Marion Parks, Jr., and Terry. Marion's my dad, Terry's my mom. I know, confusing, right?" Klimut focused on the closing ships. "You need my uncles, too?"

"Tell me at Urkuk."

Klimut held his spear vertical, bisecting himself. The longboat bore down. If he was hoping to intercept them, it wasn't going to work. Parks could make out the keel, and the woman carved into the prow, hair and dress flowing back to either side as she leaned out over the waves with her mouth agape. Beneath her, a plate of greenish metal formed a shoe that ended in what looked like an I-beam at the waterline. It peeled up the water menacingly on a line with the kayak.

The hunting ships passed to his left but he didn't have the luxury of watching them. The longboat looked more like a destroyer from here. He wanted to ask Klimut for instructions, but he knew by now these people just ignored any requests for clarification. If nothing happened, he decided, he was going to veer left. They should know to veer left, that was basic boating. Unless they were trying to run him down. Then they might veer right, their right, knowing he'd veer left, in order to crush him. He could hear a voice somewhere on the ship ahead shouting out strokes for the crew. No puny coxswain. It sounded big and mean. The words were unintelligible to him at first. He'd assumed they would speak in tongues. It took a moment to realize that the orders came in English.

"Pull! Pull!" Came across the water in a thick accent he couldn't place.

It passed the skerry and swung round the spinning eddy. The curved prow rose above them like a cobra as they crossed the line between the longboat and the hunters. Klimut held his weapon motionless. They were only a few long strokes away from being buried under the statuesque woman, who Parks could see was carved as if wearing a sheer wet fabric, her nipples protruding, eyes empty of detail. At that moment, Klimut's spear dropped and pointed left of the vessel. Parks wasn't sure if that was a direction, but he was happy to take it. He dug hard on the right side and slipped just off center as the ship cruised over his wake.

"Oars up right!" The man on the aft deck shouted to the back-facing rowers. They raised the long oars and turned the blade toward the kayak, so Parks had to veer even harder to avoid being clotheslined. The man in back glared at them from behind a spear that sprouted vertically from the deck. He wore leathers, and a short, coarse black beard going gray, his head near fully bald. Klimut was close enough to slap at the oars with the haft of his own spear, shouting and shaking it. There was a small round shield mounted at the side of each rowing station, but none of the men were concerned enough to raise it. Parks squinted at their faces in utter confusion, as they did his. A bunch of hard-ass ethnically-ambiguous white guys, maybe some South American stock. Anyone non-native must have been "his people" to Klimut. One man near the middle secured his oar and raised a bow, but by that time they had passed. The longboat spun sharply toward land. The swell and an extra stroke or two from the left side altered their course when the right raised oar. That must have been Klimut's intention with the drive-by.

The rowers pulled hard to regain their bearing on the hunting boats before the grip of the rock became too strong. They were less than concerned with the kayak, which could be held at bay with not more than an oar if it ever came close enough for a second pass.

"Again," Klimut shouted. Parks felt the kayak speed up. Dead ahead, the eddy snarled at him and threatened to swallow them into the rock. Parks was shocked to feel its pull even before they came to the white froth, but the kayak was a leaf sliding over bare ground. He spun the craft with a few desperate strokes and hurried straight for the cliffs, perpendicular to what felt like a rip current drawing him to the rock. The direction of the surf gave them a bump, and finally, they were free.

The hunting boats didn't even make it a hundred yards past the skerry before they gave up flight. Both swung seaward. The one on the inside track came all the way around to face the longboat and ran back as though to reach the safety of the channel. The other took a wider "U" and lifted their paddles. Adrenaline flooded his arms and he turned back away from the cliffs toward the others. It was a different boat now—light, agile, responsive with a little water behind it. Klimut didn't need to tell him to keep to the cliffs, clear of the toilet bowl around the rock. Here, the channel worked behind them as he hacked away at their distance. The maneuver hadn't done much. The longboat nosed in to cut off their path, momentarily obscuring the hunting boat, then swung around so they were pointed away from the cliffs and ready to row clear. The natives charged, but their path seemed more of a repeat of Parks' own run than an attempt to slip by. They were counterattacking. The men on the starboard side of the longboat, nearest the cliffs, locked their oars and lifted the shields. Klimut urged him forward, and Parks complied. What exactly he was going to do when he got there, he had no idea. Throw a stone spear and shout insults? That arrow would be waiting for him next time. He frowned as the absurdity of it dawned on him, then shook the thought away.

The port rowers pulled one to turn so that the hunting boat would pass starboard. Now he could make out two tiny figures, fore and aft. Parks couldn't believe the whole "hunting party" whose return they dreaded was five men with nine arms in three craft that even Foster's people wouldn't set foot in if they ever saw a body of water to begin with. The faster of the two—the one seaward—should have made a run for it once its buddy gave up. Instead, it resumed it's "U" around the far side of the longboat, which fixated on the first pair of hunters, now yards away.

One of them set down his paddle and raised a bow. He fired a pair of shots over the top of the shields that caused the rowers on both sides to take cover. They let the momentum of their drift spin them parallel to the skin boat. The hunters drew broadside just beyond an oar's length and stopped cold less than fifty yards from the skerry. The man at the stern traded his paddle for a bow, as well. A pair of archers from the port benches of the longboat crouched behind the shield wall as the vessels bobbed side-to-side. The hunters leaned against either side of a mound of seal carcasses in the middle of their little boat, taking away the angle of an archer from each half of their enemy's boat, respectively.

A three-pronged hook flew over the shield wall and into the boat. Who-ever was at the other end yanked, but it didn't snag. He reeled it in. The natives' arrows trained at the top of the wall, waiting for anything to pop up. The boats drifted closer still. Another grappling hook. This time, it sank into the skin hull, under the rail near the bow. The man nearest lowered his weapon and yanked it free. As he tossed it into the ocean, an archer rose from the longboat and fired a shot into his neck, pinning him to the seals. In the same split second, the other hunter loosed into the archer's chest. His com-panion tried a shot, but the hunter at the stern ducked behind the seals, drew, and rose immediately. All of the targets had disappeared, but they had seen that the man shot fast and didn't miss. They knew the next man out of the shields was also dead. Another hook, and another snag near the rear. It was too far to remove, and the remaining archer would be waiting. A third hook followed. The hunter drug the tip of his half-drawn arrow across the nearest rope to cut it, but the other two were well-sunk. The crew of the longboat patiently reeled the lone hunter closer to ship. He looked at his companion, still alive, eyes alert, but choking and bleeding out through the neck, without the strength to remove the shaft that held him. He didn't struggle or flail. His was the patience of a man who waited hours for the head of a seal to surface for the brief second it took to deliver a kill.

Parks closed in behind the hooked boat. The lines drew it within a few feet of their attackers. One of the shields lowered, and a black-haired young man, short and stringed with muscle, exposed himself calmly. The hunter did not fire. They had themselves a Mexican standoff, Parks thought. As soon as that arrow flew, the other archer would finish him off before he could reload. If he didn't fire, the men would come aboard. The hunter moved to the middle and leaned back against the pile of seals, mere feet away from the young man. His arrow pointed to the last place he'd seen the archer.

The kid opened his mouth. Parks realized he couldn't have been more than a teenager.

"Two more comin' up." He warned his crew about them.

"Board!" Came the voice that called the strokes.

The kid grabbed a short spear and put his foot on the rail to leap over. He was met with an arrow through the heart. His archer rose and fired. The shot went through the hunter's bicep as he tried to nock another one, right into his chest cavity. It must have missed anything vital, because he dropped the bow and grabbed his own spear with his off-hand, undaunted. All of the shields came down, and two men jumped aboard with short spears. One engaged the hunter. They slapped at each other's weapons for an opening. The other man drove his point through the one pinned to the seals and joined his companion. The archer took his time, and leveled an arrow into the left chest of the hunter. Then another in near the same spot. He went down to a knee but kept his spear up. The nearest man slapped it aside and plunged his own into the hunter's torso. The archer held fire as the two boarders stabbed again and again.

"Shields, port!" The voice yelled. Parks could not see over the longboat now but he knew the second hunting boat was making a run at the seaward side of the attackers. The men there went to shields, and the archer switched sides. Klimut took up both of his weapons under his right arm. He didn't need to speak for Parks to know the course. With more than half the crew distracted, he raced up to the bow of the hunting boat. When he was a few feet away,

Klimut jumped aboard. The kayak rocked and twisted. He dropped the toggle harpoon and quickly cut the two remaining ropes. With the butt of the spear, he shoved off of the longboat, trapping the two boarders with him. Their companions shouted encouragement.

"Cut his fuckin' arm off and fuck him with it!" They laughed.

The boarders grinned and approached slow. A hook reached for the boat to regain it, but Klimut flipped it away with his point. He pierced the belly of his dead companion and drew it across, spilling slippery guts over the center of the boat where the men would have to cross. Parks knew from his own boat that the footing in there would make it hard enough to stand or walk under the best conditions. Klimut alone seemed comfortable with his balance. The boarders climbed over the pile of seals. The first hopped the guts. As soon as his foot hit, Klimut made a hard thrust that was more of a push than a stab. The man was driven back a step. His foot slipped momentarily, his knee hit the deck. In the second it took him to right himself, he had a spear through his eye. Klimut steered him overboard and yanked his point back. The second man was more careful. While he stalled Klimut, more hooks captured the boat and began to reel him closer. The man refused to engage, choosing to wait for reinforcements.

Parks floated mere feet away. He felt helpless. This didn't look like his kind of fight. It didn't look like anything he'd ever seen before. He wasn't sure if Klimut expected him to join in, or wait like a getaway driver with the engine running. Everything in his gut told him he'd die if he left the kayak. And everything else made him feel a coward for staying. He heard thumps, arrows pounding into shields to keep the other side occupied. Fuck it, he could do something.

Parks pulled up against the boat and ran his toggle harpoon into a seal. He gave it a yank, and the shaft flexed where it was joined in the middle. An eyelet came loose, and he found himself holding the haft with nothing else attached. The rope ran into a tangle at the bottom of the kayak. He dropped what was now a useless stick and wrangled the end of the line free, then tied a quick knot around the brace at the stern of the kayak. When he looked up, the skerry was closer than he remembered it. The current should have run them away, but now he realized it was strongest near the cliffs. Even with the rock, some strange magnetism of swell and eddy and channel and water rebounding off the coast was sucking the whole tangled mess of ships backward. He paddled furiously straight for the cliffs. At last, the harpoon line went taut. But the men on the longboat had only to pull a rope. He was in a losing game of tug of war, though at least Klimut was caught too far away from the longboat for anyone else to leap aboard. They hauled against Parks' strokes.

He felt like a tiny fish flailing helplessly against a line that reeled him to his end. It was one paddle forward, three feet back.

Klimut moved with feet sure of the balance in the skin hull. The boat swayed wildly now, pulled from both sides. His enemy teetered and struggled to keep his feet, used to wide planks of wood. Parks was losing fast now. The hunting boat jerked between them, and Klimut tossed the spear to himself from a stabbing to a throwing grip and sent it the second his hand touched. It found home in the man's stomach. He doubled over, and Klimut delivered him into the ocean with a foot to the face.

The shields to port went down, and Parks saw the other hunting boat emerge behind them, and make a hard U-turn seaward before the skerry. Their strafing run was done and they would return for another pass, but it was excruciatingly slow. The archer had a moment to switch sides. Klimut grabbed his toggle harpoon and dove behind the seals. There was little place to hide as the boats inched closer. The moment they were close enough, two more men jumped over. Parks realized he had lost, and turned his kayak back toward his new ally. Klimut used the nearest man to shield himself from the archer's line. This man was more cautious than the others. He squatted for balance until his friend climbed atop the seals and slid down the other side, at a right angle of attack.

"Down!" someone shouted from the other boat. The man across from Klimut suddenly dropped. Klimut matched the maneuver, and an arrow flew right over them. They scrambled to their feet as the second man launched a side attack. Klimut parried him into his partner, but he gripped the shaft of the harpoon. Klimut had to let go to dodge a thrust from the other. He backed weaponless to the rail. The one who'd disarmed him looked at the stone weapon and tested the weight. He handed his shorter spear to his friend. Kimut drew a stone knife from his belt, his last resort, a few inches of blade against the long harpoon. He tried to slash at the probing tip. His attacker took a big step forward and rammed the point into Klimut's midsection. He held the hunter firm at haft's-length while the other man circled around to finish him off. Klimut saw there was nothing he could do. He twisted his body to dislocate the toggle point, and dove into the water with the leather rope trailing back to the hunting boat.

The boarder picked up the other end of the line. The crew of the long-boat found it wildly funny. They roared at the one-armed native, pierced in the water with their man holding the rope like a fisherman with a desperately hooked tuna. The taut line vanished beneath the water. The boarder let it all play out, then gave it a firm yank. That brought more laughter. Klimut floated up to the surface in agony, thirty feet away.

"Shields up!" Came the call, and Parks knew the second volley of arrows would buy him a reprieve of attention. The first arrow thumped against wood on the far side. He tested the weight of the spear he had left, and aimed for the man attached to Klimut. They saw him, but had nowhere to go. Parks leaned back in the kayak from point-blank range and unleashed. It wobbled over their shoulders and bounced harmlessly off the hull of the longboat like a wounded duck. The crew laughed again.

"Well thrown, fuckin' twat!" Someone shouted.

"That was a warning shot, faggot." He said. They laughed at him again. "Don't fuck with America's Navy." His cheeks flushed with anger, as though he traded words with someone in a bar who he knew could whoop his ass, caught like the hunting boat between pride and retreat.

Parks paddled over to the leather line halfway between Klimut and the harpoon, and wrapped a loop around his wrist. He tried to tug the other end free, but the man held on tight. Keeping the grip, he scooted to where he still had his own line wrapped around the stern. His big hand closed on it and yanked back and forth. The hunting boat rocked violently. The men on board could barely keep their feet. As the harpooner stumbled, Parks yanked again on Klimut's line, and the rope came free, floating atop the water. He untied his own harpoon line to let the other boat go, then pulled in the one trailing out of Klimut and wrapped it around the same brace at the stern of his kayak.

Parks paddled hard as the shields on the port side came down again. He worked to put yards between himself and the archer, steering toward the cliffs and the channel. What he could see of Klimut kicked up a small wake and slowed him considerably. Over his shoulder, the second hunting boat made a sharp U-turn, so close that it passed directly beneath the carved woman on the prow. They swung wide out to sea and prepared for another strafe. These native bastards were a lot braver than smart, he thought.

The two boarders in the hunting boat began tossing seal carcasses to their companions. Parks noticed just how far and fast the boats had drifted. Both hunting boat and longboat were nearly pointed directly at the cliffs as they spun, unable to row. The skerry growled menacingly behind and to starboard. They must have seen it too, because the seal throwers began chucking in overdrive, eager to cut the boat loose and get back on their oars.

Parks headed straight for the cliffs to again clear the tug of the twisted waters just off the skerry. The current picked him up and swung the nose of the kayak around. Parks used it to sling a full 180, then paddled perpendicular to the current, back toward the other boats. Klimut, eyes nearly closed, made a brief contact with him as he passed. The line curled between them, then went taut again and yanked the wounded man along. There was an audible groan.

"Sorry, bud!"

Between his load and the crossing waters, it felt like two strokes to hold position and one to lurch forward. It was some kind of luck that the boats, bound together and unable to maneuver, drifted back his way. The flow out of the channel once more caught them and spun the ships so they faced away from the skerry again, though they appeared to travel in reverse. The same current that reoriented them also kept them out of the channel and in the bone-white fingertips of the eddy. The meat thieves had taken what they dared. A few seals remained, bloody and brined, but the skerry was near upon them. They leaped to their own ship and cut the lines. The empty hunting boat accelerated toward the rock as the longboat's oars gave a mighty pull.

For the first time, he saw it close up, in totality. The tall mast rocked overhead. Both ends rose well above the heads in high curves, the bow more rounded by a hair. Water ran off the blades in rivulets as they arced for another stroke. It looked like something you'd find hanging precariously overhead in some history museum, or docked downtown for a school field trip, but these men were real, and they had killed two, going on three for a pile of seals. He looked back at the bobbing shape behind him. What was the plan now? No one ever told him anyway, but he felt particularly lost without anyone to so much as ignore him. At least there was always a brownish man nearby who he could follow without quite knowing why. The oars on the port raised again to go to shields, at the worst time for the longboat. Arrows thumped. To his left, Parks saw the empty hunting boat collide with the rocks with surprising gentleness. There was almost no mass to it. It bounced, spun, and got lodged in a depression. Each wave tried to stick it farther into the rock, and each ebb, to pull it free.

The other hunters were fucked, he thought. As soon as the longboat broke free of the current they'd do the same or worse to them. His best bet was to again turn and grind upstream through the channel, paddle downshore a ways, and look for a place to land. Find Foster and Tunguk. He winced for Klimut, floating ten yards away. If he wasn't dead yet, he'd be hypothermic within the hour, maybe less with all the blood loss. Were there sharks here, he wondered?

Still, inexplicably, he found himself paddling toward the longboat, now broadside to him. The wooden woman leaned hard away from the skerry, but found herself drifting back as arrows sailed into her shields. One arced over the boat to splash near the kayak.

"Hey, friendly fire, yo!" He couldn't imagine anyone heard. The men to starboard sat, oars ready. They locked onto him, perhaps deciding if he was a threat, or who to kill first once they made it free of the arrows and the drift.

He closed, like a leopard seal awaiting its chance to attack. With what, he didn't know, only that he wanted very much to fuck these bastards. The strain on the kayak eased. It felt a part of his body, some amphibious beast they had not meant to reckon with. These were his sovereign waters, his hunting ground, his breeding ground. Something rose in his chest, loading up like a massive swell. Then he saw it. The carving on their boat stirred. Her arms moved, her breast heaved. Terror filled him. He blinked hard to clear the shitty genetics from his eyes. It wasn't the woman. Someone was hanging on to the carving, below view of the deck, dug in like a rock climber. And he was waving. Waving, to get his attention. Foster's tender hand flapped. His ass hung in the water to take some of the load off the rest of him. On the other side, Parks could just make out the white wisps of Tunguk's hair. The runs of the hunting boat, the tight turn under the bow—they suddenly became clear. He still didn't know what the plan was. But he knew they should not be spotted until it was done.

The longboat was desperate to row. With one side under fire, they were left to the mercy of the currents. The hunters were out of view, but apparently parked to hold them in place.

"Attention, nut-knockers!" He called. The kayak drew alongside, and the black eyes of the skipper fell upon him. "I am Parks, the ranking naval officer—" He stopped. Sounded like something Carabiner would say. "They call me the Leopard Seal. You know why? Cause I'm the most dangerous predator in the sea."

"Hard to port!" They ignored him. The oars on his side plunged in. He could see they meant to turn straight at the hunting boat to break their archers' angle.

"Now you might be wondering what the most dangerous man in the Southern Ocean is doing in a kayak. Why isn't he running a destroyer? Or a carrier group, even? Granted, those are dangerous ships. But it isn't the ship you need worry about. It's the man at the helm. I could drown every one of you by hand off a boogie board. You step into the water with me, you'll be dead before your dick shrinks."

It earned him a disinterested chuckle from a few of the men. Parks closed on their oars.

"Are you running? Wise decision. Most would call you a pussy for flee-ing a lone man in a kayak, but I'm not among them. I would accept all manner of insults a man could heap upon me to avoid a fight with The Leop-ard Seal, were I not he. Run, bitches!" Parks pulled alongside. He slapped at one of the oars with his paddle to disrupt it, then tried to get a hand on the blade. The man gave it a flick, and Parks' world flashed black for half a second. There was a roar of laughter, and only then did the pain in his face well up. Blood ran down into his mouth.

"Follow us out the current, cunt!" One man yelled back.

Parks pinched his nose and his hand came away red. His sinuses throbbed and it hurt to shut his left eye. The embarrassment turned to anger. He searched the foulest part of his imagination for what he would do, given half a chance. Beat their faces to bone meal. Feed them whatever he cared to sever. Above it all rose the memory of his responsibility, snapping back like a leash. He didn't dare look at Foster, or at Klimut. All he could hope was to hold their attention.

"Good idea! Better gain the tactical advantage before facing a single man in a kayak. Not worth the risk."

"We'll skin you soon enough, fat fuckin' seal." The men were getting riled, but the skipper remained uninterested. His were the only eyes directed forward. Parks drew even closer.

"Hey, who's that woman without an oar? Is that the whore the crew bangs when they're out of dead marine mammals?" No one dared laugh, and he knew he had something going. "She's purdy. Can I have a go?" Nothing. "Hey, Faggot!" Parks tried. The man was unbothered. Enough of this, he thought. Parks slapped his paddle, sending splash of water into the man's face. He made a few recovery strokes and did it again. "How does my sea water taste?"

His head turned. "Archer." A man near the bow pulled up his oar and reached for a bow. Parks was barely an oar's-length away from the longboat. A sure shot. The skipper smiled at Parks. "Good day to you, Leopard Seal." As the man drew, a flash from the prow. A hand set a spear on the deck. Tunguk swung his tiny frame up behind it. All eyes were turned back to Parks. Eskimo Joe reached his blade around the archer's neck. The arrow flopped down and the head hung off the back by only the spine. He picked up the spear and plunged it into the base of the skull of the nearest rower.

"Arms, forward!" The captain pointed at Joe.

By now the longboat pointed at the hunters, putting an end to their peppering until they could get a better angle. The men locked their oars and scrambled for weapons. Foster's right arm and left leg clasped the deck, but he stalled. Tunguk dragged him up by the collar, then took a position to the middle and above the crew. The quarter deck stood several feet over the narrow lane between benches, so that they could only come double-file, tripping over cargo, and already two bodies mangled the footing. The spear caught the next man as he tried to arm himself, once, twice, a third time in the neck. He fell choking and gushing blood.

Foster motioned Parks closer. He paddled with authority. What did this unarmed and one-handed redneck have up his sleeve? Foster scooped up a long coil of rope near the bow. He let out the slack, took a step, then heaved it side-arm to Parks. It landed perfectly across the kayak.

"That way!" He pointed, then tied off his end around the prow.

The skerry. Parks secured the line to the kayak and paddled like mad for the rock. No one was at oars. They lined up to pick their way over the bodies of their friends toward Joe and Foster. The first strokes were immense in weight, but in moments the ship turned hard to the coast. The captain saw it.

"Aft, to oars! Foredeck, cut the line!" He grabbed his own weapon, a short, straight spear, then pushed men aside to get into the fight.

"Cut the line!" The men hesitated to engage Eskimo Joe. The front of the column slapped spears a few times, searching for an advantage. Joe rolled his point around to ready each time. The next attempt, he pulled it out the way and pushed the top of the man's spear down for a split second slash across the face. His brow, nose, and lip opened up like canyon walls and blood gushed into his sight. The old hunter gave a quick thrust of his point that broke the windpipe and sent the man to his knees gasping for a breath that would never come.

Foster camped over the rope. Parks had taken a good angle, and the bow turned most of the way around. The oars in the water were without command, nervous of the unseen fight going on behind them. They splashed disjointedly, hurting as much as helping.

"Get the fucking rope!" The skipper shoved a man forward. He stumbled in the heave and rolled toward the quarter deck while Joe fended off the man before him. As the rower raised his spear for the rope, Foster gripped the haft. He had no strength in his other hand, no shot at winning a protracted tug of war. All Parks needed was seconds more. He clamped his elbow to his side. The spear locked in as part of his body. Foster threw himself overboard. The rower came with him into the cold waters.

The skerry seemed to rise and fall like a dog pulling on its chain in anticipation. The kayak brushed the edge of the eddy. It whipped, and only a panicked effort and slack on the line allowed Parks to cut a sharp angle out, paddling between the turning longboat and the rock, aiming seaward as the ship spun closer to disaster.

On deck, the captain came to the fore. Joe slid out of the way of a big slash and dove overboard after Foster. The man severed the rope that towed them around and shouted, "Starboard only!"

Parks tiptoed the narrow lane between the furious swirl of white water and the longboat. The starboard oars, now directly between the crew and the rock, slapped his kayak in their attempt to find purchase in the sea. He snatched at one, and managed to yank it free and toss it into the white churn.

The kayak shot free of the convergence of the longboat and the rock into open water. The oars found their rhythm and were able to turn coastward, saving the woman on the prow from a direct collision. They tried to shoot the channel inside the rock, but the port rowers entered the water too hard and turned them back. A swell reverberated off the cliff wall and lifted the boat. The starboard side slammed into the rock, smashing oars and sending one man tumbling over. The boat tilted violently, but did not tip. The wave sucked it off the rock again, and they paddled and pushed to clear it. The stern dipped into the eddy and swung around, smashing the rock a second time. It seemed less violent than the first, but the scramble of men on the benches told otherwise. They bore down and at last caught the middle of the channel to shoot past the skerry, but Parks spotted a limp. The mast was already listing. Gored and taking on water. Men bailed it over the side as fast as they could while others rowed. The captain glared back at the kayak.

They were afloat for now, going nowhere fast. Parks recalled the way the *Qarapara* filled so slowly. Gave them a hope of rescue, or escape. There was nowhere in these cliffs to make land. No life rafts or emergency beacon. He knew the cocktail of fear and irrational optimism of which they drunk, and he knew the waters they would meet before they suspected. He hoped they were fighters, so they could die of creeping hypothermia instead of the quick mercy of a lungful of water.

A sick feeling stabbed through his gut. *Klimut.* He steered so close to the rock—had he bashed his Reverse-Eskimo pal in the maneuver? The braided leather line of the harpoon stood out beside the heftier one of the ship. The former snapped against tension in the bobbing swell and disappeared beneath the water. Parks spat out the blood pooling on his lips. He had the sense to reel slowly, not to let the weight get dragged well beneath the surface. A white shape appeared, then broke the wake. Klimut had a death grip on the line. His eyes were shut and he lie motionless, sleep or rigor, Parks didn't know. He brought the man with great care alongside the kayak. Air bubbled on his lips, and he coughed. A mouthful of salt water ran down his chin.

"We meet again, my sea amigo," Parks said. "Let's see if we can do this without capsizing this time." He lowered his weight. It made perfect sense now, the leverage points, the center of gravity, the subtle lean he had to take. He scooped his arm under the stump and oriented Klimut, chest to the kayak, straight up and down. His big paws pinched the ribcage. He leaned back and brought the torso over the side. Klimut groaned in agony. Right, Parks thought. Stomach wound. He gave another tug and rolled him onto his side, then his back, then over again onto the deck. Klimut was the gray of a drowned ghost, but his chest rose and fell.

Parks glanced up to see the other boat haul Joe aboard to join Foster. They paddled to the man Foster had disembarked, treading water. He looked up at the hunters without a plea or a final slur. A man free of expectation. One of the natives Parks didn't know drove a spear straight down behind his collarbone. He died without a fuss.

The kayak slid up beside the larger boat.

"Gentlemen," he addressed the hunters. "Pleased to make your acquaintance. I have one of yours here, a man called Klimut, perhaps in need of a witch doctor, or a good leeching. Well fought, by the way. Condolences on your friends, but I saw them die, and they did it well. One of the better naval battles that my friend and I have been a part of." He nodded to Foster.

"It is a good day when Tunguk can be of use," one of them, a bony man in his forties, replied.

The three natives laughed. Even Klimut managed a couple of coughs. Parks guessed that passed as a burn to these people. "Come," the same man continued. "We get the boat." He indicated the drifting hunting vessel, miraculously afloat and still skipping off the rock.

The longboat struggled down the coast. Their fight was beginning. Even in sight of his enemies Parks felt a calm. "Good idea, let's delay medical care so we can unstuck the boat." No laughs. He wasn't sure he and these natives had the same brand of humor. "Anybody got any healing herbs, at least? No? Hot tea? OK." He gave up. The hunting boat moved past him. He wrapped around and paddled up beside Foster, who shivered lightly. The call of sea birds cut the silence. They looked to the cliffs. A thousand little outcrops teemed with white feathers and wings tipped with silver. He had neither heard nor seen them before, an audience gathered for a great drama, unnoticed until the actors finished their lines and looked out from the stage. Now they sprung into it. Shrieking and flapping into a cloud, they tore out over the hunters then turned hard after the longboat.

"Hey, Fucker," Parks said as he watched.

"Hey, Brother." Foster warmed his broken hand under his armpit.

"Know what I realized?"

"What's that?"

"We're never going home."

5

FIVE BATTLES

The tops of the huts appeared in the distance. Maybe that would shut Parks up, Foster hoped. He dipped and jerked the rope higher on his shoulder. A line split off the bow of the kayak to either side, and another from the stern. He and Parks bore the front, while the two hunters took the rear. Klimut lay still inside as they trucked it over land like a stretcher. Or a coffin. For miles the leather cut into his trap. It slid, he yanked, again and again. Having one hand to hold on to the end didn't help his situation. Tunguk led without a word. The hunters carried without a word. Klimut even had the decency to die quietly. Only Parks could not bear the silence.

"The bigger they are, the harder they fall. This biggity boy's a diggity dog. I have 'em like Miley Cyrus, clothes off twerkin' in their bras and thongs, timber. Hang in there, sea amigo. We got civilization dead ahead." He resumed his song.

The village reappeared. Foster felt a knot cinch in his gut at the sight of the dark little knobs below. Tunguk insisted they help the hunters back. He was less committal when Foster asked for assurances that their help would earn them a pardon. The old man didn't like to make statements about the future beyond which foot he intended to step with next.

It seemed like every soul was about. If there was a listless ease when they first arrived the previous evening, the morning's events had shattered it. One of the huts lay in a neat pile of bone, its leather covers rolled nearby. A group of men busied themselves striking the next one. Women gathered materials into neat bundles, staged outside the dwellings. The meat rack was packed. A handful of children ran gleefully between the bone frame as soon as the cover came off. At the center of the huts, two long shapes stretched side by side, wrapped from head to toe. The activity came to a halt as soon as someone spied them wrestling the kayak down the hill.

"I'm slicker than an oil spill. She say she won't, but I bet she will, timber. It's going down, I'm yelling timber. You better move, you better dance. Let's make a night, you won't remember. I'll be the one, you won't forget."

The villagers left their work to gather around the crew as they bore their vessel to the middle of the crowd. Foster expected to see weapons drawn any moment. A flurry of concern. Instead, they formed a loose semicircle. No one asked a question, in any language. Tunguk motioned, and the four men lowered the kayak. Everyone gathered to examine Klimut. A woman spoke a word in her tongue. Four of the elders—Ingut and Gjardukut included—took over the ropes and carried him to one of the huts that still stood, as two women followed. Foster glanced at the one at the end of the row, where they'd spent what passed for a night. The rock in front was brown with blood. Above all else, he felt embarrassed.

Parks groaned and rolled his shoulder back in circles that failed to unkink it. "So we haven't been entirely honest with you," he told the hunters in a low tone. "Not to go into detail, but just be aware you may have to kill a few people to keep us alive in the near future." They looked perplexed. "I know, akamonika's a bitch. Don't go too far."

The men returned from the hut. Foster thought they would address them, but they walked past, and took up leather sacks. Everyone in the village, it seemed, followed. Only the young woman remained with her baby, and they vanished into another hut. The other children—three girls and a boy, ranging from about four to eight—ran unattended.

Foster started to open his mouth, but Tunguk interrupted. "They will bring the seal."

"Oh, thank God." Parks exhaled.

Foster didn't voice it, but he'd been a bit worried they would have to double back and carry the carcasses to be processed. Almost half of the hunt had been lost, and while it seemed like there was a lot left, he suspected they wouldn't see it the same way. At least no one was trying to kill him at this particular moment. Their reception should have surprised him, but he was done being surprised. His efforts to rationalize anything that had happened since the ship hit ice pealed like an endless bell in his head and threatened to shred his sanity. Or a dream that made perfect sense, as long as he remained asleep.

He tested his hand again. The fingers were almost completely stuck in a "C" shape now. The knuckles of his pinky and ring fingers were swollen larger than the other two. He wanted nothing more than to rest. Another round of water and meat, like before. But asking hospitality felt like sacrilege at this point.

"Looks like they're packin' up," he remarked.

"They must move camp before sleep." Tunguk glanced at the two corpses, as if it were an explanation.

"We should go. Before they get back."

"Please." One of the hunters motioned toward an empty hut. Foster's throat stuck. He remembered too well what it took to leave the last time he went in on of those things. But Tunguk nodded in acceptance.

The natives dipped through the doorway, and Foster knew they should follow. Tunguk pinned the flap open so the sun could poke its head inside. There on the floor the men helped themselves to water and meat. Soon, his greedy gulps brought the shivers back from the inside out. He wore only the sleeveless shirt and overpants, both clammy from his swim. The rest of their clothes remained on the cliff, under a stone to keep the wind from stealing them.

Foster chose to sit in the shadow. The weak light wasn't likely to warm him, and the dark had become rare. Precious. Four in the afternoon, he thought. He didn't know if that was true, or if so, how he knew, but the rhythms of the day began to seep into his skin. The sun whirled around them like some carrion bird praying for a slip-up. In the southern latitudes, it seemed like time and light were the same thing. It migrated here like a flock, covering every inch of bare ground and fluttering with activity. Whether it was 4 p.m. or a.m. hardly mattered. If there was daylight, you could do it. There were two days crowded into one, so that even going without sleep didn't make him as tired as it should have. He thought back to the morning, the boats. It already felt a month past. The charter was ages ago. Only the shade slowed things down for him. He took his bearings on the edge of the little sail of light that came through the doorway. Detail vanished around it, as though ducking out for a break from the constant press of light, and time. A man could get ancient here in an instant. He wondered, then, if the winter night was endless.

"Tunguk, will you sing first?" One of the hunters asked.

"Sing what? Are we singin'?"

"We will give our battles," Tunguk replied. "I am no singer. I will say mine in the common language so all can have it."

"What, like, tell each other what we just did?"

"Yes," Tunguk replied.

"I mean, we were all there. I was brushin' ass with you the whole time."

"It is then that it is most important. There are six battles. One we will not hear. The rest will be told so it is one, and it will be ours."

"Let Joe tell his story, Fucker. What else have we got to do?"

"I don't know. Sleep? Run away and never come back?"

"Maybe he's got stuff he needs to get off his chest."

"That's what I'm afraid of."

"Come on. You know how old people are. They just need to corner you and tell you things you already know to feel important. The man saved our asses back there. It's the least we can do."

"Are we saved?"

Parks didn't have an answer. Tunguk waited, and when no more voices were raised, he began. "I am called Tunguk. No man is my father. My uncles are Wakanat and Hawe, Uppinikuanatuk and Junnlauk, Gunnlauk, and Akawake, and Piktuk. I waited for boats to return with two spies of the sea kings, who have akmanuak. Then Klimut came and said boats were trapped by men at the place we call Faragat. The man called Brother went to Klimut to paddle, for Klimut was tired. I ran with Fucker to the cliffs at Faragat.

"When Brother and Klimut came, I jumped with Fucker. We went in the boat with Rumit and Kullunuk, who had many fur seals, and a young spot seal that was fresh, still with its guts. There were good hides and plenty of blubber, a good hunt. We lie with the seals so we could not be seen. The other boat, with Ginnikut and Osak, went first and offered for a fight. There was a ship. Many men with oars and steel. It gave battle, and Ginnikut was killed, then Osak was killed. Klimut joined and killed his enemies, until they were too many, and he was struck and forced into the sea.

"Rumit and Kullunuk shot arrows to steal the eyes of the men. I went into the water with Fucker, and we stayed with the woman of the boat until it was time. Then we went up and had a fight. I killed those who fought me. Fucker gave a rope to Brother, and he towed the men into Faragat. At this time, I left the ship with Fucker, and we returned to the hunting boat. We took the seals that remained, and towed the boat of Ginnikut in to be repaired. Most of the harpoons and spears, we also salvaged."

A pause told them that was all there was to his story. Another voice rose in the dark hut, shadowed from Foster's view.

"I am called Rumit. My fathers are Cabor, Junnlauk, and Gunnlauk. My uncle is Akawake."

"That's quite a family tree," Parks interrupted.

"Aye. Now I will sing my battle in Mattakatan." He launched into a rhythmic chant in his mother language, rising, falling like a wind that gusted and settled, and as intelligible as a wind to the foreigners. After a few minutes, Foster felt he knew what part of the tale Rumit was on. The song hardly changed, but the syllables were of a different character. Shorter and less flowy. He tried to imagine what the man had seen, having been in the same boat for most of the event. Maybe he could pick out where the boat turned for another pass, or an arrow struck a shield. At one point he heard "Brother," he was sure of it. And later, "Fucker." But the song defied him. He was hidden deep in the hull, and what Rumit saw was not the same as what Foster imagined. They weren't even English objects, and they didn't meet the way his language did. The bursts took a different pattern than what he would expect if he were simply inflecting a story the same as he would in English, but using nonsense words. Maybe the way they sung was different than the way they would have spoken. He could not correspond it to Tunguk's account either. The song was much longer. Soon he gave up trying to relate it and just listened. He figured if he stopped trying to think too hard, the rhythms of the consonants and the breath of the vowels would at least move him in a certain way. This, too, never happened. Not as he expected. It could as easily have been a story about Rumit's experience at the middle school dance, or a whale he once killed, for all Foster could make of it. He gathered only the fact that another man in the same boat fought a battle that differed in blow, and in kind.

Rumit intoned his last note.

"It is well sung," Tunguk remarked.

"Well sung," Kullunuk repeated.

"Dope." Parks added. Foster muttered in agreement.

Kullunuk continued: "Tunguk and Rumit, you have given me much room for my battle. I pray that the same is said of me by Brother and Fucker. I am no singer, so I will use the language of Brother and Fucker, since it is good for describing battles. I am called Kullunuk. It has always been this way. My fathers are Cabor and Piktuk, and perhaps Hawe. My uncles are only Akawake, and Turinakiwatankamun."

Foster wrinkled his brow. He didn't care to pry into the sordid lineages he was hearing, but several names kept coming up. It reminded him of his laundry list of "cousins," many of whom shared no blood, yet were as-cousin or more than the verified ones as far as he was concerned.

"We were returning from the hunt with a good many seals, when Osak saw a ship, far off. It was not known to us the nature of the ship, but we thought by the season it is troubling, so we paddled for the place called Faragat. There we stopped. It would overtake us if we continued for the landing. Soon, we saw it was as we feared, and the sail came down. Klimut left to bring word, while we waited. It was much to keep the boats off the rock. They were heavy with good catch, and Cabor found a spot seal for us, small enough to fit in the boat. We prayed the men would grow tired, but they remained. It was Ginnikut who said we should throw the catch over, so the men would not want us. I thought it would only make them angry. We stood for it. The boat of Ginnikut and Osak would sacrifice the seal. The boat of Rumit and Kullunuk would fight. It was thought that Klimut would fight.

"We waited until the birds were disturbed. Osak thought it strange, and when he looked he saw the face of Tunguk, and of the foreign spy called Fucker. These men came into the water so they were not seen. We were favored when they chose our boat, for Ginnikut and Osak were chosen to make battle. At this time, we also saw Klimut return, with a big man from the far seas called Brother.

"Of the fight, what is there to say? We shot many arrows, but the men hid. Ginnikut and Osak fought well, but they were defeated. Then Klimut joined the battle, and made it fierce. Tunguk and Fucker left us at this time to board the men's ship, and Brother made insults to anger them. It was then that Tunguk boarded, and killed many men. Fucker gave a rope to Brother, who towed the ship into the rock, where it was smashed, but did not sink. It took water, and made for land, but there is no land. We left them to drown. One man fell out with Fucker, and I gave him mercy. In the hunting boat, there were seals they did not take, though we knew we must hunt again soon. We took it home, and carried Klimut to the women. Once he dies, the battle will be at an end."

"It is turning into a good battle," Tunguk said. The others laughed. Foster faked a chuckle, but he never quite knew when one of these fools was making a joke or a statement of the utmost gravity.

"Is it my turn?" Parks wanted to know.

"All you," Foster offered. He heard his friend take a long inhalation, then a quick exhale and a "*Hah!*" followed by a wet clearing of the throat. There was the sound of a spit, and a splat, and Parks cleared his throat again.

"I, too, am a singer," he began. "And I will sing in the language of my people. We have heard many stories. This one is mine."

Good Lord, thought Foster.

"*Wellllll*.....they call me Brother and yall know my dad. Gary and Frank are the uncles I have." He rapped in an early '90's style. "I was chillin' on a rock with my two best bros, a redneck named Foster and Eskimo Joe, we was fresh outta prison, young jocks on a mission, you might say that we was fishin'…for some huntin' gear."

Foster realized that Parks had ignored Rumit and Kullunuk's stories so that he could prepare a rhyme in his head, and that he had memorized it to a degree. He also knew that Parks was not a good enough rapper, or rememberer-of-things in general, to compose an entire song in minutes and perform it by heart. He waited eagerly for the moment Parks would be forced to freestyle.

"When along came a nigga by the name of Klimut, a-paddlin' up, and I cain't believe I seen it, he had one arm and his face was steamin'. Said, 'Some hatin' motherfuckers got my niggas locked down, I need some bad sons of bitches to help me go to town, we gonna make 'em drown, they shorts are gonna turn brown.'" Parks beatboxed for a few measures.

"We had one knife between us and three hard bones, I said 'Klimut, call ya niggas on the Eskimo phone, tell 'em there's a posse gonna bring 'em home, them thievin' motherfuckers they as good as gone.' I got in the kayak, but my balance was whack. Klimut fell out and he gave me flack. I said, 'cut some slack, cause we back on track, now hand me that paddle, we on the attack.'

Any minute now, thought Foster. The natives sat in silent reverence.

"When we rooooolled up, we saw a biiiig rock, we saw a big ass boat, and our niggas was caught, by that big ass boat, the likes I never seen, in all my Navy travels or in my dreams. A boat full of honkies with blades of steel, and a scary old bastard sittin' at the wheel. 'I said Klimut, my gringo, my one-armed sea amigo, how you think we are gonna win at bingo?' He said, 'Nevermind fool, you just follow me, follow me, follow me right through the sea, in our little tiny boat, we gonna get the goat."

A satisfied smile crossed Foster's lips in the dark.

"The other boats made a break from cover, and I paddled hard if my name is Brother. One got caught with grappling hooks, by some hard ass honkies who don't read books. And it was hard to see, it was hard to watch, but they shot an arrow right in his crotch, except it wasn't his crotch, it was just his neck, and the other Eskimo came to protect. He pulled out his gat and he fired a shot, and wouldn't you know, he *got*...a man. He killed him dead. Then some other motherfuckers stabbed him in the head. That's when my boy Klimut said, 'Pull on up, these weak ass bitches are about to get cut.'

"So he jumped on board and he killed a man, or maybe it was two, I can't remember, if they came on board later, when their boy was dismembered. Anyway that shit ain't important, Klimut got stuck by his own damn harpoon. Let me back up, I forgot a part. I done had a rope to the other boat. And I saved his life when I gave it a yank. Those bastards thought they had him in the bank. He fell overboard but I grabbed the line, I said you can't have Klimut, his ass is mine.

"While all this shit was goin' down, My other dudes here were goin' to town. They kept the enemy occupied, and under the boat, that's where I spied, who but my old friend Eskimo Joe and a boy named Fucker, 'bout to get bowed. They jumped on deck and they had a fight, then Fucker said, 'Brother, won't you take this line?' So I grabbed that rope and I gave it a tow. I ran at the rock in my little bitty boat. Them fools tried to paddle, tried to disappear, but I had them like your mama grabs you by the ear. And I paddled and pulled, and I took that ship, right into the rock where it got ripped. Apart, that is. Then my boys over here whose names I forget, went and got my friends and pulled them in. There was one young gun still left to kill. They foreclosed on his ass and sent his mom the bill. Yeah we lost two guys, but we killed a bunch. All of this shit, we did before lunch."

The natives waited a moment to make sure he was done, then Rumit said, "It is well-sung."

"Well-sung," Kullunuk echoed.

"Well-sung?" Foster said in disbelief.

"Thank you, thank you."

"Parks, that was trash. Is it my turn to talk?"

"Hey, let's try to keep this a supportive environment."

"We will hear what Fucker has to say," came Tunguk's voice.

"Trash. In fact, I don't understand what the fuck is goin' on here at all. At first I thought this was some kind of PTSD, get it off your chest bullshit, and that's fine, I'm all about that. But none of yall even mentioned half the shit that went down. Rumit, my apologies brother, maybe you did and I didn't catch a word of it. My gut tells me otherwise. Tunguk, I know you're old as fuck, but you forgot half the damn details. Then you completely glossed over all the important shit. 'We went and had a fight. It was good. Then we left.' What kind of a story is that? You spent more time talkin' about how many dead seals were in the boat than how your boys fought their asses off and died like fuckin' Vikings. Klimut 'killed some men?' He boarded a fuckin' vessel under attack to save his friends, and he 'killed some men' with one arm. How about him gettin' towed around in the water by Parks by his gut wound? 'Rumit and Kullunuk shot some arrows'? If you was at D-Day, you'd probably say, 'Some men came on the beach, and there was a fight. Then the enemy left.' Is that how you remember losin' three friends?"

Tunguk spoke in an even tone. If he was offended, there was no trace of it in his voice. "A battle is remembered many ways. We share ours so that all may see as we saw. We will hear your battle too, then it will be part of ours."

"Yeah, buddy. I think everyone did a pretty good job of recounting what happened without disparaging anyone else. Except maybe Rumit, we'll never know for sure. But if you're so offended by what we forgot, enlighten us," Parks challenged.

"You wanna be enlightened?"

"I sure do."

"You wanna hear exactly what I seen?"

"That's literally what I am asking. I'm not sure what part of that isn't clear."

"Now before I begin, Rumit and Kullunuk: the way I understand it, it might be said that we saved your lives. Is that accurate?"

"It is so," Rumit said.

"And to my understandin', in doin' so, you, like Tunguk here, also owe us akmanuak."

He regretted it the moment it was out. A heaviness hung in the the air, as though the structure itself held its breath. At last, Tunguk spoke.

"You are foreigners."

"What does that mean?" This time, it was Parks, a new edge on his voice.

"You are not of the clan."

The two hunters remained wordless. Foster's face burned with the notion that he had committed some great offense, yet they were too polite to point it out directly.

"I don't understand," Parks said.

"He means they don't owe us shit."

"Yeah, I got that. Wait. I'm super confused. Joe, do you still owe us shit?"

"Yes."

"But they only owe you."

"No."

Foster thought Parks was being dense, but now he frowned. Was Tunguk no longer a member, either? There was no way they could have known. He'd been with the hunters every step. No one said a word to them.

Rumit spoke. "Tunguk has much help. He does not need ours."

"We don't have to help him, he has to help us," Parks clarified. "Right? Foster?"

"I don't even know which end of my dick to piss with anymore."

"It is well. We will hear your story," Kullunuk urged him on.

"Hang on now," Parks said. "Why were you clarifying who had akman-whatever before you told your story?" Foster didn't respond. "I think maybe you should run it by me first."

"You know what? Fuck it. You said you wanted to be enlightened."

"Changed my mind."

"Nah. I just watched somethin' I can't even believe happened, and yall got me thinkin' I lost it. None of what anyone said had anything to do with what I saw. Yall wanna share battles? Cool. You ought to know exactly what we just shared. Now, I know yall were off huntin' so you didn't get a chance to speak to any of the other members of your tribe, clan, what-have-you. But my story starts a lot earlier than Tunguk and ol' Brother, here. I, for one, am glad we don't have akmanuak, because to ask the smallest favor of you would be more heinous in my mind than anything those dudes in the ship were gonna do. I'm not even sure that I shouldn't go so far back as to tell you how we ended up here, but I'll save that for another time. Suffice to remind yall that Tunguk is also pledged to defend us with his life. He's done a real good job of that, although now that I think of it, every time we need defendin' in the first place is because of somethin' he did. We were brought here to eat and drink, only to be sentenced to execution. Tunguk busted us out, and if you noticed a couple ol' boys are missin' from class, there's your explanation.

"We had to run for it, which meant we would have to hunt for ourselves if we wanted meat, which meant that we needed some gear—some weapons, a boat. That's why we were waitin' there on the rock when Klimut pulled up. Our plan was to ambush you as soon as a boat put ashore. We were gonna kill Klimut, and whichever two of you who were unlucky enough to be the next boat in, so we could steal your seals and your spears. Cold blooded murder and robbery. Come to think of it, you'd have found yourselves down three brothers same as you are now."

He paused for effect. No one spoke, but he could feel Parks squirming.

"But lucky for I-don't-know-who, yall were attacked, and Tunguk for reasons beyond my comprehension decided we should help yall fight your way clear. Parks here, who yall call Brother because that's what I call everybody and Tunguk heard me say it, he flopped into the water like a fat walrus and went to paddle for Klimut. I remember thinkin' how glad I was that I had a broken hand, and he had to get into the cold-ass ocean instead of me. Then Tunguk made me run at the pace of whatever snail crawled up his ass for miles and miles until I was ready to collapse. When we got there, he told me to jump off a fifty foot cliff into a strong current and climb into one of the very boats that was under attack without bein' seen.

"I don't know for sure, but I suspect yall must've realized that whoever picked us up was gonna have the easy fight, and the other boat was bait. That wasn't no accident. How yall or those other two guys felt about that is a part of the story I would like to hear one day. But those men who yall say 'had a fight' or whatever made a conscious choice to row out from safety and stop so the pirates—which by the way, what the fuck is even goin' on at this point? So the *pirates*, who were really just tryin' to do the same thing that we were, could kill them. And they did that. I didn't see it, because my face was buried in a bloody seal coochie at the bottom of your boat, but then I didn't need to see to know what was gonna happen.

"I also didn't see Klimut, who everyone has failed to mention was fightin' with one arm, one goddamn arm, after paddlin' for his life, got on there and started lightin' fools up. Which by the way, if I've learned anything from Antarctica, it's don't fight anybody, at all. Not an old man, not a cripple, not no one, because all of 'em will cut your throat faster than you can say, 'I'm a little bitch.'

"And I didn't see what Parks did, but contrary to a lot of things I would have thought about the man prior to today, I understand he acted with balls.

He fought for Klimut like that man he was about to kill a few hours before was his childhood best friend, and if he manages to pull through, he has Parks to thank.

"But he also has Rumit and Kullunuk, who didn't 'shoot arrows.' They maneuvered a heavy-laden skin boat like gangsters, at the perfect range, makin' and takin' accurate turns and angles with relation to a movin' target in a strong current, while layin' down effective suppressin' fire that allowed Parks to avoid catchin' an arrow to the face. What's more, they rolled us out without bein' seen, cause if we had been, we'd be dead.

"And then I thought about how glad I was that Parks had to get wet earlier when I was sittin' in the freezin' water for ten times as long as him, with my balls crawlin' up into my taint never to be seen again. And I thought about how long he had to spend in the water when we went overboard, if he's rememberin' correctly and honestly. Survival suit or not, I'd be dead. And I remember holdin' on the carved titties of a woman, wonderin' why on earth anyone thought to put that on a boat, and why on earth a wooden rowboat was committin' acts of piracy in Antarctic waters to begin with. And knowin' any second I was goin' up top with no weapons, to do God-knows-what, because Tunguk never plans any farther ahead than which foot he's about to put in front of the other. Though I do admit it seems to work out.

"And I tried to figure how the hell I got here. I don't mean the story that I'm tellin', either. I mean why did I join the Navy? Why did I spend nearly all of my twenties listenin' to dudes spankin' it in the top bunk in the belly of an aircraft carrier, to the point that when I got out I had one narrow skill that I was sick of doin', and not a penny to my name? Why did I talk Parks into crewin' a civilian ship with some douchebag we used to know, when I hated the Navy and had never been on anything between a canoe and a fuckin' Nimitz-class carrier? Because all those decisions put me under a lady-carvin' on a longboat, gettin' ready to board and try to kill people I'd never met, cause they were tryin' to kill people I also never met, and was just about to kill a few hours earlier.

"I also remember that you can't just jump up on a boat. You need a certain amount of pull, and it's hard to get with a broken hand. So I had to be yanked the rest of the way up by an old man, who had also tried to kill me earlier. I watched him cut down big, strong, young men like one of them Japanese hibachi grill fuckers who cooks the food right there in front of you. Oh! And another thing none of yall mentioned. All of this maneuverin' and stallin', distractin' and turnin', was, at least I thought at the time, a brilliant and intentional ploy to use the one advantage we had, which was maneuver-ability in the vicinity of a big ship-smashin' rock. I'm now beginnin' to wonder if that was the plan at all, but there it was, so I threw the line to Parks. Then a guy tried to stab me, so I just grabbed ahold of his spear and jumped overboard, because Parks was towin' her for the rocks. Tunguk jumped over, too, and Parks set that bitch down right on the rock, like a pro. Again, say what you want about the man, or his character or general disposition, but I respect the way he handled that whole fight. So the boat got damaged, and it was takin' on water, but we let it go cause Rumit said there's nowhere to run to around here but the bottom of the sea. Then he killed that one guy I pulled out. I got zero kills, and I'm fine with that.

"That was it. It wasn't a little casual fight, or some joke of a rap song. Nor was it anything noble. Yall were gonna get fucked in one hole or another. You know what? Even if you did have to protect us, I would absolve you. I'd let you stab me to death. I feel nothin' but deep, deep, deep embarrassment and shame at the moment. I'm prayin' they don't try to kill us again when they get back with those seals, because then even more people are gonna die on my account, when I could've saved everyone a lot of trouble by drownin' from the get-go. As it stands, my—I don't wanna say 'friends'—my employers, and associates, are dead. Your clanspeople or whatever you call them are dead. Whoever that was in that wooden ship is dead. And I don't know what the fuck is goin' on here. Because last I checked, nobody lives on Antarctica, cause it's covered in fuckin' ice."

His words hung in the tent, and he tried to imagine their faces, but the dark concealed them even in his mind. There it was. Laid bare, he felt that it *was* a battle. Not the one he expected, but it couldn't remain within him. Now the apprehension he felt the entire time, running with Tunguk, hanging on to the ship and shivering, carrying home a man who they were supposed to kill—it hung plain for all. Whatever reason brought him there, and wherever his way bent him, it was signed and stamped. He realized up until that moment, it could have been anything he chose. Anything he said. Even two things at once, if he kept his own version and gave them another. Now it mixed with the others, complementing and contradicting. The stale air hardly moved, except at the opening where cool, fresh breaths lapped in.

"It is well-told," Rumit said. "Thank you for your battle."

"We have heard five battles. If Klimut lives, we will have one more. The place of the battle, we have called Faragat. Now we remember it another way. It is up to him who showed himself during the fight to name this place."

Was that it? Foster wondered. He had the sense there would be a bit of a fallout from his version of events, but Tunguk was business as usual. If he expected the hunters to move against the men he had to protect, he didn't let on.

"Brother," Tunguk said. "What will we call it?"

"Who, me?"

"Yes."

"Oh. Uhh…I didn't really give it much thought. Am I renaming the rock?" Parks asked.

"Yes."

"Shit. Ahhh, hmm. Let me see. Are there any rules for how it should be called?"

"No."

"OK. Huh. I mean, I'm just spitballing here, but what about…Pirate …….*rock*? Cove. No—rock. Pirate Rock?"

"The place of the fight is called Pirate Rock."

Foster scoffed. He pushed through the opening and into the gray light. His eyes throbbed to adjust, and he had to look at his feet for a few steps. No one was outside. He could see the four children scampering across the ridge they'd come in over. These people left men who by any definition were their enemies in their homes, with their young ones, unguarded. Trust, stupidity, forgiveness—he hadn't a notion of where they stood. Foster walked up the hill that he scrambled earlier when Tunguk put a quick end to the singing contest. He shook his head at the absurdity of it. From the top, he could see a ways, but only gray rock and lighter gray horizon. Peaks inland. No birds called, no life stirred. Clouds forming offshore and a bare breeze were the only movement in the land. The only thing here he could imagine looking forward to was leaving. Or death, which was still leaving. This was daylight. Tunguk's people—former people, he didn't know—would be here at night-fall. The temperature couldn't stay this warm. There would be no seal hunts in the dark. There hardly seemed anything to do during the day, but it could only be worse, much worse, when the sun peaced out for half a year. Where was the fresh water he'd been drinking even coming from? His eyes turned up to the white caps atop the peaks. Did they melt during winter, too? If not, how did they get fresh water, except to climb a mountain in darkness and carry snow to melt against their bodies? He didn't know whether to expect hospitality or hostility, but he cared for neither in this place. Parks didn't think they were going home. If not, he would go somewhere else. Where was home from here?

His hand reached instinctively to his belt for the map he kept in his waistband. His heart skipped, until he remembered that it lay a few hours' walk with Parks' map and the rest of their clothing, where they stashed it before he plunged into the ocean with Tunguk. If he had to, he thought he could find his way back there himself. Follow the grade until he hit the coast, follow the coast until he hit his stuff. Foster's first instinct was to abandon it—too far for worn out feet. But that little pile was all he had in all the world. And the map. That shitty map was the only thing he had left from the ship. The only object that could give him some sense of relation to what he left, even if it was only a mental image.

He closed his eyes and tried to remember the details. Foster spread it over the table in the galley of the *Qarapara*. Parks had the good one. The one that showed the entire western hemisphere, from Europe to South America. His own was much more limited. The Horn, the peninsula, and a good half of the southern continent. *Terra Australis*, he remembered the heading. Lines crissed and crossed, not just in the neat grid of latitude and longitude, but also radiating outward from certain points like spokes around a hub. As long as he'd been on the ship he never caught a glimpse of it. They were too precious to unfurl for his eyes. The couple of glances in the past day or so was not enough to burn in any kind of detail. The only thing that stuck out in his memory was the sea monster, and he couldn't even remember where exactly it was.

The peninsula was wrong—that much, he knew. There were too many islands to map, anyway, so it wasn't liable to be of any help if he did retrieve it. He might as well guess where he was, and head north. North was the way home, whether he was on the last little refuge before the Drake Passage, or smack-dab in the middle of the long chain of undersea mountains that yawned up for a breath. Useless, but his chest ached when he thought of the loss. The sun was already on its way down, but he could walk all night if he needed.

Then what? Tunguk wanted to hunt, presumably until someone came along and murdered them for a few seals. That was a non-starter, and those little hunting boats were no match for the open water. Even that big wooden sailboat looked miserable. Hanging around the coast and waving at passing ships didn't have as much appeal as it had earlier that morning. North, but in what?

"Wanna hear my theories?" Parks' voiced boomed from behind. He creaked and grimaced as he lowered himself to the ground beside Foster. "You're trying to figure out where we are, right?"

Foster nodded. Parks glanced around. "Somewhere along the Antarctic Peninsula. But that's not the issue."

"It's one of the issues."

"Not the big one. What does it matter if we know where this is," he pointed his finger at the ground between them, "when we don't know where *this* is?" He waved his hands to encompass the horizons.

Foster's eyes welled up. It was a shadow he felt creeping over him since they landed. So far, there was enough going on to ignore it. Now, he realized Parks felt it, too.

"I'm listenin'."

"You said it back there in the wigwam. No people, lots of ice. That's what *this*," he did the hand motion again, "should be. It's what we were looking at for the past few weeks, and it's why I had use a fucking search pattern to find my shriveled dick through three layers of pants every time I needed to take a leak in the middle of summer. Would you agree that something has changed?"

"It's pretty warm."

"Indeed it is, and I've been asking myself why. There's nothing else to do here. This is literally the most boring place possible on whatever planet it could conceivably be on. It makes the carrier look like Vegas. Even when people are trying to kill you, it's just so goddamn boring that I can't help but think about anything else, like what the fuck is going on?"

"So you came up with some theories."

"Two theories, entirely different, but equally plausible."

"Can't wait." He tried to sound dismissive, but something in him prayed that whatever Parks said would give him any kind of sense of anything.

"Theory numero uno: A tear in the space-time continuum."

"Uh-huh."

"Think about it. The storm somehow opens up a gash in the fabric of space-time, and we're thrown overboard, right through that gash, into an alternate universe."

"How's it a tear in space-time if we're in the same space we were already in?"

"Fine, a tear in the fabric of time. I'm calling it a time gash."

"OK. How does a regular-ass storm open up a time gash and send us and only us into an alternate universe? Do storms do that?"

"I was also not aware that they did, until now. Hear me out. So scientists have these theories, called quantum theories or something like that, that all possible universes exist side by side—"

"Next theory."

"Dude, just hear me out. And we happened to be transported to a universe where it's still the stone age. Men and probably even woolly mammoths roam a continent that in our time would be covered in ice."

"How's it the stone age if people got steel blades?"

"Fine, we can just agree on 'the past'?"

"Why can't it be the future?"

"Theory number two. This is my favorite. You ready for it? You ready?" Foster made no move to answer. "We're *already dead.*" Parks' eyes widened and he grinned in anticipation of what was sure to be a reaction of incredible surprise followed by praise of his brilliance.

Foster studied him for a moment, then smiled. "Parks, I don't want you to take this the wrong way. It might sound like I'm bein' sarcastic, or tryin' to cut you down so's you don't even realize it's happenin', but I promise that's not the case." Parks' expression remained unchanged. "I love you, Brother."

"Love you too, big guy."

"I mean it."

"No homo."

Foster stood. "Let me know if you come up with a couple more theories."

He found Tunguk holding open the door flap to one of the huts—wig-wams, Parks called them. As he approached, the old man said something to someone inside, then let the hide fall closed. By the time Foster joined him, he was busy untying the hide coverings from the next one over. He didn't even turn to acknowledge the company. Foster preferred it that way. There was no pressure to make small talk, to ease his fears or his temper. A moment with him could become an eternity, and sometimes that was preferable to the constant back-and-forth that Parks required. Instead, he took note of where the knots were, and started in on the other side. It looked like a complicated mess of leather, but as soon as a few knots fell, the elegance impressed him. They were set up not unlike shingles, with the higher layers overlapping the lower, and the tie-offs were easy enough that two men stripped the wigwam to its skeleton in a matter of minutes. By then, he had come up with some-thing worth saying.

"I finally got my days and nights." Foster didn't need a response, and didn't get one. "When we first got here, I figured you for a traveler. Some kind of nomad. But I don't guess you've ever been off this continent.

"Where we're from, the sun goes down every single night, and comes back every single mornin'. That's how we tell time and figure out what we're gonna do when. Ever since I got here, I haven't known what to do with myself cause there's nothin' but light, all the damn time. But I been watchin' it, and I think I got me a system. See where it's at now?" He indicated the sun. "Droppin'. I realized it never goes all the way up or all the way down, but it drops and bounces like a ball. Whenever it's droppin', I call that sun drop. Whenever it's bouncin', I call it sun bounce. I reckon noon to midnight it drops, and midnight to noon it bounces. But you can get even more accurate if you divide each of those in half. From midnight to 6 AM, that's bounce, but 6 AM to noon, I call that sunrise. Afternoon to six PM, I call sundown. Those are terms we use anyway, but now I got four six-hour slices of pie in a day, and I can more or less fit my schedule to it without feelin' like the whole day is one big blur. Now, at least I know when to go to sleep."

"Sundown," Tunguk repeated. He began to untie a strap that lashed what must have whale ribs together.

"That's what it is right now. Just past what we call four o'clock."

"In Summer."

Foster nodded. He worked at a lashing on his side. "That's right. In the Summer season. That's how we divide a year."

"We do not have the hour. Or the year."

Foster chuckled. "Must be nice, not havin' to keep track of how old you are."

"Seventy-nine days. I was born in what you call sun drop. Others say 'evening.' For the Mattaka, it is denankikumak—fire-king-grows-weary."

"If a year is a day, what do yall call what we call a day?"

"We do not name it. There are six times. In your tongue: when Sun returns, fire-king-is-born. When Sun leaves, fire-king-dies. When Sun is in his reign, it is fire-king-finds-many-lands. When Moon is in her reign, it is tide-queen-steals-from-fire-king. If Sun fades, fire-king-grows-weary. If Moon fades, tide-queen-flees-king's-return. There are times the king and queen change often, and times when one rules for long."

"Fire King, huh?"

"It is 'king' to you. Mattaka have no word for this."

Foster nodded. From what he'd seen, that would make sense. "So how do you know if someone's talkin' about a time tomorrow, or next Summer?"

"Only a fool does not know."

"I must be a fool, then. That's confusin' as fuck."

"For Mattaka, it is hard to learn to cut the day. It is only sleep that divides it. No two are the same. We think, 'Blind man! Do you not see Sun is elsewhere?' It is only the same the next Mattaka day—the next year."

Their straps unwound, and half the structure clattered at their feet. Foster and Tunguk caught the other half, and held it up as they worked the lashings.

"So how do you say, 'I'll meet you here in thirty days?'"

"It is you who must count everything. We find one another."

"But you know how old you are."

"In your tongue. Mattaka have numbers, but there is no seventy-nine. No eighty. Only important numbers. For important things."

Over the ridge, the first figures appeared, carrying the spoils of the hunt. They trickled in with dressed seal parts, or pelts. If the rhythms of their lives had been disturbed by his coming, Foster saw no lasting sign. Certainly the people of Antarctica had different a temperament, and their own sense of anger and grief and forgiveness that he seemed to benefit from without understanding. They didn't even count the days and years like he did, so why would he expect them to count their enemies and friends the same?

They finished separating the bones, and Tunguk showed him how to roll and tie the pelts, and lash the frame together for carrying.

"One day I'll take you to North Carolina. Show you how often the sun sets."

"I have seen the lands of day and night," Tunguk said. He walked off some ways, and lowered himself to the ground with care. Foster was exhausted. He couldn't imagine being an 80-year old who just had a heart attack, followed by the kind of 24 hours he'd had.

Mattaka. At least he had a name for the people streaming into camp with quartered flesh and sides and hides, weapons, whatever they could get from the boats. They didn't bother to process it further. Every hand busied itself striking the remaining wigwams, and tying small goods into sacks or rolls for transport. For the most part, they ignored his presence. The children wandered back, and with nothing better to do, they took a shine to Parks. They'd gather in a huddle, inch closer with curious apprehension. He let them get within a few feet, then threw his arms in the air and roared like a monster. They scattered, squealing, but came back soon enough. This time laughing, almost taunting him, until he did it again, and gave chase. They rounded a throng of adults and stopped. Parks stopped too, turned, and ran away with the kids in pursuit. Every time they rounded some obstacle, the chase reversed. Foster was worried the adults would take it as an act of aggression and carve up Parks like a seal, but they showed no concern for children or visitors. Eventually, he limped over and settled with Foster in the center of the village. They were as in-the-way as possible, yet the clan flowed around them like ants on a task. None of them seemed in a hurry. They hardly communicated. But the work got done fast. The little village lie around them in neat bundles, separated at every joint. He felt the pang of looking at the bare walls of a room, packed to vanish for good as one home turned into the next.

As they finished, they settled on all sides of the two men and chatted amongst themselves in their own language. Rumit and Kullunuk joined, across an ill-defined circle, and the singer took the center. There was no formal call to order, and several folks were still working when he begun his song. The audience seemed to half-pay attention and half-banter, though something told Foster they were more engaged than it seemed. He didn't understand a word of it, but he knew by the rhythms he was singing the battle as before. This time, the words were different. Only the basic meter remained. The verse shifted and expanded, drawn longer than an Antarctic day, but familiar in form. Now and then a face shot their way, and a few times he heard a name. Tunguk. Brother. Fucker. He sang for what had to have been an hour, a breathless hour, with no water, no break, no loss of rhythm or proportion. When it was over, Foster and Parks clapped. No one joined them. A few words of acknowledgment, and the circle broke.

They lifted the wrapped bodies of the two young men, and started again in the direction of the coast. Foster's instinct was to follow, to pay respects. Maybe help bear the load he created. But Tunguk hung back. He and Parks joined him. There must have been a question on his face, because for once, he got an explanation.

"They must see them off before we move, so they do not find us," he explained. Only a pair of older women remained kneeling over the kayak. A blanket covered all but Klimut's sweating face as they sang to him in low tones. "He is stubborn," Tunguk said. "Better to go to Urkuk with others. Four strong men. He will have a long paddle alone." The old man's eyes glazed as if he were envisioning the scene. He laughed to himself.

"Come. We will find your skins."

It took hours to retrace their steps to the place where they leapt. By then the sinking sun and the breeze bouncing down out of the mountains made them grateful to find the stone still held their things, flapping at the edges in a halfhearted effort to tumble free into the ocean. Foster shivered as he pulled on his parka, and marveled that Tunguk still carried his own spare articles in a bundle. It had to be in the upper 30's now that it was night—or whatever Tunguk would call this. Short-sleeve weather, apparently.

Foster couldn't resist a glimpse over the edge, and a terrifying flashback to the moment he flung himself into those icy waters. It looked like madness, now. Pirate Rock stirred the waters below as if it had already forgotten the men who passed through that morning.

They ran into the clan on the way back, heading south, he reckoned. The entire camp was slung between them, or over shoulders, or squeezed against a chest. He and Parks hurried to relieve three women struggling with a rolled wigwam. It was light enough for the two of them to manage—and only that light. He saw his sun bounce off the water before they headed inland to a little valley, shielded from the coast. There, he and Parks collapsed while the people got to work setting up camp. They were too exhausted to help, or wait for shelter, if it would even be offered. Tunguk spread out his coat as a mat and lay down beside them.

They slept like dead men for the first few hours, but soon the cold woke Foster. His companions didn't seem to notice it. By some luck, Parks ended up in the middle, where he enjoyed the body heat of both Tunguk and Foster, while Foster bore the breeze for the three of them. He realized why Tunguk had chosen the position he did, and after an hour of fighting in and out of consciousness, he switched to the far side, exposing Parks. The benefit was minimal, and he didn't sleep for more than ten minutes at a stretch. At last, Tunguk rose and woke Parks.

"Come."

Parks moaned.

Foster was so sleep-deprived he felt nauseous, but he struggled gratefully to his feet. Now he noticed three small bundles piled near them that weren't there when they lay down. Tunguk abandoned Parks and picked up one of the bundles, then began to walk away from camp.

"Parks!" Foster kicked him. "Yo. He's leavin' us." Parks only moaned again. Foster grabbed both of the other bundles and dropped one on his friend. He grabbed him by the collar and yanked him to a stream of cussing that ultimately lead the big man to his feet. They hurried after.

"Where we goin'?" Foster asked as they caught up.

"To the boat."

"Boat?" Parks yawned. "Do we have a boat, now?"

"Yes."

"Fuckin' A! Are we going hunting?"

"Yes."

"Sweet, so we're officially in the clan again?"

"No."

"My guess is we're banned for life," Foster said.

"Better to give us a boat than try to kill us," Tunguk clarified.

"Wait," Parks stopped. "So we're not going back?"

"No."

"Wait, hang on. Can I go say goodbye to those two guys? Those dudes we saved?"

"No."

"But I feel like we bonded. You!" Parks remembered. "You saved their lives. You have akuwhack."

Tunguk shook his head. "Rumit and Kullunuk do not accept akmanuak."

Foster wrinkled his brow. "But you accepted it for us. You made it sound like there's no choice."

"It is different."

"I don't get it."

"It is a good luck. I owe them no more."

Now it was Parks' turn to be confused. "They're the ones that would owe *you*. You saved *them*."

Foster felt the gears turning. Suddenly, they caught. "It goes both ways."

Tunguk gave a half-smile. "It is the rope that binds men. You are tied. I am tied. It is the same."

Parks nodded. "We have a word for this in our culture. We call it 'the three-legged race.' Two men tie their legs together, and they have to run as one person at some kind of family reunion, or company picnic. So if you pick the fat, slow guy, you're fucked."

"Yes. It is like that."

"But you got extra-fucked, didn't you? Cause we don't even know how to feed ourselves," Parks went on. "And there's two of us. Two idiots. Not just one. A four-legged race."

"It is a curse. You must be careful who you tie."

"Wait. Five-legged race. Right?" Foster interjected.

"Four. I counted it before I said anything because I didn't want to sound like a retard who can't count."

"I can see how this could make it complicated come fightin' time if you got too many of these akmanuaks. What if they're conflictin'? Let's say me and Parks start tryin' to kill each other? Or what if on us tries to take you out?"

"It is said Barduk once retreated from a battle that was won, because his enemy saved his life."

"What happens if we don't honor it?" Foster asked. "What if I say, 'Fuck it'? 'To hell with Tunguk. Let him die.' I just walk away. What happens to me?"

"You fall down," Parks shot in. "Three-legged race, bro. What happens if your guy falls? The fat ass lands right on top of you. You'll have a broken leg, probably a bruised ball sack. Are you gonna win the race now? Hell, no."

"I wasn't askin' you."

"It is as he says. You are wise to see the dangers. Many of the people believe they avoid them if they only honor the bond among their clan. I have seen enough to think not."

"Are you sayin' we should help those dudes back there, even if they don't think so?"

"It is not custom to remain near one like a child. If they send for you, you must do all in your power. But they will not send for you. You must not send for them. They will not come, and it is to their harm."

"Got it," Parks said. "Don't ask, don't tell—anyone to help you."

"So if we ever get to the point that we're not completely fuckin' help-less—if our lives are no longer in immediate danger—you'll leave us." Foster noticed how closely they trotted at his heels. He imagined a rope that shack-led their ankles.

"I do not think I will live so long." Tunguk grinned to himself.

They came to the beach of smooth black rock where Foster waded ashore in his bright suit. He shivered from the memory of the cold. That man thought he would never see another soul from the ship again. Thought that rescue would come within a few days, at most. It was difficult to recall a single expectation that came to pass since he tumbled into the water.

Above the high tide line sat the boat they salvaged off the rock the previous day. The three youngest wives from the clan busied themselves rubbing every surface and seam with some kind of grease. They must have been here for hours. There was no sign of damage. The oilskin he cradled in his arms had to be their doing. No shortage of hospitality when you were facing either execution or banishment, he thought.

Beside the boat, a thin pole of bones lashed together and braced at the joints lie on the ground. Another shorter one folded up off the main length, and between the two, there was a sheet of leather. Coils of rope stood by.

"Are we *sailin'*?"

"Where we go, it is not likely. But if a wind favors us for a short time, we will be glad to rest."

"You can't possibly be thinkin' of tryin' to go north in that thing." The short ride Foster took the previous day had not been confidence-inspiring.

"No. We go first to a big boat."

"How far's that?" Parks asked.

"Only to Drummoc." Tunguk looked at them for a reaction, and smiled. He approached the women and inspected the work, then threw his bundle aboard as if to certify its seaworthiness. They stepped away, and between them lifted the mast and placed it along the bottom, then stowed the ropes. Tunguk nodded to the men, and they placed their oilskins under the seats— rectangles of leather suspended between the gunwales by straps.

"Sup, ladies?" Parks edged by.

The sea hissed through the round stones as the tide stretched up the beach. It was a boat, Foster figured. That's what they wanted. It was as though some smart ass genie hung around just out of sight, granting his wishes with the most unpleasant technicalities. Land. Help. Now this. It would take a few more for that thing to make it anywhere he cared to go.

Before he realized it, the women hoisted it between them and stepped awkwardly for the water. "Hang on!" He hustled to grab a piece, with Parks right behind him. The vessel was unbelievably light, even with gear and a mast. They probably could have carried it without the women's help, but soon she bobbed in knee-deep surf. Tunguk threw a leg over and swung himself into the aft seat with a stumble that Foster couldn't begrudge someone coming up on 80. The women held her steady, and he and Parks boarded from either side with considerably less skill. After some flopping, in which he was sure his foot was going to burst right through the leather hull, Foster claimed the forward seat, with Parks in the middle.

"You must sit here," Tunguk pointed to an oilskin bundle between him and Parks. Foster wanted to protest, but he was sure there was some reason that would never be explained as to why he had to crowd into toward the stern. Once he crawled across Parks, the women pushed them farther out. It was a blow to his Southern chivalry to see them slipping over rocks and taking breakers to the face on their behalf.

"Thank yall!" Was all he could think to shout over the roar.

"Ready to row," Tunguk calmly told Parks. There were two oars at his feet. He found where to brace them, and turned to face Foster and Tunguk. Once the water crossed their waists and the waves forced them to leave their feet, one of the women moved from the back to port. The young mother with the tattoo on her chin planted her hands on the gunwale and swung herself over next to Parks. She scooted past and planted herself on the bow seat, and took up the second pair of oars.

"Row." Tunguk said. Foster was aghast. Only now did he realize there was a fourth bundle already in the boat.

"Is she comin' with us? That's even more fucked up," Foster said. "I thought she was just shovin' off, or I'd have helped. Ma'am, I'm sorry, I was not informed of the plan."

"Sweet, we're taking the chick," Parks pulled at his oars. "Hey, where's your baby at?" He looked around the deck of the boat. They lifted up over the next little wave, and were free of the breakers. The skin boat glided into open water, and Tunguk lashed a steering oar to the starboard stern.

From his low seat, Foster had a crotch to either side and little view of their companion, where they were headed, or where they came from. Even Tunguk seemed to tower over him.

"Ma'am," he said in frustration. "I would take them oars from you, but my hand is fucked." She probably couldn't even hear with a wall of Parks between them. "Tunguk! No disrespect to the lady, but what's the deal?"

"Kjartke must leave before her husband dies. We will need a woman to sew clothing and clean what we kill."

Foster batted away Parks' arms as his clumsy stroke flashed near his head. He gave the name a try. "Kjartke. Do you speak English?"

"They all speak English," Parks said. "I can tell by the way she scowls at me." He smiled over his shoulder at her. "Hey, girl. What happened to your little guy? I couldn't help but notice you were breastfeeding."

"Klimut's son is with Klimut." It was all she offered.

Foster again swatted at the careless oars as one glanced off his temple. "Sorry, dude," Parks offered. He did his best to match the woman, and the occasional half-glance back told him when he screwed up. They rowed in silence until they had a half-mile cushion from the coast, then turned in the direction that Foster recognized as the same they had taken to the help the seal hunters. South, as best he could tell by the Sun climbing toward the opposite sky.

"Hey anybody mind if I turn on the radio?" Parks swung his oars wide over Foster, splashing Kjartke as they arced back.

"Yes," Foster said. The others ignored him.

"Anybody else? Yes? No? OK, radio it is."

"As in, yes, I mind." Foster repeated.

"I heard you. And we got two No's, so radio wins."

"They didn't even vote."

"Right, silence means they don't mind, so three-to-one. Radio."

Foster shook his head in disgust, but it didn't stop Parks.

"Don't be fooled by the rocks that I got," He splashed away. "I'm still, I'm still Parks from the block. Used to have a little, now I have a lot," Foster turned sideways and hunched uncomfortably. "No matter where I go, I know where I came from."

6

Two Places

Water.

He used both hands to dip a bone, hollowed into a tall container, into the bottom of the boat. It filled most of the way before he flung it over the beam. Foster hated water.

Even after two weeks, his hand was no good on an oar. Parks and Kjartke took turns rowing from the aft position, a couple of hours at a time. The oars were short, and the boat wide. Their course put the swell coming in off the starboard bow, and he threw it back to port. The bilge—if the bottom of the boat qualified as that—was a constant slurry of freezing water. Every rope and spear and bit of sail had to be secured clear of the deepest part, which was his permanent seat. Their bundles turned out to be little more than their clothes, plus an extra oilskin coat that he never took off. The sack itself was intended to be a waterproof sleeping bag. When it was used as a seat, and sat in water, the oil tended to give way and allow the sea to soak the leather through. As the only one who sat on his own kit, his was particularly compressed and spongy. His allotment of seal jerky, which he was told "make last," rode right beneath his butt in the driest quadrant. Each night when they made landfall, he gnawed more than he should and shivered in wet clothing, inside a wet bag until by morning the sun could dry them out, only to be pickled again when they shoved off.

The brine sapped the very water from his flesh. Each had a bladder to drink from. A liter or so of fresh liquid. Since he couldn't row, and wasn't trusted to hold the steering oar, he was expected to fill all of them every time they made land. Tunguk and Kjartke seemed practically immune to thirst. They only accompanied him on the hike if it was short. Despite the fact that they were rarely out of sight of the coast, or at least some island, there were precious few spots a boat could come ashore, and fewer that also had flowing melt water. Tunguk knew them all, and a work day was the distance from one to the next, be it six miles or thirty. By then, he would be too parched to swallow. Melts being melts, they tended to move from the last place an old man swore he remembered them decades prior. It was rarely close to sea level.

136

Hours of searching and a quick ascent would leave him with a throbbing headache by the time they found a modest trickle. He and Parks gorged themselves until they were sick while Tunguk scolded their greed.

He hated staring at the bladder on his lap all day, rocking in the chop and trying to force himself to go just a little longer than the day before. He hated the cold spray in his face. Water was both his burning desire and his tormentor. It was the place he squandered his youth, and the cruel mother that spat him out here—wherever this might be.

It was his highway, home or somewhere. After three days of grinding against wind and swell, watching Parks shrink before his eyes, and even hard Kjartke faltering into a late landing, they finally cleared the island group into what seemed like open ocean. Tunguk turned them hard port, and another long paddle put the land directly behind them. Like a breath from God, the breeze that chapped their faces or threatened to take them out to sea swung around and for the first time, he saw the face of the sail. The mast came off the starboard side and angled hard forward against the backstay. Dark leather sheets sewn together angled up in a claw as the boom unfolded well-short of horizontal. It was the simplest imaginable rig, yet he was lost in it. He learned soon enough what a shroud was, and how to move the knots on the sheets that tuned to the wind. For days, it felt like they walked, sometimes backward or sideways, grinding for every foot. Now an inconstant gust let the rowers sink into their seats as they thumped along at a brisk stroll for hours at a time. The mainland peninsula disappeared into clouds to port. Foster had never seen it, but there was nothing else it could be. Here in the shadow of land, the swell was shiftier but less insistent.

It came with its own problems, though. The tilt of the vessel meant a lot more bailing, and Tunguk's instructions were usually one word that meant nothing to either of the "sailors," though they were in plain English. There was always a pointing negotiation and a bit of guesswork involved before the old man would settle back on his steering oar.

Once, the wind shifted out of the east. They must have sailed three miles sideways and out to sea before they got the mast stowed. The wind was more than happy to take what it could of the beam and push them further while Parks and Kjartke fought it back with the oars. For once, they could not make land, and rowed through the night in shifts without water. Even Tunguk took a couple of turns while Foster held the course in what felt like an annoyance that crept into a dire emergency. When it finally let up late the next day, they scrambled ashore exhausted and dehydrated. The Mattaka thinned their rations to a quarter pound a day, and allowing for size, Foster added a little more to his. But they could see Parks would not make it on so little, and after a day of rest, Tunguk set them on the hunting grounds.

The bounty of the men they rescued led Foster to believe that killing a seal was simply a matter of course. There was no shortage. At times, a great herd of them could be seen lurching through the water so near that he could hear their barks and the swish of their tail fins. They seemed to know exactly the range of a harpoon thrust and veered well clear as if pushed by an invisible force that ran ahead of the bow. It was a casual evasion. At times, it felt more of a taunt.

They tried to slide up on rocks where they sunned themselves, or corner them on a beach that looked like an all-you-can-slaughter buffet. He soon lost count of the failures. It would have been comical if it weren't for the fact that they would starve at some point. The seals just glanced at them every now and then, and slipped into the water. A sentry would sound the alarm, and a beach of what seemed hundreds would clear in minutes. Tunguk said it would be better with a second boat to drive them. Still, there were chances. A group who took the warning without spotting the threat swam nearby as Tunguk shouted at the rowers and Foster grappled with the steering oar. He wouldn't throw, for fear of losing a weapon. The bone shafts didn't float. Though he never blamed him, Foster could feel his irritation with the other three every time he missed a thrust. But as fine as he was with his feet beneath him and a man at the other end, there was a clumsiness to the way he went after game.

Worse was scanning for whales. Foster didn't see the point. No one bothered to explain to him the logistics of killing one from a rowboat. He didn't imagine it would actually be possible, which was fine, because they never saw more than a rare and distant spray. Their only luck was when Kjartke shot two sea birds on a rock. They ate them raw, and he still wasn't starving-enough to like it. She used the guts to bait a hook and snared two more the following day. It did little to lift morale. Tunguk was unconsoled. It was large game he wanted, and when Foster pressed him about the place they were heading, all he could get was that it was "A ways, yet." The woman should have been a bright spot, but for two weeks, she refused to speak a word to either one of them. When Parks tried to high-five her kills, she glared him down, and only spoke to Tunguk when necessary: short sentences in their tongue.

The three seats in the boat were unevenly spaced. The rowing stations more or less cut it into thirds, with Tunguk's steering position pressed all the way to the stern. That meant Foster could occupy a cramped space between the long reach of Parks and the old man, or the more spacious berth between Parks' back and Kjartke's short arms. The choice was obvious. In that respect, he was usually ballast, shading to whichever side needed more weight. There, in the steam of her breath, he spent many an hour trying to figure out just what the fuck she was doing with them. He knew damn well she spoke English, but her first demonstration was also her last, and his efforts at friendly small talk withered before they made their first landfall. This woman was not related to Tunguk. No one told him that, but their sparse interactions maintained a distance of polite contempt—she was treated as little more than a servant girl, and him, an old fool. The way they felt one another out, preferring to engage only in the business of piloting a boat from one point to another, allowed that they were on unfamiliar terms. It didn't seem that she wanted to be there, or that Tunguk held her in much esteem.

Parks, on the other hand, was not so easily dissuaded. He tried on the daily to weasel something out of her, the way a child seeks attention even if it has to be a whooping. There were times Tunguk let him badger her in what Parks thought was a good-natured teasing and Foster, an overestimation of his charm. Others, their apparent captain would issue some order that would force him on to better uses of his time. His friend clearly had designs on her, and if history held, it was for his preferred virtues of proximity and availability. They bickered once when Foster, seasick and exhausted, made the mistake of telling him, "She ain't into you, bro," in front of the entire crew. Parks joked his way out of it, but there was an edge of hostility to his accusation of competition, and Foster had to assure him later as they chugged icy water that he could have first, second, and eleventh crack at her if he only spared them having to hear it. Truth was, he was usually too nauseous to even consider it. When he did steal a glance—most of the time he sat under her watchful eye—he waffled back and forth between whether or not she had a strange appeal, with her high, wide cheeks, her grease-black hair and cracked hands. Or if he was only trying to talk himself into it. Her underfed frame of sinewy-yet-strong muscles was not to his taste, and though it was true of all of them at this point, his tumultuous stomach could not get past the smell that wafted over when her stroke passed his face.

He threw another boneful of water overboard. They sat less than a mile off the island that would house them for the night—a tiny, steep rock just high enough to hold snow at the top, with what seemed like a scoop taken out of the seaward side in one smooth pull that left a rare beach flat-enough to wade ashore. Tunguk had his harpoon handy while the rowers rested, waiting on a whale or a wind. All but Parks were on constant watch for spouts or wayward seals. It was a routine that Foster came to dread as a pointless waste of time. The sea was miserable. It never turned up a meal, and every minute here sapped moisture and heat from his flesh. The only benefit was that he could made headway on their standing water. The *Qarapara* had a massive pump system to keep them afloat. For the most part, he forgot that water ever ended up in a ship at all, except to shower and drink. The skin boat was only dry when they turned it over on a beach. At sea, she was always always in one of the various stages of sinking. Even when it was calm and nothing came over the beam, hand-stitching leather to be waterproof proved an impossibility. It hardly seemed to bother her seaworthiness, and in fact a small amount helped them feel less like a bath toy.

The overcast of the day was gone. Foster noted a dim moon, near full, peeking out from behind them to see that the sun still maintained its course above the horizon. The only sound was the occasional splash from his bailer, and a groan from Parks as he stretched his back over the thin seat. The mainland ran like a spine east of them, and he could see the ocean west and south studded with little rock islands. It seemed like a field of treasure compared to the usual sight: a single distant point if they were lucky, a gray screen and a long desert if they were not. Tunguk insisted that these places were woven thick with sea mammals feeding, sunning, guiding their young through the first summer paces. All Foster knew was that he was hungry, and there was at best two days food in his hobo sack, if he could once again stand to bed down half-full. And he was barely flicking his arms. Parks was spent. There was a cost to every movement. Even sneaking in on seals at a glide was work—so far, unpaid.

This was not his first subsistence hunt. He grew up accustomed to stretching meals at certain times of the month, but one time in particular, while his mama was out of work, she walked into the kitchen and flatly declared that no one was going to eat until somebody got out there and harvested a deer. As the man, he knew who she meant, never mind that he was the youngest at twelve. His sister Barbara came with him, at least. It was out of season, but they both knew where they could do it, and neither had any notion of how many times they'd shot one before. It felt like a terrible responsibility. For a day and a half until they got a chance to go, he shredded his stomach to ribbons with anxiety. Completely lost his appetite. Never once did it cross his mind they might starve. He just didn't want to be the reason the Foster women went hungry. By the time they started into the woods, though, he couldn't even think of what he was doing. Old trails took him and set him down where he needed to go. When the young buck appeared after hardly any wait, fully cooperative in profile, there was no drama to the moment. He just laid it down like nothing else in the world could have happened. Barbara gutted it and helped him drag it off the mountain, and that was it. This day might have been the first or second time he even thought of it in all the years since.

The air in the boat was entirely different. He knew not a damn thing about hunting seal or whale. Couldn't even imagine how it might look. Something in him still insisted it wasn't possible that they would starve, but now it sounded like he was trying to convince himself. It should have fallen to Tunguk. It would be him who knew the first thing about this business. Even Kjartke was probably more qualified. But with Parks splayed over his seat trying to perform chiropractic adjustments on himself so that he could take up the oars once more, somehow, Foster felt responsible again. If he died sloshing water overboard, it would be unspeakably shameful. Ignorant as he was of the strategy to killing sea mammals, he could see plain as day when a thing wasn't working.

"Is there another place where the whales might be?" Foster asked. It was as polite as he could put it.

Tunguk considered the question. "The whales go many places."

"Is there one where they go more often than here?"

"Many places."

"Maybe we should go there, instead."

"We are here."

"I think that my friend is saying," Parks rolled off the bench and stretched out sideways, shifting the hull shape so that the water hurried to the seat of his pants, "is that if there are hunting spots where the odds of spear-fucking a whale are higher, that might be our best bet."

"It does not matter where we go, but if the whales come."

"Yeah, but they come more often to some places than others, right? People go to bars because there's food, and sexual opportunities. If I were looking to wet my whistle, I wouldn't hang out in a Hobby Lobby parking lot at midnight in the winter. I'd go to a bar on Spring Break. Better chance of success."

"Your people talk of chance, but I have not seen it. My people talk of the wise hunter and the foolish hunter."

"The wise hunter goes where the whales are at." Foster said.

"It is not known where the whales are at. Some places, they have been many times. The wise hunter goes to this place. Other places have not seen whale. The foolish hunter goes here. One day, the whale does not come to the wise hunter. He comes instead to the foolish hunter. Then he is wise, and the wise hunter is a fool."

"Well my people have this thing called probability," Foster said. "It works because it works most of the time."

"How does it know where the whales go?"

"It don't. But if you can tell me all the times they've been everywhere, I can calculate which one has the highest probability. Usin' math. So if we got an 83% chance to see a whale or a seal at this one spot, we go there, instead of a 26% chance somewhere else."

"And the whale is always there?"

"No. It's there 83% of the time."

"How can you know? You have never hunted whale."

"I don't need to, I just need someone who *has* to give me the data. How many whales, where, when, that sort of thing, then we can figure it out."

"You want stories of whales?"

"I don't need the stories, just show me on a map where and how many."

"And you will know where they are now?"

"Probably."

"Yeah, I don't really get the math either," Parks admitted, "but what he's saying is we can run the calculations, and we're less likely to waste our time staring at water. Or, maybe not us personally, but it's possible."

"And if the whale goes somewhere else?"

Foster threw up his hands. "Look around you, brother. This *is* 'somewhere else.'"

Tunguk nodded. "Now, we are the foolish hunter. My people do not know chance. We make a choice. From there, it follows."

"What I see followin' us is trouble and starvation. Look at this man," he indicated Parks. "He looks good. Almost ripped. If you'd have known him before, you'd know that means there's somethin' seriously wrong. Wise hunter, fool hunter, I don't care. We just need to eat." He let it sink in. "I'm sure you know a lot more about whalin' than I do." He thought he heard Kjartke scoff. "Maybe back in your day, the whales used to love this place. But we tried your way. All I'm askin' is one shot. Let me make the call tomorrow."

"Well, now, hang on. I don't know if that really solves anything," Parks said. "I think what we were saying is we want *you* to choose," he turned to Tunguk, "based on the odds, rather than at random or whatever it is you do. Foster doesn't know shit about hunting."

"The hell I don't. I killed my first deer when I was seven." He pulled the map off his belt and spread it out before them on the deck.

"Fair enough. If you see a deer, kill it. All I'm saying is if we're stuck with nothing but Antarctic sea creatures, We should let Joe pick. He just needs to pick better."

"Show me where we are on the map, and I'll show you where we're goin'."

Tunguk and Kjartke glanced at his map and burst out laughing. Foster leaned back stung, the more because he had no idea what imbecilic thing he had said. It was the first time he saw anything like a smile on the woman's face, though soon the corner of her mouth settled into a sneer of amused contempt.

"Where is the bird who drew your map?" Tunguk said. Foster wrinkled his brow. Tunguk ran his finger over the lines. "It is how a bird sees the land."

"It's an aerial view. Yeah. So we can see things."

"When you fly?" Tunguk laughed. Kjartke managed to pull it together and return to her cultivated disinterest, but the old man was clearly enjoying himself.

"Yes. Sometimes we fly over shit. Or we sail or we walk. It don't matter. This way we don't have mountains blockin' our view of everything."

"You say you were shipwrecked. All you would save is your bird maps?" Tunguk's laugh settled to a grin.

"Someone else saved 'em. Anyway I don't see how it matters. Why, what the hell do your maps look like?"

"Mattaka do not draw maps. We see them always."

"Yeah, well, that don't really work when you've never been somewhere before. Can you read the bird map?"

"Yes."

"Then show me."

Tunguk's finger fell without hesitation on a curve of the arm that reached toward South America.

"See? That was easy. No need to heckle me or anything." He looked up in the direction that must have been roughly south, their course of travel.

"Where will we hunt?"

Foster folded up the map. "Let me think about it."

They didn't land on the big scooped-out beach as he expected. Instead, Tunguk steered them into the lee of the island, what seemed like a forbidding wall of inaccessible rock pressed into sheets and turned sideways in near-vertical pillars, cracked and broken off at intervals. The landing spot appeared out of nowhere: a flat shelf accessible at high tide. There was less than a hundred yards of uneven ground before the back wall, on which he could see the black mark where the storm waves pounded. It made little sense why they took the more difficult place. Tunguk must have been confident they'd be gone before the ocean came that high again. Foster didn't question it, though. No one who visited this place for the first time, or even just casually, would have passed up the easy harbor or even known there was another. Whatever he thought of the man as a hunter, there was a method at work he could only let run its course.

The climb to the ice was no picnic, either. It, too, only appeared when they were upon it—a stairway out of hell, the steps of which had to be scaled at times. Everyone came, scrambling after Tunguk's lead. Foster hesitated to continue more than once, not because he couldn't make it up, but because if he did, he wasn't sure how he would get back down. He helped steady Parks up the way. As soon as he was out of the boat, the man became a lumbering zombie, and every fear that Foster had about his ability to keep them moving came to bear. A rest with the boat would have served him, but he was too parched from his pulling to get by with a single bladder of water. When at last they found the smallest trickle, it was accessible only by Foster hanging on to Tunguk's hand, with the ball of one foot on a four-inch outcrop, while the other leg stretched and pressed into a sheer wall and the free hand held the mouth of a bladder under it for a fill that took several minutes. He pressed his cheek against the cool black rock and let the trickle of water hold his attention back from doubts about the old man's ability to hang on. The maneuver had to be repeated until he lost count, with short breaks for them to empty their bladders, and a final top-off for everyone.

They rested before starting down. There was no worry of losing the light, though their perch hid in the shadow of the little mountain. Foster pulled the map from his belt to an apathetic glance, and spread it over the rock between the four. His was the one with the detail of the Antarctic coast. Next to it, the consulted his own—the spot where he recalled Tunguk's finger— and searched for the equivalent. Even on the more local version, only the top half of the continent under the Western Hemisphere was depicted. A handful off large islands dotted the entire length of the peninsula, though they passed dozens in a couple of weeks. Not exactly a coast pilot.

He looked out over the water between themselves and the mainland, then turned south, where he could make out two distant shadows that must have been islands of a similar size, along with a third that he couldn't distinguish from a low cloud. Tunguk looked amused.

"Are you ready to choose where we hunt?"

Foster shook his head. "My maps don't tell me what I need to know. There's shit missin'. And I have no idea where the huntin' spots are, or how often the game comes."

Tunguk slid close for a look. "Nowhere to hunt here. It is a map for those who pass by."

"What about out there?" Foster looked at the shadows on the southern horizon. Tunguk suddenly turned away. He ran his fingers over the ground, and gathered a number of pebbles into his palm. Then, he lay a large one on the map. His finger rose and pointed to the east-most island, followed by another pebble. And the second. And the third—it *wasn't* just a cloud. With some deliberation, there were soon more than a dozen pebbles littering their way, shrinking as they progressed farther out. At last, he pressed the first one, the largest.

"That's where we are now," Foster ventured.

Tunguk nodded. "And here," he tapped the nearest pebble, and pointed to one of the dark lumps to the south.

"But we're not on that one, we're on this one."

"To know only the place you are is to be lost. You must know two places."

"Fair enough." He wasn't sure it made sense, but it sounded like one of those things that might be true if it mattered at all. "Which of these has the most game? Most seals and whales?"

The bony finger found another pebble, all on its own to the west-southwest. "Seals go here often."

"Done. That's where we hunt."

Tunguk shook his head. "Nowhere to land. No water. If the weather turns, it is difficult to come back," he indicated the direction of the peninsula and the thicker cluster of islands.

"So which of these have game, *and* water that we can get to?" Tunguk touched fewer than half of the pebbles. "Cool, so let's clear the rest and talk about these."

"We need them," he stopped Foster from removing the other markers. "These help us find our way."

"Fine. Whales, then. Out of the water islands, where do whales go? I mean, fuckin' *love* to hang out?"

He pointed to a pair of pebbles, so close they touched and just a short distance beyond the farthest of the islands in view.

"Is there water?"

"Here," he indicated the landward of the two.

"Perfect."

Tunguk shook his head again. "Unless we find wind, it is two of your days to row. No water."

"You said this one has water," Foster pointed to one between them and the pair.

"Yes. It is well-known. Tall ships go often, here," he pointed, "here, here," three places in total. "These they do not stop, but it is good wind," he said of the pair with the whales. "Best to go," he pointed to a successive string of just three islands.

"Well shit, if that's the only choices, they're all lined up! We have to hit all of those anyway to get water."

"Yes."

"So what am I even choosin'?"

Tunguk sat back, satisfied he had made his point.

"What's the game situation at these? Anything?"

"There are times a wise hunter finds game."

"And the tall ship ones? More, or less game?"

"More. But it is the foolish hunter who is soon robbed."

Foster pursed his lips in frustration. "But this little pair here has the most whales, enough water, and nobody stops there. They just pass by. They're like me. They got this map, and they just wanna get where they're goin'."

"It is true the tall ships do not know this place but Haqawa know all," he swept his hand over the entire field.

"Who's Haqawa?"

"It is the people, but best to avoid them."

"Fuck it, I still think we go here. If these Haqawa know all, that's a wash. We don't even consider it. There's a high chance of whale, and a near-zero chance of anybody else."

"It is two of your days to travel, with no sight island. What does chance say of weather? If we are clouded, we will drift until it clears. How many days will you drink this?" He held up the little bladder. "How many days will they row?"

Foster looked at Parks and Kjartke. He realized it was their skin he bargained with. But Tunguk's method was not a choice, as he said. It was a route. A safe one, to safely starve.

"What about this: we check the wind. That's all I'm askin'. Tomorrow, when we set off, we check the wind. If we can get somethin' out of the sail, we go my way. If not, we go yours."

"You think if a whale comes, it always comes. If a wind blows in the morning, it will always blow. It is a good chance, you say. I do not see the difference between your way and mine. But I will let you choose. We will see where we arrive."

When he woke, Kjartke was already rigging the mast into place, ready to hoist at a moment's notice. Foster wasn't sure if Tunguk ordered it, if she felt it her duty—or if it were a silent voice of approval for his plan. Maybe she was just sick of rowing. Their captain was already down at the water's edge, admiring the swell. From his position, Foster couldn't feel if the weather was cooperating. At least he was never hungry in the morning, not even with his foot off the gas coasting into starvation. Later in the day would be a different story. He found the once formidable sack that held the remainder of his food, rolled up on itself. It was light. Even his broken hand cold bear it. He rummaged for the remainder of his dried seal, and produced the last pound or so that had to hold him until they put a spear in something.

Parks was slow to rouse, slower than usual. His body seemed to refuse to do anything it didn't absolutely have to. Foster didn't know what his friend had left, but it had to be even less than his own share. Do it now, before you get hungry, he told himself. He tore apart his chunk of meat and extended nearly half of it. Parks gave a look to make sure, then tore into the breakfast. There was no point in spreading it out. He'd likely need all of it and more before they even made the next island, whichever way they went.

"Fuck, I hope there's wind." Parks absently shoved layers into his sea bag.

"There's always wind. We just gotta hope it's blowin' the wrong way." Foster knew by now the prevailing breeze came out of the west, usually turning north when it hit the peninsula. The only time they had it at their back was when there was a weather system swirling through, or some local gust created by land features. Otherwise, it was a row into the teeth of the elements. He realized the "wrong way" had a second meaning. "I just keep thinkin' that every mile we go," Foster tilted his head in their direction of travel, "we gotta cover again to get home. I hope this goddamn Drummoc comes up sooner than later."

"Mm-hm." It was a distant grunt, from a distant spirit.

"Come on, brother. We got this. Hang with me a little longer. We come too far."

Parks gave a lazy nod. "Got what?"

"This. All of this."

"You still thinking about sailing home?"

Foster's eyes widened in disbelief, bordering on offense. "Uh—yeah. You ain't?"

Parks shrugged. He squinted in Kjartke's direction. "What about her? We dropping her off, bringing her back…what?"

"Don't know, don't care. We gotta think about the long-term."

"Based on what I've seen, she might be the best option either of us are gonna get."

"You wouldn't be singin' that tune if you had to sit close enough to smell her."

"Oh, I've smelled her."

"You know what I'm talkin about, fool. You're the one with all the theories. I aim to find out which is which, and no matter what, get us somewhere that we don't gotta sit in a fuckin' canoe whale watchin' while we starve to death." Tunguk saw what he cared to see, and turned from the shore in their direction. "Besides, you're talkin' about a woman who tried to kill us. Which I admit seems to be the best way to make friends around here. But nevertheless, tried to kill us. Who just abandoned her dyin' husband, and her *infant child*, and don't seem too broke up about it. That ain't a long-term prospect. That ain't a short-term prospect. If there is any such thing as a red flag on God's green earth, it's gotta be that."

"She smoked those birds from three times the distance. What I saw was someone who couldn't bring herself to shoot me."

"You can't be serious."

Parks stared at Foster in bewilderment. "Dude," he shrugged his hands around them at the bare rock, bare of game, of life. The sea, freezing and empty. The sun that never set. "Who gives a fuck?"

They stood as Tunguk approached.

"What's the verdict?" Foster asked. "Sail?"

Tunguk looked to a gull out over the water. It flapped and spun to face the way they came, then stopped and held steady, going nowhere in the headwind, wings still. After a moment's rest, it made a slow turn and swooped with effortless speed until it disappeared from sight around the point, as if to reply, 'Isn't it obvious?'

"That's a start, anyway." Foster managed to contain his optimism. "Whale. Drummoc. Ship. Home. Dial it up, Cap'n." Foster felt the twinge of discomfort when he couldn't tell if what he said met with approval. "Bet you'll be glad to be rid of us."

"It is a way, yet."

The breeze found them as soon as they cleared the island's shadow. The rowers got to face forward for a change as they skipped along at a good clip once the sail dried. When the rigging was up, the little boat became even more of a clusterfuck. Foster kept busy crawling around and over his crewmates to trim the sails to Tunguk's orders. By now he had the basic principle, and working the knots even with his left hand at half-capacity was easy enough. The old man—maybe for the want to avoid insulting him—began to abbreviate his commands to a nod, if he gave one. He preferred to let the wind do the cursing when Foster made his mistakes, to the point that he would adjust bearing with the steering oar and watch quietly as Foster scrambled to get the sail around to compensate. The overcast sank to water-level, and the islands they saw so clearly the day before vanished though they had to be nearing them. It wasn't clear what they were orienting to, but all the adjustments were too precise to be simply pointing in a compass direction. He puked only once, which was an improvement over the last time the sail was up. There was nothing to it but bile. Despite the stiff wind snaking through their wet clothing, the bumpy ride, and the empty stomachs, the mood aboard was the brightest he could remember. Not that anyone spoke. Parks folded his arms over his lap and lay his forehead on them like a kid in class. Meanwhile Kjartke forcefully lifted their legs and yanked the boots off their feet to mild protest, then settled in her bow seat to mend them with a bone needle. There was no rush to her pulling, though their feet numbed to the cold water coming over the beam. She seemed pleased to be able to look at something besides the three of them.

Sometime in the afternoon, the wind shifted over the starboard bow, and they hove-to. Tunguk said if it didn't change, they would soon row to the nearby water island—the one he wanted all along. But within a few hours it worked back around, a bit more of a seaward than before, and they were once again underway. Foster bit off little sips of water all the while. Parks was less judicious. It caused him a fair amount more concern that Tunguk hardly touched his at all. The gray curtains darkened as the sun sank west of them—it was impossible to tell where, beyond an enormous slice of ocean that was somewhat lighter. At last, Tunguk ordered a course change towards the darker section. Within a couple of hours, the boat was rocking in disturbed waters that seemed to come from both angles while the frail remainder of wind nursed them along. Again, they paused. Tunguk pulled in the steering oar, lifted his bladder, and took a long pull.

This was night. No sun, no moon. A bank of clouds, not quite dark or light. The breeze skipped in over the port beam, cold enough that Foster debated climbing into his bag. To do so at sea meant that it would sit in the damp of the boat with his extra clothes in a pile between his feet. Nothing beneath him and the skin deck. It would be impossible to get comfortable, and everything would be soaked by morning. It was his watch, and he preferred to shiver with a few dry parts. The others kept their bags stuffed as cushions as well, and curled into whatever awkward positions they could find. How they slept was beyond him. Between the cold, the cramped space, and working up enough saliva to swallow, there didn't seem to be any hope of sleep. He wasn't even going to wake Tunguk for his turn, but the old man roused himself.

Foster nodded politely, and Tunguk smiled. He must have sensed his unease as the boat tottered in a wobbly circle, because he didn't try to compel Foster to rest.

"A young man comes on a boat for the first time."

"Is that your version of, 'a guy walks into a bar?'" He'd been on boats. It didn't feel worth it to correct him.

"There is much to learn. If he stays long, he will be an old man. If he looks, he will see much. He will feel the sea. After many days, he will know something of it."

"Yeah, well, I hope to not be here for that long."

"Are you the first man on the sea?"

"Hm?"

"Why you do not ask me of these things? A young man will look until he is gray as me, and he will learn what an old man can say in a word. Boats do not sail by young men. Now, it is easy. I do it for you. He must find an old man, if there is one who will talk. Ask him of the clouds and the birds. The waves. The wind. How to sleep at sea. You will learn if you live, but you can have this now. It is good to have an old man in your boat. Better to carry him with you," Tunguk touched his own chest. "This is what I mean that boats sail by the old, even if the crew is young. Many men watch the sea, and they speak of it to others. In one man, there are many more. A boy might see as all of his ancestors. This is a secret that is guarded. All men know it, and that is how it hides. There is much more than I can say."

"Right, people pass down knowledge. I get that. You want me to ask you about sailin'?"

"You must be sure you ask an old man. Not an old fool." Tunguk chuckled to himself.

Foster rolled his eyes. He looked around at the featureless clouds blotting out the horizon on all sides. This was night, because he should be asleep, but it was something different to Tunguk. "Fine. What did you call this again? This time of day? Or year, or whatever the hell it is?"

"Denankikumak."

"Denankikumak," Foster repeated.

"Fire-king-grows-weary."

"That's right," he nodded at the memory. Foster could hardly blame the old fire king. Rest was hard to come by here, and the both of them would be on duty for a while yet. "Do you know where we are?"

Tunguk looked around. "I think yes."

Great, Foster snorted to himself.

"Do you know this wave?"

"What wave?" The sea was a little choppy, but not anything he would call a wave.

"Cloak," he pointed over the bow at the water.

"Cloak?"

"Give me your oilskin. I will show you how it was shown to me."

"I'm cold. Can't you just explain?" Tunguk seemed to mull it over. Foster let out a heavy breath and peeled the garment off. Tunguk caught the toss.

"Arms are gone," he held it up and waved as if to make them disappear. "This is a cloak. You watch." He spread it out completely flat and held it behind him between his outstretched arms. When he was sure Foster was paying close attention, he slowly pulled it until it touched his back and the two sides wrapped around to close in the front. For a moment Foster thought he had been scammed out of his warmth. But the old man looked at him in quiet expectation. All he got was a furrowed brow.

"You have seen. Now you feel." Tunguk slid over the middle seat where part of Parks was sprawled to sit on one of the ribs beside him. He held the oilskin up flat behind him, paused, then slowly brought it around Foster's shoulders until it wrapped over his chest, the arms dangling free. It felt like a tender embrace that a parent might give a sick child to warm him, and it took Foster a second to bring himself back to where he was. Tunguk removed his hands, leaving him with the coat and no more of a clue.

"Now you do." Foster would have assumed he was the butt of some hazing at this point, but something stirred in his gut. Somehow, the simple act had taken him out of the overcast sea. It was almost surreal. Tunguk seemed eager with anticipation. Almost proud of whatever he was up to, like some sort of magic trick that required audience participation. Foster imitated the gesture, spreading the oilskin behind him, wider at a tilt of Tunguk's hand, until his shoulders could go no farther behind his body.

"You are the island," Tunguk said before he could move. The image of a tropical paradise entered it head. In fact, he *was* a sort of island. The only thing poking up proud over the water. "Cloak is the wave." He motioned for Foster to proceed. As he brought it forward, he felt how it first bowed against his spine, then curled around him until it overlapped, covering his arms and folding over his knees.

"I think we are in the cloak." He touched a point of fabric where it ruffled together. "Here." Foster saw his tropical paradise again. A low, slow wave hit the shallows and curled around either side until it sloshed together in the lee of the island. He looked ahead, but the water only seemed confused. Tunguk must have sensed he was close.

"If we sail into the sea, the boat will tip, first bow, then stern." Now he noticed the rocking motion—the same one they felt all along. The water hit first off the starboard bow and tipped them, but before they could totter back the same direction, a more subtle movement came from the port bow and lifted the vessel the other way, causing what felt like a strange figure-eight that changed period due to the uneven forces. He thought they stopped for the night because the sea got choppy. It was still too hard to visually discern what Tunguk was trying to show him, but in his mind he saw it clear, and felt the undulation. Through the dim gray skies ahead of them, something invisible loomed. The rough open water vanished, and instead became the welcome mat of their destination. The world before his eyes never changed, but from a formless smear came lines and shading, detail that gave him a sense of place, even if it was mostly imagined. Something downloaded itself into his brain, so that he knew it with every bone in his body. Every part of the scene seemed to shimmer. It was some time before he could think, and only then did he realize he still held the oilskin around like a cloak.

Foster shoved his arms through the sleeves and secured it again. "Thanks." It felt like a stupid thing to say. "So someone taught you all of this, too?" Another stupid thing. What else could it have been?

Tunguk nodded. "I look very wise," the wrinkled face curled . "Only when I sit beside you." He laughed.

Foster grinned. "Yeah, well, I'm known to have that effect on people. Still, I'm impressed. In this weather, I'd have passed that island right up. Your old man teach you that? The cloak thing?" Tunguk seemed confused by the expression. "Your father."

He shook his head. "An old fool."

The morning brought a fog and a trickle of wind from the port stern. The sail took what it could while the overcast hung dead and the sun glowed through it, back at the beginning of its ellipse. Within a few hours, though, the breeze was gone and the clouds burned off to leave a thick shadow on the horizon. The mast was stowed, and Parks and Kjartke had to take up oars. The former was out of water entirely. Foster's head throbbed from dehydration and his mouth stuck to itself. He couldn't imagine trying to pull, but neither could he imagine giving his last precious sips to his friend. This was *thirst*, thirst. No fucking around. The sea air seemed to pull the moisture right out of his skin. A few hours ago, he would have done the right thing and offered his up portion, knowing a refill was just a few miles out. It was easy to imagine how noble he would be when he wasn't quite suffering. Now, he was afraid of what might happen in between. Foster already justified it, reminding himself Parks made his choice. He was too big. No way both of them would live if it came down to it.

It looked like they would arrive any minute, but the island kept its distance for most of the morning. Gradually, it peeled in two—a smaller nob with flat heights lie toward the peninsula with a big sister seaward and a narrow channel between. He figured they would head right into it, but Tunguk steered them wide of the larger one. It proved a wise move. By noon, a breeze picked up directly out to sea. It was all they could do to keep windward of the larger island. Had they angled in for the channel, they may have blown clear of both islands altogether. Instead, they had a battle to avoid being driven into a rocky shallow. The leather boat had a habit of surrendering to any blow that came its way. Tunguk ordered the mast readied again, and Foster understood that if they couldn't keep windward, he would get as close to the islands as he could, then turn to the coast at the last moment and use the sail to try to shoot the channel.

"Come on Parks, you got this, bro." Foster was far more encouraging than he otherwise would have been. He was sure it was out of guilt for how quickly his survival instinct kicked in, before the water was even gone. At last, the wind slacked off and they managed to draw even with the island in the early afternoon. To their left, a sheer cliff wall rose up to a peak that formed the highest point. There wasn't a speck of snow. Sea birds covered the entire face. They squawked in private conversation, under no threat from the hunters. Kjartke couldn't afford to lose an arrow firing from aboard. The rustle of feathers lifted Foster, a distant reminder of the clamor of port. Life and voice called out to him, and he was overcome with a homesickness for human contact. Tunguk worried there may be others here, and elsewhere along the way. Secretly, Foster prayed for it. Not everyone could be the kind of assholes they met in the longboat. Hell, they were going somewhere with people and ships. Why couldn't there be folks to trade with? To share a drink of water and a seal steak?

As they skirted past, the birds' cries grew into a cacophony.

"Breedin' grounds?" He shouted over it.

"No more eggs," Tunguk anticipated him.

Foster wished he had a pair of wings to soar over the islands and scout for game. For some frame of reference. He had no idea where they were, in more ways than one. So far, his world was twenty-feet long, population: four. Resources: zero. This place wasn't even on his map. If there was any truth to Tunguk's claim that you needed two places to not be lost, he was in trouble. He didn't even have one. If the birds had drawn these, they weren't interested in the same things as Foster.

"Dude, I don't see any whales," Parks leaned into his oars. It was only then that Foster noticed Tunguk's eyes followed the line of the island, instead of scanning the sea for signs of game. He thought they were circling to look for prey. Now he wondered if it was something else.

"We just got here. I thought you were on Team Probability."

"I'm on Team Cannibalism if we don't find something real quick."

"Better to say when you were fatter." Tunguk didn't even look at them. It took an audible sniff from Kjartke—dangerously close to a chuckle—for them to realize he was joking.

Foster considered his captain's advice the previous night. "Besides, it ain't time to hunt, yet. What should we be lookin' out for?"

"Boat."

"If you ask me to fight another ship right now—fuck. I'm too tired to even kill myself," Parks groaned.

"No ship. Small boat. Like this."

"It's a water island," Foster thought aloud. "I reckon if you're goin' up and down this coast, you gotta hit almost every single one. Mattaka people never heard of bringin' a cooler."

"It is the other where there is water." He seemed distracted as he said it. Foster followed his eyes to a squabble of wings. A couple dozen birds of various sizes hovered and swooped over a spot near the cliff. Tunguk motioned for them to row where the swarm was growing. It reminded Foster of air battles for scraps that went on behind a fishing boat. Their approach annoyed the larger birds, but did not scare them off. Something white floated in the water. A seal, but it wasn't moving. The birds landed on it and pecked at the carcass. The rowers guided them alongside and Tunguk waved a spear to move the birds off. One stared at him in defiance and screamed. Tunguk skewered it and brought it aboard. He handed off the bird kebab to Kjartke, who was already processing it. He motioned for another spear, and got it from Foster. The birds shifted a few feet away and screamed in protest, but refused to stray far. Tunguk gently rolled the body over. It was chalky gray, swollen to immense proportions, but Foster recognized it as human. He and Parks recoiled in disgust.

"Nope. I am *not* eating that," Parks gagged.

"What's up, bitch? Team Cannibalism," Foster taunted.

"I can't tell if that's a man or a woman."

"Man," Tunguk said. None of the features were distinguishable. Foster had no idea how he knew. "Drowned. One of your people."

Foster and Parks glanced at each other. By now they knew that meant anyone other than a native, but Foster had to wonder if it couldn't have also been one of their actual people. They'd have been in the water long enough to bloat and float a ways. To finally meet land, and be finished by the birds. But this far? They must have been over a hundred miles from where the ship went down. He questioned the figure as soon as he thought it. It was impossible to tell how fast they were going at any time, unless there was an island. Then it was the island that seemed to move while they sat still. He thought of the life raft that drifted free.

"Who turns the face of a drowned man will soon drown." Kjartke broke her English silence. The Americans were taken aback. As if a witch had just uttered a curse.

"For your people," Tunguk said. "For my people, it is good for hunters. The birds were given a feast. It is a sign we will have the same."

"Who are your people? These?" She tilted her head to the sailors.

"Yeah, us," Foster said. "But I'm with Parks. I ain't eatin' that."

"Not this. It is a sign of game."

"I wonder how long you will live without Tunguk," Kjartke said. Foster was bewildered. Not a word to them for weeks. Maybe it was thirst, or lack of food. Something had given her the courage.

"I wonder how long you will," Foster said. They glared at one another. Kjartke skillfully slit the bird and tossed the entrails into the water, to the delight of the rest of the flock.

"Nobody has to worry about that," Parks interjected. "It's a good omen, like Joe said. Our people have the same tradition. When we find birds eating a drowned man where I'm from, it means we will have a nice steak dinner, and make love to a woman."

Tunguk said himself that their "people" didn't know about the water here. What he feared sounded more like rival natives to Foster. His hunger vanished as his insides turned with possibilities. *Man*, he thought. Three men went down with their ship. It was unlikely they would surface and drift. Then again, he had no idea how drowned bodies behaved. He knew well-enough that the wind and current usually moved *up* the coast of the peninsula, opposite their direction of travel. It couldn't have been the raft, then. But he had seen the wind shift countless times, and the currents were equally baffling. Depending on how far they were…the possibility excited him. Though it meant he may be staring at a dead companion, if anyone at all was here with them—he didn't know what it meant, but it was at least something.

I pray to God that's Carabiner, he thought.

They left the birds to their meal. By then, Kjartke had finished cleaning the enormous bird. She separated a leg from the carcass and held out the raw morsel to Parks. He grimaced.

"Eat," Tunguk urged.

"It is…very kind of you," he accepted the only acknowledgment from a woman he'd received in weeks. Holding it between three fingers, Parks turned it over, looking for a way in. At last, he stuck his teeth well out from his lips and worked them around a loose bit of flesh. She didn't bother offering a cut to the others. Kjartke placed the rest on Parks' luggage in the center of the boat and returned to rowing while he sawed off a delicate bite. After a little chewing, his face relaxed.

"How is it?"

He nodded along. "Mostly a texture thing. Could use a little more time on the grill." Parks held it up toward Foster.

"No, thanks. I'm more thirsty."

"Same." Parks set it down with the carcass and turned to help row. Immediately, he thought twice, reached behind him, and transferred it to his lap. Now and then, he took a stroke off to work in a bite. They soon rounded the southern edge of the island and steered along the width, much shorter than the side they just crossed, though still without so much as a reckless landing possibility. The little sister came into view, and there Tunguk again had them ready the sail but not raise it. Under oars, they peeked into the channel. The water turned greenish-blue over the quarter-mile stretch between the islands. In the middle, the sheer rock on both gave to gentle slopes and shallows that promised a beach on either side. The two were in truth a single mass, the low center submerged, and not by much if the bright waters were any indication.

Tunguk spotted it first. A black lump broke the water and disappeared. Foster held his eyes on the surface like rifle sights, waiting for movement. Again it appeared with a spout, and glided at the surface for a while before rolling under. Over and over, it breached, circled, and disappeared. Foster wanted to whoop with joy, but a whale in the water was a long way from supper. But whether or not they starved, there it was: vindication. Game where game should be—between them and a narrow channel, at that. If ever there was a place they might catch up to one of these giants, it was here. He scanned the rest of the boat for a reaction. No one was quite ready to applaud. However disgusted Parks was at his chicken leg, he sure used the pause in action to stuff a good chunk of it into his mouth.

It seemed to work its way around the same spot. As they neared, they heard its moan. Foster was no expert on whale song, but it seemed unsettled. They soon found why.

"Mother," Tunguk said. And nearby, a calf. Foster thought it was a rock at first. It lay barely moving above the surface of the water between the two islands. Beached on an unexpected shallow. The mother swam back and forth, trying to coax or cajole it to work its way free, toward the deeper waters from which the hunting boat approached. The calf either didn't understand, or couldn't pull it off.

Mama whale grew into a giant. Foster couldn't believe that a creature could be so large. He'd never seen anything so close, and it didn't seem like it had the wherewithal or energy to worry about them. Covered in big lumps of white crust, nearly black, she seemed scarcely faster than the paddles, but that wasn't the problem. She was ungodly huge. The tiny bone and stone spears looked like toothpicks in comparison, and he had no idea where they would put any meat they took if they could somehow manage not to enrage a woman who was already having a pretty bad day. One roll or flip of the tail and they were sunk. The harpoons had leather ropes, but the notion of them holding on to one end as if it mattered while the beast dove was insane. How did people kill whales back in the day, he wondered? He knew Eskimos did it. Old wooden whaling ships did it. Apparently, Tunguk did it. It just didn't seem possible with the gear they had on hand. Not to mention he felt more than a little vexed by the idea of slaughtering something that just wanted to save its young, right in front of that young, who would die of being beached. And to waste literally tons of flesh that they could never eat, haul, or anything else.

Then he saw it. Tunguk motioned the boat toward the shallows, protecting their approach with the bottom. If the calf grounded, the whale had no chance anywhere near it. She knew it, and kept a good distance out. They weren't going for the mother.

The big whale spotted them. She turned their direction, and Foster froze, imagining the huge body leaping from the water and collapsing across the vessel. But she veered before it got too shallow and swam at pace parallel to them. The higher-pitched cry of the little one skipped over the water, and Mama came into detail as she raised her head to answer. Foster was horrified. It did not look like a creature that belonged on this planet. He'd seen whales, but never like this. The grotesque white mounds sprouted like bone-hard boils on her face. A big black eye pleaded with them from beneath the incomprehensible curve of a mouth. Her face looked like it was on upside down, with the upper jaw a thin wedge and the rest of the head, including the eye, beneath her strange smile. There was no feeling of threat now. It was as if she thought this new animal might have come to help.

"Spear," was Tunguk's command.

"Damn," Foster hesitated. "Ain't no fish and game laws in Antarctica, I guess."

"Fuck the fish and game. I wanna know how we stop that thing from pulling us under," Parks said.

"We're goin' after the little guy."

"Fucker is the wise hunter," Tunguk stated flatly.

"I don't wanna be the wise hunter. I want a goddamn Taco Bell drive-thru, not baby whale sushi that I slaughter in front of its mom. Who, by the way, if she's anything like my mom, will hunt you to the ends of the earth and kill you if it takes eight decades."

"It's a fuckin' whale, bro, not Liam Neeson."

"So you're just fine with this?"

"Fuck no, I'm not, but a man's gotta eat. And I paddled, so you gotta kill it, not me."

The water beneath them grew lighter. Foster could see the shelf, the calf on the edge. They hugged it as they worked around toward the flank. The mother pitched and spouted, and he wasn't sure, but he felt her cries deepened. Her child moaned back. She couldn't and wouldn't get any closer. He saw that the little whale had the same white crusty scabs. They looked like warts, or calluses up close. What caused it, even in the young, he couldn't guess.

"Is it diseased? Can we even eat this?" He probed for an excuse.

"It is the nature of this whale," Tunguk said.

The tail fin flapped and sent water spraying past them, but it was a heartless effort to free itself, exhausted and resigned. The boat eased alongside. Foster looked into its big black eye. It seemed to plead with him, a creature of intelligence. He was no hippie, and he never begrudged a hunter his kill. But he was used to taking deer from range, not stabbing something with more intelligence than Parks however many times you needed to spear a whale to kill it. He tested his left hand by opening and closing it. Better than the first few days by far, but he still couldn't dream of squeezing anything with any force. It was true, though. Parks and Kjartke had paddled their asses off for days while he sat limp-dicked on the cold skin deck weighing down the boat and eating their rations without serving the least of a purpose. More than anything, he hated feeling useless. He hated people waiting on him, taking care of him, doing things for him that he should have done himself. Even though Parks rarely missed an opportunity to shit on him about his injury, call him a pussy, or the one-armed man, he could tell the big guy was holding back out of sympathy. The barbs lacked venom. Parks did just enough to draw attention away from his own whining and griping, but not enough to entirely throw his friend under the bus. And that sympathy drove Foster nuts.

He reached for the spear at his feet with his right hand. Probably better this than the toggle harpoon, he thought. The rope would be useless and the point stuck after one thrust. They would need more than several to do the job. He had no idea how they were going to butcher it. He felt embarrassed to do it in front of the mother. Like robbing a cradle. A kill they hadn't even earned. This place was his choosing, though. Hobbled as he was, his pride was undamaged and weeks of letting an old man, a new mother, and a guy who cried about a shin bruise like a broken leg had gotten to him. He'd have taken any other opportunity to man up. Fighting pirates, spearing seals, anything. Killing a stuck calf didn't seem like it earned him much reprieve, but here it was. The only meaningful thing he could do.

The paddlers brought the bow up to the whale. Tunguk raised a spear overhead and plunged it halfway into the side with both hands. It screamed in agony. He gripped the shaft and used it to leverage himself out of the boat and onto the back on the beast. Tunguk stood, turned, and motioned to Foster. Foster rose with his spear and tried to steady himself as he stepped past Kjartke, bracing his forearm on her shoulder.

"Spear," he repeated.

"I'm comin'."

"No. Spear."

Foster paused in the bow. "You don't want me to spear it?"

"No." He motioned for the weapon.

"I don't understand."

"You are no whaler. I will do it fast." Foster should have felt massive relief, but it was as though the spear found his own heart. After pep-talking himself into the last thing he wanted to do, now he wasn't allowed to. The only thing worse than being willing to be a turd, was to be willing and still unable. Reluctantly, he passed the spear to Tunguk.

The old man aimed for the spine just below the skull. He drove it down with a thud, worked it side to side. Foster heard the vertebrae crackling. The whale barely made a sound. It faded as though someone with a hand on the volume twisted it off. The fins moved involuntarily a moment, then they were still. The mother must have known. She let out a sound that pierced Foster's internal organs.

"What can I do?" He asked Tunguk.

"Tie the boat," he indicated the spear still protruding from the side.

Foster secured the bow line to the shaft. Kjartke was already shoving past him to climb on top. She and Tunguk drew their knives and cut each a shallow slit in the skin. They pressed their lips and drank of the blood that ran out. Tunguk saw Foster standing beside the whale looking on in horror. He opened another nearby.

"Drink."

"I'll wait. You know, for the water."

The old man took another pull, and Kjartke smeared the blood off of her chin tattoo. Their thirst quenched, Tunguk worked his long blade deep though the blubber to open a line down the length of the side. Kjartke lay on her belly and used her U-shaped blade to separate the blubber from the flesh. Once they peeled back a lip of more than a dozen feet, they climbed down into the boat again. Foster was still standing. To sit would have resigned him to uselessness, but now he fled back out of their way. Parks was silent. Their eyes met, then he looked away to the mother, still circling, calling out to her young. Tunguk pulled the boat parallel, and they each made a vertical cut on their ends so that the side hung down over the boat. Then he pulled the spear out, peeled the flap down, and drove it in again to deep red flesh. The odor of blubber hit Foster's nose and turned him from the kill to gather himself. When he looked back, Tunguk had cut a hole into the thick strip and tied off a rope. With a little more work, they freed the long rectangle from the side, pushed back, and let it splash into the water between them before guiding it behind the boat and out of the way. Kjartke climbed back up top, where there was still flesh to stand on, and began to peel more skin free, this time leaving as much fat as she could. Meanwhile, Tunguk sliced into the meat. He motioned to Foster, and Foster guessed by handing him one of the now-empty sacks that held their rations. Tunguk cut hunks of flesh and tossed them one after another into the bag. He noticed Foster staring, and handed a piece to him. It reminded him of fresh tuna in the way it looked. Famished as he was, the frenzied butchering left him ill at ease. He would have to wait before he got the nerves to eat the thing. Another spout reminded him that the mother was still present and persistent in her grief. Parks watched him closely. His face was gaunt, sparse stubble turning into a patchy beard beneath sunken eyes. The rest of him looked strong—only because of the size of his frame. There was a good thirty pounds unaccounted for. It could have been a photo from his high school football team sitting on that bench. This was not someone Foster had ever seen in eight years of company. He handed over the piece of flesh. Parks seized a bite and chewed out of duty. After some consideration, he gave a shrug, and tore in.

While Parks feasted, Foster helped Tunguk fill the remaining three bags with meat. There had to have been a couple hundred pounds of food all told. Kjartke finished stripping the flesh she wanted, folded it, and handed it down. Foster assumed they were done, but Tunguk simply moved over and began to throw more meat directly into the boat. Kjartke went to work carving out vertebrae near the tail. The boat was fast becoming a stinking mess. The gunwale was already coated slick with oil. Cured of his appetite, he wanted nothing more than to be off the boat after more than twenty-four hours at sea. He held on to what skin he could find, lifted a foot on the spear shaft as a stepladder, and vaulted clumsily onto the top of the whale. Something told him it was going to be a while.

Foster turned toward the smaller island. All he cared for now was the water that supposedly ran there, though it wasn't high enough to hold ice. Two weeks, he thought. The sheer amount of energy it took to keep a wet mouth and find a meal was heartbreaking. For all his talk of probability, he knew it was dumb luck they came across a beached calf. There were likely whales here, alright, but the chances of taking that big one in the open water in their condition were nonexistent. How could Tunguk not see that? He wondered how much farther this port was—the place they might find a real ship heading the right away. And how many times they would have to pull this off again.

Below, Parks looked marooned on an island of flesh as Tunguk's pile grew to ridiculous proportions. Half of their gear was already buried.

"Dude," Parks held up his second steak. "This is way better than the chicken. No offense," he added to Kjartke. "Honestly…" he seemed to think it over, then yanked the bird carcass free of the whale meat and flung it sidearm into the water. It hit with a dull splash. Kjartke stopped her work cold. She fixed on the rippling pool where it disappeared, and did not move. Even Parks sensed the shift. "I just feel like we need to make room," he back-tracked. "Foster's got no place to sit." Whatever ran through her mind was a mystery buried under a steel face. All Foster knew is it made him uncomfortable as fuck.

He tried to bring his attention back to the island, hoping she would resume her cutting soon. There was a flicker. Two black shapes moved in tandem from the direction of the channel. He shielded his eyes from the glare. Whales, he said to himself, and knew better. Even with his meager experience, the movement of the silhouettes registered in his mind.

He called to the crew. "Boats."

The two Mattaka stopped cutting. Tunguk gave a short order, and Kjartke climbed down off the whale to sit in the boat. He clawed his way up to see for himself.

"Should we skedaddle?"

Tunguk watched for a moment. "We stay. In the boat." Foster scrambled down first, and Tunguk after him. Kjartke was already sitting in Foster's spot on the deck. He took it to mean he should sit on her bench. "Friends?" He asked.

"No."

"Enemies? Tourists?" Parks said through a full mouth.

"We have found here many things we expect," he gave Foster a wry glance, then took the piece of whale from Parks. "Haqawa," he answered. "Appear as though with a full belly."

"That bad?" Foster asked.

"They are foul people. Thieves. They hunt sacred waters. Kill many Kapadak."

"I don't follow all these words. Is Kapadak them people we were with? The ones that kicked us out?"

"Yes."

"Then who is Mattaka?"

"The people."

"All of 'em?"

"All of our people," he looked to Kjartke.

"Don't worry, Joe. We're your people now. We can call ourselves," Parks searched for a word. "The Slappadick clan."

"So why aren't we runnin'? Are they gonna try to kill us?"

"If to them, we look weak, they will take the whale. If strong, they will leave."

"In other words, bow up. Look hard as fuck, Foster." Parks flared his elbow in a quick flex. A few bites of dripping flesh seemed to have exhumed his spirit.

"They got two boats. That's more than we got."

"You will sit tall. Look to have little concern when they approach. They will think you are whalers."

"Act like a whaler? What the fuck does a whaler act like?"

Foster got no answer. The occupants came into view as they closed. He counted three heads in each. Younger. Long black hair. Tunguk spun the bow to press into the carcass in plain view, broadside to the oncoming traffic. To show numbers, and a lack of fucks given, Foster imagined. He thought about taking a posture that looked both hard and unbothered, but he figured whatever he did would just betray his unease, and let his shoulders slump instead. He didn't dare look back at Parks, but he prayed he wasn't posing like a rapper on an album cover. If his eyes left the boats it might show a lack of confidence. He decided to hold a stare like folks in the mountain give you when they're sitting on the porch and you walk up the drive.

The boats back-paddled to stop at a distance and surveyed them. Neither side moved for several minutes. Then they resumed a slow approach. Now Foster could see detail. He imagined war paint at first. Some Last of the Mohicans shit. Every one of them was done up different, but the general pattern registered. Face tattoos. All six of them were women.

They stopped again ten yards out. One of them shouted to Tunguk in their language. He gave a curt response.

"What did they say?" Foster whispered to Kjartke without breaking his gaze.

"Do not question me in front of them," she scolded. Foster clammed up, wondering what taboo he broke.

"They want the whale," Tunguk said. "They say it is too much for our boat. They ask to take what we cannot."

"Do we get first dibs?" Parks asked.

"I do not know 'dibs.' If it is to fill our boat before they do, yes."

"That mean they decided not to fight us to the death over some blubber?" Foster asked.

Tunguk huddled them up for a private conversation. The women must have been at least in danger of understanding English.

"It is a hunting party. When women hunt, it is bad. Trouble for the clan."

"Because women suck at hunting?" Parks ventured.

"There are no men to hunt. It is what your people call 'take ram.'"

"'Take ram'?" Foster frowned. "That's not our people."

"It is when you cannot outrun or maneuver. You take the enemy's thrust, that you may board and have a fight. If you kill them all, you have a boat. If not, you sink. Last try for victory before defeat."

He smiled. "Hail Mary."

Tunguk continued. "The kill belongs to all of us. Our people have a way to choose. If there are three, all will say what they want. If two say to deny them, or if three say it, we will deny them. But if one says to deny them, and two say to share, then it is shared."

"Ah," Parks nodded. "We have a similar system. It's called a 'vote'."

"We will have a vote."

"Cool. I say have at it," Parks said. "We literally have a metric shit-ton more than we need."

"You vote to share. Haqawa have stolen from me many times. I will deny."

"Harsh, brother. You gonna make these ladies starve over some old-ass grudge?"

"Your say will choose it."

"What about her?" Tunguk and Kjartke looked at him in confusion. "Never mind." Foster shrugged. "Chivalry might be dead or never born in Antarctica, but where I'm from, you take care of neighbors even if you don't like 'em. I vote share."

"We will share with our enemies."

"Hang on. If they see me and Brother here tryin' to clean the whale, they're gonna know we ain't whalers." Kjartke and Tunguk laughed. Foster turned away annoyed. He seemed to be a constant source of idiotic amusement for them. *Like to see how they get along in the Blue Ridges*, he thought.

Tunguk said a string of words to the women. They didn't respond, but Foster sensed a secret ripple of elation through them. They didn't seem to expect it. The old man leaned in to Foster so that only their boat could hear. "If Kjartke speaks a word to them, kill her first." He handed him a spear. Foster's eyes met hers. She betrayed nothing. The order was as much for her as it was him.

She and Tunguk resumed work on the carcass. Foster and Parks sat eyeing the women. He imagined they were acting as guards to avoid having to pretend they had any kind of skills, or posed a threat, whatsoever. A quick scan of the faces put them in a range from 20's to probably 40's, though he knew by now these people aged gracefully enough that everyone under fifty more or less looked the same.

"I wish we had a secret language," Parks muttered.

"Why?"

Their tattoos all varied, but they ran anywhere from below the cheekbones to the chin, and some, around the sides of the eyes and brow, hard brown eyes and never wavered. Nothing on the forehead, the nose, or the cheeks, themselves.

"The Reverse-Eskimos can talk right in front of us without us understanding."

"Mattaka," Foster corrected.

"But their English is too good. We can't conspire in front of them."

"Don't say 'conspire,' they can hear us."

"I doubt they know what the word means."

Foster turned to him. "They don't know what a lot of our words mean."

Parks snorted. "Retards."

"They probably don't know what a retard is."

"Nincompoops."

They laughed. "Hey Brother, you ever played that game Taboo? Where you gotta make your partner think of somethin' but you can't say certain words?"

"I crush it. I lather my balls in my opponents' tears."

"That's our language."

"Taboo?"

"No, retard. The taboo words are the obvious one. They don't know our figures of speech, or our culture."

"I don't know your culture, or what the hell you're saying half the time."

"I'm serious. Check it out. Which of the last Mohicans is your Beyonce?"

"Huh." Parks grinned. "I think I follow. Fleur-de-lis is behind my door number one."

Foster looked them over. Sure enough, one of the women had an arrangement of thick dots and lines on her chin with a center pike extended on to her bottom lip, and two branches that curled to either side—an upside-down approximation of the symbol. "Nice." He and Parks smiled at one another.

"Took some Spanish in high school, by the way."

"Not me."

"I guess English would have been hard enough."

"Too close to South America anyway. Let's try another one. Reckon you—no, wait. Why reckon you, *Tampon*, becomes *shish-kebab* by *Dixie* if *eak-spay ig-pay atin-lay*, then *Gettysburg?*"

"I have no idea what the fuck you just said, but that's a good idea. We can just use Pig Latin. Ink-thay you-way…Abertits-say?"

"We're not usin' Pig Latin."

"*You* just did,: Parks protested.

"I mixed it in. What don't you understand? I thought you were good at this."

"I'm extremely good at clue-giving, not interpreting dumb clues that don't make any sense."

"Gettysburg is from the Civil…thing, many Yankees' and Dixies' final tango."

"I know what fucking Gettysburg is. I'm not retarded. I meant your whole clue sucked fat whale taint."

"My clue was fine. Your solvin' needs work."

The nearest boat of women took a few strokes to draw closer. In the front sat the oldest—a thin, muscled woman with an intricate design tattooed in a crescent around her right eye, four square dots in a diamond formation on her chin, and the left side bare skin drawn smooth over high cheekbones. Behind her sat Fleur-de-Lis, the youngest, and another woman whose entire bottom lip was a black bar over a symmetrical design of lines and dots that flared up to either side just past her mouth.

"He would not give us kill," she nodded toward Tunguk. "It is you we thank."

"Not a problem, Darlin'," Foster answered.

"You are whalers."

He nodded. Foster could feel Kjartke and Tunguk listening. He wanted the women to go away. A wrong word on his part, and they might chance a fight. Or one on theirs—or Kjartke's—and Tunguk would start it. Their getting closer to thank him was an excuse to better size him up.

"You are from shipwreck."

Foster squinted. "How'd you know?"

She laughed. "You look like others."

"What others?"

"You not know?" He didn't answer. "Then I repay you for your gift. Your mates, there." She pointed to the smaller of the sister islands, the one with water. "Long time. They say, pay great price if we bring home. We not think so. We not like whalers, so we leave them." The women laughed.

"What did they look like?" Parks asked.

"You."

"How many?" Foster challenged her.

"Two. But they say more."

"How many more?"

"We not care. If they die, is better."

Tunguk shouted something at her in their language. She smiled, and turned the boat back to join the other.

The rest of the afternoon passed in silence as Tunguk and Kjartke disassembled their kill. The long strip of blubber and skin they peeled earlier was cut into manageable sections and set along the open space in the bottom of the boat. More strips of skin were cut, and meat wrapped in them. Eventually, it was piled on top in thick slabs, completely unprotected from the elements—hundreds of pounds that seemed like it would spoil as soon as they began taking water over the side again. There was nowhere to sit but where they sat. No room for moving about, and already, everything was slick with a foul-smelling grease. The rigging couldn't even be stowed properly. It rode atop the pile as well, across one side of the hammock seats. All the while the Haqawa women waited like jackals just beyond the kill, while the mother whale held her vigil at the entrance to the channel.

They turned over the carcass to the women without a word. Foster had to assume Kjartke's oars and make a show of rowing. Tunguk was worried that any sign of weakness would cause trouble for them, even if these were the last six able-bodied members of a clan desperately in need of meat. And they would have it. The far side of the whale was still untouched, and there was plenty of good meat left on the one they worked over. He hoped they were too focused on their scavenging to notice his rowing technique. Every pull sent an electric pain down the side of his forearm to his elbow, and he could barely maintain his grip on the slick oars, though he swore he never touched the fat. The left blade skipped over the top of the water as he failed to dig it in. His face flushed as he struggled to get them beyond earshot of the women.

"We're goin' slow as fuck. I might as well have her sittin' on my back like a stool and rowin' for all the convincin' we're doin'."

"I'm with Fucker. Let the woman row, I'm doing all the work."

"Good for healing. Tell hand it is needed."

Foster grunted. "They didn't seem that bad, anyway."

"No need to be bad. We gave them food."

"Which you voted not to. You sayin' they would have tried to kill us if we told them to fuck off?"

"They would wait until we leave, then take food."

"Then why bother voting?" Parks asked.

"We must choose."

"Same either way."

"It is different: share, or leave behind."

"Like I said. Same difference." Parks spat a dry glob over the side.

"I see the difference," Foster said. "We shared, so they did, too. They knew we were shipwrecked. They told us where we could find survivors."

"Haqawa lie."

"Why would they lie?"

"They are Haqawa."

Foster shrugged. "Well, I'll guess we'll find out. That's where the water is."

"We have had our drink of whale's blood. Filled our skins," he touched the water bladder. Foster hadn't even noticed him do it, but he was disgusted at the notion. "It is best to find water at the next island."

"Next island? Hell, *we* didn't drink any blood," he motioned at Parks. "Fine, let's vote on it."

"How far are we talking?" Parks asked.

"If the wind favors us, one of your days."

Parks pursed his lips. "I think I can make it."

Foster was beside himself. "You don't *have* to make it. There's water right *there!*"

"And people we don't know."

"The fuck, brother? The lady said there's survivors of a shipwreck who look like us. There's no advantage to lyin', I don't care what Tunguk said. He acts like all his ex-wives were in those boats, but they're just girls who wanted to pay us back for helpin' 'em out. And all we gotta do is swing by and see whether or not one of our people managed to drift their asses to land. Maybe they some other natives who brung 'em there. Or a thousand other scenarios. If we survived, someone else could have, to."

"It is not your people. It is no one. Or they send us to enemies."

"Dude, the boat went down way the fuck north of here. How would they even get there?"

"I don't know. How did *we* get here?"

"I mean, I don't doubt it's possible. But who the fuck do you wanna find? She said two men. What two men? Everyone else on the ship got blindsided. I don't even think they had survival suits on. Only two men for sure made it off. You wanna find Carabiner and that map-faggot and put 'em in a boat that's already too full, that I have to paddle because you have the grip strength of a wet twat?"

"She said there might be others. Maybe the women survived, too."

"Good! I hope they did. So what? We gonna kill Carabiner and the map-faggot and take the women?"

"Look, fuck Carabiner. I don't care about them any more than you do, but you don't abandon a crew member because they annoy you."

"It is not your people," Tunguk reiterated.

"Listen to the man. All this whale sushi is quenching me. Why risk it?"

Foster looked to Kjartke. "What's your vote?"

"She does not choose," Tunguk said.

"I say she's crew like anyone else. She done more than I did. She paddled us here, she cleaned the whale. I wanna hear what she thinks." No one answered. "What is she even doin' on this trip? She's got no say? Is she even here of her own free will?"

"She travels to Drummoc."

"Why?" Tunguk held eye contact, his patient expression unchanged. "You said I should ask you questions."

He seemed to consider it, then gave a little snort of amusement. "It is what question you ask that chooses what you learn."

"And I'm askin' why Drummoc?"

"There, we will find the best value for her."

Parks cut in. "Value? Like we're gonna trade her for spoons or some shit?"

Foster glanced at Kjartke to see if her face betrayed anything about Tunguk's relegating her to trade value. It did not, and she struck him as having few fucks left to give about anything that didn't involve her immediate survival. But the remark didn't sit right, and for different reasons than Parks'. He turned it over in his head. "Best value. Is there somewhere else, with worse value? Somewhere closer?"

Tunguk paused. "Yes."

Foster's eyes bulged out of his head in frustration. "You realize that our home is *that* way?" He pointed the direction they came from.

"I know where you come from."

"I truly fuckin' doubt that."

"It is best for you. You want your home? You must go far from home to get there."

"How far?"

"Drummoc is the last place."

"Last place?" He processed it. "On *Earth*?" Foster threw up his hands. He looked to the woman. "And you're OK with this?" Kjartke stared back, unmoved. "Fine. Fuck all yall. If yall are are afraid of an ambush, just drop me off and I'll look myself."

"We're not worried about an ambush, we just don't care. We're not wasting the energy," Parks explained.

"Parks. Come on. How many times have I had your back? You and me, Brother. We gotta stick together. This ain't our world. We ain't whalers, we ain't Reverse-Eskimos. You know what we're lookin' for. If there's any chance of it—any chance we might even get one little step closer, we gotta take it."

"You wanna swim over there, that's fine, but I'm rowing where Joe tells me."

Foster drew his oars from the water.

"Come on, bro," Parks said. "Don't be a bitch."

"Tunguk." The old man watched the distant Haqawa, tiny dots on the black lump of whale. "I know it's stupid. But if anybody understands stupid for the sake of loyalty, it's you. You killed your own clansmen on a blood-bond with some white fuckers you just met. We got you banished for life. Then when we were about to jump Klimut and his boys, you risked all of our lives to help them because they were in trouble. You're bonded to save us, but you put us in harm's way for people who didn't want nothin' to do with you anymore. Why?"

"To help you, we need boat."

"Nothin' to do with the fact you wanted to help your friends?"

"Strangers. Who is on that island is not your people."

"You don't know that."

"Yes."

"And even if it ain't. Code of the Sea, brother. You don't let a man be stranded if you can help out. That might be you one day."

"It is *your* code. Not mine."

"It isn't our code, either," Parks shot. "We actually have a very well-defined code, with bylaws and shit, and that's not one of them."

"Then it should be."

"If there is a fight," Tunguk faced him. "You will not win."

"Fight's the last thing I'm after. I just wanna see who's there. You say it can't be my crew. They had a boat, better'n this one. They had provisions. If we could make it this far in bone and leather with barely a drink and a handful of jerky, you never know."

Tunguk picked up a piece of whale and took a large bite. "It is a good luck to be crew with Fucker," he mumbled through his chewing, flecks escaping down his chin. "But it is a curse to tie akmanuak. If I help, I am bound."

Foster dipped his chin, then gazed across the channel at the still island.

"But your people do not have this," Tunguk continued. "It is up to you if you help, and if you are bound, it is up to your gods."

"It's up to you, brother. You got the vote I need."

"I will not help. If I am there," he pointed to the shore of the seaward island, "I cannot help."

Foster grinned. "We can drop you off and take a look."

Tunguk stared at the island pair. "I will go to shore. You will see if your people are there. Fill water. Then you will return to me. There is room for one in this boat. If it is two, or many, you must choose."

"Goddamnit," Parks said.

"Each will say. Go with you, or with me."

"I can go by myself. Won't kill me to paddle a mile or two."

"Shut up, faggot. You know I'm going, too."

"Haqawa tell the truth," Kjartke broke in. "I go with these two." Tunguk cast her a look.

"What if they see us drop you off?" Parks indicated the Haqawa women at the whale.

"Their boat is full. They do not want an old man."

"So we're safe?"

"From them." Foster could feel Kjartke's eyes on him. They would be without their fighter, their guide. And in the company of someone who he did not seem to trust.

The sailors guided the boat to the shore of the smaller island. Tunguk waded up the beach with a handful of meat, a drink of blood, and a spear—emergency provisions. He would have no water unless they returned for him. From that, Foster gleaned two things. He gave them a good chance of survival, or else his bond would have required him to help. And he placed a great deal of trust that they would honor their end of the bargain. Kjartke took his place in the front, while he slid to the steering oar. Why she cared to help them, or if, was beyond Foster. He recalled Tunguk's words from earlier. Under normal circumstances, he wouldn't strike a woman for the best of reasons. If this one said or did anything that felt off, he intended to plunge a spear through her neck.

7

MUTINY!

Kjartke hopped over the bow and drug the boat shoreward. Foster and Parks swung over the sides into the icy channel. The bottom was solid rock, slick with algae, and the three of them fumbled with a different beast of a vessel than they were used to. Swollen with whale meat, they guided her through the shallows while they clung tight for footing. There was no sea to speak of in the harbor. He had chosen it from a distinct lack of choices—the only place low enough for a landing on the channel side, at least as far as he could tell. Foster scanned the heights ahead in anticipation of life. There was game where he said there'd be. Was it too much to be right twice in the same day?

He was captain, now. Not by any explicit agreement, but he noticed when he made a suggestion, they just did it ever since Tunguk went ashore. Kjartke turned over her bow on command, though he let her keep the odd little knife, and Parks gave up humming early-2000's Top 40 hits. A few days ago, that request would have been a sure way to turn up the volume. Either he understood why silence was advisable, or he obeyed out of habit. A sailor looks for orders.

Not even the cold sea could take his spirits. It was incredible what the smallest bit of say in his fate could do. His vision skipped, light from dehydration, but his steps rose high out of the water, out of proportion to the energy he should have to give. The hull scraped over wet rock with a sound that made him cringe. Kjartke lifted the front while he and Parks gave it one, two, three great heaves to clear their ride of the lapping water. It was as far as he dared haul it for fear of a puncture. He wondered what Tunguk would do.

"This high tide, or low?"

Kjartke shrugged. They looked around the rocky shore. There was a clear storm line well ahead, but nothing obvious to show were the tide came to rest. He thought to the whale, stuck on the bottom hours before. If that was a receding tide, it would be coming in by now, if not peaking. Before he could decide, Parks lumbered ahead. He groaned and stretched like a man stuck in a tiny boat for days. A few yards inland, he lifted his seal skin. They heard the unmistakable hiss of liquid on rock.

"Yo," he called back, his voice dry gravel scraping against itself.

Foster came over to him. Parks pointed while he shook loose the last of a paltry stream. A man lay ahead, stripped to the waist on a low, flat boulder facing the landing. His head, arms, and legs had been severed from his torso and placed in their standard positions, a few inches off the joint, arms straight out to the sides and legs angled like some anatomical drawing. His bare chest was decorated with an arrangement of slashes and notches in a deliberate pattern. He was white—not from exposure. A fellow Caucasian, and young. Late teens, most likely. Not someone they recognized.

"The fuck is that?" Foster recoiled inwardly. He was careful not to show physical alarm. His first thought went to the Haqawa women, but the eyes were missing, and the soft flesh around the face bird-pecked. This was many days old. He felt his hopes of seeing someone he knew, alive, leave him in a gut-punch. Already, he wished he hadn't pushed for this. Tunguk should be with them. There should be no hope of rescue, for anyone.

"It is a bad luck," Kjartke joined them. She walked over to the body, then knelt, leaned over, and hocked deep from her throat. Carefully, she dropped a glob of spit over his right eye socket, then his left, and rose. Parks and Foster exchanged glances. "I watch the boat," she offered.

"I don't think the tide'll get much higher." Foster was far from certain of it. Before he saw the man, he probably would have suggested someone stay back to make sure. "We stick together," he said.

For the first time, with him or anyone, she offered a dispute. "If we leave, they take boat. They watch now." Their eyes darted up the rock ahead of them to the interior of the island, with its two small peaks of sharp, ice-carved rock, though the ice was gone. Not a soul stirred.

"If we leave you, *you* take the boat."

"I vote we all take the boat. This isn't one of ours, and you know our people didn't do this. Mystery solved. Let's get Joe before we're attacked by cannibals." Parks was right, and he knew it. The smart thing now would be for all of them to turn around, grab the old man, and gut it out for another day on a few sips of whale's blood and the moisture from the raw meat. But he felt settling for anything less than fresh water now would be utter defeat. Worse. He fought them tooth and nail for this. To flee the second he arrived on the field, the first day in ages he moved under his own power, would destroy any good name he had left. And as low as his hopes fell, it nagged him that he might turn in fear with a living member of the *Qarapara* huddled up there somewhere, praying for a miracle.

"Even if our people didn't do it, they might still be here," Foster said. "Besides, would you really put it past Carabiner to lose his fuckin' mind?"

"I'd rather spear-fight cannibals than deal with Carabiner on a psychotic break. There might have been a .22 in that emergency kit."

Foster examined the body. "I don't see a bullet hole."

"You wanna be the one to flip him over?"

"Kjartke…" Her look told him not to push it if he didn't want to risk public dissent.

"Pow wow," said Parks. They stepped away and leaned in to whisper. "Look, dude. We don't know what we're up against, and I trust her about as far as my dick can reach."

"Agreed," he whispered. "Kjartke! Come with me. Parks got the boat."

"Not what I meant. If we can't all go in, we all go out."

"I didn't come here for survivors and water to find neither. You got the boat, but we launch you. Whoever did that," he thumbed the disjointed man, "is shipwrecked. They can't get you if you're in the water. Float off the coast there and come grab us when we're done."

"Who's gonna help you if she decides it's strap-on time?"

"You act like I've never fended off a strap-on." Foster walked to the boat and took out a spear and the bow. Kjartke extended her hand. "Pfft!" He laughed. "Nah, bitch. You'll get what you need when you need it." He slung the quiver over his shoulder. Kjartke fished out a pile of the whale skin she'd been working, and a little sack of other stuff. Foster pulled it free for a peek inside: a jumble of leather thread, bone needles, and a hollowed-out vertebra fresh from the whale.

"Water," she could tell he didn't know what he was looking at. "Very big."

Foster nodded as if it made sense. He wasn't sure how much time they'd have for arts and crafts, but he handed it back.

They launched Parks. Foster hoped all that scraping hadn't opened a hole under the pile of meat. It would be too late to bail by the time it became apparent. He rowed north around the bend and out of sight. If Foster and Kjartke weren't back within 24 hours—when the sun was once again hidden on the horizon by the westward island—he would row for Tunguk and return with help.

"You are leader," she said. "I walk first, or you?"

"I figure a Haqawa woman knows how to get around these parts better'n a West Carolina boy." She flashed what was he closest thing he'd seen to a smile since they'd met—only for a moment.

"You are wiser than the fat one."

"Don't try and flatter me. A retard could see that those are your bitches back there."

"Haqawa is what Tunguk calls us. We are Jargadak."

"Jargadak."

"And you are 'retard,' to put your mate out with my people near."

"You said yourself their boats are full. We ain't got a thing they want." It hit him as soon as he said it. "Except another full boat."

Kjartke stifled a laugh. "You can hope they are grateful. They are not afraid."

Parks would be back to check for them in an hour or so. He thought about running up a ways to try and signal him back right now. Abandon the entire search, like he probably should have done as soon as he was voted down. She must have seen it.

"You worry. Do we drink now, or sail? It is a fool to wait."

She was right. Standing around debating the matter was only drying them out. "What are the chances your people go after him?"

"Your people have chances. Not mine."

He looked back on the channel, and could see neither Parks nor the Jargadak women. He glanced from the body to the unmovable woman before him. Then he pointed the spearhead. "Lead the way."

Kjartke moved with confidence to higher ground. Her speed was almost reckless. Based on Westerns, he was surprised that the Indian guide didn't kneel to taste the ground, or decipher from a fragment of a footprint how tall and fat of a man came through, exactly how long ago and how fast. She didn't even seem to look around, much less slow enough to spot anything. All he saw was bare rock, with smaller rocks scattered over it. Nothing soft enough to leave an impression. He didn't know what he expected her to find, but he did expect something.

She rounded a boulder large enough to hide a fair-sized ambush party without caution, and hopped up on a spur that lead into the central heights.

"Hey, girl, be careful! Whoever cut up that body could've been right there waitin' to jump our ass."

"They wait near the cliffs at the far side."

"How do you know?"

"Birds."

He craned his neck across the cloudless sky. "I don't see no birds, or hear no birds."

"When we land, we hear them. Soon after Brother put in, we walk. Their call turns short. Someone moves to the cliffs. This is the way up. We find fresh water near the top."

"That don't mean we won't get waylaid along the way."

She paused in confusion. "Wayalay?"

"Waylaid. Attacked. Pieced up."

"I have you to protect me." Foster began to get a sense for the native sarcasm. He wasn't entirely sure she wasn't fucking with him about the birds, either.

They cut switchbacks for half an hour. The birds she claimed to have heard were not apparent. Whenever they had opportunity to regain the top of the spur, he got in the habit of scanning for the Jargadak women. It sent hollow pangs through him when he couldn't see their boats, but even the whale was hard to pick out—not more than a speck and a possibility based on memory—and they would be on the far side. He consoled himself that it took time to cross the channel, and he would see them if they did. Hopefully, Parks had the good sense to keep his eye there too, and run for Tunguk if he saw anything move his way.

The grade began to flatten and widen, dotted with small wind-smoothed rocks. The lichens up here were slightly different. That's as much as he could make of it. Foster kicked a rock over and noticed the underside was much darker in hue than the rest of it, as was the spot it vacated. Not from moisture. It was dry as a bone. That rock must have been in the same spot for years. Thousands of them. Maybe millions. No one had any business here, and anything too heavy for the wind would sit until it evaporated. He gathered it with his foot and nudged it carefully back in its silhouette. His eyes probed the rest of the scattered field. A dark spot, or a rock dark-side up might show him the trail someone else had taken.

Kjartke was leaving him behind. He jogged to catch her, hopscotching over anything he might kick. Foster wondered how many signs he'd already disturbed before he realized it. A pair of birds he didn't know glided in from the sea, close to the rock. They floated well ahead in a smooth line on the wind, took a sudden sharp turn, and flapped furiously down the side of the little mountain.

Kjartke pointed and whispered. "Someone waits."

Foster gripped the spear in his good hand tight. He couldn't see what she was talking about, or how she knew for sure. Her eyes locked on a short rise ahead. There was no sneaky way to approach it but up and over, and no way of knowing the terrain or who "waits." She held out her hand towards the bow.

"You trust me?"

"No." He kept it. She started ahead. "Wait," Foster caught up and cut her off. "I'm not sendin' an unarmed woman in first."

His imagination filled in the worst of the details for him. The memory of Tunguk scolding him for how he saw his "battles" irked him. But every effort to run through reasonable and pleasant explanations for the welcome mat left for them went foul. If it was his people, they were in terrible shape, though he felt willing and able to spear any of them who required it. They crouch-walked to the lip of the rock and paused to listen. Nothing, not even the squawk of a bird. "Wait here," he whispered. "If you hear me say 'clear,' I want you to follow me. If you hear me say 'pleased to meet ya,' that means run back to Parks and let him know what's up. Don't get seen. Don't move til you hear one of my commands."

Foster put his right forearm on the top and leapt from his left foot over the rise in one motion. It was a flat expanse that lead to the another elevation gain and the peak farther up. He couldn't see anyone right away. There was a small rock formation a few yards ahead, the only place anyone could hide. He crept to his left in a wide circle. Around the line of the formation, something appeared. A stack of five flat rocks, manmade beyond a doubt. They marked a point in a circle of smaller rocks. As he crept on, an inner concentric circle came in to view, then another cairn about 90 degrees around from the first one. The design took shape with each step, and a third cairn. Almost like he was looking at three-fourths of a compass, or a map of some sort, arranged around a center point: a pair of rock piles, each with broken eggshell on top. Foster swung wider and raised his spear.

A fourth cairn on the perimeter closed the circle, and behind it sat a boy, no more than sixteen, wisps of facial hair making their best efforts on his jawline. He was shirtless, drawn out and thin, with leather pants and boots. His skin was a sunburnt light brown, but not the tint of the Mattaka. He looked almost European, though his dark hair and eyes could have been South American as well. Beside him on the ground lay his leather shirt, and on it, a piece of rock knapped sharp on one side, and an ornate silver bottle, wide at the base and narrowing to a wood-plugged top, embossed with fine figures and polished smooth.

"I surrender," the boy said with a wry smile.

"How many others on the island?" Foster held his ground. He hadn't yet decided what he wanted to signal to Kjartke, but his eyes darted to his periphery as the boy spoke.

"One."

"Only one?"

"On this island."

"What does that mean?"

"It means there is only one other on this island."

Foster couldn't quite place his accent. It wasn't Spanish or anything else as obvious, but his English was excellent. "OK. How many on that island back there?"

"It depends on how things are going. I think less and less."

Foster's heart sank. They'd dropped Tunguk off alone with someone else. Several someones. Kjartke rounded the formation and joined him. So much for waiting for his command.

"Where are the other two?" The boy asked.

"What other two?"

He waved his hand at the rocks arranged before him. "There should be a crew of four."

"I ain't followin' ya," Foster played dumb.

"He is what you call a 'grim,'" Kjartke offered.

"I don't call nothin' a grim. What is this, some kinda witchcraft shit?"

"It's a calling circle. I called for a boat, and four to crew it. Here you are. Don't tire your arm." Foster let the butt of the spear rest.

"Well, you got a crew of two. Beggars can't be choosers."

"There will be two more."

"Why you so hung up on four?"

"Enough to crew a small boat. Few enough we might kill them if they won't help. Easy, mate. That was two weeks ago. There's no fight in me now."

"Shipwrecked?"

The boy nodded. "There's water there if you want." He tilted his head up a ways. Foster *did* want, but he didn't let on. He sized up the ornate little bottle.

"What you got there? A genie?"

"Ambergris perfume."

Foster frowned. "More valuable than whale meat," Kjartke clarified. He reckoned by the way she said it she meant *all* the whale meat.

"That's the one thing you decided to save from a sinkin' ship."

"And you saved a bird map," Kjartke fired. Foster was taken aback. Whatever quiet deference they enjoyed from her had turned to straight-up backtalk.

"Give me passage to the continent, and I will give you one of every ten from the sale."

Foster and Kjartke looked at each other. "How 'bout I put a spear in you and take the whole thing?"

"It would be done if you would do it. You ask after someone. One of ten, and I help you find him if I know."

"The ones on the other island. You know 'em?" He shook his head. "But you know they're there. So you saw 'em. Or you saw a ship go down."

"One of those things. I will say when you agree to my terms."

"What does it matter if I agree? I got the spears. Ain't nothin' bindin' me."

"I can see you are honest. Even if you lie about the rest of your crew. You do it to protect them."

"I need to talk to your buddy before I go signin' any legal documents."

"He will be back. Can I trouble you for water? It is nearby."

It was. Shy of the first peak, they stared down a crevasse six feet wide, at a dark pool between ten-foot walls of sheer, smooth rock.

"How the fuck do we get that?"

"It is deep," said the boy. "I jump down and drink. Then I put my foot on that edge and reach your hand. You lie on your chest to catch me. You pull. I pull. Not as easy as it sounds, but you grow used to it."

"And hope your buddy don't decide to leave you down there."

"He would be mad—there is nowhere else to drink. And when you're half-dead of thirst, you take the chance."

Foster turned to Kjartke. "Well looky there. A young man who appreciates probability." He heard a splash. The boy was already treading water. He lowered his lips and sipped from the surface. Foster stepped back from the edge and leaned in to whisper. "Is it just me or is this kid full of shit? I got half a mind to leave his ass down there til he drowns, go interrogate his friend, then we fill up and get the hell out of here."

She didn't bother lowering her voice. "What is the word when a man not do as he says?"

"A liar?"

Kjartke shook her head. "When his heart is weak."

Foster foraged through his vocabulary. "A pussy?" She offered no confirmation. He could only glare off at the distance. Water splashed in the crevasse.

"Pull me up before I lose my bollocks," the boy called.

"You heard the man," he tilted his head to Kjartke. She lay on the edge and dangled her hand. The boy found a tiny fingerhold. He placed his foot on a shallow ledge, a couple of inches at most, just above the water level. With a leap, he caught her grip. His other clasped around it. Kjartke struggled to her knees and backed up while he walked his feet up the wall until he was able to get his armpits over the top. He came up shivering. The water had to have been ice melt trapped too far from the meager sunlight to evaporate in summer. Kjartke didn't wait around for permission. She dropped her stone chopping blade and stepped over the edge without warning. When she had her fill, she signaled to Foster.

"Get her up," he said. The boy shook his head.

"Too weak. Did you say you had whale meat?"

"Bullshit. How you been pullin' your buddy up?"

"We were stronger before. I am thin. He has not had a drink in near two days. The last time he went in, only by a miracle did I get him up."

Foster rolled his eyes. "Alright, son. Go stand your ass way over there," he pointed to a sheer drop where the boy wouldn't be able to run without crossing back his way. If I see you flinch, I drop her ass and I run you through. I been carryin' this spear way too long, and I swear, I'm gettin' itchy."

"Of course." He backed away. Foster lay down his weapon and got to his stomach, his head turned to face the boy. He was careful not to put weight on his left hand, else he reveal the injury. His right dangled over the edge. Kjartke made the leap with ease. Foster moved to back up but electric pain shot up his arm into his neck. He stopped, and adjusted on to his forearm, which gave him the leverage to squirm back with the grace of a wounded beetle. There was no way the kid didn't notice.

"Damn girl, you're heavier than you look," he tried to play it off.

"I'll stay here while you go," the boy offered. Foster considered the pair he had available to extricate him from a hypothermic death.

"Let's get movin'. I wanna find your friend."

"Aren't you thirsty?"

"No," Foster lied. He wanted to kick himself for not getting Kjartke to fill his bladder while she was down there. His position was unraveling around him. It was just a kid, he kept telling himself, but somehow Foster felt he knew. He knew about the hand. He knew just how well he trusted Kjartke. How he wouldn't spear a child for a bottle of perfume. How he cared about whoever he was looking for. Probably, he wasn't even holding the spear right. Helpless as the kid seemed, he knew Foster was a pussy. "Now where's your friend?"

"It depends."

"On what?"

"Where yours are. If you mean to help us, we need to hurry."

"I don't like the sound of that."

"He will be watching them. If they look weak, he will look to cut their throats. He's a good mate, but a bit cold-blooded. One of the meanest knife fighters in the fleets, and he has a knife. If your crew drops their watch for a moment, they will smile from their neck before they can blink, and if they do see him coming, they will be consoled to know they are dead ahead of time. I would sooner charge the two of you unarmed than the three of us take him on with shield and blade and helm, each."

Foster's grip tensed around the spear. "You said you trust my word. I give you my word I'll kill you both if he tries it."

"Mate, you did not bring enough men to kill him. I can stop him if they are not already dead. If you promise to help us."

Parks bobbed in a little cove beneath a cliff, where the waves and current gave him a respite from constantly correcting his position. He was closer to the shore than he would have liked, but nothing was pushing him any closer. A boat full of a thousand pounds of whale meat turned out to be a lot harder to control by yourself, especially with his mouth shriveling like a raisin. At first, the moist sushi had quenched him, but now every additional bite seemed to move him in the opposite direction. Whatever Foster was doing on that island, he needed to hurry the fuck up. If he didn't get a drink here, then by the time they could snag Joe and head for the next watering hole, he might not row another stroke.

Now he found himself replaying Foster's words over and over. Was it, "Check back in twenty-four hours, and go for help if we're not here," or was he supposed to keep checking repeatedly, and give up after twenty-four hours? Because that would involve a hell of a lot of up-current paddling to the meeting spot. He would be constantly either going to look for them, or returning to a safe waiting distance. That didn't sound like a reasonable intention, but he wasn't sure if Foster had intended to be reasonable. Probably, he had Parks confused with an outboard motor. He *had* gotten significantly stronger and more efficient over the past several days, but he was thirsty, and the lingering taste of raw whale made it worse.

Maybe he would check once before the twenty-four hours was up, and again at last call. The sun would have circled well-toward the west, nearing its night domain. Of course, he couldn't actually see it from the cover, but he had an inkling of time. Agonizing as the wait was, it couldn't have been more than an hour or two since he dumped them on the beach. Worse than the separation from modern comforts, from anything familiar—even a sense of where that might be—the boredom got to him. His voice was shot from days of singing the verse-and-a-half and a chorus that he knew of just about every song in his repertoire. The privacy had been a bit of a blessing at first. He'd been able to masturbate for the first time since the shipwreck, and he was already contemplating a second pass. But it was wasted on the memory of a Thai prostitute, and only after did he realize that he would have much preferred the thought of Kjartke. Hers was the only Reverse-Eskimo name he could even remember.

A bird shit plopped into the water beside his canoe. He glanced up at the cliffside, covered in nests and brooding mothers with their fledglings. The whale meat was already spotted white here and there. It was probably not the most sanitary place to sit, but it was the only one that saved his arms. They'd gone berserk squawking and shitting everywhere when he first arrived, and kept it up for a good half an hour, until they were certain he wasn't trying to raid their nests. He'd been forced to knock a few of the larger scavengers into left field with the oar when they tried to land on his meat. By now, he and the birds had an understanding. One that did not cover appropriate places to shit.

If Foster had sent him out so he could bang the girl, Parks was going to punch him in the dick. He picked at the wet scab on his shin. It held where he thought it should give, so he dug his nail underneath—too hard. Most of came free in a painful tear. Fresh blood leaked out. It was for sure going to leave a nasty scar if he could stay dry long enough for it to close up. A tender press of his forefinger told him the bone bruise hadn't gone anywhere, either. Bone bruise, according to Foster. He would make it a point to make a point that it was a hairline fracture the next time he saw him. Not having to walk on it should have at least helped that, but he also couldn't stretch out his legs. When he tried earlier, both his calves cramped so bad he would have preferred a double amputation.

Parks looked around to make sure only the rocks and the birds were watching. For some reason, even in the absolute isolation of Antarctica, he felt self-conscious when he pulled it out from under his sealskin tunic. Like someone was bound to appear just as he and Kjartke were getting through the setup dialogue. He turned to his right and put his left foot up on the side so he could hopefully do a better job of making it overboard this time around. The birds began to shriek as if in protest of his indecency.

"Yeah, you like that? This is for shitting on my whale, fuckers," he called over his shoulder.

One cry cut through the rest, deeper and doppling closer. By the time he recognized it as a human scream, it was too late. The water exploded a few feet from the gunwale. A flash of a shape disappeared beneath the splash and the whirling foam that broke the stillness of the cove. Parks froze mid-stroke. His eyes fixed on the epicenter. It seemed as if it would calm, as though whatever had caused it was done, and content to be beneath the waves.

Then a head breached, a flame of red hair coughing violently. The man flailed more than swam until he caught hold of the gunwale. A hand came over, then another hand with a knife. That was all he could manage. He spit up water, doubled over as best he could. The pale face was already beet red. Parks glanced up at the cliff. It had to be eighty feet from the lowest flat point.

"You jump from way up there?" The only answer he got was more coughing. "I'm no cliff diver, but that looked like a belly flop." The man, near his own age, gained his senses enough to take a horrified look at what Parks still held in his hand.

"My bad, dude." He shoved it away. "Caught me pumping the bilge water."

"Help me, cunt," the ginger spat. Parks keyed in on the blade.

"Were you trying to bushwhack me?"

"Fuck me, I think I mashed me innards." His accent was a thick slurry of unrecognizable material—like a foreigner who learns English in Ireland. Parks picked up his spear and leveled the point at the man's throat. "Ah, come on. I'm tryin' for a rescue. Been stuck on this squat for weeks."

"Trying for a rescue with your knife drawn, eh?"

"You never know if someone's a cunt or not. You seem like a nice cunt. Help me in." Parks touched the tip under his jaw.

"Knife."

He groaned and let it slip from his fingers into the pile of meat. Parks unhooked the tip of the toggle harpoon and wrapped the line around his wrists a few times, then passed figure-8's and tied off the point. He hitched the other end to the shaft of the harpoon.

"Is that fuckin' necessary?"

"You interrupted my wank, wanker. You're lucky I don't defile your corpse." That earned a sputtering of laughs and half coughs.

"Ah, you're alright." He tried to haul himself the rest of the way up. Parks raised the shaft connected to the line and steered him back into the drink. He came up coughing again. "Shit bastard!"

Parks held the pole so the slack was too short for him to swim within reach of the boat. He angled it high so the man was suspended from his hands, all but his chin underwater as he egg-beatered to stay in the oxygen.

"I like you right there."

"I'll fuckin' freeze if I don't drown."

"Easy, bud. I'm not gonna let you die. I just want you to have a little hypothermia and nothing left in your limbs when I'm done asking you what I need to know."

"You'll have your answers when I'm in the boat."

Parks let the pole droop and he plunged under. He raised him again. The man sputtered. "I was gonna kill you and take your fuckin' boat. You moved at the last."

"I don't recall moving. Maybe you just jump bad."

"I jump fuckin' banger."

"Were you planning to land *in the boat*? Because I'm pretty sure me and a bunch of meat would have been about as soft as asphalt."

"I wasn't aimin' for the boat."

"Then how'd you think you were going to make a big splash and swim up on me without me noticing?"

"I don't fuckin' know. What else am I gonna do?" Parks studied him. "Fine! I was aimin' for the boat."

"Well that's just dumb. If you fell on me from up there, we'd both be dead."

"Praise the fuckin' gods," he said sarcastically. "Didn't have to float Manhas on your cock." Parks steered the line over so he could cling to the gunwale.

"What is this, whale? It's fuckin' slimy."

"You have a potty mouth."

"Come on, mate. I'm gonna catch me death. I been once in the water already and I don't care for it no more."

"Shipwrecked, huh?"

"Nah, bit of a mutiny."

"Hate those. Did they make you walk the plank?"

"Plank?"

"You know. Captain takes a long walk off a short board."

"I'm not the captain, cunt. I'm a fuckin' mutineer."

"Oh." Parks raised his eyebrows and grinned. "Do tell."

"I been honest with ya. Let me in the boat while I can still talk," his teeth chattered.

"As the acting captain of this good vessel, I don't feel entirely safe letting a confessed mutineer on board my ship. That said, as a man who's been overboard in these waters, and felt the icy fingers of that bitch Hypothermia, I don't think I can let a man die like that."

"Thank fuck!"

Parks swung the rope around until he could get his wrists over the side, then paused. "But don't think I'll have an issue skewering you if you say or do anything that I perceive as subversive to my ship or my captainhood."

"Me oath, cunt. Now pull me in, me limbs are numb." Parks grabbed his collar and lifted his torso over the edge far enough for gravity to do the rest.

"Sit facing the other way. If you turn around, I run you through."

"Can I have some of this meat? Been weeks."

"As long as you chew with your mouth closed. Glad to meet a man who knows what a week is." The shivering ginger dug his fingers into the whale flesh until a generous hunk cleaved free. He was lean from starvation, but his wide shoulders betrayed a strength that would return in time. He wore leather pants and shirt. An actual shirt, in a more Western style welcome to Parks' taste.

"They call me Brother. Son of Marion, Jr. and Terry. My uncles are Gary and Frank. Who the fuck is in my boat?"

"What are you, a fuckin' squain?" He said with his mouth full. "I'm Gionn."

"A squain?"

"Do you rate me an imbecile? Come off it." When he realized Parks had no answer, "Would you have me believe you don't know the squains?"

"Uh…"

Gionn swiveled his head around. "This is a squain boat, in squain waters. That's squain clothes you got on. And a squain spear. You talk like a squain, but you're white as me bare arse. Were you stolen by those thieves?"

"I was not stolen, I came here and was warmly welcomed by a great people, whose name I forget, as a noble ambassador of my land, which is obviously America. Everything about me screams America. From sea to shining sea."

"Never heard of it," he spat out a piece of gristle.

"Where's home?"

"Bottom of the sea. And what hull keeps me from it."

"Answers like that get your body tossed overboard."

"It's true," he protested. "I'm too bashed up to lie," he knocked the side of his head with his palm a couple of times. "Can't keep 'em untangled."

"A Son of Neptune, then."

"Why are you so fuckin' interested in who me parents are?"

"Anyone else alive on the island?"

"Me mate."

Parks took a long look up at the cliff. "One guy?"

"Aye, here."

"What does that mean?"

"Means there's one just here."

"Has anyone else been through?"

"Squain bitches."

"No more whites?"

Gionn considered the phrase, then took his meaning. "White-arses don't come here less they got good reason."

"Like a mutiny."

"Somethin' like that." He raised a piece toward his mouth, but Parks speared it out of his hand. "*Hoy!*"

"No more until I get what I need. How does a mutineer get stuck on an island with his mate?"

"Ah, fuck. I knew it'd come to this." He said with audible regret.

"What don't you want me to know?"

"All of it. It's fuckin' embarrassin'."

"Out with it," he jabbed Gionn lightly in the back with the spear tip. "I'll allow you to deliver it in the form of a song, if you like. A rap, or an Irish jig, or whatever kind of music you listen to."

Gionn grumbled something—Parks caught "idiot" and "rescue." Then he fell silent in a way that Parks knew meant he had given up, and was mustering the courage to admit it—or cooking up a lie.

"You know how it is when you're full up. Worst time to be a captain."

"What business you full of?"

Gionn paused. "I can't make your sort." Parks offered no help. "Whaler," he went on.

"I hear you, bro. No leg room."

The man shook his head to clear his utter bewilderment with his benefactor. "Aye, and shares and all. Too much easy huntin'. Not enough fellas dead in the process."

"Shares? Like investments?"

"Are you truly not ticklin' me arse, cunt?"

"Huh?"

"Have you no berth at all in what I'm sayin'?"

"Whaling, right? I admit I've never read *Moby Dick*, but as you can see, I do alright for myself."

Gionn shook his head again. "Am I alive? Are you a shade, havin' a go at me?"

"I'll be the one asking the questions. Explain yourself, or I'll answer that with my spear."

"I'll assume you're an idiot then. Where were we?"

"Assume away. Shares."

"Aye. Full up. Starts you wondering how else to divide it. Captain's boat means captain's share's half. So's you want a bigger share, you can rid yourself of a bunch of woodcocks thinkin' the same about you, or the one guy."

"I fuckin' hate captains. Except my last guy. He was good guy. And my guy right now, which is me. And before that, Eskimo Joe. And I guess Foster. Actually, I've had a pretty good run lately."

"Aye, mine was good, too. Maybe the best I had. That's why we was full up, and he lasted long as he did. Smart captain starts givin' out shares the fuller he gets. He don't give enough, he knows he goes. Give too much, you're a fuckin' twat, and you go anyway. I think he struck it right, down to three-to-one parts. We was just too rich."

"So you hatched a plot."

"You don't hatch no plot on the whalers. Nowhere to hatch it, everyone hears every wank. You must be off somethin' bigger."

"Carriers. Biggest that ever sailed. Everyone still listens to you beat it."

"So we had one of them eyeball agreements. You know. You eyeball the guy, not too long, so's captain doesn't notice. Then the other guy. You get enough of the right eyeballs, you know you got the numbers. Had a sister ship, too. We knew they was for it. Captain's brothers were runnin' her. You can always count on a brother for a bit of a mutiny—why he put 'em on the other ship. We got it started like usual. Bastard didn't take it well, though I can't say he was surprised."

"What's the usual way?"

"Have you never done a mutiny?"

"Nope."

"Come on, cunt! Not even one?"

"It's frowned upon in my circles."

"It's fuckin' frowned upon in mine, too. Ah, don't worry, you'll get one sooner or later."

"'Preciate the vote of confidence. Let's assume I don't know how things work on your fleet."

"Safe to say. Can I turn around? I can't tell a fuckin' story out me arsehole."

"You're doing great."

Gionn sighed. "The fellow with the biggest bollocks stands up and declares himself captain."

"Not you, then."

"Fuck, no. Even if the crew's for it, they might not like you and kill you where you stand for the crime of mutiny. And you don't know for sure how many men's loyal to the captain. The boat's too tight for a fight right away, so then you wait till all the shy cunts have a chance to stand up or not, so's you know the lay. Then if it's worth a fight, you fight, dependin' on the numbers and where you're sittin' and all. Smart captain puts loyals and mutineers in a proper jumble so if it's split, maybe they call it off cause everyone's got enemies fore and aft, and it's a bloodbath if you go through with it."

"Smart."

"Aye, but if he moves rowers too much, it shows fear."

"Which was your guy?"

"Smart enough, but everyone stood. And the sister ship, too. He started spittin' curses at us. Felt sorry for the bastard. He was a good captain. Good to his men. Knew where to hunt. We was well-tossed every port. I thought for sure he'd have more support. You get none, you're either shit or the best, nothin' between. Nothin' to sell, or too much for your own good."

"Gionn, you rapscallion." Parks tut-tutted and shook his head.

"Victim of me circumstances. I stood last, not cause I was afraid or nothin'. I wanted him to think I was thinkin' it over, but the numbers forced me. Doubt he believed it, though." The big shoulders slumped and he rubbed his arms for warmth.

"In other words, you're the biggest pussy on the boat." Gionn nodded. "So you made him walk the plank?"

"Got no planks on board a whaler, dumb cunt!" Parks jabbed him. "Ow!"

"I'll have your best manners on my ship."

"Sorry, mate. You big ship cun—cocksu—ah fuck. You…*captains* are heartless bastards if you put a man to swim Manhas. Nah, dependin' on whether or not you like him, you put him ashore or cut his throat."

"And which were you?"

"I was with the throat-cutters, of course. Should've been an easy throat-cut, no decision to be made. But some of our cunts and most of the other ship were shore-putters. And that includes his two brothers. Came a fair fetch of an argument over that, it did."

"Gionn, Gionn, Gionn," Parks *tsk*-ed. "I was fully expecting you to lie your ass off and leave out as much as you could to make yourself look like a semi-decent human worth rescuing from a desert island. I have to give you credit, though. You have defied expectations."

The mutineer held out a timid hand. Parks replaced the hunk of meat. "Thanks, cunt. Captain Brother. Stupid name, but where was I? Yeah, the shore-putters," he ripped off a big bite. "It's against the Code of the Sea."

"You have a Code of the Sea, too?"

"Everyone does. Problem is, it's different for each. Way I see it, Code of the Sea says it's a fuckin' malice to put a good man ashore so's he dies slow of thirst or has to jump a cliff to kill himself. Wouldn't strand me worst enemy. Or, least not a middle-of-the-list lad. Throat-cuttin's the only honorable way. His brothers agreed, which is why they wanted to put him ashore."

"So there was a fight."

"Nah, we put him ashore. They had the numbers. But soon as we did, a different fight broke out over how to break up his shares, and if the shares he already gave should stand, or if we broke them up, too. I thought we was goin' to murder one another. But then we settled that easy enough. And no sooner did the first fight, between the shore-putters and the throat-cutters, come bobbin' up again."

"What did it matter at that point?"

"It didn't. I just…thought it violated the Code of the Sea, that's all. Wasn't tryin' to start a fight, I just needed to call a few cunts a 'cunt' and be on with meself. Some of them took it a bit personal, and then it was all blades."

"Actual blades, or words that cut like blades?"

"Blades, captain. Words don't cut nobody. They was carvin' for guts. Shore-putters on me boat had a bad time of it, until the others boarded us. Like I said, they had the numbers. Saw it wasn't goin' me way and decided to grab what I could and swim for it."

"And that's what landed you here."

"Aye, and them there." He pointed to the sister island.

"Why would they go there?"

"I don't know, it was one of the two and I suppose they wanted to avoid the captain. Someone put both ships to fire in the melee. Ours went down direct. The less fiery one made it most of the way over there."

"Still there?"

"Maybe. I saw 'em float a barrel ashore—swimmers did. Don't know what's left. We got our own source, here. We'll outlast 'em."

"Unless they swim across. That's maybe half a mile in the channel."

"Your sailors swim?"

"Like fishes."

"I'd've pegged you for a sinker. Most of ours were sinkers. There's a few made it, of course, but that's a long take in the current. Wouldn't be much of a fight in whoever managed to crawl up on shore."

Parks thought back to the beach where they left Eskimo Joe. There were no signs of life, but it haunted him that he may have delivered their only guide and protector into the hands of men like the one who sat before him. The image of his captain, standing solitary at the edge of the water as he watched them fade across the way left him ill at ease. Like he was disconnected from a vital organ that before long, he would need to live. A thought struck him.

"And your mate on this island." Parks grinned. "Is he still pissed that you voted to take his ship and cut his throat?"

Foster lit up when he saw the little leather sea monster round the point. Parks gripped the steering oar with a spear braced under his other armpit. In front of him sat a wide back under red hair, somewhere between them in height. He tugged at the oars with bound hands while the stone point hovered near his breast. Foster glanced at the boy for a reaction, but if he was surprised or defeated, he kept it well.

"Ahoy!" Parks shouted. "Did someone here order sushi with ginger?" They waded out to meet the vessel and dragged it ashore. The red captive scrambled over the whale, still leashed to Parks. He looked pleadingly at the boy.

"Sorry, mate."

"*This* is the guy?" Parks said. Gionn nodded. "Shouldn't you be in school?"

"I'm impressed, Parks. Didn't know you had it in you to capture the baddest knife fighter in the southern hemisphere," he spat the last words at his young prisoner.

"And you got yourself a captain," Parks congratulated him.

"Captain of *what?*"

"A ship. His ship." He indicated their new acquaintance.

"This lyin' little fuck is a captain of grown-ass men?"

"He's got bigger sack'n all of us," the man interjected on his captain's behalf.

"Maybe so. But my shriveled balls are 'bout to head out on that boat while yall starve to death on this shithole."

"Don't leave us, cunt. Tell him, Captain Brother."

"Captain Brother, huh?" Foster chuckled.

The boy locked eyes on Foster. "It's clear that this man is the captain," he corrected. "I am Oduy. Gionn would call me Oduy Grassbender. I have lied to you to save myself and my crew. Now I speak captain to captain. You came here searching for your mates. Would you not do the same for your own crew?"

"Hang on. What makes you think he's the captain?" Parks said.

"He's tryin' to drive a wedge between us. Even now he's plottin'."

"We mean no harm. Do you want to know what I do if I harm you?"

"I'm guessin' that," Foster pointed at the man unburdened of his head and limbs on the landing.

"It's just a ward," Gionn deflected. "And not a real one. He was drowned when we cut him."

"It's a bad seat we're in. We are not your mates, and we have a bad look. No strength to fight, or swim. So I will give you a gift. Maybe you like it, and you repay the kindness."

"I don't give a fuck about your perfume."

"No perfume. I will tell a story, and if you listen, you may live."

"We don't have time," Parks cut in. To Foster: "There's a bunch of mutineers on that island with Eskimo Joe."

"My story is short, and that's part of it."

Foster considered him. "You got ten seconds to catch my interest before you catch my spear."

Oduy wasted no time. "You will not stab me soon or ever. You are a twat, and a shit sailor. I do not say this to hurt you. I say it because I see it, and other men will see it, too. I watched your boat approach. None of you belong on the sea. You hardly know where you are, how to steer, how to land, how to bring ashore. The ward is a fake. No power to it. But it gives me your reaction."

"I don't know what the fuck a ward is." Foster felt his cheeks burning red at the boy's dress-down. He considered running him through, but his body refused to comply.

"It's the fucking dead cunt right in front of you," Gionn said.

"Your face was fear, and you did not know what you saw. Only the woman. You are more afraid of her than she is of you. You have never fucked her. Neither of you. She is in your charge because she cannot row the boat herself, otherwise she would have killed you already. It would be easy, because your hand is broken, and this one limps from a small cut as though his leg were broken."

"It's a hairline fracture, bitch. I wanna see you put over 200 pounds of solid muscle-weight on a broken bone."

"You hold the spear wrong when you threaten with it. You do not trust the woman, at least you are that smart. But you defend her. You are loyal to her without reason. No one is the captain of your boat. I know this because you argue openly with your slow friend. You cannot cooperate, but you would die for one another. His mouth is big. I knew enough of your troubles before he told me that your captain is on the island with my brothers. You are not mutineers, so you left him there with intention of picking him up. I do not know why, but he does not know about the others, and they will kill him if we do not hurry."

"I've heard that before."

"I lied about Gionn. He is fair in a fight, if it suits him. But far from a name men fear. Biggest mouth, I will grant him. The men on that island are not like Gionn. Your captain is good, because he got you here, and your cargo is full. Probably a squain. If he falls, you will die one of a thousand ways. If you are seen by anyone with that cargo—anyone at all—you will die. No one will help you, because you have nothing to give that they could not take. If you were a man to reckon with, your crewman would not speak to you as he does. This woman would slink in fear for how many times you have beaten and raped her. And you would have killed us the moment we met." Foster's jaw tightened in defiance, but he had no reply. "A good luck has brought us together in our condition. Now you have one thing. You have a kindness you can show. If you help us, I will get your man. I know my brothers, I know that crew. I know the fastest way to get there, I know how to find him, and how to kill my enemies. If you do this for me, I offer you a seat on my crew."

Foster and Parks met gazes. Their faces broke, and they snorted with laughter. "A seat on your fucking crew?"

"You are dead men without me, but you are strong enough to row, and you do not have it in you to mutiny. I will help you sell your whale, and the bottle of perfume. You keep all of the shares, and divide the crew's half on future cargoes. It will not be long before I get us a bigger boat. If your captain likes, he can join my crew. If he does not, I give him passage to a port. I also promise not to rape your woman, but I do not promise not to seduce her. She will go to port."

Foster smiled. "You know what? You're right. I'm a fuckin' pussy. I'm not gonna stab a starvin' man in cold blood. But I will leave your ass here to finish starvin'. Come on, Parks."

"You can't do it!" Gionn said. "It's against the Code of the Sea." Foster studied him. "Cut our throats if you'll leave us. You can't let a man to starve."

"He might have a point, Fucker." Parks admitted.

"What, now you suddenly got morals about leavin' people stranded?"

"I mean, yeah, that too, but I was talking about the little captain fella."

"You can't be fuckin' serious."

"What part of what he said was wrong?"

"We don't need him. We got Tunguk."

"If he's still alive."

"If anybody's dead, it's probably every other man on that island."

"He's one old man, dude." Foster grimaced. Parks was still giving Oduy information. "You wanna risk being on the sea with just her?"

Foster shook his head in frustration. There was no point in trying to hold anything else from them. "Even if I wanted to take them, even if I trusted this guy, which I don't, Tunguk says there's only room for one more. We bring 'em both over there and find Tunguk, then we gotta leave at least one—Code of the Sea or not."

"Then let us make our cases there," Oduy said with his eyes on the island. "I don't know how many of my crew made it ashore, but it was more than stand before me. If there's a fight, you'll need both of us. If your man lives—and if we do—he can decide which of us to take."

"Or cut our throats. None of that strandin' shit," Gionn insisted.

"Alright," Foster looked them over. "Let's vote. Parks?"

"Take them."

"Kjartke?" She was again surprised to be included in the decision. This time, she thought it over.

"We cut throats."

"You've convinced me," he said to her. "I was all set to say the same, but if you want 'em dead, I reckon it's in your interest and not mine. Way I see it, we need at least one fella on board who you know will kill your ass if need be." He turned to their captives. "Gentlemen, you just got a ride to the island." Gionn smiled. "On the condition that you help us get our captain back, and that one of yall's gotta stay behind when we're done. I'm sure Tunguk'll be happy to cut whichever throat he sees fit."

Foster couldn't find anything in Oduy's assessment to disagree with, but it stung him. A child had just told his ass that he was the lesser man, soft of heart and skill. He'd compensated by forcing them all to march back up to the water, without food, and sent Oduy into the cold drink to fill their bellies and their bladders. It was nothing more than a face-saver, and he knew it. He wondered if Parks thought the same about his leadership. At least the big man was able to paddle. All Foster could do was bark at people who knew he wouldn't bite.

He watched in awe as Kjartke made quick work of stitching and greasing the seams of a large whaleskin bag. She pulled the flesh through the opening of a vertebra, then folded it back on itself and sewed it to make a neck for the bottle, with a bone plug coated in more skin. It looked good for at least five gallons of fresh water to hold them between stops. If they'd had it a day earlier, he could have left this shithole the second the butchered body told him he wouldn't find the people he was after. The former captain was sent down once more, and the bag hauled up dripping with ribbons of priceless silver, the only thing he cared about in that moment.

He decided to keep the two whalers unbound after Gionn forfeited his knife. The whalers tore into the flesh, unconcerned with the white dollops that Parks said was bird shit. Gionn ate so much that he vomited, and had to start all over. Meanwhile he and Parks no longer had reason to hide their thirst. They drank themselves listless under Kjartke's disapproving stare.

Only when his stomach gurgled in protest was he able to turn his attention across the channel. What if Tunguk were already dead, or died in the rescue, he thought? Would this little bastard honor his agreement? The only value Foster had to him was that he was lost on his own, and too weak to be disloyal. Or was he talking a big game like when he made Gionn out to be Jason Bourne? Maybe their previous differences didn't matter. Parks had filled him in on the mutiny. The former captain didn't seem too pissed. Gionn was useful to him, and use was deserving of forgiveness. Parks pulled hard, and Kjartke's merits were obvious. That left himself.

Foster's eyelids sagged. "It is not night here. But it is time to sleep." Oduy said. Foster shook his head.

"We gotta get goin'."

"Best to sleep when night would fall. All men here do it. The men we are going after will do it. We will be stronger for a fight in the morning, and they will be one day weaker."

Foster checked the circling sun. He'd been up a hell of a while. What time was it, anyway? He wasn't even sure how low it had left to sink, but it nestled toward the horizon.

"Alright. Parks, you and Kjartke sleep first. I'm gonna stay up. And so is Oduy. We switch in two hours."

They didn't take any convincing. The boys were snoring in no time. Kjartke moved away from the rest of the group to take a spot in the shadow of a rock. Foster felt ridiculous with the glut of weapons in a pile beside him—three harpoons, bow and arrows, knife, and the spear that lay over his lap. Parks slept with his own spear. Full and exhausted as he was, no part of Foster could have slept. Somehow, he couldn't imagine sharing a boat with these two—maybe not Kjarkte, either—without utter hostility between them. Fearing ambush every time he lay down or turned his back. Not without Tunguk's guidance. And though he had a seat to give, it was hard to justify taking either of these sons of bitches aboard.

"We got some time to kill," Foster told Oduy. "What are you gonna do with him?" He tossed his head toward Gionn. "If you end up our captain?"

Oduy smiled. "You think I should kill him for mutiny?"

"He done it once."

"Now who's trying to drive the wedge?"

Foster grinned. "You got me. Not that he needed much help."

"No, Gionn is as predictable as you and your friend. You are predictably soft, he is a predictable murderer. You, honest and loyal. Him, a jumper who will save his own skin. It is no matter a man's acts, as long as I know what they will be. I knew he would never mutiny unless his hand was forced, and I knew he would be happy to cut my throat if it meant the crew would not cut his. It is rare, that consistency. I can take a consistent man and make him worth something."

"That's a back-handed compliment if I ever heard one."

"Not at all. Do you know I never saw the sea until three years ago? I grew up on the high plains of Qachunxta, barely a thing to eat and a cloth to dress me. My older brothers took me to the coast to find work in the fleets. I knew about as much about the sea as you do. But I learn fast. And I found consistent men. Not always the strongest, or the smartest, or the most-skilled. But if I can know a man, I make him my mate. The fast-changers, they have no mates. Not for long. One moment, they have one thought, and another the next. They sail into the wind. But two men are always stronger than one. So I worked, I stayed alive, and I made consistent mates."

"I'm guessin' you didn't save up all your leftover money and buy a boat at the boat store."

"To buy a boat is for rich men who never sail them. If you want a boat, you work them, and soon enough, there is one without a captain," he smiled. "Then another, and another. You learn that a man does not need money to be a captain, only mates. If your mates are happier than the rest of the crew, they support you. One day, you are captain. Getting the boat is easy. Keeping it, that is the trick."

"Did Gionn help you get the boat?"

"Aye. He is a sailor's sailor. Charming, and funny, and not better than anyone at anything, so they do not come to resent him. Even the fast-changers like him. He helped me get a boat, and keep it more than once. Maybe he will help me get one more."

"And your brothers. They consistent men?"

"Consistently stupid, selfish, jealous, and backstabbing, aye."

"We had guys like you in the Navy."

"I have a hard time believing you were in any Navy."

"Believe it, brother. I saw enough manipulative, psychopath brown-nosers who'd call anyone 'friend' and step on the same guy to get what they wanted."

"Do you think I do not consider Gionn a mate? A 'friend,' as you say?"

"You consider him a tool. If it came down to your life or his, you'd always choose yours."

"Of course. As would he. I consider the man a friend, not an idiot. It is the duty of friends to align their interests. I would be dead without him, and he would be dead without me. And I do everything in my power to make sure we want the same things. I love the man more than my own mother. But I do not expect him to commit suicide for me, and neither does he."

Parks back rose and fell in a soft snore. If there was anybody on any Earth he would fight for with suicidal enthusiasm, this must be the one. But he recalled how easily his thirst refuted him earlier.

"Me and my captain, we got this thing called 'akmanuak'. You know it?" Oduy shook his head. "It's an Injun word. Mattakan, I guess they call it. Means when you save a man's life, you're bonded to him for good. He's gotta do everything he can to keep you alive, even if it mean his own death. He may not like your decisions. He may cuss you into a concussion while he's savin' your life, but he'll do it. Best interests or not. Hell, I don't even know what my interests are. Where I'm from, if we call you kin, or friend, it's damn near akmanuak. I hate my one uncle Jeff, but if some boys was rollin' up on his property lookin' to give him trouble, I'd haul ass over and give 'em a fight."

"It must be a great consolation to know that the first time any one of your friends makes a stupid choice, you are all dead."

"I reckon it is. All I know's yours put your ass on an island to die."

"We'll be having a talk about that tomorrow."

"You like our chances?"

"Don't know how many's left. With luck, they have been killing each other off for the last of the water, and starving the same as us. If they are smart, which they are not, they took your man alive and are waiting for you to get him. I will be hoping he is dead, that way both of us get a seat without a fight."

"He won't be."

Oduy curled up on his side and closed his eyes. Foster glanced over at the island silhouetted in the sun. Even if Tunguk was alive, and they got him unscathed, he was still stuck in a boat going the wrong direction, if there was a right one to begin with. His most likely prospect was hunting whales—with one captain or another—until anyone decided to kill him. Even the women here were manlier than he was. Or he'd drown in a storm. Or die of thirst, or hunger. Home felt impossible. Victory felt like barely surviving to try it again tomorrow. Day and night obliterated, cold, wet, and alone but for Parks. The kid had been a captain, and now found himself at the mercy of strangers. Kjartke. Tunguk. The clan they'd left. The whaler women. Everyone he met was a fingertip away from going over the edge at all times. Yet they seemed to be taking it in stride. The only thing that kept him from walking into the sea was the fact that he had as little to lose as to gain.

The birds found his whale. He pulled himself to his feet in no particular hurry and swatted them away with the spear. They landed a few yards off and set their beady black eyes on him, waiting for his efforts to flag for any one second.

8

THE CODE OF THE SEA

Tunguk stood on the rocky beach and fixed his unblinking gaze across the channel on the other island. Calm waters lapped the shore. Nothing moved on the horizon. No black dot bound his way. It was as still as the man who watched it.

A sparse-bearded youth in his late teens arrived beside him and scanned the same horizon. He was pale brown, dressed in leathers showing the wear of being soaked and dried a thousand times. A short, steel-bladed sword hung from his belt. He wrapped a hand around it as something moved through his head, then leaned over on his knees for a moment of rest, his flesh drawn tight around the angles of bone. His stare was the more determined of the two, as though with enough strain he could pull something from the morning shadows. Neither man acknowledged the other's presence.

"Any sign?" A voice called from behind. The younger one straightened up as five companions joined him. The one who spoke, a few years older, had the same look about him. A bronze pommel protruded from the scabbard at his waist where another short, heavy sword hung. The rest were a mixed lot, though all but one in the prime of their youth. The stoutest of the men wore a short-cropped gray beard and a balding head to match. Each carried his own steel, and nothing else. They gathered behind the first youth on Tunguk's flank.

"If they are coming, they are in no hurry." The coast watcher replied. The older of the two checked the sea for himself.

"What about the squain?"

The first shook his head. "Must have been a mutiny."

"I saw the ones did it," a young man with vaguely Mattakan features offered. "No mutiny. He is a scout. They will be back."

"You sure they went to Oduy's island?" The first man challenged.

"Aye."

His older brother clapped him on the shoulder blade. "You are being a wet cunt. He is dead. There is no water there."

The man looked sideways at him. "What if there is? And he got the boat? Might not be coming at all."

"If he got the boat," the older one answered, "He will come." The group studied the waters in silence a moment. "Split up, make another ring and meet on the back cliffs. And do not fucking kill him!"

The men parted in opposite directions, leaving Tunguk alone to contemplate the sea.

Foster barely slept. Even when it was his turn, all he could do was squint against the sunlight invading his eyelids and mull over his options for the rescue mission. Oduy seemed content with the deal he'd made to leave the men's fate in Tunguk's hands. That struck him as rather more haphazard than the boy's personality would indicate. Foster considered that there was nothing on the other island that could be good for the two castaways, no reason for them to go there other than compulsion and the small hope of being the one Tunguk chose to carry—if he even gave them that consideration. If it was Foster in their position, he'd take his chances when it was two on three, during the ride across the channel. Two on one able man, one injured man, and a woman, none of whom were experts on the water.

He felt like a middle school teacher, trying to figure out the perfect seating arrangement to make sure the troublemakers didn't have a chance to make trouble. Oduy held his only possession, the bottle of perfume he'd put up if Foster made him captain. Foster wondered briefly what it was worth. He had a hard time imagining what currency he could get for it, or what he could get for that currency. He didn't even know what he would ask for if a genie popped out and gave him three wishes. Something told him he should hang on to the few things he had: a bag of water, a spear, and a boat.

Over his shoulder, Parks and Gionn laughed about something. They were hitting it off like long-lost frat bros. He looked for Kjartke, and met her eyes where she squatted to piss in the open. He turned quickly away, as if he'd invaded her privacy. If it came to a fight, she would be unarmed as always, having not earned Tunguk's trust, and by extension, not Foster's. Two unarmed men against two with spears. But Parks would be rowing. He'd have to drop his oar to arm himself. That meant the weapon would be near at hand, and that meant he couldn't have either of the hitchhikers sitting near Parks, or it would be a toss-up as to who got it. He thought about making both Oduy and Gionn row at spear point, but he didn't know the water like they did, and he was afraid if they could coordinate, they would be able to work some advantage he hadn't guessed. Capsizing the boat on a wave, running it aground, or even just using the oars as clubs. He preferred them empty-handed.

The size of the boat meant the rowers needed the benches, leaving the cargo space in the middle for two passengers, and the back seat where Tunguk steered. If Kjartke and Parks rowed as usual, he could put them both in the middle—a terrible idea—or split them, buddying up himself with one and leaving the other to steer. Neither appealed to him. He also had to consider the rowers faced back. The rear position, then, would have three people behind him and only be able to see the steersman, close enough to knock knees. There wouldn't be a full spear's-length between any two people the way he figured. It was a cruel brain teaser puzzle. There didn't seem like any way he could have both of them covered at once and still have some control over propulsion.

"Ready when you are, Captain," Oduy addressed him. Foster gave the boat a long look, as if staring at it would produce some solution. "How would you like us?"

Kjartke rejoined them. Parks and Gionn meandered over, deep in conversation.

"Come off it, cunt!" the ginger protested.

"I'm serious, You should try it."

"Just out, and then right back in?"

"Yep, but it's all in how to come back in."

"I don't see the purpose. Are you practicin' your shipwrecks?"

"Practicing my shred."

"You got your odd uses for a board, don't you? Mutinies, now this. You must think me an idiot. You can barely stand in a boat, much less on a bit of flotsam."

"It's not that kind of board. Polyurethane, fiberglass…plenty of walking room on these suckers."

"Parks," Foster interrupted. He didn't seem to hear at first. "*Parks!*"

"Yeah buddy?"

"I need you rowin' up front today."

"Why don't we make this big lug row? Free labor."

"We're happy to earn our place," Oduy added.

"Speak for yourself," Gionn shot in. "I'm fuckin' half-starved. Need me strength for the fight. And me knife."

"You're gonna have to do it on half-strength and unarmed. You're rowin'. Aft position."

"Fuck's sake, cunt. Gimme half a fuckin' chance. I didn't just survive two weeks gnawin' bird bones to kill meself on the cunts I swam here to get away from in the first place."

"Take what you get or stay here." Gionn grumbled some kind of acquiescence. "You're with me midship," he said to Oduy.

"Honored."

Foster deliberated over his pile of weapons. He picked up the jumbled mess of rope that snarled the toggling harpoon. Parks never reset it after he tied up Gionn. Foster shook it loose and turned to Oduy.

"Hands." Oduy looked confused. "Put out your hands with your wrists together." He bound the slender arms.

"Won't be much use like this."

"That's the idea. You'll get 'em back when we make land. Parks, you got the ginger's knife?"

"Yeah." Foster waited. "What? I have to give you that, too? Why are you the only one allowed to bear arms? Are we Americans or what?" Foster didn't blink. Parks pulled the knife from his belt reluctantly.

"Kjartke." He held out a spear to her. She didn't seem to know what to make of it at first. Her hand wrapped around it, and she tested its balance. "You steer. If this fool takes one stroke you don't like," he indicated Gionn, "put that in him."

"Pretty good," Oduy offered. "Hadn't thought of that. Can I make an observation?" Foster let the quiet be his consent. "I told you before that I mean you no harm, and I prove it by telling you what I see. What other men see, too. You could do this one of a few ways. If you have no trust whatsoever for the men you are about to rely on to fight beside you, and if you don't intend to build any, the way you done it is right. You're a smart captain, but not a popular one. It works as long as you always outsmart everyone else. As long as you have all the blades. In my experience, that never lasts. Should you find yourself in need of help, better to be popular. And you will find that soon enough."

"'Preciate your honesty. Wanna know what I see? I can bet this a couple ways, like you said. If I bet we get Tunguk back, this is the safest way to do it. Now if we don't, maybe I fucked myself. Maybe you end up captain like you said, and you stick me and toss me over cause I didn't pay you no courtesy. But maybe, you don't take it too personal, not as long as I'm useful to you. This fucker mutinied your ass, and you're gettin' along just fine, cause you need him."

"You think you can be useful, then?"

"I don't think popular is any use to you at all. In fact, I think it's a problem. You don't need popular crew. You need men who are consistent. Who can't whoop your ass in a fight, or run a boat on their own. You just need to know where they stand at all times. Here's where I'm at: I'm never gonna be your friend. I don't like you. But if you can help me get the things I need, I got no problem helpin' a brother out in return. All I got to do with you is make sure the thing we both need most is the same one. You said that yourself. Well, right now, you need a boat. I need my boy Tunguk. Those things are different. I put us on an island of hostiles, the thing we both need most is to get off alive. Now we're buds again. Once we get that, we need to find somewhere to unload this fuckin' whale. I don't know what's between us and that, but if you start killin' off crew and run into someone who wants what you got, odds ain't good you'll get there. I can't row much, but I can stab a motherfucker, so you need me til we make port. After that, who the fuck knows? Figure it out when we get there. For now, if either one of you tries to commandeer my goddamn vessel, I'll set you out for the birds."

Oduy grinned ear to ear. "Now you're a captain."

Parks settled on the lone silhouette standing on the low, smooth rock where they dumped Eskimo Joe. From halfway across the channel, he couldn't make out any features. His world had grown remarkably smaller and fuzzier without glasses or contacts, but he was learning to interpret the shapes and shades beyond the few yards of clarity in ways he didn't expect. He found that if, instead of straining his muscles to focus on a single spot, he relaxed his eyes, he could expand to something he thought of as "landscape view"—an expanse of colors blurring into one another in a way that reminded him of a painting. Once he had it, he could get a broad focus on any general feature he liked.

His first weeks were spent in grayscale. It was the only thing he saw anywhere. Now he picked out ribbons of green, blue, purple, pink, yellow, more shades than he'd imagined could ever stripe such a dull landscape. "Black," he thought to himself, and at once all other colors faded a bit and every black line and swatch became more prominent. He could do it by color, or even object. "Rock," he thought, and the sea and sky faded. He saw all outlines of rocks, none in any detail, but the sum of which gave him a picture of the island. "Bird," and three smoky specks he hadn't noticed flashed through the upper left of his field. "Black," he thought again. It was the color of the man on the beach. He knew right away it was not Eskimo Joe.

"One of yours," Parks said to Oduy, who sat sideways facing Foster, their legs extended between one another's.

"How can you tell?" Foster squinted.

"My eyes," he did his best Eskimo Joe voice. "They tell me many things."

"Then it'll be bad news for your man," Oduy said.

"Parks don't know shit. He couldn't see his dick in his left hand," Foster said. Gionn snorted.

"You want us to row right up to the enemy, Cap'n Crunch, or is there a Plan B?"

"It is not him," Kjartke confirmed.

"I can't see shit either," Gionn said, "Never thought I'd say the words, but I trust the squain bitch. Squains can see for days."

"He's waiting in plain sight, then. Wants to be seen," Oduy contorted his face in an effort to distinguish the lone figure.

"We ain't sneakin' up on nobody. We get closer to make sure," Foster stated.

"Shall I tell you the three reasons he would be there?"

"I could tell you a thousand reasons, and I don't give a fuck. We need to get visual confirmation."

"These men are not clever enough for a thousand. He might be there to try and scare us to a different landing. More likely, he has your friend, or wants us to believe he does, and intends to bargain. Either way we should head round for another spot before he makes our number."

The mention of it made Foster slink low in the boat. Parks thought the kid made a lot of sense most of the time, and couldn't understand why his friend had to be such a dick to him. Probably because his presence made it clear what a shitty captain he was. It was liable to get them killed, though. The kid was no dummy, and Parks had already decided to vote him as captain if Joe turned out to be waiting for them in Eskimo Heaven.

Foster waited an appropriate amount of time to make it clear he begrudged the help. "Kjartke, head around to starboard. Keep her wide enough that guy can't see what they're up against."

A quarter of the way around the island they found it hidden in a recess of cliffs: a low rocky cove where they might land. Sixty yards into the water, a scorched prow and the remains of a single mast titled from the surface where the ship had come to rest. This was where the men on the island made landfall. The walls around the cove rose steeply. Along the left side, they extended well into the sea at a 45-degree angle, then rose straight into the highlands. It wasn't clear how many ways, if any, there were out of the cove by foot, but at least one of the survivors had managed it.

"Don't even fuckin' tell me that, 'Oh, they're watchin' it, they'll slaughter us if we go there, blah blah blah,'" Foster got it in before Oduy could speak. "I'm not retarded."

"You weren't hoping to get your man without a fight, were you?"

"Tie up on that mast." Kjartke eased the boat alongside and Parks secured a line to the flame-licked trunk.

"Lunch break." Parks dug his hands into the nearest slab of whale. Gionn was ravenous as well, but Oduy made no move. His attention was on the quiet shore.

"They want off the island, they're gonna need a boat," Foster announced. "Boat stays here, with her."

"Is she expected not to fuck off and leave us all to die, then?" Gionn said.

"You're gonna have to trust a squain bitch again," Foster answered.

"Then how are we getting ashore?" Parks fumbled another fingerful of whale into his mouth.

"How the fuck you think?" Foster spun the harpoon's rope free of Oduy's hands and replaced the point in the toggle, then secured the pin to the lower section before neatly coiling the rope. Gionn stowed his oars and extended his hand for Kjartke's spear.

"Hell, no," Foster caught it. "Darlin', I'm gonna need you to wait here. Anybody but me, Brother, or Tunguk swims up, you put that thing in their face. Reckon this boat's too heavy for you to get far on your own. Give us a day. Whatever that is. One sleep, and if the sun gets back where it is before we do, toss whatever meat you need to make this thing move, and go somewhere you feel like goin.'" She didn't say anything, but he knew it was taken to heart.

"What am I going to do for a weapon?" Parks mumbled through a full mouth. Foster thrust the toggle harpoon into his hands, and tied Gionn's knife to his own belt. Then he took up their other spear. "So you and me gotta swim ashore, then stab everyone ourselves after we get hypothermia again? I mean, I've just been rowing for weeks on almost no food and water, but I guess a Stone Age suicide mission is worth a shot."

"They ain't done us wrong, yet. If they're smart, they'll bargain." He peeled off his long sleeve, leaving only the Eskimo tank top.

"For what, mate?" Oduy said. "You don't have enough boat for the two of us, much less whatever they got."

"We'll figure somethin' out."

"Nothing doing. We kill them, or they kill us, and try to swim out here, and probably get a taste of spear. No way the woman bargains if they capture us alive. If she stays at all. The captain should be with the ship. Let the crew get your man. If they take us prisoner, you can decide if you like the terms. Go it alone if not. That doesn't help me, either way. I'm trying to help *you*."

"'Preciate your pretendin' to care. I lead from the front." He rolled over the side backward like a scuba diver, then bobbed up. "Oduy next, then Gionn. Parks last."

"Fuck's sake, mate. We won't have no bollocks left to fight with when we get there." Gionn watched Oduy go in without a word. He followed, and spat water and curses as soon as his head cleared. Parks glanced at Kjartke.

"If we don't see each other again, just know that you're the only beautiful woman I've never beat it to." He winked. "M'lady."

Parks hit the water with the grace of a walrus. The cold barely took the wind out of him, as though he was nearly used to it. Ahead, he heard Foster swear. The blur ducked under the water and came up a few times, then swore again. Parks turned over onto his back and took a deep breath, then kicked his feet while he held the harpoon across his chest. When he checked again, the others were halfway to land, though not the cove. Foster was making a line for the outcropping at the edge that extended well into the surf. Did he expect them to climb that? He faced the sky and kicked to catch up. They would already be cold and tired, but if Foster wanted them to scale a fucking rock before the fight, he might as well swim back to Kjartke now and have eight brown babies and live out his days as king of the Eskimo Islands. He craned his neck and saw their movements change. Shoulders lifted and sank, and the splashing stopped. They were walking now, not swimming. Parks turned and spun his legs for the bottom. No luck yet. A few more kicks and he scraped it. It was still chest deep, but better than nothing. He let his body dip back until his knees were bent and only his head showed, like the others. Stealthy as fuck, he thought. Like a SEAL raiding some unsuspecting jihadi beach party. It occurred to him that the past couple of weeks were a thousand times more action-packed and bad ass than his eight years in the Navy. He had not signed up for the action. Parks liked the confidence that came with living in the deep belly of a carrier, fighting guys whose biggest payload was a shoulder-launched RPG. He knew plenty of dudes on the boats who had been roped in, thinking they'd be SEALs, and ended up in some bitter check-list-checking reality once they got a little cold water splashed on them. Not Parks. He had his sights on boredom and a paycheck the entire time. He'd meant to do his twenty years and retire with full benefits. Foster had sworn they could take their skills back to the civilian world and *not* have to deal with piss ants like Lieutenant Carabiner. Now he was doing Navy SEAL shit for free. Fuck Foster, he thought.

The rocks were easier to scramble than Parks expected. No one had been of much a mind to wait for him, which was annoying since he had half their armaments. The others were well up when he got started. The outcropping led toward the heights of the inland, and none of it was smooth. It looked like some giant had randomly chiseled big chunks at sharp angles, which made for a convenient climb. The others finally stopped right before it joined the main peak. Parks huffed up.

"Stallone is here with his big ol' spear—"

"*Shhhh!*" Foster cut him off.

"It's a *Cliffhanger* reference."

"Shut the fuck up," Foster whispered. He pointed below. Parks saw how the cove dead-ended at a wall. The only way out was a light scramble up the sharp rocks. Thirty feet below them, three men crouched behind cover waiting for whoever had to pass their way. All three had steel spears, on a short hardwood shaft—none of the chipped stone bullshit he was carrying. They couldn't see the cove, much less the water, from their hiding spot, but they would have been perfectly placed for a high-ground ambush had anyone come up that way. A wood barrel sat not far from them—no doubt what was left of their water supply.

Only then did he notice Foster was empty-handed.

"Yo, where's your piece?" He got no answer. Parks really, *really* hoped they didn't make him fight all three of those dudes by himself. They looked hard as fuck, if a little starved, and all better-equipped. Foster caught his eye, and must have seen it. If he'd planned to send Parks in there before, he thought better. Foster motioned them to climb down a few feet for sonic privacy. He kept his voice to a low whisper.

"Let 'em wait. We find Tunguk and slip out of here."

Oduy shook his head. "My brothers are not with them. We have high ground and surprise. It's unwise to fight them later."

"It's unwise to fight them at all."

"If my plan works, we won't have to." Oduy scrambled up before Foster could stop him. He stood on the rock above them in plain sight. "*Hoy!*" He shouted. Their eyes filled with fear. "I have a crew and a ship, anchored off the coast. It approaches on my order." He turned to his companions and motioned for them to join him. Reluctantly, they stood by his side in view of the men. "I forgive your crime of mutiny. If you can't trust me, fight us. On the very low chance you win, my boat leaves you here to starve. Or you bring me my brothers' heads, and we fill our holds before the season ends."

The men looked at one another. The oldest one, bald and wide with graying whiskers, spoke. "There'll be no debt?"

"Aye, there's a debt. Gionn carves the 'M'." They seemed to consider it, but not for long.

"Aye, Captain."

The men climbed up to meet them where the rock flattened into something walkable. "This is not a mutiny on my part," Oduy lowered his tone to Foster. "Your ship, your crew. But we need to pretend if this will work." Foster looked more than a little displeased, to Parks. The three ambushers made the top and looked over the "crew." Parks did his best to look intimidating, but they seemed to reconsider when they saw the state of their weapons. He thought for a moment there would be a fight. Oduy was unconcerned.

"What about Gartuk?" The same one asked.

"Gionn," Oduy said. "What say you? Shall we allow Gartuk to rejoin the crew?"

"I'd rather Gartuk than Unnar," He spat. Based on the reaction, Parks guessed that was the bald one. "Fuck it, I say kill 'em both." Unnar's hand tensed around his spear.

"Easy. Unnar's back in shares, now."

"Gartuk's not. Let 'em fight, then. Maybe we get lucky."

Oduy nodded. "I owe Gionn a debt. Gartuk will have to die with them."

"Are these cunts supposed to help us? They're unarmed," Unnar complained.

"We'll help if we can, but the work's yours. Price of forgiveness." Oduy said, unwavering.

This must have been one of those eyeball wagers Gionn spoke of. The three before them made up their minds without a word of debate.

"Fine," Unnar spoke for them.

"Where's the old man?" Foster demanded the second they started up the slope. Oduy shot him a look, but let it go. The crew turned to their captain.

"The first mate asked you a question."

"Don't know."

"Who does?" Foster continued.

"Don't know."

"But he's on the island."

"Don't fuckin' know."

Foster opened his mouth but Oduy placed a hand on his shoulder to stop him. "My mate will keep his patience," he paused, "if you tell us what you *do* know."

"Can't find him. Gartuk's waitin' to tell you we got him, but we don't. Not unless they caught him since we split up."

"Seems like a rather small island to lose someone."

"We been over it. No sign of him. Are we to kill him, too?"

"No," Foster blurted.

Oduy stifled whatever expression nearly flashed across his face. "Just lead the way. We'll worry about the old man, you worry about Inaq and Olan."

"And Gartuk," Gionn added. The group filed along the trail. Oduy dropped back to Foster in the rear, with Parks' big body separating them from the others.

"These men are cooperating because they're more worried about what *I'll* do to them than my brothers. If they sense I'm not in charge—"

"I know how this works. You get them to kill those guys so you don't have to, then you got a crew of five against me and Parks."

"And not one will make it to the boat. I'd be a fool to escape starvation on one island to do it one over."

"Then how do you figure we get rid of 'em when they smoke the other dudes?"

"With any luck, whichever side 'smokes' the other, will be half-dead and bloodied. Give me the harpoon, I'll finish it myself."

"When I give you an inch, you take a foot. I don't trust you with anything sharper'n a finger."

"You don't have to trust me, remember? We both need the same things."

Parks did his best to ignore the murmurs behind him. He was tired of the two of them measuring dicks against how wrong everyone else was. He much preferred the company of Gionn—vulgar, insubordinate, too dumb to look out for his own welfare. That was Parks' people. He didn't know what the "captains" were up to, but he figured it best if the bastards in front didn't get wind of it. "Gionn, you ugly fucking cunt," he said too loud for their distance. "You pimple-backed ginger potato-eater." Parks hadn't yet figured out what he was going to say.

"Aye?" Gionn responded.

"I have a question for you, you 'roided-out leprechaun faggot."

"No need to flatter me, cunt."

"What does it mean when he says that you'll carve the 'M'?" That earned him turned heads and sidelong looks from everyone. He suddenly felt stupid for asking, but it was all he could come up with to divert attention from the plotters on short notice.

"You don't carve the 'M' on your boats?"

"Depends on what you mean by that."

"I mean when a man commits mutiny, don't you find some some cunt who has his letters and make him cut a big fuckin' letter 'M' into a man's face, because 'M' is the first letter in mutiny, and even dumb cunts without their letters knows it?"

"Ahh," Parks smiled. "See, we just make 'em walk the plank."

"What do you mean his face?" One of the men, browner than Oduy, called back.

"I told you, cunt, there's no fuckin' planks. No room on the whalers for anything you can't fuck or sell, or both."

"What do you mean 'face'?" Unnar echoed.

"So's everyone can see it," Gionn snapped back.

"'M' is carved on the arm."

"Says who?"

"Every 'M' I ever seen is on the right arm."

"You ever seen one carved by me? Yours will be an improvement to your ugly fuckin' face."

They stopped and turned on Gionn and Parks. "We didn't agree to that. Arm was the bargain."

"Captain never said where, he said Gionn carves it. Gionn is me, so I'm the cunt who picks."

Unnar grew red. "You mutinied same as us. It's arm or no deal. Captain!" He called to Oduy.

"Not same as you, cunt. I can't carve it on your arm, I need the space to carve 'shore-putter'. I want all your future mates to know you abide by no code. You'll set a man to die of thirst for the crime of makin' you a little too rich."

Oduy stepped in between the men. "'M' is for the arm, Gionn. All is forgiven when my brothers are dead." No one spoke, but that seemed to ratchet down the tension a notch, and only that. Oduy rearranged the line so that Unnar led and Gionn trailed behind. Parks found himself next to the quiet one of the three as they picked their way down the slope toward the channel side of the island, switching back to avoid a slide down the bare rock. He was the youngest, except for Oduy. Late teens, heavy scars on his hands and forearms. "What boats you from?" He said without turning.

"Beg your pardon?"

"With the planks. What boats?"

"Navy. Former, anyway."

"Which navy?"

"Not at liberty to say."

The kid nodded. "I know the one. Is it big, then?"

"Your mom tells me it is."

"Hm?" The kid said in confusion.

"Is what big?"

"Our ship."

"Ohh. The one we're going on. Yeah, I mean I'm not in the Navy anymore, so it feels small to me, but you'll probably think it's big. We have have one whole plank on board. Well-traveled."

Unnar stopped and pointed to the beach. Oduy joined him. A man stood alone at the landing, facing the water, indistinguishable from the height. "Your brothers will be among the rock," Unnar gestured to the boulder-strewn slope. "They'll see us comin' once we start down the spur. No way to surprise 'em." The group waited while Oduy considered their move in silence.

"A ruse, then." He circled round the group to Parks and Gionn. "You two will stay with me. First mate, give Gionn your knife."

Foster stalled. He clearly didn't intend to part with it, but he was wary of contradicting Oduy. "You men will march down with Foster. He came ashore alone looking for his man. The others are anchored off the coast. They will have to bargain for the ship. Once they relax their guard, kill them and meet us at the cove where you set the ambush."

"Takin' a foot," Foster said. Parks didn't get the reference, but he suspected Oduy understood. "If they see me or Gionn, it's up. Could send Parks, but none would take him for a captain. Unnar does all the talking. All we need is a moment. If they buy it long enough to turn their heads, they're dead. That's our surprise. You men time it right, you won't even take wounds."

"I don't like it," Unnar said. Oduy glared. "Captain. With respect. We all go. Say we took all of you. You're unarmed, so they'll believe it. Then we got seven to three."

"You'll take Foster."

Unnar nodded. "We can say we captured the harpoon, then." Parks gripped his weapon tighter out of reflex. "When the time comes, I toss it to him. Then it's a proper four to three fight."

"First mate Fucker, gimme your knife." Gionn held out his hand.

"Unnar, I suspect you haven't eaten in a while. Your head is slow. That is why you seem to have forgotten what a captain is. The harpoon stays here, you go with Foster."

"Knife, cunt." Gionn's voice grew insistent. Foster didn't move. Parks wasn't sure what was going on, but it felt off. He glanced at the harpoon in his hand, and for a brief second he thought it was a trident before his vision focused to a single point.

"Apologies, captain. Forgot myself," Unnar said.

"*Knife!*" Gionn shouted. Foster froze in bewilderment. He seemed about to reply, when Gionn cried, "Fuck it, *run!*"

He grabbed Parks' collar and yanked him away from the group with such force he thought his neck was liable to break. They took off in a full sprint the way they came. Parks didn't know what moved his feet, but he found them turning over so fast he was sure he hadn't hit that speed since high school. His shin didn't even hurt—as though he barely touched the ground. There was a clamor of shouting behind him, but he stayed on Gionn's heels. The mountain clawed at his breath and tried to drag him back down. The same slick footing he'd tip-toed one way somehow held firm under his pace, and not once did his foot slip. They charged until a voice behind them commanded a stop. It was Oduy. Parks turned. The three men came to rest and collected their hearts from their throats. Below he saw four figures not far from where they started.

Foster never had a chance to take a step. Before he figured out his boys were high-tailing it, a hard tackle sent him to the rock. A hand ripped the knife from his belt. He turned onto his back to see a spear point in his face.

"I'm the only boat captain on this island," he said before it had a chance to get any closer. "And it don't come unless I call it."

The mutineers hadn't bothered to chase them. Parks stood with Oduy and Gionn in plain sight a few hundred feet up the slope. His heart sunk at least a half-inch in relief when he saw they were walking Foster downhill instead of stabbing him like a potato before going into the microwave. Still, there was no denying the turntables had turned against him. One friend captured, another missing, and six armed bilge-pumpers to fight with nothing but a harpoon and two men's fists, neither of which had much incentive to want Foster back. Now there would be room on the boat, if only Kjartke let them. *Kjartke,* he thought. She probably would have killed all of them herself if she'd been here. Parks loved him a good old-fashioned nightmare woman.

He could see the three men below move to join their comrades. *What would Foster do?* Probably try to bully Oduy and Gionn into a rescue mission against the threat of stranding. There would be a rescue mission, though, he was sure of it. Foster wouldn't leave his ass, and he would abide by the Code of the Sea as he saw it and do the same. Parks was no Navy SEAL. He sucked at close combat, planning tactics for close combat, and chessmaster strategies. His first instinct was to try to convince Gionn they should trade Oduy for Foster. A prisoner exchange. But maybe Oduy was his friend now, too, and that would be a code violation. Besides, these men didn't care about prisoners as much as boats. Already a fatal flaw. Parks was terrified whatever he settled on would have a similar cat in the engine that would cause it to fall apart when it was too late.

"I don't suppose I can talk you into swimming back to the boat," Oduy said.

"I wouldn't blame you if you tried. I'm gonna get my buds first."

"The squain bitch would blame us," Gionn protested. "I've already called her a squain multiple times right in front of her. I'll get a third eye socket. Or a second mouth. Or a face-cunt. Call it what you will."

"If she's not left, yet," Oduy reminded them. "Best bet for me and Gionn is to get him back alive, hope the old man's dead, and we both get off the island."

"They can't kill him if they want off, either," Parks said.

"The things they do to him will not be fatal. Not at first."

Foster looked over his shoulder at the three distant shapes studying him from the slope. He was at once glad they got away, and pissed that they left him. The conversations played back in his head as he searched for what tipped them. Probably Parks talking about planks. Or maybe it was him and Oduy whisper-fighting earlier. For all he knew, they'd intended a double-cross all along. They were mutineers, after all. His hand had hit the ground hard when he landed, and it was throbbing like a teenage lump at the high school dance. It was all he could do to not clench his eyes and whimper.

Yerban and Opiq. That was the other two—a mutt in his twenties and a brown scarred teen, they deferred to Unnar. Opiq shoved him along. Most of the way down, a pair of men emerged from the boulder-strewn base at the beach. Men in this case meaning a pair in their late teens or early twenties, one a little older than the other, both Oduy's senior, and neither remarkably similar in appearance to him or the other. The man farther back on the beach that they'd seen from the channel kept his distance, kept a watch on the waters for a sign of the boat that brought them. That would be Gartuk. Foster had read in an online article once that if you know people's names and say them, it strokes their ego and they'll be less likely to murder you. He was shit with names. Usually forgot them before the person introducing himself finished the last syllable. Now, he was intent on giving it a try.

"You must be Inaq and Olan. Unnar here tells me yall are kin to Oduy. My condolences." It didn't earn him so much as a grin. "Who the fuck is this?" The older one said. Inaq, Foster thought. Oduy'd name the older first.

"Captain of the boat," Unnar said.

"Which is where?"

"Settin' a healthy distance out to sea with the rest of my crew," Foster offered. The man looked at Unnar, who nodded to affirm. "How many in the crew?"

"Didn't get a look."

"Gartuk said it was a smaller boat, probably squain. Suspect four at most." Olan added.

"And my brother?"

"Him and Gionn are alive. They got away with a loose one, up the slope a ways." They all turned to look, but the men were out of sight.

"Him and Gionn are mates again, eh?"

"That's the look of it."

"He thinks the arse-cunt is his brother," Olan said. "I swear, Gionn could cut off Oduy's hand and slap him with it, and he'd find a way to forgive him, blame us, and make the dumb fuck think it was us who put him up to it."

"You gonna tell them the rest of the story?" As soon as Foster said it, he felt a pang of regret. Not for what he was about to do. For the fact that a little over a day with Oduy had turned him into a conniving bastard who measures all the angles and works them instinctively at every turn.

"Speak again without permission and it'll be your hand left off," Unnar said. Foster thought it a bluff, but he kept quiet. He knew the seed was in.

Inaq looked at Unnar. "The rest of the story."

"Don't know what fuckin' story he's on about."

Bad move, Foster thought. You had a chance to get in front of me, now I got a lane. Inaq turned to him. "What story?"

"We made a deal with these fellas. They'd kill the three of you in exchange for a ride outta here. They changed their mind when old Gionn got 'em pissed about carvin' an 'M,' whatever that means."

"Lies. They got the jump on us, so we told Oduy what he wanted to hear. We were set to kill 'em soon as we met with you, just needed the numbers."

"You gonna believe a man who's now committed mutiny twice?"

"Against Oduy? Aye. Try to turn us again and I'll have your cock off instead of your hand."

"He'll be doin' work on us if we wait too long," Olan said. It felt like he meant Oduy, not Foster.

"We don't need to fuck with him," Inaq said. "This captain orders the boat ashore or we start taking parts he don't need til he change his mind. Oduy can starve."

"Damn. I got the sense he was a bad motherfucker for his age, but I guess I didn't realize to what extent." Foster paused for a moment, and continued when no one cut him off. "He's a fuckin' kid fresh outta diapees, but his crew is so scared of him, they surrender without a fight even though he's unarmed. They turn on their own, then they mutiny again once they realize Oduy's outmaneuvered 'em. Then his *older* brothers, even though they got numbers and six-to-one on weapons, decide they're gonna run from his bad ass rather than risk a fight."

"I'm cuttin' somethin' off." Unnar started for him.

"You so much as trim my fingernails, I'll tell the boat to leave us all. Hell, if it comes, you'll just kill me and my crew anyway. Only way you get off this island is if you surrender to me right now. I'll take you as captives to the nearest port, where you can stand trial for mutiny. That's my best and only offer."

They stared at him for too many beats of his racing heart. Then every one of them burst into laughter. *Fuck*, he thought. "*And!*" He spoke up over them in an attempt to salvage something. "I'll let you kill Oduy. Hell, you can have Gionn, too. But you bring me my other friend unharmed, and you help me find my old Eskimo buddy. If he's dead, I want his body for a proper burial at sea."

"We'll kill your crew if they come. And you'll kill us if we surrender. What's left to do but cut your throat and swim for the boat?" Inaq's eyes were set hard, but Foster sensed in them a glimmer of desperate hope. A rhetorical question pleading for an answer.

"I'm not your brother. When I give my word, I keep it." *And I gave my word I'd let Oduy or Gionn come with us, both if Tunguk's gone,* he reminded himself. He would have to break it to someone. The men consulted one another with looks alone. "Yall haven't harmed any of mine yet, and I ain't harmed yours. We got no reason to be enemies. I don't wanna strand yall no more than you want to be stranded. My boat's small, but we'll ferry you two at a time to the other island. There's water there, and we'll leave meat." Their eyes caught fire at the thought of food. "Then two at time, to the nearest port."

"Could be weeks to port. Weeks back. You can't make it three times. Any delay and we winter in this shithole," Inaq said.

"Maybe we'll scrounge up a bigger boat and get the other four all at once, but if we need a third trip, we make it."

"Why?" Olan asked.

"What do you mean why?"

"Why would you help us?"

"Why the hell wouldn't I? If I were in your shoes, I'd want the same."

"Mate, nobody does that."

Foster shrugged. "I ain't nobody."

They looked to each other again. Something in the distance caught Unnar's attention. "What's Gartuk doing?"

The figure on the beach was crumpled on the ground. "Bring him," Inaq said, and they shepherded Foster toward the coast. The entire rock expanse between the channel and themselves lay exposed, with hardly a pebble until the boulder field at the foot of the highlands. They crossed the smooth rock at a trot. He could tell by the way Gartuk was slumped that he was dead long before they got close enough to see that his throat was cut several inches deep. The Mattaka youth had fallen exactly where he stood scanning the channel for an approaching boat. The mutineers looked around in disbelief.

"Oduy," Olan said.

"Oduy's in the heights," his brother corrected.

"You know what I mean."

"Don't be a fucking nitwit." He looked around furtively. "Someone's in the water. Got to be his other mate," he thumbed at Foster. Unnar held him while the men fanned out to study the surface of the still, dark water that lapped the edge of the rock.

"He will have to be up for air," Inaq insisted.

Unnar's grip tightened, and for the first time, Foster realized it was surprisingly weak. A thick man with sausage hands should have crushed his arm, but he felt hunger in the grasp that did only enough to prove it was there. As tired, as battered and thirsty as he was, he'd eaten that morning, and the day before. What felt like the brink of his physical capacity was still more than these men were working with.

The mutineers's eyes darted across the glass surface for minutes. Foster's heart raced, hoping that if Tunguk was there, he would somehow have a chance to get a breath. Nothing. More minutes than any man could go without a gulp of air.

"We need to get off this fucking beach," Olan said. "Before he does it again."

"Mate, if it's your man," Inaq said, "call him off, or you die here."

"Tunguk!" Foster addressed the water. "If you can hear me, chill. Them and us only get outta here if we cooperate."

"It's Oduy," Olan repeated.

"Shut the fuck up, it's not Oduy."

"How do you know?" Yerban chimed in.

"He sank us, you know he did," Olan continued.

"Gionn fuckin' sank us. Don't be paranoid."

"Gionn is Oduy's hand."

"I don't care who did what, he does it again, I kill this one and we all starve," Unnar shouted to no one in particular.

"Calm down, all of you. You. Captain. What's your name?"

"Foster."

"You offer us safe quarter to port? On your word?"

"I do."

"Let's stand for it," Inaq addressed the men. "Three and we take the offer. I say aye."

"Oduy's between us and the cove. There'll be a fight." Olan said.

"What's terms?" Unnar asked. "Spare his mates?"

"That's what he said."

"He has to help us kill Oduy," Opiq said. "To make up for Gartuk."

"And Gionn," Unnar added.

"Too much trouble. If we turn Gionn, it's all of us against Oduy." Olan suggested.

"Gionn won't turn."

"Gionn'll turn his arsehole to anyone for anything that saves him a moment's trouble," Opiq said. "No need to fight the big bastard."

"Alright, we'll hear it," Inaq said. "Aye or Nay on Gionn." There was a string of "ayes," and Unnar begrudged his own to the consensus. "Gionn gets the chance to turn. Foster! Will you help us kill Oduy if we honor the rest of your terms?"

Foster was taken slightly aback by the practiced efficiency of their decision process. "I'm unarmed."

"We'll have to trust him armed eventually. I say arm him," Inaq proposed. A chorus of ayes came back. Unnar tossed him back Gionn's knife. "You're armed."

"In that case, I'll help yall with Oduy if you spare Parks, Tunguk, and Gionn, and surrender to me on the condition of bein' brought to port to stand trial."

"Good enough for me." Inaq looked around the circle.

"Who goes to port first?" Yerban asked.

"I add the terms that whoever deals Oduy's death blow sets the order," Inaq said. Ayes followed. "And to the main question. Do we surrender to Foster on the terms set?" There was hesitation. But he saw beneath it a desperate hunger for any chance to be anywhere else but here. These men were not the villains he'd set them up to be. They were scumbags, sure, but not unreasonable. They were hungry, they were afraid, and they wanted to live.

"Aye," Olan said. Each man followed in turn. Inaq added his own perfunctory aye to the tally, then turned to Foster. "We surrender over Oduy's body. If Gionn won't turn, we kill him, too. If any one of us suspects for one moment we can't trust you, you're dead, and we're to follow."

Up another mountain. Everything here was water, coast, or crag, Foster thought as they hiked the slope back toward the cove, the only path where anyone might be. His stomach was in knots over how to communicate to Parks the new situation before he could set up an ambush that ruined everything. Mostly, he felt ashamed that he had to give up Oduy. Foster liked him a lot more than any of the five in his company, and he hated the idea of having to strand either him or Gionn. He equally hated the fact that he'd agreed to row these men to port, if it was as far as they said, and as many trips. He had no concept of where he was, the size of the place, the time to travel it, and he feared he'd overstepped his capacities. Still, one man dead was better than five, and it seemed the right thing to do to step aside and let them work out their family differences.

He kept his knife in his belt for now, though the others were all ready for a fight at a moment's notice. Foster had agreed to help, but he figured they wouldn't need it, and it was better for his safety and his conscience to stay out of the fight altogether. The low sun sent long faint shadows across their path. Most of the route was open, no chance of encountering anyone yet. They would have to, eventually, and every yard was one closer to that moment. Leaving Kjartke in the channel had turned out to be a saving grace—luck, more than brilliance. He hadn't foreseen any of this, but now anyone who wanted off needed his help. It was safe to assume everyone wanted off.

The mutineers huffed up the hill at a slower pace than Foster was used to. He realized what a toll the hunger must have taken on them. If Oduy was smart, he'd make them walk as far as possible before jumping their asses, and Oduy was smart. That let Foster relax as they entered the flatter section near the top. Plenty of places to hide in the outcroppings, but he knew it would be a while yet. They climbed down onto a steep, smooth slope and half-walked, half-crawled sideways to avoid a narrow section where two men wouldn't be able to pass side by side. It was tiring, and on the other end they saw that no one had been waiting anyway. Every corner now was a bundle of anxiety that only let up until the next one. The men scanned high, low, and behind. The expectation was worse than an actual attack, and soon they prayed for it. As the mountain flattened out, they got their wish.

Oduy sat ahead—well ahead—on a rock across an open area. Parks and Gionn were nowhere in sight, and he was too far for any hope of surprise. He was exposed, and meant to be. The column stopped. Inaq stepped forward. Halfway between them and Oduy, two large boulders lie to either side of the open path, like a pair of pillars. He looked them over.

"I know they're behind those fuckin' rocks."

"I'm unarmed and alone. I've come to deal." He showed his hands.

"Bollocks. Gionn! Show yourself!"

"Gionn and Parks are with the woman. We hold the boat against any chance of swimmers. I'm here to repeat my previous offer. Unnar, Yerban, Opiq. Turn your blades on my brothers and Foster will give us passage. Aside from that, you have no chance."

Inaq laughed. "Foster's dealt with us. Gionn and Parks, come out. I know you're there. You're spared, and we all get off without a fight. Oduy dies, and we surrender our weapons to you and Foster."

Oduy looked to Foster. "That true, mate?" Foster swallowed hard and nodded. "Parks, if you're there, it's true. They get Oduy, we get their weapons."

"For fuck's sake, cunt!" A voice called from behind the left slab. Gionn stepped into the opening with the harpoon. Parks joined from the right, a pointed rock clenched in his fist. "We had a rescue all set. Why'd you have to go and deal with these cunts?"

"This is the way with the least bloodshed. You and Parks are safe. Stand aside."

Gionn looked back at his captain, then to the crew. "Eh. Don't think I will."

"You won't kill five," Olan said.

"I'm sick of all this dealin' and double-crossin'. I can't even keep straight the whos and whats of it. I stand with Oduy, and I'll kill the first through."

"Parks!" Foster snapped.

"That's fucked up, bro," he replied.

"Captain's gotta make tough decisions."

"Yeah, well I decided somebody's 'bout to catch a rock to the dome. I stand with Gionn."

"Goddammit," Foster muttered. He took Inaq's elbow. "I don't care about his fuckin' rock, anyone harms Parks, no one leaves this island."

"Then you better grab him, mate."

The five advanced toward the stone gate, measuring their opponents' reactions after each step. Unnar with his short spear slipped forward toward Gionn, who readied the stone harpoon. Olan kept at his flank. The space between the slabs was big enough for two men at a time, and all knew it. Oduy rose and approached the middle. He scooped a small rock, the size of a strawberry, and hurled it at Olan. It bounced harmlessly off his chest. Then another, and another. Oduy pelted their hesitation. One found Unnar's finger, and he howled in pain.

"Gionn was right, we should've cut your throat!" The moment he said it, something smashed into his face. Parks had hurled his skullcrusher. Unnar's brow split open and blood poured. His hand came to his eye and he blinked hard to realize his brow hung down in a flap. In that instant, Gionn plunged through the opening and rammed his point below Unnar's collarbone. He kicked Unnar back, and the toggle head came off inside, unfurling the rope.

Gionn barely leapt out of the way of Olan's slash. "What a shit weapon!" He cried as he retreated and twisted the rope around his forearm, yanking Unnar with it. The bald man screamed and clutched the line, unable to pull the tip free. Olan charged for Gionn, essentially disarmed. Parks caught his arm as the short sword raised. Gionn turned the bone shaft and brought it down like a club on Olan's forehead again and again until his knees buckled. Parks pried the sword free and raised it. Olan's eyes widened at the giant. As the blow came, Foster drove a textbook tackle into his ribs and brought his friend to the ground. He lay on top and pinned the arm with one hand and the wrist of the broken one.

The rest of the men stormed forward. Gionn threw his bone at Unnar, an insult more than an assault, and turned. He and Oduy fled farther along the path back to the cove, easily outpacing the men. They gave up pursuit.

"Dude, we were winning!" Parks protested.

"You were a half-second from dead if I hadn't slung one back and wrapped your ass up," Foster barked. He got to his feet and snatched the sword, handing it back to a dazed Olan. Unnar worked his way to a sitting position, and they gathered round the red-painted face. The point was deep, but apparently had deflected north of the organs. His shoulder was useless, and his leather shirt darkened and clung to his chest. Inaq knelt and gently tried to wriggle the harpoon out. Unnar and groaned at the slightest pressure. He slapped Inaq's hand away and stood.

"Can you fight?" Inaq asked.

"I don't care who gets Oduy. Gionn is mine." He tried to cut the line with his spear, but his hand trembled and he couldn't keep the rope taut. Inaq drew his sword across it. *There goes one of our hunting blades*, Foster thought. He gathered the shaft and the rest of the line. Maybe Tunguk could fix it if they got the point out. If they found him.

"I'm not going to help kill Gionn," Parks stood.

"We don't need your help," Inaq said. "Just stay out the fuckin' way."

Parks fell in next to Foster as the others passed. "We switched teams, huh? Just like that?"

Foster shook his head. "You're on my team, and I'm on yours. Same way it's always been. We just switched prisoners."

Gionn stood on the quay at Jarrahil with his hands clasped behind him, the evening breeze that brought the big sixty-seater to port till prominent in his hair. Her crew wrangled her ashore at the landing for what he expected would be a short provisioning. To his right, three late arrivals mimicked his posture. Just lads—brothers, he figured—maybe 13 to 18. They had the look of inlanders, dressed in scraps, their features a mix of whoever would have passed through their mum. More and more of these types made for the sea each season, and he didn't fancy them as crew mates. Never knew their way around a boat. Never knew how to swim. These ones looked malnourished, at that— no good on the oars. No doubt sent to the coast when their family ran out of ways to feed them. They carried nothing, not a sack of belongings or a small blade. He was probably the first sailor they'd ever seen. If he covered his face with mud and wore his shirt on top his head, they'd probably do the same. It was no small luck that these were the only others to petition the rosters so far, in a place like Jarrahil. His chances were high if there were seats open. The crew had seen them, and would take their time, make them wait.

"You cunts ever been on the boats before?" He called.

"We born on a boat," the youngest one lied.

"Good swimmer, then?"

"Aye."

Gionn nodded. He walked over to face the lad, who gave him the hardest stare he could muster. He was at best half Gionn's weight, and he felt lighter when Gionn scooped him up onto his shoulder. He calmly paced to the side of the quay and tossed him in the water. His brothers screamed in protest and ran to the edge, where the little one flopped and splashed and struggled to keep his head up. "Aren't you gonna help your brother?" He asked. The lads froze in fear. "People think the boat has to sink for you to drown. Not so. Cunts fall overboard all the time." The lad was quickly losing the battle for oxygen. His brothers pressed themselves to the wharf and tried to reach out their hands for him. "Grab on!" The oldest cried.

"There's storms. Waves. Fights. Drunkenness. Bad balance," he continued. "Cruel bastards such as meself."

The middle one jumped to his feet and pounded his fists on the thick torso. "Get him out!" Gionn was unmoved.

"Shocking how few cunts know how to swim, really. They hear the stories of how the whalers make filthy rats into rich men, and they forget the hazards. That's why there'll be seats on this one. There's always a seat. Cunts like you don't know what you're oathin' up for." The lad disappeared beneath the surface for good.

Gionn shoved his brother off and dove into the water. Moments later he surfaced and passed a blue and motionless body to the brothers. Then followed onto the dock and turned him face down, pounding on his back until he coughed up water in a violent fit.

"Easy, little cunt. You're alright."

"You near kill him!" The oldest shouted.

"Wasn't me nearly killed him. The sea did. And it'll do it again, when one of you goes in. Not if. When. And not a man on that boat will be goin' in to save him, even on the off chance he swims. If his own brother can't get him—if he can't get you—best to ply your pretty little faces in the brothels." The little one opened his bloodshot eyes onto Gionn's face. "You'll make near as much, and though you may feel like you're drownin' a time or two, you just spit it out and take your pay. Boats are for men."

They turned to see a short figure approaching, curly black hair to his neck and a thin beard. He had the northern brown—Cathay, or Elna perhaps. They all scrambled to attention, the little one still gasping and coughing.

The man surveyed them in amusement, two of them dripping wet and the others still quivering from the ordeal. "Is this all I have to choose from?" He gave a charming smile. "Maybe we wait a few days and see who else turns up."

"We better crew, you no find," the oldest one struggled with what was surely a recent tongue.

"That so?" He studied the little one. "And why is this one all wet?"

"I was teachin' the little grassbender how to swim," Gionn said. "Important skill for the whalers, that."

The man laughed. "Not if you stay in the boat." Gionn had a few smart comments that he thought would be quite appropriate but he held his tongue in favor of potential employment. This man would not be the captain. Too big a boat for the old man to bother himself with harbor rats. First mate, at best.

"Any of you ever worked on whalers?"

"Aye," Gionn said.

"And why have you found yourself crewless?"

"I'm a really good swimmer," He said. That earned him a laugh.

"As I said, not important. The big girl do not take seas like your rafts."

"No rafts, mate. I know single oar, double oar. Know me knots and me nets and me blades are whet."

"Very impressive. You know your letters, too?" Gionn hesitated, then shook his head. "Too bad. That, I can use more than someone who is good at jumping ship."

"If the seat's open, I'll claim it. These cunts don't know which end of their cock's for the lady."

"Three seats open, as luck would have it." Gionn let out a smile. "You brothers?" He addressed the lads. "Aye, sir," the oldest spoke. Little Grassbender still coughed up water. The first mate knelt before him. "And you. You know how to pull an oar, I'll bet." He nodded. The man stood and went back to Gionn. "Let me see your kit."

Gionn drew the knife with his left, a half-foot of steel with a swollen wood handle. From a scabbard, he pulled a short sword, the grip wrapped in leather, with an ornate bronze guard and pommel. The first mate let out a low whistle. "Where did you get such a beautiful piece?"

"A man's blade's only as good as the blade of the best cunt he's disagreed with." The first mate laughed again. He looked over his shoulder as the rest of his crew made their way down the dock. "These boys are without sharp," he added.

"Indeed they are," Gionn said.

"Give them yours."

"What's that?"

"Give your sword to the big one. And your knife to the middle one."

"Why for a bleedin' arsehole would I do that?"

"It is as I said. Only three seats. They will find more use for them at sea than you will here."

"It don't fuckin' belong to them."

"Do you figure to be the best cunt I disagree with?" A half dozen men approached him at this point, and Gionn did not expect he would be disagreeing with only the mate. He glared as long as he dared, then threw the weapons on the ground. The first mate said to the brothers: "Welcome aboard, boys. Collect your kit and make ready to stow at first light tomorrow." The two older ones hesitantly gathered the blades.

"And what to do about you?" He asked the youngest. "Captain's rules, every man carries his own blade. How would you cut a line? Or your dinner?" The lad's eyes hung. A shadow crossed Gionn's face. The mate smiled to himself, as if giving it consideration. "Maybe I'm a fool, but I think you will be better sailor than this one over here. I will stand for you." Grassbender nodded enthusiastically. "First light!" The man and his crew shouldered past Gionn.

Grassbender looked up at him, his clothes dripping. "It is a good day to learn. I learn to swim," he said, his accent thick. "You learn to shut up." The brothers giggled.

"Stupid cunt. You think I learned to shut up?"

"Wait here. When I am captain, I take stupid men like you. Strong cowards who do as I say." His brothers laughed again.

"You know what it means?" Gionn let the bewilderment sink in. "If a man's got no experience, no skills, he can't get work in the fleets. Not unless someone stands for him. Normally, people don't do that, because it's his arse if you fuck up. And you can bet you'll take a beatin' every time you do. Better not happen too much, though. If a man takes back his word, you'll be disembarkin' at the next wave, and we seen how you swim. In fact, you'll be doin' everythin' he don't wanna do himself. You'll tie and untie lines. You'll cut his food into little bites, and give him yours if he wants it. You'll stand up so he can lie down and sleep. And when he tires of pullin' his oar, well…let's just say you'll be pullin' it quite a bit. No women on the boats, you know. Gets real lonesome for some fellas. Course, some don't mind as much—the no-women part. In fact, they prefer it. Let's just hope he's very selfish. Not the sharin' type. That would be much worse, stuck on a boat in that situation. You'd hate to give him any reason to be unhappy. To take back his word." Gionn smiled as it dawned on Grassbender's face, and the lads fell silent. He lowered himself to the dock and reclined on his side. "Guess I'll be sleepin' here, in case anyone changes their mind and decides to run as far inland as their little legs can carry, and never smell the sea's salty cunt again."

"You try to scare us."

"Aye. G'night."

The brothers bedded down on the opposite end of the quay, determined not to miss departure. Gionn listened to the sounds of Jarrahil, of the pavilions, and the little huts that served as sometimes market, sometimes inn when the occasion called for it. Near sixty men with fresh pay and too much time at sea sent their voices pealing through the harbor: a boast or a laugh or a wail of pleasure, the hasqa songs, heaving like waves between a fight and another fight. He shivered though it was summer, uncovered on cold wood. It would be worse if he got a seat. He hadn't oilskin nor bag—nothing but his blades, recently departed. All that for this: those bellows behind him robbing him of sleep. Months of work, where—he knew not, to end in nights like these, and a scramble on the last of his shares to find a place worth wintering, that he could do it all again in the spring. He hoped to hear their little feet stealing away on the planks. Then he could follow them, and kill them and take back the only things of value he had left. That would make it easier to find work. But they whispered, they shifted, they stayed put, awake with apprehension rather than noise. That was something he was used to feeling, to the point that it no longer kept him up. It settled like a layer in the parts of his body against the wood, tingling like an old wound, until his eyelids sank and the drunks lulled him to his usual shallow dreams.

Footsteps slipped in, and grew close enough that he didn't confuse them with his sleep, though he kept his eyes shut. He heard a moan. "Up, boy!" A man's voice, and more feet scrambled over the wood where his ear lay. He squinted to see the someone drag the little one from his stunned brothers. There were no torches harborside, himself not more than a dark lump on dark ground. Ten yards off, their silhouettes stood against the half-moon sky.

"You are too young for sleep." It was the mate, and Gionn could imagine how his breath smelled in the lad's nostrils. He rose. The movement caught the grassbender's gaze. The man had him by the wrist. He faced the water, toed the edge, and untied his pants.

"Mate," he called. The man continued to fumble. The brothers held his weapons. He saw their heads shift furtively from himself to their brother.

"I need to piss," the first mate slurred. "Hold it for me."

"*Mate!*" Gionn said louder. The man looked over his shoulder without turning, saw who it was, and went back to his business. The brothers were frozen. "You'll tell me if a fourth seat opens up?" He grunted something. "Didn't catch that."

"*Aye*, I will tell you. Fuck off and let a man piss." The lad pulled back with all his might, but the man was too strong. He wrenched the arm, and Grassbender cried out. He looked to Gionn, who strolled over. Gionn smirked and extended his hand. Grassbender didn't understand, but he reached with his free arm. Gionn grabbed his wrist in his meaty grip, placed his left foot on the first mate's lower back, and gave a casual push.

He slept through first light, and second if there was a thing, secure in the assumption that the men he heard last night would be lucky to pry themselves up and out to the dock by midday. By then, he stood with his hands clasped behind his back. The three brothers did the same. A slow parade of hungover sailors trickled past them, oblivious to their presence, the last few stragglers from their revelries. He was glad to see the captain was as fair as him. A few years older, he had a good head of sandy hair. Captain hair. A small group of the crew conferred with him. They broke and approached the recruits.

"Looks like I got four seats."

"Splendid," Gionn said.

"We found the mate floating in the harbor with his pant round his ankles this morning. Good timing, that, right when we had one less seat than recruits. Don't suppose it was enough to wake none of you."

"Aye, captain. I was awake."

"Were you then? Maybe you can tell me how a man who's taken a thousand pisses in storms somehow falls into the harbor from dry land and drowns. Bad balance, was it?"

"Nah. I pushed him." The men were taken aback. "The arse-cunt made a pass at me and dropped breech to show me his tusk. How was I to know he was a sinker?" There was a long pause, and it was all Gionn could do not to try to melt between the planks into the harbor.

"You swim, then?"

"Aye."

"Experience?"

"Ten seasons, til I stopped coutnin'."

The captain looked him up and down. "Rule on my ship is every man's got his own blade. What if you get caught in a line?"

"Temporarily dispossessed. But I got me letters."

The captain drew his knife and passed it handle first to Gionn. "Let's see 'em." Gionn took it and knelt. He carved a few shapes into the dock. *GIONN.* The men bent over it. "How do we know it's real letters? Not just scratches?"

"It's me name. Gionn."

"We don't know that."

"Would you know your own name if you saw it?" The captain smiled. "Course. Guil." Gionn nodded and knelt. He worked the blade back and forth for a few moments, then stood for all to see. Beneath his own name, the plank read "*CUNT.*" The captain squinted over it, then nodded his approval. "Can you carve the 'M'?"

Gionn started to kneel, then stopped himself. "Won't need to know that one, will I?"

"Right man," the captain smiled. "You and them two's got seats. Head into town, ask for Abo Ic Abo-Te. He'll sort you, show you what you carry. We'll be stowin' two days, then I want it done. No drinks, no girls for you lot. That's earned. You'll have your chance." The little grassbender looked up at the captain expectantly. "Sorry, lad. You got no blade. No experience. Your credit's gone."

"We stand for him," the oldest brother said. Captain shook his head. "Can't stand for family. Anyone want the lad?" He called to his crew. They snickered and looked around at each other, but no one stepped forward.

"I stand for the little cunt," Gionn spoke up.

The captain looked him over. "And you know what happens to the both of you if he don't work out?"

"Nothin' happens me. I see that Grassbender goes for a piss with your mate."

The captain rubbed the missed sleep from his eyes. "Stow, then." He and his men headed to the boat. Gionn faced the brothers. "Give me back my shit."

"Fuck you," the oldest with the sword said. He stalked toward Jarrahil. The middle one followed, leaving Gionn with his new charge. Grassbender stayed put. "I do as you say?"

"That's how it works, mate. Don't worry," he slapped the back of the boy's shoulder. "Your tits aren't big enough for me." He headed after the others.

Oduy watched Gionn pile small rocks on the beach of the cove. He'd amassed quite a collection, checking each time he stooped to see if the others were coming down the pass as he knew they would any moment. The former captain stood calm, preparing neither to fight nor flee. He double checked that Kjartke was still there with the boat. She'd certainly seen them, but made no effort to approach. Beyond her, the nothing of the ocean. A last dot of rock before the expanse of the place he'd fought so hard to live. There was no tinge of regret. He knew life on the high plains would have been shorter and more miserable, and if he died here today, at least men had called him captain and cursed his name, and he'd been rich at times. This wasn't even the worst spot he'd been in. Not within the five worst. It would be near anticlimactic to succumb now, but he did not feel Gionn's frenzy for life. The fire in his skin that made a man feverishly grab anything that might hurt another, any small chance at living another day for whatever reason Gionn had decided he should live. Oduy didn't feel the dejection of his first mutiny, or the hopelessness of this last one, alone on an island to die having not garnered a single measure of support or mercy. Now, he was content. Had the situation been reversed, he wasn't sure he would have stood with Gionn. Not unless he lost himself for a moment. He owed the man nothing. Whatever Gionn had done on his behalf in the past had been repaid many times over, and his sleights all forgiven.

Had his brothers wanted the big ginger, offered him even a day of survival, he was sure he'd have taken the deal. Oduy needed no guarantees, no stability. A day at a time was enough for someone like to him to earn a second, then a third. Gionn was not so clever. Sly, maybe, but his stubborn arrogance always came through like a tag-along virtue he could never bring himself to strand. It got him into the next fray even as he was getting out the previous. A moment of reflection would have told him where he stood, why he should have made the token gesture of handing over a man they would get anyway, but he was too thick to put aside an affront and do what was best for himself. Oduy felt sorry for him, but if this was the end, it felt good to have what Foster would have counted a "friend."

"Mate, put your cock up and get some of these rocks."

"Yerban and Opiq. You recall if they swim?"

Gionn paused to give it a thought. "Never had occasion to notice. They made it here from the wreck somehow." Oduy waded out to his knees. "Unnar'll be useless with that wound you dealt him. Wasn't much more than a splasher before. Same as my brothers. Assume Yerban and Opiq swim. None of 'em like you, though."

"We can't swim out there without Foster."

"And they can't swim out there without passing us."

"That's their plan, cunt. Seven on two. Pass through us like a sword."

"Unnar's no threat. Without him, I count two short swords and two spears. We get chest-deep, swords are hard to swing, and we can slip below if we need. The spears, we'll need to watch out for."

"Foster and Parks swim."

"Foster and Parks are predictable. Parks won't fuck us, and he may turn if he gets a chance. Foster will prefer to let others fuck us. If we fuck them first, we're in a position to renegotiate."

"So I gathered all these shit rocks for nothin'?"

Oduy's expression drew Gionn's attention back to the beach. Inaq and Olan filed down, followed by the others. Unnar brought up the rear with Parks and Foster.

"Throw your rocks. Then join me for a swim. Not too close, though. Separate, but close enough to get closer if I call for it."

Gionn smiled, "Aye, Captain."

The mutineers spread to a wide line and walked at an even pace, with Parks and Foster behind them. A rock sailed. Yerban blocked it with his forearm, and yanked it back in pain. Another just missed Inaq's head.

Foster grabbed Parks and moved away from the line of fire. "Yall are on your own here. We don't do rocks. Price of a ticket on my ship."

The men shielded their faces and weaved, a rock here or there cracking into a torso, a leg. Gionn was a shoulder broader than any of them and his throwing arm was a sling. He found Unnar's cheek, and the struggling man went to a knee.

"Aha! Fuck you, Unnar, you ripe cunt! Out of the fight already?" Gionn taunted. Unnar took his time getting back to his feet. A rock bounced off of Olan's chest. He picked it up and threw it back, nailing Gionn's arm.

"Ow! You little shit!" He now directed all of his fire at Olan, who had to crouch and cover. The other three closed the distance quickly. Gionn fled his dwindling pile and high-stepped out into the shallows. He and Oduy tested the bottom until the calm water found their ribs.

Foster and Parks followed them to the shoreline and stopped. "Probably don't like water either, do you?" Inaq said.

"Nope," Parks replied.

"Alright. What's the ruse, Olan? You know he's got one," Inaq said, turning his attention to Oduy.

"He plans to swim around and tire us."

"Switch with me," Inaq held out his sword to Opiq's spear.

"Fuck, no."

"He'll separate us, too," Olan added.

"Let's just kill Oduy first. All together. If Gionn swims off, I say we strand him."

"Aye," they answered in turn.

They made their way into the freezing water, shading to their left, Oduy's side, with an angle to avoid Gionn altogether. Oduy backpedaled as they swung out into a tight semicircle, shielding him from the shore and the rest of the shallows. He could swim seaward, or towards Gionn only. Instead, he stayed put. Their steps were belabored, water rising past their hips, elbows flared to stay at the surface. Unnar now waded tentatively up to his knees, far trailing the others. His left arm hung useless, every movement seemed an effort. He took up a post to block the way back to the beach.

"Hang on, cunt." Gionn abandoned Oduy and headed for shore. The four in the water paid him no attention, tightening the formation. The brothers shaded between Oduy and the shore, the shallower water where they could get more of a swing to use their swords. The spears kept even with him, closing parallel to the shore. Close enough to one another that he didn't stand a shot of grabbing one and wrestling a weapon free without immediately taking steel from another. Oduy bent his knees and lowered his chin to the surface, making the target small as possible. His former crew now loomed over him like giants. Just before they came in range, his head dipped beneath the water entirely.

Yerban approached the ripples he'd left with care, and jammed his point a few times into the area. It came up empty.

"Stay close," Inaq said. "Press this way. Don't let him swim between us." They probed the bottom with their feet and closed like a patient net.

Their attention occupied, Gionn made no effort to conceal the fact that he was headed straight for Unnar. The graybeard readied his spear for a thrust. He retreated a few steps to shin-deep where he'd have better balance. Gionn strode up like one who was just leaving a nice swim to collect his towel from the beach. As Unnar tensed to lunge, Gionn flicked his foot, sending saltwater into his face. The small distraction was enough that he sidestepped the thrust and wrapped up Unnar in his big arms, tackling him into the shallow water. The weakened man screamed in pain when his shoulder hit. Gionn shoved his face under with his left hand and yanked the spear free with the other. He posted on the back of Unnar's head to stand, then brought the spear down again and again with great speed. The water went inky red and Unnar stilled. Gionn turned back to the crew.

Inaq spotted him, but he was interrupted. "There!" Olan said. Oduy surfaced for a breath thirty feet away, the same distance from shore. He stood and waited for them. Behind him, the rocky spine that marked one side of the cove grew closer, another barrier that threatened to herd him to the fight. The four moved to corral him. Inaq called back: "Gionn, fuck off."

"I'll fuck where I please."

"He's not worth what I'll do to you."

"I'll take me sword back now, you fuckin' gull."

He was hopelessly behind, though. They ignored him and pressed toward Oduy. Drifting ever nearer the rock, his exit to deeper waters was outflanked. It was shoreward, or into the fight. Fifty feet or so separated them now, and Gionn was triple that from the mutineers. Oduy retreated to the rock and searched for a hold to climb out. He got a foot up and slipped back in. It was too steep close to shore. The bits he could have scaled were all farther out, eclipsed by Yerban and Opiq, his brothers ready to pursue him if he ran for the beach.

Gionn chugged as hard as he could, but the water was a thousand hands pulling at him with every step. He looked at Parks, who held the bone harpoon shaft but made no move. His pace wasn't helped by the fact that his lower extremities were numb. Couldn't blame the fat cunt. Rushing in with a glorified stick to bludgeon men with real blades on behalf of a kid he just met was best left to idiots like himself.

Oduy tried once more to climb and slipped off the very first handhold.

"Kill him fast, Gionn's coming," Inaq warned.

Oduy saw the tuft of red over their shoulders and smiled. He imagined what he would miss. His friend was no great warrior, but he was too stubborn and big to die without opening someone. Maybe two. With any luck, they'd die of their wounds. With a bit more, it would be one of his brothers. If they were sufficiently cut up, maybe Foster would just betray them and kill them as soon as they surrendered their weapons. No, Foster wasn't the type. If anything, he was swimming for the boat right now. Oduy glanced out, half-expecting to see a pair of heads and the wake of the two leaving the whalers exactly where they would have been had they never happened across the islands. But it was just Kjartke, her tethered boat. He looked to the shore and saw only Parks, who for some reason had chosen this moment to make a sprint for the fray with a bone in his hand. Too far to matter, that one was as dumb as Gionn.

"Hey, Brother!" A voice brought him back. He looked up and behind. Foster stood on the rocks above him. He must've gone around and walked down the way they'd come up. "Catch." Something dropped into the water in between him and his former crew. Oduy didn't see it but he knew what it would be, and he shot under seconds before Olan could bring down his sword.

His hands swirled madly, praying for contact. He brought his torso near the bottom to evade any blows that might come from the surface, and could hear the movement of feet nearby. Something tapped his knee from above. Oduy lashed at it and closed his hand around the blade of Gionn's knife. It sliced his palm but he didn't let go until his left hand was secure around the handle. The water was clear. He could make out legs, and he was sure they could see his figure now that they were close. He grabbed the nearest one he could and slid the blade across the tendon on the back of the heel. It rolled up the leg and someone fell under. Oduy wrapped his arm around them and began stabbing as many times as he could. He saw a spear point flash before his face and miss, then again. He rolled so the body would block it, and the next thrusts found whoever he'd cut. His lungs were ablaze and he was already shivering, but the thrill of spilled blood warmed him. He pushed off the bottom, gave a few kicks through the hole in their net he'd created, and surfaced ten feet away. Olan bobbed up after him.

Gionn was close, but Parks had closed faster without the deeper water's resistance to slow him. He splashed forward wielding his bone, then hesitated when Inaq raised his sword. Foster leapt from his perch and crashed his elbow down on the top of Yerban's head, driving them both under. Energized, Oduy sprang forward at his brother. Inaq swung a wide blow, all he could manage at this depth, but Oduy easily leaned back and closed on the miss. Inaq raised both feet and kicked him away, propelling himself back. As he stood again, Parks' bone slammed into the back of his head and sent him face-first into the water. Oduy grabbed his hair and stuck the blade in the side of his throat to the hilt, then flicked it across, opening half his neck. Gionn was on them now. Foster surfaced with Yerban in a bear hug. Opiq saw the numbers had shifted and backed up. It was Gionn's spear that ended Yerban, just under the arms of Foster, with a rip that sent his entrails floating up. They turned to Opiq.

Opiq brought his spear around and extended the handle to Foster. "I surrender to you, Captain. I am your prisoner and your crew, and I ask quarter." Foster took it from him.

"Problem is, I only got one seat on the boat, and my ass don't feel like makin' multiple trips."

Gionn grinned, and plunged his tip into Opiq's throat.

Foster realized Oduy and Gionn were both armed now, and both between him and Parks. It would be a hell of a fight if they wanted to make it that. Oduy held out the knife to Foster.

"Believe this is yours, Captain." Gionn snatched it. "Actually, it's mine." He tossed his spear to Foster. "You can have this, because I've got *meeeeeee*" he leaned over and felt around with his foot and his hand. "I've got *meeeee*," he gave a dramatic pause as he fumbled beneath the water. "*Sword!*" The bronze pommel and guard raised triumphant.

"Every bit as rich as when we first met," Oduy quipped.

"Swim home, Grassbender. This is my captain now, Captain Foster, a fine cunt if I ever smelled one."

Oduy grinned. "Aye."

"Now let's get out of here before your squain friend shows up, else one of us'll have to stick around."

Kjartke held the spear ready when they returned. Foster reached the boat first and stopped, treading water. Their eyes met for a moment. He hesitated, then he threw his arms over the gunwale and kicked hard to propel himself on board. She lowered the weapon but made no attempt to help.

Once everyone was aboard, unbound and armed as they were, Foster gave the order: "Circle the island. We ain't seen most of it, but there ain't much to see. We'll pass close to shore and call his name."

"Aye-aye, Cap'n Crunch," Parks replied.

"How many times are we gonna circle around hopin' the cunt appears?"

"Until I'm satisfied he won't." Either they finally deferred to him, or were too tired for any more fights. Foster had them swing the boat back into the channel, starting with the only other safe landing spot he knew of. If he had to trade Tunguk for Oduy and Gionn, he would consider it a loss, but not as great of one as he would have a day prior. Still, one man was bound to protect his life, and the others had a similar pact, each with himself.

He probed the coast, every corner and shadow of gray rock, for any flicker of movement. They cruised close enough for someone to hear them yell, but far back enough to see as much of the heights as possible. The main beach was deserted except for a black patch that he knew was Gartuk. For an hour they floated there and called, with no answer. Reluctantly, Foster moved around the south side of the island. The side his map told him was toward the pole, anyway. The familiar square of cardinal directions was deceiving here, as any line south also brought him significantly west or east—far enough, and those last two directions would have no meaning. That side of the island was a steep slope that fell right to the sea, no place for a boat or a man. On the seaward side, the same storm of birds protesting their presence with varying degrees of enthusiasm, nesting by the hundreds anywhere they could find a place flat enough to host their downy young. The corpse they'd been picking a couple of days earlier was gone, resting in those bellies, seeding the next generation of squawkers. The cliff bristled with dots of white and gray and black, as though the birds were its eyes, hundreds of them, blinking suspiciously.

There was no more luck at the cove, either, though a commotion of feathers already gorged itself on the fresh food. Hours of circumnavigation and sore throats brought them back to the burnt-out hull of the brothers' ship. They decided to come ashore to refill their water from the barrel they'd seen, and to scout the immediate area. Bladders full and empty-handed, they launched again.

"Good on you, mate. You done all you could for your man, there," Gionn said. "Code of the Sea, and all that. South is the way, much as I hate all things south. That'll be the nearest port with something like a building or two, and a few less-squain-y cunts runnin' around. We can tell this whale meat to fuck off."

"I'm starting to think 'squain' is a bad word," Parks said. "Like 'cunt', or all of the other words Gionn says."

"My guess is it's like callin' someone 'nigger,'" Foster said.

"I'll try that one sometime, but I like squain. Simple. Has a nice sound to it."

"Do you think the lady likes you sayin' that in front of her?"

"Lady? You mean the squain bitch?" Kjartke didn't bother to look at him. "Nah, you'd never call a squain a 'squain' on land. Or alone at sea. Or if there's so many cunts around that no one's lookin' what the other ones are doin'. Only if there's no immediate benefit in murderin' you. Anyway, sorry about your old squain friend. I don't like the smell of 'em, and I like sittin' in boats, so I'm glad he's gone, but it's sad for the two of you."

"If it was us, he'd make another pass." Foster's eyes refused to stray from the shore.

"Maybe two, but he'd order this little fella to take over for me so I can rest," Parks suggested.

"I think you're right."

"You got to be fuckin' me." Gionn whined.

Oduy had been quiet, but now he spoke up. "If you've never been to Hiade, Summer's not as long as the sun says it is, and Winter's night, and death. It'll cost a day and sleep to do it again. I'll row it if you say. But you should know that port's weeks yet. And this is not a working boat, not to anyone but her people. If we get there too late in the season, the kind of boats that get you cross the Autumn storms to the continent will be gone. No one who doesn't have to be here for night stays—for the *real* night."

"I doubt a day makes a difference."

"A day makes all the difference."

Foster looked at Parks, a moment of weakness, he realized, to consult a crew member with a glance. "He's there, dude," Parks rested his oars on his lap. "Eskimo Joe's a fuckin' survivor. Where else could he be? He's just a lost dog, maybe scared, maybe alone, waiting for his owners to call long enough that he can poke his head out and run up and lick their faces."

Foster considered Oduy's warning. Was it the same kind as when he warned them about Gionn, the ninja assassin? Or a credible problem? A big boat to anywhere else was exactly what he wanted. He knew the storms—they were bad enough in a modern diesel workhorse. This dinghy wouldn't do. Nor was he sure what "big" meant, based on the ships he'd seen since arriving…wherever this was. The question lingered: what continent was he hoping to make it back to, anyway?

He considered Tunguk, the old man who'd tried to kill them and was now contractually obligated through some fortuitous cultural taboo to preserve his life. Would he help them at all if that weren't the case? It didn't matter, no more than it mattered why Gionn insisted on fighting for Oduy despite any obvious reason to the contrary. This place—Hiade, Oduy had called it—this desert of rock and ice, was not one where a man could afford to turn down the smallest favor for any reason. The margin between life and death was too thin, and those margins were everywhere he turned.

"Row to the beach on the channel side. We haven't been aground there yet, and it's the only other place where a man can stand up. We rest for the night, then we make one more circle. Just one. Tunguk would do that much for us." If Oduy was disappointed, he hid it well.

"Aye."

Gionn looked around, trying hard to meet the eyes of everyone on board except Foster.

"No," Parks scolded.

"No what, cunt?"

"No, you know what."

"That's not what I was doin'. You seen it wrong. I was just gaugin' how the crew felt about Captain's call. Just gettin' the feel."

"Don't make me rustle up a plank," Parks dug his oars to start them for the beach. Foster caught on and glared at the mutineer.

They plowed into the channel in silence. A wind coming from something like west pushed them away from the beach until they got close enough into the shadow of the island. Parks wasn't as sure of his support for his friend as he made it seem. He actually thought Gionn was a pretty chill dude, and it was true that Foster could think his piss was moonshine from time to time. Regardless, this was about Eskimo Joe, not who was in charge. If your crew was your family, Eskimo Joe was his cool grandpa that always carried knives when there was no reason for it and got on your mom's case for letting you be a pussy. Maybe in time, Gionn and Oduy would be his brothers, too. And Kjartke his sister. Actually, step-sister. Wife, if she was lucky.

Blue, he said, and the hundred hues of water and sky came into blurry focus, the island itself disappearing into the part of his perception that he reserved for background noises and things he was supposed to do—present, but just beyond him for the moment. Black, and the shadows of rock yawned to life, stripes and triangles on the near-invisible gray rock canvas. A pair of lines on the beach, one horizontal, one vertical. He knew the first to be that Gartuk character, the same shape he'd seen standing on the beach when they first approached and veered, because it was the wrong one. The other jabbed his memory like a spear point.

"Eskimo Joe."

"Hm?" Foster said.

"There." They all squinted beyond the tip of his finger.

"I don't see shit," Foster said. No one else seemed to, either. Kjartke gave him a look as though trying to determine if he was crazy, or retarded. She spun back, and a second later added her finger to the line of sight. "There," she echoed. Within a few seconds the others caught on. Not ten feet from the slain man, an unmistakable shape, standing just as he had when he watched them paddle away after he was dropped off. Foster let out a whoop. "How the fuck did your blind ass see that?"

"Must be all the whale meat. Probably high in vitamins and shit."

Foster was first out of the boat and he didn't bother to help them drag it to shore. His arms wrapped around Tunguk and squeezed a grunt out of the old man.

"Where you been, brother?"

"Hiding."

"I can see that." The others joined. Parks lumbered up and lifted him into the air, spun around a few times, and set him down. Tunguk weathered the storm. "Buddy! How you been? We thought we lost you."

"I am found." He nodded to Oduy and Gionn. "And your friends." Foster thought about correcting him, but he went on. "It is not these men."

"These men are our friends, now," Foster explained.

Tunguk nodded. "Which will you choose?"

There was a long pause. "I'd like to take both. I know it'll be cramped, but I can't justify leavin' a man here after what we been through."

"No strandin'. Cut our fuckin' throats if you must."

"Don't worry. Nobody gets left."

"It is good to see you well, Fucker. I would have seen you before, but it was not needed. And Brother. Your skill on the water has grown."

"Thanks, bro," Parks said.

"You have learned in some ways to keep safe. There are others you do not yet know. Is it still your wish to return where you came?"

Foster and Parks met eyes. "It is our wish, great genie," Parks spoke for them.

"Then we must cut these men's throats, as they ask."

A look of horror fell over Foster's face. "You said we could bring a friend."

"These are not the men from your ship. Not the ones you searched for. But it is true, we agreed you could bring one. If you are wise, you will choose not to."

"We can make room. You know room? Space? They can sit on the meat."

"When we left, there was no room for Kjartke. We took her as cargo. These men are not cargo. I will honor what I said if you wish, and let you choose one. You must honor what you said, and leave one behind."

The elation of their victory over Oduy's brothers, their discovery of Tunguk, dropped like a rock in their stomachs. Foster and Parks looked at their new companions for a reaction. Kjartke leveled a spear and Tunguk held his knife ready. They signaled that they half-expected a fight, and that it would not go well if the men made that choice. If both rushed them, Foster thought, they might both get off, but they'd probably die or be badly wounded, and it would take cooperation. If one hung back, or even sided with him and Parks, he would get to go once the other was dead. Instantly, he realized they understood that as well, and there would be no fight.

"So we're votin' on it, then," Foster said with resignation. Tunguk shook his head. "It was you who sought your friends, it is your choice alone."

Oduy nodded. "If that's the way it is. I suppose we make our cases for who gets the seat."

"You go first, cunt. You're the clever one, I should get to hear what you say. Otherwise you'll twist me words and make it come out in your favor."

Oduy smiled and stepped forward. "Gionn should have the seat," His proclamation was met with stunned silence. "He got me my first seat on a boat, when he didn't have to, and he got me this last one, when he shouldn't have. I'm a captain. You'll look at me and think I earned my rank early, but I paid more for it than most." Gionn lowered his eyes to the side, replaying the memory of whatever Oduy meant. "Never once did I beg, though, or fail to repay a favor. Gionn could've left me to my brothers. If I die today, at least I saw them off as a captain. You've already got one of those," he looked at Tunguk. Then turned to Foster. "Maybe two. That's where my skill lies. I'm not a big rower, not a rough barrel. I read situations better than seas. And as Foster knows, I'm not as honest or as loyal as this man, mutinies aside. Where you're going, Gionn is your choice."

Foster's face narrowed. He hadn't expected Oduy to just give up like that, and now he wasn't so sure that's what was happening. It wouldn't be out of the question for him to try to mindfuck his way into the boat, knowing Foster didn't trust him and was just as likely to do the opposite of anything he said. But maybe something really had come over him. His world and his ways had got him here, and it was Foster's that had got him out.

Gionn stepped up behind and placed a consoling hand on his shoulder. "Thanks, mate. Is it me turn?" Foster nodded assent.

In one motion, his knife sliced a deep channel across Oduy's throat. The boy clutched at it and fell to his knees in shock, then rolled to his side. He wheezed and gurgled blood as his face turned a rich purple.

"I agree with this cunt."

9

THREE SHIPS

Gionn lay hog-tied, something other than enjoyment on his face where it pressed the rock. Kjartke stood over him with a spear pointed his way in solemn prayer that he make any effort to free himself, wiggle, scratch his nose.

Some feet removed, Tunguk huddled with Parks and Foster. The latter held the short sword and knife he'd confiscated when he bound the prisoner. The weapons changed hands without resistance—they'd have to credit him that. The rope, he took with a measure of relief. Had their decision been firm, it would have been spear that came calling, instead. One trial past. The hard one. He could not see the little grassbender's body, but he knew it lay not far, gazing upon his loyal mate. Even now, he squirmed under those penetrating eyes. It was not wise to linger in the presence of one scorned—especially not one of his ilk—but Gionn knew his luck was nearer. These would not have been his choice, but it would be the beggar's bowl for him. Once again, the calamities had aligned themselves on his behalf in that unmistakable way that eased the worst of his dread even as it gnawed at the loose corners of his flesh. Would have been his preference to do it on the boat, rather than strand the lad, as such. Still, better than Parks' cruel cunts with their planks. His eyes closed fast on their own.

It was a mistake, and once the vision came he couldn't shake it from his head. He had looked back as he leaned for a long stroke out of Jarrahil on the *Orquas*, and sworn for the briefest moment he saw the brothers still on the quay, though he knew them to be struggling with an oar each somewhere forward. In his heart, he knew the omen, though he turned it over to mere memory as it did not concern him, and soon lost it altogether until this day. Got the boat wrong, though.

The little squain daille swelled at her seams behind the three trunks that rustled with his fate. At first the voices had been heated, but he could tell from the low tones and limp hands that the tide had turned to discussion. He let it run for a few minutes, let them have their arguments, whoever may have argued on his behalf. There was someone, that was for sure. Had it been unanimous, the woman would have been happy to carry out the deed. Parks again, almost certainly. It was only his big arms that saved Gionn from rejoining his former crew sooner than he allowed. Wasn't sure if he could suffer that Foster cunt, but he'd pull alongside Parks on any boat. Most boats, anyway.

"Cunts!" Gionn called. "Cunts! Over here!" Heads turned. "Allow me to say a few words in me defense."

"You already had your say," Foster spoke.

"I invoke peers."

"You are not a member of the crew," Tunguk explained. "Fucker will choose. There is one who speaks for you."

"What the fuck is 'peers'?" Foster asked.

"How is it that I'm subject to the justice of a bunch of rockhumpers?" He scoffed. "If a man is accused of a crime by the captain, and believin' as he does the captain to be unfair or otherwise contrary to his interest, he can invoke peers. The men of the crew will say his fate, and all must agree, else it returns to the captain. But the captain's got to honor their say."

"This is only at sea. Only for men of shares," Tunguk reminded him.

"I'm crew. Foster said he'd take one of us, and the other cunt gave up."

"Well I don't see what difference it makes. I'm not the captain," Foster said. "Still my call."

"Are you not?" He smiled inwardly. The bewilderment painted across the men's faces was alone worth the move, but it was not from Foster's hands that he wanted to remove the decision. The old man could say it was the nitwit's choice, but if so, there were two-too-many in his ear. If nothing else, the ancient squain knew the ways of the boats and seemed to abide with them.

"No. And I just watched you cut the throat of your only friend in the world."

"Aye, he was me mate. It'd be a cruelty to strand him, nor would I turn the cut over to you filth. It was me job, and I did it."

"Huh. He does have a point," Parks said.

"See? This is why I need to make me own defense. The dumb cunt defendin' me don't think of things."

"Another fine point," Parks added.

"'*Ayes*' from those who'd make me crew and allow peers."

Foster shook his head in disbelief. "What is all this parliamentary procedure crap? Are we in 4-H Club?"

"I assume you're referrin' to the simple request for a sound-off. If even that be foreign to you, perhaps I should let you cut me."

"Code of the Sea, bro," Parks tried to help.

"Wrong, lobcock. The Code runs deeper. I'll start at the beginning for your thick benefit. A boat is a small piece of flotsam on a vast bit of water, with lots of sharp things aboard. Have you no way to keep order? Air your grievances?"

"You'll have to forgive me if I find it ironic that this is the seventh time I've heard one murderer or another call for a vote on some triflin' issue like a bunch of lawyers."

"Feel free to think it over. I'll remind you that a man of his word said there was a seat to be had. That another man forfeited his claim on it. There bein' one left, that fellow had good cause to think himself crew, actin' in good faith."

"Just 'cause he gave up don't mean I wouldn't have picked him. Maybe I like a guy who gives someone else his seat even when it means he's dead."

"That would make a very fine quality in a man. If you ever meet that man, make him your first mate and marry his daughters. But if you can't find it—and I warn you it's rare—go with the honest man."

"*You?*"

"Aye. I will tell you with all honesty I'm a liar, and a horrible one. You'll never believe an untrue word of it. I haven't got the craft. I pull oars and cut throats, and I stand by me mates—if they're mates, and it's not too hard on me. You have before you a man without ambition who honors the Code."

Foster stood fast a second. Something about the phrasing rang an old bell. It was almost as though he repeated something he'd heard too often to doubt. As though he'd borrowed a script from Oduy. Or was it the other around?

As brazen as it was, Foster had to admit—quietly, only to himself—that Gionn was right. What upset him is that he thought he saw two men who would do anything for one another. Who would stand unarmed against family, prepared to die beside one another. And later, willing to go right back to maneuvering, to betrayal out of self-preservation. There was Parks, the only thing keeping him afloat here, his only friend and reminder of where he came from, where he intended to return. The thought of becoming like Oduy and Gionn—the captain and the follower, the plotter and the muscle, pitted against one another and at the same time, the other's only salvation against the world—was too much. He'd stood across from his friend for a few terrifying moments, and he sensed the resentment brewing over his orders. All of this was his choice, his headstrong will to search the island, deal with prisoners, plan rescues, choose who lives or dies, and he feared the day when either one had to wonder if the other really, truly had his back. No one else could drive a wedge between them, he thought, but he might do it himself.

"I will make you crew on one condition."

"Not suckin' your cock."

Foster shook his head. "Tunguk is the captain, not me. I'll make you crew, if the captain charges you with mutiny, and allows you to invoke peers."

Every face was cast in confusion. Tunguk considered it, and nodded his assent. "You are charged with mutiny. If you do not wish for my choice, the crew will say." Gionn was speechless. His head spun trying to catch up to Foster's angle. Foster turned to Parks.

"What do you say, Brother? It has to be unanimous, else ol' Tunguk calls it." Parks lit up like a kid at Christmas.

"I mean, he clearly committed mutiny, but I feel like he kinda had to."

"What's the normal punishment for mutiny?"

"Death," Tunguk said.

"That seems a little harsh," Parks said.

"Agreed. As does strandin' his ass."

"Maybe we slap him with a censure. A stern reprimand. Next time he mutinies, he walks the plank."

"I think that's a good first step. But I had somethin' else in mind."

"Yeah?"

"I'll give you a hint: it begins with an 'M'."

"Fuck," Gionn said.

"An 'M'? Oh. *Ohhhh.*" Parks' eyebrows raised. "Huh. Not on his face, right?"

"Just a little scratch on the arm."

"Just on the arm."

"We in agreement?"

"That sounds fair. He did try to jump on me with a knife while I was spankin' it."

Foster cringed in disgust but decided not to pursue a line of questions to which he didn't want answers. He looked to Kjartke, hovering over their prisoner with the stone spear. "And what about you, darlin'?" She glanced at Tunguk.

"She is not crew."

"She single-handedly held the boat against attack while we were on the island. If not for her—if she had come ashore, or just fucked off altogether—none of us would be standin' here."

"She is not crew," He repeated, and though his tone was unaltered, this one felt final.

Foster nodded. He set down the sword and raised the knife. "Gionn, you're reprimanded, and everyone you meet from this day on will know you once killed your captain." Foster started for him.

"Ah, come on. Is that necessary?"

"No," Tunguk spoke. "It is a long paddle to Nunoc. He will need his strength."

"Ha! Right-o, captain. No sense cuttin' the arms that move you."

"There, you will carve it."

Travel to Foster was something that happened while you were doing something else. Aircraft carriers steamed across oceans while he worked on aviation electronic systems, filled out forms, ate, slept, showered, masturbated, chatted with friends, lifted weights, read, played games. Or a car moved him while he listened to music and twitched at the wheel and tapped pedals beneath his conscious awareness. Whether the featureless ocean or the Blue Ridge mountains, travel could well have been teleportation for all he saw of where he passed. The time was on the clock, and space was a nuisance that would disappear soon enough.

There was no such travel here. The little boat laden with meat and men required an action to move even a few feet. When the winds fell, Parks and Gionn—or Tunguk and Kjartke, if they were tired—had to stick an oar in and pull it. When it was the relief team, Foster became pretty handy at the steering. There were fewer corrections from the old man's watchful eye, and when he first set the course without guidance and lashed it in place without Tunguk saying a word, he beamed with a pride that, like the summer sun, refused to leave him entirely. More often, it was sail.

With no keel to stop her drifting sideways, the little bag was helpless in anything resembling a headwind. They once had to drop sail for nearly two full days at sea when the mildest breeze sprung up off the port bow and just refused to quit. Tunguk kept the steering oar into the swell, and they had to battle their way back to sea every time it eased even a little to avoid being swept into the peninsula. But when at last it swung around, they filled their sail most of the next five days, as if accepting an apology from the wind. As Foster understood it, the prevailing westerlies should have come in off the starboard at all times, driving them into the peninsula like a freight train through a fly. But the next headwind only left them three days on a water island before they once again found a friendly gust. It seemed that anytime they began to take it from the wrong quarter when at sea, they only had to head for the peninsula to find a calm that could let the oars loose, if not a glorious blow astern. The thin projection seemed to confuse the wind and set it after its own tail. The same was true of the currents. The main swell fought them toward ruin on the rock, so they stayed as far out as they could while taking advantage of the sail. But local streams welled up constantly, washing them in some direction Tunguk only half-anticipated, so that when the mast was up, there was hardly a moment's peace between the ropes and the bailer as they jockeyed for position in the wandering pockets that held them on their course.

Kjartke's whaleskin water pouch turned out to be a blessing and a curse. It was good for an easy three days of fresh water, and more if they rationed it. The rowers never flagged. Sleeping at sea was miserable, but it no longer carried the prospect of death. Not by dehydration, anyway. It also allowed Tunguk more leeway in chasing fortuitous winds and currents, rather than taking the shortest, most conservative route to the next island. It was there the curse began. Foster felt sure they wouldn't have been caught at sea that one stretch had the old man not ran inland and off the course of the next rock after a current that was supposed to be there but never showed up. It was fine, if you didn't mind the enduring misery of trying to sleep on a pile of meat while everything rolled beneath you and freezing water lapped on your soaking skins. No matter how good the sea, how fast the travel, they still never missed a chance to stop. The old Mattaka knew every piss puddle between them and the South Pole, and he never set off for an island that should have taken a day to reach without a full bag.

The worst part was the taste. The skin hadn't time to cure properly before she made it into a vessel. The first days were nauseating. Every sip tasted of rank blubber, and they would always empty it entirely when they found a new water source in an effort to flush it clean. There was no problem drinking only what they needed for basic survival until the end of the second week, when either it leeched itself clean, or they just got used to it. It was still his job to fill up. He tried to row once, and though it only hurt a little, he was worried the repeated strain would make things worse. Part of him knew when he winced and shook his head that he could have gone, but none of him wanted to.

So his job was to sleep when it was calm enough to row, and keep watch while the rowers slept. Day by day, the sun pulled additional slack into its tether. Nights came with something near twilight now. If they went down short of Christmas, he reckoned it was late January, though any notion of a date dissolved into the hazy surroundings. He began to understand why the year was one long day to the Mattaka. There was little to mark the borders, and it felt like a single series of tasks to prepare for a time when there would be nothing to do than sit in silence in a cold, dark place. For now, the sun made false threats of disappearing completely without ever following through. There was plenty of light for him to monitor their position relative to land, and wake the others if they drifted too close or too far.

The weather was at least good, according to Tunguk. His version included a day when the seas rose behind them ten and fifteen feet, enough to make the sail stutter when they dipped into the valley. Each time one of them loomed, he swore it was their last. Thousands of gallons of water would break over the little old man and swamp the boat, this time without a bright insulated layer to float him to some unforgiving shore. His heart stopped as the stern lifted, but every time, just as he resigned himself to his end, she would bob gracefully over the top, every rib shifting under the weight of the cargo, and slide down the back with barely a drink over the gunwales. The man at the steering oar bore the brunt of it, and it looked easy enough until it was Foster's turn. By then he was wretched with seasickness. Parks already lay amidship moaning and vomiting over the side in alternation. Neither of them could keep food down. When the first freezing splash anointed his head, he thought of begging Tunguk to take his place, of claiming any kind of malady necessary to get out his shift. Although he rarely had to touch the oar, his four hours at the helm felt like an ordeal surpassing all but his swim from the *Qarapara*. Even that was so distant that he was tempted to count it easy in comparison, if only because his stomach wasn't in revolt. Parks took a full day to recover once it calmed—a far cry from their running a marathon just a few short hours after landing. He wondered if things were actually getting harder, or if there simply wasn't as much left to give.

The others took it in stride and swore it was good luck. A real gale would have kept the little boat beached as often as moving and devoured it if they failed to anticipate a change in weather fast enough to get to shore. The hunting boat wasn't meant for open water, as Gionn was fond of reminding them—only a squain would be mad enough to even go as far from land in the best of summer days without a keel, or at least an outrigger.

In fact, there was damn near a course in comparative primitive boating to be had in all of Gionn's complaints. Hardly a detail escaped his annoyance. Foster learned that on the big ships he'd be taking home, there was a place to stand, a place to stow. More places to tie off the ropes, which were stronger, and less-prone to slipping, being ungreased by blubbery fingers. That he would be able to smell his foul shipmates in the absence of the same grease, which was fouler still. Everything from benches to stitches to the pitch of the mast was unconscionable shit. He learned about the inferiority of bone as a building material, and that the sail shape was all wrong; that wood oars wouldn't flex at the lashings, leeching a man's power, because there were none; tholepins shouldn't wobble; what a tholepin was. They sailed in, at intervals: a whale's stomach; a leather bucket; the standardship of Iopsen; a wrinkled old cunt; a fine funeral shroud; Uinab's foreskin; a parchment raft;

a squain's purse; a squain's bladder; the seal mother's meaty arsehole; flotsam; wreckage; a larder; a wet lung; the crone's gift; and the Fairest Squain Flower of the Southern Seas.

At least better days seem to lie ahead. Foster clenched his jaw to avoid one-upping him with the floating city they were accustomed to. He always regaled his old civilian friends with horror stories about life aboard the carrier, sharing a bathroom with more than a hundred men. Here, it was an acrobatic feat to shit and piss over the sides and splash their asses with freezing water. Privacy never existed in any phase of his life, from four sisters to dozens of bunkmates. He was used to it, but it still bothered him that the woman had no qualms about staring at anyone as he dumped over the edge.

In his spare time, Foster made a pretense of studying the maps. He knew he had no bearings, and Tunguk understood where they were better than anything a picture could provide him, but it grounded him. The maps did not show the current, or the wind, or the preferred routes of other ships. Nothing ever came where he expected it, or to scale. As the only one incapable of propelling the boat, it was his job to scan the horizon for rocks and shoals, islands, and especially movement. Food was hard to come by for ships coming and going, and a small boat full of meat would be treated as a fortuitous buffet, so any sign of an approaching vessel was a direct threat to their lives. They'd mostly be going this time of year, appearing over the bow, which is why he missed the huge tall-masted outrigger—sidecock, as Gionn put it— that appeared like a gray ghost speeding past them only a few miles out to sea. If it saw them, it wasn't interested.

One Job, Parks had taken to calling him after that.

"One Job, do you mind passing me some water, if it's not too much trouble?" Parks stopped rowing. "I can ask Kyort-key," Parks again tried to roll his R's and inflect the way she and Tunguk did, and butchered her name in a new way every time. If Foster wanted nothing in all the world but to find his way home, Parks settled on another destination. Foster knew it from many port calls past. He was under the impression that mispronouncing native words with great confidence while making naive cultural references with the right eyebrow movements was the best way to seduce local women. "Thank you, One Job," he stopped pulling as he got his drink. That, and getting them hammered. He held up his water in offer to Kjartke, who had her own and knew how to ignore him by now.

Gionn pulled the cap off the ornate perfume bottle and took a long swallow. It shouldn't have shocked him when he found out Oduy and Gionn had dumped out whatever contents may have been of enormous value to use it as a water bottle during their stay on the big island, and its barter value had been somewhat overstated. "Anyone about to murder us, cunt? Have a look around while I rest me arms."

Foster did his best Kjartke impression and acted as though he were in an entirely different boat than the rowers. To Tunguk: "If they keep callin' me One Job and Cunt, does that change my name from Fucker, or am I still Fucker?" He'd long tried to grasp the Mattakatan naming conventions with little luck. Parks had called him a dozen different things since they met the old Reverse-Eskimo, and vice-versa, but it was still Brother and Fucker to him and the woman, though Gionn had no problem adopting whatever floated up from his bile ducts into his mouth.

Tunguk chuckled. "A name is a sound. That is what your people think. They take now one, now another. For Mattaka, it is no less alive than the one who bears it. It is the shape," he swept his hands to indicate Foster's figure. "They are not given with ease. How can I take you apart, and build you again like a boat? I can no more change your name."

"So whatever 'sound' somebody makes first, you're stuck with for life."

Tunguk shook his head. "Many keep their name, but many others will change once. It happens the man outgrows his shape, so must his name. It is a good life to change once. More, is very good. Or very bad."

"You can't just do me a solid? Help a brother out, and call me 'Foster?'"

"All must agree. If one Mattaka knows a name, you must say this when you meet, or be proven a liar. It is when all see another that a new name is birthed."

"And who gets to pick it?"

"No one. It will choose."

"Great. Lots to look forward to."

"If you are in a hurry, all men receive a new name when they die." He smirked.

"Goddammit, Parks," Foster lamented.

"I like Fucker," Tunguk's eyes glazed into the distance. He returned. "It makes me laugh. When a man cannot laugh, he waits for death."

"One Job, fill me up again," Gionn handed him the bottle and turned to have a piss. Foster dipped his arm over the side and let the icy sea water burble into the neck, then capped it. No one seemed to notice. He slumped on his seat—his gear-stuffed sleeping bag that sagged and lumped in all the wrong places. If he took out his warmer clothes, he would rest on what amounted to a leather blanket atop raw meat, so he chose to shiver. The lashings of the gunwale groaned against his lean, and he only relaxed once the slack was out. There was no stomping, tossing, or turning when every joint and seam felt poised to quit. His legs alternated between Kjartke's, opposite of him. They sailed almost as much sideways as forward. The wind inched around closer to the terminal point when it would be back to oars. Three weeks, or thereabouts since they left the Isle of the Unburied Dead, and the crew seemed to have an unspoken agreement than none shall ask how much farther. He was positive the woman had never been so far from home. Gionn, maybe, but the lack of whining about Tunguk's courses led Foster to believe the prisoner had only a conceptual knowledge of where they were—an empty space between precious few known points.

It wasn't clear whether it was the result of their landward drift or a curve of the peninsula, but a white-gray shadow darkened over the water straight ahead, boxing them on two sides. Given the wind and the lack of urgency, their captain must be angling for a mainland stop. There didn't seem to be any other way around. Where the usual water islands poked out like knees above the surface, the mass ahead towered until the tops disappeared into the haze. It projected out from the peninsula for miles, and he already felt the misery of waiting for a really good wind before they could beat around it. This one goddamn-well should have been on the map, yet the gentle curve of the drawing refused to acknowledge any such feature.

Kjartke said something to Tunguk in their native tongue. They went back and forth a few lines, then he spoke. "We will go to shore before the storm." Foster looked west, whatever direction that was now that longitudes bent to a single point. A few scattered clouds failed to hide the sun. Some were thicker, one in particular rising high and counter to them, but he didn't see whatever they were seeing. Despite their wide leeway, the old man was determined to milk the sail for whatever forward movement he could get.

Water was at two days. Not urgent, but he knew if the breeze turned, they could end up staring at land for that long or longer without gaining an inch on it. If that was their stop, the faster they got into the shadow of the giants, the sooner they could go to oars if needed. His neck tingled with more than the cold. Foster could almost swear the light fell on the faraway land in an imperceptibly different way. It felt like walking up a stranger's long drive, and all his stomach wanted to do was go around. The talk of a storm made his queasiness return. It felt like something large and inhospitable lumbered their way, but he was at least as sure that he was making it up based on what he heard.

Gionn disappointingly did not take another sip of water, electing instead to insert his hand into a hunk of the whale and scoop out a meal with his fingers. The beautiful red flesh had turned to grays and purples. Every bit of it had been splashed, stepped on, slept on, and shat on by passin gulls who weighed the risk of a meal against the stroke of a sword. A few pockets here and there looked better than others, and for more than a week there waged a secret battle to pull one's share from the least-foul places without showing a preference that would draw anyone else to the prime cuts—at least among him and Parks. The Mattaka didn't even bother to scrape off the disgusting outer layer of brown mush to get to the more appetizing middle. The whole mess was brined from sitting in the bilge, which could be pleasantly salty, or spat right over the side depending on where it came from. He was sure all of it would have been spoiled by now. But somehow, the cold water and the refrigerator temperatures kept it in a state that was at least arguably fit for human consumption, while the wind dried the exposed parts—if they could go long enough without a boot squashing them. Even then, a huge amount of their cache seemed ruined. It once felt like they would never need to hunt again, but with hundreds of decent pounds to go, Foster could see that the whale didn't have to be eaten to be depleted. There was still plenty of blubber, at least. The Mattaka saved it like a delicacy. None of the white boys could stand to gnaw on strips of rubber that oozed lamp oil. Tunguk forced them to take a minimum each day. He claimed a man could whither on whale flesh alone. Foster knew the old man was right, even though he probably didn't understand why: they needed fat to survive. The meat alone was too lean.

Foster huddled in on himself for warmth as they poked toward the steep landmass, always steep. Hardly a sloping beach down here, much less a gentle valley. Everything stood up jagged like a wall, topped in the forbidding ice that dared to stretch farther down from the peaks the more they traveled. Still a far cry better than his weeks on the tourist boat, navigating a minefield of icebergs calved from the sea ice in the summer. The land would have been white, and the whiter shades of blue and green. At least here, he had the bare stone.

Twilight came as the horizon shaved the first few slices off the sun. He'd never spent a winter in this hellhole in his former life, as he'd taken to calling. Everything was a mad rush between the first sign of the ice receding and the first of its return. He'd never once set foot on land. Storms happened topside. Night was something they expected to show up after they left. He trembled at the thought of it getting even more miserable. It was cold now. Especially when wet, which was a permanent feature that varied only in degree. But cold meant well above freezing. He wouldn't have lasted a few hours in the Antarctica he was used to, not in a boat or on land, sure as hell not the water. No one would have been within a thousand miles to feed him, to find him water, to move him from place to place. The survival suits seemed like a joke during their orientation. Survive a few hours for what? To die slightly later? Even the rafts, with several weeks' supplies, wouldn't hold much chance of a rescue if they managed to stay upright in the kind of seas that set them sailing to begin with. His misery would have lasted days instead of hours, and death still assured. If staying alive was something he wanted to do, this was almost better. For the lack of easy food and water, at least he had company. Company was often someone trying to kill him, but here he was, weeks later, alive. In no immediate danger of freezing, starving or succumbing to any other natural process. A much better place. If, again, staying alive was something he wanted to do.

It occurred to him maybe this was just a worse version of a life raft adrift off a frozen continent. Maybe now he would survive months instead of days and weeks. Then what? Not a minute of this was easy or pleasant. It was a constant act of will. He didn't want to say it, not even to Parks, but home was a foggy notion that had begun to shed its detail. Success, then, meant finding meat and water in the nick of time, again and again and again. Steering clear of hostile men and weather. Rowing or plodding somewhere, always. How long would he need to do that for in order to justify his efforts to continue drawing breath? How long after an ordeal does somebody have to survive in order to say they survived? If home and safety were the deciding factor, he could end up not-surviving for years to come.

"Fuuuuck," Parks moaned. "This seat is killing my back. Remind me to explain 'lumbar support' to your people someday," he said to no one in particular, then slid off and nestled in sideways between Kjartke and the suspended bench. The space was tight enough that his shoulder pressed firmly into hers as he leaned back into the gunwale and wiggled to loosen his spine. His long legs trailed well across onto Foster's side, stirring up meat with a squishing sound. "You can have the seat, Fucker." His arms spread out over the side, one of which was behind Kjartke. "Don't worry, we'll let you know if anymore ships go by."

Before Foster could move, Kjartke pushed herself up and sat on the vacant bench facing Tunguk—her back to the men. Parks shrugged and spread out, crossing his arms behind his head. At least he seemed to be adapting to the circumstances a little better. Foster wanted nothing more than to talk to him alone. He wasn't sure why he hesitated to discuss where they were, or how they got there, or where and if there was a path home. It's not as though they'd believe him, or care, even if they did. Gionn would make fun of them for something, the other two would shut the fuck up, none would have a solution or a problem. Yet he couldn't get the words past his throat when they had company.

Foster wished his biggest concern could be flirting with the woman in front of him. Parks was either sure he'd make it, or sure he didn't care. More likely than either: he hadn't thought any farther ahead than what was necessary to get some.

"Remind me to explain women to you someday, brother."

"Love to, Bud," he clasped his hands behind his head and shrugged. "Think we might have time now."

Foster nodded. "When they don't talk to you, or look at you, in my experience, that means time to move on."

"That's what a lot of people think." He locked eyes on her. "Or they meet some girls from Jakarta, or Rio, or Reverse-Eskimo land, and they think, 'these girls are not like the ones back home. They're just not attracted to the same things.' They'll meet a girl who goes stone cold on them and think she just doesn't have emotions, or she doesn't want to show them, and they don't know what to do next, so they give up. You know what I think? I think they're too used to easy pickings. I can assure you, no women has ever taken one look at me, listened to a few charming words, and jumped into bed. Look around, bro. You see those glaciers?"

Foster humored him with a glance over the bow, now pointed at the land. "No, I just see some little patches of ice up high."

"OK, well there are probably glaciers other places. And you've seen glaciers before. You know, geology? Have you heard of it?"

"I'm passin' familiar."

"They cut the Great Lakes, my friend. You know how? Pressure, and time. No need to rush it. Enough pressure and time, you can make coal into diamonds. Ain't that right, girl?" He smiled at her back.

"Just a few million years to go, I guess." Foster settled on the unyielding coastline. "Besides, even if you succeeded, where would yall fuck?"

"What, do you go soft if someone's watchin' you, Fucker?" Gionn piped in. Foster didn't respond. Against the dark gray of the coastal peaks something moved. He saw first the two in the middle, then two more before and behind. Six shapes hugged the shore like black insects crawling over the port bow.

"Boats!" He said almost too eagerly, maybe afraid someone else would spot them first and speak. It was hard to tell if they were small and near, or large and far. The profiles disappeared behind the swell and rose again. The others followed his gaze. He realized their sails were pitched the same as his.

"Hunting party," Kjartke said without hesitation.

"Mattaka?" Foster recognized the size and shape of the craft. She nodded. Tunguk leaned on the steering oar as he watched. "Too many," he said. "This many will keep greater distance to hunt. They are whaling, or it is trouble."

"Headin' in from the same storm we are."

"Yes. But another trouble."

"Headed for that bay," Gionn offered. A deep curve disappeared into a section of rock miles wide.

"No bay. It is a channel. An island. Your people call it Yunoc."

"Ah, didn't recognize the cunt! Are we already to Yunoc?"

"We should stay on the outside. So they don't see us," Foster offered.

"The storm will take us. The channel will be calm. We will find water."

"And trouble?"

"It is to be seen. Here, the storm will take us."

So far, there was hardly a breeze or a sea to herald the weather that the natives expected, though Foster did notice the sail begin to flutter a bit as a gust occasionally spun from the starboard beam.

"I'll take 90% fucked over 100%," Parks voted. "We got two Reverse-Eskimos on board. They might play nice."

"Squains get along like whale seals. Which is to say they get along, or they kill each other. These two don't get along much, and there's no tellin' if those'll like either one of ours."

"They will not fight an enemy who harbors from the same storm," Tunguk assured them.

"Code of the Sea, huh?" Parks said. "What about when it's over?"

"It will be best if they are not enemies." He adjusted his course—the signal for Foster to figure out the complementary sail.

The rocky prominence cleaved down the middle and split like a block of wood into a channel, with the largest island he'd yet seen, and what looked like a few smaller ones nearer the coast, though it was hard to tell what was connected and what stood alone. All would have remained permanent extensions of the peninsula for Foster and his map, but Tunguk's familiarity was a key that opened features locked to naive eyes. As soon as he saw it, the western sky darkened, and a distant system billowed up as though a mighty cavalry kicked up dust that marked their advance long before they appeared. Well before the first gust, he felt the sea route slam shut. There was no way left for them but through the channel. If the wind shifted too far to starboard, their drift would take them into the peninsula. But the sail was up, the oar was set. There was nothing to do, except follow the slim line of boats and pray to duck in ahead of what was coming.

A choppy western swell ran out ahead to meet them, as though the ground shook in warning. Hour by hour, the confusion of the water grew. The closer they came, the slower the going. The wide bottom began its characteristic wobble that would herald a new round of seasickness as he lost the ability to predict which way she would bend. Now and then the stern lifted right out of the water as another swell came abeam, slapping them back down in a sudden jolt as she rode over and twisted so hard he could see a visible wrinkle in the hull for a moment. Somehow, her undulations always managed to glide out of the worst of it instead of fighting the sea like steel. At least as long as it didn't wring her apart. The water drummed the sides, and Foster thought of how he didn't even know the name of the craft that carried him. At times like these, when he was truly a passenger, it felt as though he sat on the back of an animal desperate to take him where it thought he should go. A creature who could swim a hell of a lot better than he could, yet had barely any more say against the will of the sea. He sensed her determination—and a hint of fear. It would have been nice to know who to thank, who to encourage. Tunguk already made it clear that Mattaka don't name their boats.

He fixed his eyes like darts on the rock ahead—the only way he knew to stave off the sickness was to find something that refused to move. Parks's head rested between his knees, huddled in his oilskin. They came down off the following swell right in the trough of the western current, and the modest wave bashed itself against the man's back. Water streamed over the side and hid among the mountain of mess at their feet. Foster sprung for the bailer and began to scoop and toss as fast as he could.

"Move!" Tunguk scolded Parks. "Too heavy!" He relocated to Foster's side to lift the starboard beam out of the water a bit more. Kjartke spun around. She and Gionn took each an end of a long strip of skin she had cut from the whale, and dipped it so that water filled it like a trough. They swung it back out the way it came, but the boat was noticeably more sluggish. It was an excavation to move enough things from the middle to the sides so they could even get to the deep part. Foster felt seawater over his toes, and flecks of whale meat lifted and settled as it sloshed. The three worked at a feverish pace to lighten them before the wind. Foster glanced up and saw the six boats just on the other side of a clear line that marked the wave shadow of the land. The washboard waves flattened to a short drumroll.

He couldn't see the other end of the channel or the island, and had he not been told, might have thought it was still just a bay. The first small gust ripped in from the west, flattening the sail and shaving the tops off the waves. Spray sent their faces into their shoulders. Foster made himself small, as if any part of him wasn't already wet. He was afraid that would be it for their forward momentum, but before he could even get to the ropes, it died and the gentler northwest wind filled them and drove them on. It was darker now than even at the sun's lowest point—the closest thing to an evening he'd seen yet, even in the big swells they'd so far endured. The storm had closed so fast, he knew they'd have borne the brunt of it with no hope of making land had it not been for the Mattaka eyes. It was going to be a shit-kicker soon enough.

Ahead, the channel looked as if it had been gouged smooth by comparison. The growing chop settled into tiny echoes, reverberating off one another even before they reached the landmass. The last stretch was painstakingly slow. They moved no faster than a walk, and it would have been a miserable wait if his bailing weren't plenty to occupy him. She was lightening up, but it was only a matter of time until another one came over, then another. Gionn dropped his end to bring the sail even more in-line with the vessel than it already was. The freezing water numbed Foster's hands and feet, but he ran it down until it became difficult to get a full cup in his bailer. He was so preoccupied that when they finally clawed across the line into the channel waters, he only noticed by the pitch, and looked up to find the growling sea running across their wake.

Once they passed the headland, the wind turned behind them again and picked up intensity. The landmasses caught the northwest breeze and gathered it into a funnel that drove the little boat before as if someone turned on a fan behind them. The boats ahead were already gone. It grew darker still—the sun behind the clouds, behind the mountains. Foster helped Gionn amend the sail, then he took out his damp piece of parchment and had Tunguk point out exactly where they were. He didn't mark it lacking any means of doing so, but also for the strange reason that he felt queasy about defacing a historical artifact. He made a mental note of the spot. Big island with channel: another annoying omission. His eyes traced their route back across every water hole along the way, half of them vanished from the banks of recollection. Once the image was impressed, he hurried to fold it as the wind tried to whip it out of his hands. Both sides loomed like the walls of an unwelcoming castle, and otherwise made no attempt to keep anyone at bay. 'Come in, Fucker,' it said. 'What's mine is yours. What's mine is rock and ice and death.'

"Do you know a story about how your ancestors came to this place?" Foster leaned back so he could see Tunguk around Kjartke's shoulder.

"To Yunoc?"

"The whole thing." He drew a circle over his head with his finger. "What's it called?"

"Ajatse," Kjartke offered without facing him.

Tunguk nodded. "Yes. It is not told during a storm."

"That's fine. I was just wonderin', did they come to some other place first? I mean, humans used to be apes in Africa. So at some point, they decide to pass on outta there and find some better stompin' grounds. I been a lot of places, man, and all of 'em are better'n this one. What on God's green hell made yall keep goin' until you found the coldest, darkest, most barren goddamn wart of a place and then say, 'Know what? I think this is it!'"

"There are women who charm a man because they are kind," Tunguk explained. "They prepare food and clothing, and tell him he is a great hunter when they make love. They take care of his children, and are at peace with the family and the clan. And some," he looked at Kjartke, "charm a man because they are none of these things."

"Wigwam!" Parks suddenly came alive from his stupor and pointed at nothing at all on the shore of the island.

"Wigwam?" Foster tried to follow.

"Right there, dude. Up on the little bluff."

"What the fuck is a wigwam?" Gionn snorted.

"The little house thingies they have," Parks explained.

"You seen one of those skin igloos we were in at back in the main camp?" Foster asked.

"I didn't 'seen' it, bro, I'm pointing at it right now."

"Point somethin' less fat than your finger, I don't see shit," Foster came back.

"Nor I," Gionn added. The way Tunguk and Kjartke scanned it was clear that no one did.

"Parks is blind as a vagina at anything but bangin'-distance."

"The black circle-y thingy up there. Joe, you see it."

"I see rock."

"Yo, girl! Kjartke! Right there." She shook her head.

"Fuck off, mate," Gionn took up his oars. The sail fluttered as the once-sturdy wind disappeared at intervals. Clouds creeping over the peaks told them that the storm wind out of the west had blown out the weaker breeze. Kjartke gave up her seat and sent Parks to his position with a look. It was manpower from here, though they left the sail up in case any stragglers came by to aid them. The surface of the channel was rippled glass, flowing weakly against them. Parks took one more look at the top edge of a rough dome, setting behind the edge of the bluff. Distance ate it, and then he wasn't sure if he'd seen it at all. Admittedly, everything was a blur to him, but the blurs were different colors. He dug on.

The others seemed to think he was a piece of equipment. Just crank him up whenever the wind died. He remembered his first paddle—the kayak with Klimut, then-husband of his one true love. It had only been a few hours, but the fatigue afterward had trucked him for days. He didn't know how anyone did it. Then he got stuck on an even bigger, heavier boat and the paddling never stopped. The first days, he thought it would simply kill him. Soon, he found something like a low gear, some kind of diesel that he could hum along with, almost to no end, as long as there was whale and water. He was a different animal by the time they found Oduy and Gionn. Then weeks on the nearly-open sea sent him right back to wishing he had broken an arm instead of a leg, so he wouldn't have to do it anymore. Though that wouldn't have stopped Klimut. The seasickness whittled away a little more, and now his big arms were tender noodles. What had been a fair amount of body fat had melted to thick muscle, giving him the appearance of the boat motor, he assumed, but none of the power. His lower back ached with every stroke, and his hips and knees locked up from lack of movement so that whenever he did switch off, which meant lying sideways for a brief stretch, he as often went into agonizing cramps as relaxation.

Gionn cursed him til he got the cadence. Eskimo Joe couldn't be bothered about coxswain duties, and facing away from his partner, it was always a bit of a crapshoot. Usually, Gionn just matched whatever Parks could put out, and it was Parks' job to make sure that was the least amount possible. This was a get-there pace. No one wanted to be on the water much longer, even though the island to his left would keep them from the worst of it. As usual, he had no idea how much farther he had to keep it up. It was soul-crushing: the sheer size of everything he could see—the imagined proportions of the places ahead and behind—against the slow drag of the hide blade, a few feet for every mighty pull.

Where Gionn's two islands were barely more than bare rock jutting from the water, this was an ice-capped giant, the curves of which made it impossible to see either the entrance or the exit of the channel. Every time they rounded a bend he expected to glimpse the hunting boats again, but they were either miles ahead, or safely ashore. He wondered now if Joe planned to have them row throughout the storm, only in the channel as opposed to the sea. He'd expected to find a suitable landing and rest it out, but it occurred to him that they could make forward progress, albeit slow, the entire time and maybe find a camp at the far end, ready to emerge as soon as the wind favored them. He had no idea how long this island was, but it passed at a walking pace.

It surprised him the first time it happened: the fact that you could doze off uncontrollably in the middle of extreme exertion, but by now he was used to nodding off like a driver at the wheel midstroke without his arms betraying any more than a hiccup. Heavy blinks interrupted by splashes, or sprays of salt when a gust found its way down on of the steep ravines. While he couldn't see Gionn's face, he was sure the ginger fell victim to the same fate now and then.

If it got bad enough, if real sleep threatened, it came with the strangest of dreams. Sudden flutters of voice, or the image of a face, like a flock of birds spooked to flight. Seconds long, forgotten as soon as it jarred him back. One moment he looked into the sea, crystal clear, at a mirror that showed the hull of boats. Then Foster spoke to him in bird squawks. His parents admonished him for not returning their calls. A Brazilian girl laughed at one of his jokes. He shook his head so hard his brain hurt. The blurry grays faded again and he was on the *Qarapara*, Foster pointed and explained to him a chart showing the rookeries that dotted the coast. He woke again when his paddle slipped from his grip and clanged to a halt with his heart in the tholepin. He knew now that bone didn't float, and if it went over, they would make the replacement from his femurs and his back flesh. He cringed as he recovered it, expecting the tirade to come any second. But Gionn was turned halfway around, his attention fixed forward.

"One Job, why are not shoutin' 'boats' you bucket?"

"Because everyone fuckin' sees 'em, and it's the same ones from before."

Parks tried to lean around the heads but couldn't make it out.

"Aye, but when the boats go from movin' away line-ahead to movin' at us line-abreast that's worth a fuckin' remark." Whether sleep or his vision, it took a moment for the shapes to form. Six hunting boats bobbed their way, a half-mile up, lined up side-by-side with ample space between.

"Should we be haulin' ass outta here?" Foster asked.

"Prey runs. It is our people's way to run them to greater strength." Tunguk said.

"Nothin' back that way."

"Nothing we see now."

"If we are weak from long travel, and they are not, it is also strength," Kjartke added.

"Well I don't feel like fightin' six boatloads of squains with you worthless cunts. I say we surrender and hope they like redheads."

"We row to them. They will see we do not run or save our strength for a fight." Tunguk snapped off something at Kjartke in their tongue.

They slowed their pace to one of resignation. Parks sang the strokes, as he often did when he wanted to sneak the cadence lower, and Gionn ignored, as he always did.

"*Pull…Pull…Pull…*dip yo paddle and *pull…*" He beatboxed a descent into a verse. "Well, my name is Parks, I don't mean to entertain you / I got my niggas Foster, Gionn, and a squain or two / came down hot but I didn't sink / dropped like an ice cube into the drink / picked up little mama and I caught some swell / it's hard to beat meat when you ridin' on whale / fools try to kill me, but I don't play / my spear is harder than N.W.A.

"*Pull…Pull…Pull…*dip yo paddle and…" the chorus continued.

Oar, cunt, Gionn corrected to himself.

He snuck a glance over his shoulder as he leaned back into the stroke. Bare pole, under oars. The one starboard splashed a bit to stand off the coast, her bow angled to sea while the other two pointed directly at them. It seemed an odd lot, but he hardly got a look before he recovered and sunk the long wood shaft once more into the sea. They were becalmed and rowing by threes—his luck had it that the other two shifts could gawk while he had to imagine his demise based on the commotion aboard.

"Jarrahil!" Someone cried.

"Hold course! Look a-soger, lads. Wait my command. It'll be all-hands to oars." The captain's voice boomed from the stern.

"Aye, but which way?" Gionn heard a man behind him mutter to another.

"North," came the response. "We no meet, is too many."

A thorough annoyance crept through his veins as every man who wasn't pulling stared and weighed their words. Again, he craned to see and only caught enough to whet his curiosity. He didn't care for north, but there was no move yet, and if it was a run they were in for, best done sooner. The captain was still taking the measure of them, perhaps of himself. The voices became louder, and though they were addressed within the crew, the more tongue-heavy among them began to reach for the captain's ears.

"If we give wake now, they won't come after," another said in rising tone. Louder still were the exotic tongues who were quite sure most didn't share them, lobbing fears and boasts they would never have to answer for. The two older brothers takka-takked between themselves somewhere among the forward benches. Probably debating whether to shit themselves or jump. They couldn't know what was before them, though they had eyes on it. Everyone in front of him yanked their necks between the ships ahead and the tall, fair man on the steering oar. It was a fine enough show, how long he remained abaft without concern. Now the big square-rigged cunt took his march forward, at last roused from his position. Voices died and arose to life in a wave before and behind him as he moved to join the new first mate for a look. There could be none more torn than he, but he stood it well. Hardly a leak in his trousers as he brushed by the bent head of red hair and thumped up to the fore deck.

"Guil'll crack 'em!" One shouted from the aft benches. "Never seen him run!" Gionn rolled his eyes. The favored seats were for the barrels whose anvil was wave and skull—and the arse-ticklers. He cared for neither. A fair luck, as he found himself thrust among the wankers and the takka-taks in front.

"Ram!" Another called.

"Mad fuck, can you not count to three?" Said Olred from midship. "And each a tighter turn than ourselves." Gionn didn't like anyone yet, but he was considering Olred. The old salt knew more than the first mate and the second, yet he was a one-share man on account of his grumbling. He couldn't wake on a ship alone without finding the sun an idiot for the way it rose, and saying as much, though it was always with a wit. He spun the best tales, full of idiots doing idiot-things to other idiots, and himself always caught between them. Yet he spared no barb at his own expense—all the world was too terrible to be upset at, and none became cross with him as it was his own pride he cut up first.

"We'll run a day and go round to sea," Olred stated flatly.

"They'll overtake us," a man named Daios claimed. Several more expressed their agreement.

"If they bother after us, I'll throw meself over to lighten the pull," Olred offered, his head half-turned toward the captain as he rowed.

"'Course they'll bother," Daios said. "They're here to stop ships. You think they'll say, 'Ah well, that one's gone. Hope the next one hails?'"

"Guil don't run!" The man near the stern shouted, and most of his peers hooted. It was fast shaping up that the midship favored flight and the aft, a good toss. Gionn and the forward men kept their forward mouths shut, except the one. Gionn didn't need to look to know it was Teague. "Fuck 'em!" The sparse fellow shouted with such effort that his voice broke. He didn't specify who. For reasons unknown to himself, Gionn paid the new lads the kindness of pointing out, on the eve of the first day, each and every man they should take pains to avoid speaking to. To this one, he added: "Don't look in his eyes, nor glance past him. If he walks, move. Don't touch his gear or his garments. Don't rest your foot on his bench when he's off doin' a shit. Don't look at the back of his head, or yawn his direction. Quiet when he sleeps, and if he goes over, you never saw it." The mad cunt kept long periods of brooding silence, broken infrequently by terrible shouting that need not mean anything to anyone else. When he did manage a word of communication—yet more infrequently—he came off well enough, which was even more unsettling, because it was clearly not the case. The tension of waiting for another of his stone silences, or that maniacal laugh, was too much and few men had a word for him. He was the only man not rowing who remained seated and facing abaft. No other could take his eyes from what lie ahead. It was telling that the benches immediately before and behind him were assigned to the two youngest grassbenders. Gionn hoped he would drown soon.

The voices grew rather heated now, the runners and the fighters, and among the runners, the forward, back, and go-rounders—even a hailer, midship. Some captains would tolerate none of the advice. Guil was of the other nature: all had their say and nothing sacred. Gionn found it made for a merrier ship, as long as the last word belonged to the captain. If he didn't act soon, there would be a new one.

The gut-wailing of the crew was enough that at first, he didn't hear the small voice that begged his name. The second time, he found his swimming pupil crouched beside his bench, staring up with big gray eyes.

"You're supposed to be rowin', Grassbender."

"Who are they?"

"Now you've gone and made the sides unmatched. We'll be makin' circles widdershins if I don't even it up." He shipped his oar. "Captain won't like it a bit, but don't fret, I'll explain it was your doin'." He rose and stretched as wide as he could, then turned and placed a foot on his bench to have his first good look at what lie in wait.

"Who are they?" He repeated.

Puraba, the man one bench forward, overheard and answered: "Out of Jarrahil." Gionn squinted. An odd lot, indeed. The one at center was without a doubt of Jarrahil build.

"Why? We leave Jarrahil behind. Why they stop us?"

"Checkin' letters, I suppose," Gionn said absently. It was a fine excuse to see for himself, but he realized his mistake when the other two brothers left their benches to crowd around. They'd all get it soon as the captain turned. The other idle shifts saw free movement aboard, and men began to drift.

"It is good," the oldest said. "You make letters."

"Eh." Gionn grumbled doubtfully.

The hailer from midship approached. "The lad is right. Should be no concern if this one did as he said," he plead his case.

"Your letters—they are good?" Puraba questioned.

"Me letters are fuckin' perfect."

"Your face is lie. Look to his face! As if he smells something he no like!"

"How certain are you it'll pass?" The hailer asked.

"Well, it's not as though I put a mark through 'north' and wrote 'south,' cunt. Mine's crisper than the one we threw over."

"Aye. Then we hail. No good cause to tire ourselves or kill ourselves if the letter's good. And if it ain't, we kill this one first!" The men in their vicinity cheered the hailer. Gionn studied the ships in silence. Grassbender bent ahead and spoke under the others.

"You worry. Why? You make oath the letters are good?"

"Not that simple, simple cunt."

"It is simple to make oath."

Now the hullabaloo caught the attention of the new mate, who turned on them in a fury. "Back to your posts, you fuckin' wankers! Every arse on a bench before I stitch a sail from your hides!" He stormed down the middle as it cleared.

"Cap'n said 'look a-soger!'" someone shouted to the amusement of all as they scampered off under a volley of threats from the mate. "Row!" He backhanded the smallest lad as he passed, but went by Gionn as if he didn't see him.

"Forward says we hail," the hailer claimed as he returned midship.

"Fuck forward!" Someone aft said.

At last, the captain made the slow pivot and followed after the mate to midship. The men fell silent. The only sound aboard was the slosh of oars and the creak of wood. They pulled as slow as they could, and it seemed eternity before Guil spoke.

"Well? What of it?" No one knew how to answer. "I got captain's ears. Not an arse may whisper on me ship that I don't know it, and I heard a fair number of 'em. Just as well, I say. You pull an oar for me, you're a full-share man—even if you're half the size of one," he looked at Grassbender to a ripple of laughs. "If I want it back, I'll put you over the side, but until that day, I don't care if you're half-wappa, half-squain, or half-bucket. If you got a word of the tongue, I'll hear from the crew. What say you lads? Fight? Or run?"

It was all the invitation they needed. Every throat pealed at once in a melee of boasts and curses. Gionn pressed his lips tight and glanced back—only the little nuisance kept his quiet. The captain let it fly across the benches like so many arrows until he sensed a lull of fatigue, then inserted his fingers in his mouth and loosed a shrill whistle over everyone. Even then, it took a few moments for some of the voices to wind down, until only Teague was left shouting something incomprehensible.

"Teague! Shut the fuck up!" The mate ordered, and the man shouted a few more words, then muttered himself back to wherever it was he came from, grinning ear-to-ear.

"Enough of the monkey calls! I'll hear one man from each. Mate!" The first mate straightened up. "Will you speak for fight? Or Run?"

"I stand with the will of the captain."

Guil almost smiled as he nodded. "Second mate?"

"Will of the captain."

That farce out of the way, he looked about the deck. "Who will stand to run?" At first, no one flinched, though plenty of voices had called for it. "Is it to be a fight, then?"

Olred moaned as he creaked to his feet.

"Olred will speak for run. Any runners opposed?" No one answered. "What say you, Olred?"

"Captain. It's certain that we run. Only a matter of direction. Either way, a pull is a pull. But these young lads aft are thriftless. They would row a part of the mornin' and quit to their deaths, while meself, I'm willing to work all summer."

"Is your blade timid, then?"

"Aye, like a cock in the cold when I mark them at a hundred men to our sixty, and three rams to one."

Guil smiled and nodded. Daios was already on his feet—a thick lad with rust-colored hair who always seemed to be leaning backward even when he stood, his arms curved away from his sides as though his elbows had never made the acquaintance of his ribs. He looked around, and when no one objected, he said, "Olred sees it wrong. Them's faster. It's a fight either way. We got the bigger ship, the greenheart crew, and a fuckin' barrel captain. I say fight goin' forward!" Whoops of approval shot through the benches.

"You forget we're empty," Guil pointed out. "And more rowers by weight. You don't think they're undersheeted to catch us?"

"Fuck, no."

"We'd be a lot faster if this lad could manage to find the water with his oar," Olred said. "Even then, they're two of 'em undersheeted, and all three undermanned, and they're like to know it of their sails better than this twat."

"That it?" He surveyed the crew. "Is there a man here who thinks Olred and Daios have not done it well? Anything unsaid?" He was met with silence. "Thank you, lads," he nodded for them to sit. "But before I make me decision, I'd very much like to hear from me new hands. Let's find what kind of idiots we've oathed up." Guil headed forward to Grassbender, who still had not resumed his pulling. "What of it, me son? Where do you stand?" The little one looked over at Gionn, who refused to return his glance, then back. He put on his bravest face.

"Run."

"You'd have me run away?"

The lad paused again, then nodded. "It is because I got no blade."

Guil laughed. "A practical bastard, this one!" He called to the crew. "He's got the best argument I've heard yet!" The captain frowned past the madman and approached the older brothers.

"And yourselves?"

"Fight."

"Fight," came the echo.

Guil spun and stood over Gionn's shoulder. "And you. Is this your shift?"

"Aye."

"Then why aren't you pullin'?"

"The little cunt across the way stopped. Just squarin' the sides."

"Is he your equal then?"

"No, captain."

"Or do you take every other stroke off to account for it?"

"No, captain."

"Then why don't you pull?"

"Eh. Wanted to see the fuckin' ships. How can I say where I stand if I don't know what's the lay?"

"If the both of you don't have oars in the water before I finish me sentence, I'll have to answer your mutiny by lightenin' the bow." They frantically fumbled their blades into the water and searched for the time of the stroke. "Mate!"

"Aye!" The first mate answered.

"Tell the present shift what lies ahead."

"Three light navy of Jarrahil. One local, forty-seater, she's the standard. Call it a darraig. One abiama of Ampos, thrity-six seater. One Mabhani river thief, looks thirty or forty."

"There it is, me son. Which way do you row?"

"If they're as he says, and out of Jarrahil, I say run."

"And why is that?"

"Olred's called it. Even if they catch us, wouldn't be all at once. We'd have a fair go, if a bit of a pull. And as the Grassbender mentioned, I, too, am without blade. None of that matters, though. You've already made your mind to fight."

"Have I?"

"Aye. You asked the two runners to give cause, but not the two fighters. That means you understand why it's fight, and want to figure if we're idiots or jumpers."

Guil lit up with a warm smile. Gionn didn't know yet if he was a captain, but he looked one, through-and-through, and he couldn't hate the man as much as he would have liked.

"Let it be known," he announced. "The letter-forge may be prone to loll about, and may yet jump, but he's no mongrel. A good, crimson lad, this one." Guil rubbed his hair. Gionn had long ago made up his mind to throw the first cunt overboard who engaged in that particular sailor's charm, and now that he let it pass, there'd be hands on his scalp as often as a man climbed the rigging or raised a spear.

"Our trade is south. If you'd shirk a patch job of a Jarrahili 'fleet,' you have two choices. Remove yourself from me vessel at the next port—and there will be one—or name your captain now, if you think you got the numbers." Gionn had to admit to himself he was a little impressed. The men were allowed to yell anything they wanted so they got it out their stomachs. Nowhere did Guil allow them to stand for one or the other, or get any kind of count. It was impossible to say how many would stand for run, but it was less than before, and there would be no one for mutiny.

"You're the captain, Captain," Olred conceded.

"Slow and steady, lads. When I give the order, it's all hands to oars. Soon as we're within range, I'll call the mark, and it's lean-ho. Don't let up til you feel the ram hit the mast, then it's hop bench and back before the other two can turn on us. We run south. If they stop to help their sister, we're off free. If not, we got the numbers, and once the winds pick up, the weather-gage if we want it. Look a-soger, and you other shifts, don't touch a fuckin' oar til I say the word."

Cheers erupted, mostly from the back and middle thirds. Though no man moved, a fire of anticipation rippled through the crew. Even the dissenters seemed lifted by the orders, and he knew well that no man is thrilled to run, let alone as the first act of the season. It was incautious, but it was a captain's maneuver. Through-and-through.

"Hang on, there," Gionn shipped his oar. Grassbender looked at him like some malefic ghost who had suddenly appeared on deck. Guil turned, and his eyes boiled over. "We haven't heard from the hailers." The officers were too stunned at the gall to even curse him. "You there," Gionn pointed at the man midship who earlier had drooled on them trying to win hands. "Didn't you say you wanted to hail them? Thought highly of me letters, didn't you?" The man retreated into his leathers.

"Aye," Guil said. "I did hear somethin' of hailin'. You know me decision. Would you still speak? I'll allow it, if you think it wise." All he got was a shaken head. "And you! If your oar comes out—"

"I speak for hail," Gionn said quickly. "Can't do it while I row. Makes me all out of breath." Guil ground his teeth.

"Speak fast. If you think it wise."

"Captain, I have never done a wise thing in me life, and it has served me well and found me here. This cunt over here, if I may sum his argument, made the point that we can simply hail as they ask, present me admiralty letter, and be off without trouble."

"You're the only one thinks that letter'll pass," Daios shouted.

"Oh, she'll pass. She'll slip us right into any port in the kingdom. Captain knows it, too. He don't know his letters, but he knows the look of one. Captain, have you ever seen a finer hand than me own?" Guil was too irked to reply. "But this cunt," he pointed at the hailer, "is an idiot." Gionn rose. "I tell you cunts, we got a clever one at the helm. Captain is right, no ship of Jarrihil will be fooled. Do you know why? Aye, some of you do. I can see it in your faces. And just as clear, I can see the idiots stumblin' over their thoughts. You're first mate now, cunt! You'll want to listen up. No ship of Jarrihil will let us pass, though we just come from their port without trouble. The reason is not me gorgeous, unbruised flower of a letter. The reason, you who call yourselves sailors, is this: b*eads!*" He let the stupor work its way through the bulk of the men.

"Aye, beads. The Jarrahili, lacking any men of vigor or originality, keep the same practice as their Amposi cousins. I should amend me earlier remark: the letter's good in any port in the kingdom *not* held by Ampos or Jarrahil. Those will of course want to see it, but they will also demand our beads. In every backwater of theirs from Aqu to Hiade, there is a lowdown, jungle-smellin' bead cunt. Though I didn't see it happen, I imagine that when we sailed, our fine captain received not only an admiralty letter, but a little strand of beads, is that so?"

"Aye," Guil confirmed.

"And while it's well enough to fix the letter so we might steer south, I haven't a fuckin' notion what any one of those beads means. Do you? Anyone? Does any man here know the beads? No, I thought not. If that's a detachment from Jarrahil posted to check the traffic, I can assure you there will be a wrigglin' worm of a bead cunt on board. Now, I don't know for certain that the beads contradict the letter. Could be a simple cargo manifest. Maybe they say 'sixty handsome cunts bound for glory.' Maybe, 'kill these cunts on sight.' But it would be a bad look if our letter says we're bound south, and the beads, otherwise. By then, we'd be sittin' with o'er a hundred men around us, ready to board."

"Couldn't have said it better meself," Guil interrupted. "If I were explainin' exactly why we should, under no circumstances, hail. Now that you've thoroughly convinced everyone what a confused idiot you are—"

"Hang on, cunt. Not done. I speak for hail, and hail it is, if we're wise. More so now that I've taken up all the time we might have used to scamper north. Jarrahili fleet's manned by cunts like them," he motioned at the brothers. "They're worth their weight in shit. Can't row, can't fight. Bunch of loafers who wouldn't be able to trade past the river if the Amposi hadn't taken to their lovely port—brilliant place for it, that. When I heard Jarrahil, even before I turned I had no concern for which way we went, and I'd happily wet me ram for the good captain if he asked it. But me luck was with me, and I got a brief glimpse that spared me the slobberin' report of the dumb cunt mate.

"While it's not beyond conception that the King of Jarrahil might have sat three ships a few days south to check that clever bastards such as ourselves had not rearranged our plans, somethin' did not sit with me. It's an odd lot, but it weren't that. I've seen fleets cobbled from worse. But those ships, in that place…" He squinted in frustration. "For a moment, in me confusion, I was prepared to take up oar again. But then I looked at these three little cunts. Three brothers, or close enough to it, of very questionable bloodlines. And I thought, what a sight! These cunts on a ship. They'll never last, of course. All dead by winter, my guess. Just have a go at them. Seen plenty like 'em in my travels—but never on a ship. There's nothin' about them that belongs here, in this place, and so it made me wonder why the fates wove 'em our way. Then I decided I didn't care, but that in turn made me wonder about our companions over there. And I knew not what to make of 'em. Glad I gave pause, or we'd be rowin' to our deaths."

"And you've got little enough tact to make me ask. If this isn't the best explanation I've ever heard for mutinous behavior, we'll be parsin' your share soon enough. I haven't got time for dissent, cunt. Out with it! Or take it for a swim."

"Ah, come off it! Let me have me moment. I've never had the opportunity to save the lives of every man aboard me ship. Probably won't again. I ask no thanks for me heroism. Only to enjoy the moment I see your dumb faces turn when they realize what a clever cunt stands before you, and just how close you were—"

"*Out!*"

"What makes you think it's Jarrahil?"

"Standardship's out of Jarrahil, and who else waits three days out of Jarrahil to hail?" The first mate offered in defense.

"Aye, that's the look of it. You're right about one thing, and only one: the ship in the middle is Jarrahili. Whether she bears the admiral's standard, we shall see. I can tell you that Jarrahil runs a square rig, though, and that's a claw."

"It's so they can chase close to the wind if we run," the mate sneered.

"I know what it's for, and that the Jarrahili Navy would propel themselves by pole if they could reach the bottom. They don't run claws, and barely sail accordin' to the loosest meanin' of the word."

"The claw comes from Ampos. If they can get an abiama, why can't they get a sail?"

"Enough of your riddles, Gionn. Tell me who sits before me," the captain demanded.

"Pone."

There were a few chuckles of disbelief, and twisted brows trying to put it together.

"Pone. You think the Ponic navy sits off a hostile port, with captured vessels from two enemy kings, wavin' to those who go by?"

"No, I think Pone sits with two of their own, and one Jarrahili bob that they couldn't stand, not even for the purposes of deception, so they re-rigged it. Our most-benefic mate says that's an abiama of Ampos. Bet me share he don't know where the Amposi stole the design. The one-and-a-halfer was born in the yards of Pone when she was a fair power, and much copied up the coast once the advantages were known. You might wonder why she fell out of favor, and she didn't. There were few enough warships of any kind built in Pone for better'n a hundred years after the fleet took their leave at Gessimala, but never did they stop producin' some version of the abiama, which is called the 'adhu' by their wrights for the same reason. Again, you'll note the claw, which the Amposi, at half-sense, rig about half the time, though it's the only sail in Pone. If the adhu escaped your attention it's because for quite some time it's been confined to the local waters due to lack of gold and good timber, both of which are beginning to trickle back south. But I assure you, she never ceased to sail.

"What marks the adhu from the claw-rigged abiama is really one thing: a deeper keel. If it can't sail close to the wind, it's useless in those waters, and none on the sea is faster into a blow. See how still she sits? Hard to make, but I would except an abiama to pitch just a cock-hair's breadth more. Aye, if we ran, that one would have us thrice over. But I wouldn't be surprised if she was second to reach us."

"What, the Mabhani?" The mate scoffed.

"There's your standardship, hidin' in plain sight."

"The *Mabhani?*"

"Once more, I'll admit she has the look of the new sort comin' out of Mabhan's murky ship-hole. Have you seen them, yet? They're actually quite good, contrary to all expectation. Sturdy cunts. It's said a ram finds them as appealin' to penetrate as a squain whore, and they're fast-enough before the wind. The bane of Ampos, or they would be if there were anyone to crew 'em. When your land is a filthy assortment of lazy, bark-skinned—actually, eh, before I go on, there wouldn't happen to be anyone from Mabhan on this ship, would there?"

"I am from Mabhan," a dark man behind him said.

"Ah! Perfect example! Lazy, bark-skinned river draggers—flat-footed howlers like this one—well, what can you ask?

"Regardless, they can run close-hauled well-enough, and they're a pleasure under oar. The fore and aft decks are shortened and the bulwarks raised to sate their preference for archers and their utter terror of bein' boarded. 'I thought Mabhan devised the raft to improve the seaworthiness of her navy,' I can hear you thinkin'. 'How did such a competent vessel find it's way out of their shipyards?' Because they didn't build it! King Watirochtep hired, at great expense, the finest shipbuilder in Pone—a man named Ughocha—to pump a load of vigor into his whimperin' fleet, and that he did. For all Ampos' efforts to take ports and molest trade, they could have done the thing in a stroke had they sunk whatever ship carried Ughocha to Mabhan."

"You think they captured one from Mabhan and Jarrahil each, then?" The captain sounded skeptical.

"No. That's not one of Ughocha's. My guess is some crisp apprentice of his, working back home in Pone. It lacks somethin' of the grace you'd see were it from Ughocha's own hand, yet I dare say it's a better ship. Mabhani sailors haven't the same skill. They would have forced concessions of the master builder to suit their capabilities. That's why you don't see the high bulwarks. My guess is there's plenty of deck, too. Pone loves a good boarding fight. But see the way she sits?" Gionn pointed at the ship closest to the coast, turned nearly broadside to them, as if begging a ram. "The mast hardly moves. Flip her over and you'll find a good deep keel, like all of 'em would have had if the Mabhani could tie a knot. Might be the most beautiful warship I've seen, if only because it's virtues lie just beneath the vulgar eye. *That*, me cunts, is where you'll find the admiral and his standard.

"They are at this moment praying to every god they know that we try to ram them. Man for man, there's no better rowers and sailors in all the kingdom, even if there are few enough. Their least-disciplined slob of a bucket will row any man aboard this ship to his death, and me twice. Them thrice," he pointed at the little lads. "They're smaller, tighter on the turn as Olred said, and vastly better crewed. We'll have a ram in each side before we get out pants down. And if we run, two'll catch us and turn circles til the third arrives. I don't know any of you lads. Never seen you fight. But I know enough of how that lot does that I don't care to do it short forty or fifty hands."

He could barely contain his smile as he watched the doubt spread over the faces of the crew.

"If it's Pone, why would they bother hailin' ships out of Jarrahil?" Guil challenged, though Gionn could tell he was only giving permission to finish convincing him.

"Because they fuckin' hate Ampos, and Jarrahil by extension. An honest ship of those waters that hails will be slaughtered and scuttled. A dishonest bastard who runs will not be wanted in Ponic waters anyway, and they'll find the same treatment. They know we come out of Jarrahil. The only way through is to hail of a neutral. The admiralty letter lists us for a merchant. They don't have bead cunts in Pone."

The crew launched in a flurry of argument—hardly short of a panic. It took both mates to shout them down so the captain could be heard.

"Even if that's true, we're empty. Headin' south."

"Aye, I agree. It's a bad look."

"It's a look that'll get us killed just the same."

"Forgive me delay, captain. That's why it took me so long to speak up. Come with answers, they say. Not questions. I asked meself what by the limp spear of Hadalis have we got to pass as cargo? We're a cog with a ram. A load of timber would look fine, long as it's not Hiade-bound, but better yet a barc close on our heels. Then I thought we could claim to be a hire of hardy men from some sea king, sent to retrieve his daughter he married to some cunt down that way, or in possession of a very important message that they could not have a look at. But wouldn't that be convenient? Problem with those kind of tales are there's no way to call 'em false. I've never heard a truth that fit. There has to be just enough that don't make sense. Just enough of a surprise," he pinched his fingers an inch apart. "Part conviction and part calamity. I asked meself, what about us just don't fit? What don't fit with the the truth, or the one we want them to believe?"

Gionn stared down the three plains lads. "Here, captain, is our charge. Three fair princes of Begere. Look at those lovely eyes, not a wappa brown among 'em. Did any of you men know that shortly before we sailed, King Ekti-Pamanau of Begere learned that his cunt brother Outri had just sailed from exile in Lanoas with more than a beggar's fleet, intent on taking the standard? That the king sent his three young sons, disguised as sea hands, in the charge of their illustrious tutor, appropriately unarmed, in a hired cog bound for Hiade, where they shall wait word that the false claim has been sunk?"

"Who, them?" The officers laughed.

"Aye, them. Just look at that sword the oldest has. There's two ways to get a sword like that, and but one to keep it. Does he look like the sort to take it? And if he were a beggar, would he not have lost it by now? Course, we all know there's nothin' short of twenty men waitin' for the chance to get it off him, meself first among 'em, but to the common eye, it doesn't fit the lad at all. Nor an unarmed man as resplendent as meself, able to recite his letters and name every sea king, every builder and his ship."

"Pone hates Ampos. If we're bound for Hiade—"

"All the better. There's no ill between Pone and Begere, and if we were tryin' to shirk our way out, why would we name our intended port as one belongin' to their bitter enemy? It don't fit."

"Then you're prayin' they've heard news of this King Ekti when none of us have, nor could we name him a moment ago."

"I pray nothin', because the only true word of it's the man's name. Don't even know if he's got a brother. Or sons. But neither will anyone from Pone."

"You're mad."

"It would take a madman to hail a fleet from Pone in our situation, and they'll be surprised enough when we greet 'em as such, thinkin' they were so clever to pass as Jarrahili bead cunts. They won't fear Begere, which is why it's a poor choice for a lie—they could kill us all or not. But why anger King Ekti-Pamanau if you needn't do it? They can look us over hide and hair, and every one of us but me and the lads might say our true names, and our fathers' if we know 'em. Those cunts are droolin' on their laps, thinkin' they know just who rows their way. But what they'll find is somethin' halfway between a lie and a truth, and they won't know what to make of it."

The captain held Gionn's eyes in irons. "Any man who thinks it's Pone that waits for us…on your feet!"

Gionn stayed up, while both the first and second mates sat, in case the captain had yet to change his mind. No one moved. It was a clear choice, and here they were twisting their necks like it was a mutiny. Measuring one another, as though the time at-arse and the order in which they stood up were the difference between facing a blade behind or in front. He knew better, and it felt that way even to him. His stomach curdled, and Gionn realized that Guil wanted it that way. The first up would be marked, and the second. A rush of blood stung his face. It was all he could do to remind himself that if he didn't get the numbers, they would be dead soon enough. That kept him upright, and he may have looked more sure than he felt. Eighteen oars swished onward in somber duty.

Idiot cunt, he told himself. *Three days was all you could manage?* That was enough to turn every man against him. He was right, beyond a shadow of suspicion. It was a great kindness he had done them. Spared them, if a man among them had the bollocks to take it. More than that—it was a sacrifice. No one held favor for a smart cunt, not one who made them look a fool. Yet without him, they were all dead men. Ungrateful corpses. Even if every bench rose, he was ruined. The luster of being right and being alive had drawn him to overstep. He loathed every dull, sun-stained face before him. There weren't two wits among them. The ship was wormed through with mongrels and madmen, shirkers and slinkers, slipping under the beams of every bright light in the kingdom to profane the sacred waters. Worse than beggars. They would cut steaks off a dying man if their bellies were full. He was an idiot cunt to appeal to their good sense. There could be none among them. Masters of the one-hand craft. Their sight stopped at the end of an oar. They could serve none but themselves, and they'd no idea how. These loathsome cunts lived all their lives as the man in the tale: awaiting the late arrival of a friend, they turned away Balgan himself from their fire, and it would be to the same fate. He wanted to shake them in his rage until their necks snapped, until their heads fell overboard and reddened the sea.

It would be little surprise if they killed him now. But there would be some small satisfaction in watching the sailors of Pone cut them to bits if he made it that long. Maybe he could jump, and seeing that he shared an enemy, the Ponic arseholes would pluck him from the waves and enlist his help. He could be a first son held at ransom; an unwilling pilot; a tutor! A tutor prisoner, forced by knife to make letters for ill-purpose. His eyes darted to the chest beneath the mast. If only he could get to the right pennant, he could signal. Wave it and jump, and wave it again. It was a shame he hadn't got himself a weapon to cut one on the way off.

Me luck is with me, he repeated to himself in alternation with quiet curses for signing on this merchant of imbeciles. To think he worried he wouldn't qualify! His vision went faint, and he blinked it back. *Can't have that when I jump*, he thought. He leaned his broad thighs against his oar to steady himself without drawing attention. It looked as though the boat spun beneath him again when he saw movement on the port side, but it held its shape, and he was still upright. He found a pair of pale gray eyes, the gray and the glint of steel. Grassbender was on his feet.

Gionn's chest lurched. The captain now wrinkled his wide mouth into a smile. "It's unanimous among the unarmed!" A few of the crew laughed nervously. The lad went around the mad cunt's bench to his brothers and lashed into them in his grass tongue. They tried to ignore him, but he boxed them about the ears until they cowered, whereupon he took the middle one by the forearm and began a tug-of-war to drag him to his feet.

"Let them sit if they would sit," Guil bellowed. The lad turned on the captain without fear.

"He is right! We hail. We hail. He make—his words, he is good. He knows as it is," he struggled. "Please. Wise captain. Please. This man, he is good."

The captain got a good laugh, which only deepened the crease on the lad's brow. "You!" He pointed in the face of Teague. "Up! We hail! You will see he is right." Even Gionn recoiled as he latched on, pressed his entire shoulder into the drooler's back. A hard slap sent him to the deck.

"Fuck you, you fuckin' cunt!" He leapt up to hover over Grassbender. "I don't like it! I don't like it!" Teague turned back around, but seemed to go into one of his stupors. He remained on his feet as Grassbender joined him, out of breath. The Mabhani frowned, then stood with his arms crossed.

Renewed, the child set upon his brothers again. This time, he held off the abuse, and drove them up under the shrill break of his voice.

Splendid, thought Gionn. The worst cunts on the ship sided with him. Now the pair of rowers nearest the bow—a couple of wappas staked under the sharp watch of the mate—set aside their oars and looked for the first time at the three ships. They faced the captain and did not sit back down. A fresh stir came over the deck. One of the two positions with none to their back had committed, as the mates had gone amidship in their stupidity.

"Stand!" Grassbender shouted. "A child can stand. Three childs. Are you men? Stand with Gionn!" The row immediately in front of the wappas stood. The wet benches, they called them. Captain's bane. The fore deck rose like a slow wave. Gionn had to catch himself on the shoulder of the man in front of him when it passed and his knees buckled in quiet jubilation. He held his breath as it reached the captain, and indeed several kept their seats, but enough stood that the numbers were in. There was a hesitation as it reached Olred, and it seemed as if it may wash back, but the salt not only took his feet, he rested one high on his bench and leaned on this leg as though enjoying an idle moment. There was the signal that he was confident it was a casual measure, that weapons would stay in their place, and there was no stopping it as it swept the ship and splashed back, lifting the stragglers on the return to the mast. The captain nodded at the two mates, the last to rise, then he looked at Gionn with a charming grin. He placed a big boot on the nearest seat and stepped up so that he towered over the crew.

"Aye! Prepare to hail!"

The crew erupted in a cheer. Gionn wanted to retreat into his own skin. Hands clapped him on the arm, on the back. He gazed up at the sun, coming on noon and squinted. The ship pitched beneath him, and he returned to deck to find Guil holding court over the celebration—it was as though they had already decided he was right, that all was well. That Pone would stand aside. They loosed their kind words, their praise of wisdom on the captain, and made ready with a new vigor. Somewhere deep, Gionn was sure that Guil, too, was glad it went the way it did. It was not easy, a captain's job. More to consider than just a course. Though he showed a high spirit, Gionn knew the man was wise enough to know they were far from through. He barked men into position with a light charm, as though they had just stood to confirm a share. For his own part, Gionn wasn't even sure he could speak if he tried, and the lads still needed a good tale that he himself didn't yet have. He waved them over, and hesitated. There was no use in thanking Grassbender. It would only build him up. He wasn't sure this was even what he wanted, but his eyes did linger with the little one. And when they turned again and caught the gleam of the captain's smile, he knew it was not gratitude that sent it his way.

Gionn was fucked.

"*Pull…Pull…Pull…*dip yo paddle and *pull…*" Eskimo Joe signaled a halt. Their momentum carried them forward as the hunting boats curled around in a semicircle. Parks turned around on his seat to get a better look, putting him face-to-face with Gionn, glazed over, for once at a loss.

"These men receive us," Joe leaned around Parks to speak to the ginger. Gionn's eyes raised, then he turned in his seat to face the Reverse-Eskimos. There was an awkward silence, and something told Parks he should just keep singing. "Can I hear from the west side?" He pointed at the boat to starboard, and answered himself in falsetto: "*Westside!* Can I hear from the eastside?" He pointed to port. "*Eastside!* In the middle…in the middle…in the middle, yall lookin' at a sight that you never seen / I know what you thinkin' but I must intervene / Eskimo Joe is not a crook / he's a balls-deep native by name of Tunguk / captain of the ship and he mean no harm / we just tryin' to find shelter from the mothafuckin' storm / Gionn on the oars, when shove come to push / he red up top and down in the bush / Foster at the midship, he got a good heart / my lady up front, and my name is Parks." He got blank stares all around. Each of the boats had only two men, better odds than he'd hoped, but all of them looked tougher than saltwater taffy. A paltry handful dead seals lay in one of them. It felt like their eyes were slicing off filets of his flesh. No one on his vessel spoke, and the agony had just about spurned him back into song when one of the men addressed Joe—"Tunguk" was the only word he caught, and Joe repeated it back. He recognized the general sound of some of his uncles' names. The speaker said something else with his eyes on Parks. Joe glanced back, then gave a short response. All of the men burst into laughter. Parks was relieved to know they appreciated his sense of humor.

The conversation went on for several minutes. At one point they consulted Kjartke and she gave a single curt sentence in reply—it seemed to satisfy the question. A few more minutes of negotiating, then the men rowed on in their original direction.

"We cool?" Foster asked.

"They say we may shelter at Yunoc until the storm tires."

"Sweet," Parks said.

"Then we stay, or return to the arm. We may not pass to Nunoc."

"Wait, I'm confused," Foster said. "All these fuckin' names sound the same."

"That's because the fuckin' places are different warts on the same arse-hole," Gionn said.

"I forgot why we were even going to Nunoc or Yunoc or Moonoc to begin with," Parks said.

"Boats," Foster reminded. "They got big boats that can go back north. Accordin' to Tunguk, anyway."

"That's right," he nodded. "And now we're doing what?" Parks knew he should feel crushed, dejected, but he was exhausted. He had a hard time imagining hope, or feeling the stab of despair, in the same way as Foster, who seemed to row to and fro between them. The real oars had a way of taming the extremes that Parks had energy left to feel.

"We're sittin' in this channel til some keel or sidecock comes through, and we're gonna somehow kill every man aboard and raise a crew and go north before it gets dark," Gionn said.

"None will come through."

"They come through here all the time."

"They are being driven past."

"To what?" Foster quipped. "Greater strength?"

"If you are not seen, it is also strength," Kjartke said.

"So we're fucked. We can never go home."

"We will spend the night here. At day they will leave, and we will go on to Nunoc."

"Fuck that," Gionn said. "I'm with One Job. Cunts like us," he seemed to indicate himself and the sailors, "don't winter on Hiade."

"We stay as guests. I have given the whale to the people as a gift. To run, we die before we reach the end of the channel. If we are favored, and we escape, we starve."

There was no escort. It was understood if they tried to pass south they would be killed, and it wouldn't be difficult. Why, Foster did not know. The storm was reason-enough not to make the attempt, though south and only south lay a way back north to the place where home should be, if it still existed. He was there, on a real boat, off a frozen shore, having left out of a real port in the Strait of Magellan, by way of North Carolina as he recalled it. At some point, he crossed a line, fell in a hole, whatever you might call it, to end up…*here.* No telling if it went both ways, but he was damned sure going to find out.

The stone clouds came over them and brought a dusk that seemed to be the true face of the continent—not that everlasting sun. Nothing fell from them. Nothing that reached them, anyway. But the scream of the wind over the peaks and the cold that dropped into the channel told him that even in the miracle of this sheltered position, he couldn't rest. The waters chopped from some distant disturbance that snaked its way behind the island, and the oars struggled for purchase. The gale buffeted the island and stripped wide rivers of snow from the peaks, sent them racing overhead toward the mainland at a speed that would've polished their skin to a red shine had they not ducked into the shadow of Yunoc.

There didn't seem to be anywhere to "pull over." The peaks butted right up to the water, as jagged as monstrous waves frozen in time. Foster's good hand tested the weight of the short sword. He didn't want a fight, nor expect one as long as they did what the men asked. Still, Gionn's determined insistence that this was no place to spend the next six months freezing your pale white balls off made a good bit of sense to him aside from his impatience to either find his way back, or know that it could never happen. He hadn't trusted the throat-cutter with a weapon since they'd left. Good as Foster was in a scrap, though, he knew there was more to a sword than swinging it like a sharp stick, and he wasn't liable to figure it out in the heat of the moment. Tunguk wouldn't let them come to harm. If for any reason, it became more desirable to leave than linger in Tunguk's protection, he decided he would arm Gionn. The ginger wasn't as predictable as Oduy had insisted, but Foster could at least trust him to want to leave, and do whatever was in his interest to facilitate it.

The bow skipped and slapped through the turmoil, hugging close to the shadow of the island. Tunguk seemed to know exactly where they were going. He never scanned desperately for somewhere to land the way the Englishmen did, as Foster had come to think of lighter-skinned speakers of his native tongue. Even blind Parks squinted as if he could squeeze a resting spot from the sharp folds of the mountain. It was Tunguk's ship again. His own charge had been short—successful, in his opinion. But he didn't know anything. Not where they were, how the storm would act, the best way to orient the boat to the changing patterns of water—he reckoned if he could even row it would look like one of the spoiled kids in his bunk trying to operate a broom for the first time. Shit would get swept, at the cost of his dignity. Every time he fumbled with a line or didn't seem to understand why they needed to do something a certain way, Gionn was beside himself with irritation. He was convinced that Parks' and Foster's tale of experience on massive ships was akin to some virgin kid talking about how many women he's had. Living on an aircraft carrier, even when you spend time on the flight deck, had taught him less than nothing about boats. The fact that the deck was for flights and not every other kind of deck activity was telling. The Antarctic boat he worked on for all of a few weeks had filled in some gaps, but little of it applied to bone and leather driven by human arms. Meanwhile, Tunguk treated Kjartke as though she were lucky to benefit from the kindness and skill of the men who gave her passage, lucky enough to forfeit her rights to ask for any additional consideration whatsoever.

She knew a hundred times more about this world than Foster did.

"Wigwam!" Parks called. This time he really saw it. Foster reminded himself to stop drifting off into thought so that the lookout was the last to see anything. The corner of a black hut poked out from a little inlet, and disappeared as the rock took an angle on them. Tunguk directed them to turn. What looked like a wall was, in fact, a tall projection—a narrow mouth several hundred yards across opened up into something too small to be called a bay. The little hide structure perched like a sentinel on the point. It didn't look like a very comfortable place to hang out. A young man came into view on the backside, swinging his arms in a particular pattern as he faced into the cove. Tunguk steered a wide right to put him off their starboard.

As soon as they cleared the the gate, the land erupted with life. The seal-skin wigwams dotted every spare foot of ground in a half moon that sloped quickly to the heights of the island that shielded them from the gale. There wasn't much flat. Most of the little huts were set on slopes as far up as practicality would allow. Nearby, a dozen hunting boats and as many kayaks were hauled ashore and lashed together against the lift of the wind. It was exponentially calmer here, though still strong enough to turn the fleet into an airborne raft had it not been anchored with heavy rocks on all sides. The edge facing the mouth of the little bay—the most likely entry point for the wind—was guarded by draping skins over the front of the canoes and setting large stones on them to prevent it from getting under the hulls and tearing them free of their rigging. It took a second for Foster to recognize the shapes as sails.

Dwellings still rolled into view to port as they cut inside. At once, in the most-protected area, three massive outriggers rose from the surface like giant spiders, over 100 feet long. They were perfectly symmetrical bow to stern, so that he couldn't even tell which way they faced. A tall, bare mast rose from smack dab in the middle of the deck. The sides of the hulls were dotted at intervals of a few feet with little round openings, shut tight from the inside—each a home for an oar. They lay at anchor a few football fields from the wigwams, and he could see men milling on the decks, though they appeared to be more on-watch than at-work.

Foster estimated half-a-hundred wigwams in what looked like a camp that had been up for a minute and not expecting to move soon. The six boats they'd followed were already being hauled in, and they made for the same point.

"*Fucker,*" Gionn whispered over his shoulder. "*Don't say 'squain.*"

"What is this?" Foster said loud enough for all to hear.

"Nothin' good and proper, I'll tell you that. Too many—of their people —in one place. And coal ships. Correct me, wise captain, but aren't your lot banned from crewing any deep water vessels except under the tight supervision of officers of the kingdom? I don't see any alabaster skin."

"We forget our manners. Please take our apology to the farri." Tunguk laughed alone at his own joke.

Parks and Foster watched from shore as men in kayaks surgically dissected and removed their cargo like a line of ants. The boat was incredibly light unladen, but with the fragile leather hull, it was both too heavy and too risky to haul out until it was empty.

No one took their weapons, no one even spoke to them. The sliver of wind that made it into the bay chilled them and sent flurries of detritus and snow spinning in eddies. None of the precipitation came from the thick cloud cover. It was swept off the mountains above or the ground below and redeposited in their faces. Parks blinked hard as another shard of ice slapped his eyeball.

"'Scuse me fellas," he raised his voice to the men unloading. "Can I trouble you for the use of a wigwam, so my amigo and I can get a bit of a respite?" They ignored him. He looked around but couldn't find where Tunguk and Kjartke had disappeared to. A blur twice as thick as any Mattaka told him that Gionn was squatting for a shit. Someone yelled at him and flapped his arms—probably he wasn't supposed to drop a deuce in that particular spot. He gave a dismissive wave and kept shitting.

Parks craned his neck at the high walls that surrounded them. He felt secreted away from all the world. Like a kid crouched inside a fort he built of blankets, couch cushions, and dining room chairs. The outside seemed to ripple around and over them. And within it all, he and Foster stood as a version in miniature, safe and unseen. Miserable as he was, he could not peel himself away from the men at work on their little vessel. The ice swirled around him as though a great hand shook his little snow globe. A perfect little scene. More people than he thought he would ever find in one place again. The biggest boats since his tumble overboard. And though most of them were tucked away from the descending storm, a bustle of activity rubbed together like hands on a frigid day. A glance at Foster's face revealed his companion didn't find it quite as magical. His red nose leaked into his thriving mustache, but it seemed like something else drew his brow into tight lines. They stood for some time without speaking. The entire place defied comment. All he could do was watch it move, anchored to Foster the way the boats huddled against the wind for something familiar that could hold them still.

A cat's paw swiped across the water in their direction from the channel-side wall, and reached them as a bitter wind—a hole slipped in their impenetrable fortress. It was bound to have found them eventually. They turned their backs to it and watched the men in the kayaks scramble for a hold as they were blown like leaves.

Parks looked the other way at the huts and shivered. "Might just have to pick one and barge in."

"I don't know what these people consider rude, but I do remember ol' Tunguk's reaction when he thought our greeting was some kind of insult."

"Doubt *he'll* be too concerned about that," they watched as Gionn marched toward the little village instead of rejoining his companions.

"Good. If he don't get killed, we'll just go wherever he goes." They left the men to wrangle their boat and headed for the camp.

A handful of people moved between the dwellings, all with a sense of purpose. A group three generations thick filed like ants with a wigwam parceled out and loaded on their shoulders in pieces just the like ones they helped the people move when they first landed. His crew were the only recent arrivals. These must have been relocating campsites—from where to where, and why, he had no clue. Two of the younger children held long, straight bundles that had to be a fierce set of hunting weapons, and a little girl dragged a big bag like the one Kjartke used to carry her sewing. Last was a teenage boy, two big whale ribs strapped to his back, and a large whaleskin bladder bear-hugged to his chest. Parks wondered if every sip these people took their entire lives had the flavor of decomposing flesh. He envied Gionn's little genie bottle.

They stopped to let the procession pass along the perimeter of the camp. If you couldn't carry it in one trip, it wasn't yours, he grimaced at the sight. No fires burned, no light, no smoke, nor had he seen one since he found Foster on the beach. Not a scrap of wood, either, except the hulls, masts, and oars of the three big ships at anchor. He wondered for a moment where they got it. Even this warmer-than-expected climate hadn't produced a single tree as far as he'd seen. Just a few desperate animals, and whatever they could make from each others' corpses.

Gionn wove in and out of the haphazard arrangement ahead of them. All the door flaps faced roughly the same direction—toward the towering masts—and that was the end of rhyme and reason. There was hardly enough room to walk single file between them, and no one bothered to arrange the wigwams into neat lines and lanes. Often, they had to step over the corners of two dwellings that overlapped at the stone that anchored them. Where they lacked stones, the frames were guyed to one another. He imagined that if your neighbors two doors down were thumping the headboard, you could follow the particulars in the flap of the wall.

The greasy red crown appeared and disappeared ahead as the variable height of the structures allowed. It was a good thing there was no fire here, because escaping from the center in a blaze over guy ropes and terrified Eskimos would have been a nightmare. Despite the cold, the smell of close packed leather, well-seasoned, hit from all sides. It felt like they were crawling over the bumpy back of a sleeping giant, his loose flesh rippling in the breeze. His toe snagged a line, and his shoulder fell into a rib. The wall sagged and for a terrifying moment, the entire shape twisted and deformed, then sprung back as he righted himself. Parks hurried on. The wind had effectively dried his upper third, but he felt the familiar dampening of the dark reaches within his pants. The wigwams radiated their own heat between them, so that it was a good twenty degrees warmer at his crotch.

He dipped a finger into his sleeve and scratched loose the last of the chilly whale fat, and smeared it on his fissured lips. Did Eskimo Joe give away their fat stash, too? He said "food," and it technically was a personal hygiene product the way he was using it. Or was it "whale"? *Fuck*, Parks thought. Did Reverse-Eskimos chap? Had to. All men did. But if the remedy was foreign to them, he could do quite a business in this weather if he could get his hands on a good stash.

They closed distance as Gionn stopped to consider one of the wigwams. He threw back the flap and disappeared inside.

"Yo! Knock knock." Parks tapped the skin with his knuckles. Foster knelt and lifted the corner to peer under.

"In or out, cunt! Stop lettin' the wind have it!"

The darkness was near total. The top hole had been covered by a tied-on patch that flapped and inflated but limited the air to a cold draft. Parks tied the entrance behind him. "Gionn?"

"Aye, Brother Parks. Fucker," came the voice out of the shadows. "Welcome to me quarters."

"Hello? Is anyone here?" Foster called.

"I just told you I'm here, dumb cunt."

"I meant anyone *else*."

"These ones are on watch at the ships. Flap was tied from the outside."

"Are you sure?"

"Well, no one screamed 'takka-takka' at me when I came in. And there's no rubbish on the ground. Squains never leave good rubbish behind when they're just off for a piss."

"These people don't believe in light, do they?"

"I don't even know if my eyelids are open," Parks complained.

"What, do you not enjoy sittin' in the dark with nothin' to do in a hellish wasteland during a massive storm? If you want to share a wank, I'll never know so long as you don't whimper too much. Go ahead, arse-cunts, if you don't do it now, you will soon enough. This is midsummer. Come winter the only glimmer of light you'll get is when the weather unfucks itself long enough for the moon to peek out. Then you can freeze your fingers off watching the green ladies dance. Meanwhile the ice creeps down farther every day. It don't rain much, which is good, but every time the wind blows the salt spray turns to snow and whips you like a mess thief. Care to guess how often the wind blows? Soon you'll be walkin' on it, sleepin' on it, cuttin' it loose just to get out the door. Welcome to Hiade."

They heard a gurgle, followed by something that sounded half like spit and half like vomit. Gionn fell into a tremendous coughing fit. Foster burst into laughter. Gionn composed himself between hacks to let out a staccato string of expletives. Metal bounced somewhere near Foster and skittered across the floor, stopping at Parks foot. He picked it up and recognized the feel of the fancy perfume bottle. A quick sniff and a nip of what was left clued him in as to who must've filled Gionn full of salt. He joined in the chorus of laughter.

"Fuck you cunts, I'll drown us all. Cut a hole in the boat while you sleep," he choked. "Guard your water skins, you black-bottomed buckets. Guard 'em day and night, for the rest of your miserable lives, or you'll taste a potion of spunk and blood and poison, and the foulest crust of a dead man's arsehole, scraped and saved for the moment your eyes dim. Every time you part your lips from this day forward, let it devil you that this may be Gionn's sip." He paused while they cackled. "Meantime, we might just get along."

When they were done heaving, Parks curled up and heard the others do the same. The wind dragged the bank of huts like a spoon across a washboard, rolling every corner and frayed end, and pounding the parts pulled tight like the skin of a drum. None of it stopped him from falling asleep out of sheer exhaustion. His dreams were strange, as if they were projected onto the black walls of the hut instead of pulling him into their own world. He couldn't remember any of it, but he knew that nothing was familiar, and he was unable to find anything from the past. No tool or trapping of civilization, not an old friend, or a memory, or even Foster. When he woke, shivering on the cold rock, he was sure he'd slept for days. The ceiling of the little wigwam could have been a foot overhead or as far as the night sky—he had no sense of space, and no light found him. The wind settled to a steady thump. He instinctively reached for his water bladder and found it tied to his belt as he'd left it.

"Yo. Foster," he whispered sharply. "You awake?' No response. He repeated the name a few times, the volume rising.

"Shut the fuck up," Gionn moaned.

"Is Foster here?"

"How should I know?"

Parks couldn't remember where the door was, but he remembered that Gionn's voice was straight across from him, and Foster to his left. He felt for the wall, and crawled along the edge. Pain shot through his gashed leg. His knees swelled from all the cramped sitting, the sleeping on hard surfaces. It was always cold, now. Whether he woke wet at sea, or damp in a shelter. Always he shivered, no fire to warm him. And it was impossible to wear all of his layers in anything but a full blizzard without drenching himself in sweat. He thumped around the edge until his hand hit something. A leather tunic.

"Are you tackin' for a cuddle, arse-cunt?" Gionn snapped.

"Sorry, bro." He retreated along the wall, and encountered no one. Partway back, along a spot he'd passed before, he noticed a seam. His fingers found strap, and untied the opening. Gray light tumbled in, dim but blinding for a moment. He closed his eyes so they could adjust and plunged out. Nothing but wigwams. Tiny flecks of ice skipped across the maze of huts. A fresh dusting. He stood to see over the tops. It was as as blurry as always, and the sting of the wind and the snow made him squint. Which way had they come from? Parks had no idea, and it wouldn't have told him where Foster went. He scanned for movement, for people, but no one seemed to be out and about. Missing out on such a gorgeous day, he thought as he tried to draw his arms into his tunic. The parka was entirely too hot inside, and since not even the smallest of little girls wore one out here, he left it with Gionn out of shame. Did these people even feel cold? Chances are they just didn't give a fuck, same as they didn't give a fuck about blankets or hot meals or personal space.

The masts of the three ships tottered above the huts in the bay. It was the only thing he could recognize, so he stumbled in that direction. The rocks securing the wigwam walls constantly nipped at his toes and heels. Parks imagined the elders of the clans gathered around a big fire, listening to him teach them the ways of straight lanes between buildings—hell, proper buildings— clothing, tools. He'd invent the backpack to carry things, none of these hobo bindles. And the compass. They listened in awe as he single-handedly drug them by the scruff out of the Stone Age, and showered him with their whiskey, which he taught them to distill, and with their daughters. If he was going to stay here, he'd have to do something for work, and a cushy consulting gig on dry fucking land sounded right about his speed. King Parks, noble regent of whatever they called this place. All of the words these people used sounded like clucking to him. What had Gionn called it, "takka-takka"?

There was Foster, clear of all of the dwellings, shoulders hunched on the shore. He couldn't make out any features, but he'd never seen any of the Reverse-Eskimos huddle against the cold. The winds careening over and around the wigwams joined forces as soon as he was clear, and physically shoved him forward several steps before he leaned back into them and got his balance. It hit him that the random layout, while a bitch to walk through, broke the main force back on itself and drove it up so that it shook the perimeter and little more.

Overhead, it must have been gusting at gale force. The main drift from the peaks raced hundreds of feet above, while little bits separated themselves from the stream and fluttered to earth, making it feel almost calm in the gusts at ground level. His broad back acted like a sail, his feet barely tapping the ground he had to make between him and his friend.

It wasn't hard to follow Foster's eyes. Unsure of what to say, he elected to make up a song until someone else did something. "Three big ships in the harbor / Three big ships in the sea / One's goin' near, one's goin' far / one's a-comin' to get you and me."

"Coal."

"Hm?"

"That's what Gionn called 'em. Coal ships."

"A fine American resource. Keeps the furnace hot, keeps the lights on…hell, it'll even get you where you're going a lot faster than these guys," he flexed his biceps and quickly recrossed his arms. "Pearls before swine, here."

"I don't guess you know how to build a steam engine out of thigh bones and seal pelts."

"Buddy, you put me in the right machine shop, I'll Wright-Brothers you a motherfucking airplane out of foreskin."

Foster grinned. "You change tires on helicopters."

"Also one of my many talents."

"What are we doin' here?"

"You tell me, I was fine in the wigwam," he rubbed warmth into his arms.

"You know what I mean. *Here,* here."

Parks nodded. "Far as I can tell, spending the next six months or so not letting our standards for what counts as bangable dip as low as the temperature."

"Here," Foster said. "Whatever they call the place that this place is in."

"You can't remember either, huh?"

"I remember where we came from."

"Pretty sick, wasn't it?" He watched the decks pitch and thought of the men who must be dealing with the same weather on a tossing surface. "Stuff to do. Cool people. Easy."

"You wanna go back, right?"

"Oh, I want to."

"We haven't even talked about it in weeks."

"I don't know. I never feel right bringing it up in front of the murderers we hang out with."

A smile crossed Foster's face. "Let's agree now, no matter what happens, I never murder you, and you never murder me."

"Even if there's a woman involved."

"Especially, then."

"What's on your mind?"

"What's on my mind is you act like this is it. Me, I'm plottin' and schemin' all day to get us any hope of a chance to make it back north to maybe figure out a way we don't gotta be penguin-pokers the rest of our lives. I'm not seein' the same sense of urgency out of you."

"Urgency to do what? Say we get a boat north. Then what?"

"I don't know," Foster shrugged. "We see when we get there."

"That the whole plan?"

"More of a plan'n you got."

"You know, it's not that I *want* to freeze to death in the dark. It's more like, I don't really see another possibility."

"Maybe not yet, but even if all we got is a sliver of a slim chance, soon as we stop tryin' we got none. I got to keep movin' and hopin'. I got to keep busy, or I'll lose my mind."

"Try rowing," Parks suggested.

"I got me a better idea."

All the wigwams looked the same, and they interrupted a couple of groups of Mattaka who cussed them back outside in the king's English before Gionn's "fuck off" told them they'd found the right one.

"Wake up, you Irish faggot," Parks bellowed. "Me and Foster have a proposition."

"No to your proposition. What's 'Irish,' is it a terrible thing? I'll have to remember that one."

"You're gonna like it," Foster said.

"Why, does it involve elevatin' me own lot through various kinds of scumbaggery?"

"It involves gettin' your ass off this island."

They heard him sit up. "Cunt, before anymore words roll off your cock-polished tongue, I will point out that it's quite dark, and lazy or conniving natives may have snuck amongst us while I slept."

"Uh. Hello? Anyone there?" Parks called.

"Don't be a drip. Feel around."

"Hang on, we need a system. So they don't slip by us. Gionn, follow my voice and meet me at the wall. We'll go opposite ways til we meet again. Parks, you lay down in the middle, and kinda just fling your arms and legs around so nobody can pass without you touchin'."

"Like a snow angel?"

"Up in the air, like a bug on its back."

"I see your madness." Gionn headed for the sound. Parks crawled on tender knees to what he imagined was about the middle of the circle, and lay down. He half-heartedly flung his arms and legs in the air, imagining some sneaky Reverse-Eskimo trying to hop over him to avoid the others. "Marco!" He called. No one answered. "Marco!"

"Is that you, cunt?"

"Yeah," Foster answered. "Parks, you clear?"

"Polo-free."

"Keep your voices down. These are skin walls. I could hear you comin' even over the wind," Gionn scolded.

"We need your help," Foster almost whispered.

"Is this a proposition or a favor?"

"It's a plan that requires all of our combined expertise."

"Sounds like a shit plan."

"What's the one thing we all want?"

"To be respected by our peers," Parks guessed.

"To go home. We're rowin' to that other island hopin' to catch a boat rowin' back the way we came, back up north, and these fools want us to spend the winter here, instead. Ask yourself, why do we need to wait half a year, then get back on the water in that dinghy and hope we don't capsize so we can maybe find a seaworthy vessel willing to take us?"

"Oh, gods. No."

"There's three good ships sittin' right outside our front door."

"No." Gionn repeated.

"And we're gonna steal one."

10

THIEVES

"No."

"You're the one tellin' us how shitty it is to spend the winter here," Foster countered.

The wind trotted over the tops of the wigwams, snapping the thick hides at intervals. Gionn waited for the gust subside to avoid raising his voice.

"Aye, the winter's shit, but I now know beyond a fathom what I have long suspected: that you two tramps are lyin' your arses off about having ever sailed anything but a litter. Perhaps you rode here on one, full of hardworkin' salt-swillers. Perhaps you managed to fall off. Or had some help. But sailors, you lot aren't."

"Are you tellin' me the same man who faced down a posse of armed killers for no reason but the principle of loyalty to a friend, whose throat he later cut, is now opposed committin' theft against a bunch of strangers?"

"How dare you, cunt. I'm not opposed to thievin'. I'm opposed to dyin' in the effort."

Foster adjusted the hilt of the blade that hung from his waist so that it didn't prod his thigh. It was his Siamese twin ever since they took the bastard aboard, little as he wanted it. A reminder to both men that however they might treat one another, Gionn was still a prisoner. One whose interests weren't as precisely aligned as he hoped. An escape attempt seemed unlikely, but captivity didn't mean cooperation. Not when the man could simply stand back and allow his keepers to get themselves killed.

"They're lightly guarded," Parks said. "A few dudes sleeping on the deck at best. If we can get over there in one of those dinghies, we catch 'em by surprise and put 'em over in the boat we came in without hurting a long black hair on anyone's head."

"Dumb cunts," Gionn laughed. "Those are sixty oar vessels with big fuckin' masts and sails that'll capsize you in a storm even if you know what you're doin' and do it a moment too slow. Besides the rowers, those rigs probably take a crew of a dozen sailors, split between the two watches. Then there's a captain, and at least two mates, though I would say more, a

282

drummer, and a coxswain. I'll allow you do without that last cunt, and the crew works the sails when they don't row. Let's just pretend they know how. The bare minimum to get her out the bay, down the channel, and into the winds is twenty good strong pullers. Then you're prayin' to whichever is your sea god every time you shunt across the wind, passin' through the worst seas in the world in a race to beat the Autumn gales. Speakin' of which, can you organize a proper shunt? Never done it meself. I understand the gist, of course, but I'd not trust meself to call the ropes.

"By me count, there's three of us, and only one who knows his paces. You're lookin' to convince nineteen squains to help you steal their own ship and take you to a part of the world where their kind don't go. Where they're like to be executed upon arrival for thievin' and crossin' open waters. And as soon as we pull the third stroke everyone knows the ship's movin', and a proper number of arms heads to the other two, overtakes us and boards before we're halfway out the channel. You know what squains do to enemies captured in war? They cut out your jawbone while you live, so's when you go to their land of the dead, you're without speech to negotiate passage to your next life, and you're known to their ancestors, who hunt you all your days and nights."

"Solid points," Parks said. "Foster, your rebuttal?"

"I don't hear a better plan outta you."

"I don't make plans. Not very good at it." Gionn insisted.

The flap peeled back and voices screamed in Mattakatan. "Get the fuck out of our tukit," one switched to an English not as accented as Foster expected. The men crawled out to face a trio of natives carrying their bindles. The weather greeted them with a gust.

"It's fuckin' windy, mate, and we are your guests."

"Not *my* guests."

Foster looked them over. They didn't seem properly dressed, and carried no weapons. Nothing at all, but water bladders and one parcel wrapped in leather that must have been a ration of whale.

"Chill, brother. We're goin'. Where do you want us to set?" He pushed past Foster without a response.

Gionn caught the arm of the last man. "What is that black shit all over you?" The men's face, hands, and clothing were all smudged.

He laughed in contempt. "You don't know firestone?"

"Coal?"

"As you call it."

"On watch, then? Do you need us to relieve you?"

"We have been relieved." He followed the others in.

Foster furrowed his brow. Gionn indicated with his head for them to follow. He led the sailors the way they'd come originally, clear of the—what had he called it? Tikuts? He wasn't even sure how to pluralize the word, or if it needed that. They crossed the open rock to the raft of upturned boats, their own lost somewhere in that mix. Gionn chose the leeward side and plopped down against a hull and slumped so that no part of him protruded above into the wind. The others did the same.

"That's interesting," he said.

"What is?" Asked Parks.

"It's coal on board."

"I thought we knew that. You called 'em coal ships before," Foster reminded him.

"Aye, but coal ships carry coal or coke. Same ships, cunt."

"Coke?" Parks grinned. "Well I'll be a monkey's uncle. I didn't know these boys partied."

"As in, cocaine?" Foster clarified with Gionn.

"I don't know what a cocaine is, but I did say coke is *not* the thing on those ships, which is bloody interesting."

"Surely you don't mean 'a-cola,'" Parks said.

"All of the words you two say confuse me. I'm referrin' to the shit you make from coal that goes in the forges so they burn hot. Must I explain the entire iron trade to you provincials?" Their silence answered that. "It is interesting that they carry coal, and not coke. I don't make plans, but someone who did might find that useful. This whole fuckin' scene is interesting. I don't know what these dregs are up to, but I guarantee you it's highly illegal no matter who you call Farri."

"If you want us provincials to see anything more than a pile-up of Antarctic Eskimos, you're gonna need to explain."

"Fine, cunts. Well, none is this is allowed, innit?"

"Why not?"

"Have you never heard of First Deluge?" He got blank stares. "None of these moaners has tied you to a rock for three days while he sang you the song of Barduk?"

"I think someone tried once," Parks said.

"Fuck's sake. I don't got time for all that, but let me pin up me bollocks and do me best minister of law. Squains cannot assemble in large numbers, except when bidden to do so and overseen by a representative of the farri. Squains cannot possess or pilot oceangoing vessels, except in the previous situation. Squains cannot own or carry weapons in iron or steel, and bronze is only permitted in the previous situation, though squains who crew coal ships may not carry so much as a stone knife. And neither squains nor anyone may steal coal. Since no one sends coal ships to this shithole for any reason, we can guess the nature of its transit. Even scoundrels don't steal coal. Ruins things for the rest of us."

"So why do you reckon they did all that?"

"I'm not done, loud cunt. If you've noticed, these are southern squains, not from the arm like your woman there. We know because they carry coal that they were bound for Nunoc. It's coked there, and most of it never leaves the forges. Only things that come north of Nunoc are forged metals, spare coke, and perhaps some seal pelts and whale bits to ballast the holds. Had they made Nunoc, that would be their cargo. I know only this: those ships left Drummoc under King's Navy, no doubt with regulars on the sails and a complement of Marines to keep order. They are not in Nunoc, and I only see squains."

"And you think that there's a plan in there somewhere."

"Don't know, cunt, I don't make 'em, I just ruin 'em. If you get a good one, don't tell me until the last moment. And even then, only me own part." He scrunched lower and wrapped his arms around his knees.

A gust stampeded over them and rattled the boats. At once, a corner lifted, and the wind snapped the leather bindings like string. Half a dozen peeled free and began somersaulting toward the water. Foster leapt up and ran after them. He folded over from the wind at his back, though it gave him the acceleration he needed to catch the gunwale of a kayak. It shot free from his weak grasp and tore apart on the rocks. Behind him, a crash, and another came free. It spun along its bottom right at him. Foster sidestepped and simultaneously snatched at it, catching the bone. His broken hand lit into him, but he held his grip. The wind slipped inside and lifted both boat and Foster like a kite, several feet off the ground. His legs flailed and came down running. He rolled inside and flattened out to weight it down. The little ship resumed its sliding. Leather ripped beneath him as he headed for the water, no oar, and by now bound to be leaking if not heading straight to the bottom.

It slammed to a stop as if yanked by a tether. Parks' big hands clutched the gunwale, and he collapsed to his side to keep the weight low. By now people were scrambling from the wigwams to wrangle their boats before they were swept into the water, and to secure the raft before anymore got away. A flash of recognition hit him. It must've come a second sooner to Parks.

"Isn't this ours?"

The storm lasted another full day and change before it was possible to get out and inspect the damage. In the meantime, Gionn earned them a shelter of their own by barging in on family after family, demanding hospitality and being run out, until they became enough of a nuisance that a place was found for them at the very back of the windward side of the settlement. It was the wigwam of greatest elevation, meaning the last one the natives could reasonably fit on the steep slope. The rock beneath them tilted at least thirty degrees, and though the cove cradled them from the worst of it, whatever wind they did get rattled their skins with its full fury. None of the Reverse-Eskimos opted to stay with the boys, so this was either a place for honored guests, or the biggest shithole they had.

When at last it lulled, people poured from their dark refuges like bees on a Spring day. The sky still hung dark, and it blew in ragged bursts that were uncomfortably cold, but the chatter of voices drew Parks and Foster out and down to the harbor. Almost every boat seemed to have suffered at least some minor offense at the hand of the storm. Theirs lay splayed open before Tunguk and Kjartke like some rotting autopsy that sent Foster's heart plummeting. One of the ribs lay aside, snapped in two places. Several sections of their hull amidship were shredded for a length of four or five feet, as though some wild beast had got hold of them.

It would have been a fatal wound, but that two other boats went for a hell of a tumble before anyone could get a hand on them. They were deemed beyond repair, and Tunguk managed to secure a replacement rib and several yards of good leather, which he and Kjartke set to stitching and lashing into place.

Parks and Foster watched, as useful in this task as any other.

"Lot more women and kids than I thought," said Foster as he surveyed the people milling about, mending boats, talking, playing. Two young boys sprinted near enough for their legs to feel a slap of breeze. "You know what that means, right?"

Parks squinted. "Potential hostages. It'll have to be a bluff, though. I don't think I can kill a kid. Maybe Gionn can."

"No. Although you do have a point. I'll backpocket that one. No, Gionn said they sailed these big boats here full of coal, so I doubt that they were carryin' anythin' other than hard-ass sailors. These little boats come and met 'em. Families, probably. Friends, tribes, whatever."

"So?"

"So I don't know. I'm just paintin' by numbers here. Seein' what I got."

"Bringing the loot to your homeys is a risky move."

Foster nodded. "This bay ain't just for hidin' from the wind. I'll bet they got lookouts on either end."

"Smoke signals."

"Or somethin'." He looked up behind him at the mountains. They seemed too steep and icy for much foot traffic. "If I can find a way to get one of them boats out the bay that don't involve nineteen Mattaka—and if I reckon on a minimum 20% chance of survival—I'm goin' for it." Parks nodded along. "I know you don't think there's a way out of this. Not out of this bay, or this fuckin'…place, wherever we are."

"Nope. But I agree with you on one thing: it's nice to have a project. I'd rather die stealing a ship with my bud than from boredom in a dark leather cave."

Foster smiled and clapped him on the shoulder. "Attaboy. I'm gonna do some sniffin'."

"And I'm going to use my charm and my statuesque frame to inspire nineteen strapping sailors to join our crew."

Foster spotted a line of men trudging upslope with leather bags. He snatched up the ship's water reservoir and Parks' bladder.

"What're you gonna do?"

"Get me a bird map of this place," he jogged after them.

From the get-go he saw no way up, but fell in line with the Mattaka who had to know he was there, but didn't acknowledge his presence. Every time he thought they were blocked from moving up to the level of the glacial ice, the line bent down a switchback of a couple of inches of rock level-enough for a man's feet, or they clambered up and over a boulder and found the trail. Though "trail" was a generous term. It had not been carved by any human effort. More so a failure of the mountain to consider that a man might still figure out a way to pass here. His heart pounded and he prayed the wind didn't return on the exposed rock, where any little poof might send him tumbling eight hundred feet with no hope of arresting his fall.

They hit the ice line, and poor footing became impassable. Half of their progress required crawling, or scooting backwards on their butts to get enough traction. Foster considered the huge sack he carried, no handles or straps. It was nearly empty and easy enough now, but he wasn't sure how he would reverse this trail down, or even whether it would be full of ice or liquid. Fuck inventing steam engines for these people, he thought. A backpack would be a better start. It wasn't until they dropped their gear at a flat section that he dared to look down.

They were well over a thousand feet above the floor. He still couldn't see over the rocks that blocked the settlement from the channel's view—only the tiny mouth of water that lead to it, and the land on the other side. To either direction, the mountains were shrouded in a low cloud. He had about a quarter-mile in each direction. If there was any signal system in place to warn of ships entering the channel, it was weather-fallible, or didn't involve lookouts up here where the worst of the winds that had sailed over their heads would pummel a man. The calm and the pressure drop felt foreboding, like it wasn't done, but for some reason it was pacing, catching its breath, waiting for them to finish so it could kick back up.

The men were excited to find liquid trickling down. It disappeared behind an outcrop and probably spilled down the steep side, but here it ran, and Foster let them fill up first. He studied the ships from afar, and didn't see anything he couldn't have noticed much closer. How long would this water be water? How long before the only way to drink it would be to melt it? And do it every single time, all winter long? These people made his Appalachian family look wealthy, and he had no desire to fuck them any harder than they were fucked by taking a third of their heat source. If only there was some way to unload it, they could keep their "firestone" and he would have a lighter ship, easier to row, faster to sail—maybe fast enough to outrun one that was loaded down.

It had to come ashore eventually if they were going to use it. Could he volunteer to help ferry it, and take the first ship they emptied? Or would they only remove it as needed, or too late for him to make a run north through the ice fields?

Then there was the nuclear option. If he could get a skeleton crew, they could burn two of the ships as they took the third. No one would catch them in skin boats, or be able to do anything if they did. That would leave them well-stranded and likely to freeze or succumb to hunger. The food situation seemed the worst. He knew they were short, if the little addition of their meat was so welcome. This was the first chance he got to see the group, and it looked like a solid 300 people, give or take. Mostly young men, but a good number of women, children, and old folks. He knew little about their ways, but hunting through winter didn't work much anywhere, let alone this place. If they were like everyone else outside the equator, they would need to lay in food to feed the whole lot for several months by the end of Fall. Anything less than several tons of fat and meat, and it would be 300 corpses that thawed in Spring. The thought made him shiver.

Those boats were enough to get them out to better grounds if things got dire. And they were big enough to carry all the food and fire these people could want. But he reminded himself that he was effectively their prisoner, and owed nothing to no one but Parks and Tunguk. If there were an easier way, he'd take it. Regardless, he planned to winter in North Carolina.

"And you're sure there's nothing I can do to help." Parks sat Indian-style watching Kjartke and Tunguk pass bone needle and wet sinew through skin, and pull it tight with a snap. Nineteen thieving volunteers, he thought. The first two ought to be easy. The Navy had taught him many times, in many ways, to try the easy things first. There were too many Reverse-Eskimos scurrying around to broach the topic openly, so he figured he'd use the time to build a rapport before he pitched the sale.

"Your arms must be getting tired. Not even a shoulder rub?" That woman was a tough oyster to shuck, but Parks knew if he kept pestering, eventually he would get a violent response, from which he could charmingly retreat, and then the lines of communication were open for development.

"I accept," Tunguk said.

Parks grimaced. "I would, but I'm afraid these big strong hands would pull the flesh right off those old bones. No, I was talking to the lady. Shall I take your silence as a yes?" She stopped sewing. Her gaze didn't lift, but the way her fingers tightened on the needle, he decided to reinterpret her silence. "That's cool, no worries. Just to clarify I meant the offer only in the most platonic terms. I know you recently lost your hubs, probably not quite ready to be vulnerable again. I feel you. I've been there. My advice? Take your time, do some things for Kjartke for a change. It's super sweet of you to do all this woman's work for us, but just so you know, I don't see you as stuck in that role by any means. If it helps you grieve, you go for it, girl, but just know that we're all on the same team here. We've all lost somebody. In my case, it was all the somebodies I ever knew. I'm not gonna pretend that wasn't hard. But you know what? Here I am, doing what I can. Same as you, same as everyone. You take your time. Enjoy the single life, whether that's running through a few, or just a really cool sewing project you've been meaning to start.

"I know my boy Klimut probably needed a lot of help, with that one stumpy arm and all, but—" he waved both hands in the air. "I'm good to go. I mean, we do need you to finish up the boat, cause me and Foster have no fucking clue how to do that, but otherwise we're all grown-ass men here. Don't think you have to take care of us. The world was made for men who can have a hand in two places at once. It is—" he searched for the word. "It is our oyster, and we may shuck it. But I feel like the least I can do for a buddy who I served with, in direct combat, who lost his life as a result, is to be kind to his wife. Whatever that means for her. Just, be there for his—"

"War wife," she interrupted. *Score*, he thought. That was all the opening he needed.

"War wife, huh? Sounds pretty bad ass. How does a man go about…*earning* himself a war wife?"

The needle stopped. Her obsidian eyes rose to meet him. "Go to her village. Kill her father. Kill her brothers. Throw her baby in the sea. Take their weapons and their pelts. Break the…*sapak*—" she looked to Tunguk.

"Story shirt."

"Break the story shirt of the family. What you cannot carry, throw also in sea. Then take her home, and make child."

The bone needle moved again, a quick jab through the seam. She flicked her wrist and the thread seated with a snap.

The storm returned, as Foster expected, after a day and a half in which they just had time to stock up on fresh water, repair the boats that had been damaged in the earlier gusts, and lash them down again. Half the rations he received consisted of whale meat that tasted very familiar, along with a glob of some unidentified fat, a slice of blubber, and a dried fish.

He didn't know how long that was supposed to last him, but so far he'd been stuck in a wigwam with Parks and Gionn for three days straight while the wind and the driven ice flurries made standing outside miserable, and sailing impossible. He'd eaten everything but the fat and the blubber, both of which were disgusting. There didn't seem to be anyone coming around with more, and he reckoned that going door-to-door asking for seconds wouldn't be much use.

"Dogshit slope," Gionn rolled over and complained again. Between the stampeding wind and the grade, there wasn't much in the way of sleep. Foster often resorted to cracking the flap and sticking his face out in the elements to bathe in the gray light until his nose froze, or one of the others yelled at him that he was letting the cold in. Otherwise, the wigwam was a cruel experience in sensory deprivation. Nothing to see. Nothing to listen to, but the weather and a pair of voices that dragged even as they tried to raise to be heard. The smell of leather and old farts. It became difficult to tell, in moments of exhaustion and hunger, whether he was asleep or awake. At times, it was the belly of a ship, tossing in a storm, and his seasickness returned. Or he dreamt the snow piling at the door, until the panic of claustrophobia sent him clawing for the opening. A few minutes of the scouring wind was enough to put him in retreat, but it reset him. To know there was still a world outside eased his breath and made him grateful for the stinging cheeks. The others had no such need. Foster reckoned that meant he would be the first go if they spent the winter here.

The hut, at least, was surprisingly warm. Almost stale. But the cold, the noise, the slope, the dogshit slope, colluded to sap his energy until pulling his boots off felt like weightlifting. He was glad for the darkness that spared him from having to see his own withering flesh when he changed clothes.

"Anybody wanna trade lunches? I got fat for fish," Foster called into the blackness.

"All I've got is a piece of blubber that tastes like kerosene. Are we getting resupplied or what?" Parks' voice answered.

"I think we were the resupply."

"You'll be right, fat cunt. Soon as it lifts and a hunting party gets out. Otherwise me and Fucker'll have to eat you raw."

"That last hunting party that led us in didn't hardly have shit between 'em."

"Coal squains are shit hunters."

"So why are they here?" Foster demanded. "I wanna get out and look around. Talk to some folks. But if I'm the only dude wanderin' out in a gale, it's gonna look suspicious." He had never seen another soul in his brief forays, though he hadn't gone far.

"Everything about the two of you is suspicious," Gionn reassured him. "You're tryin' to decipher the squains, and I'm wonderin' who I share a fuckin' tent with. You look well-bred, and you're useless, which means you're probably in charge of useful cunts somewhere, not from any virtues of your own. Good fathers, and good assignments. I'd believe you were Navy—you're shit enough to lose an entire crew and somehow slither away un-harmed—but you know too little even for officers of the farri. No, you're here to look at something, or someone, and report back to someone. You got good maps and no clue how to use 'em. Good heads, and no more fight in you than a couple of rich lads who grew up with sisters. Question is, what are you spyin' on? Squains? Sea Kings? You here to make sure the Viceroy at Nunoc don't lose count on a few things movin' through his port? And what are you worth? Would they come lookin' for you?"

"We're as Nobody as you are," Parks said.

"I'll bet you are. Well anyway, I owe you cunts me life. Which is worth-less to me, so fuck you. Just know that if you have important friends and a profitable trade, I work for very little and require no respect. If you're filthy spies, just remember that my name is Gionn and I have dark hair, very grace-ful features, and a pleasant manner." He rolled over again, found a tolerable position, and was sawing boards in no time.

For two days, Foster disappeared in and out of the wigwam at intervals to sit in the gray light and the gale. Parks joined him once, but it was impos-sible to have a conversation, and the cold gnawed on his bones. His friend would close the flap behind him, huddle around his knees, and sit right in front of the hut, squinting and basking in the ability to see the things around him until he could no longer stand the cold and retreated to shiver it off for the next few hours. The light was nice, but not worth the discomfort to Parks, nor Gionn apparently. For the first time here, he felt lonesome. Not for home, or family, or a woman, but for Eskimo Joe. The old bastard's presence reassured him more than he realized. It was both security and a sense of place. Now he felt like he'd wandered off the tour and fallen in with with a suspect element. Every day, though he didn't know where they started and ended, he expected to see the wrinkled face poke through to check on them. Between Joe's conspicuous absence and Foster's forays into the weather, it was borderline abandonment. He remembered the time his parents lost him for over two hours at the California State Fair. Some massive carnie woman fed him pickles and held him at her booth until he assumed he would just belong to her from then on.

Now Foster had been gone for twice as long as usual. His tolerance to the weather seemed to be building, but it wasn't like to him to be out for more than an hour. The wind had dipped to a murmur, as it did on occasion, and he could hear something other than the flap of leather. Voices. He closed his eyelids tight—the last time had taught him that to pull open the flap, even to the dull gray light after hours of blindness, was the same sensation as stabbing yourself in the eyeballs with a pencil. The backs of his eyelids turned a dim red, and he paused in the entryway to let it filter through for a few minutes. Then a crack, and the grays and blacks and browns of ground and wigwam material bled through in a wet slurry that he blinked down his dry cheeks.

Parks stood, the tallest man in the world, he thought. Over the tops of his neighbors he saw heads bob, many dozens of them. They traded words he couldn't make out and moved through camp at an easy pace. It took him a minute to notice the lack of the windchill that had become his assumption. The sun wasn't out, but it came through the clouds a little more than he remembered. His stomach growled to remind him that he hadn't eaten more than a few sucks of blubber oil. The ground around him smelled of piss. They were supposed to go way from camp, but none of the three men cared to more than poke it out the flap. Lucky they hadn't eaten enough to need to shit.

He slipped and tripped downslope into the camp until the ground leveled out enough, then started left—the direction of the skin boats—before stopping. That way was open space. The memory of Tunguk and Kjartke sewing the hull stung him. He'd retreated without a word, and hadn't seen either since. Parks decided to veer right where the sound of voices was clearest. Watercolor blobs bled into focus as people coming and going from a certain spot. He let a woman and her son pass with a polite wave and caught a whiff of stale meat. The zigzag path over rocks and tent skirting brought him closer to bustle and noise. It was the same method he used to find the best places to spend several months pay on a weekend of shore leave. Where people move in the same direction, or from the point they scatter, that's the money spot.

A hand squeezed his tricep. "Brother! You are done hiding," Eskimo Joe said warmly. He remembered the big woman's words when his father appeared: "This one looks like yours." Both of them did their best to conceal their elation as they began the search for his mom. To the Parks men, the only appropriate response to anything of gravity was a bad joke.

"Sup buddy? Can you point a mole to the cafeteria?" Joe didn't respond. "Food. Is there food? I'm fucking starving."

"It is here," he motioned to a group of huts where all the traffic converged. "Did your servants forget to bring it?"

"They forgot to bring it, or to tell me it existed in the first place, or where the fuck it was. Is there some sort of a 'You-Are-Here' map of this place that shows you where everything is? I can't even tell which dick is mine in this clusterfuck."

"I will show you," he guided Parks forward to a growing mass of bodies piled outside what he imagined was the mess hall.

"It smells suspiciously like that whale I've been sitting on for the past few weeks."

"It is our food until the hunting party returns."

"Does that mean the forecast is clear? No more wind?" He clarified.

"The wind you knew has blown."

"It is you who killed the whale?" A woman who could have been 35 or 65 interrupted.

"Yes, ma'am, indeedy. I am the great white hunter known in these parts as the Leopard Seal. For I spare no prey, and my friends are always full." She threw her arms around his waist and he returned the hug. "Thank you! I say, 'We will not starve.' Poye say Nune is fertile. I do not think she mean you! You are big son!" She laughed.

"Uh. My pleasure, m'lady. Tell you what: I don't want you to have to crawl into that dark old wigwam. Why don't you just place your order with me and I'll bring it out for you?"

"Oh, thank you, thank you!"

Parks waited for the current diner to exit then plunged in with her leather sheet and wrapped a big hunk of meat. He shoveled a handful from the pile in his own mouth, and it tasted, if anything, less foul than it had when it was constantly drenched. A few days to dry out had firmed it up and replaced the soupy sour with a near-pleasant tartness.

"In fact," he called out. "Why don't you folks just hand me your baggies and I'll fill 'em up? It'll go a lot faster than everyone crawling in and out." He greeted each person who came, Brother, known as the Leopard Seal, whose father is Marion, Jr. and whose uncles are Gary and Frank. He listened carefully for their names and shut his ears down before they named their families, knowing he'd forget everything if he tried to remember everything. In between, he took little bites of his own. It still tasted too funky to gorge himself. The Leopard Seal always takes care of his friends, he reminded every fifth or sixth person. Almost all of them knew enough English to trade names, and most knew quite a bit more. The older women, especially, seemed to take a shine to the big man. The young men were respectful, though he noticed a bit less warmth. It was mostly women of any age who came to him, some carrying away meat that was obviously for an entire family, if not several. This, despite the makeup of the camp being overwhelmingly able-bodied males—the opposite of what he'd seen with Tunguk's people, and the tat-faced women who shared in the whale, which at this point he felt equally responsible for killing as Foster and his Reverse-Eskimo companions. After all, they never would have gotten there without his oar. It must have been the women's job to see about food. His stomach sank at the realization that the next face that appeared to him at any moment could be Kjartke's.

But she never came. He stayed there for the next few hours, schmoozing with the men, flirting with the old ladies, and maintaining polite deference to the younger ones, not knowing what the custom was regarding other men's wives and not wanting to find out. The pile of whale dwindled terrifyingly fast. It had seemed like food for a lifetime when they killed it. Weeks of daily meals, and the many pounds lost to the soaking waves, and now shared out, and he realized if everyone who came today were to return and ask for the same they'd taken, there would be no more whale meat. There was still a nice mound of fresher seal, as well as baskets of something old and dry, like jerky. Stiff mats of fish stacked in layers. But it wasn't the storehouse he would expect for so many people. How many days' rations were they hoping to get out of what they grabbed? Even at a stretch, they would be back to sucking on hard pieces of blubber in a week.

Eskimo Joe had disappeared. The center of activity at the mess disintegrated into a few dozen smaller bubbles and people passing between. He had nothing to wrap it in, so he carried the chunk he cut on his forearms, trying to steady it against falling apart. Half of it, he deposited in their hut. While he didn't make a search of the dark, it sounded like Gionn's snores and Foster's incessant rustling were both absent.

The other half he took on a meandering pattern through the wigwams, passing each group of people he found close enough to distinguish faces. Some of them acknowledged him now, where before the entire camp had cold-shouldered him and Foster. They remembered him from the mess hall, and he greeted them in return. He'd passed through the entire camp and given up, when on the return, through a section he'd crossed before, he saw her stowing away the satchel of fat that she used to regrease the hull whenever it hinted at drying or damage—probably finishing up the repair of their boat. She saw him, too, and considered him for a moment, then went back to her work.

Parks was never much good at knowing what chicks were thinking, or how to un-piss them off. He tried to think of what to say to her, but his gut kept his mouth shut. Instead, he knelt and lay the slab of whale a few feet away, turned, and left without a word.

The last thing he wanted was to go sit in the dark wigwam, so he picked his way through camp to the shoreline to look for Foster or Gionn. Neither one was liable to be hanging out with the natives, so they would be on the edges—either the flotilla, the shore, the big ships, or wandering up the mountain for water. A glance around didn't uncover anything in the field he could distinguish. Right away he felt bored and awkward standing alone and staring at the water. For the first time since—what would he call it, being shipwrecked here?—he missed his phone. Something to scroll through mindlessly in case anyone else looked at him. On the carrier he'd mastered the art of looking busy, but none of the familiar tools of his trade were at hand. He pulled out the square of leather he'd folded tightly around his map and tied with a strap. Splashproof, if not waterproof. Then he uncreased the old rectangle. That guy who had chartered them here would have a conniption fit if he saw that Parks had folded up the artifact like a piece of paper, which brought him a smile. It was holding up remarkably well. Or maybe not remarkably, since it had survived hundred of years already, though he could feel how the repeated wetting and drying and saltwater was beginning to make it feel less pliable. Maybe Kjartke could give him some grease to supple it up again.

Parks pretended to study the features in earnest. Foster had one too, and if he recalled correctly it was stranger and less valuable. It only depicted *Terra Australis*, the part of the Antarctic coast that faced the Atlantic, the peninsula, and a large stretch of coast extending to a huge crescent bay, as well as a number of inland details that his own would be missing. He can have Antarctica, Parks thought. I got the all the shit we need. The peninsula stretched from the corner. Maybe that's what Gionn kept calling "the arm," where they'd first washed up and found their Reverse-Eskimo friends. It didn't depict a fraction of the islands he'd seen, but there were a few bigger ones. Surely this had to be one of them.

The most prominent was too large to be accurate, probably stretched to accommodate the symbols drawn in its borders: a high ridge, a rock of some sort. The whole outline was drawn in the shape of a curled four-legged beast with a smooth head and sharp fangs. Medieval cartographers didn't seem to mind taking artistic liberties at the expense of accurate navigation. A smidge to the north, there lay a second island, unmarked but close to the mainland, split by a narrow channel. That had to be it if it was there at all.

"*Doot* doot doo, do-de *doot*-doo," he hummed whatever was stuck in his head. It felt familiar but he couldn't place it. A ram-horned monster drooling fire drew his attention farther south, to a crescent nearly off the page, as though he guarded the bay. Nearby where land gave up at the edge, an angel woman held a sword in her left hand, angled down to a point on the ground, and raised her right palm aloft in prayer, her eyes closed in concentration. Glad I'm not a sailor back in the day who had to rely on somebody's acid trip to avoid sailing off the edge of the world, he thought. The song came back to him—it was his own. "One's goin' near, one's goin' far—" he lowered the map in time to see Foster paddling across the bay in their boat, straight toward the anchored ships.

Every stroke made his hand sing, but now it was at least bearable. On the mend. He figured there was a 50% chance that no one would give a rat's ass if he paddled leisurely up to the ships, and with any luck, they might let him on board for a tour. If not, at least he would know how close he could expect to get before what kind of reaction took place. It turned out to be swifter than he hoped.

By the time he was halfway across, the men aboard the nearest one were already lowering down the long wooden boat that each carried. It wasn't shift change, he knew. They were fresh on the job, having relieved the sixteen soot-black and miserable souls who rode out the storm on each vessel. That was the foul weather compliment. Now there were only eight, and half roped down into the little boat. He held course, his excuse already prepared. It would look far more suspicious if he veered, so he was playing dumb when the boat intercepted him.

"Where you going?" They backed water and turned broadside to him. All he could think was how he wished he had that thing, with its stout wood oars, when they came down the coast.

"Just scootin' round the harbor. Our woman just repaired the boat after the wind gashed it, and I wanted to test it for leaks." They seemed to not mind that answer. "Thought I might check out them big outriggers. I've seen outrigger canoes before, but never anything like that." The apparent leader, a flat-faced man in his early twenties, glanced back at the ships. "Amu."

"What's that?"

"The outrigger. We call it amu."

"Amu," Foster mispronounced it. "Can I check it out?"

"No. Test your hull over there," he pointed to the waters near the hauled-out boats.

"My apologies, brother. Didn't mean to offend you. There's just not much to do around here."

"Do not-much over there." His companions laughed.

The gears in Fosters head spun as he paddled back. That and the cold numbed his throbbing hand. Took them five minutes or so to launch the intercept vessel, starting at about halfway. From now on, he could expect them to spot him sooner. There wasn't much of a night yet, but it would probably be easier to creep up then, though no excuse would fly. Nor could he haul the boat over land to launch from a closer point without carrying it past every single wigwam. But if he could get them to launch with a diversion and do a quick end-around, he'd only have four men to overpower on the deck. The amu seemed to be made of tree trunks, fitted and lashed, covered in something like pitch. Three wooden arms extended from the deck level and curved down to join it at the middle and each end. Over the flat part of the arms, there was a second deck of planks without any railing, which almost doubled the main deck. He reckoned there was a cutout in the middle of it from the way the men appeared and disappeared at the gunwales from about any point they chose, like a high school track running around open grass.

There must have been small gaps between the planks of the false deck for water and rope to pass through, because a line of wicker containers covered in leather sheets were lashed to the part nearest the ship, probably for balance as much as extra stowage. He hadn't seen the wood boats before the storm, but now they, too, were stored upside down on the false deck—one per ship—so they probably got pulled on board and secured when the weather was rough.

He could also see that the sails weren't just down, but stowed away entirely. Foster didn't know the first thing about rigging sails, but he assumed it took at least three times longer than however long he assumed. That meant that not only must they escape the bay under oars, but they wouldn't have an opportunity to raise sail and get a boost from the wind until there was no one pursuing them, because every hand would be needed at an oar, while a pursuer with a full crew might spare the hands to get under sail without having to pause the chase.

Gionn was right, he smiled to himself. *I'd make a damn good spy.*

Parks met him at the landing and pulled the prow in. "Thought you were paddling to North Carolina without me."

"Just checkin' if she's seaworthy."

"Ballsy move. Are we fucked?"

"Not fucked. Just can't fuck the way we started out wantin' to fuck."

"Never been a problem in the past, has it?"

"Balgan bless your appetites!" A voice called over the din from the steps of the open air pavilion. Gionn turned far enough to be unimpressed and went back to sucking the bones of his fish. His fire red hair and broad shoulders had an unfortunate habit of attracting characters like this to conversation even in crowds, so he did his best to slide a little more of his frame under the table, at least until someone humored the man, or stabbed him. No one else seemed keen to attract his attention, either. Even the toothless creature sitting beside him knew better. Dark brown and small even by his people's abbreviated standards, he'd sat himself down in a manner that told Gionn none of the crew from his own boat would have him, and since then hadn't managed a communication more complicated than to smile too wide and nod between Gionn and his plate. Maybe he was trying to make friends over the common ground that both were eating fish, same as everyone else. When a ribbon of drool dangled from his open onto his lap without him realizing it, Gionn had said something to the effect of, "Smile at me again, and I'll put new teeth in your mouth so's I can knock 'em out." He went mopey after that. It was unpleasant enough that Gionn was about to get up and move benches when the newcomer came prowling through.

"How's the hasqa here?" He asked a man who ignored him. "Finest tavern in Cantare, this," he remarked to another. Gionn tracked his slender frame and sharp features out of the corner of his eye. New leather and new steel on him. Rust hair and not a whisker on a face that likely couldn't grow much anyway, despite his thirty-some years. There was a hint of tan to his skin, the only thing that undercut his otherwise distinguished presentation. Over a hundred men crowded every available seat, and the latecomers sat on the floor. All he had to do was keep his mouth shut as the man drew closer.

"Look at this specimen," he stopped behind Gionn. *Fuck.* But the hand fell on the toothless creature's shoulder. His eyes lit up and his smile returned. The stranger had found one who didn't dare ignore him. "Tell me, lad, are you the captain of them fine ladies in the harbor?"

"You'll find no oars here, cunt," Gionn blurted out before he could catch himself. Apparently everyone had been as keyed in as himself, because the whole pavilion erupted in laughter.

The man smiled. "And who said I'm lookin' for oars, me son?"

"You know this ugly bastard's not the captain of the bucket he shits in. I gone through all the trouble of wipin' the toothless smile off his face and now you've squalled me efforts." More laughter. "Tell him, Gionn!" Someone called from across the way.

"Gionn. Pleasure to meet you, captain."

"You know I'm no captain, as well. Off with you, now."

"I believe me fleet has had enough," A short, thick man with a great gray beard and only stubble left on his head stood.

"Then you're the man I'll talk to. Huighan's the name. What can I call you?"

"Aye, Huighan. Fuck off. You'll not find crew among me fleet."

"It's not crew I seek, captain. Or is it admiral? That's what I'm accustomed to callin' a man with as many boats. No, I come addin' ships to me own fleet."

"Your fleet?"

"Aye."

"I only see three good whalers in the harbor, and all's mine."

"Then you're anchored next to me."

"What, the fishin' boat?" The crew laughed.

"That be she, and a fine one she is."

"You call one boat a fleet?"

"You call three a fleet?"

"Three's two more than one."

"Ah, you're right. I'll need at least four before I have me fleet."

The captain laughed. Gionn slunk farther, sitting as he was directly beneath a man who might be set upon at any moment. "You think I'm gonna join up with a fisherman?"

"I'm a terrible fisherman. But I was steersman for Paladris." The room feel dead silent.

"Lots of cunts was this or that for Paladris."

"Not yourself. And I was not steersman in his fleet, but for the man himself, on the *Oulba.*"

"I can tell you the chance of that bein' true." A few timid snickers returned to the men. The captain smirked.

"You would see soon enough, but perhaps if you won't take me hospitality, you'll offer your own. Would you have a fourth boat in your fleet?"

"A fishin' boat?"

"Aye, and twenty-five good men."

"The fuck do I need with a fishin' boat?"

"Fish." Huighan let the room have a laugh at his expense. "I'm sure that you've caught plenty under this man," he addressed the pavilion when it died down. "Have there also been times when you came up empty? Have you rowed days on an empty stomach? Had to dangle a line, or make land to forage when your bones barely pull? I was steersman for the great Paladris, and yet I've been without food a week at times. You take me on, all you do is whale, and eat. No starvin' or scramblin' for your meals."

Gionn had not heard of such an arrangement. Often enough, there might be one to trade them food, but a member of the fleet? Despite the grins that surrounded him, he could tell the notion had a certain appeal to more than just himself. Rewan was unimpressed.

"If you were steersman for Paladris, what the fuck could you know of fishin'?"

"Nothin'. As I said, I'm a terrible fisherman. But I know every wind and current from Thaibe to Hiade. I know every rock in every port, every reef and shoal. I know the trade routes, and the thieves' ports, and where the Navy hides. I can navigate months in a cloud, and above all, I know every tactic Paladris or anyone he ever fought ever used. Every word of Eandus' *Tactics*. Me crew, on the other hand, are all Chalxalwa tribesmen, who've fished since they were old enough to wade into the surf. They know lines and nets, and they harpoon dolphin, dive for lobster, bait seabirds, and dig oysters. It's said they breathe underwater. They catch the food. I'll move your fleet."

There were a few timid whoops of approval. A sign of amusement, at least, and that Rewan would have to respond in satisfaction.

"Me fleet moves fine as it were," he bellowed, then softened his tone. "But if your crew can do as you say, we'll stand to see you attached. At least as long as you keep our bellies up."

"How many shares?"

"Five."

"Each?"

"Among you." The look on Huighan's face said it, and the room crooned at the insult.

"Ten."

"Agreed, if half the crew stands for it."

"Outta whose fuckin' purse?" Gionn blurted, and cursed himself under his breath as soon as he did.

"Outta yours, Gionn, if your tongue wags again."

"A fine offer, and one that fairly acknowledges me skill. I've no doubt that a man you supposed a liar would get carried down and dunked for his troubles. If I may ask, ten shares from how many?"

"Two hundred and forty."

Huighan smiled politely. He raised a finger and seemed to jab it at each head as he scanned the pavilion. Rewan rolled his eyes impatiently. "Hundred and nineteen," he saved the guest the trouble.

"The other half bein' yours, I suppose."

"Mine, and me captains'."

"And if I may ask again, how many belong to your fine captains?"

"You may not ask, and it don't concern you. Your offer is ten for you and your crew, if you don't tire me first."

"Of course, none of mine. And I won't put you out by askin' you to make a count. I'm certain there's a man in Cantare who can square it for you." Gionn cringed at the insinuation that the captain could not handle his numbers well enough to take ten off and know the sum, and hoped Rewan would not take the gist. "I only wanted to be certain I was not takin' me shares off one of your stout captains, or if it be so, that it would be a smaller number. Four from yourself, three from each of them, that would be ten, and naturally the admiral should bear the generous portion."

"You'll leave that to meself and the captains, fisherman."

Gionn glanced at Acabulo, who he did not think would appreciate the suggestion that he give any of this shares to a fishing boat.

"Ah, there's one," Huighan gave a curt bow to Acabulo. Must have been more than a few cunts looking for the same reaction—the one Huighan no doubt followed. "Me apologies, sir, it has never been me intention to take your shares."

"Nor fuckin' will you," The Amposi barked.

"Nor fuckin' will I. I think it should come out of the admiral's purse."

"Aye? And you've lost the offer," Rewan waved him away. "The fuck am I talkin' to a fisherman for? I've lost me head. Off with you now, me son."

"But you haven't heard me counteroffer."

"Gionn, stab this man," Rewan ordered. Gionn didn't budge. Why couldn't he have asked for "someone" to stab him? Why did it have to be "Gionn?" Now he was mutinous if he didn't, though he was very much inclined to listen to the argument of a man who knew his numbers and might spare him the trouble of starving.

"You would kill a man at supper?" Huighan protested playfully.

"You barged in uninvited and you're not eatin'."

"It's still under hospitality."

"Aye, you made sure of that didn't you? You're right, I'm no madman. That's why Gionn will do it. Gionn!" He repeated.

Huighan looked at him. "Me son here looks strong as a bear, and he rows on his belly. It's a shame you put him in a spot to choose murderin' a tradesman at supper or betrayin' his captain. Not to worry, lad. There are more here who feel as you." He turned back to Acabulo. "Captain, perhaps you'll hear me counteroffer. There bein' a hundred twenty or so among three captains, I assume you and your mate hold thirty apiece, and sixty for the inhospitable man across the room."

Acabulo snorted at the notion. Gionn saw clear through Huighan, showing off his numbers again.

"No? How many?"

"None of yours, you crazed fuckin' bastard." Rewan started over. Several crew jumped up to block the lane.

"It's courtin' a foul luck, Captain," one said, and though Rewan fumed, he held his place. Captain's wrath aside, no man would violate the threshold laws before he sailed. Rewan slapped away one of the hands, and stepped back. They eased into their seats once more.

"Ten," Acabulo answered.

"Of *a hundred-twenty?*" Huighan said in disbelief. "And your other captain? Ten, as well?" The trick worked and he followed the eyes of the room right to Iras, among his crew opposite the pavilion from Acabulo.

"Aye, do you think I give away me ships to beggars?" Rewan turned a familiar red. "Had they joined with their own wood, might be different. But every man here knows me crews come in fat. Ten shares of not one, but three holds. You don't think I see your ruse? You think you'll get me captains to trail along after your fish gutter? Any man who thinks Rewan is unfair is welcome to fuck off on the trawler. But the ships are me own, and I'd advise you lot to sail before the sun comes up."

"I'm sure you cut a fine deal to acquire them. I'm willin' to pay you the very same." Acabulo laughed, and some of his men with him. Huighan went on. "Perhaps it was a poor choice, to make an offer to men on a full stomach. How soon they forget how they felt on your oars! A poor choice, but I wouldn't dare stand here on the offer of a few fish, and I *do* believe you've misunderstood me. I don't ask your men to leave you, but the very opposite." He let the silence sink into the room. "I shall take your berth, and these two men will keep their ships. *Their* ships, free to leave if they please, though once they sail with me, I doubt it'll come to pass. Thirty each, and another thirty for meself. The Chalx-alwa deserve twenty among them, and though it means little to you now, you men will be as full as you care to be as long as we sail. That leaves ten. One each to the first ten men of me fleet who stands out to me eye."

Stand, Gionn thought. Clever cunt used that word intentionally.

"Are you tryin' to mutiny, on *land?*" Rewan laughed. There was a desperation to it.

"Best place for it. I'll let you walk away unharmed."

"You're a fuckin' shirker. You hide behind the gods. Even if you get off tonight, on me oath, you'll find me close on your stern."

Gionn stared into his bowl. He'd been outmaneuvered by the steersman. Idle under orders. Rewan would not accept a lesser apology than a knife in this man's ribs. With painstaking effort, he unwedged himself from his seat and rose beside the interloper. The pale blues met his without fear. Then he bent and picked up his bowl of wet whitefish, and cursed Uinab under his breath as he marched the lane between Huighan and the captain. Rewan was confused, but his face seemed to lighten as he realized a man of his crew was moving away from the one who would steal his berth from beneath him. After what seemed a mile, he reached his captain and paused before him. Rewan placed a hand under the bowl out of instinct when Gionn pressed it to his chest.

"You're gonna need this more I, cunt."

Foster and Parks followed the stream of people to the far side of the camp, where they congregated in a half moon around an older woman who sat on a fur seal blanket. It felt informal enough that they could intermingle, and it was close to the landing by the big ships, which allowed Foster to politely take the rear of the crowd and steal glances without arousing further suspicion. He figured the anchor point was a two hundred yards from shore, if you set out from the nearest spot. The only boats that put in here were the ones that changed shift. Those came directly from the ships, and returned there with fresh bodies. He'd already watched the first one, about a half day from when the storm watch was relieved. Four men paddled up, got out, and four more got in and paddled back. Another four remained on board. Foster assumed that meant a shift was twenty-four hours, with a staggered crew of four coming in every twelve.

"How many you got?" Foster said in a gruff whisper.

"How many what?"

"You said you'd get oars. Tunguk and Kjartke is two. How many of the other seventeen you got?"

"Negative two. I haven't asked them yet."

Foster rolled his eyes. "We'll talk about it later. There's Gionn." The ginger shuffled up. When he spotted them, he stopped and joined the crowd.

"Is he mad at us?" Parks wondered aloud.

"Fuck him if he is, we're gonna stand right by him. He ain't wormin' out of this." They walked over and took up either side.

"What is this, some kind of a town hall meeting?" Parks asked.

"I don't know, cunt. I'm not a fuckin' sss…clan…people—one of these cunts."

"Scuse me, ma'am?" Parks put his hand on the shoulder of the woman next to him. "Now didn't I see you at the lunch line? The whale meat?"

"Aye," she smiled. "Leopard Seal!"

"You remember me."

"Who forget you?" She laughed. Foster rolled his eyes.

"Do you know what's going on here?"

"She read the bones. Full moon pass during storm, so we wait to hear until now."

"Read the bones?"

"It's the divination, then," Gionn explained. He could see the blank looks. "She'll cast the fortunes for the group each moon cycle. My prediction is sittin' on arses, shit weather, and death by boredom."

When she felt enough had gathered, she rose. There was no ceremony to it. Apparently whatever needed to be done had been done in a dark wigwam prior. The crowd fell quiet. Foster hadn't seen anything like the whole gang gathered, so he counted heads as best he could. When she spoke, it was in Mattakatan.

"Goddammit," Parks said. "Gionn!"

"Do I look like I speak babble?"

"Ma'am?" She hushed him and listened intently. The woman's voice grew in volume as she made a proclamation. A murmur passed over the group, almost a collective sigh of relief. She went on. This time she spat in a staccato and jutted her chin as she finished. Everyone—every single person present—turned and stared at Parks, Foster, and Gionn. They froze. The woman went on, and heads began to drift back to her. A few more quick words, and she gathered her blanket and left. The crowd broke into smaller groups, chatting and dispersing at what Parks had come to recognize as a Reverse-Eskimo pace. The woman who spoke to him was gone, and no one else seemed eager to make their acquaintance. Foster meandered away, still studying the ships. Gionn's vice grip caught Parks' arm and pulled him aside.

"I saw the stunt he pulled. I don't want to know the plan, but you got to be honest if it starts to look like an inside-out arsehole. Much as I despise all the people and things within a thousand miles of here, I prefer to live miserably than die valiantly." He wandered off toward their slanty wigwam.

"How long do you reckon it takes to raise an anchor?" Foster rejoined him.

"I don't know. Based on pirate movies I've seen, it usually involved a bunch of guys walking in circle around a big wheel to pull up a massive chain, which has to be long enough to reach the bottom, so I'm guessing somewhere around a long-ass time?"

"That's what I'm afraid of. I forgot to think about anchors. These folks ain't got chain and metal things that look like your tattoo. I'm guessin' they drag up a rope by hand, probably some kinda rock on the end."

"Slows down the getaway a bit."

"Unless you just cut and run, in which case it slows down the pursuit. But then you gotta know for a fact you got spare anchors and line on board, because you gotta anchor eventually."

Parks could see the big wheel in his head tugging at all the difficulties of the plan. "I hate to be the Debbie, but it's at least a little bit possible that there's no way to pull this off without getting us killed. We'll be lucky if they just cut off our hands."

"If there ain't a way yet, we're gonna make one. Come on."

"Come on, where?"

"We gotta call in the big guns."

They found Tunguk well off by himself on the far end of the camp. He sat Indian-style and stared into the mouth of the bay. Parks wondered if they just called it "Reverse-Eskimo style," or maybe just "sitting". The ratio of stuff-to-do to time available was about like the Navy, which meant that some people never rested, and many others spent the majority of the day doing things like staring into space, especially if they were too old to masturbate. What these people lacked was the complex culture of diversions. It was a wonder they hadn't lost anyone to suicide.

"You want me to help steal a ship," Tunguk said as they approached. Foster looked around to make sure no one was within hearing.

"How'd you know?"

"The poye. Her bones say that the weather is good. We will have troubles from thieves. And a voyage not all return from."

"Which was the part where everyone looked at us?" Parks asked. Tunguk smiled.

"There is also a trust, then a betrayal. Or a betrayal that turns to trust. It is not possible to know the order, and the way the bones fell, it can be both."

Foster clenched his teeth and gave it some thought. "So you don't think it's a good idea to steal a ship?"

"It is not possible to steal a ship. But if you steal a ship, I will help you."

Gionn, too, must have known why he came, because he made Foster crawl around the wigwam with him to search for stowaways the moment he arrived. "I know it's gonna be harder with the whatever-you-called-it."

"The divination? That's the least of your troubles. How many oars have you got?"

"Including you? Two. But Parks is rummagin' around for some more right now."

"Fuck's sake."

"Problem is, they're all expectin' a theft, so we're tryin' to pull this off in plain sight."

"You can't expect a divination to go assumed like that. There's so many different kinds. Different strengths and weaknesses in what they can predict, and how well. And all of them depend on the skill of the one doin' it, which is the biggest fuck-factor. No doubt these squains have seen them get cunted up before." He paused. "Although that one was pretty fuckin' dead-center."

"Let me run one by you. My biggest problem right now, before we even bother countin' how we're gonna pull anchor, raise sail, or row the thing, is how we get on the damn ship to begin with when everyone's watchin'. We launch from where they keep the boats, it's too slow. They'll see us. And there's no boats to launch from the closest spot. I'm thinkin', once we got enough crew, we use the little sliver of dark we get every day. The amu's the weak spot."

"Amu?"

"The outrigger."

"The sidecock?"

"That. It's low to the water, and the boards on that second deck have room for lashin's. We can easily loop a rope and climb up. We just gotta swim a couple hunnerd yards, cut the anchor lines to the other ships to cause a commotion, and slip on board. There'll be a full eight against us, but if we come with enough to row, that'll be the easy part. We might could even use them as hostages to prevent the others from chasin' us."

"Swim two hundred yards in waters that freeze you in minutes, then try to climb out under our own power and win a boarding fight?"

"In the Navy I used to work for, we got guys who do that. Called SEALs."

"I'm guessin' you're not one of 'em." Foster's silence answered for him. "Besides, I told you not to tell me your plan ahead of time. If there's one thing I'm good at, it's findin' a way to ruin anything that benefits me in any way."

"That's exactly why I *need* to get you involved. I didn't even consider it might be too cold for us to swim. Or that you need twenty dudes minimum to row out to the winds. Without you, me and Parks would be standin' on that deck alone with no clue how to get goin' while the whole Mattaka nation laughed at us and sharpened their knives."

"Looks like it's goin' to be a long winter, mate."

He could not see it yet, but somewhere the first beams of sun absent more than a week slipped through a hole in the clouds, and poured at a slant through the mouth of the bay, glinting off of silver specks of ice that swirled in the dawn breeze. It looked as though the angle revealed a shimmering veil otherwise invisible when the sun was anywhere else. Between the cloud cover and the coming winter, it had been close to real night. For a few hours, he was able to enjoy an astronomical twilight sitting in the wind shadow against the high slope before the glow seeped back through to stir the camp to activity.

Foster saw Kjartke from the moment she left her wigwam to trudge up the grade. She was in no hurry, and strangely, nor was he. It was chilly. He was a little thirsty, not for lack of water but finding the taste of leather unappetizing so early in the day. A little hungry, as the whole camp had scaled back on rations until the hunters could return. None of it was much of a bother. He could feel the Mattaka winding down with the sun, the weather slithering over them as if returning to the continent to coil up for a winter's rest. Below, he could see the remnants of the gutted the flotilla. The hunters had poured out the mouth of the cove in a dozen boats with a kayak accompanying each pair. For how long, or to where, he didn't know. They would find out soon if it would be possible to survive the winter here. If he waited, and they came back lacking, he may not need to steal a boat at all. Every man, woman, and child would be forced to continue north. But if they came back stocked, telling of fertile hunting and fishing, then he would have missed his chance to make a run when the enemy was undermanned and insecure about their chances of eating.

"Tunguk say you wish to speak," Kjartke sat beside him overlooking the camp.

"Did he tell you what about?" She nodded. He let it rest at that, and for a long moment neither made a move against the silence. "Nice, innit?" Kjartke reclined back against a rock as if she expected to be there a while. "Know what's funny? I woke up in the middle of the night like I usually do. Since the Navy, anyway. But it wasn't outta sweats or terrors. I mean, I could actually die here. *Soon.* I feel like this whole continent is just barely puttin' up with life, til it gets the chance to do somethin' about it. In the past month, I lost my crew and the place I came from. I seen guys get killed, nearly got killed myself a half dozen ways, and now I'm faced with either shiverin' through a winter half-starved and frostbitten, or maybe gettin' killed makin' a run for it to nowhere in particular on a ship I don't know how to sail. But you know what? Here," he shrugged. "I'm chillin'. Back home, I'd have to smoke two bowls every mornin' just to get out of bed. In my warm house, with nothin' out to get me. And don't even get me started on crowds. I worked below decks. Never even took fire in the Navy, but I sure as shit came out with PTSD."

Her furrowed brow begged an explanation.

"You know, like anxiety? No? You know the word?" She shook her head. "OK, well. Thanks for listenin'."

"We cannot steal the ship."

"Look, I hate askin' you to act against your people—"

"These are not my people."

"'Cannot.' Does that mean it's hard? It's forbidden? What?"

"It is both."

"And when you say 'hard,' do you mean 'impossible?'"

"There are men who can do it."

Foster leaned in. "Do they have names like…Foster? Parks? Tunguk?" She grinned. "Then what do you suggest?"

"I do what you do."

"I'm askin' if you have any ideas of your own." She shook her head. "I get that you're not used to people wantin' to hear your opinion, but I'm fuckin' serious. I'm outta rope. I don't even know how I'm gonna get on the ship, who's goin' with me, what we're gonn do once we're there…all I know is I can't stay here. And that I don't understand this place well enough to do it myself. If you got somethin' decent, I'm all ears."

"I do what you do," she repeated as she rose.

"Five," Foster said to Parks as they hiked the leather water resevoir up the switchbacks. He knew the way by now, and it was easier to conspire here than by constantly meeting in hushed tones.

"You got three more?"

"I got Kjartke. Fuck what Gionn says, if her and Tunguk count as rowers, I'm countin' us too. We ain't tryin' to play violin in no orchestra. You and me can figure out how to pull oars."

"Make it seven."

Foster stopped in disbelief. "You actually got people?"

"Damn skippy."

"And they know what we're plannin' to do, right?"

"'Course."

"I'm just worried you might have phrased it—I don't know, in a misleadin' fashion."

"I'm as eloquent as the summer day is long, dude. There were no misunderstandings."

"Who'd you get?"

"You know those guys who've been hanging out by the skin boats all day?"

"The little eight-year olds?"

"I'd put them at malnourished twelve-year olds. You could practically smell the sea in their blood."

"I'm almost one hunnerd-percent positive they posted those kids there as lookouts to let them know if I try to launch another boat. And you told them we plan to steal a ship."

"Don't underestimate the lure of the open water, dude. They seemed very interested. Brothers, I might add, or at least half. They have the same father, and a great many uncles, none of which I can remember."

"So you recruited two elementary-school snitches with tons of family here."

"Did I miss where you said you signed up the Stanford rowing team? Because I'm doing my best with what the Good Lord gave us. What is it they say? Start where you're at, with what you got, lickety-split?" The sound of feet shuffling on the trail quieted them. Four Mattaka men rounded the rock. They carried stone hunting spears instead of water reservoirs.

"You come," one said.

A crowd gathered around their wigwam by the time they arrived with their escort. Profanity and the sound of a scuffle spilled out, followed by Gionn. "Rude cunts!" He yelled back at someone, pulled himself to his feet, and surveyed the scene. Tunguk and Kjartke arrived, apparently under their own power, to complement a good portion of the young men and several onlooker families. "Is this how you treat a guest?"

One of the men with spears stepped forward—about 40, with close cropped hair flecked gray along the sides and the little mustache that many Mattaka tried to grow. "It is not our way to be rude to guests." He seemed more than a little miffed at the accusation, and Foster suspected that Gionn knew the reaction he would arouse.

"It is not me understandin' of hospitality to be rousted from me sleep and cast into the foul weather and filth of this camp for no good reason," he said of the mild breeze. Behind him, two more men crawled out and shook their heads to the escort party.

"It is not rude. The matter is urgent and all are needed."

"Rude," Gionn muttered.

"There has been a theft." Gionn's eyes darted to Foster and Parks for a split second and shot away.

"A theft of what, me kind host?"

"Food is gone from the tukit."

"Perhaps it was eaten."

"All the food is gone."

"*All* of it?" The man gave a single nod. "Why would I take hundreds of pounds of disgustin' whale meat that I've been fartin' on for better of a week? I can't even stand the little bit I have."

The man looked to Parks and Foster. "Farting is an understatement. We didn't take it, either, and I'm more than a little disappointed that you automatically assume it was the white guys. Isn't that reverse-profiling?"

"Search every tukit. Under the boats. Have the watch search the ships." He turned to his companions. "These men were on the water path. Take others with you, search the entire route." People scattered in all direction. A handful remained.

"Let's try this again: Foster. Son of Dawn. Don't feel like listin' uncles."

The man hesitated. "Lenet."

"Pleasure to meet you, my brother. Can I safely assume you're the leader of this here operation?" He swept his arm over the camp.

"No. If these people listen to me, then I'm honored. We are free to follow who we choose."

"Well, they're listenin' now. I know it looks bad when outsiders show up and shit goes missin'. But let's remember, we're the ones who brought you most of that shit to begin with, and we're eatin' our corn off the same cob, here. None of us can take down..what, with the shit we gave you, plus what you already had, gotta be at least two-thousand pounds of sushi? Maybe more? And we'd have to know that if we stole enough to be noticed, we'd be the first motherfuckers you blamed. In fact, it don't make any sense for *anyone* here to do it. What could anyone have to gain by starvin' the whole camp?"

"Spies of the Viceroy would gain."

"I stand for these men," Tunguk said. "They are shipwrecks without skills of spycraft or fighting. If not for akmanuak, they would be dead. He who cannot, did not."

"You were seen walking the camp very early."

"Couldn't sleep. Thought I'd watch the sunrise." Lenet considered his response. "Besides, how'm I gonna move that much weight? My hand is broke. I can barely grip an oar."

"With help," Lenet said.

"My leg hurts," Parks picked a bit of debris off the bruised gash on his shin.

"And I'm far too lazy to carry off so much without cursin' the whole camp awake," Gionn chimed in.

"You, I believe." Lenet motioned to his companions. "If someone plans a voyage, it will be on the ships, or near." They headed that direction.

Gionn moved close enough to avoid being heard by any of the stragglers searching the wigwams. "Bold move, mates. Bit obvious, though. Should've got the crew before the provisions."

"You know good and well it wasn't us," Foster said. "My money's on you."

"Guys, if we start accusing each other, we're just perpetuating racial stereotypes that the white man steals from the poor natives. If, on the other hand, we apply a little old school detective work and solve the crime—"

"No good findin' the cunt," Gionn butted in. "If there's no food, the whole camp breaks, and us with 'em. Whoever did it, did us a favor. Not sayin' it was you, but…well-played. Tell me where not to look so's I can pretend to look."

"It was for *sure* you." Foster started off.

"Where you going?" Parks called.

"They're gonna have eyes on us 24/7 at this point. Might as well try your idea and go help Lenet." Parks followed.

Gionn hollered after them, "I'll pretend to look under boats!" Half a dozen Mattaka shot him a cold stare. "What? I said 'look.' You've a poor grasp of the language if you heard otherwise." He marched toward the skin boats and several of the searchers tagged after him.

The bustle of activity reminded Parks of his childhood hobby of stamping ant piles and watching the frenzy of assault, evacuation, and repair. Half of the men fanned out up the slope at the ice line, not much larger than ants from this distance, scouring every walkable stretch in case whoever took the food had the courtesy to refrigerate it. Other than in a wigwam, all of which would be checked, Parks couldn't see anywhere else to hide it besides buried in a snow bank way up high. The camp level was bare rock except the boulder field near the ships, which men and women alike probed. Lenet and several more men waited at the shore, Parks and Foster near at hand. The three skin boats he'd sent for were being hustled down the shoreline by others. It was amazing how light they were. One man could've carried them if not for the bulk, so two was sufficient. Most of the activity was ringed around the wigwams. A handful of others seemed to be searching door to door, from the center outward. Even in daylight they'd have to crawl with their little ant-feelers to find anything, but he figured it would be hard to miss the smell, let alone the presence of that much meat.

The boats arrived, one of them carried between the two little rowers he'd recruited. Foster was right, they did look eight, but Asians always looked younger due to being Asian, and possibly vitamin-deficient—he hadn't seen a vegetable yet. In general, Antarcticans looked close to Asians, so they probably followed the same rules, he guessed.

"Wonder who it was, saw me walkin' around at sunrise," Foster nodded to the boys. The watch crews on the ships had all been alerted somehow, and they stood eight abreast on the false decks waiting for the search parties. Lenet's group pushed forward, ready to board the boats as soon as they were in the water.

"Lenet," Foster got his attention. "What can we do to help?"

He gave it some thought. "Stay close, and do nothing." Foster said something in protest, but Parks didn't feel like talking those two. He watched the men piling into the boats, six each. Lenet and the others were distracted by Foster. He saw the boys—what were their names again? No matter, he would give them fine nicknames. Parks had a hard time imagining his new friends and recruits would betray their trust.

"Hold on! One more!" He waved to them as they were about to shove off. Parks threw a gangly leg over the gunwale and toppled in. One of the boys—he would be called Grom—gave it a push with the oar, and they were away. It was almost fifty yards to sea before Lenet and Foster noticed, and though he couldn't make out their exact expressions, Parks was pleased with the way he imagined them.

Being on the ship reminded him of being at a bar in high school. His football frame and fake ID were plausible enough to get him shooed in, and despite the fact that all of the adults knew he wasn't supposed to be there, none of them cared. Except the two who were waiting on the shore.

Being blind to distance, it was the first good look he could get at the source of all their hopes and troubles. From the moment two hands helped him over the outrigger and onto the false deck, he felt his whole world shift. The gentle rock, the clonk of the wood underfoot, and the gaps that let the sight and slosh of the water through took him far from the frantic camp only yards away. Everyone here was chill. They greeted each other in their friendly tongue, and seemed more interested in telling stories than conducting any kind of search. Parks could see why. Despite the fact that it dwarfed the boat he paddle up in, there was very little to the ship.

It was symmetrical bow to stern, and if not for the outrigger, it would've been side to side, as well. He hopped down four feet from the false deck, which ran into the gunwale, onto the main deck of the boat. It covered the entire ship, except two square cutouts fore and aft that lead to the hold—a little under thirty feet wide, and four times as long. There was a large mast dead center, though the sail must have been stowed below.

Most of the rest of the deck was covered in some kind of containers, stomach high, all covered in sheets of oiled leather and lashed down to wooden protrusions set into the deck for the purpose. The outrigger was to port, and the load was shifted in that direction to keep it weighted, with some of the cargo spilling onto the false deck. Or at least he thought it was port. The more he looked, the less he could tell which end was supposed to be the bow. The main deck was covered in more containers. Narrow walking lanes left enough room to access all sides of the ship, the hold, and the masts and stays.

"Should we start checking under these tarps?" He caught the attention of one of the men who'd arrived with him.

The man shook his head. "It is firestone."

"What if the thief dumped out a container and hid the meat there?"

"The watch crew says no one has come aboard. Someone is awake on deck at all times."

"Leonard didn't send us out here to have cocktails at the yacht club." He raised his voice to everyone. "There is no food. Food gone. We look everywhere. No firestone unturned."

"You want to spend hours untying and retying lines because Lenet lost the food?" Another man asked in much better English than Parks had imitated.

"Me? No. I don't know how you tie those things down. I want you to do it. Do you really think if we go back after a quick glance around the deck, we won't just have to paddle over and do it again?" Their faces sank like sailors who just got assigned to clean the head with a toothbrush, but they knew he was right. "I'll be conducting a Western investigation into the theft. That means I'm going to need to interview everyone who was on duty at the time. Please form a very quiet line. No talking or making up alibis. If you have any captain's logs, or private journals, I'll need to see those, too. I'll take any hesitation or lack of cooperation as an admission of guilt." They exchanged confused looks.

Nevertheless Parks interrogated all eight of them. Who was where on the ship at what times? Did they see anyone coming or going? When did their shift start and end? He even went so far as to ask if they'd heard rumors of discontent, or if anyone had been acting suspicious. Whenever anyone protested, he accused them of sympathies to the Viceroy, whoever that was, and it got them talking again in no time. It was fruitless if you were looking for a thief, but he got every detail of the watch routine, down to who slept away from the others because he snored too much. One by one, he released them to work, uncovering what ended up being great wicker baskets of raw coal.

The other ships busied themselves checking their cargo, as well. With everyone occupied, Parks decided to take a tour below deck. A ladder in the aft hole led him below deck. The musty smell overwhelmed him, and it took a moment to acclimate to the low light streaming in from windows on the sides, and the two hold openings overhead. His head bumped one of the braces that held the deck up. None of the Reverse-Eskimos would have had a problem walking tall down here, but he exceeded the lowest clearance by a good couple inches, ducking alternately as he crossed each rib. In the center, there were more baskets on boards that spanned the bilge, with openings for men to access it if it needed bailing. The sail was rolled and tied, and he saw a length of extra material and rope at the high points where water wasn't likely to soak them. To each side, rows of plain wooden benches met the hull. There were thirty on both sides. Each had a window out of which an oar extended. Those lay perpendicular across the tops of the benches, and blankets laid across in a few places told him people used them as as elevated cot.

One of the sides was nearly completely shaded by the false deck, and the oars had to maneuver beneath it. Nowhere did he see a cozy place to sleep, a toilet, or any other accommodations for living things. It was a ship for coal. In the stillness he saw how storms washed through the windows and rained down from above with every wave. Men with buckets scurrying from the bilge to the window and back as fast as possible. The smell of shit. They probably pissed right into the bilge if the weather was bad. Sprawled out wherever they could find a patch of open wood after they were worked to the point of exhaustion. All of it seemed like Heaven compared to paddling around in an open skin boat.

"Leopard Seal!" A voice called from above. It was one of the boys. He climbed down carrying a leather cylinder in his hands, and presented it. "Here is only papers on board."

"Thank you, Grom." Parks untied it.

"I am Ulpit."

"Grom."

There was a rolled piece of parchment, sealed with a purple wax stamp. "Don't break it," the kid warned.

"Why not?"

"Admiralty papers."

"What's that?"

"It means the ship has arrived."

Parks figured he wouldn't get anywhere asking for clarification, so he tucked them back into the cover and returned them. "When the men are done searching the cargo on deck, have them check this crap," he waved at the stuff in the center.

"The watch is to change."

"Very well. You and Blowhole take those four back, then return to the ship. When we're done searching, we'll stay on with one more to take a watch shift. The rest of the search crew can return."

"Who is Blowhole?"

"I think you know." Grom nodded. "You remember our secret mission, don't you? Loose lips sink ships," Parks waved him away.

Lenet and four fresh men helped the boat ashore when the watch returned.

"Who relieved you?"

"Brother. The one who calls himself Leopard Seal."

He motioned to the replacements. "Then we will relieve Brother."

"Has the food been found?" The watchman asked.

"No." The watchman gave Lenet a long look that Foster thought would have bordered on insubordination if it weren't for the fact that these men had no leaders.

"Hello, cunts," Gionn greeted the men returning from watch outside the entrance to their wigwam. It was the same one they'd been run out of when they first landed. "As you can see, I've waited outside the sanctity of your home to ask a small favor. I've gone and done a stupid thing. Ate the last of me whale. What with the theft and all, it isn't likely to be replaced. Would you be about to sit down for supper?"

"Not with you."

"That's unfortunate." They started in. "You see, we searched every one of these skin castles, and mine thrice. Didn't find no meat, but I did notice that one in particular had a certain odor about it. The woman I was helpin', she noticed as well. Lucky I was able to convince her that before we go castin' accusations, the owners should have an opportunity to explain. Over supper."

Parks and Foster waded through the mess of wigwams as the sun once again threatened to disappear entirely. When he was sure no one could see them, Foster clapped Parks on the arms and gave him a loving squeeze. "Fuck yeah, brother!" They arrived at their wigwam. "Can't wait to hear the full report." He waved Parks in ahead of him, then tied the flap tight.

"Where's Gionn?" Parks' voice asked.

"Dunno. Don't care. What's the intel?"

"Should we do a quick squain-check?"

Through the dark, from the back of the wigwam, came a third voice.

"You will find one here."

11

Two Camps

A roller from the following swell lifted the stern of the ship and broke through the oar ports and the bailing hatches over the Mattaka rowers. They spit and shook wet hair but held their stroke. Lenet sat in the middle of the hold, facing aft. His stick fell with effortless force on the drum head that beat the rhythm of their oars, steady though he expected a command soon. The seas were growing too high for oars, and at the least, they should have to close the three windows on either side, just large enough for a man, that allowed them to bail when needed, and breathe when it was calm. Most rowers preferred the occasional dunking to the thick, stifling air, but since they left Drummoc that morning, the captain had pressed them to make time until the winds could be of use. He checked the bilge level with a glance—also one of his tasks—and it was still short of needing attention. They wouldn't want to sacrifice oars to the task just yet, so he expected they would be stifled.

Ardhan, the coxswain, was a fortunate draw for this trip. A tall, clean-shaven Navy man whose head flirted with the upper deck, he was content to sit and let Lenet determine the stroke at all but the most critical junctures, when he took commands relayed down from the main deck, usually by the second sergeant—the Navy's equivalent of the second mate. It was the captain's orders, but when the ship was under oars, it was the second sergeant's commands. As the only one who could see the water, he coordinated the major maneuvers, and decided which and how many shifts rowed. He gave one of the four paces, or the marks between them. But it was the coxswain who interpreted that, and who decided when the shift was relieved. Some of the coxswains on the firestone route would row men half to death, and even when they didn't, they were more inclined to command and heap abuse than their abilities should dictate. They were the only man who could not see the water or feel the stroke—answerable to the deck, and whose small station gave them a tendency to exaggerate their own importance. Ardhan was the rare man who understood his position as a messenger. He commanded the four marines of the watch below, and let the stroke fall upon the bone stick of Lenet's drum. His arm knew the paces, and he could beat them with his

317

heart if he had to. There was nothing more frustrating than a coxswain screaming at him, "Faster!" when he knew the rhythm was perfect.

For it was also his job—unacknowledged and never thanked—to look after the rowers. To ease the pace without calling attention when he felt them waver late in a pressed shift. All of them were Matttaka, and it was just the opposite for the crew on deck, though sometimes Mattaka were hired to fill berths among the sailors, and on this voyage there were four. It made for a trying run. The usual complement of four officers, eight marines, and twelve sailors already made the Navy nervous, outnumbered as they were by the sixty-one Mattaka below. When they started giving up their knot men for Mattaka, it was worse.

Not that any of the men cared to make trouble. Every practice on the ship was a time-tested and well-drilled result of the disadvantage in numbers faced by the crew. Besides the personal consequences for as much as the rumor of subversive behavior, which were sufficiently terrible, there would be worse for his family back in Drummoc, or one of the hunting camps. Most of the men chosen were family men for that reason. Sons, husbands, fathers. It was uncommon for Lenet to have earned such a trusted position while unattached—though it always came with the ire of men in harder roles. The sailors would be like him, he thought. No one behind to answer for them. There was only one reason a Mattaka signed up as a sailor on a coal ship, and that was to vanish at Nunoc, or beyond if he could, to seek an unsavory berth.

Until then, none of them would speak to one another except to repeat loud orders. There was no hope of any man below coming up the ladder unless the ship was hauled ashore, nor one of the four sailors finding shelter below. Theirs was the worst position. They would be worked when the work was done, even when the other sailors rested, and no task that might send a man overboard would ever fall to any but them. The Navy knew why they came, and would get their full use out of what was like to be a one-way trip. Even a dog rower had it better.

Especially under Ardhan. This was Lenet's first turn with the officer, but his reputation was well-attested. A blessed name among the people, often cursed as a light-touch among the Navy, though he kept good order and always turned into port ahead of time. The greatest danger in his hold was that the ship would run too smoothly. The men would remain fresh and spirited. If the other two boats in the fleet were not as well-managed, they would lag behind. Their coxswains would have their ears lashed from above, and they would push men who were already overtried beyond what they could do. Two rowers had died on the *Kalpa* and another dozen wasted two seasons prior, it was said trying to keep pace with the lead ship and with Ardhan. He did not care for the responsibility of also "adjusting" the speed for vessels he could not see. Lenet prayed for wind.

"*Huuunnnnhhh,*" one of the rowers groaned.

"Shut up," Ardhan said without enthusiasm.

"Shut up," Lenet repeated to the man nearby. Muk, they called him, because his name was Mennetungiliamuk. Being from one of the older Drummoc families meant he was prouder, and so made more trouble than one with such a large family ought to. But he was not one to complain, so the second time he let out an involuntary moan under an even pace in fair conditions, Lenet grew uneasy.

"Shut *up,*" Ardhan had to work hard to make it sound like he was more irritated with Muk. His stroke lagged a quarter beat behind the men around him. "Lenet!"

"Shut up," Lenet repeated. Muk made brief eye contact, then looked back to his work. Now in his late-thirties, Lenet was old enough to be the father of half the men, Muk included, but he was a father without authority, and often earned whatever rebellious behavior they couldn't risk directing toward the Navy. And if he didn't exert enough discipline on his charges, the responsibility in the eyes of his employers would be his. So his heart leapt when Muk took both hands off his oar and let it shudder to a stop at the oar lock with a bang. The younger man rose and stepped into the aisle facing Lenet, blocking his view of Ardhan.

"Back on your oar!" Lenet shouted, which alerted Ardhan, who uttered a string of curses under his breath as he got to his feet. Muk collapsed in a heap on the deck and quivered violently. Lenet dropped his drumstick and slid down to cradle the man's head on his lap. "Keep rowing," he shouted to everyone. There were side eyes from some of the men, but no one betrayed more interest. The young man was heavy. Shorter and thicker than most, he made up for his height in the unmeasured brutality of his pull. Lenet pressed a hand to his flesh. It was warm, and the blood returned fast to his fingerprints. The light dew of work gathered around his collar. It was too early to ail from the things that would find them once they left the Attavaik Sea.

"What is it?" Ardhan called from abaft.

"He holds his stomach. Must have eaten a foul bird before we left."

"Get him back on his fuckin' oar."

"Aye, sir."

Lenet tried to guide his shoulders up to a sitting position, but Muk was dead weight. He didn't have to explain the consequences of a sick berth to the man. "Back to your bench! Turn up if you must. It will be good to put it out." He tried again to lift the stocky little man. The dark eyes closed and his head arched back as Muk wailed something unintelligible at high volume. Then in a softer tone, he spoke short and quick in Mattaka: "Lenet, my brother," from a man who'd never had a kind word for him. "Let my words pass." He wailed again, as Ardhan clomped over.

Lenet turned to stone in dread as the coxswain towered over them. The rower's breathing heaved in rapid snatches, face contorted in pain. His arms cradled his midsection and his knees balled upward to envelop his trunk as he turned on his side with a whimper.

"Up with you! What's it about?" Ardhan grew agitated.

"I don't know," Lenet protested. "If we take him to the bailing hatch, perhaps he will turn up."

"Aye, but which end of him?" The coxswain grinned. "I'll leave it for you to sort. Get that man off me deck. Have you raised an oar opposite to balance the stroke?"

"Starboard, *one oar up*!" Lenet nearly forgot. "Edriket! Oar up!" He called on the bench across the keel. Ardhan turned for his seat. Muk refused to budge.

"Hear me, great people!" He yelled in Mattakatan to the entire rowing deck in what sounded like an excruciating cry, but his words did not match his shaking and his tone.

"Are you mad?" Lenet spat in Mattakatan. "You're going to get us all killed."

"Shut the fuck up!" Ardhan stomped back to pair. "No Mattakatan! No Mattakatan! On alert for mutiny!" He pointed to the two marines fore. "On alert for mutiny," to the two aft.

One of them clambered up the ladder. "Lock oars, face bench!" Ardhan commanded. The crew secured their handles and knelt facing the hull. They lay their chests and faces on their benches, as the original marine came down the ladder with four more. They fanned out in pairs, back to back, steel-spears at the ready. Within moments, both hatches closed behind them, taking much of their sun and sealing them below deck. Lenet hoped Muk was only seeing visions from his illness. If not, whatever he trouble he cared to make was already quelled. Even one as reckless as this would know it.

"If I may have one to help me lift him, I will take him to the bailing hatch. Air will do him good," Lenet plead as much as offered.

"He will lift himself, or it's a sick berth for him," Ardhan said, now an alternating form of man and shadow in the crossing light from the oar locks.

Muk winced and let out another cry: "I have eighteen on this ship who will take it," he clawed at his stomach.

"Translate every word!" Ardhan snapped. Muk panted. Through a narrow opening in his eyelids, he watched for Lenet's answer. "Translate it!"

Lenet stuttered. The marines poised their spears to rain on the unarmed rowers. Eighteen of them, if he said one thing. Perhaps more, if he said another, not to mention their families. How he wished to take up his stick again and sneak the pace a beat lower!

"It is nonsense. This man is very sick."

"As many on each of the others," Muk kept up his writhing.

"Translate!"

"His—his mother."

"What about her?"

"If I am brought to deck, we take the hold."

The life-breath went out of Lenet, and he felt the walls of the hold squeeze like a great hand. If he were armed, he would kill the man himself. Perhaps it would be taken into account. At least, for him, though he could say nothing of the crew. A desperate thought of squeezing the thick neck with all his might fluttered past. It was no wonder nothing had been said to him in advance. Only a boy and a fool could have such notions. Only an arrogant Mennegur would make him choose between the lives of his crew and their families, or sparing them at the price of a knife from his own people as soon as he returned to Drummoc, if not sooner. It was haste that freed his lips. Were it not, he was sure he would have spoken otherwise.

"His mother has not prepared the seal fat." There was a shift in the shoulders on his lap. Something unseen moved over the hold. He wondered if the rowers were as surprised as he was.

"Then we rush the deck and signal to the other ships to do the same."

"Not enough seal fat for winter. He babbles. It is takka-tak."

The ship felt as though it spun around. Lenet knew better. He wiped the dreams from the backs of his eyes. Listened to the slosh of the bilge. The lap of the swell against the creaking frame. Little shafts of light ran like spears through the hull to illuminate dust in chaos. The quiet seemed eternal. When no one moved, Muk wailed again.

"We will get the people from the hunting camps."

"Maims," Lenet said quickly. "He says there are maims beneath the ship."

"In Spring, we will take Drummoc."

"They grabbed his oar." Lenet's chest became the drum.

"If all stand," Muk coughed and heaved for air, "if all stand…if all stand…"

"He says there is no wind…there is no wind…I think he cannot breathe."

"They will sing of us."

Lenet shook his head and looked up where he knew Ardhan's face should be. "It is more nonsense. This man needs air," Lenet trembled as he said it. "Let me bring him above."

"No. Get on his oar. Back to your oars!" He called to everyone, then turned to a pair of the marines who came from above: "Haul him up and let him breathe. Then it's a sick berth for him."

They lifted Muk, who moaned and gasped. His show was becoming less convincing, Lenet thought. It seemed too jerky, and Ardhan might sense it. "Two of you stay down here." A marine pounded on the bottom of the hatch.

"What of it?" The first sergeant's voice came.

"All clear! Sick man, comin' up," was the answer. The bolts turned, and the hatch lifted, on one side only. The marines were barely able to coax Muk up the ladder. Hands from the deck assisted, and with great effort, he disappeared topside. Lenet held his breath, expecting to see the hatch close behind them any moment. He heard the word—"Hatch." Knew the sound it would make, the way the light would vanish. Instead, the forward one opened, as well.

It was not clear what Muk intended. Maybe the others knew. He didn't wish to upset them. If it was to be this way, best to step back and let the men show him their intentions. No one below could fault him any longer. But he was unsure of what went on above. Muk was not one for subtlety. He had fooled a soft-touch in a dark hold, surrounded by his people. It was far from certain he could do the same for long in the sunlight, among the officers. Lenet weighed it. Only seven below, but if they were able to bunch up and call for help, it would be a bloodbath between them and the support from topside. As they stood, there were two each fore, mid, and aft.

"Back to your oars!" Lenet barked for Ardhan. A number of the men looked to him expectantly, but slid back onto their benches. The marines' forearms slackened against their weapons. He could see the rowers droop. It was tempting to guess the ones Muk had referred to. But just who it might be, and with what kind of spirit, he could not know. Another wave caught them on a pitch and broke through the starboard windows, right on the bench he was to take. Lenet watched it run off in ribbons and race to the bilge. He drew a full breath of sea air through his nose and let it soak his lungs until they tingled before it dropped in a sigh. Instead, he moved to his drumstick and tested the heft in his hand. As far as he dared to look, everyone returned to work as commanded. There was more than him who needed convincing, and that was if Muk spoke the truth about the numbers. If it was more than just the dream of one madman. It was a fine show, and none could say he did not put himself in the front of his men. But for the best thrust of Mennetungiliamuk, it may have fallen short.

Lenet felt it was a strange hand that tapped out a soft rhythm, rising steadily in tempo and power.

He heard his name from across the hold. "You'll have to bark it. You're on the oar!"

He held his beat, and imagined the sound thumping the deck above them, setting the officers at ease. He wondered what Muk thought as the boards beneath him pulsed. The crew seemed to hesitate. One young man went as far as to turn around at his bench and stare at Lenet, a question in his dark eyes. Lenet grinned, and spoke in a flat Mattakatan.

"Quietly! So they cannot hear you above the drum." His stick fell harder.

"No Mattakatan!" Ardhan yelled. His patience was wearing. The coxswain turned again in disgust, and marched straight for him as a father for an insolent child.

"Sorry." Lenet meant it.

The young man slammed into Ardhan and smashed him into a coal bushel. A hand clapped his mouth, and a second rower's fists thundered on the pinned officer. A dozen arms closed around the spear shafts of the marines before Lenet, and as many bodies could fit in the space swallowed them up. A scuffle behind, and the slam of something hitting wood. Lenet pounded harder as a voice cried out and was muffled. The stampede of bare feet was raising too much noise, and he wanted to silence them, but dared not raise his voice. How much would reach the deck and be noticed, he could not say. He had never stood topside while men rowed. The loudest work could have died at the hatches, or they may have heard every scrape and creak. Lenet nailed his eyes to the aft hatch. As long as there was light, they might live. Seven men were stilled in six measures of the six-beat time. He was glad he could not see what they were doing to the men with such force. Then there were spears in hand, and fine knives. Not many, but already there were only two marines left topside, where there was always a man over each hatch. Any Mattaka who may have wanted otherwise was now committed. Despite their numbers, every man knew that his life depended on making the deck. All of the food and water were stored topside, and it only took a single spear at the hatch to hold the ladders while someone sealed them in to die of thirst.

The noise died. Every man held as still as the pitching ship would allow. They waited in the cloak of the drum and listened for hasty footsteps, or any sign that someone up there knew what was happening below.

"What now?" One of the men whispered to Lenet. He was taken aback. Had Muk thought nothing of this in advance? The eyes of the crew fell on him, though each and all knew he had no part in it—not until he did.

"We go up both holds at once, as fast as we can. Protect the openings. Don't rush them until we have numbers. Don't let them beat you back," he said in Mattakatan. The man regarded him for a moment, then held out the short spear. There were only a half dozen of these, and he knew the sailors up top would still outnumber them in arms—three officers and eight hands on deck. He considered the weapon for a moment, then turned to the man beside him.

"Listen." He nodded to his drum. "You will take the stick." There was not a little fear in the man's eyes as he studied the rhythm. "One, two, three, four, five, six," he counted. "One, two, three, four, five, six. In three measures." They counted together in a whisper. Lenet backed off and held his arm long so the man could move into the space. His palm opened, and as the last beats thudded on the tight leather, Lenet hung up the stroke. The rower snatched the stick and brought it down. A half-beat late, but perhaps only Lenet would notice. He took the spear.

A palpable exhalation passed through the hold. Lenet crouched up to the ladder and twisted this way and that, trying to get an angle to see the man he expected to be standing over the hatch. Only gray cloud showed itself through the square. Three of the spears lined up beneath the other ladder, and the other two behind him, followed by the few knives, and the braver of the young rowers. He tested the first rung with his left foot, and wondered if he should creep up the ladder, or race with all his might. Another look from the second rung told him the man was keeping clear of the sight line, but there was no way to learn which way his head would be turned the moment Lenet's black hair crested the surface. One more tentative step. He glanced back over the expectant faces behind him, then up at the doubtful sky. It was not Pikte he called upon, nor mighty Hapaput, but Eridukne—the boy god who held his arm steady on the drum and kept the time.

With a shove, he bounded up, missing rungs. His foot slipped on the last one, and his chest and arms caught the deck. He knew he had to clear the ladder for the next man at all costs. His legs flailed. He rolled onto the deck and out of the way, expecting to feel the first spearhead any moment. Then he was on his feet, with no memory of how, and the spear clutched under gray knuckles. To port, against the gunwale of the false deck, the two marines stood at arms with their backs to him, while the first sergeant and one of the Mattaka sailors crouched over Muk. Lenet froze in disbelief as he stood astride the deck entirely ignored. Another sailor looked up from where he dressed the big rolled sheet that lay lengthwise over the deck, and paused in confusion. He didn't seem to know what to make of the sight. Another rower got his feet from the other hatch. The captain glanced over from the stern where he was giving orders to a pair of sailors at the steering oar. Another lie napping on a coil of rope, and the rest were scattered, no more than a pair to any part of the deck.

Rowers streamed out of the hatches to fill the mid-deck. By now, every man in turn noticed the crowd seeping up, stranding them in separate pockets. No one spoke. Their eyes hung, or darted between one another. Lenet leveled his spear in the direction of the first sergeant, though he was still fifteen feet away. What he envisioned as a storming and a bitter fight had become a calm assembly. The Mattaka sailor who was probably translating for Muk stepped up onto the false deck and backed away from the Navy men. There were arms somewhere up here. None of the sailors made a move for them. The dull thud of the drum under his bare feet came to rest, and the man who took over his stick pulled himself up, the last of the crew.

Lenet could see resignation—but not fear—in the captain's eyes as he strode forward. Although he wasn't sure of the man's name, his reputation was decent. A patient sailor, not one to take undue risk or lose his temper without reason. He halved the distance to Lenet and sighed. "Don't suppose I can talk you out of it?"

Lenet smiled apologetically.

Muk sat bolt up and beamed at his crew, miraculously recovered from his ailment. "They will sing of us!" He whooped.

The first sergeant plunged his spear through Muk's spine.

Peither descended the ladder to the rowing deck of the *Maraigh*. Before his feet hit wood he heard his son say, "Captain on deck!" A deep chorus of "Aye!" came from the rowers, who weren't expected to interrupt their work to snap to order like the marines. Heath clapped his left hand to his hip and extended his right arm sideways, palm forward beside his leg—the Mattaka gesture of unarmed deference that the navies operating in Hiade had adopted generations ago, since the normal raised hand salute was too similar to the way the locals preferred to declare personal warfare. Peither nodded it off.

"Everything alright down here?"

"Aye, sir," the young coxswain answered.

He looked the rows up and down. "Gimme oars up."

"Oars up!" Heath ordered, with some confusion. The rowers raised them from the water and held them parallel to the deck, awaiting command.

"*Queen Taral* just stowed oars and halted." Some of the rowers glanced at one another nervously.

"Why?"

"I don't know. But I don't want to come on her too fast, in case she's good reason." The rowers muttered to one another under their breath. "Quiet them down."

"Quiet on the benches!" Heath yelled.

"Do you recall if that was Ardhan or Caise, the coxswain?"

"Ardhan on the *Queen Taral.*"

"It was oars went up, then they started down, then came up again."

"Hailin'?"

"Aye, but that's not the procedure, is it?"

"Let me have a look." Heath approached a bench. The rower didn't immediately take the hint, so Peither shouted at him. "*Move,* squain, let the boy have a look!" The man stood aside to allow Heath to the bailing hatch. He hung his torso out until he could see the *Queen Taral,* half a mile ahead.

"She's droppin' oar again."

"Had to sort somethin' with the rowers?"

Heath didn't answer right away. He lingered a moment, and popped his head back in. "Pullin' at thirds now, I'd say." He watched a moment more, then came in. "She's turnin' about."

The crew looked around at one another. Peither frowned. "I'll need you up top. See what banners she flies." He started for the ladder.

Heath poked back out. "Don't see none yet."

"Up top," Peither said calmly, though there was an edge of urgency to his tone.

"Aye," the lad called from outside the hull. "She's comin' round." The man who stood for him to get to the window locked eyes with one companion, then another. He reached his arms overhead one at a time to stretch his tired muscles, twisted his stiff back one way, and then the other, a luxury they rarely had when moving. A quick crack of his fingers, and he grabbed Heath by the ankles and fed him through the window into the sea.

"I have come to join your crew," the voice came again through the pitch black curves of the wigwam. Foster looked to about where he thought Parks was, and wished he could see what his friend was thinking. Was it just the one? He hoped the big man would come up with something clever to diffuse things, but it became clear that he was too embarrassed for one of his usual barbs.

"What crew is that?" Foster tried.

"The food is well-hidden. Ready for a voyage, I think."

"Lenet. I done told you it wasn't us."

"We will search again tomorrow, but I doubt we will find it. Camp will have to break if the hunt is poor. Before then, I will help you steal your ship."

"I don't know if it was Grom, or Blowhole, or who told you we plan to steal a ship, but I just want to point out that it's not only false, but racial profiling, and rude to guests."

"I will not insult you anymore, then, if you do not insult me."

"Fine," Foster said. "I ain't confirmin' or denyin' anything, since it won't do me no good. But maybe you can explain me this: why the hell would you steal a ship from your own people?" Foster's hand slid to rest on the hilt of Gionn's sword under cover of dark.

"There are two people here. One has family on Drummoc, and must stay hidden. One has family here, or no family, and would go north."

"And you're the second kind."

"I have no family, but we must stay hidden. We think it was the original plan."

"You think."

"The one who made it cannot say. But assurances were given to men who left family. If they find out the ships did not reach Nunoc, there will be examples. It was difficult to convince the men to winter here and return to Drummoc in the spring, but when we had food, they were willing to stay. Now, they are restless again."

"Well if yall ain't headed north, I'm not entirely sure we're on the same side." He paused to give a chance to convince him, then went on. "My undertandin' is Drummoc and Nunoc are pretty apart. How would they even know if you made it or not?"

"Every ship that leaves Drummoc for Nunoc carries a traffic log. When we arrive, we give the admiralty letters to the Viceroy. Every ship the rest of the season carries the full report of arrivals and departures, in case any are lost. It isn't strange this late in the sailing season for us to be delayed, or for confirmation to be delayed over winter. But when the first ship of spring arrives, if these ships are not confirmed, it will be bad for the families."

"Bad, bad?" Parks asked.

"Many who are related to those on the ships will be killed."

Foster was unsure of how prolific these folks were at breeding, but if they were anything like every other poor folk he knew, that would be quite a body count.

"So how's hidin' here gonna help you?"

"We think it was the plan to hide until spring. We chase the ice to Drummoc, and see to it that the first ships to arrive are ours."

"Won't they still be pissed?"

Lenet laughed. "They will be 'pissed' when we take their fleet in the harbor and overwhelm them on land. But unless the food is returned, we cannot stay. To leave Yunoc this early in the sailing season, it is certain we will be seen no matter where we go, and word will reach Drummoc. Most do not care. Their brave act is done."

"Why do you?"

"I am responsible for the family of Mennetungiliamuk."

"Akmanujad, huh?" Parks guessed.

"Guilty conscience."

It all sounded plausible. None of it could unknot Foster's innards, though. If Lenet was being truthful, there was no way he could ask around to corroborate the situation without tipping their hand. And if not, Foster would be confessing to theft.

"Classic road trip dilemma," Parks interjected. "Am I right, Foster?" He didn't respond. Any time that mouth opened, he knew they teetered on the cusp of disaster. "The old 'Which way do we go, George?' We've been through this in our boat already. You're the Foster of our people. Or Fucker, as your people call him. He was willing to leave everyone else behind and row to a highly questionable island all by himself on the off-chance that someone we knew might be there and in need of rescue. That's what you're talking about, isn't it? Leaving all your bros behind if they won't just agree with you. What I don't understand is how that would help? Let's say you convince us to join your crew."

It was a nice evasion at least, Foster thought. Maybe Parks was sharpening his craft.

"Let's say you steal a boat. So what? How does that help you? They'll still go north. They'll be seen. You got a third of the ships, and everyone knows you're missing. If there's one thing we learned—I *hope* we learned it—it's that you gotta stick with your homeys no matter what. You might have good ideas, but so do your bros. Just cause you want it, doesn't mean it's possible."

Foster gritted his teeth. It wasn't lost on him that Parks was planting the seed of aborting the whole thing.

"If we cannot be the first three boats in spring, we will be the last boat before winter. Most of the camp will not agree. They have their people. Or they lose heart. Their fight ended when we took the deck. The loudest, we sent hunting, because we feared the ships would be gone if we went instead. Those of us who go south, we are the same as Fucker. Our fight has yet to start. We will go alone, if just one of our family members can be saved. I have enough loyal men to get one under sail. It will be a hard trip. A hard battle, if we make it. We only need food to start the journey, and arms to pull an oar, and raise a spear."

"We definitely have some pretty good arms, me and Foster, but we don't have your food."

"How many men are we talkin'?"

Lenet hesitated. "We numbered short of two hundred when we landed at the hunting camp to gather as many as we could. More than half have family who remain on Drummoc. But of them, I think half again do not believe it will come to anything. And of those, fewer will steal a ship from their brothers."

"How many?"

"Twenty. Maybe thirty."

"I don't know the first thing about no Drummoc, or who you expect to fight there, but that don't sound like a lot."

"If the people rally to us, it may work. We will have to show signs of victory first."

"What's the opposition?"

"As the Mattaka say, 'six-hundred,' right now." Foster felt there was a joke he was missing. "But in winter, three. Perhaps four."

"Four hunnerd. Against thirty."

"It would be better if all came. But we cannot wait. If the hunters don't come back with food, there will be too many who oppose us."

"Was it Blowhole, or Grom?" Parks interrupted.

"What?"

"Who told you?" Parks insisted.

"Shut up," Foster said. "Nothin' to tell. How do you know it wasn't the men who want to break camp and go their own way who stole the food?"

"I have considered it. If so, there is no choice for us. I pray it is you. Do not leave us behind. The others will promise to take you north. I cannot give you a reason to go south with me. But should you go, many families will be grateful."

A rustle told them Lenet was moving across the space. The flap came open, and his silhouette disappeared into the twilight.

The little bay played host to every remaining kayak and hunting boat come morning, circling like eager predators. Gionn kept their vessel relatively still while Kjartke tugged on a braided fishing line that seemed like it would never end. Arm over arm, after several minutes she stabbed her hand into the mouth of a big silver fish and flipped it unceremoniously into the boat. Parks watched from the shore like some seventh grader whose crush was dancing with another boy while he clung to the wall. They'd been at it since before he got up, and the fact that Gionn hadn't come home the night before had his stomach in knots. He could even see her mouth moving. Words. It wasn't easy to get her to say words, but somehow the most abusive of them had been the one she asked to take her out fishing, and now she was having the closest thing to a conversation he'd yet seen while she piled up fish after fish.

Most everyone who had a line was doing the same, with similar results. He wanted to commandeer a kayak under some pretense of needing to talk to Gionn, but interrupting them seemed like a worse idea than brooding. He was confident that if he left Gionn long enough, he'd manage to screw it up himself.

"How is stealing?" Eskimo Joe stood behind him. Parks looked around quickly.

"Shush, you. No one's stolen anything." He looked back at Gionn and Kjartke. "Yet."

Joe followed his gaze. He clapped his hand on Parks' back, then shoved him into the bay. The cold hit him like a truck and knocked the wind out of his lungs. It was all he could do not to reflexively gasp while underwater. He flailed and flapped until his head broke the surface in a scream for oxygen. Joe reached out a hand, laughing.

"The fuck, bro?" Parks wiggled back onto dry land shivering.

"Cold water is good. Make you forget."

"You're supposed to save my life, not drown me," his teeth clacked.

"Practice." He extended his hand.

Parks shivered in his wet leather with the old man for another hour before the pair in the boat headed for shore. He realized that while they had whale left, Joe was as eager for fresh fish as he was. Between the two of them they ripped the bow from the water and held it for Gionn and Kjartke to disembark.

"Quite the catch," Parks said to Gionn.

"Aye, it'll be a few more days til we starve. Unless we catch the thief, but he's proven himself too clever so far." He thrust the oar into Parks' hand. "Bring me a fish once the woman cleans 'em," Gionn strolled off. Parks helped carry the boat out. Kjartke lay a sheet of leather on the rock and threw fish after fish onto it—twenty of the same kind. It would be sushi, same as everything else. He noted to himself to show these people how to batter and fry them if he ever got the chance. Parks would be the greatest inventor the Reverse-Eskimos had ever seen, if he could just live long enough. Joe rolled them up and hefted them onto his shoulder, then left towards his wigwam.

A few others were coming ashore as well, so they carried the hunting boat out of the way and secured it without a word. There was nothing to say to her at this point. Maybe he could apologize, but he hadn't meant any harm, and he figured that type of woman would have more respect for a sea slug than a groveling man. Her face tattoos set her jaw even firmer than it would have been in a frame of black hair as she snapped knots into place. All he knew how to do was hold the hull still so she could work. When it was done, she stood and faced him.

"That Gionn's an interesting character—"

"Lenet sends a message," she interrupted. "Fifteen men will go with you. There are others who will not oppose."

"Well, now we're talking. Do we know where the food is?" She shook her head. "Foster thinks Gionn took it."

"Many think you took it."

"Can you catch enough fish along the way to feed a whole crew?"

"Way to where?"

"Does it matter?" He evaded. "You're pretty good from what I saw." She scowled him down.

"Well, good talk."

Kjartke caught his wrist. "What is your reply?"

"Uh," he clacked his tongue. "Tell him, thanks bro, standby for orders. We don't acknowledge any impending crimes or malfeasance, but per our previous conversation, and the terms established at that time—fuck it, tell him I gotta talk to Foster."

"He said thirty," Foster complained through a handful of sushi as they climbed the trail to collect water.

"'Others will not oppose,'" Parks repeated.

"How many others?"

"You know, she didn't say."

"So if we somehow make it out of here, it's on the agreement that we help fifteen men launch a fuckin' amphibious assault against 400 Navy personnel because that's what the majority of our crew wants to do. Meanin' it ain't our crew. And we gotta get there on starvation rations."

"I hate to point out what Lenet already pointed out, but fuck Lenet. Why don't we just wait til everyone decides to abandon camp and hop onto one of the northbound boats?"

"All those poor bastards in whatever that place is are gonna get curb-stomped."

"You say it like there's something we can do about it."

Foster brooded a moment. "Call her up here." Parks turned and waved at Kjartke, who had been following a polite distance back. "Darlin', be honest with me," Foster said. "Do you think Lenet is just tryin' to catch us in the act? Is any of that shit he fed us true?"

"I cannot know his thoughts." Their faces drooped. "But the ships are stolen. There will be pain for the people."

"All that shit about half the camp wantin' to run and the other half fight."

"I do not speak with them."

Foster nodded. "Fine. Tell him we wanna meet tonight. All fifteen. I wanna look at their faces. Everyone who's goin'. You, me, Parks, Tunguk, fuckin' Gionn. I want a team meeting tonight at the trailhead. Parks, bring your little fuckers you recruited."

"Dude, we can't have that many people meet anywhere, much less in plain sight."

"He is right," Kjartke confirmed. Parks beamed a little inside. "Lenet send me to talk. He cannot be seen with you."

"The element of surprise is fucked sideways at this point. If there's really two camps to this camp, we don't need to surprise 'em. We need a show of confidence. If those men want us to fight with 'em, they're gonna have to put their balls on the table. I'm gonna make those wishy-washers choose sides. You tell Lenet if I don't like what I see, we break camp with the rest of 'em. Now go on, git," he waved her off. Foster turned back to Parks. "I need you to bring me that thief."

Parks stood guard outside the mess hut. The people were generous with their catch, but it was all stored in private hands at this point. None trusted the place where a gazillion pounds of meat had vanished into thin air. Grom and Blowhole arrived with the witch woman who had predicted the theft.

"Here is the poye, Leopard Seal."

"Very good, Grom. Does she speak the King's tongue?" The woman babbled something. "She understand what you say," Grom confirmed. The woman spoke again. "She already try to find the thief. He has protections."

"What sort of protections?"

"The kind our people place," the translation continued.

He mulled it over. "Is the loot protected, too?" She shook her head. "What did you tell Lenet?"

"She says she does not answer to Lenet, and he does not ask."

"In that case, I humbly request that you use your witch powers to locate the food." She shook her head and explained something to the boys. "The moon is wrong. Questions to recover what is stolen are for Sunken Moon. In Falling Moon, it is questions to discover guilt or innocence."

"But the guilty have protections." She nodded. "Can you find out if a specific person is innocent?" She nodded again. "OK. Run it on me." She said something else and laughed.

"The poye says she know you are innocent, you are too stupid to deceive."

"Guilty as charged, but not everyone would agree. Maybe if you told them…"

She smiled and unrolled a leather sheet. In it was a bag tied with thin leather. She loosed the knot and shook it while she spoke in Reverse-Eskimo. There was a rattling within. The poye tipped the bag and continued to shake until a bone fell out onto the leather. On it was a carved a symbol. She repeated the process until two more tumbled after it, then arranged them in a line. Whatever she saw earned him a crosswise look and a grin.

"You have protections, too," Grom translated.

"Bullshit. Are you saying I'm the thief?"

"No. Different protections. You are innocent."

He frowned in confusion. "Can she do more people?"

"Depends on what you have to trade."

"I have no material possessions, but I can offer you a lustful evening with one of my associates here. Hell, you can have both." The boys gave a look of disgust.

She answered in plain English: "Fish!"

Tunguk rolled the tiny bone bead in a pool of fish blood he'd dripped into a cavity in the ground, then rubbed it clean and held it up for inspection. A pink tint remained over the small symbol that looked to Foster like an equal sign with a diagonal from the beginning of one line to the end of another. The old man smiled, as if waiting for a comment.

"Cool, brother. What is it?"

"Sapak bead," he answered. Kjartke rolled her eyes while she cleaned fillets and lay them out to dry.

"He want you to ask him about sapak." She said.

Foster nodded. "What she said."

Tunguk crossed his arms and grabbed the bottom of his tunic, then peeled it overhead. His bones protruded at all angles of a sunken chest, hairless and spattered with scars. The leather frame hung from his neck and tied around his back at the bottom. It was covered in beads of various colors, and carvings, though all more or less fell into one of three shapes: a round sphere, an oval, or a straight bar, nearly rectangular but rounded again at the ends. The new addition belonged to this latter shape. Some were alike, showing up frequently. It was hard to tell, with a good many of the symbols shifted around to face his skin from the general chaos of movement. Small knots held them apart like punctuation marks, with some running together, others completely isolated. A wrinkled finger indicated the empty leather strip where this one would make its home.

Foster had seen it a few times already, and felt it under his hands when they first approached him, collapsed from his heart attack. It never felt right to ask. Parks arrived with Gionn and beat him to it.

"Joe! Put your guns away. You're making me feel small. What is that thing?"

"Sapak bead," he repeated.

"Quiet about your necklace. Parks thinks he knows the thief," Gionn plopped down.

"Indeed, I do. I'll be needing four of those fish."

"We don't need to see you act it out with fish characters, just tell us," Foster said.

Tunguk ignored them to fiddle with the knots that would allow him to attach his latest carving.

"I'm not doing fish theater, Fucker. I need to pay the witch woman. She charged me one per question. Lucky I got it in four." All except Tunguk perked up. "First, you and I are clear," he said to Foster. "I've got Grom and Blowhole spreading the news around camp. By the way, you don't have any protections."

"What does that mean?"

"I don't know, but apparently, I do. Just thought you might find that information useful. Because the thief placed protections against discovery over everyone in the camp, except us. A cloud of confusion, if you will. We were exempt, by accident or on purpose. I found this out when I asked if Lenet did it and she couldn't tell. It wasn't until my fourth question that I got my answer."

"OK," Foster nudged him on.

"No need to reveal that. The important thing is that the trip is a go."

"That does *not* seem like the important thing, cunt. How do you know this?"

"I told you, I asked four questions of a witch woman."

"Excellent. Let's trust our fate to her with no explanation."

"If you can't trust it to her, trust it to me."

"You fuckin' twat. You said yourself that there's protection on the whole camp but the two of you. How can you know?"

"Through a stroke of genius. I'm doing the thief a favor. By not revealing him or her, I create goodwill between us, and I can confirm beyond a shadow of a doubt that we will be rewarded by that person providing enough food for our little cruise. So we don't need to point fingers. The plan is a go. Foster, tell us the plan."

"I ain't got one yet."

"Are we not havin' a meetin' of conspirators tonight?" Gionn asked.

"We are."

"Perfect! Who needs a plan, or food?" Gionn threw up his hands. "We'll just trust his interpretation of a senile old cunt's interpretation of the future!" He huffed off.

"It is many days since I add a bead," Tunguk spoke, tying off the knot. "I think not many more will come."

"You're gonna tell us about it even if we don't ask."

"Yes. It is my story. When something happens, I carve a bead."

"Is it just for decoration?"

"To remind him of shit he's done," Foster corrected. "Where he's been, what he's seen."

"It is men of the north whose beads remind. They are my eyes, my nose, my ears. It brings me to where I am. So you must take care what beads you carve. Not too many, or too few." His fingers closed around a pair. "Some are my pride. Others," he traced a line of five, "hateful." His fingers fumbled for another group. "My courage." He went straight to another and pinched it: "A woman departs," and another, lower and to the left. "Or arrives. I wear them all." He held up the latest carving and rolled it between the pads of his thumb and forefinger. "It is my song," he said, then threaded it onto a strip of leather. A grin spread over his face. "And for decoration."

"Sounds pretty gay, even for arts and crafts," Parks said. Tunguk pulled his tunic on and extended four fish. "Answers to questions," he addressed Parks, "do not fill." The old man departed.

Kjartke let out a little snort.

"You got somethin' against my boy Tunguk?" Foster squinted.

"Tunguk does not know a sapak. He is—what you say when one who lives now follows old ways he does not understand?"

"Ah," Parks said. "We call that, a 'hipster.'"

"Aye. Tunguk is a hipster. Sapak is not for a man to wear. Not for him to make. To carve the beads for himself, it has not been done since long before the grandfather of his grandfather. The sapak belongs to clan. It is passed from ancestors, too sacred to wear except by elder of clan during ceremony. Tunguk has no ancestors. No family to pass it. A song?" She laughed. "Only in his ears. Old man who mutters. He has no medicine. Tunguk is Tunguk."

Foster stood a polite distance from the wigwam with his hands folded in front of his hips, as he'd been for the past half hour. The family glanced his way at times to see if he was still there—mostly the young ones. The women kept to their mending. Always mending something, the Mattaka. It reminded him of his own grandparents' stiff refusal to throw anything away that could somehow be jury-rigged to almost do the same thing, or converted into something else. In this case, at least, he understood. These folks in particular were wealthy by comparison to their peers. A great assemblage of fishing line, tools of bone and stone, and piles of skin in various stages of use covered the ground outside their dwelling. Their clothing was a bit warmer and a hell of a lot fresher than the bachelors he'd seen walking around in what amounted to a tank top and nothing but a water bladder on their belts. Just in the time he'd been here, two different people had stopped by to return stone knives and offer a cut of fish or a scrap of clothing, which was refused in true Southern American fashion several times in what nearly became a heated argument before the loaning family gave in to the token.

That was the last he'd seen of the gentlemen who did the speaking, a man in the second half of his thirties whose deep-set eyes regarded him with suspicion before disappearing inside. Now it was an old man, much the junior of Tunguk, who presided over the scene, though he did no work himself. He was another one of those porch-setters. The ones who'd carve you with their eyes if they didn't know you. By now, Foster was well-filleted, but he was rooted through flood or fiery hail as far as he was concerned. At least, until it got too cold. This was Kjartke's advice. She never mentioned how long he should expect to wait.

The first few minutes he thought he would be wrung bloodless by impatience. After cursing them sideways in his head and running through every Appalachian custom that seemed to convict their rude behavior, he at last settled in to the pace of Antarctica. It took a whole year for a single day to pass, and eons for the black rock to well up from the ocean. Might just be that his timelines were as reliable as the map on his belt. Once he accepted it, he felt something melt like a stream of ice water running into the ocean. He no longer wanted them to acknowledge his presence. He would stand among these wigwams until they rotted on their frames. Until the wind sanded the peaks down to shoulder-height. He imagined these people's descendants stopping in this cove on a hunting trip. Resting in the shade of Foster Rock, a permanent feature of the landscape. As comfortable going nowhere as anything else around him.

So it was a mild shock when the man stood before him wearing a polite smile.

"Will you share a meal with us, mate?" He asked. Foster blinked himself back.

"Oh, uh—thank you. No. I'm just here to speak to the head of the family."

"Then you have what you came for. Please, we have caught much today."

"I'm really OK. We had a pretty good catch, too. Just wanted to have a few words, if you don't mind." That seemed like enough refusal, so when the man insisted once more, Foster pretended to hesitate, grimaced in defeat, then nodded.

He found himself seated within, though none of the other family members joined them. The man would not hear a word of his business until he had eaten what he thought was an unforgivable amount of their food, especially given the rationing. Only after the women came to take away the bones did he exchange more than names with Vekret, who carefully avoided naming him in return since he'd introduced himself as Foster, and no one here would call him anything but what Parks christened him the day of the shipwreck.

Foster took a long swallow and water and wiped his mouth. "I reckon you're wonderin' what particular cultural misunderstandin' brought this idiot to impose on your family." The man did not interrupt. "Like I said, I was just hopin' to speak to the head of the family. I feel bad acceptin' your generous hospitality, because for all I know, it ain't you I should be buggin'. From what I hear, there's two different camps. One of 'em seems to look up to Lenet. I know there's no leader, but he's about the closest thing I can see. Which made me wonder: if he speaks for the Mattaka who aim to head south first thing in Spring, who is it that speaks for everyone else?" Foster let the man mull it over, but he still didn't get a response. "I happen to know that the folks who want to go south are rowers who left family behind. The reason I'm harassin' you has nothin' to do with anything but the fact that you seem to have four solid generations here. No reason to go riskin' anything on a fool's errand. Now, you may not be the big chief, the Northbound Lenet, but at the very least, I'm bettin' you can tell me who is."

There was enough of a silence that Foster worried he would be in for another geological wait. Then Vekret spoke.

"It is good that my family caught your eye. Of the many here, it means we are a fine sight. You are right that all are here. But it is not so simple."

"What's not so simple?"

"It is true what you say. Many rowers wish to return to Drummoc for their families, and many who have them are ready to depart. But not all. I have spoken to men who left wives, children. Who think it is no use to return. No good will come of it. And there are men from the firestone ships who gathered their people, and are prepared to return that their crewmates can do the same."

"In that case, I apologize for bein' presumptuous. I didn't mean to suggest you didn't care about your shipmates."

Vekret laughed. "I am no rower. My son pulled for the *Queen Taral*. These others you see lived with me at the hunting camp on Drummoc. Even among the families, though, it is divided. We left many of our mates, our people. The ones who have no family on the ships will suffer the same if the Navy learns we deserted the camp."

Foster blinked in amusement. He remembered his mama's reaction when he and his buddy Vince showed up at the house with three Xbox games they stole from that douchebag's locker. Their narrow survival. He couldn't fathom rolling up on his family with three coal ships in open rebellion. While the particulars of the geopolitical relationships eluded him, he got the impression this shit had more consequences than even the Mattaka cared to acknowledge.

"But you're not one of 'em. You want to go north." It was difficult having all these conversations in a wigwam too dark to read the other's face. He hoped Vekret took it in good humor. "If you were with Lenet, no way you'd be talkin' to me."

"Hm!" Vekret gave a chuckle of admission. "It would be one story if we had seal laid up for the winter, and for the trip. I understand why the men want to return."

"That changes things, don't it? Not the seal. Goin' back. Your boy stole some ships. I'm sure that's bad, but if Lenet gets his way and yall show up like an invadin' army…Would you even have a chance?"

"We do not—"

"I know, I know. Your people don't believe in chance. You know what I mean."

"I was saying, we do not fear battle. If we go to the hunting camp, and get the ones who were afraid at first to leave, the numbers are good. We would perhaps find the fleet in winter shape. Dry dock, if the gods are good. But it is not courage we lack. It is far. There is not enough food for hundreds of people to make the journey."

"Even hunting along the way?"

"There is good hunting, but a ship that hunts does not sail. Without provisions, and with so many people, we would spend all our time searching for whale and seal. If we must kill our food as we go, I do not think we could travel farther south than Nunoc, or north of the Orin, before we would have to stop. But now it is my turn to ask something of you."

"Ask away, brother."

"Your boat sailed south when you stopped. But it is known in the camp you wish to go north. What would do you to make it possible?"

"You're askin' if I would go so far as to steal the all food and a ship? Absolutely. I know yall won't believe me, but someone beat me to it. I just want to make sure if one or all of those boats goes my way, I'm on it. Whatever you need me to do. And if you're not in charge, I'll be happy to speak to whoever is."

"There is no man who leads us, but I will make it known. The loudest ones are hunting, and they will make their finest effort. But if they come with full boats, there will be yet more hunts needed to have enough for winter. I think the ships will go your way."

"How far? If we support yall, will you promise to spare one of them ships to take us all the way where we came from?"

"No. We go to the arm, then hunt for winter."

"Not good enough."

"There is no meat for the voyage you want. Perhaps in another spring, or two more. Not all will find the arm hospitable. If you are patient, you will have little trouble to win a few restless boys for your crew."

"You're talkin' years. Days, whatever you call 'em."

"It is years, as you do."

"I can't wait that long."

"Do you think you will arrive sooner if we go with Lenet? If all agree, there is still food to gather, weather to favor you. Then there is a battle to win in the spring. Then you must provision for a long sail with what ship may survive, and what crew. If there is damage, it will be difficult to repair. The timber comes from Ampos, if it is not enough in the yard. Then you have many miles to travel, and counterattacks to fear all the way, not just from Nunoc. If you desire to go north, it is best to be on good terms." He heard the rustle of the man rising to a crouch, the sign that supper was over. Light spilled through the flap. "A man of many enemies travels hard."

"This whole place is just connectin' flights from Hell," Foster muttered to Parks as they searched for the next step in the broken moonlight. His mind was one degree more at ease with a potential hedge in place. At least now, they could look at what stood before them and decide to walk away. As far as anything solid, though, he was picking his way forward one foot at a time in more than just the physical sense.

The meeting spot was plausibly out of sight, though he had no illusions that such a group could assemble unseen. His boatmates were there, minus Gionn. Whether he decided to bail, or still didn't trust himself was unclear. A long dark snake moved behind the farthest wigwams in their direction. The silver strands that filtered through the clouds glinted off the stripes that were Lenet's men, all fourteen of them, making overtures of stealth as they settled in behind the fleet of hunting boats. The ones Parks called Grom and Blowhole strode up without any such effort.

The men were left to his imagination. It was difficult to make out their features, but the silhouettes were short and sturdy. Not a posse that he would want to tangle with, except that half of them were unarmed. He remembered what Gionn said, about how they weren't allowed so much as a knife on the ships. That meant the weapons Lenet planned to use for assaulting Drummoc would come from whatever they stole off the decks. He'd seen just a handful of steel spears running around. The stone ones probably belonged to the hunting camp, and weren't going anywhere. One more wrinkle he failed to consider.

"Is this enough to man a ship?" Foster whispered.

"Maybe," Lenet replied.

"It is not," came a voice, and then a mess of red hair, followed by four more men—the watch crew whose wigwam they had originally borrowed. "But this is."

"How did you get these two?" Lenet motioned to a pair.

"He extorted us with lies and starvation." A ripple of quiet laughter washed over Lenet's men. Lenet explained: "Each shift has two who would return to Drummoc, and two who would have us leave for the arm, so four of every eight on watch are opposed. This is the way we decided, that no one would steal the ships."

"So if we get these four on board, six out of the eight are our guys." Foster reasoned.

"We can take the ship without a fight."

"Not everyone say 'thank you' at once," Gionn retorted. No one did.

"Parks says he knows who the thief is."

Parks nodded. "I'm not going to cast blame, but I can confirm that the thief is among us as we speak, and we will have the food when the time comes. It's been confirmed by the witch doctor."

"You cannot put too much cargo in the words of a poye," Lenet said.

"If you know who it is, tell us," one of the watch shift said.

"My grandmother used to do embroidery," Parks explained, "and she liked to make pillows with inspirational sayings on them. I remember one she kept on her couch even when she would rotate the others, depending on who she expected for company and how she wanted to shame them into changing their ways. It said, 'a harsh word withheld outweighs a kindness paid.'" He was met with blank stares. "I'm not revealing the thief because I know he, or she—not saying it's you, Kjartke, I know you're the only 'she' here. Just being gender sensitive. He or she, but probably he, will appreciate not being thrown under the bus, which is like a big ship with wheels—never mind. That person will give us the food, because that person will starve if we leave without it."

"And you got this from the poye?" Gionn asked.

"The witch woman. Yes."

"Well, she's a dumber cunt than you are. You know how I know?"

"Because you stole the food."

"Aye, I stole the fuckin' food. None of these fucks would be standin' here prepared to row for you had I not, and you'd never have got within a shit's throw of the ship, because this whole camp puts too much cargo in the words of witch women. They were on the lookout for a thief, and their eyes were on the ships. So I done you a favor. I gave 'em somethin' else to look at. Besides, men row on their bellies, and starvin' cunts row far away from the shitholes that starve 'em. Tell that one to your fuckin' grandmother."

"It's a bit long for a pillow."

"And how the fuck did you find out? I was to understand that I had protections."

"You just told me."

"Aye, because the poye fucked me."

"She didn't know." Even in the dim silver light Parks could see Gionn's face go as red as his hair.

"You bluffed me." Foster beamed with a smile and slapped Parks on the shoulder. "You fat fuck. You didn't even ask her those questions."

"I did, but I realized I couldn't ask her who the thief was, so I used my fourth fish on the next best thing. The only reason we needed to know the identity was to find food for our trip. Turns out she'll only answer certain kinds of questions depending on the moon, and it's a Falling Moon, so that mean questions of guilt or innocence. But it also means questions about departures and the fortunes of voyages. We can't make it where we're going without food, so I asked whether we would arrive safely according to Foster's plan. And she said—" He motioned to the boys. "I can't remember. How did she phrase it?"

"Fucker will arrive at the place he seeks with three distinguished friends," Blowhole offered.

"That could mean everyone starves to death but him and three others, probably me being one since I stand out like a cock at the shrine of Agata."

"Give us the food and we won't have to worry about it."

"Can't."

"Why not?"

"I threw it in the water."

"You what?"

"I said I threw it in the water! Thought I could just shuffle it between the huts after they searched, but it was a pain in the arse. So last night, I weighted the bundles and threw it all in the water. Good riddance! If no one's gonna appreciate me efforts on all our behalves, I hope we all fuckin' starve. Ungrateful cunts."

Silence hung over the group. One of the watch stepped forward, one of the two dissenters, apparently. "I will not row to my death on an empty stomach. Sorry, Lenet. The hunters return tomorrow, or the next. Then we take what we have and break camp." Lenet nodded.

"When's your next shift?" Foster asked. "When do you go back on watch?" The man looked at the sky. "Soon."

"I got me a plan, but we go tonight."

Four men stood on the false deck and scanned the shore. The pale outline of the camp was visible under a thin, clear moon, but the relief shift had disappeared into the night's black hair. The slosh of oars came first, slipping over the surface well ahead of any shape. Soon the prow appeared, and the relief party pulled abreast of the deck. One of the hands caught a line and wrapped it around a cleat, then arms reached for arms and the men were hoisted one by one. Last of all, the boat came up, and those who rowed it stowed it.

That meant the work was done and they could return to their sleep. Aset wasn't sure why he lingered, stone spear in hand. His watch was more to prevent the small clan of Lenet's mates from trying a trick, as theirs was for him. Tonight, he stared at the water as it lapped against the amu. There would be no storms to snap their anchor lines, or sweep them into one another. No one daring enough to enter the tiny bay at night. His family were hunters, though—his rowing conscripted. They didn't need to understand what changed in the current, the air, the ice, to know that it was different, and that other creatures knew this, too.

He walked a quiet lap of the deck's edge, its hard right angles. Not until he came to the fore side, closest to the bay's mouth, did he notice what he knew he didn't know he was looking for. A faint slosh. One of the many fish that had arrived so suddenly breaching in the night. Or more likely, a seal exploring the flurry of activity. Then another. Too rhythmic. He knew he was hearing a single paddle as the sound grew. A quick shadow and a wake creased the narrow band of moonlight on the water.

Aset yelled an alert to his companions. They all joined him in time to see a giuk emerge, heading around the ship a hundred yards from the bow. The person—he was sure it was only one—was indistinguishable, but they paddled with all the grace of a whale seal slapping its enormous girth across wet rock. No Mattaka paddled that way. He knew it was one of the visitors.

"I will tell the others," one of the new watch said in Mattakatan, and disappeared back onto the main deck to signal their sister ships. The man in the giuk seemed to be going nowhere. He turned around and paddled back the way he came, then did it again, splashing circles just out from the ship. "What is he doing?" Aset asked.

"I think he tests us," one offered.

"They are mad," another disagreed.

"Mad enough to steal our whale and our ships?" The first said.

"Board us from a giuk?" The other man laughed. "Aset, you are best with arrows," he continued. "We will be prepared if he attacks." They all laughed. Aset grinned, and scampered onto the main deck, down into the hold to retrieve his quiver and bow. Back topside, he looked around for the man who'd gone to light the signal fire. He could see neither man nor flame, but the cargo blocked most of his view to starboard. He shrugged and climbed onto the false deck, jogging back to the spot where they'd watched the pale man in the guik. His friends were gone, and the man, now clear only yards away, headed straight for him. He fumbled for his bow and turned to look for his companions. On the far side of the false deck, Rukuk sat cross-legged in submission—his fellow sympathizer in his watch group. Behind him stood the other six men of the watch, and eight more with spears, including four of the guests. The fifth drew his giuk close enough to talk in a calm tone.

"Sorry, Brother," Foster said. "You mind givin' me a hand up?"

He couldn't understand why two of the men who were supposed to oppose Lenet's suicide were now helping him, but Aset lay down his weapons.

They lead him to the main deck in time to see the faint outline of more boats slipping with soundless strokes up to the false deck of the next ship. A rope secured it, and shadows streamed aboard while the watch bided their time on the main deck. Two more boats moved between them, and Aset knew the third ship would fall, as well.

Lenet drove the flint down over the bowl of powdered coal, where it sparked on the whale oil and quickly filled the container. Several lumps were added, and he raised it above the deck, issuing flame and black smoke into the night. Two more joined him, each from the other ships. It was an hour before someone in camp noticed and roused the others, but just before the early dawn, the entirety of the group gathered on the shore. A boat was launched with four men. It would have been easy to guess who had the ships and why. They would represent the interest of those whose families were present or safe, those who wished to go north to hunting grounds, rather than south to battle.

The boat drew alongside the false deck. Foster stood with Lenet, the flaming bowl between them. Behind, the rest of his crew and several of Lenet's loyalists. The delegation looked them up and down—among them, Vekret, who did not seem surprised or disappointed.

"What will you do without food?" One spoke.

"We're responsible for the theft of the whale, and now of your ships," Foster said. "Now I ask your trust. I have enough men here. We could have burned two of your ships and taken the third. But I have no intention of harming you any further. I just don't wanna spend the winter freezin' my balls off. My buddy Lenet here says he has a promise to keep. You say you got yours, and you wanna get out. If I let yall fight it out, half of yall's gonna be unhappy no matter what. So I have a proposal. No one's been harmed. I will allow you to keep *all* of your ships, and to decide for yourself where you go and when you do it, under two conditions." The men waited for him to go on. "Condition one. You release to me enough food and men to travel somewhere near Nunoc, and from there we five launch our little dinghy and go on our separate ways. The ship returns here."

"Why Nunoc?"

"Seems to me your problem is that you're expected. If you leave and get spotted, Lenet's dudes are fucked. And he has to show up with perfect timin' and no resources for a helluva fight. Otherwise, the families yall left behind are dead. What if they didn't expect you?"

There were bewildered looks all around.

"We don't have enough food for a trip to Drummoc by my understandin'. But with the fish we're catchin', and if the huntin' party has any kind of success, we'll have plenty to get most of the way to Nunoc. From there, we drop our boat over and go on our own. My boys are tired and they don't feel like rowin' the whole way. When we get there, we hand them those admiralty letters you got. Say we came across three coal ships wrecked on the shores of…wherever you want me to say. Most hands are alive, but the ships are firewood and the people request water and food and provisions to make it through winter, or better yet—rescue. They asked us to deliver their letters to prove their case and send for help."

"They do not care about the people if the firestone is lost."

"That's what I'm countin' on. They'll take the letters, mark you accounted for, and let you starve. Then you can do whatever the hell you like. No one's lookin' for you. No punishments or retributions. We'll get our northbound ship from there, maybe even as a favor for deliverin' the ships' message. You can overwinter if the huntin's good. You can fuck off if it ain't. You can wage war across the seven seas for all I care. We part on good terms, no one gets cut or ripped off, everybody's happy."

They considered his proposal for a moment. Vekret spoke up. "You said there was a second condition."

He nodded. "Every last Mattaka man, woman, and child from pole to pole has to agree to stop callin' me Fucker. My name is Foster."

12

THE THIRD CAPTAIN

The man on the quay paced with his hands clasped behind his back. He wore a worried smile on his dark bronze face, smooth as bare rock with what seemed an unusually large pair of almond eyes. Now and then he would attack an itch in his black hair with indignant intensity. It fell just past his jaw line on all sides, though the middle was bald but for a sparse tuft. His long sleeved tunic was leather, modestly adorned with red patterns around the cuffs and the seam in the front. He wore a tight bead necklace in a single strand, and his ears held round gauges of red-dyed bone.

Now and then, he shivered as his bare feet padded the cool rock. His hands waved in front of him as if in a bow of deference, and he mouthed something polite to someone imaginary. Every few steps he nodded graciously or touched his palms together in front and held them out as if to allow someone to pass with a few kind words. His lips moved, but no sound came out. There was no one to talk to. In the distance, buildings of timber and stacked stone rose in a neat line. One-story, rarely two, they packed tight against one another a quarter mile from the water. To either side of the pacer, permanent pillars held up wooden platforms in a U-shape. Most of them splintered and crumbled, some clearly for a long time, but a half dozen still elevated large ships with deep keels and hole after hole where oars would appear. They were braced underneath with beams and rocks, and they rested on long rollers, their masts stowed somewhere out of sight. Farther off, smaller ships lacked all but the supports that held them upright on land. Nothing sat or stirred in the natural harbor, and it was rare that someone moved between buildings.

The man continued to rehearse his conversations, occasionally checking behind him to see that no one approached. Whatever was going on, he handled it with grave dignity. He shivered again and squeezed his elbows to his sides. Out to sea, a sleek shape appeared in the gray distance. His big eyes grew bigger, and he scrambled for a sack nearby. A rectangle grid of leather strap emerged, the top strands dotted with beadwork. A quick yank sent dozens of beads skittering across the ground.

The man scrambled to pinch them one by one back into the sack. He gathered the loose ends of his creation and sifted through the pile underneath—a jumble of leather strips and beads, some raw and some prepared. His slender monkey arm fished out a handful, and he sorted through in a hurry, tossing back the ones he didn't want, then he lay the rest on the rock before him in neat rows beside the bead grid. The ship was far off still, but he fixed his feet beneath him, clasped his hands behind, and rocked gently heel to toe, his smile the same mix of beaming excitement and apprehension.

Perhaps realizing how long it would be before the ship reached port, he looked around, knelt before the water, pressed his chest to the quay, and reached every inch of his long limb down to dip his hand. His arm recoiled and flapped. He rubbed it for warmth as he resumed his posture and composure. Again the lips moved, less now.

For the next half an hour, he squinted to make out the vessel. As it came into view, he gathered a specific bead and slid it on to the end of the open strand. More careful study, then a second joined it; a third, dismissed into the bag. The longship was the single mast variety. Sleek and with a shallow draft, it moved entirely under oars. As soon as he could count them, he added another bead and checked them against the previous ones—an exact match, separated by a single knot. He tied two small knots after the last addition. The ship was nearly to the quay now, and he smiled with a little more ease.

When it spun wide to come alongside, his eyes bugged out in horror. Another boat. Attached to the first with a tow rope. It was one of the skin models the natives used along the coast. He scrambled through the beads he had in front of them, finding them inadequate, then hurried into his sack. Fingers fumbled for whatever he was after while he checked the arrivals' progress over his shoulder. They were nearly in. The man grabbed a handful and set them gently among the others, brushing off a few that stuck to his firm, sweaty grip. The rowers expertly maneuvered sideways to sling the skin boat toward the quay, then released the tow line that it could drift home under lazy oars. They set out for the landing, where they could carry their own boat ashore.

A quick head count gave him five passengers, a mixed lot. The redhead at the prow threw him a line, and he guided the boat in and tied her down.

"Welcome to Nunoc!" He extended a palm low and out from his side, the acceptable greeting of Hiade. "I am Barzos, First Assistant to the Assistant Viceroy of Hiade, the White Jewel of Ampos." A roar of laughter from the longship drew his attention. A man stood on his bench and stomped up and down like a fool, and humped the air with his hands behind his back. When he saw Barzos look, he raised a rude gesture to another chorus of laughter. Barzos fumbled for his place. "The White Jewel of Ampos."

"Can you give your speech when we're out of the fuckin' boat, cunt?" The redhead extended a hand.

"Profuse apologies." Barzos grabbed it, and nearly yanked himself into the boat on the first pull before he recovered and helped the man ashore. Barzos scanned their faces for signs of rank—probably the one ashore already was the captain, and it was important to help them in order of importance so as not to offend anyone, but they offered no hints. He passed over the two Mattaka faces and fell on the fair ones. His hand shot out to Parks. There was no sign of protest, so he continued down the line, until finally the woman was ashore and the boat raised from the water. Only then did he continue.

"It is my pleasure to be the first to greet you in the rich port of Nunoc." Foster and Parks looked around at the windswept dry docks and the plain stone buildings. "The Viceroy extends his warmth and hospitality, and the Assistant Viceroy also extends his warmth and hospitality, but not as much as the Viceroy, who is of course the most generous of men. Uh…" he trailed off. One side of his lip curled and his eyes glazed and widened before they lit up again with a smile. "Oh! Will you be wintering with us?"

"Fuck, no," Gionn spat.

"Ah, very good. I understand it is cold." He slipped a bead over a piece of leather.

"What's that?" Foster asked.

"Sorry. Records."

"What do you mean, like whose' comin' and goin', with what?"

"Very right, sir." He tied it off after a single addition.

"Don't you need to check our cargo or somethin'?"

"Uh…aye. Of course." He leaned around and looked inside the hull, then nodded.

"And you know what all those mean?"

"Of course, sir. Many say, Barzos, he is dumb, he hasn't got his letters. I say, it is true, but do you have your beads?" He laughed nervously.

"We don't either," Gionn blurted. "Got our letters, I mean. None of us. We are simple sailors, seeking only employment on a northbound vessel."

Barzos lips stretched tight. "Very sorry, the Viceroy has closed the trading season. The last of the coal ships left a week ago. Waves have turned very early in the Orin Sea."

"What about Navy?"

"I anticipate the last Navy ship will leave soon. Passage north is quite expensive this time of year. Perhaps you would prefer to sail in Spring?"

"I would not."

"The only private vessel left to depart is the dog ship. You would be paid for working passage, of course."

"Perfect," Gionn said.

"But it is going south to Drummoc."

"Fuck off, cunt. Why would anyone want to go south right before winter? We'll pay the passage north."

"Ah, very good. It is the marines who must sell their spot."

"How much?"

"Difficult to say. I understand Five—perhaps ten—silvers?"

"*Silvers?* We could buy a whole fuckin' ship for that!"

"Per seat. The winter here is rumored to be unpleasant."

"Do you have a brothel?" Gionn changed his tack.

"Aye, though I must warn you it is a bit understaffed, and not at all inexpensive."

"Good. How much for the woman?"

Barzos's eyes lit up. "Oh, my apologies. I assumed she was a wife, or a daughter. Very good! She will do well. But, uh, the owning and selling of persons in Hiade was banned some generations ago. She can perhaps work and share her pay with you?"

"It is better she works in Drummoc," Tunguk interjected.

"Very fuckin' good, indeed. She can get fucked and the old man can rot. We," he waved to include Foster and Parks, "will be enlisting in the Navy."

"Sorry, sir. The Navy is not accepting enlistments at the moment."

"They are, they just don't know it, yet." He brushed past Barzos toward the settlement. Barzos turned back to the others. "Profuse apologies for upsetting your captain."

"That's guy's, like, fourth in command at best," Parks said. Barzos' eyes bugged out in confusion.

"Look," Foster stepped forward. "I understand the situation. But maybe the Viceroy will make an exception for us as a thank you. Considerin' we bring urgent word from three of his coal ships."

"Coal ships?" The smile once again turned nervous. Foster produced three leather wraps from his belt. "Admiralty letters. From the *Queen Taral,* the *Maraigh,* and the *Pallaia.* I'm afraid they were caught in a storm and shipwrecked." Barzos nodded grimly. "We came across 'em huntin' for seal. The ships are firewood and the coal's almost all underwater, but a lot of the rowers made it ashore. They got water and food for a month or so, and no good means of shelter for winter. If yall don't rescue 'em right away, they're straight-fucked."

Barzos dug furiously through his bag of beads. "Terrible news… *Captain?* I will inform the Viceroy as soon as his honeymoon is over." He found what he wanted and threaded them on.

"Does that mean you've recorded them as shipwrecked?" Foster pointed at the crafts project. "Aye, sir."

"And you'll deliver those letters to the Viceroy?"

"As soon as his honeymoon is over."

"Which is when?"

"Difficult to say. His new bride is quite lovely and full of fire."

"You listen here, man!" Parks said with a bit too much bluster. "Those men—those mostly Reverse-Eskimo men, all of the important officers are dead—they're depending on a speedy rescue." He took Barzos' shoulders in his mitts. "Lives hang in the balance. I don't care that there's no valuable property to recover. You need to—"

"*Parks,*" Foster barked. "You mean we've done all we need to do, then. To make it official. And it's in the hands of the Viceroy."

"Aye, sir. The King of Ampos thanks you kindly for this great service. I will petition the Viceroy to allow you passage north on the Navy ship. If he finishes his honeymoon before it departs."

"That ain't gonna work for me. I need a guarantee, now. Did you say there's an Assistant Viceroy?"

"Aye, sir. He left for Drummoc on the Viceroy's ship."

"Drummoc?" Tunguk laughed. "He must have made a woman of the Viceroy's dog."

"No, sir. He volunteered to inspect the mining operations and act in esteemed capacity as the voice of the Viceroy in the hinterlands." His beaming smile returned. "Can I sign you on to the dog ship, then?"

"Not just yet," Foster said.

"Aye," Tunguk gave him a look. "It is as we agreed," he nodded to Kjartke.

Barzos grinned. "Very good. Captain."

The men of the patrol ship hauled out and braced her early in the day, quite satisfied that they were no longer needed after spending the morning towing in a small squain boat they found struggling against the chop—for weeks, or so he had claimed. It had taken only a day or so to sail from where the *Queen Taral* dropped them off cleverly south of the harbor. He never thought he'd be glad to see Nunoc. It was common on the ships to hear, "a bad lot for one who can't imagine worse." Usually from some cunt in a slightly better position who would be as happy to whinge if the task were turned. Trifle though it may be, Gionn thought it a fitting compliment for this place. The prospect of a winter in a squain camp made it an effort to hold down his joy, out of caution. He could not help but notice the past several weeks' course steered him from the utmost of misery to mere rubbish. It was too early to celebrate, though. Though he was quite sure the squain ship had come unseen, it could always be intercepted on the way back to its crevice. The hunters had come the morning after they took the ships, with a fair enough catch to provision the voyage and have rations left to hunt again. It did not matter a whit whether their camp were found and slaughtered, except that it would be a bad look for him given the story the two idiots planned to tell. Fair as Nunoc was by comparison, this was not a place he meant to linger.

It was plain enough which Navy vessel the monkey referred to. The others were already wintered in. The black docogon, fresh with pitch, pointed her ram down the slope toward the quiet harbor as if to savor the sea air in anticipation of her release. She was as deep as she was calm, this harbor. No anchor would find bottom very far from the natural ramp where they ran ashore. He understood it was once a much longer haul, waters being what they were now. Tucked in the north and the east side of the island, the mountains took the winds off the sea and smoothed the surface, while the channel of perpetual ice between them and the mainland meant that ships could only approach from one direction. Easy enough to blockade, but it would be the weather and the food that broke a siege here. Nunoc had all the seal and water they cared for, and any blow would imperil the besiegers and torment them away. He saw nothing of the dog ship, but that would probably be at the squain harbor, where the coal ships brought their loads to be coked. There, a long river of a glacier spilled right into the sea, and it was the ice the dogs needed to move the loads in the summer. Gionn looked for it after they started round the northwest side—wouldn't be far off with the smithies here—but had not seen it. Probably another place to make this one look cheerful.

Two darraigs and a long-dry abiama. That was all he saw available for patrol. A wonder that so much blood had been spilled over this place, yet the winter garrison amounted to three meandering lads with short spears, such was the difficulty of doing her any harm. Besides, the real fleet would come from the north when the ice lifted. These were here to have something afloat. It was one of the former that hailed them so close to the harbor, he thought they'd make land uncontested. By the time they were seen, they'd lost the part of the ruse in which they arrived from the south where the coal ships were "wrecked," except for their word on it. He was a bit worried they weren't disheveled enough for the trip they claimed, but then Nunoc was never a place where stories needed to add up. The Navy men shrugged off interrogation and tied them up not out of kindness, but so they wouldn't have to row in circles for hours escorting the only traffic for some time to harbor.

As with any time he met a new ship, he'd hunched low and scanned for familiar faces, as no faces familiar to Gionn meant anything but trouble. He recognized the sort, but not the same. Now if he was to enlist before the next and likely last ship went North with those the Viceroy couldn't pay through winter, the obvious place to start was with those who had already done him the service of a ride. He knew that the more a man was allowed to aid him, the deeper the habit of aid was carved. But he didn't quite trust that these were accustomed to him the way that Foster and Parks were. Better to find the tavern and make mates with those cunts. These men would be by shortly to bolster his case. To make first thrust of mateship with men before you know you'd be recognized by others—that was an even better trick.

He veered far from the dry docks down the row of buildings marshaled like an army. A very lazy one, with a confused jumble of helpless, frightened cunts behind the one line of brave ones. For the architecture belonged to the farri—tight mason work and timber, simpler than in Ampos but no less skilled, dating itself back to times when such skill was available here. But the town behind the thin van was classic Mattaka. As with the camp, the only regularity to it was the doors that faced opposite the prevailing wind. These ones were at least made of jagged rock, fitted as close to the familiar dome shape as skill allowed. Otherwise, the little piles huddled together with no rhyme or meter. Between them, barely enough space for two feet to pass, or a piss pot to empty without hitting the next wall. They believed that it confused both winds and evil spirits, causing them to flee. He certainly wanted no part of it.

Though no one milled about that he could see, the feeling of the place told him that one out of every three buildings held anyone at all, and probably fewer the farther into the maze you went. Not wanting to be stabbed by some soot-choked coke hauler, he walked the row that stood at public attention until he found what he was after—a black plume feathered out from a stone vent near the roof of a stout hall with a heavy door of red Amposi wood, as old as the stones that held it. On the stoop, there was carved a horizontal line, with two more descending at angles, left and right from its midpoint.

"Balgan be fucked!" He slammed the door behind him. It didn't get the laugh he hoped. "You pious cunts," he reprimanded the hall of thirty or so men of deeply mixed origin who quickly returned to their drinking. Most were huddled in patches the way men do when there's someone to avoid. Probably still in their crews from whatever working ships had turned blue coat. "Is there a girl, or do I serve meself?" No one bothered to answer. "No matter. I'll be leavin' soon enough. Soon as I talk…" he worked over the faces again, ensuring there were none he knew. Come in quiet, and they all spot you before you have a look, he thought. Come in blustering, and they stay down so you have a fair chance to turn wake before you're recognized. He'd never been to Nunoc, but the sea had a way of sending him its worst in the least likely corners. So far, his luck held.

"…to *this* man!" He settled on an old carrion-sack eating alone. Not the old of dignity as distinction. The one that dribbled out the corners of its mouth as it gummed its food. A bald head and thick white sideburns glanced up with blue eyes that fled before attention of any sort. Gionn reminded himself to be careful not to underestimate him. There was no luck that would grow a man old in his line of work. But the ritually slumped shoulders and imprecision of his fingers as they pinched and dropped boiled fish made him reasonably confident that whatever threats the man once posed had been reduced to odor and blubbering.

He let his muscular shadow fall over the frail hands. "Eatin' alone, I see. Fair and blameless, from the look of these," he thumbed at the rest of the room but spoke so that everyone for several buildings over could hear him. "Can't say I could stomach their manner meself. Beg your pardon, sir. The obnoxious monkey whose name I didn't bother listenin' to informed me that I should speak to the officer about enlistin' me services to the good king and whatever unwanted in-law he made Viceroy." Finally, a chuckle from the crowd. "You're clearly he, judgin' by your age and your noble appearance, at least by comparison to these wave-beggars. Recite to me the oath of allegiance and I shall repeat it back to you."

"Fuuuuck you," a bored voice called, followed by more chuckling.

"Are you gonna let your tiller grabber speak to me like that, sir? How many lashes shall we give him?"

"Lash me cock with your tongue," the man cried back. "You know very well that bucket's no officer." Gionn smiled and approached the speaker's table. His was a motley crew of whites and browns and all shades between, not more than half of which could have actually been Amposi. The man himself would have been. His wide nose and skin of tanned leather contrasted with the hazel eyes that could only mean a noble family, or a mother fortunate-enough to be in a town sacked by one. Gionn parted the shoulders of a pair of men and squeezed onto the bench opposite the officer.

"Beg your pardon, sir. You also have a noble look about you. I simply hadn't noticed due to all these ugly cunts crowdin' around you like flies on fresh shit."

The officer grinned. "I like you. Bet you're a good man to have on certain boats."

"Aye, and I'll be every bit as good on yours. The one goin' north in a few days, as I understand it."

"Certain boats, I said. Not Navy boats. Navy's gotta follow orders."

"I follow all the best orders."

"Even if you had Navy experience, which you don't, the lists are full."

"These are the best sons of all the finest families then, are they? Groomed from an early age to helm a ship?" The officer grinned. Gionn went on. "If the lists are full, they're full. I'll swear as a Marine if I need. Or your pilot boy." The crew laughed. "And if that list is full as well, maybe you can have a think at those names and pick off just one you'd find less use for than a strong, good humored cunt like meself. A man in your position has the authority to do such a thing. If he wants."

The door burst open and the crew of the patrol boat blustered in. "It's the slowest oars in the kingdom!" Gionn shouted to them. "Had to spend all mornin' pushin' these cunts into harbor with me rowboat!" They laughed and muttered a few curses back. "One of you forgot your dancin' girl on the quay. What long, beautiful hair she has!"

"Barzos?" The officer laughed. "You'd best make friends. He'll keep you warm all winter."

"He has one for that," one of the new arrivals remarked. "Ripe young squain."

"That so?" The officer raised a brow.

"She's yours for the price of a single oar. I'd rather fuck Barzos."

"And I'll fuck me wife."

"A wife? *Here?*"

"Aye."

"Doesn't it get boring?"

"Aye, but if I don't fuck her, one of these peltasts will." They laughed and slapped arms in agreement.

"I shall do my best to repel her seductive advances," Gionn promised.

"What're you doin' travelin' in a rowboat with a squain?"

"Two squains," one of the patrol corrected. "And two more halots."

"I know a good story when I hear one," the officer said.

"And hear one, you shall," Gionn smiled. "Soon as your wife pours me one of whatever's in those cups."

The Seal Mother, Tunguk had called it. For some reason Foster expected a sprawling metropolis. Bustling harbors, cargo moving in and out. Torchlight and signs of trade, of sailors and women, local merchants, kids running the streets and beggars begging. Maybe it *was* during the tourist season, but now, as the stormy curtain that separated Antarctica from the continents began its slow fall, the place felt like an old man bedding down for Winter. A column of black smoke billowed from one of the low, plain buildings that lined the row, and the ping of two distinct hammers traded blows on metal from within. Beyond that, there were few signs of life. Here, a roof caved in. There, a rotting frame once held a door. Though he didn't know what a sign of occupancy might look like, two of every three felt like a husk waiting for a breeze to take it.

He and Parks followed Tunguk until simple stone piles gave way to a more impressive line of mostly two-story affairs, the second always a smaller rectangle on top of a larger one. Here, the stone was cut into precise blocks instead of stacked raw and jagged, and a more liberal use of timber framing—almost unnecessarily so—told him these were once meant to impress. The wood looked old now, and he knew in this cold, dry climate that time had a way of standing still, of lending youth freely that all things were older than they seemed. Tunguk led them to the front of a building that hardly looked different from any of the others. No signs or distinguishing marks. Barzos had sent them to what he called the "Dog Charter," Though he hadn't bothered to explain where that was. The old man paused before the heavy door, then cut down the alley beside it and stopped at a short stone hut that only the two Mattaka among them could have entered without ducking. Foster checked over his shoulder to ensure that Kjartke was still following.

"This it?" Parks asked. Tunguk let out a *"Howw-Hoooooowww-wwwww"* sound of a dog baying. He laughed, as he often did, alone. His flat palm slapped against the keystone over the leather flap. A long minute later, a Mattaka man peeled it aside. After a glance at Foster and Parks, he spoke to Tunguk in Mattakatan.

"You stay," the old man instructed them, then followed the native into the what he could have generously called the shed, indistinct from the dozens or hundreds of other Mattaka dwellings that crowded behind it.

"Bro," Parks pulled Foster aside as soon as it closed. "Am I wrong that it sounds like Eskimo Joe is Kjartke's pimp?" They looked at her. She squatted at rest, her face angrily bored as ever.

"It did sound like he meant to take her south to a more lucrative whorehouse."

"And what's in it for her?"

Foster shrugged. "Freedom from her husband? Ability to work from home? I don't know. Not my bitch, not my problem." He lowered his ass to the ground and plopped the map open in front of him. His finger found what had to be Nunoc. The little icon could have been a dog or a seal, yet somehow looked like neither. For weeks of brutal travel, it seemed as though they'd hardly budged from the spot on the peninsula where Tunguk had shown him they first washed up. Beyond Nunoc, his Antarctica disappeared off the bottom, though he seemed to recall Parks' map having more details. When he turned to ask, the big man was already most of the way to Kjartke.

Parks squared his feet beside her and gingerly lowered himself into a squat. As soon as his hips sank below his knees, he began a slow-motion tumble onto his ass, then stuck his legs out in front of him. He had no idea how Kjartke could sit on her heels with her feet flat for hours while she worked. Too much leg muscle, he told himself. Too strong, buddy.

"The Lord's work, huh?" He asked her, and paused for the expected silence. "That's what we called it in the Navy. Saving the souls of wandering sailors. I respect it. Essential support personnel." He waited again. "If Eskimo Joe is forcing you—"

"No one force me. It is my bargain. I prepare food. Mend clothing. Mend boat. I help, Tunguk take me to Drummoc."

"Why don't you do that, then? Be a cook. Or a clothes mender, or whatever. I'm sure there's tons of job opportunities for people with your talents right here. Or in Drummoc. Maybe you could get work on a boat." She looked at him with an unreadable expression. "Just something to make ends meet. Other than…*making ends meet,* if you get my drift." He raised an eyebrow. She didn't seem to catch it. "I have no husband or children to care for me. I work while I am young. Then maybe I have children to care for me when I am old."

"I have some pretty sick business ideas," Parks carried on. "Maybe you can work with me when I get my start-up going. Backpacks with straps. That's gonna be my first invention. You can work for me as a seamstress. You already know how to make the backpack part, whether or not your realize it. I'll teach you the straps. Foster wants to go home, but I don't think it's possible." He grimaced as he looked around. "Besides, there's just a ton of entrepreneurial opportunities here. Give me a decade, I'll be tootin' around the ocean on a multi-million dollar steamship. And don't think I'm the type to forget my first seamstress."

"Foster speak true," Kjartke said. "You should go home." He met her gaze at the furrowed brow poring over his stupid map, thick bearded by now in a way Parks could never grow one. For all his talk, he felt the rising hollow in his stomach whenever anyone mentioned that particular cardinal direction. Home may no longer lie to the north, he thought, but north had come to mean home. He wished he could pack all five of them into a big cutter—even Gionn—and sail right into Santa Cruz to the shock of both onlookers and crew. Maybe all they really needed to do was cross the equator, or the date line, or find some whirlpool portal that would spit them into familiar waters, familiar ports, familiar brothels where he'd been restored to the stillness of land, time and again.

"Just out of curiosity, how much—"

Joe opened the door and Foster sprung to his feet. Kjartke rose to join them, and Parks followed with reluctance.

"Dog ship will take us. It is working passage. Those who can row, will row." Joe looked straight at Foster.

"I'd rather find one north," Foster said.

"I have agreed to bring Kjartke to Drummoc. It is best if we all go, so I might keep akmanuak."

"And what if I find us somethin'? What if I refuse, and go north anyway?"

"I cannot help you if you flee. It is best if we first go south."

"Who said flee? You're invited, motherfucker. You tryin' to get rid of us?" He looked Tunguk over. "Will our lives still be in danger if we go north without you?" He knew the answer, and Tunguk did as well. He was starting to get the hang of this akmanuak bullshit. "I acknowledge your advice, and choose to ignore it, but we still need your help. Look, I like buildings and streets," Foster said. "I don't much care for ships unless they're takin' me someplace less shitty than the one I'm at. Can she go on her own from here?"

"I have to agree with both of you," Parks said. "We should stick together. *And* we should all go north."

"There are no boats north. We will be paid to go south. In spring, when the cost is less, we buy passage north."

"When's it leavin'?"

"Three of your days."

"I'll tell you what. If I ain't got anything better by then, we'll do the dog thing. But if I do, you gotta come with me."

"We will not help you steal the ship."

"Why the hell not?"

"We must bring the dogs to port. Four teams have not returned from training. Good dogs. We must find these, and bring them to port with the rest."

"I see what you're doin'. I can't steal a ship if I'm runnin' after dogs."

"Not you. Kjartke. And me. We are not fit for oars. We bring the dogs."

Foster nodded. "So three days. Me and Parks. Unsupervised."

Joe grinned. "Wait for us."

Gionn practically trotted down the lane of buildings back toward the harbor. The bounce in his step came in part from the excitement of how clever he could be when he wanted to. An easy man to make miserable, but near impossible to kill. It also came from an urgent need to intercept his boatmates before they had a chance to speak to anyone else. His hope of finding them wandering the main street lost didn't land. There was a mild feeling of panic. Maybe the old man had stashed them in some low ruin in the interminable maze of streets. They could already be talking. Telling different stories than the one he needed.

So he was greatly relieved to find them heading not into town but toward the dry docks of the harbor and the bare bones of the winter fleet.

"Just the cunts I wanted to see," Gionn jogged up. They were eyeing the big warship that would be the last to leave the waters before they were choked with ice, with ear-splitting wind that beheaded the swell.

"You're just the cunt we wanted to see, too," Foster said. "What do you think it'd take to shake one of these loose?"

"By shake loose, do you mean steal, or convince to go along with your bollocks schemes? Because either way, the answer is the complete cooperation of the entire Amposi Navy."

"My bollocks scheme got us this far. If you don't wanna help—"

"Before you say anything that might indicate to me you're considering the commission of a crime, I must inform you that as a sworn sailor of the Navy of Ampos, I am oath-bound to report illegal acts to my commandin' officer, and to collect a reward for doin' so."

"You're in?" Parks grinned.

"Aye, mate. In, and out in under a week."

"Nice! Put 'er there, bud!" Parks raised a palm. Gionn imitated in confusion, and Parks slapped it.

"What did you do to me, cunt!" His nostrils flared. "What was that?"

"Relax, bro. That's what we do in our culture to commemorate the sharing of awesome news."

"Did you just fuckin' curse me?"

"It's a high-five, bitch. Parks is congratulatin' you on fuckin' us over. Because I'm assumin' you didn't manage to enlist us as well."

"Ah, yeah. Didn't really try, but I assume it would have been a lost cause."

"I still think it's cool." Parks assured him.

"Thanks, mate. Can I try the high-five again?" Parks raised his hand. Gionn gave it an awkward slap. "It's a pleasant sting, innit?"

"As I was gonna say earlier. If you don't wanna help, I'm more than happy to keep my end of the bargain we made back in that shithole island. You didn't forget that you're our prisoner, and we spared you on the sole condition that you face charges for your crime as soon as we got to port, did you?"

"I did. Recall, that is. Which is why I needed to find you before your tongues wag themselves into trouble. I know the story we settled on about the squain boats bein' shipwrecked and all is very important to you. Can't have those squains and everyone who ever met them bein' slaughtered on account of a slip up. So I made sure to tell the entire tavern exactly the thing you told me to say if anyone asked."

"Get to the part where you fuck us."

"Gettin' there, impatient cunt. Fair turn for your mates, they believed me. Every word I said. I can be quite charmin' after a drink or two. They also believed the other words I said, in which you are sailors from a powerful Navy somewhere north of here, with large ships and extra planks, who were the sole survivors when your vessel was attacked by thieves whilst on a diplomatic mission to open up the coal trade to your rich nation in exchange for much gold, which obviously is lost. It's very important that you remember all that. If our stories collide, all five of us and the entire squain camp will be dispatched in short order."

"Uh-huh."

"In this story, I'm not a murderer, but an honest merchant. A whale trader, who along with his poorly-paid squain guide and a toss-piece to keep the cold out, was scouting new whaling grounds for the followin' season when he happened to rescue the two of you and offer to take you to Nunoc, where you might secure passage home.

"The reason that fucks you is because only by agreein' with me do you have a credible story behind your presence. Try to tell them what you told me and they'll take you for liars and have you before the court. Accuse me of bein' a murderer, and they may believe you, but then all the good things I said about you and your mates are now beyond trust, and men who know the right questions to ask will ask questions. Do you know the kingdom well-enough to lie your way out?"

"Fair enough, brother. If you put half that brain to that much use half of the time, I'd hate to be your enemy."

"Good on you, cunt. If you need me, I'll be nowhere to be found by you or anyone else, which is where it's easiest to keep me mouth shut and me cock dry and generally avoid ruinin' what I think is a pretty fuckin' brilliant maneuver, circumstances considered. Many thanks for the ride." Gionn gave a little salute and headed back toward the town.

"Welp," Parks shrugged. "Dog ship?"

"Barzos. That guy on the dock. With the beads and the strings. You think he's reliable?"

"He seemed like he wanted to be."

"I know he said he'd give over those letters, but I'm startin' to worry. Especially with Gionn floatin' stories. If you came across a big shipwreck and you were responsible for gettin' a rescue mission goin'…if you looked all those people in the eye, and told them you would see to it, beyond a doubt, that someone came for them, would you hand a letter to the TSA faggot, dust off your hands, and head for the bar?"

"Dude, I tried to act all indignant about it and you got pissed."

"You're a shitty actor. All I'm sayin is, if we're long gone when that Viceroy's done gettin' his honeymoon on, and he sees a few letters, is he gonna shrug it off like old Barzos? He gonna believe some guys who flew in and out without ever meetin' with an official, or makin' any kind of serious effort to get a rescue together? Or is he gonna find that suspicious? Like Gionn said. There's people who know what questions to ask, and we won't even be here to answer 'em."

"Maybe we should talk to the Navy. Barge in there and demand a rescue mission in such an obnoxious way that they won't grant it."

"Can you keep an eye on Gionn?"

"What are you gonna do?"

"Fuck the Navy. I'm gonna talk to the Viceroy."

Barzos stood dutifully on the quay, hands clasped behind his back. His smile was fixed on the empty distance, the horizon beyond the point that denied the harbor to the northwest swell. Foster decided not to interrupt right away, in case he was deep in thought. Some important bead counting, or contemplating what threads pulled such a strange creature so far from any-where that might have been his home. Instead he looked at the same spot, or the same direction, at least, because there were no spots to fix on. The vision lost itself in a blur of grays that inevitably turned him back into his own thoughts in search of any kind of distinction.

It was minutes. He wondered if the man was so committed to his task that he would stare until the sun flirted with the horizon. Or if he was day-dreaming, and what people like him daydreamed about. It may have been a matter of etiquette. Foster imagined Barzos was not allowed to speak to him until spoken to, and that he may be wondering the exact same things about his new company.

"Why do they call it—"

"*Baaaah!*" Barzos jumped in terror and clutched his chest.

"The Mother of Seals?" Foster finished. Barzos grabbed his shoulder and panted a few deep gasps before he managed to speak. "Profuse…apologies… Captain. I did not…see you arrive."

"My bad, Brother. I'm not a captain, remember?"

"No, it is me who is bad."

"I hate to bother you."

"It is no bother. I do not know the answer to your question, but I will find out."

"Not about that. It's those ships. I can't get it out of my head."

"The coal ships? Do not worry sir, they are accounted for."

"I mean the people. I had to look them in the eyes and tell them I would send help. Men who were cold, starvin'. Who knew for sure they were dead until they saw us. Then the way their eyes lit up, like I've never seen before. No woman, no best friend, not even my own mama's ever looked at me like that. They're countin' on me to get them outta there, and—" he trailed off. "Look, I know you're good at your job, and you're gonna alert the viceroy the moment he's available."

"Aye sir, it is very terrible. You can rest assured I will personally deliver word of your friends."

"I just don't know if they can hold out til he's tired of fuckin'. I'm sure he won't mind a brief interruption if it's a life-or-death matter." Barzos eyes bugged out again.

"Of course, sir." They stood waiting for the other to speak.

"So are we goin'?"

"Aye sir. As as soon as he is through with his honeymoon."

"I appreciate that you're under orders."

"Not to disturb."

"Not to disturb. But you can at least show me where he lives."

"Ah, of course. I know the way to his estate. Er, what will you do?"

"If you don't know, he can't blame you." Barzos puffed up his cheeks in frustration. "Barzos. Come on, buddy. Let's go for a walk."

"Sir, it is my order also to monitor all ships entering and leaving the harbor, and reporting them to the viceroy."

Foster looked around. "How's the viceroy gonna know if you take a fifteen minute break?"

"It is the assistant viceroy who has assigned me this task, and also the task of noting quietly to myself any interesting persons or cargo, which I am to report to the assistant viceroy in the spring."

"The one who's in Drummoc."

"Correct, sir."

Foster took another look at the empty waters, the motionless ships on rollers. "I think we might just have time to run down there."

The viceroy's estate was the last great building on the main drag, and run he did, to keep up with the fleet-footed accountant. There was no use in trying to talk him into slowing down. An armada of rich cargo ships hellbent on avoiding customs procedures could dock illegally at any second, especially in the last hours of the day when customs officials least expected it. In the long twilight they huffed up to a two story stack of blocks, timber-framed and built of cut stone, no bigger than any decent two-story home he could find in North Carolina, but majestic in comparison to the other structures he'd seen here. While the Mattaka made their huts of natural rock, knocked here or there to fit on top of the other and domed like their wigwams, there wasn't a curve to be found. Even the roofs were tapering stair steps that must have collected thousands on pounds of snow over the course of winter.

There were no windows on the ground floor, but on the second, a bank of open squares were filled with form-cut wood shutters that could be removed for light and air. All were closed up tight. The door was heavy amber wood. Before it, a low burlap sack filled with small, jagged rocks held a spear that had been planted tip-down.

"Please, sir. I advise that you wait."

"Thanks for the advice, brother." Foster clapped him hard on the back. Barzos let out a moan and recoiled. He tried to wriggle away as Foster grabbed the tail of his leather tunic and pulled it up to his neck. Long, dark brown stripes crisscrossed his back, scabbed over in most places and turning to puckered skin where the scabs peeled.

"The hell's that?"

"Amposi law. The maximum lashes a man in the service of another may receive for punishment is seven each cycle of the moon."

"You must've fucked up good."

Barzos nodded to the spear. "It is a marriage tradition. The spear is planted in virgin soil that has never been pierced by tool or root. I was only able to find these small rocks."

"Virgin soil?" Foster laughed. "There ain't a speck of dirt for a thousand miles."

"Aye, sir."

"Fuck." Foster approached the spear, and looked up to the closed windows, then back down. He wanted to walk right around it and pound on the door, but the object fixed him. His vision went a little lightheaded, and thin threads of moonlights danced before his eyes for a second before he blinked it away. Another step. Stomach bile filled his throat the way it had at junior high dances. It was probably good enough, what he did. Handing over the letters. The story. Foster knew the hollow ring of the lie that tried to coach him away. He wanted it to be sufficient, so that no man could say he was lacking in his diligence, and he might sleep the rest of his nights with whatever happened to the people huddled on that steep rock. Enough that he didn't have to cross the short strip of ground and speak to anyone else. The same still voice, or one that sounded the same, told him otherwise. He had fulfilled his promise, word for word. It would be good in any court of law and by any definition. Yet he knew that when men have to bring up the definitions, it meant there was more to be done. Probably, no one would question him. Parks would be fine with it. Maybe even Lenet wouldn't begrudge him. Theirs weren't the questions he feared. Foster also knew there were times in his life he had acted with conviction. They were few enough, but had the wide nations of the world cast doubts on his actions he would have stood by them without a second thought, and died on that line if need be.

It was plenty, and he knew there was more. Still, nothing he could tell himself could move him beyond a stick in a bag of rocks to knock on the amber door. He felt Barzos exhale a palpable sigh of relief when he turned back for Nunoc.

It was a half-mile walk to the tongue of the glacier where it lapped at the sea. Blue-white ice turned gray at the edges and spat rock carried from the deep mountains of the island. The man they followed was Rawet. He took them to the dog camp—a half dozen tukits clustered on the ice itself. Not one of the three spoke before they arrived.

They were greeted by the yip and whinny of dogs jumping at leather lines anchored by stakes in teams of six all around the camp. The biggest dogs just passed a man's knee, and their thick coat gave them credit for more girth than they had. Sharp ears pricked up and their long muzzles bayed the arrival to all who hadn't noticed. Kjartke hung back and eyed them with suspicion. Tunguk smiled at her reticence as Rawet disappeared into one of the tukits. As if to prove a point, he strode up to a lunging pack and stood just beyond the tug of the leash. It seemed like the dogs would tear the flesh from his bones if he were but inches closer. He held his ground for a long time. Then he stepped forward. The lead dog hunched its shoulders and shrunk. Tunguk extended closed knuckles for him to sniff. He let out a bark. The old man made a burst of clicks and placed his hand on the nape of the dog's neck. He settled to his belly, and his group sniffed at his hindquarters, as though to catch the scent of the man by some transfer. One by one, they ventured close enough to sniff at his fist and the cuffs of his clothing.

Tunguk motioned to Kjartke to come closer. She didn't move. "First dogs?" He laughed. "I will introduce you." The wind gathered her hair across her face. She tucked it behind an ear and held fast. Rawet emerged from the hut with another man.

"Ulmar will show you. It is his nephews with the dogs." Tunguk rose and greeted the man.

"You can both drive a sled?" Ulmar asked.

Tailing the ginger was straightforward-enough in the beginning. It amounted to a bit of distance and a prayer he wouldn't turn around, as they were the only two souls on the main drag. His was the only splash of color against the drab surroundings. But Parks nearly lost him when he turned into the maze of stone wigwams. As in the camp, the streets were not arranged in some neat crossroad fashion. It was always a curve left or right, terminating at a wall and splitting in two, three, sometimes four directions like the staggered branches of a tree. He traveled along alternating arcs, a little wider than the ones between the skin wigwams. No line held for more than a dozen yards, if that, and several times he had to take a panicked guess which way to go before he caught a glimpse of red disappearing into the next curve. What's worse, the huts were just high enough to obscure his view of the two story buildings up front as twilight deepened. Were it not for the mountains the settlement nestled against, he would have been hopelessly turned around.

Gionn changed direction again like a stream slipping down a gorge. Echoes of activity—of voices and tools meeting—snaked through the structures but the sources never quite appeared. After three more turns with no sign, Parks was sure he lost him, and though all the buildings looked alike, he recognized a bronze-colored stone in the bottom of a wall. It had to be the same he'd seen earlier. Everything else was shades of gray and black, and this, a cornerstone for the entryway, had been placed for a purpose. Or maybe lots of people did that, provided they could find the material? Was it just the Reverse-Eskimo version of some suburban door ornament? He slowed his pace, ready to abandon the search, when a familiar sound caught his ear. A woman moaned, followed shortly by a man. Every few seconds one or both would punctuate the silence. He crept up on the source, another indistinct one-room building, and strained to listen. As his mind turned after its tail wondering how the dirty bastard had manage to work so quick, the red hair shot between a gap well ahead, and he abandoned the chorus with some reluctance.

It was no use. Within minutes all sightings ceased, and he wasn't even sure how deep he was into the settlement. If the mountains had been on his left when he entered, he only needed to put them on his right and keep going. And to concoct some story for Foster about how he tailed Gionn to a hut and waited for hours before giving up for the night. It would have to be a hut he couldn't recall how he found.

Something spun him around to the empty lanes behind him. Still no one there. Or maybe some passerby gone on his way. But it gave Parks the heeby-jeebies. When he started back up he made sure to walk quieter so he could hear footsteps if there were any. If Gionn had somehow figured out what was going on and managed to turn the tables. He rounded a building, and instead of making the obvious curve, kept going for nearly a 360, just short of the path he'd come on. Moments later muffled footfalls passed where he'd been. He doubled behind them at as close to a right angle as he could manage. A woman lighting an oil lamp in front of her hut nearly gave him a heart attack. It would be dark soon enough, and lamps dotted up here and there, to help those who were out find their way home when work days or drinking binges were done. Now the shadows followed him, too. It felt like early evening, but he knew by now not to confuse the sun with the time. Twilight here was stubborn, and with each degree of latitude, it refused to budge more and more. Once again he hurried his step, then stopped abruptly. At least two more feet on gritty rock sounded behind him before stopping as well. Parks quickened.

His eyes fell on another lamp as he turned again, and he had to blink away a temporary blindspot of bluish-purple in his field before he could see where he was going.

A thin man, probably half-something, but dressed in the leathers of a sailor slid through the streets. On his belt he wore a knife that nearly disappeared in its deep sheath, and a small satchel. At every juncture, the man would stop, listen, scan the options, and pick his turn. The next one held him up. He heard nothing, and had to consider each of the three alternatives twice. Settling on the one thickest with shadow, he rounded a building to a lamp at eye level, and squinted hard against the sudden glare. When he shook it, before him stood a giant of a man, sparse red-blonde beard and a wispy mustache, his white skin aglow in the light.

"You following me, bro?"

The man laughed. "Following you?"

"The act of walking in another's footsteps, on the same ratchet-ass streets, with no destination other than my backside?"

"Don't be a fool. My destination is same as yours." He pointed ahead. "You're going to the brothel?"

Parks squinted at the building beside them. He'd grown so accustomed to the same sight that he failed to notice this one was just a bit wider than the rest. The hut behind it was not a separate hut at all, but another room connected by a short, low passage. He grinned.

"Lucky guess."

"Where else would a man be his first night after landing?" The accent was thick but confident. More sing-songy than the Reverse-Eskimo one, which always reminded him a knife chopping on a cutting board.

"How do you know I just landed?"

He laughed again. "If I never seen you, you just landed."

Parks stepped aside and waved his hand for the man to pass. "Locals first." The man nodded and slipped past.

The time it took him to reemerge was impressively short, even by Parks' standards. He pressed his shoulder into stone and watched the man peel off in another direction. An older woman saw him off. She lit the oil lamp out front and vanished into the brothel.

The door was not for men of his height. It was covered only by a pair of heavy leather flaps, one outside and one inside. He swooped his arm through and ducked inside. Oil lamps dotted the dank interior. Four piles of skins on the floor must have served as beds. All were empty. Clay jars of all sizes lined the floor by the wall. Woven baskets held sticks of dry herbs whose perfume was welcome in the musty space. The woman, probably in her sixties, sat cross-legged on the floor, braiding strands of some thin twig. She tied them together at intervals and worked her way up. Her eyes acknowledged him, then returned to her work.

"Slow night," Parks remarked. "Maybe you can help me. I'm looking for a friend."

She shouted something in her tongue. "You will find here." Three women emerged from the back to form a line. Even in the seediest places he'd visited, he could count on a certain effort in the cosmetic department, and either their finest or most-revealing outfit. These women had no such concerns. They didn't dress any better than Kjartke, who'd been on a boat for weeks on end, nor did they look more recently-washed. One was obviously pregnant, and another almost certainly. The only one he knew was without child was not much younger than the old madam. None seemed enthused to see him.

"Got your Tuesday lunch buffet crew, I see. Sorry ladies, the friend I'm looking for is a heavily muscled man with red hair."

"We have girls. No man."

"I'm not looking for a boy toy. Just wondering if my friend fitting that description has visited your brothel-slash-potpourri shop."

"You are first customer in long time."

"What about the man I just saw walk out of here?"

"This a medicine shop. You need herb? We heal you. I see no one come in. I see no one leave."

"Did no one have red hair?"

"You want girl or not?"

"Sorry, no money."

"You try for free. You get money, you come back." She nodded to the middle one, the youngest and less-pregnant. The girl crossed the floor and linked her arm around Parks'. He recoiled a bit. "What, you no like bump?" She motioned to the older woman.

"No, no, no. Bump is good. Bump is good. It's just, I'm supposed to be meeting my friend. The ginger."

"I no see him. Maybe you come back with money, I see him," she laughed. The girl gave his forearm a hard squeeze—not a seductive touch but a sign to shut up.

"Free girl, right?" He changed the topic.

"You be back," she gave a gummy smile.

The girl led him through a narrow opening to what amounted to a small room partitioned with curtains of delicate leather dyed red or purple, hung from a scant wood frame. She tugged his arm to the farthest one, and shut the curtain behind her. A small pile of clothing, a bowl, and what he recognized as a crafts bag similar to Kjartke's told him this was where she lived.

"I was afraid you were gonna point me to one of those beds out there." She shook her head. "Summer, it is busy. More girls. Winter, it is only for the sick."

"Classy," he rubbed the curtain between his fingers. His voice lowered: "Is there something you wanted to tell me?"

"What you like me to tell you?" She smiled and stroked his hand with her fingertips. He pulled it away.

"Are you sure you should be…working so hard, in your condition?" He nodded to her belly. In truth, he didn't find her that attractive. She seemed thin, her face wide and flat, though easily the best of the bunch. For a second, he thought he saw something like shame cross her dark eyes, and it stabbed him in the stomach.

"There is good money in winter." He imagined for a moment being stuck on a frozen, windy rock in near total darkness for months at a time. Men probably didn't take much convincing to part with wages, no matter who was working, or how hard.

"I'm sure a girl as beautiful as yourself will be a queen by the time the sun's back." He thought he saw her dark cheeks flush.

"It's your wife. On the boat?"

"How did you know about her?"

"When boats come, we hear."

Parks shook his head. "A friend. Like the red head. Have you seen him?" It was her turn to shake her head.

"I will look."

"If I come back with money."

"If you come back with money." She grinned. "You try?"

"I would like very much to try," his voice trailed off.

"Why not?"

"How do I put this? You're great, you're like, one of the hottest Reverse-Eskimo hookers I've seen so far. I mean, I know exactly what that guy was thinking," he pointed to her belly. "It's just…that woman, she's not my wife, but she's not just a friend. You know?" The girl nodded. "And she gets really jealous. She's got a crazy sense of smell. Not that you smell bad or anything, but there's always a smell. And I really do have to find my other friend. Who is *only* a friend, nothing going on there."

"To kill him?"

"What?"

"Your friend. He betrayed you."

Parks took a second to process what she was saying. "Yeah. I guess he kinda did. But not to kill him. We just need to get on a boat north before winter."

"Who will go? You and the woman?"

"Hopefully. And the other guy like me. The pale face. And the old man."

"To Ampos?"

"Not to Ampos. Home." He beckoned her closer and lowed his tone still. "You see, people think we're from around here, but we're not. The place we came from, it shits all over this place. No offense. It's just so much better, I don't even know how to lie about being from around here. We told the little dude with the beads we're diplomats. We're not. We're just men without a ship. The red head? He's not a friend. No mate. More of a…what's the word? A cunt. He's a bit of a cunt."

"You are no diplomat. Whaler?" He shook his head. "For the firestone?"

"Nope."

"Then why you come to Nunoc?"

Parks looked around at the curtains separating them from the rest of the room.

"We have privacy."

"Can you keep a secret?" She nodded. "Of course you can. I'm a secret operative of the Navy of the Kingdom of America. My real name was taken from me at birth. They call me the Leopard Seal. My faithful assistant—who pretends to be of slightly higher rank to throw people off—he and I came to these waters in search of a ruthless murderer. A cutthroat mutineer, from our own Navy. He's wanted for staging a rebellion that resulted in the death of a great knight of the high seas, Sir Elton John. Beloved by his men. His family put up a tremendous reward for whoever brings the man to justice."

Her eyes lit up. "You come for bounty on the red man."

"No. We're crack Naval operatives. We don't get rewards. Our Navy also sent us, because we may not know shit about sails and rowboats and all that gay stuff, but we're the best man-hunters in the fleet. There are others who would kill us to take our prisoner and collect the reward. We do it only for the honor."

"But you come in rowboat."

"Yes. Our ship was sunk in the battle with the traitor's. We barely escaped with our lives. But a Reverse-Eskimo man named Joe took mercy on us, and he gave us his akmanuak." She squeezed his hand with excitement. "There's more. After we caught the bastard, on our way here, we came across a shipwreck. Three coal ships. Mostly your people. They're stranded south of here with very little food or water. There were too many for us to help, but we promised to bring word of their situation to the Viceroy, so he could send out rescue ships before the winter kills them." A look of horror crossed her face. "I know, right? Titillating stuff. So we're in the unfortunate position of trying to alert the local officials of an emergency, while at the same time transporting a deadly prisoner, and hiding the fact that he's a prisoner, so that the bounty hunters don't find us and kill us. I told Foster—that's the other dude—I told him, if only we weren't such nice guys, always doing good deeds and shit, we could just cut his throat, or turn him in for our own reward, and say fuck those shipwrecked fools. But no. That ain't us, girl. And now the lying little shit has slipped our grasp and enlisted himself in the local Navy, no doubt to try to seize power again in another rebellion. And all we need to prevent it is emergency passage north."

She took both his hands and pulled him to his feet. "You must go now."

"We would, but we don't have a boat."

"From here. Through back door."

"There's a back door?"

"It is a brothel."

Parks nodded. "You promise you won't tell anyone?"

She kissed his knuckle. "This way, Leopard Seal."

It was a troublesome sign. He untied the leather strip that reduced his eyes to a pair of narrow slits and squinted at the dark shard that trotted across the field ahead. Tunguk blinked and allowed his eyes to widen a little. The light was little enough now that the mask was unnecessary. Some distance ahead, Ulmar veered. He had seen it, too. His snowshoes lifted higher out of the sticky powder as the frontrunner marched the column up the glacier, the needle, toward the jagged blue-black ridges that towered ahead. This must be the what he called the eye—the impassable center of the loop that ran the edges of the flow all the way to the mountains and back to the point they stood, many sleeps' journey. It was to the right that the course began, yet the lone dog came from the left. Emerging from the end, but going where? And without his team.

The six dogs that fanned out from a single hitch on the lead sled took the direction of their leader, as they had since the three of them left camp. Behind them came the sled with the trail tukit, and tied to that, the second one, driverless as well, with half of the food, and the woman riding on top like cargo. Tunguk's own dogs sensed the change and once more filled with spirit as they jerked after the others. He stepped onto the runners. It was difficult to keep them from racing the slower team ahead. Many times now he had to overturn the load to stop them, and wait for the others to regain the lead. Now there was no use. He would let them tire. Catch Ulmar, before he stopped them and listened to their howls of resentment as Kjartke's sled again overtook them. The whip had not come out of it's resting place, and would not, he thought.

At least they knew which way to search for Alakset and his boys. There was a storm on the glacier not long before the boat landed. A running wind, and much snow before it. Ulmar was unsure how far the other Vjarku had traveled before, and since. This was no small matter. The course around the eye was too much to start the wrong way and still return in time to board the *Juhketappat*. They needed to find signs of which end was nearer the family. It was here that they should have found Alakset, too, waiting for his sons. They were too young for the eye, Ulmar insisted, but news of the *Kurrhatet-giuk* had forced Alakset's hand. He took not only the oldest, but the younger brothers as well to try to "break the pups"—to work the new dogs in preparation for the coal season, and to give the boys trial as drivers and men. It was a man's feat, to be sure, but the family had discussed it and allowed them to go together due to their ages, instead of trying it alone. Alakset could do nothing but wait to confer the initiation. Yet he was not here.

"Dog!" Ulmar shouted into the calm air. The second time the voice reached the animal, and he stopped in his tracks to consider those who approached, still far. It was not to his liking. He turned and quickened his step over his own path. Ulmar veered again, and Tunguk's team followed left. He looked over as he drew even with Kjartke, and met her scolding stare. There was no way for those six to pull faster than his, and the pair of sleds were slow to respond to their efforts. He put his feet down and struggled to steer right to avoid a collision. The dogs did not care what happened to the things they pulled. But there was no way to move a team that did not choose it. They brought the sleds as close as warships set for boarding. He leaned away as the dogs drug him past her. The far right dog of Kjartke's team noticed the pack coming up, and turned to snarl. Rewa, the biggest dog in Tunguk's team, abandoned Ulmar and bounded straight for the rival. Four of his dogs tore at one of Kjartke's before the rest of his team turned on them. Tunguk upset the load, but it was too late. The leads tangled and jerked as the packs gave battle. Kjartke did not move.

The old man entered the thick and grabbed Rewa by the lead and the scruff to pull him from his victim, buried under the teams. He turned and snapped at the wrists that held him, and Tunguk struck him hard on the nose. Rewa cared nothing for it. He returned to the fight as soon as the hand drew back. He put himself between the outermost dogs as best he could, turned his back to Kjartke's team, and flung one of his dogs aside. It sprung back and tried to go between his legs to get at one of the others. Now it seemed to the team that Tunguk was being attacked by their rivals. No matter how he beat them about the ears, they pulled with ferocity to get past him to the other dogs in defense of their master. Something hit his knee from behind and sent him to his back. Two dogs climbed on him to snap at one another. With both feet, Tunguk gave a kick that launch his dog back into the sled. He did not dare touch the other team. It would only excite his own. Ulmar's voice barked at them as he ran to help. The two men struck and pulled the animals, bleeding from tooth and fist, until at last the teams were separated, though the threats between them continued unabated. They feared no voice, and no pain. Only the blows of a brute could drive them off once they set upon something. The two men glanced back at Kjartke, unimpressed by the affair from her seat on the second sled.

Across the glacier, the lone dog continued his trek with as much interest in the teams as the woman. They would have to let the dogs work out their fire now before they could right the loads and give chase, or it would be another fight. Ulmar and Tunguk panted. In the failing sun, something caught their eyes. There was now a second dog. It appeared as a ghost with the first, a lighter color, some ways ahead. Both moved in a loose dance in the direction from which they surely came.

The sun had long slipped behind the northwest mountains. A deep blue reminder of light defined the black shadow of the range under the early stars, and gave Foster the next several steps along the avenue. When he asked Barzos where he could find the naval headquarters, he said only, "You will know it," before he scurried off to whatever bureaucratic exercise he felt compelled to do. This had to be what he meant. The only one with a pair of oil lamps burning on either side of the great door. The thick walls thundered like a muffled drum. If the viceroy was indisposed, he figured the next best thing would be to speak directly to a naval officer. They'd be the closest thing to law enforcement. That would allow to him to report the ships missing, and if anyone could give him something going north, it would be them. He steamed a little at how Gionn had outplayed him so that reporting him would undercut his own credibility. Oduy had underestimated his friend. And while the captain's death struck him as less than tragic, they had an agreement. He didn't find the man half as predictable as advertised, nor did he plan to make the mistake of letting him hang around longer than absolutely necessary. Not by his side or even a thousand miles—even a universe—behind.

"Halt! Who goes there?" The voice made his stomach lurch into his throat but he managed to hide any physical response.

"Eat a dick," Foster answered.

"I might see if they have something better on the menu." Parks joined him.

"At naval HQ?"

"Does that sound like HQ to you?"

Shouts flooded the landing as the great door threw itself open. Two men, arms around each other for support, stumbled past and down the steps laughing. The sailors slipped in before it could shut. Every seat in the hall was full, and men crowded every open walkway between tables. Little cells shouted over their neighbors, clanged elbows, split and reassembled. There wasn't a cupless hand among hundreds. Younger men prowled the room with ceramic jugs in measured horror. Thirsty men—all men—pounced on them for another pour and cussed them off to refill their pitchers if they couldn't hit the brim. There was no bar, no area distinguished from any other. The men themselves wore whatever they pleased, and it was a wide range that pleased them. There were men like Gionn, and at least half a dozen more ethnicities that they could distinguish. There were even a Mattaka or two scattered about. It was impossible to tell navy from civilian, and officer from crew. They stood paralyzed within feet of the door. Few noted their arrival, and quickly returned to their shouting over shouting.

"We need some music up in here," Parks noted.

"What?"

'I said '*we need some music up in here.*' Where do you get those cups?"

"I ain't stayin' long. Once I find an officer, we're out."

"We can turn in Gionn."

"Not no more."

Parks nodded. "I took care of it. In twenty-four hours, no one's gonna trust him."

"How?"

"I'll explain later." Foster grinned and bumped his fist to Parks'. He snagged the passing arm of a jug boy. "Hey brother, who in here is Navy?" The kid gave him a bewildered look and snatched himself away.

Parks felt the tingling skin of eyes upon him. He snapped right, and caught a glimpse of a man moving through the crowd, the same walk that moved between the buildings on his way to the brothel. The crowd closed behind him to obscure the view. The big man, a head taller than most, pushed after him. Foster hurried to catch up. A throng of foul-smelling bodies and hot breath blocked the lane.

"'Scuse me. 'Scuse me, coming through," Parks tried to pry them apart. The nearest man glared and made no effort to move. Parks wedged his two hands between a pair and nudged them gently outward. A squat man with wide eyes and a flat, gray-brown face waved at him and probably cursed in a strange tongue. Parks tapped him once more on the shoulder, and his reply was a quick punch to the nose. He recoiled and pressed his finger to his nostril, turning to Foster.

"He hit me!"

Foster regarded the group, who resumed ignoring them. "Yeah, I'm gonna have to let that slide." The finger came back with a mixture of blood and snot. Another jug boy passed, and this time it was Parks who grabbed him. Rather than asking for directions, he placed both paws around the vessel and tugged. The boy fought back with surprising vigor, not an unfamiliar battle by any means. A size thirteen foot planted itself on his chest and shoved the kid into the pack, who laughed with glee. Parks raised the jug far overhead.

"Officers only! This jug is for officers!" He headed back toward the fray, shouting and stretching it beyond their short arms. "Move, fuckers, this is officer booze!" One by one they shuffled aside, and Foster pressed close behind in his wake before the crowd could close again. Parks kept up his cry, "Officers! Thirsty officers!" He felt like he was kayaking a current, slipping between rocks, being swept this way and that, changing course at the last second as one opening closed and another appeared, all along the length of the tables to the heads, where he hoped important men sat as they did in his own mess hall.

"Officers, who needs a drink!"

A cup shot up. "I'm an officer!"

Park glimpsed the man heading the other way. "Let me see your cup." The man reached it out over several shoulders. Parks took it and threw it across the room. "If you're an officer, I'm Barzos' twin brother." He hurried away while the man's profanities merged with the crowd. A few more twists and he saw his quarry slip into an opening on the benches, a few feet from the head. All of the men at this end of the table were the same light brown, the same short, straight black hair.

"Officers! Drink for officers!" One of them raised his cup. Parks yanked the top and tilted over a reddish-brown liquid that filled his nostrils with some of the most pungent booze he'd never smelled. "Are you gentlemen officers of the great Navy of Ampos?" They looked at him but did not answer. "We are foreigners, far-flung from the noble shores of America, and we have news of great importance for the commanding officer of the garrison." The man next to the one at the head motioned him in. He leaned his lips to Parks' ear and screamed, "Too fucking loud!" The burst of air rung his bell and sent his finger twisting in the earhole. The officer indicated the wall nearby.

"You wait. Quiet soon."

They pressed their backs flat to the wall to avoid the brush of traffic. These men had no sense of personal space, never mind personal hygiene. The room was thick with fish and booze, and the cool weather did little to suppress the aroma of a few hundred people who toiled and sweat every day where the water was barely above freezing and no one cared to bathe in it. Foster had to wonder what the man meant by "quiet soon." No one called for it, and there was no sign of voices winding down or people making ready to leave. Nauseating as it was, his stomach rumbled to remind him he hadn't eaten since the night before. The only thing available seemed to be a watery soup—fish, by the smell—that men scarfed in between cupfuls of unrecognizable alcohol. After a moment, he measured the traffic and pushed himself from the wall at the right time to slip between to the table of officers.

"Hey! 'Scuse me. Do yall wanna just step outside?"

"You wait!" The same man screamed. "Too loud! You wait!" Foster scowled and retreated. A boy passed with three bowls balanced one each arm. He spun impossibly between the crowd, somehow managing to avoid any more than a slosh. Foster stepped in front.

"How do we get this? Is it free?" He seemed puzzled by the question.

"Free for Navy. You are Navy?" They looked at one another and nodded. "I come back, you give me your bowl."

"We don't have bowls."

"You want I pour it in your hand?" He laughed and squeezed passed. It was too loud, that much was true. They didn't even bother a conversation. Both men busied themselves with people watching. Foster searched the crowd for red hair, or any sign of Gionn, and found none. Sailors, in his experience, were those too foul and uncivilized to be kept on the land, where they might cross paths with ordinary folk and cause harm by the fact that those they protected would realize that such people exist. Confined with others like them, other teens desperate to leave home, they had no choice but to match or exceed all neighboring behavior to avoid being plowed over by it, and as the detachment from the tempering effect of the land and its society grew, it became easier to forget and more necessary to escalate the arms race. Things boys were supposed to grow out of took on adult proportions. People got fucking weird. When they did make land, the extreme difficulty of months at sea without movement, or a drink, or much more than a familiar sock, exploded into port and spent every dollar of pay and ounce of energy until they stumbled broken and broke back to the boat to repeat the whole affair. It was these men who made it impossible for him to handle the others when he finally bounced. These ones drove him back to boats, back to the sea, where he least stood out. But the men in this room made his fellow sailors look like a goddamn Navy marching band parading at the White House.

He'd seen the boats these men sailed. Ridden there on one, in fact. The carrier was a cruise ship in comparison. And what was there at port to let off steam? Nunoc was not Singapore. If these men ever had a chance to begin with, it was lost once they signed onto the boats. There was no choice but to go mad. It occurred to him that this is how a polite civilian might feel if you dropped her into a Southeast Asian bar filled with sailors after three months at sea. His heart thumped and he began to feel claustrophobic. These wretched souls were the ones he was praying would take him north, on one of their garbage-ass ships—his last and best hope. The crowd pressed around him, and his vision stuttered and skipped ahead to catch up. The tingling came to his face and neck first, then spread out to his hands and feet. The noise made his ears ring like the moment tinnitus dials back the speakers at a concert. If he said the wrong thing, looked at the wrong person, he could die here. If he moved at all, he could die.

The next thing he was aware of was his sweat smeared on Parks' big forearms. Sausage fingers dug into his ribs under his far armpit, and his friend slipped a shoulder under the near one. Their height difference caused Foster's left foot to leave the ground momentarily before they steadied.

"Fresh air," he managed. Parks surveyed the room. They were lodged against the far back wall opposite the door.

"Not possible. Deep breaths, bud."

"Fuckin'…I gotta go…Get me out."

He reached his other arm around and cradled Foster. "I got you, dude. There's nowhere to go. Breathe it out."

"Crushin' me."

"In and out. Just breathe like you're back in them-there Nawth Carolina hills."

"You're crushin' me."

"Shit, sorry." Parks loosened his grip, and the two of them slid down the wall to their butts. Foster closed his eyes, but could only manage shallow heaves. "Fresh…air," he gasped. Parks wasn't even sure they could stand up. Boots and bare feet alike slammed into their toes, heels stepped back and if they found something, stayed planted. He gathered Foster's shins in to avoid the melee, but his own legs were too long to be helped. "Can't breathe."

"You're breathing. Stop psyching yourself out. You're breathing right now." Foster shook his head. "Sorry, bud. There's nowhere to go. We gotta wait it out. Breathe. In… two… three… out… two… three." Foster made no effort to match the pattern. "Come on," Parks repeated. Shallow squeaks were all he could manage. "I'm not gonna lie, I have no idea what I'm doing. For all I know, breathing's a terrible idea. Maybe you should just pass out so your body can reset itself." Foster's eyes looked like they wanted to laugh, but it only sent him into a gasping cough. The hacks grew in intensity, until Parks was sure he would break a rib. Then came weak little bursts of dry air, until his breath settled on a shallow but steady pace. His head collapsed on Parks' shoulder, and his eyes shut, though nothing as kind as unconsciousness found him.

Parks watched the knees of the terrible creatures swim past. It reminded him of being a child, in a sea of adults, all of them more powerful than him, drinking to some mysterious occasion that would end when they said it ends. The strange flux of the room at first fascinated, then terrified him, until he was bored of terror and baffled of the rules, praying to be whisked away my familiar legs at any minute. Only Foster gave him a sense of presence, and then only because he figured his friend would be trampled to death if he didn't have a conspicuous shoulder to slobber on. He was not rescued, though. No Kjartke, no Tunguk, or even Gionn stood over him to extend a hand. It was minutes. Then it was hours. Gaps began to open in the crowd, though he couldn't see the door open and shut. Many of the revelers didn't even bother to stumble home, if there was such a place. They curled up on or under a bench, along a wall, in the middle of the floor. Then there was a little space to weave between tables, mostly at the edges. Where sailors had blocked his view, he could see the officers now, mixing and chatting, some leaving. They wore nothing of distinction but the way they carried themselves, yet seemed to keep only the thinnest of barrier between themselves and the men. No behavior seemed to shock them, and it was as often as not they who shouted and shook out cups.

There was plenty room to leave now, but Foster could at least breathe for himself, and it didn't seem worth it to wait all this time only to bail before they got what they came for. He wondered if they had forgotten about them. If they had ever intended to speak at all. Just as he was about to prop his friend against the wall, the man from the brothel approached. A shrug of the shoulder alerted Foster. A tilt of the head told them to follow. Four men remained at the table, including the brothel visitor. The one at the head, oldest and tallest, still had most of his coal-black hair. If any of them had a uniform, it was him. Like Barzos, his tunic was fringed with geometric decoration, but he also had thick stripes down the arms and across the waist—maybe an insignia of rank, though at least of wealth. No others wore it. His gaze stayed fixed on his cup, which he nursed without concern for the visitors.

The man to his right—the same shade, with a wide nose and hazel eyes—spoke for them. "I will do you a great favor, me sons." Parks was surprised to hear speech more like Gionn's than whatever he imagined would come out of one who looked like this. "There is only one boat north, and you won't be on it. There are no more seats, as I've given the last to your red friend, and me own to a young captain more suited to the task."

"That does sound like quite the favor," Parks said.

"It does, when you know that the poye has predicted doom for the ship."

"Poye. That's a witch lady?" Foster managed.

"Aye, and here she is also the healer and mother of the brothel, as you well know." He smiled at Parks. Foster opened his mouth but Parks held up a hand.

"My friend and I have different priorities. He'd like to tell you that your ships are wrecked. The coal is fucked, and the crew will be too if you can't get to them before winter."

"And your priorities?"

"While I appreciate your concern for our safety, it really is important that we get home. Maybe a few more of your boys wouldn't mind giving up their seats on the ship of doom if we had something valuable to give you in exchange."

"A damn shame you arrived so poor."

"It's true that our gold was lost, along with our lady attendants, as well as all of our fine clothing and perfumes, and our friends. But I have something even more valuable. The one thing that doesn't sink with a ship." He paused for dramatic effect. "Information." They seemed unimpressed. "It may interest you to know…that there is a murderer among your men." All four officers regarded each other.

"A murderer. In the Amposi ranks?" His lips tightened off a smile.

"That's right. A cutthroat. A danger to any honest and god-fearing sailor."

"I pray you tell me his name, lad, that we arrest this fiend at once."

"What if I told you, you just gave him the last seat on the last boat north?"

"Not the red lad! Well. He'll be drowned in a few days."

"And you're still sending the ship?"

The man shrugged. "There's enough willin' to take their chances. Squain seers aren't the most reliable lot."

Parks nodded. "It would be best for us if he survived."

"It's your main concern to spare the murderer, then?"

"Spare is a loose word. Concern, too. I would say, we have interests in the temporary survival of our friend."

"Kind of him to save your lives from the shipwreck."

Parks chuckled in response. "Shipwreck. Yes, that was kind of him."

"Coal contracts are all spoken for. That's what you are, right? Coal traders? From…where is it, again?"

"The great kingdom of America."

"Never heard of it."

"You will."

"What is it you were hopin' for?"

"A luckier ship. Pointed north. We'll take the man to our kingdom, and your ship will return as heavy as you like it. You're free to accompany us, if you like. Make sure your compensation is appropriate."

"Your king thinks highly of two sailors and a murderer."

"It's very important to him that everyone is properly compensated. You, me, Gionn…that's what he said his name was, right?" The officers looked at one another. A shadow fell across their demeanor.

"Gionn is a man of the Amposi Navy. He is not subject to crimes under foreign powers, and we do not release him from service. He'll be deployed accordin' to the interests and priorities of the Viceroy. You might want to find warm quarters, lads. There's a winter goddess, unkind to strangers."

"What the fuck was that?" Foster seemed to have regained some of his faculties as soon as they hit the cool air. The sun had already begun to turn back the starlight.

"Bro, that was fuckin' art. I was like fuckin' Picasso in there. Or Steph Curry. You have no idea how hard I just mindfucked those dudes. We're gonna be on a boat to the goddamn Outer Banks with Gionn bound and ball-gagged by this time tomorrow."

"Really. Cause it kinda sounded like he didn't give a rat's ass about anything you said."

"It did. And that's because they're trying to figure out just how much they can get out of us. Did you see how their eyes lit up with, fuckin', whatever the currency is when I said the word 'compensation?'"

"So they're gonna give us a crew and a boat. And what exactly do we do when we get wherever we're pretendin' to go and there ain't no gold doubloons or whatever you just promised?"

"One puzzle at a time, my friend."

"And what the fuck was that when you reported the ships wrecked? He didn't even acknowledge that you told him."

"I'm sure he took it into account."

"Took it into account? Look, I'm fine with fuckin' Gionn over. I'm fine with goin' north. But if we have to let that bastard sail off into the sunset and spend a winter freezin' our dicks off to make sure those fuckers don't get wind of what's goin' on with Lenet's crew—to make sure they don't slaughter hundreds of women and kids and old folks and little cousins—that's what we'll do. That was the one thing we absolutely had to get across, and you went straight to some bullshit that don't even make sense," he ticked off a finger, "is a hunnerd percent not true," he tapped another, "and they probably wouldn't fall for if it was."

"I didn't see you offering much help."

"Bitch, you hand-silenced me. I thought you had a plan."

"Did, and still do."

Foster stopped in his tracks. "They could barely avoid laughin' when you told 'em there's a murderer in their ranks. We're a joke to them. Nothin' we say carries the weight of my cold right nut."

"That's what I'm counting on."

"It is half a mile, that way," Ulmar drew a bladed palm up from the foot of the nabak in a line that cut the twilight. The stone man faced the same, piled up over their heads and covered in most places with fresh-blown snow. His twin would be a full mile beyond, both erected to gaze upon the mother, where they would find a cache. Both posted to collect wandering sleds and point them to the place they could easily drive past in a storm.

"It is late."

Ulmar nodded. The distance would be little for the dogs, still fresh from a light day, but it would take too much time to locate it. In the dusk, they might come within feet of the manabak and remain unaware.

"The woman will make the tukit," Tunguk added where Kjartke could hear him. She slid her legs off the load and began to untie the straps that held their dwelling on the first sled.

There was no sight of the two dogs, long vanished. The teams had approached the place from an angle, turned, and wove the trail until Ulmar found paw prints that left their mark here and there in the icy layer of the recent storm that already began to harden to the pack beneath it. Soon, these were lost, as well. But by then the nabak loomed clear ahead. It was a new build. Ulmar said they always broke these men when their duty was served, to avoid confusing themselves in journeys to come. No boy had done this, either. It was the work of Alakset, after the storm had passed. To travel this way around the eye was ill fortune, and he would not have done so without cause. His food would be at the manabak when they woke, and with any luck, so would he and his sons. Neither man said it, but the boys' uncle seemed to hold as little expectation as Tunguk. One did not cache his food to remain in place, but to travel faster. If he intervened in the ordeal, the initiation would be spoiled. Perhaps Alakset saw the same dogs, and thought his sons in peril.

Tunguk watched as Kjartke lashed the tops of the six ribs together. The men offered her no help when she climbed inside and fought to raise the center. With her head between two of the bones, she brought the ends to the snow, and kicked each one out in turn until they caught the lashings at the top. After a few more kicks to set them, she began to lash the crossties between them.

"Much of this day, Kurrhatet was my uncle," Ulmar said as he staked the dogs for sleep. "I did not think we would find help so late, when it was most needed. Perhaps now, he is my father." He nodded to the woman, already near the end of the bone frame.

"You would think not, if you saw the other two."

"The halots?" Ulmar grinned. "Are they less than an old man and a Jargadak?"

Tunguk could only manage a wry smile.

"Afraid of dogs, I know. As the rest of them. I do not care. If they can throw food across the deck, it is enough."

"We will see. They have not met dogs, but they fear the things they shouldn't, and brave the things they should fear."

"Pups!" Ulmar laughed. "Pups do not fear other pups. They will do well with my nephews." Ulmar took a seat in the shadow of the nabak and craned his neck at the figure. "Alakset is a kind father." Tunguk took his meaning. "It would be difficult to wait."

"It is good they have uncles like us."

"Aye," Ulmar perked up. "It is not so easy as it was."

"Does the firestone draw well?"

"There is firestone-enough to build a pyre for every generation of the people, before and to come." He looked over to the teams, where they curled in a mound of fur. "It is dogs they forget. Dogs pull the people. Even the ones who will not touch them." Kjartke threw the first of the skins over the skeleton. "Your steel," Ulmar tilted his head at Tunguk's waist. "Theirs," he nodded into the blue haze in the direction of Nunoc. "What is firestone without pups?"

They broke camp before the sun straddled the glacier. The dogs sensed there was a purpose to the run, and they pulled with spirit for the short distance to the manabak. The dark, jagged rocks of the woman were too well-fit to have been gathered in haste. These were gathered over many days, raised and struck down over and again as needed. The one who built it knew where each one should rest on another. In this weather, impossible to miss. As they neared, a pair of heads raised in their direction. The two strays rested under the woman. High, short howls challenged them as soon as the teams winded their companions. It seemed they were resentful of the dogs' freedom, and were eager to help the men bring them under the leads again. But the two young males took off at a relaxed pace well before they had a chance. Ulmar did not bother to give chase.

"They aim for home," he noted their path.

It was plain what brought them here. The mound of ice blocks and snow at the foot of the structure lay gashed. It was not the careful hands of a man who uncovered the seal meat, but the greedy claws of the roaming pups. Tunguk judged by the empty leathers that an impressive amount would return with the two dogs. What they could not stomach was scattered around the opening. There were signs they had gorged themselves until their stomachs turned up, then eaten it again.

Tunguk upset the load to anchor his team, and knelt beside something that was never covered. He levered up one end of a great whale rib so that Ulmar could see it. Five more lay at his feet.

"The sled will be fast," the old man remarked. "He took only the skins. Food for the trail."

"Do you know these dogs?"

Ulmar considered the retreating animals. "Of course. But I think you ask if I know who drove them. It is hard to say. There would be pups in every team."

"It will be hard to catch a father who drives for his sons," Tunguk remarked. All of them knew well the dog ship would not wait.

"Do you have sons, grandfather?" Ulmar gave him the traditional name of respect. Tunguk's lip curled. It was one he had not heard in days.

He shook his head. "Nor you?" Ulmar shook his, as well. He judged the glacier ahead of them. A gentle breeze already swirled the loose top layer that had not yet frozen from the recent storm. There would be no tracks.

"Can you find your way to the camp?"

"Aye. If the weather holds."

"It will hold for half a day. After that, you must turn back. Bring the team to the ship. It will have left our harbor, but you will walk the dogs to Nunoc and meet it there." He bent to work on the strap that connected the two sleds. "The woman will stay. I will drive ahead with your team. You take the young ones. Keep me only in sight, half a mile or a little less on your left. We will meet at the place we call the narrow. You will return with what dogs we have found. If we are favored, it will be none."

Tunguk stood over his new charges. Ulmar had given him the finer dogs when they set out. Seasoned by firestone, and by the glacier. Now he had two older females, and four pups who were here for the same purpose as those they meant to bring back.

"You think they are beyond."

"At Gjeplate. The crevasses just around the curve of the eye. It is the most difficult for a team. But when there is a long blow, it is worse. They are hidden under many snow bridges. Very thin. Even for a man, it is bad. For Alakset to drive against the course and break the trial, he must mean to take the boys through."

The door was long gone. The two youths paused in the frame of early morning light, searching the room first with their eyes. Then into the dim workshop, long abandoned and stripped of all wood and iron but otherwise pristine. The Amposi went first, his dark skin fading once he'd gone beyond the light of the only opening. The fairer one followed, his spear at the ready. The floor was empty. Holes pocked the wall where metal hooks had once held tools. Even the door to the furnace was gone. The round bulb rose chest high before it tapered into a tube and disappeared out the ceiling. He wondered how the old Mattaka smiths could see what they were doing. But there would have been a fire then, and oil lamps. And their people spent half their lives in the dark.

He clapped to get the attention of his companion. A shrug of a spear, a shake of a head. The other man pointed his weapon at the furnace like a question. The halot turned to the opening. He banged the wooden butt against the rock and turned back. The Amposi came and over and repeated the gesture. Then he probed his blade into the hole. It seized up fast. Something tried to pull it away. He screamed in Amposi to his partner as his feet slid toward the opening, and had to repeat it before the halot guessed what he meant and grabbed hold of the shaft to help. Whatever had them was losing grip. A foot on the furnace thrust them back, and out of the hole spilled a pale man covered in old soot.

"Chill, brother! I surrender!" Foster dragged himself up coughing with two points inches from his chest.

"Come out!" The English-speaker shouted to the furnace.

"Who you hollerin' at? Ain't nobody but me in there."

"My spear will tell me."

"Alright, alright," came an echo. "Hold your dadgum horses." Two oversized feet wiggled out, followed by the rest of Parks. He was as black as Foster. The speaker made a head gesture that looked like he intended the other man to cover him. Then he tousled Parks hair. His locks, normally more blond, were tinted brown by the soot. The halot rapped his spear on the furnace again to no answer, then jimmied it around inside to the clank of bare stone. He frowned at the two men, then he and his partner walked out without a word to join the crews moving building to building.

They watched them go, then walked the short distance to where Barzos stood vigil on the quay. He regarded them with some horror. Foster knelt beside the water and splashed his arms and face, then his chest. There was a hollow splash, and he looked up to find Parks bobbing naked above the surface. He shivered in panic and flapped for the side, where he caught a hand that helped him back. Barzos' eyes widened and shot away.

"Top of the m-morning to ya, B-B-Barzos," Parks' lips shook.

"Good day, sir," He avoided the sight line. "Captain," he nodded to Foster.

"I'm not a captain."

"It is well, sir. I am sure it will be your fortune." Foster rolled his eyes. "I am most relieved to know it is not you they are looking for."

"So am I. You haven't seen the one they *are* after, have you?" Foster asked.

"I am not certain." After a pause, "The red one?"

"I ain't too sure myself, but I have a hunch Parks knows."

The big man pulled himself back into his leathers. "Never trust a lady of the evening," he winked. "That said, we should probably find him first."

"What happens if they beat us?"

"Ideally, they drive a hard bargain and turn him over to us with a ship and a crew. But if someone goes poking around a little too hard with their spear, or Gionn acts like Gionn, we might lose the only reason anyone would want to help us. In which case, we either end up on a dog boat, or executed for espionage." Barzos tried to blink away what he'd just heard. Parks went on. "So should we split up?"

"Yeah," Foster replied. "But I got another meetin' to get to before I worry about that motherfucker." Barzos squirmed when Foster settled his gaze on him.

Parks leaned against the wall across from the back door of the tavern. If there was any activity inside, no evidence seeped through the thick stone. Here and there beyond the maze of living quarters huddled behind the main street, he heard voices echo orders to one another in a variety of languages. They were still searching for Gionn. A few hundred men. It didn't seem likely that they had missed a building or a furnace in it, yet he hadn't been found.

Not unlike the food on what's-it-called—Yunoc? He doubted they would be so lucky that he threw himself into the sea like so many pounds of whale meat. The sudden bounty of fish in the cove made sense in retrospect. The rush of being the one who caught the redhead never fully left him. Not Lenet, or the Reverse-Eskimos, plowing through dwellings like the Navy men were now. Not Foster. It was him who outwitted the bastard. He felt like something of an elite criminal profiler, at least as far as this one dude was concerned. The way he handled the meat theft—when they finally cajoled the story out of him below deck on the musty *Queen Taral* during the long, dull weeks of passage—was a perfect illustration of his character. Clever enough to see the value, and to orchestrate it. Ballsy for the effort. But with as much foresight as a sailor on shore leave. In the end, capable of any crime, so long as it wasn't too much trouble.

He claimed he first moved it under cover of dusk to the nearby hut owned by the men of the watch, while their shift kept them on the coal ship. After a few loads, the magnitude of the work dawned on him. Whatever his original plan may have been—Gionn took pains to avoid giving particulars— it shifted faster than his loyalties. If he even pulled it off, he would have to shuffle it again, during the inevitable search. The rest of the meat went straight to the water in sacks, weighted by rocks that braced the wigwams here and there.

It was luck, not planning, that the search was a dog and pony show. The Reverse-Eskimos threw themselves into whichever place they thought it would be, with no systematic effort, and no coordination, so that some dwellings were searched several times, and others, none at all. In the midst of the chaos, Gionn managed to transfer the rest of the meat to the water a little at a time, right under the searchers' noses, so that when they did eventually crawl into one of the last places they expected to find it, they in fact found nothing. At least, that was the story.

So he waited behind the big hall. Partly, it was that he knew that Gionn would again follow the easiest and most self-serving path. Partly, it was that he didn't trust himself to find his way into the thick of the town and out again. Gionn wouldn't, either. Something told him that he would seek one of the first places searched and last to be rechecked. One where he had a chance of intercepting food scraps or a jug of water on its way out to the stores. Parks had just arrived, but not a soul stirred near the tavern that was the hub of all movement just the night before.

It wasn't long before his hopes dropped as a column of Navy searchers filed dejected down the back lane. If Gionn was nearby watching, this would keep him low for a good while longer after they passed, which meant more waiting. The head of the line locked onto him as they approached.

"Stop right there!" He pointed. Parks continued to lean. There were sixteen or so in an array of different clothing, with weapons ranging from spears to knives, steel to stone. About half the men wore hard leather helmets strapped below the chin, and some of those sported leather chest armor and straps across the forearms.

"He's got red!" The same man called. The column fanned out before him, points pointed. "Is that him?" Another said.

"I'd call it more of a dirty blond, with a little rust that looks red in the light due to the luxurious shimmer I get from my natural oils."

"Is your name Gionn?" A gaunt, gray man in his forties challenged.

"Good idea, cunt," another voice rose from the ranks. "Just ask him if he's the one we're after, and we'll let him go if he calls himself Darell." The others laughed. The man stepped forward, heavily muscled with helmet pulled tight to his brow. "That's hardly as regal a fuckin' red as it was described to me. More of a beggar-dog brindle. And if he's 'stout,' I'm fuckin' Euphor."

"Aye, he got the wrong look," said an Amposi in full armor.

"We've checked everywhere he's like to be," the first man to spot Parks protested.

"Have you searched the captain's wife?" The muscular man said to a ripple of amusement.

"Aye, we checked her early," he replied.

"You check her cunt?" The men laughed. "I hear it's a proper thieves' harbor."

"She said she'd not seen him."

"Did you ask, or look?" The first man hung his head. "Fuckin' idiot. I bet her mattress bleeds when you spear it."

The Amposi shook his head. "We got to get him alive."

"Then spear *her*."

"Alright. We check."

"Are we gonna eat first?" The gaunt man asked. The Amposi answered by marching toward the quarters. The others followed with obligatory strides. They disappeared around a building, and after a moment, the vocal man in the helmet reappeared. He pressed against the wall and watched where they'd turned for a minute, then joined Parks.

"Well-played, shit cunt."

"And yourself, rojo."

"I don't know what you said to 'em, but I know it was you, and not your mate Agata the Unfucked." Gionn wedged his fingers under the helmet to rub the blood flow back to his forehead. "Fine way to treat one who's been with you through thick and thin."

"You lied about us to save your own ass. I don't know what you said, either, but it wasn't what you told us, because I doubt they follow shipwrecked sailors through the streets at night."

"You were gonna turn me in for murder. That's a violation of the Code of the Sea."

"Is it? I would say that murder is the violation."

"In what world, cunt?"

"Mine, I guess. How'd you get the outfit?"

"Found a cunt who didn't need it. Lucky, the captain's wife wanted to save her own arse as much as mine." Gionn scratched a bit of crust from the tip of his spear with his fingernail. "For her sake, I hope they don't check under the mattress."

"So the whole staying away from drinking and women to keep out of trouble until the boat sailed…"

"I'm a ruiner, cunt. Don't need cause for it, but if I can get a mediocre toss as well," he shrugged. "Anyway, we'll use your lie. What am I pleadin' to?"

"You'll go with whatever I say?"

"Got no choice now, have I?"

"Gionn," Parks smiled. "Hand over your weapons. You're under arrest for murder. And also, high treason."

They held before the spear planted in the gray pebbles. The windows were still boarded and the heavy door to the Viceroy's estate stood fast. Barzos gave him the pleading eyes of a dog but Foster brushed them aside. He felt himself grow an inch taller as he strode past the ornament and up to the red wood fitted with green copper. Once more he glanced back. He'd no intention of being turned away again, but something made him look to the trembling bureaucrat, as if to allow one last chance to talk him out of it. Not a word or a breath came from the stiff chest of Barzos.

Foster banged the side of his fist three times, the slow hammers echoing through the interior. It was half a minute before he heard the creak and crack of a board lifting, and a grim face appeared in leather armor and helmet. The man had the look of a soldier more than a servant or official. He didn't speak. His appearance was the question, and Foster understood.

"The name's Foster. I got an urgent message for the Viceroy that has to be delivered personally, regarding three coal ships—" the door slammed in his face mid-sentence and he heard the board lock reengage.

Barzos gave a beaten shrug that had too much relief in it for Foster's liking. He walked back to his guide, who had managed to change breaths before his brown skin turned completely purple.

"Do not worry, Captain. I have recorded your passage, and your message will be delivered. I believe the Viceroy will act to send ships to the rescue of those found, and they will be very grateful for your efforts."

Foster looked up to the window that he knew must be the man's suite. A clothesline ran from it to the building beside with a leather tunic and pants, dyed something between red and purple and faded to different shades. Intricate bead work framed the lapel and the tail, and more beads of every color and shape were embroidered in geometric patterns across the tunic so that there was less leather visible than bead. The pants were only a notch less ostentatious. It reminded him of rhinestone jeans and bejeweled t-shirts. That a man thought himself important enough to rest and fuck while people froze and died of thirst made his blood boil, and he had to remind himself that no one was really shipwrecked. If the Viceroy searched for it, he'd find nothing and probably distrust the story. If he didn't believe the story to begin with, he'd search and find the coal ships. Lenet's people stood no chance besieged in the small harbor. No, the man had to believe the story, and he had to have reason to let them rot.

Barzos must have sensed something, because he tensed up again. "Captain Foster," he said and waved a hand for him to lead back the way they'd come. Foster gritted his teeth. It was no use arguing titles with the man. He spun on his heel, marched up to the spear, and ripped it from the basket with his good hand, sending pebbles across the ground, then took two steps toward the door. His arm coiled, and he launched it with a snap into the heavy wood. The shaft wobbled but the point stayed fast. Not bad for the first time he'd ever thrown the weapon, he thought. It took much less time for the man to appear now. He cracked the door, glanced at the protruding spear, and closed it again.

There was no sound of the lock this time. Instead, heavy footsteps crossed the floor and disappeared. Foster grinned to Barzos, who didn't share his enthusiasm. It was minutes before anything moved. Then it came from above them. The board in the window hole shifted and disappeared within. A head and a pair of shoulders appeared, bare-chested and bald except around the sides, where his thin graying hair was cropped clear of his ears. His features were fairer, and his skin was a shade more ghostly than Barzos' and a few decades older, but it was clear they were of the same people. Nothing about his hook-nosed scowl seemed happy. Foster thought he was going to bellow, but when he finally spoke, it was in a rich, even tone.

"I would not normally interrupt my honeymoon to conduct business, but I admit I am very curious what you thought wise to foul my hearth spear over."

"My apologies, Mister Viceroy. I mean you and your bride no disrespect, and I wish yall many happy years and happy kids. I wouldn't have done it, except it's an emergency. Matter of life and death."

"Very much so."

"Less than a week ago, me and my crew came across a shipwreck. Three of your coal liners, splintered on the coast south of here. I'm sorry to say the officers drowned and the cargo's lost, but quite a few of the crew managed to get ashore with some supplies. They ain't got much, and not a stick of shelter for winter. If someone don't get to 'em soon, there won't be nothin' left come spring. I promised them I would personally deliver their message, along with their admiralty letters, to the Viceroy. And if there's one thing you'll learn about me, I'm a man of my word."

"Barzos."

"Aye, Most Excellent Viceroy of Hiade!"

"Did you take this man's report?"

"Aye, sir! It is recorded, and it is as he says."

"How long do you think they can survive?" The Viceroy addressed Foster.

"Few weeks at best before the fresh water's gone."

He nodded. "I will send a ship to look for them." Foster tensed his mouth and held off swallowing. The Viceroy went on, "as soon as I have finished my honeymoon."

The door of the house opened, and three men emerged—two with spears, and the third, the man at the door, a leather whip.

"Barzos, see to it that this man is lashed to his final breath, then leave him in the harbor for the birds." Foster froze and quickly weighed his chances of fighting as nil. The men stepped forward as the Viceroy started back inside.

"Wait! Sir," Barzos added. "Uh…" he searched for the words. "Oh! This man is in your service. Under contract to the dog boat leaving for Drummoc. Amposi law states that a man may lash one in his service at most seven strokes each moon—"

"I am aware of the law." He let out something between a sigh and a grunt. "Seven strokes, then," he called to his men. "And Barzos."

"Aye, sir!"

"When your moon returns, have these men give you seven more."

It was not possible to keep pace with Ulmar. Tunguk's pups pulled with uncertainty over the ice plateau now that their frontrunner was gone. He did not have the shoes, or the youth, to go ahead. Even the snap of the whip above their ears did little to sway them until he gave them their first taste of leather. After that, the sound was enough to urge them on. He could still see Ulmar's sled, now and then, fighting with the sticky ice on the far side of the course and well-ahead. Tunguk drove near enough to keep the notched blue wall of the eye in clear view to his right, that any movement beneath it would not go unnoticed. Nothing lived up here but man and dog, and both were wise to keep a distance from the ice falls and the foul kaim who haunted its steep faces. Still, it must be searched, because lost boys and dogs may seek its form to guide them through the narrows ahead, where the unbroken white of the glacier's plateau pinched in suddenly for miles, and the edge was difficult to tell from the plain hundreds of feet below. This was Ulmar's course. For miles, he watched the distant team curve inward until they were nearly straight ahead, and from there, his dogs made ground despite the shallow grooves that snagged the runners every few yards and called for a younger Tunguk's strength to shake free. The sun neared its height, and he knew Ulmar waited at the place he would turn empty-handed to push downhill for Kjartke.

The sled slammed to a stop as it wedged the left runner into another shallow notch. The dogs lurched at the resistance, and doubled their efforts in a madness to clear it. Tunguk tried to rock it and lift, but as long as six beasts yanked at the leads, the runner only dug harder into the lip that held it. Perhaps Ulmar could have freed it. The try was not worth the grunt. He shouted at the dogs to stop, though even the two females in the middle of the fan—the calm, trail-hardened pullers brought to teach the young ones by example—refused. He thought they must have wind of Ulmar now. They were not eager to drive along with an old man they did not know if there was one of their kin ahead. He would have to go round front to still them. If the sled freed itself, it would be good if they only ran off, and left him to walk. Were he in front, he would be trampled under the heavy runners.

There was no other way but to hope it held. The sled rocked side to side as they scraped for solid ground under sliding claws. The dogs nearly crawled on their bellies to move the load. Without haste, Tunguk went around until he stood before the little pack. One of the females, Ila, stopped as he placed his hands around her muzzle and spoke the command. The pup beside her bounced against the lead, which pulled him sideways and into her. She tore free of Tunguk with a snarl and set upon him. Though the male was bigger, he was too young to know this, and soon showed his belly. Now the rest settled, and Tunguk returned to the rear. With much effort, he was able to draw the sled back out of the ice and tilt it over.

"Up, up!" He called. The dogs now lay still, panting in the sun. "Up, up!" The young male smiled back at him, but made no move. He gathered the whip out of the hollow and began to untwist the lash. At the sight, the same dog bounded to his feet and drove with all his might, moving the sled under his power alone. The others sprang up to avoid being run over, and before Tunguk could get a foot on the runner, it was gone.

His belly heaved with a soft pulse, and his lips drew tight as he looked at the whip in his hand. A gentle bout of laughter rolled after the animals. He looked down at the ice that stuck to his thin boots. Already he could feel where they shredded free and the cold numbed his feet. The late summer warmth was enough to dampen the ice so that it clung to itself and built up in stubborn knobs on everything it touched. It was good he had only himself to see through this. He must have looked the spectacle for the local spirits, a man alone with a whip and nothing to drive.

Tunguk's head snapped right. The brush of eyes on his skin brought his focus to a small thing framed against the wall that marked the center of the glacier. At first he thought it a trickster, luring him against Ulmar's warning, but the dog took shape, so near that he was ashamed he did not see it before. There was nothing to hide it but a slack attention. He looked back at his team, and saw them snagged again far ahead, with no interest in freeing themselves. It was a shorter distance to this new one. He considered the whip in his hand, then stuck the butt in the ice so he might find it later.

The animal did not budge. He thought it was a female he approached. In a younger day, he would have been sure. This one was not spooked like the pups they found earlier, nor full of mischief and bent on the smells of a strange place. Her panting tongue retreated into her mouth and her ears raised to study the man before her. When he was still some way off, Tunguk paused, and held her with a gentle stare. He tilted the palm of his right hand out to the side. It was enough. The dog broke her hesitation and started his way. Her coat was lighter than most—white on the underside, pale grays atop dashed here and there with darker ones. The blacks that many of the animals wore were missing, and a thin stroke of light brown marked the areas around her eyes and mouth, and the shoulders where the white met the darker shades. She stopped yards away to think him over. Tunguk did not dare move toward her. She would be gone long before he could arrive.

"I am Tunguk," he said in a flat voice. "No man is my father, but I bring tidings from Kurrhatet. Will you come home?" He knelt. The dog resumed her patient walk and stopped to sniff his outstretched hand, buried her nose in his sleeve, then leaned around to check his waist. Her hopes were high that this man had food for her. He stroked her head with the other hand, and lifted her snout to examine the brownish color that stained the bottom of her chin and part of her chest. His fingers probed the area for a wound that may have bled down from her throat—a tumble with one of the other dogs—but she was unharmed. The seal meat they fed the animals was long past bleeding. This one had tasted something fresh.

He lifted the short length of leather that dangled from her harness and stretched it out. It measured just the length to her mouth, where she gnawed herself free of the lead. The harness, too, had tooth marks but she had given up trying to remove it. His hand wrapped once through the little trace of leather, and he stood to bring it taut.

"Hungry dogs." Her mouth narrowed again and her eyes locked on his. It was the phrase Ulmar repeated as he fed the teams. Tunguk had nothing to give her yet, but when he began the trek to reach his sled, she offered no fight.

With the other sled to run to, the dogs made a good pace. Ulmar did not seem pleased when he spotted the new girl. They trotted up with her tied from the back—it was ill-fortune to run a team of seven, though not as bad as five. It was plain that the other team's search yielded nothing.

"Pregnant," Ulmar spoke as soon as they stopped. Tunguk looked at her again. Only now could he see what the driver knew from a distance. "Alakset would not send this dog with his sons. Did you feed her?"

Tunguk shook his head.

"Good." Ulmar untied the lead and wrapped it around his palm. "Will you remain a little longer? It will be easiest. Your dogs will wait for us here. I will go in front with her. Keep my team in my tracks. The narrows are easy to drive if you know them, but there are many soft edges and folds that deceive the eyes."

Tunguk took hold of Ulmar's sled, and the man pulled the mother ahead of them. He looked down at her. "Hungry dogs!" She twitched with excitement. Ulmar motioned with his gaze into the white expanse ahead. She burst against the lead.

It was an easy pull keeping up with the frontrunner. Again and again the sled snagged, but it gave Ulmar time to regain his distance. These were rich with experience, and he needed only free them and give the word. They were promised food at the end of this, and they spared no enthusiasm. Ahead, Ulmar stopped and turned. He motioned his arm inward, toward the eye, to direct Tunguk off a line before resuming his stride. When he drew near the spot, Tunguk looked left to see a clean powdered hump vanish into a gash. There was little steering to do with the target of the man leading them, who had only to coax the mother forward.

They passed several more, and soon Tunguk could spot them even before their lines became visible by the way the man and dog before them seemed to curl around the edges where the notches cut sharply into plateau across their path. They would know each one, though they traveled them in reverse. When at last the mother became animated and refused to veer, the frontrunner stopped and awaited the sled. It seemed less severe than many they managed to avoid. The snow dipped in a shadow and sloped gradually back up the other side in a wide chip that looked as though some god had inserted his fingernail straight down and scraped out a field of ice before them. Ulmar motioned for Tunguk to overturn the sled. He joined them at the lip. For as far as they could peer, there was nothing but new ice. Ulmar yanked on the lead and the mother started around the edge with the men on her heels, their heads cocked left as the bottom of the wash came bit by bit into view. It was shallow, no more than twenty deep at the bottom, and far less remarkable than many of the steep grooves. If approached from the far side, it seemed almost a hospitable place where one might tuck in to shelter from a wind. Neither man spoke or changed their pace when the wood appeared, one runner jutting at an angle parallel to the ground from a bank.

With care, they picked their way down the opposite side toward an unmoving pile that took shape as a sled on its side. Just behind it, a thick dusting of snow covered most of the dark brown leathers. A trail tukit, missing the ribs, pulled across the ground and humped in the middle. The mother dragged them forward to sniff at the edges. Ulmar jerked her away, and passed hold of the lead to Tunguk.

"Forgive my intrusion," he called to the dark shape, then knelt to take the edges on his hands. The frozen snow on top resisted his attempts to pull the leathers free. With each jerk, the ice broke in sections, until at last he peeled enough to free its resident.

The dog staggered back at first, then pulled again to sniff as near as Tunguk would let her. Alakset lay huddled on the ground. His neck stood open with jagged edges, much of what was inside, missing. The soft flesh around his lips, his nose, his eyes, was gone. Ulmar looked up at the rise twenty feet above them, and back to the sled. Then he resumed trying to break the leather free of the ice. Tunguk tied off the end of the mother's lead to the front of the sled. He lifted the stiff traces for Ulmar to see. It was clear which had been gnawed. The other five were cut clean near the end that met the harness.

"He loosed them for us. Kept this one, in case he needed to eat."

Tunguk batted away the mother as she tried to sniff her driver again. It was curiosity. Perhaps concern. The portion she took was small, and it was not to her liking, or they would not have found her on her way home. Tunguk helped free the cover from Ulmar's brother—or was it his sister's brother? They looped their arms under Alakset's and drug him free of the tukit. His body was stiff as a sled. As they set him down again, something gave to Tunguk's touch. He felt around a soft spot on the left chest where the flesh yielded. The men cut open his tunic. The blue gray flesh was stained with a deep bruise covering most of his left side. A rib poked out of his torso. He survived the fall long enough to free the dogs and crawl into a shelter with one lung. They stretched out the stiff sheets and wrapped him in the manner of the Mattaka. After they pulled him up the slope and tied him to the sled, they returned below. The mother tugged at the lead and whimpered when they picked their way down the slope again. She sat on the ice, and turned her ears toward them in anticipation. Ulmar looked long at the dog.

"It is late. We will salvage the sled another time."

Tunguk freed the knot, and she pulled with such spirit to climb the slope that Ulmar had to take the lead from him so the old man could keep his feet. They glanced back at the edge.

"He drove to head them off before the storm lifted. Alakset knows this course better than I. It is the only way he could miss it," he said of the wash.

The old man allowed the plateau ahead to fill his vision. Here was the mother of the dog families of Nunoc. She bore them—man and animal—as this one carried her pups. Every one of them made their turn around the needle. The ice in its many faces, the cold and wind, pressure and flow, the pressure ridges, crevasses, the narrows and the false bridges, the hateful kaim. There was no other way. Nothing another could do on one's behalf.

"It is hard to know when they are ready," Tunguk said.

Something must have sparked within the deep lines of his face. Ulmar followed his eyes to the distance. A mile yet, maybe more. The movement was unmistakable against the untrod layer of new ice that glistened over every surface. The dark speck veered right without slowing, and it became two speck. Then three. A close line of many-headed beasts raced downhill in their direction.

"We must hurry," Tunguk said, and took a step back the way they came. His companion frowned. "They have had no help. It is still their course. Shameful, if they came so far to follow a couple of old wretches home."

Ulmar grinned and clapped him on the shoulder. They quickened their step toward the sled.

The patchwork Navy stood aside as they paraded down the narrow lanes. "Make way, mateys!" Parks wore the leather helmet loose on his head and urged Gionn on with his own short sword. "Make way for the infamous Scabwarts, the rebel assassin. The Leopard Seal always finds his prey." The red head hung and sulked along, his hands wrapped before him in leather strap. He was doing a fine job of pretending to be stewing with rage, Parks thought. "This prisoner is now the property of the great kingdom of America. Don't be fooled by his stupid demeanor or gay appearance, this is a criminal of the highest order. You're lucky I snagged him before he was able to charm his way into your ranks. To work his intrigues and turn you on one another, until the kingdom of…whatever this is, ravaged itself, and in its hour of weakness, allowed the red demon to swoop in and sit upon the throne.

"Unlikely? I can understand how it would seem that way. You have no idea how close you came to disaster. With men like this, a foot in the door leaves the house in ashes. Be sure to thank your gods that you had the Leopard Seal on your side." Their faces were as baffled by the speech as the sight, but the strange collection of men that passed as their armed force did not intervene. Confusion was his ally, because Parks knew he had nothing that couldn't be taken in a heartbeat, and he still needed these men and their boat if he ever wanted to get his crew off alive.

His crew. He was every bit as capable of enterprise and leadership as Foster or Eskimo Joe. And without ever having called a squad his own. One had delivered them from the elements and the Reverse-Eskimos, the other from a hellish winter on an island of refugees. It was his turn, and him who would get them where Foster dreamed but couldn't go—not on his own. Each man had his time at the helm. But the Straits of Bullshit they found themselves in now were his, and his alone.

They cleared the onlookers and made for the empty workshop where he and Foster had spent the previous night. "Trim your sail a bit, cunt. I've enough reputations without yours."

"Relax, Broseph. All part of the ruse. We'll be out of here in a day. Two, tops."

"Aye, and when your ruse is rused, I plan to be a free man again, trampin' me way through the ports of the profitable world, same as these cunts. I don't need a man in each who calls me an escaped traitor and schemer of devious crimes against the most powerful men on the fuckin' sea."

Barzos skidded around the corner in front of them, regained his balance, and sprinted up out of breath. He tried to speak but only air wheezed out.

"Find your wind, cunt. Have you forgot to count a flea on me arsehole?"

"Where's Foster?" The Leopard Seal melted back into Parks.

Barzos' residence was indistinct from the others on the outside. No address or potted plant or indication of his office. No door. He pulled aside a heavy leather flap on the outside, then pushed an opening in a second inner flap for the men to slip through. A single oil lamp burned in the corner of the room, where on a rug a heap of man curled and trembled uncontrollably. Parks didn't even recognize the shape, criss-crossed with brown smears of blood from the black stripes across the naked torso, but he knew instantly it was his friend. He let Gionn's blade clatter to the ground, and ignored his protest, "Watch me bevel, ripe cunt!" Pain shot from his foot to his knee on his gashed leg as his shins pressed the ground. He peered over, and saw that Foster was not trembling from cold—he was sweating profusely.

"Buddy, can you hear me?" Foster made no attempt to respond. Parks looked at the wounds—at least they were clean. Long, thin, shallow. For someone who liked to rattle on about his mama's switch growing up, it seemed to him that his friend's reaction was a touch dramatic, but the vacuum of action drew him in as it always did when Foster wasn't present or ready for the task.

"Boil some bandages," he said to Barzos without knowing if that was what you were supposed to do. When he didn't move, "cloth bandages. Tear some cotton into strips and boil them to sterilize whatever garbage sweated off your back."

"What are you on about?" Gionn interjected. "Tear good cloth and waste good coal to boil it? Is he gonna eat it?"

"Sir, I have only two garments. Both of leather. I will happily tear them if—"

"Never mind. Uh, ok. On a scale of one to ten, how bad does it hurt?" Foster managed to raise a middle finger. "Nice. He's still with us."

"It is quite painful, sir," Barzos added. "If the wound remains open, it may sour."

"And where does a man go for his medical needs?"

Foster dangled between the shoulders of Parks and Gionn, blinking at the fire across his back, now throbbing into all parts of his body and convincing his legs to rebel. They stood before an entryway that pawed at Parks' memory.

"So that's where the brothel is. Couldn't seem to find it with this cunt on my tail," Gionn indicated Parks.

"How can you tell?" Parks said. "I've been here before and it still looks like every other outhouse on this island."

"It's always marked if you know the mark."

"My apologies, Captain," Barzos addressed Foster. "I understand the Navy doctor was killed and the replacement has been delayed in passage."

"How much longer?" Parks asked.

"Hard to say. Five years since the request was placed, I am told."

The two pregnant women reclined on mats in the main room. The poye looked up at them as they pushed through the door, then nodded for the women to retire to their quarters, where the third was already imitating screams of ecstasy. Parks smiled at the girl he'd spoken to, and she turned away quickly.

The two men lay Foster on his stomach on the bare ground. "New viceroy is good for trade!" The poye laughed.

"Can you fix him?"

"I fix. Can you pay?" Parks looked pleadingly to Barzos. He grimaced, then nodded to the poye. "I look," she knelt beside Foster.

"I wouldn't trust these hags with me worst enemy's cockrot," Gionn confided a little too loudly.

"She's alright," Parks kept his voice lower. "Offered me a free sesh with one of the gals."

"Offered. Then you turned it down?" Parks braced for the abuse. "Smart man," Gionn said. "No such thing as a free toss."

"I give you herbs. Barzos knows," She rose from Foster's side and laughed.

"And will these herbs make him seaworthy for a long voyage north?" Gionn asked.

"How long?"

"Well it would have been Ampos, but thanks to your shit divination, that boat's off. Too many cowards refuse to go on a doomed voyage."

"Divination is good. You lucky, you die at sea. Sail only Urkuk."

"Manhas," Gionn corrected her. "I'm no squain, and squain divination is known to all sound persons to be bucket filler."

"It is good! Better than halot!"

"Oh? One word: Barduk." She clammed up and fumed.

"Guys, guys," Parks stepped between them. "Herbs for the man with the whiplash. Please."

The poye took a basket brimming with a dried gray-green leaf crumbled to small chips. She produced a large, flimsy sack and emptied the entire contents into it—a massive amount by Parks' reckoning.

"Chew, she placed a pinch in Foster palm. No swallow. Put in wound."

"The whole thing?" Parks frowned at the foot after foot of open flesh.

"Much to chew," she said and nodded at Foster. He fumbled as much as he could into his mouth, crumbs caking his beard. After a few seconds his face went white and he began to spit it out furiously.

"Chew!" She shouted.

"Tastes like shit," he managed. The poye handed him more. This time he lasted a bit longer. Then again his face turned, and he vomited everything onto the floor to a cacophony of indistinct screams in Mattakatan.

"Can I chew it for him?" Parks offered.

"No. Each must chew his own." She extended a pinch to him.

"What's this for?" The woman pointed at the gash on his shin. "This bad. Wrong color. You chew and pack, every day. Both of you. It taste bad, but it burn worse in the blood. Burn out all the bad blood. Pain will get much worse before it get better. You keep to chew, or you lose leg," she said to Parks, "and he lose more."

He took the offering and placed it in his lip like a wad of tobacco. Foster was right, the taste was abysmal, and he felt the queasy stomach he knew from the first time he tried dip, but long years of experience allowed him to hold it in until it became a mushy paste. Spit ran down his leg as Parks pressed it into his shin. He took the sack of herbs from her.

"Barzos, I'll venmo you."

A single lamp of whale oil was all Barzos would spare for the night vigil over Foster. He was able to speak and move, and take a little food now, but the herbs still made him vomit on the floor, and the stench filled the tiny space while Parks scraped it up on Gionn's blade and flung it outside. Not more than one of them seemed to manage any sleep at the same time. Barzos climbed out from under his fur blanket near midnight and scooted over to where Parks sat beside his friend.

"I worry he will not be seaworthy tomorrow."

"I'd say that's a safe bet."

"The dogs will be here in the morning. And the ship will have been provisioned at the coal harbor."

Parks nodded. "My boy Eskimo Joe bringing in the reinforcements."

"That means it will leave as soon as it receives its passengers."

"You think our Reverse-Eskimo friends are going with them?"

"You must all go with Captain Tunguk, and Captain Ostuk. Him," he nodded to Foster, "most of all."

"Not so," Gionn had been following along from his end of the hut. "I am a very valuable prisoner. They would not like to lose their cut."

"We're going north," Parks said. "Soon as we can arrange a new ship."

"The viceroy spared him because I told him Captain Foster was in his service as a crew member of the dog ship. If he ends his honeymoon and the ship is gone without him, he will no longer be in Amposi service. It will be up to the viceroy what to do."

"You don't think he'll find this sufficient?" Parks waved a hand over the bare lash marks scabbing up. Barzos grimaced.

"He is a man of firm convictions."

"How long do you guesstimate until he gets tired of spitting venom in the new missus?" Barzos' face went blank. "How long til he's done?"

"Tomorrow. Two weeks. We cannot know. But you must be gone."

"Well, shit." A stirring caught his attention. Foster struggled to press himself up on his elbow. Parks and Barzos slipped under his armpits, but he groaned and shrugged them off. With great effort, he sat under his own slow power.

"I can go."

"The journey is very rough, Captain. Strong men die of sickness in the autumn seas."

"What choice do I have?"

"The one that I bamboozled for us," Parks said. "They're right where I want them. I just need to march in there with my prisoner and demand a ship leaves tomorrow with all of us on it for the Kingdom of 'Murica. Land of the free. Bringer of death to traitors," he winked at Gionn.

"It can take many days to load a ship for a long voyage," Barzos explained. "The dog ship will be gone, and you will pray to the gods the viceroy lies in his bed."

"Yall go," Foster managed. "Put me on the dog thing. You shouldn't get fucked over me. Yall go, find a way home. Maybe you can send me a map."

"Fuck that. Parks crawled to his feet, and had to hunch to avoid hitting his head on the low ceiling. "Our boat leaves tomorrow."

"But if—" Barzos protested.

"You make sure Foster and the others get on the dog ship, just in case. Either I get us on the northbound express before it leaves, or we're all cuddling in the kennels on the frozen tit of Antarctica this winter."

"Fuck me, cunt," Gionn whined. Parks extended the straps that bound his hands.

They tried the massive doors of the tavern at dawn, but dawn in Nunoc was still too early for an answer. Parks and Gionn sat on the top step and stared north. The wall of mountain to the east protected them from the wind and the early light, though a gray-blue hue radiated from somewhere behind the rock expanse.

Parks' face contorted as he mashed more of the poultice between his teeth and slapped it on his wound.

"Where I'm from, people love this herbal shit," he indicated the wad of leaf and saliva. "Swear by it. And crystals. They buy stupid little crystals by the boatload and put them up their butts for wealth and protection and shit."

"Aye. And where I'm from."

"I don't feel a damn thing."

"Maybe it's not far enough up your arse." A lone figure caught their attention. Barzos crossed along the main drag carrying his sack of beads. "Speakin' of which."

"Where do you figure he's going?"

"Turn us in to the viceroy in exchange for mercy."

"Gionn. I think if we'd met under different circumstances—like, shipmates in the Navy or whatnot—you might be the kinda guy I'd buy a round for once or twice a year."

"I'd still hate your guts, but I'll take that round soon as you come by it."

Barzos quick-stepped with his head down in furious determination, barely able to contain his stride to a walk. The sack slipped low on his shoulder and had to be rehoisted. He glanced up at the window as he approached the viceroy's estate—still boarded tight. The spear had been replanted in the basket of pebbles, which made him snicker. No way it would work now, if it ever had. He paused with his fist raised in a knock position, then lowered it.

"Oh, sorry to bother you," he practiced under his breath. "So early in the morning—Sorry to bother you, but I have the reports. Oh, excuse me, I forgot to bring over the reports yesterday. Oh, sorry to wake you. Just dropping off the reports a little early." He smiled at that one and knocked as softly as a knuckle might. No one came. There was a wooden clank that sounded like it came from the viceroy's quarters. Barzos froze in fear. For a full minute, he dared not move, and barely breathed.

When he stepped back to gather his courage, a flash of color caught his eye. A lone garment hung from the clothesline extending out from the window—a rectangular shawl, onto which someone had crudely painted with soap the image of a turtle, a lightning bolt crack in its shell. The window was already closed again. A woman's garment, he thought. Maybe he hadn't woken the viceroy after all. Or anyone. It was probably good fortune that his wife air one of her washed items.

He tried again with more vigor. This time, a slow shuffle crossed the floor. The board latch creaked out of place and the door cracked. Barzos raised his sack. "Oh, did I wake you? I am very early with the—" The guard ushered him in with his head and walked away, letting Barzos catch the door behind himself. His sight went black. No light made it through the window closures designed to keep out the winter gusts. It took several moments before the outlines of shadows took their form, and he heard the man nestle back down in a corner of the same room where the rest of the household staff still slept on mats in the open.

His foot swept back and forth in front of him every step until his toe contacted what he was looking for. He opened the chest and his hand found the flat mat of leather strands and beads he'd filed only the day before. Barzos lifted it, and the edges tangled with the one beneath it, clinking beads. He went still, then shuffled them quietly until they came apart. It went into the sack, and another, identical in the dark, came out. He couldn't see the beads, but if his memory served, they were nearly an exact replica of the one he took. A deep sigh escaped his lungs, and the lid slipped from his hand. It slammed to a chorus of curses from the sleeping staff.

"Sorry!" Barzos half-sprinted out. As he closed the door behind him, something again caught his eye. This time, it was the absence of what he expected. The clothesline was empty. He frowned, and hurried away.

The tavern cleared of men as soon as Parks and his prisoner were led in. At the middle table sat the captain of the canceled ship, and the man who wouldn't speak to them the night before—dollars-to-donuts the big boss commander. Parks also noted the man who'd followed him to the brothel, and a small squad of regulars across the room in the corner who were probably babysitting the meeting. They took a seat on the bench across from the captain.

A long pause followed, as Parks wasn't sure who was supposed to speak first. He settled on his default: "Gentlemen, I haven't been entirely honest with you."

"Oh?" Said the captain with a great deal of sarcasm.

"But judging by the fact that you had every man on the island chasing down my red devil here, I'd venture to guess that you already knew that."

"Yet you're the one who caught him. Leopard Seal, is it?"

"Rats," Parks smiled. "Then I'm guessing you weren't after him as a personal favor to myself and my associate."

"It is just as well you have done the work," the commander spoke. "You can't leave without a ship."

"And you'll be wanting half the reward."

"Half? No. You're ineligible to collect. We'll be needing the whole thing." Parks snapped his fingers. "You got me. Can't blame a man for trying to save his countrymen a little cash-money." He nodded. "One hundred percent of the reward, but I do have one demand that must be met." Again they paused and waited for him to speak. "We leave today."

All the men at the table laughed. "You want us to load a ship for a land so far no one's heard of it, with enough provisions, and a full crew, and set sail in a matter of hours?"

"Yarrr."

They looked at one another, bewildered. "Is that 'aye'?"

"Aye," Parks confirmed. "We have staked our honor on bringing him home in the year of the crime. To be executed on the anniversary of the founding of our great kingdom. You know, for good luck."

"Rubbish," Gionn erupted.

"'Scuse me?"

"Rubbish. That, and everything else. This man'll tell you of autumn winds—secret gales that will bring a wise navigator home or blow a fool off course to his death in the calms. He'll claim the course is treacherous, full of sea monsters and private ships and hostile powers. Harbors that'll rip your hull apart if you so much as pitch to lee at the wrong moment. He'll say I'm guilty of lyin', of treachery—even fuckin' the captain's wife." The captain went red-faced with rage, though not surprise. "Anything to get you to set sail today, and on his terms. Don't believe a word of it. This man is a schemer, and I his victim. Do I look like one capable of the things his rumormongers lay blame for?"

Parks tensed up. It was all he could do to avoid cutting down Gionn with his own sword. His careful words, his craft had led him to the verge of victory—he'd even allowed Gionn's escape as well—and the worm had squirmed once more toward their mutual disaster. Why couldn't he just go along with something? The captain pushed back the bench and stood. His eyes cut through Gionn, then laid into Parks' own soul. With deliberate patience he walked toward the far end of the long table, away from the commander, and around, back toward where they sat, and came to a stop hovering over their shoulders. Parks dared not look up. His eyes dropped to the table in front of him and awaited the ruin Gionn had long promised.

The captain raised his arm, and backhanded the ginger across the face and off the bench. "*Cunt!*" Gionn screamed at no one in particular. While he cursed and clambered back to his seat, the man returned the way he came and sat down. "If it's as long as voyage as you say, you'll do well to control your prisoner."

Parks nodded.

"We appreciate your need for haste," the commander said. "You will understand why we cannot send the three of you, even with a full complement of men, to a land whose king we do not know. He is as like to thank us for our efforts and cut our throats as he is to pay us."

"I assure you the king is very honest, and those who put up the reward, very rich. It's nothing to them. Also, we have…sacred laws. The gods will destroy those who promise reward and pay a penny less."

"That may be, but it will not console the dead. The prisoner remains with us. One of you will stay to watch over him. You'll have full quarter. The other goes with our men and vouches for the trade. Your people will send a ship with a reward in the spring, and it will return with the two of you and your man."

"That's…not gonna work for us."

"And the ship will not leave for two more days."

"Well, that's even worse."

"You're lucky to have a ship at all. I assume you will be going since your man was lashed by the viceroy yesterday. Very noble of him." They all laughed. "This one," he nodded to Gionn, "would not likely trade his flesh for his honor."

"How about this—"

"The way I have said is the way. You will pilot the ship as a free man, or bonded. Since you were prepared to leave today, I am sure you know the course well."

"Uh…I know half, my friend knows the other half."

Their "guest quarters," as the commander put it, was a small stone hut immediately behind the tavern where jars emptied of drink were stored. The door was the standard leather flap, and they could see the shadows of feet where it didn't quite touch the ground, though how many personal security detail they'd earned was anyone's guess. A team had been sent around to retrieve Foster, and they were to stay put until he joined them.

"Way to almost fuck us back there," Parks said to Gionn, his wrists still bound in straps.

"We're proper fucked anyway, cunt. And I was helping, whether or not you're clever enough to see it. We may not be goin' north, but he believes you, thanks to me."

"That'll at least get my throat cut far from here once they realize there's no ransom and I have no idea where I'm going."

"And mine when they return with an empty belly."

The flap flew open and the captain entered with one of the men from outside. "Not that it matters a great deal, but I'd call it an act of good faith if you told me where you're hidin' your whippin' boy." Foster slipped them, Parks thought. And if he had, it was Barzos' work, and there was only one place Barzos would take him.

"Did you check the brothel?"

"We always check the brothel."

"Did you check your wife?" Gionn retorted. The captain glared, but didn't respond.

"Hm. I don't know, bud," Parks shrugged. "We can help you look. It would appear the ol' Leopard Seal is much better at finding people than your men are."

The captain turned to the man behind him. "Talk to Barzos. He was with them." They pushed out through the flap.

"Cunt," Gionn whispered. "How many you suppose they left to guard us?"

"I say four."

"Me guess is two." Gionn stretched out his wrist to Parks. He hesitated, then untied the straps. Gionn lay them in a pile on the ground, then surreptitiously smashed one of the jars on the leather to deaden the clink of clay on bare rock. He sorted through the shards, selected a slender one with a good point, and wrapped the straps around the backside to serve as a handle.

"I mean, I can probably guess your plan, but maybe you should fill me in just in case I'm missing something."

"Listen." Parks clammed up, thinking Gionn would speak, but his eyes glazed as his attention turned to something small and far away. Parks followed with his ears. It was at first a high, faint staccato, then another. The sounds filled out like dots appearing in an impressionist painting, until he knew what he was hearing. The yelps and whines were low and far, but rising in pitch.

"Dogs."

"There's but one boat out of here now, cunt. If we go too soon, they catch us at the harbor. Too late, and your mate is gone without us. Our timin' has to be sharper than…" he searched for a metaphor. "This thing." Gionn raised the ceramic blade. "They'll need to board the dogs, and whatever passengers they carry. Then a certain time passes where the lazy arse rowers mill about, loadin' their own possessions and forgettin' stuff and goin' back for it, havin' a chat with their ugly squain missus, goin' through inspection with that odd cunt, sewin' up beads and shit. Then the captain looks her over, which may be a glance or half a day of finnickin' dependin' on the cunt involved. Everyone squares away, and they shove off somewhere between a song and a day after they were supposed to. We have to approach the quay at that precise moment. If we make it, we die at sea in autumn passage through the ice and the gales, or we make Drummoc and wished we'd died at sea when winter comes. I needn't explain what happens if we miss our boat."

"And how do you propose we pin the tail on that particular donkey?"

"I don't know what a fuckin' donkey is. But I propose we have a guess."

Barzos stood over his bulbous sack of beads and leather as he watched the Mattaka drive the dogs onto the gangway. The biggest ones were a third of a man, and most less than that, but the creatures terrified him. Long snouts and fangs like jaguars. Long, thick fur and pointed ears. They were the color of snow mixed with rock and dirt and the debris of the Hiade wastelands. Nothing of the sort existed in his land, and if it did, his people would kill them for food or their own safety. The fact that the Mattaka worked them as slaves was as bizarre as their legend. Tricksters from lands as far north as they were south, Dog stole from Man, but he could take only food. They killed one another, and Dog lived a hard life in the cold country. He was jealous of fire, that kept Man warm. He was jealous of house, that kept out wind. And he was jealous of boat, that took Man to rich lands. One day, he approached the place where Man lived, and praised Man's cleverness. Dog offered to work for such a noble creature, asking nothing in return but a bite of food.

Man was suspicious of Dog's tricks, but he could see that Dog worked hard and asked little in return, so he invited him to lie beside the fire at the end of the day. Dog was such a good worker, Man brought him into his house in the winter so Dog would not freeze. And when he came south, Dog was on the boat, and his children inherited all the rich lands that man found.

And the reason Dog always smiles with his tongue out is that though he works for Man, Man does not realize that he works for Dog.

Few of the Mattaka could tolerate the animals—a few families owned every last one in Hiade, and these did their best to keep them from wandering off course. They were roped together in sixes and marched across the rock—no ice here to drive a sled this time of year. The handlers spent as much time untangling them or breaking up fights as moving them. Nothing that was apparent stopped them from running off—certainly not the arm strength of a handful of men, and the woman from Captain Foster's ship, who walked the sides to hem them in, but kept her distance and held no lead. The real captain handled the teams as if they were long fingers of his arm.

"Barzos!"

"Bah!" Barzos jumped. A squad of Navy men stood behind him. They cringed away from the parade of beasts, as uneasy as he was in their presence.

"Where's the man?"

"Which man is that, sir?"

"The one you harbored in your quarters after you got him whipped by the viceroy."

"Oh, that man. Aye. Uh, I do not know."

"He's a special guest of the Admiral."

"Very good, sir. I will treat him as such,"

"You'll hand the fucker in."

"Aye sir, if I learn where he is, that I will do." One of the dogs in the old man's team yanked against her mates, her belly just starting to swell with pups. She stretched the lead to where Barzos stood with the Navy men, and they circled away like a flock of birds as a predator crashes the center. She sniffed furiously at his bead sack.

"Aya-ni! Go away!" Barzos made a half-hearted kicking motion that didn't disturb her at all. The old man reeled in her lead.

"She will not harm you," he said. "Her belly is full on the flesh of man." He laughed. Their faces widened in horror as he took her back to the pack. The Navy men returned their attention to him.

"We've searched every building on Nunoc."

"The Mattaka ones?" Barzos suggested.

"Every one he might be in without a stabbin'."

"And he is not here? That is very curious."

"It is, isn't it? I doubt you'd risk the viceroy's wrath by helpin' him."

"Oh, never! I have felt the temper of the viceroy. Hm." Barzos pondered. "Maybe it was him in the boat." They looked at the dog ship. "Not that one. When I inventoried the boats this morning against my records, one was missing."

"Which one?"

"The little skin boat they came in. It would be difficult to go far alone. I cannot think of anything that would make him desperate enough to try."

"Alright." Almost as an afterthought, he added: "Search the dog boat. Once they tie down the devils." Barzos gave his most deferent smile and waved after them.

The procession took hours. Each team had to be lead aboard and secured on the deck of the big outrigger. It was similar to the favored coal ship design—a single triangular sail took the wind, on a long boom that extended out to one side of the mast. The dogs were tied up everywhere on the main deck except where a sailor might need to get at a line. It would be lighter and ride the waves more nimbly than the coal transports, and she would need it. The storm season would be on them soon. The sleds—made of light, flexible Amposi wood—lie disassembled on the false deck, covered in seal pelts to keep out the relentless spray. Casks of fresh water were lashed in the free spaces. The dogs' food would travel on the swampy false deck, secured against the water that would take only days to find its way in. There was a single wooden daille, for going ashore for fresh water, or hunting seal if needed. Barzos recalled his own terrible passage to Hiade—his first time at sea—in the Viceroy's fine vessel. He was so glad to reach land he thought he may not wish to go home. Certainly not on to Drummoc. In one of those things.

One hundred and twenty dogs, and wood-enough for twenty-four sleds, the man had told him. He was content not to count. Many would die on the voyage, and every last one would be needed in Drummoc, especially without word from the *Kurrhatetgiuk*. Those who made it would have an easy winter of sleeping and building their strength on seal, and fish, and whale tendon. Come spring, they were the only way to haul any considerable amount of coal from the mines of Camne Drumlag to the shore for shipment, or from the shore to the furnaces of Nunoc.

Barzos had only been on the job a couple of weeks, but already he'd familiarized himself with every record available for decades. The dog shipments were split up across the year to prevent the catastrophe of losing every one of them to the sea and paralyzing the mining operation for a year or more. One each season except for winter. This one was critical. The first had a terrible passage. Eight of ten dogs aboard died of sickness or were swept over in heavy seas. And the second was already months overdue at Drummoc. Several ships of all variety had made the passage back and forth without a sighting.

They whinnied as the handlers drove them up the planks. Maybe Dog wanted to share the boats, thought Barzos, but they were not kind to him, and even though many of these had never seen the water, they seemed to know what awaited them. It was his turn to inspect and catalog the shipment, but he waved the Navy men ahead. They took another hour to search the benches below and to force the crew to uncover every basket and sled to ensure no one hid among the provisions.

"She's yours," the man said as he led his bunch down the gangway to puzzle over where Captain Foster could have gone. He glared into the distance for a moment, as if to work out the direction and odds of a skin boat making it to safety with a single rower, then shook his head and left.

"I will now board to log the crew and cargo," he said to no one standing anywhere nearby. "I will need to bring my sack of beadwork, which is difficult to carry. It is fortunate that sacks *do not complain.*" He twisted the end into a tighter grip and tried to wedge his shoulder under it to lift it. It took some bending and conorting, but with a great effort, he hoisted it off the ground and immediately entered into a controlled stumble under its weight. As his foot lifted, his toe caught the gangplank and the sack slid off with a thud. It groaned.

Barzos scanned to see if anyone had noticed. The small crew was scattered about—all Mattaka. None paid him mind. He tried to wiggle under again, but found his balance teetering him near the edge, and the freezing water. "Sorry," he said, and drug the sack roughly over the walkway until he dropped aboard and once again had the leverage to shoulder the load.

"Heavy." He turned to see the old man who'd arrived with him, the woman not far behind. "Aye, Captain," he replied.

Barzos stood below, looking up at the gray sky past the ladder. He fretted, having trusted the sack momentarily to the man called Tunguk, who offered to help. His head appeared alongside Kjartke, and between them, the bag. Tunguk supported the bottom. He set a foot on the top rung of the ladder, and immediately lost his grip. The sack slipped free and yanked out of Kjartke's hands. Barzos lunged forward with his arms outstretched in time for it to collapse on top on him. He hit the floor hard. A moment later, Tunguk landed on top, sandwiching the sack between them. There was a muffled howl of pain.

The native rowers and the passengers who found themselves below all turned to watch Foster crawl out of the bag, stray beads clinging or falling from his skin. Barzos scrambled silently for an explanation, but Tunguk spoke before he could find it.

"This man is a member of the crew. It is important that he travels with us. I will wait up top," he said to them more so than Barzos. Though it was as polite as anything he could have wished for, the blade dangling from Tunguk's belt as he climbed was enough that no man attempted to poke his head above the deck.

"What's the word on Parks?" Foster brushed himself off.

"They are guests of the admiral. It will not be possible for them to turn down his hospitality."

"Then get me back off this boat."

"Not possible, Captain. I believe the negotiations did not turn out in your favor."

"Good or bad, our favors are the same."

"Not true, sir. I have reason to believe the viceroy's honeymoon will be ending very shortly. His wife is a most noble lady. This morning she hung, for a short time, a cloth with an image of a white turtle, whose shell was cracked. I believe it was a warning. Ransom or not, you will be killed, and your friends will live under his terms."

"Tell Tunguk. Did you tell Tunguk? He can do somethin'."

"Sir. I must confess. I have violated my sacred duty." Foster waited for him to continue. "I have made a clerical error. Captain Tunguk and Lady Kjartke never arrived on Nunoc. There were three men in your boat. Which I set adrift. When the patrol finds it, they will believe you perished trying to escape. The three of you will not be sought." He gave a weak smile. "And it will be harder to discover your lie about the coal ships."

Foster's throat seized up and he didn't dare move or breathe for a moment. "Thank you, Brother," he choked.

"When you get to Drummoc, can you do me a favor?"

"I'll murder women and children for you if you want."

"That will not be necessary. I ask only that you speak kindly of me to the assistant viceroy."

"Of course."

"If you should decide to offer him your services, you will have my reference," he handed Foster a pre-made strand of beads. "I think you'll find him more agreeable than his superior."

"And Parks. What're the chances you can get him to me in the spring?"

"He is bound for the Kingdom of America as soon as a ship can be provisioned. I can send word of him, and of Captain Gionn, to you in Drummoc, and pray for his safe passage. If you prefer that option."

"Is there another option?"

Gionn's ear pressed against the side of the hut, the ceramic knife clutched in his hand. "How long?" Parks whispered. Gionn shushed him and returned to listening. "Bit of a wait, cunt. I can tell by their cries of torment that they're still loadin' the monsters on the ship."

There was a stir among the guards outside.

"Good afternoon, sirs," Barzos' voice came through the doorway as he addressed the men posted. "I have been asked by the captain of the *Juhketappat*—that's the *dog ship*," he said strangely loud, "to inform you that the missing has been searched for and *not* found to be aboard. I have completed my inspection, and she will shove off at any moment."

"Fine," one said dismissively.

"At any moment," he repeated with an increased volume. "The *Juhketappat* will depart, and she will *not return* under *any circumstances* until spring."

"I fuckin' got it, monkey. Fuck off."

"Good day to you, sir." Parks and Gionn's eyes locked. Barzos voice came once more, trailing away. "Any moment!"

Tunguk stood at the aft-most line securing the *Juhketappat* to the quay. Two of the crew hauled the gangplank ashore and jumped back over the narrow gap of water between the ship and the dock where it was pulled snug against sections of timber hung from ropes to prevent it from slamming into the rock. Four enlisted men chatted on the quay were they'd been left in the off-chance that Foster would show up at the ship. He looked down the line at the others manning the ropes, and there was a shrug. Nothing moved in the distance, and it was several hundred yards of open rock between the buildings and the dock.

"Lines clear! Prepare to shove off!" Came the captain's order. Tunguk acted as though he had not heard. The other three men untied their ropes and were coiling them when the captain repeated in his ear, "Lines clear!"

Tunguk played confused. He looked around, then pointed questioningly at the rope in front of him.

"Aye, that line. Have you been to sea?"

"First time." He dawdled untying it, but even his slow movements couldn't delay the process much. Once the command to shove came, the men on deck would pole off, the oars would emerge, and they would be away. Tunguk felt the world growing very small again. It was another place he could not return. Territories closed on him north to south, as they had expanded in his youth, returning to the spirit world where they had once risen to life. He had seen these buildings go there before, but he knew this time they would stay. His heart tightened as if a rope coil shortened around it. It was the same feeling he felt right before he was bound to akmanuak. With the man below deck. With the man somewhere before him. And he wondered if he had done enough, or if it was the knot that came to claim him. To make him a wanderer in more worlds than one.

His hand moved to the familiar handle of his long blade. Tunguk faced the captain. "Hold the ship." The man gave him a strange look, but it quickly disappeared over his shoulder, drawn by something unsettling.

Tunguk followed, and the rope on his heart gave slack. Two small figures sprinted from the line of warehouses on a direct course for the port. The Navy men faced the ship, laughing about something. They had not noticed, and would not, unless they turned around. Close behind the runners, more men broke into view, moving as quickly. Four, seven, then twelve in total. Tunguk stepped to the edge to leap onto the dock, but a hand pressed his chest back to the boat.

Kjartke's touch was not forceful. It asked his blessing, and at the same time, assured him. He nodded, and she jumped onto the quay. The Navy men noticed her. Something fierce spat from her mouth in Mattakatan. They were utterly confused. She marched toward them, screaming louder and louder in her language, her face in a rage. None of the men knew what to make of the native woman, suddenly furious at them for no apparent cause.

"What's she on about?" One of them begged the group. The men aboard the ship didn't interfere. Tunguk watched as the two runners crossed the halfway point, then halved the distance again. It was as in the legend of Pikte's arrow: the master archer who the gods blessed to never miss had fired at his lover Katillike in vengeance, but her father sang a song to the arrow. It crossed half the distance to the target, and half again, as many times as the wave breaks, where it still travels across the sky at night.

The arrow left the world, and the one called Brother filled it. He led Gionn by several strides, and tore past the squad, leaping onto the ship. The men were stunned to stillness, then shattered as Gionn lowered his shoulder into the pack and sent them spilling across the ground. He tried to regain his balance, but slid near the edge of the quay. Kjartke grabbed his thick wrist with both hands and yanked him up.

"Shove off!" Tunguk shouted. He looked at the captain, who pursed his lips, then repeated the command.

"Shove off!"

Gionn and Kjartke leapt the gap as the oars widened the distance to land. The men, back on their feet, yelled at the ship to stop. Tunguk stood on the edge of the false deck in case one would make the jump, but no one attempted.

Parks and Gionn rose and gasped for air as they watched the collection of men. Parks burst into jubilant laughter, and hugged his fellow fugitive.

They spat insults at their pursuers, and Gionn waved his hands overhead to torment them.

"Here ya go, mate," he handed something to Tunguk. It was a ceramic shard, wrapped in leather, caked in blood. Tunguk regarded it as the others joined the crew on deck. He drew his arm back and tossed it underhand at the feet of the men. His people knew songs to deliver an avenging party to the weapon that harmed them. He didn't know if these men had such songs, but he suspected they would not be far behind.

13

JUHKETAPPAT

There was a moment of weightlessness. Kjartke gripped the ladder rung as the ship topped the wave and waited for the hull beneath her feet to tilt her backward, steeper and steeper, until her hold was the only thing that kept her from falling. She braced her arms when they hit the trough as everything suddenly shifted forward. It was all she could do to keep the momentum from slamming her into the rungs, and she knew she had missed her chance once more. Around her, rowers somehow managed to steal sleep amid the thunderous collision along the side of the ship. Water trickled through every window on the amu side despite being closed up tight. Three passengers—a Mattaka mother and two daughters—passed a bucket from the bilge to the one window left open to port, where everyone crowded to stay dry. A short waterfall from the deck emptied over her head and rushed into the bilge, which was shin-deep on the woman whose turn it was to fill and pass as fast as she could. All three of them performed their work surefooted and without complaint. It was a permanent task during heavy seas. Were it dire, there would be many more buckets at work.

She looked back over the huddled mass. Southern clans, every one of them. Every passenger below, every crew above. Accustomed to long travel in deep water. She could hold her stomach in a skin boat as well as any, but those would never brave seas like these. And wood was different. Skin rolled and bone twisted and swayed with the water, like a whale gliding over the surface. Wood stiffened and creaked, jumped and fell and fought the waves every step of the way. It would prefer to be smashed apart than to heed the water.

The sharp feeling clenched her stomach again—one she had not felt since she was a child, taken in a hunting boat by her father on a calm day to listen to what the sea had to say. It was when you tried to have your course that it gripped you, and when you gave up that it released. She remembered that, but did not know how to do it in this ship where the people hide from the waves the way a girl hides from her auntie's anger. For the sea was a woman, she knew. Foreigners pleaded with it by many names, all men. Even the southern clans who knew her story prayed to the god who they said moves across the surface of her body. Kjartke knew better, and did not waste her prayers.

Before it could pitch again, and she staggered to the bilge, leaned over, and forced herself to vomit into the waters near the bailing woman. She spat twice, then dipped her hands in and cupped a drink to her mouth. A quick swish, and she spat the rest of the taste free of her tongue, replaced by salt and bitter wood.

The ship started up the next hill of water. She gripped the ladder again and held firm as it leaned forward and tempted her with a quick climb. She knew better, and would not be caught near the top when the ship dive the other way. The keel moaned as the sea ran beneath them and the hull tipped the other way and tried to shake her loose. The bottom leveled them, and she waited to feel the deck tilt again. The ladder now leaned the other direction. Hand over hand, she scrambled up the gentle slope as fast as she dared. The crest would arrive soon. This time she anticipated the weightless moment, the flying moment, and lunged forward. Threw herself onto the deck and rolled clear of the hatch before she could be tossed back on the descent. Windswept spray crossed between the peaks overhead as they began the next slow climb. The black wall towered ahead of the ship, which approached as straight as it was wise, but always veering this way or that way. For the wind blew in their teeth. The captain carried as little sail as he dared—enough to give them steering, and held as close to the gale as the claw would allow. Their course was much more sidelong and ahead. Each time she took the deck, it took a moment to orient herself. The hatch found itself at the bow, with the amu to her right as she faced ahead—between them and the swell. It meant they drifted toward the hidden coast.

The captain and all nine of his sailors were locked in a fight with the lines, and she knew she had picked a poor moment to come topside. Kjartke pressed herself to the deck for balance, and so that she would not get in their way. They loosed the giant boom. It took all their power and coordination to keep its swing under control. The sailors made quick talks with the wind as the boom swept out over the starboard and the open ocean, and for a moment, the ship drifted broadside into the wave. She felt the deck tilt and lunge as a dog let from his lead after a seal pup. The entire ship spun. When she was sure this was the time it would go over, the boom crossed the center of the wind. The bow rotated to stern, the stern to bow. They angled back into the wave in the other direction just in time to be lifted harmlessly over the top.

It had happened often enough since they left Nunoc. Tunguk explained that the amu must always keep to windward, and it was the only way to cross the wind. But it was not a movement Kjartke had learned to trust. She slicked her wet hair back out of her face and wobbled to her feet, then across to the false deck—always to port, no matter which end called itself "bow". One of the dogs noticed her and let out a short bay. The chorus spread across the deck, most of them leaping to their feet. There were many signs like this that told her how the voyage was going, even though she knew little of the open sea. This one told her how many dogs were well enough to eat, and every time their number dwindled. The sailors secured the lines and spread across the deck. That one meant the ship was safe to cruise for a while.

Her foot slid every few steps. "Dog soap," the crew called it. It found its way onto every surface, greased every rope, and tracked down the ladder rungs to the hold where it fouled the air. The waves that broke over the changing bow kept the deck clean fore and aft, but between the hatches where the dogs were tethered to spare them the worst of the water, it was a muddy slurry. To walk the *Juhketappat* required ice legs.

Kjartke peeled back the cover and gathered as much seal meat as she could carry into a sack. She fed them from the farthest containers to spare the drier food for the people. The dogs did not mind that theirs was soaked through. The creatures looked pathetic—shrunk to half-size with wet fur and whimpering from the toss and the spray. Still, she did not wish to go near them. So Tunguk had given her the task of feeding. He said it would make them like her. Kjartke did not care to be liked. Only that she not have to touch them. The hunting clans in the arm had no use for dogs. It was said that they are the souls of men who angered the gods. The cruelest of the animals, returned to serve the lowest of Man, the slave clans. That the best dogs and the worst Kammatuk traded places. Either way, they moved firestone for halots.

The beasts leapt and gnashed as the first handful landed among them. Their leads tangled and tied up legs and necks. The strong ate much, and the seasick ate none at all. It was a surprise to her, as many as tended to die in milder summer crossings, that all of them were still alive. Tunguk and the three from Nunoc would be up to bring them fresh water and untangle them as they drank. She was careful not to give them too much. All on board ate from the same rations, but if the dogs starved, they could be fed to one another.

Kjartke stepped down the line near the center of the amu and rained meat upon the next group. A fur lump stirred and sat up. Foster, pale as a spirit, looked at her from under his blanket. He was nestled in with the pack for warmth, as he had been since the beginning, preferring the spray to the stale air below deck. She held up a handful of seal, and he shook his head. Little stayed down since they left, though the dogs were grateful to eat what came up. She raised it again, insistent. Again he turned her down. The whip might have healed if the sea had not broken his stomach and his strength. It was beyond her how he could stand the creatures, but weak as he was, he had no fear of them. Even took comfort in their midst. The dog she knew would die first was curled against him—the pregnant bitch who had tasted man's flesh on Nunoc. She would not eat, either. It was not her wish to give birth on the sea, and it was killing her. Kjartke feared that once Foster died among them, or came close enough, the dogs would leave not even his bones. Yet she did not try to talk him below deck. This was his choice.

She worked her way around the entire deck. Every time they lunged for her and the line went taut, her heart leapt, and it thrilled her. It was impossible to know if they adored her for bringing them life, or meant to tear her apart, but the way they swirled like furious eddies around a rock, crashing and diving and drawing back, sent currents across her skin and gave her a world that was hers alone.

Once more she climbed the false deck and stowed the sack, tied down the covers. The ship rose on the long slope of a wave, and she looked back over the tumult, dark and restless. For an instant she glimpsed it, crossing the top of a wave before it dipped and disappeared. The flash of sail was clear now. Closer than before. The storm had slowed them, but it had not turned them back as they had hoped. The gale that lashed them and spun them, lay low their crew and their dogs, and threatened at every gust to rip them to Urkuk was the only reason the sleek warship had not overtaken them.

From his bench, Parks watched Eskimo Joe lead the three dog boys up the ladder—no simple task when the ship rose and fell and pitched sideways at random intervals. Dog boys, he called, them, because only the oldest may have been a teen.

"Guess they grow up fast around here," he remarked. Gionn opened one eye from the floor between the benches where he reclined. "The mushers," he clarified, "or whatever you call them." He thought back to the young captain. "And your boy Oduy." Gionn closed his eye without a word. "When I was a kid, my biggest responsibilities were cleaning up after I spanked it and making sure I had enough herb to get me through until my next allowance came in."

Rowing hadn't been much harder. They only pulled until they cleared the harbor, and the oars had been secured ever since. He felt half-retarded on the stroke at first, and it destroyed him, but after a few hours of mimicking everyone else he had enough of a handle that at least he wasn't knocking oars with Gionn. That was nearly a week ago. The gale hit on the day before, and hadn't even made a pretense of letting up. Just as well, since he'd been seasick on and off the entire time. Half the ship had it, and none worse than Foster.

Parks left Gionn to his perpetual nap and negotiated the ladder. It was getting easier each time. He lurched onto the deck and steadied himself on all fours before finding his feet. His stomach sank in relief when Kjartke stood before him, heading for the same ladder. He'd felt the turn when she was topside, and while Foster was his excuse for being up here, his wasn't the only well-being that worried him.

"How's my boy?" She walked past him to the hatch and stopped. A rough, gray hand extended in his direction. When he reached to meet it, she clasped firm, put the other hand on top, and allowed him to support her as she took the first few tentative steps down the ladder, until she was low enough to hold the rungs herself.

The spray blasting off the waves stung his cheeks and chilled him, left him in a salt blur even worse than his normal vision. He'd wanted to ask her if there was any word on the Navy ship. It could have been sitting on the stern and he wouldn't have made it out. An unsettled belch rose from his stomach with no horizon, nothing fixed, the ocean in calamity under shifting cloud. None of it quelled the little flutter he felt when she let him help her. Did she have a choice? She did, he told himself. She totally did.

Something slapped across his back. Tunguk held out a full water bladder. "You must make him drink." He returned to the boys where they transferred fresh water from kegs into what was a soft, seal-skin bowl, for lack of a better description. These they carried to each group of dogs, let them drink, and refilled. The pliable container allowed them to clamp the top shut as they stumbled across the deck—invaluable when fresh water was liquid gold and spilling could mean dying of thirst in a week or two.

"Aye-aye, Cap'n!" Parks saluted the man as he passed—Ostuk was his name. Or something very similar. He only called him "Cap'n," as he imagined any captain would prefer, and because he was afraid he was confusing it with the word "ostrich" and it had been another word entirely. Ostuk stared as he passed but did not return the salute.

"I'm becoming quite popular," he announced to the pack of dogs. "We've graduated to consistent eye contact." Foster propped himself up on an elbow. "Go on, *git!*" Parks swiped a dog aside with his foot. "I don't know why everyone's so afraid of these little guys," he knelt beside his friend. "You just gotta have that BDE, am I right?" His fist went unpounded. Foster shook his head at the sight of the water.

"Come on, you're seasick, not rabid. You gotta drink."

"Can't."

"Baby sips."

"It'll come up."

"Then let it come up. You're whiter and wetter than these bastards. We gotta keep up your strength," he pulled the bone plug. Reluctantly, Foster brought it to his lips and grimaced as the smallest amount trickled down his raw throat. It tasted as terrible as always, but something about the sensation made him take another sip right away. "Atta bro."

Foster let out a deep sigh. "You good?"

Parks grinned in response. "Me? Magnificent. Except my shin started hurting again," he scratched at the wet scab. "I haven't been able to chew that herbal crap since we hit turbulence."

"How long til we get boarded?"

"Good question. I don't really know how boats and storms and boarding parties work. But don't worry yourself. Thanks to Barzos, they think you're dead. It's me and Gionn they want. You're sitting pretty, my friend. I guarantee you no one's going to search through a pile of dogs."

"Unless they decide to kill everyone on board for aidin' and abettin'."

"That's exactly what Joe is trying to convince the captain of."

Tunguk found Ostuk aft, at the steering oar. White foam snarled behind them where the big tree did its best to slow their leeward drift. Many times the size of the Mattaka's bone, the heavy wood was anchored to a pivot, its handle braced under a notch in the half-moon frame. A thick rope, tensioned on both sides, wound several times around the slim part of the handle to prevent it from jumping out of the hands of the three men who were needed to adjust it. Rewet and Hagalut kept watch over the great leg, ready to help their captain. It creaked under the strain as the *Juhketappat* crested another wave.

Ostuk stole a glance behind at the height. His skin was salted leather, taller and with a thicker trunk than the full-Mattaka crew. The darkest brown hair and the shape of his eyes betrayed his mixed parentage. Enough halot to get him a ship, not enough to run any but the southern crossings. Tunguk greeted the captain in a string of Mattakatan.

"Aye, still there," Ostuk replied in the farri's tongue. "I have not seen her, but the woman says she is close."

"Maybe the woman lies."

Ostuk shook his head. "Storm or not, she is fast."

"I have been on ships in my days. The crew is very good. We, too, run fast under sail. Not long to reach Galliput."

"Under sail," Ostuk dismissed the compliment. His eyes checked what slim sheet he dared carry. "And Galliput is weeks yet. Once the weather clears, we're caught."

"Will they be angry that we do not wait?"

Ostuk smirked at the trick. "No one will blame us in a storm. We have to stay on this side of the water."

"It is good," Tunguk said. "A dog captain, for a dog ship."

"You are wondering which breed."

"I do not wonder. It will be made when it is time."

"I have not yet lost crew, passenger, or dog. But there are no good choices." Tunguk nodded in agreement. Ostuk took his eyes off the waves and lay them on the old man. "When I make a bad one, it will be interesting to see who makes it with me."

The men watched the storm in silence for a few minutes. There was no flash of what Kjartke had seen between the swells. Tunguk left without a word to meet Parks as he made his way back to the hatch. Parks handed over the empty water bladder. "Any luck?"

"He will have me prepare to fight if we are boarded."

"Nice. You think we got the manpower? Advantage goes to the defender, right? It's not like they have cannons and shit. They have to climb over here and get stabbed in the fuckin' face."

"The woman has seen it close. But she does not know the crews of ships to say how many. It is less, but they are fighters."

"Yeah, well that's like saying the Browns are a football team. They might be, but they're bumbling retards compared to the Pats. I mean, how good are we talking?"

"It is no matter. There will be no fight." Tunguk pointed to three of the crew where they bent to strike a flame in an earthen oven, one of them holding a sheet of leather to block the vent from the wind. The moment it sparked, they placed a small metal pot with a rounded bottom and two handles atop the opening. "Whale fat. They will pour offering to their sea god to bring us from the storm."

"Well, God bless 'em."

"When the storm calms, we will be caught. To ask a fight is a fool's prayer. They will give you over."

"Shit," the logic sunk in for Parks. "Should we go kick over the kettle?"

"It is hard to know which sea god holds these waters. We will not anger theirs if he does. It will not help if he does not."

"So what's the plan? Mutiny?"

"Pray for storm."

Ostuk waited by the steering oar until his men made their offering. They hadn't asked his permission, and he wouldn't have given it. The old man needed to believe they wouldn't just hand over his mates, but he had to have noticed the puka they prepared. When he saw the three crewmen arguing, he knew it was over who would receive it. Filikut and Anset were animated, no doubt in favor of acknowledging Pillanuk. But Anset's uncle, Arwoset was still devoted to Hawe. It was said that when there is a great change in the sea—one that lasts many years—the gods are at war. That was enough to convince Ostuk to make his prayers to "King of these Waters," wherever he may be and who may answer. But he didn't intervene in his crew's affairs. All nine of them were full Mattaka. They may work for a dog, but they would not take council on the gods from one.

Arwoset got his way. They inserted poles into the handles and carried the steaming cauldron to the stern, feet away from where Ostuk stood vigil at the shuddering oar. It was of little help when the seas were like this, but even little things could keep them afloat. The fat spilled over, oozing off the deck into the sea. If there was a hiss, or steam, the turbid waters drowned it out. They crouch-walked over to him, shielding their eyes from the sting of the spray.

"The crew would have assembly," Arwoset said. It was a captain's right to demand assembly, and certainly his right to refuse, but Ostuk nodded his head. He was too diligent to be feared. If he were halot, he would be obeyed absolutely. If he were Mattaka, he'd be respected, but he would not be the owner of the *Juhketappat*, and perhaps not even allowed to be its captain. His job was to sail between worlds, and answer to what gods may call.

The men assembled on either side of him, leaving space for him to see the waves ahead. Arwoset watched for wanderers—the motherless travelers who could arrive from any direction—from port, and Rewet from starboard. All huddled close, as much for stability and protection as to hear over the screaming gale. Before he began, Ostuk noticed that one of the fugitives was still on deck after having taken water to his friend, camped among the dogs. The tall man stood safe to center beneath the mast, facing the waves ahead. Both of them were too far to have a hope of hearing what the men discussed.

"You have called assembly, Arwoset. Perhaps you will speak the orders."

"We do not order you, Captain," he replied without turning from his watch. "We ask what you will do when the Navy ship comes."

"What would you have me do?"

"It is not my place."

"My contract binds me to bring dogs to the mines for the King of Ampos." He paused while his men spat upon the deck—their informal obligation when no representatives of the king were watching. "My ship must arrive safe. My dogs, my crew. I am not bound to stowaways."

"Even if they are your people?" The youngest one, Ijak, thought no more of him than the rest of the crew, but lacked the manners of an Arwoset. The nose of the ship shot up the next wave, and the men before him took a few hard steps to stop themselves from collapsing into Ostuk. Hands braced against shoulders with a firmness that would have started a fight in a tavern, or earned a captain's blade, but under the circumstances the mutual strength the touch afforded was welcomed, and men could grapple mid-conversation without any bearing on the words they spoke.

"My people? You speak of my father's people. I must thank them that I can own a ship, and that it must be confined to the waters of the Attavaik. That I may not cross the Orin. It is my mother's family who raised the money to first lease the *Juhketappat,* and who raised more to help me buy it. It is her people who keep watch on my deck while I sleep. Her cargoes I carry. Her gods I sing to for safe passage. What do I owe these men?"

"Ijak will be ashamed of his speech," Arwoset assured him, though Ostuk knew he was quite pleased that Ijak had been willing to make a fool of himself for something that plagued the others' dreams as well. "We know you will give them to the king when his ship comes."

"But there is more that you would ask."

"It is said we could have stayed in port to turn them over as they boarded. Instead, we shoved off. Will they not be upset?"

"Will they not cut our throats," Ostuk rephrased it for him. He laughed. "The old man is clever. I am not surprised he spins these fears. No, my boat leaves on time. And it stops when it is hailed by the Navy of the King of Ampos."

"Then we will be safe," Anset said, though the statement hung in the air like a question.

"It is not the Amposi whose blades you must fear. We are ten. There are forty rowers, and near one hundred aboard besides us."

"You suspect mutiny," another of the more experienced men, Hagalut spoke.

Anset shook his head. "Many of these rowers have worked with us in days past. They are loyal."

"Half at best," Ostuk corrected, "and I don't know how many of them are well-armored against these fugitives' plots."

"Poikatuk, Geslauk, Alo…" Anset named, "these are loyal men."

"It may be," he screamed louder as the wind picked up and gave them a sideways jolt as they sheared over the top of the wave. "It may be, but enough are in doubt."

"Then we kill the stowaways before they make trouble," Arwoset said.

"They row for me. Care for my dogs. You would have me murder three halots and two Mattaka out of fear?" Ostuk smiled and shook his head. "We are on mutiny alert. You will watch these people. If they do not cause trouble, they travel with us until the Navy ship comes. Or if we cross Galliput, they work their passage to Drummoc. Are there concerns?" He knew there were, but the men remained silent. "Back to your stations. Rest if you can. We will run for some time before we cross the wind again." They turned, and Ostuk called after them. "Arwoset! Anset! Hagalut!" The three men remained behind.

"We will not wait for mutiny to spread. Speak among the rowers you trust. Tell them the stowaways petition the captain to fight. Tell them I struggle with the decision, and that you think if many men show their loyalty, I will be able to turn them over without asking any man to take up arms. But I fear if the rowers are loyal to these men, then we must fight, and many will be killed. Let their tongues do the work for you. And keep your ears to the wind." He motioned for Arwoset to take over his watch at the steering oar.

The sail snapped and filled as they rose high enough for the wind to take the slack. The head lurched against the halyard a little too far for his liking. Ostuk leaned his shoulder into the wind and stepped near as much sideways as forward. He drew near the tall man who had invaded his ship.

Parks pressed his palms together and bowed his head as he bellowed into the storm. "God, I'm not really religious or anything, but if you could do me a solid, maybe I could get you back at a later time. I submit to you my prayer. Wherein, I do beseech thee, make this storm a storm. Make the winds rage and the sea foam like a drink that got shaken up and then opened. But not too much. Like, not so hard that we end up sinking. And actually, if you could go easy, Foster's a little seasick. Some of the rest of us, too. But still make it suck balls bad enough that the ship that is trying to catch us, which is full of heathens, cannot get close enough to board. I have no whale fat to boil for you. But Foster is a hillbilly, and I don't think he's religious either, but a lot of his people for sure are, and that alone should make us outrank all these other barbarians. Anyway, with all due respect to any heathen gods that might be listening, you, God, are truly the king of the sea. I pray you deliver us safely home on the back of a great storm. Amen to that!"

He double-tapped his chest with his fist then pumped it in the air. Only then did he notice Ostuk waiting a respectful distance away. Parks wondered if he'd heard any of that over the gale. "Sup, Cap'n?"

"I wait for you to finish your prayer." He indicated the mast and its array of rope that held fast the sail and the long boom. *Nice*, Parks thought. The captain had finally spoken to him. Earning trust.

"Much appreciated, amigo. You carry on with all the good work you're doing here." He clapped the man on the shoulder as he passed. His heart lurched into his chest as he hoped that his appeal for the storm had been lost in the wind. The weather sure looked like it wasn't going to unfuck itself any time soon, but he decided to dry his skin below. Surely Eskimo Joe had something cooked up if it did. Akmanuak, and all.

A gust buffeted his ears and changed the pressure so that it felt like someone had box clapped the side of his head in a middle school hallway. His hands rose to shield them, and cutting through his fingers and the roar, he heard something like a gunshot. The crew was screaming and running around the deck as fast as they could move while bent in half. A sound like the hooves of the Four Horsemen tilted his neck back to find the top of the sail snapping like a bed sheet out over the starboard beam. The rope that fixed it to the mast was an angry, whipping serpent, loosed from its hole.

"Drop sail!" Ostuk shouted. The old man was already on the ropes. All hands joined him except one, whose screams from the steering oar were lost in the gale. But there was nothing on the free end to pull it in. Four of the men fought the knots on the array of lines and worked to haul it down by the reefing lines. One of the younger sailors didn't care to wait. He scaled the mast to the boom and shimmied out on the long arm to windward of the flapping sail. The captain noticed the furious handwaving from the stern, and snatched one of the men by the shoulder. "On the oar!" A vein bulged in his face as he shouted in the young man's ear. The kid and one other sprinted toward the stern. At once, Parks understood. The bow of the ship backed into the swell. They'd run so far with the outrigger to windward and to the waves, at a slight angle. Now without the drift from the sail, the rudder was pushing them head-on. He wasn't sure why it was a bad idea, but the frantic crew told him all he needed to know.

The man on the boom gave a whoop and rolled himself off onto the sail. It looked a hell of a drop, but the lift from the wind buoyed him so that for a stomach-turning moment, it seemed as though he'd roll out over the side and overboard. But he swung his legs off the side and hugged the sheet with his arms so that his feet touched down on the deck with no room to spare. Two more men jumped on it, then everyone at hand, including Parks. They wrestled it to the ground, then a pair stood and hurried to where part of the pennant still trailed over the side. They bunched it and hauled arm-over-armful to bring it back on deck.

The bow pitched upward as they took the next wave nearly head-on. A glance back saw the three men had shifted steering oar to regain their angle, but without propulsion, the ship sank into the trough and nosed even straighter under the momentum. Unprotected by the false deck, tons of water washed over the bow and ran off the first quarter of the deck while dogs scurried as far as their leashes would allow.

Ostuk shouted a command in Reverse-Eskimo, and the sailors cleared off the bundle to check its seams for tears. "Rope!" He called to Parks and pointed at a spare coil near the edge of the false deck. The big man lumbered under the wind as fast as he could, tripping over dogs, spinning, juking his way to the line. When he hoisted it over his shoulder he sank under the surprising weight of the wet fiber. A pitch shot his foot from beneath him and he felt his groin overstretch as the other knee banged into the deck. Somehow, he threw himself back to his feet when the ship tossed the other way, and leaned into the controlled stumble. When he dropped it at the mast, Ostuk joined him.

"Do you know how to rig the halyard?" The blank look must have been a sufficient answer, because the captain turned in disgust and pulled one of the men from the sail. Parks scanned the deck for something to do in nervous frustration. He jumped back as another man shot past him to help with the rope. At the stern, the three men grappled with the big steering oar to find a position that would slip their nose out of the wave. *The old heave-ho,* Parks thought. That was something he could handle. He waded through more dogs. The bow rolled up behind him and pitched him onto his face. A mighty peal of thunder sounded as if the ship itself were struck. He crawled to his feet, and nearly forgot about the open hatch in his path. With a spin, the flung himself around it, posted a hand on the ground to right his balance, and joined the screaming crew at the stern. They abandoned their post in unison and pushed past him, screaming in panic on their way to midship. A bewildered Parks approached the stout apparatus and blinked. It took him several seconds to register the absence of the long rudder that held them on their course. A section of new, light wood protruded in the middle of the brace where part of it had sheared off and shredded the rope that held the handle in a firm grip. It wasn't thunder at all. The steering oar vanished somewhere into the cobalt waters. The dog ship was adrift.

Again he nearly tripped over the hatch before he saw it on his sprint to the mast. Ostuk pointed and stopped him cold. "On your oar! Rowers to oars!" He leapt back as if he had been shoved, and scrambled below deck.

Ostuk watched the wet head disappear down the ladder by the time he realized he had given no other instructions. If there was a man with any sense below, he would feel the pitch of the ship had changed and set the oars to ease her back so the port bow took the swell. For a moment, he turned back to the sail, then caught himself. It would do little good to raise it if they capsized by then. They dipped into the trough again, and the bow hesitated to decide her course. If the amu were caught leeward, they would go over. For now, at least, there was no danger of taking them head-on once the steering oar tore itself free.

"Sail is good!" Hagalut called.

"Rig it!"

The dogs howled a blood song. They sensed the change in the crew. Now he wondered what to tell the rowers at all. It would have to be the starboard oars, and they only, but the sea might rip them from the men's hands if they didn't take care. His inward gaze saw the other steering oar shipped at the bow. Did he dare try a shunt with the rowers to give them steering? It would be difficult-enough to bring the amu into the swell, to say nothing of crossing it. And it would take men away from the sail to have the steering oar ready when they got there, where still they would await the long climb.

Ostuk started for the hatch when a white head appeared out of the hold. Tunguk looked up at the sail, then the wave ahead. Despite his claim, it was clear the old man had been on ships. Ostuk prayed he would know the orders to give the rowers. The head ducked down. It would be too much to ask a full shunt. Not yet. The veteran men raced the new halyard into position. The bellow of the storm grew so that no man could hear orders unless he shouted them in his ears. So far, they didn't need to. As soon as the rope became the work of few, three of the nine hurried forward to the steering oar they had left, to await the moment it would meet the sea. Another wave rolled under them. Whether his fortune, or Hawe drunk on whale fat, the amu swung just to starboard so that the front edge crept between the ship and the swell. The deck changed pitch and every creature upon it stumbled. Ostuk surrendered to the wood before it could throw him, and he heard the dogs in an uproar.

He spun on his knees and craned his neck at the coal-dark mast. Somewhere up there was the block that the halyard would thread. At its foot stood Rewet and Ijak, two of the younger crew—each but a season wet. They glanced back at him, and he raised a finger to the top. There was no question what the order would be. None was eager to do it, and they were begging their captain to decide their courage for them. Neither man would have been his choice, but the others could not be spared. Ostuk rose and pointed to Ijak, then up.

Rewet took the end rope and climbed with gratitude to the boom. There, he made it fast around the climbing belt. The layered ring of stiff leather hung from the mast, sewn to itself that it could not separate. Maqay tossed up a stone the size of a man's foot, with a hole bored on one end. When it was fixed to the loose tail, he joined the others who waited to receive it again. It would take but moments to run up the head, but that would have to wait for Ijak to scale a tall tree and pass his end through the block.

Ostuk watched as a small pitch at deck level sent the top of the mast several times the distance, and the gusts slammed with enough force to tear it from even the strongest arms—never mind letting go to secure a knot. The fall would kill him, and there was a great chance he would not even land on the deck. Already, Ostuk listed to himself the names he would send as each failed. He would send the entire ship if he had to.

The deck rotated beneath them. Oars must have found the water. She spun to starboard. There was no rowing in seas like this. All they needed was a dip to correct their drift and put the amu back to windward. Tunguk's head appeared again to take the measure of their stroke, then ducked below. Another good one would lay them neat to the swell, and it would be a matter of managing the angle, not least because it would make Ijak's task easier if the mast always swayed back and forth in a steady line. The oars bit again. There was a jolt as twenty blades plunged in to slow the oncoming wave.

It was too much. The bow crossed the trail—the angle he wished to ride over the sloping water—and settled near to broadside. Rowers were not meant to steer like this, and many of these were unseasoned. He hoped they got their oars out, or they were going to lose them. The sea arched its mighty back over the *Juhketappat*. There was nothing to do. They were going over.

The false deck reared up. Every man leaned into the wave as though he scaled a steep mountain. She tipped so hard that dogs slid across the deck, their leads catching to yelps of protest. Ostuk lost his feet and slid back into someone. The beam behind him sank near the sea as though to lower its lips for a drink. When he thought the push of a feather would send them over, the amu burst over the crest. For a sickening moment, it was weightless. The deck lurched back the other way when it slammed into the backside of the wave. Water rushed over the false deck and the spray crossed the entire span to land amidship. A pile of dogs crashed into the port beam, and a brief waterfall ran over their heads. Several baskets of supplies snapped free of their cleats and rolled free into the hungry wave. A few more slid across the false deck to wait the turn that would take them, too. But now the amu had weight again. She plowed with determination down the backside to bob in the wind shadow of the next giant.

The way the top of the mast snapped back and forth tore at Ostuk's stomach, though in the cloud-dim night he couldn't see the end of it. Impossible for a man to scale it, free a hand, and feed the line, he thought. The other choice was to float at the mercy of the waves, to correct the heading and keep her port quarter into the giants, and pray that no wanderers came across—perhaps for days on end until the storm settled enough to re-secure the halyard. A ridiculous measure. They would go over sideways on a prayer every third time if the rowers were excellent. Meanwhile the pounding waves could choose between capsizing them one way, or ripping the false deck itself free under the direct blow abeam. The only way out was up.

The men locked fingers for Ijak's foot and hoisted him up onto the boom. In all his years, Ostuk had never seen a sailor help another start his climb. So little was their envy of his task. Ijak sat astride the boom and hugged the mast. He wriggled into the climbing belt, tugged the line to check it, then pressed his feet into the pole and leaned so the belt took him at the lower back. A quick yank sent the other end of the belt a little ways up the mast, then a push with the legs brought him level with it. Ijak turned so that the faced the oncoming set. To take the pendulum sideways could break a man or twist him free of the belt. Again, the ship turned beneath them, but this time, a little ways back to port. A correction from the oars beneath the false deck. The crew shouted at him to pause as they approached another wave, and another severe tilt of the mast. Ijak just noticed the turn in time to square himself to the mast. This time, she went over as smooth as she could, and in the trough Ijak scrambled—scoot the belt, scoot the body, each in turn, inches at a time.

When the next wave came, he pushed with his legs to brace the mast away, took the slack out of the belt with his low back, and hugged tight with his arms. It was a dance. Were he to give in to the instincts of every man who ever climbed and wrap his legs, his hips close to the pole, the loose belt would abandon him and he would be ripped free at the next movement. Even a mere twenty feet over the deck, his thin body rocked in a wide arc as they came to the next trough. Then he shimmied again, as far as he could before the angle became too great to do anything but survive.

Ijak took advantage of the relative lull between sets to make good on the mast. Tunguk's head appeared, and Ostuk meant to get his attention. It was well enough, their heading. But the old man disappeared before he could make the sign. His eyes turned in the direction of the coast—where it ought to be. His reckoning put them out by twenty miles or more, but the only birds who braved these gales were unreliable—an albatross, if he were fortunate. It could be no more than a guess. Their drift may have pulled them far closer. He could see less than half a mile. The wait for the sail was too much for him to take, and his thoughts ran ahead to how he would act when it was up. Another shunt would give them steering, but it would run them toward the black rock that would announce itself only too late. The repairs to the lock that held the oar in place would take hours in the best of times.

He fought through the pack toward Arwoset. The aggressive ones pulled at their leads, while the pups cowered in pitiful lumps of wet fur. One dog ran across his path and stopped him cold. He'd broken his lead, the wet strap trailing behind him. Their eyes met, and the dog gave a single quick bark before moving on.

"Hold course," he shouted in his man's ear. "We will steer to sea by the sail. When you can spare the men, take them below for wood. We must have our oar before we shunt." Arwoset nodded, and left it unmentioned that the choice to spare them the rocks would bring the warship to bear as they ran more sideways than ahead. He must think beyond Ijak to keep his head, but he knew he could not stray as far as the men who lurked in their wake.

There was one and only one more steering oar below. Ostuk swore for days he would not sail with less than five aboard—the two at work and three spares. But they came from Ampos. Only the unwanted—officials and proclamations—arrived reliably. Everything that was needed must be sent for at twice the number and a year before it was required if there was any hope of having it. He once made six hundred miles on a single steering oar after the other broke, but that was northbound to Nunoc in Spring.

The waves steepened as the next set approached. It was difficult to tell how much timber Ijak had made. The wind moved from his cheek to his nose, and he knew before he could find their bearing the rowers had again pushed them head-on into the swell. Ostuk left his men for the hatch, and met the head as it protruded again. Ostuk lowered himself to all fours to speak.

"It is too much. Ijak climbs the mast. Steer to port. Only five good rowers, short dip." He worried with each correction that Ijak would fail to notice and square himself in time. Tunguk started down, but Ostuk stopped him. "All who do not row, move to port. Weight on the amu," he betrayed his fear of another heavy-handed stroke and a wave abeam. Tunguk ducked away and Ijak snuck in a few more shifts of the belt before bracing himself. He moved fast, but it would be harder to hold on the higher he went. Even now, he was a soot gray outline against soot gray clouds that made summer days into winter nights. Whatever the rowers did, it wasn't enough. They took the first of the set just off center on the port bow. Ostuk motioned to Tunguk, *again*, when he reappeared, then wondered if the man knew what the gesture meant. He did, or knew what was needed, because the next dip set them near to perfect for the next wave.

But it caught them moving, and the lift took the nose of the ship. Her drift worsened as they slid down the backside. Ijak climbed again, and Ostuk prayed he noticed they were almost broadside, though at least the amu remained to windward. A dog slid across the heaving deck and slammed into

Ostuk's legs, knocking him over her. She'd chewed through her lead in terror, and he realized that many more had as well. They clawed for footing and pressed themselves into the railing that led up to the false deck, the center of the ship's rotation and the least movable part.

"Wanderer!" Amarkuk cried from his watch on the starboard beam. It drowned in the wind, but the crew knew his signal. A long wall, half the main swell, raced toward them off the starboard bow at a cross-angle. The *Juhketappat* lifted with grace and sat down on the other side. It was as kind an unwanted visitor as they could have met, but now the contrary motion bumped the mast from its pendulum swing to inscribe a jagged circuit in the clouds. Out of instinct, Ostuk looked not to the mast but the air over the surrounding sea, expecting to see a man fly into the water at any moment. No one came. A glimmer of movement, a shadow slid above. Ijak chanced another climb. Ostuk raised five fingers to Tunguk and motioned to the starboard side. The third wave smoothed their pitch, and by the fourth, the oars edged her back toward the trail. He watched as one more container floated off the false deck, probably unmoored by the earlier broadside hit. When the old man came back up, he gave the signal to hold. It was a little off, but he couldn't trust the rowers to be so precise.

The fifth pawed at them as they came over, and again the bow drifted to starboard. The weight was off. Too much lost from the forward deck, or too many terrified passengers crowding the stern below, that the rear could not keep pace. No matter now. Tunguk didn't need the order before he descended. Number six coming, thought Ostuk. The old mariners always called the seventh wave in the set Tembet's Ferry. It was the monster that carried souls over the shallows to Juhk, the namesake of his ship. A regrettable decision, he laughed to himself.

"All hands to the amu!" It was a feeble gesture with the thin crew on deck, but they put what weight they had against the false deck with the dogs—at least the animals knew where to be without needing the command. Six, who had no name, lifted them and sent the mast whipping far beyond the starboard beam. Ostuk felt his heart drain for Ijak. "Prepare to climb," he yelled in Rewet's ear as they rode up the face. They braced for the top. The *Juhketappat* crashed over and dove furiously in the other direction as the amu skipped across the top of the wave. Ostuk looked back and saw only sea over the gunwale. He felt the amu go airborne. Water rushed off the false deck onto the main to drench hide and hair alike. The tilt of a finger could have sent it over their heads in a somersault, it seemed. A brief second of weightlessness. His body felt like it dropped out of the sky. Then the amu slapped down before them and took weight. Plumes shot up between the boards of the false deck. He knew that the sea was higher than the oar ports, and water would be racing in below, just as surf surged over the gunwale. Tunguk did not reappear right away. It was an ill sign. She leveled out in time for him to see it loom ahead, slower than the others. Tembet's Ferry.

The dogs snapped at him in fear as he raced toward the hatch. Ostuk could see nothing in the black pit. He took the first two steps facing forward, then turned his body to face the ladder. The storm made it night at all hours above, but it was nothing like the darkness below. Voices cried at one another in Mattakatan, and water sloshed. On either side, gray light here and there where oar ports were forced open. As soon as his feet hit the bottom, he stood ankle-deep in water. Dark shapes flew by him—buckets, passed furiously to bail the overflowing bilge. The cries began to mark themselves: someone calling for a bucket here, someone crying in agony there.

"Tunguk!" No answer. "Tunguk!" He called again.

"Eskimo Joe!" Another voice shouted. It sounded like the fugitive. Wet footsteps stomped his way. "Cap'n, is that you?"

"We are broadside to the wave. Coxswain to the ladder for orders."

"I got you, bro."

"*Coxswain*," Ostuk demanded.

"Gionn knocked him out."

"He yelled in me fuckin' ear!" Another voice protested.

"Fine. Five oars a side. Everyone else to port. Port oars, turning stroke on my command. Starboard, be prepared to halt if we go wide. Halot, to the ladder."

As he climbed back up, he heard the last voice say, "That's you, cunt!" It was answered with an "Ow!"

Parks' head poked up behind him when Ostuk made the deck. "Now!" The fugitive stepped down and repeated the command. The wave bore down on them as she nudged about. "Again!" He motioned. Once more, Parks went below, and the bow backed toward the wave. It seemed to gain speed as it neared, as though it sensed the moment of peril. "Again!" A final short stroke. She came to half a square from the mountain of water, then past it with a stutter.

"Halt!" It was close enough. There was no time to correct. Ostuk threw himself on the deck as it pitched back and rode up the wall near enough the trail that she stayed on the amu. So heavy was the top that it curled over in white foam to greet them. Had they gone broadside again, it would have smashed them back and over. She plowed through the short break in a burst of spray. Another torrent streamed over the forward quarter of the false deck and snaked across the main, swallowed the men at the steering oar, then fought with itself to force its way back to sea. The dogs twisted in a mass to escape the worst of it. Foam bubbled around precious cargo. Then the rain began. The burst showered them all the way to the aft hatch just as the ship pitched over the top and ran down the shallow side. Another plume of water reared up when they made the bottom, but it hardly sprayed the deck. When it cleared, he saw three drenched men, clinging yet to the forward steering lock. Across the false deck, the hand of Hawe preserved their supplies. Not a one broken, and no harm but to what improbable creature may have still been dry. The *Juhketappat* righted herself, and he looked into the clouds.

There was no way Ijak was still on the mast, Ostuk told himself. But there it was—the rope curved slack from the coil at the bow, rose over the deck and disappeared into the darkness. The rock of the ship slowed now in the break between sets. Ostuk motioned to the crew, and they ran to meet at the sail. The shadows did not tell how far Ijak had made it, or if he still climbed. They waited at the rope and measured the time until the next set arrived. The mast was not still, and never would be. Ostuk took their end of the rope in both hands and gave it three sharp whips. A signal, if Ijak still had wits. He was probably too tossed about to see the oncoming waves and pick his moment, but if it was to be done, this was it. No response came down the rope. The crew fixed their eyes on it for any shift at all—slack taken, a swing, a drop. It swayed in the wind. They could not tell if it was man or storm that moved it.

Ostuk looked at the faces around him. He realized they had turned from the rope to their captain. He didn't have an order, but he made orders because he knew the men needed to move. Move anywhere.

"Rewet, Arwoset. Watch the rope. Ijak must signal that it is done. If he falls, Rewet climbs. Then Anset. Amarkuk, Hagalut—prepare to hoist. When it's secure, Arwoset will take a man below for wood." He left the name to the older sailor, not knowing who would be atop the mast by then. "I will call the oars. Keep your eyes up! Ijak must not fall on the crew." They split to their stations with resigned silence.

"Port, dip oars!" Parks' head went down, and the ship corrected dead-on the trail up next set. "Hold!" Ostuk's attention returned to the rope, dangling limp in the wind from some unknowable point above. He thought to shake it again—encouragement. But he thought better. The battle of the last set would have to be fought again and again, like an endless army without fear of death pouring over the plain, breaking bones and spirits with each assault until there was no one left to resist. The chaos below, Tunguk, the coxswain, all of that from a single set. Ostuk needed wind to steer. He could run flawlessly in these conditions and still lose her, but wind was breath for the *Juhketappat*. She needed to breathe.

"Captain!" Arwoset made himself heard over the gale. A twitch caught Ostuk's eye. Had he seen it, or dreamt it? The men surrounded the rope. It jumped again, as though a fish tested the line. A third time. Weaker, but unmistakable. He took it in his hands and pulled, slowly adding pressure. It felt taut, but was it tied or still attached to Ijak? A signal, or a renewed climb? A wave strummed down and shook his grip.

"It is in the block!" Ostuk proclaimed.

"Where is the weight? Why does he not pull?" Arwoset said.

"He has but one hand, and he is weak. Give him line!"

Hagalut did not wait to be named. He freed a length from the coil and backed until it was slack over many feet of the deck, then took it in both hands and whipped as hard as he could to send the slack up the mast. There was a pause, then a short jerk. Hagalut gave another whip, a few more inches for Ijak to work through the block. The rope must be heavy as stone at that height, thought Ostuk. They needed only enough to get the weight running. Another wave seemed to add a foot or so, and Hagalut repositioned. He snapped it again and again, until at last it continued to move when he ceased. The line jumped out of the coil and he had to snatch it before it ran free. Arwoset came to his aid, and they fed it as fast as they dared. The rest of the men gathered below the mast and searched the clouds. They held their blood from pumping. At last, a flicker. Something bobbed in the wind. The weight trailed out over the starboard beam. It should have been plenty to ease down onto the deck, but it wasn't made to use in such a storm.

The next set approached to shield the gale, and the weight swung hard over the deck. Hagalut and Arwoset let out line as fast as they dared. It swung back over their heads and out to sea, then repeated the maneuver. The second time, Anset snatched the line with a hook and they leapt upon it like birds on a carcass. It was Arwoset who got his portion. He made it fast to the head of the sail while Hagalut set the free end.

"Up!" Shouted Ostuk.

"Running up!" A few of the men called in turn, hoping Ijak would hear and avoid the tangle of the rope. No matter. It would only be raised enough steer, with all the reefs taken in. The stained sheet showed its face to whoops from the crew. None was more joyous than Rewet, next in line to climb. They set the boom so the *Juhketappat* took the waves as she was meant. There would be no rest, though. All hands were needed to keep her on course until the oar lock was repaired. The captain worked over to the hatch so Parks could hear.

"Oars stand by. We may need you yet."

"Aye-aye, Cap'n." Parks bellowed the order down below. Ostuk walked under the mast and craned to see. Ijak was still too far, but tears welled in his eyes. He raised his hands to the tightened halyard where it led into the shadows of the tall tree. One of the loose dogs joined him and looked up to try to see what everyone was searching for, before he scurried off. At once, the seething mass of fur settled—still yelping, tugging at leashes, but no longer in complete panic. They knew the ship as well as its captain did. Or they knew its captain.

Answet and Rewet embraced before him even as they rode up the first slope. She held her course well enough that he did not risk a correction, and they took the next wave with the same ease. There were small corrections after that, but now it was in the hands of sailors, steering from the deck. Ostuk hoped that enough dogs survived for him to reward the boy above with an extra share. They took the remaining waves like a sea bird, though his stomach hurt now for Ijak, and every move of the mast brought a jolt of terror—but they were nothing like before. Then Tembet's Ferry. It was no bigger than any of the others. The crew gripped one another's shoulders to keep their feet as they went over.

"Arwoset will never let us offer to Pillanuk again," Anset joked as they dipped over the top.

"It is well," Rewet said. "Hawe still holds his throne." Ostuk nodded and grinned ear to ear. When they leveled out, he looked up for movement that he could not find. His neck grew sore, and his sight came to rest on the sail. Something was out of place. It took him some time to realize that the thick leather climbing belt rested across the joint of the boom. The men saw it as he did. Not a stitch was broken. It wrapped the mast as strong as it ever had. The man who went up in it was gone.

"Over here, cunt!" Parks followed the voice in the black hold, where shadows passed before a few shafts of useless haze spilling through the bailing ports with the slap of the sea. The *Juhketappat* had found the trail over the waves, and the oars were secured, though five rowers stood ready on each side in case they needed to steer in a hurry. She was far from smooth, but what had felt like sickening tumult before was now a reprieve from the chaos of floundering. Water sloshed everywhere, as every free and unbattered hand bailed the overflow from the bilge, which extended nearly to the feet of the benches at its worst.

He slogged through with his hands waving before him until his fingers ran through Gionn's hair and across his face, then down to Eskimo Joe, cradled in the big arms.

"He was floatin' in the pisser," Gionn referred to the open trough of water that ran the length of the ship. "Face up, if he cares to thank the gods."

Parks lifted him. "Joe. You with us, buddy?" There was a moan, and he felt the man shift in his arms, touch a hand to his forehead. "D'you hurt your noggin'?"

"Brother."

"I'm here, buddy."

"It is dark and cold, and I am not rid of you."

"Good to be alive." Parks' memory flashed. "Kjartke!" Someone sloshed over. He passed the thin bones into her arms. "Take care of my boy, Joe. If you know any native healing arts, or witch spells that can cure a bonked head, we would be very grateful."

The ladder to the deck announced itself under heavy steps of passengers and rowers in need of a reprieve. Parks joined the file. There were already a dozen people on deck, squinting against the salt spray and glad to have their sight again. The crew looked exhausted, but there was a kind of wet life to their movements. Somber, but purposeful. Three of them attacked the splintered wood of the thing that held the steering oar in place. Another set fussed over the lines of the sail like a father trying to hold his son by the seat of the bike as he ran after. Parks leaned toward the outrigger and let the pitching deck decide when he stepped and when he held. He had the sea legs of a baby giraffe, but they were beginning to work on their own. Dogs ran loose everywhere. The crew didn't seem to mind, but the passengers, despite all being Mattaka, did their best to give them a decent berth.

His heart skipped as he looked over the clusters still leashed, tugging and wondering why the others got to go free. There was no sign of Foster. His head swiveled, hoping to catch a glimpse of human limbs strewn across the deck in some pathetic pose. Nothing. He waded into the pack.

"Foster!" The dogs whined at his presence, as if he could do something to relieve their misery. "Have any of you seen a man? Beard, brownish hair, tattoos—probably puking his guts up? No? Strong southern accent?"

One of the animals rolled over, and his blurry vision managed to assemble the features. Parks lunged to the ground beside his friend. "Fuck, dude, I was afraid we lost you." Foster lifted his head from where he lay, three dogs—including the pregnant one—pressed as close to him as possible for their own reassurance.

"Wait. Don't tell me you slept through all that."

"*Slept?*" He coughed a vicious wet burst and spat out phlegm. "Motherfucker, I was lookin' around for somethin' to kill myself with so I wouldn't have to drown in that cold ass water." He spat again. "You good?"

Parks smiled. "I'm a shellback, bro. A goddamn Son of Neptune. If anything, I'm less seasick now than I was before."

Foster nodded. "Same. Almost like I needed to see how bad it could get."

"Good, cause we're not out of the storm yet." They looked over the flurry of activity on the deck. "And with any luck, we won't be."

"Nine guys, right?"

"What's that?"

"In the crew. Nine guys, plus the captain?"

"Far as I know."

"I count eight." Parks took it in. Neither said it, but they let the silence hang between for a while. They were sailors, too. Sort of, he thought. "Guess if the storm doesn't hold, our mutiny just got a little bit easier," Parks shrugged.

Foster shook his head. "You didn't see what I saw up here. Our mutiny just got damn near impossible."

He recovered his courage before his strength. Foster watched the three boys fight with the dogs for what felt like a couple of hours, then found his feet for the first time in days. It was shame that lifted him. The oldest of the brothers couldn't be more than thirteen, with the others a few years behind in turn. Thin Mattaka boys who just outweighed their charges. No one offered a hand. Over a hundred wet, frightened, angry, starved, and seasick critters belonged to them, alone. Every time the ship pitched one into another, a fight broke out. At least the logistics of making war on a shifting surface in buffeting winds put an end to most of them after a quick sound-off. They had a good handle on the animals, he could give them that. No man moved when he was in their way, no crew, especially. Foster heard it called the "dog ship." The sole purpose of the journey was entrusted—if that was the right word—to a few children. It was his understanding they'd never been to sea before. When the youngest, dragged along by a leash in each hand, leaned over his shoulder to vomit on the deck and returned to his work without pause, he had enough.

Blood rushed to his head and made his eyes dance. Silver sparks fluttered like confetti before him as he clung to the false deck, and one by one, they faded, leaving spots on a film negative. Kjartke worked with one of the sailors to re-secure the supplies that the seas shook loose. Tunguk still hadn't appeared on deck. He reached down and scratched the head of his new friend, the pregnant one who would not leave his side, the only one who looked as sick as he felt.

The debate about whether or not he should let go and try to take a step ended as the deck pitched and gave him the first few at no charge. He managed to stop himself without falling. The water whipped his face and ran down his neck, though the permanent sting of salt in his lashes had long since faded into background noise.

"Hey!" A dog stopped its scamper. "Hey! Come here." It turned and trotted off. Another sniffed nearby. Foster approached slowly, which was as fast as his body would allow. His foot settled on the chewed-off leash. He was able to pick it up before the animal noticed. At first he tugged and whipped his neck, but Foster held it firm without fighting back. He tried once more, and saw that the man was not going to let go. Rather than pull, Foster waited. The dog leaned into the slack, and coughed. After a few more half-hearted attempts, he lay down.

"Come on, brother. Let's get with the pack." Foster led him to the others and tied a firm bend in one of the severed lead. The boys noticed him, and though they did not acknowledge him, their efforts became a bit more spirited with the extra help. Still, it took hours to gather every straggler. The seas were no more cooperative than before. The crew did a fine job of keeping them angled into the waves. He was nauseous the whole time, but it wasn't the paralyzing grip of before. Just a lightness, a queasy tingle, constant burping. Every burp took him back from the edge, until he just started forcing them out almost as often as he breathed. No one in the crew would speak to him, but he felt them looking on when his eyes were on a dog, or a knot. He must've looked like a miserable ghost, haunting out of habit and wondering why he couldn't just die already.

When all was done, he started not for the hold but back for his pile of dogs. Kjartke appeared before him. He took the seal meat—wet and slimy—from her outstretched hand. It was at least easier to chew that way. Foster realized that he'd stopped walking in order to feed bite after tiny bite into his mouth. He had not felt hungry, but now his appetite was ravenous. He finished the entire portion, and could have eaten another, but she was gone from the deck, along with the other passengers.

There was the captain, stoic before the mast. The crew had worked in near silence since they righted the ship, but he felt it was the silence of a single body, each limb at its work, nothing left to say. The body was wounded.

He crossed what felt like miles of deck, the storm now little more than radio static hissing across his station. Ostuk met his eyes.

"Thank you, brother." The man didn't reply, or know what to make of it. "I'm sorry about your man. But we're all here cause of yall. We just counted. Every last dog. All of 'em made it. Every man, woman, and child. I know you'd probably trade the whole lot of us for any one of your crew. But here we are. I don't know shit about sails, or wood boats, or anything, but

I'm smart enough and I learn quick. If you need a guy, I'm willin' to earn the rest of my passage. I've seen how you work, and I'd be proud to serve."

Ostuk gave a polite smile. "It is kind of you. The crew will be better shorthanded if they do not have to teach one what to do."

"Understood."

Ostuk watched him retreat to the dogs. Eight men was just enough to swing the boom in this weather. He hoped he would not need to use the madman who slept among the beasts. Mate of the fugitives. Barzos had stood for him, and though he had met the man for the first time only weeks prior, it was good to have one like him in your debt. Or it had seemed at the time. Now Ostuk began to see the cost.

The black hold was of great comfort to Tunguk. Many times he had been on the sea without a deck to hide beneath. Many days and nights he leaned against the slap of the weather as she crossed their path on her way to Ajatse, or Ampos. Had there been a deck then, and a hold, he would not have taken it. Below was a place for women, and the sick. It smelled of vomit, and passengers relieving themselves in buckets or straight into the bilge when seas were rough. It was shameful to a youth, who searched the horizon for land or ship, eager to leap. Tunguk was no youth. Still weak from when he was struck down by those bewildering gods who protected the foreigners. He had not been on deck to tend the dogs in two turns of the sun. The dim light brought pain his eyes, and his head throbbed between sharp and dull since he fell from the ladder. The woman had brought him food, and Brother had given him a foul herb that made him vomit ever since, though he only held it in his mouth a short time. He slept, and when he woke he would ask about Foster, who had not been below, and of the sea.

Now Brother told him that he had made prayers, but his prayers had failed. The storm still blew, but it grew tired, and Ostuk said it would be gone soon. Tunguk rose with great effort. In days past, he was often hurt, and soon he would be himself again. But in age, he would never find himself fully. Each time, less and less of the man returned, and he knew it would be no different now. More and more the young man left him in his dreams, for longer and longer, and his visits came less and less. He was eager to see other lands, and this one held him like a dog's lead. There were greater pains he had risen from in the past, and the memory of those took him as far as the ladder.

After three rungs he gave pause as his head stabbed him. It played like a drum, and he waited out the beating until he could climb again. Topside, the cold air hit his face, and though the gray sky made him squint in pain, a deep sigh sent the spirit rushing through his limbs. He was able to pull himself the rest of the way. Foster was about, tending the dogs as he had while Tunguk rested. He had learned to know a sailor at first sight, by the way he sat on the bench, or where he looked first when the wind changed. He could tell a hunter from a warrior by how the hand closed around the spear. Many people, he knew in ways that they did not know themselves. Not in his youth, but now that his reactions slowed—when there was no time left for mistakes, or wandering.

He did not know this man, Foster. No sailor and no warrior, that was clear, but he had never seen a man so unaccustomed to rope and blade take the dogs like he was one of them. No hunter, or fisherman, either. This man must have lived on wealth won by others, but he moved like a beggar of no status. Yet he had manners, and customs, and a code—not one that Tunguk understood, but it was the same at all times. He had letters, but knew nothing of lands and kings whose stories every peasant within a hundred miles of the sea could tell. Perhaps it was as he said: that he fell into this world from the dream world, where it is like the world in many ways, and beyond reckoning in others.

He had angered many gods—even before he was born, he suspected—but thought that they had begun to forget him in his last days. Now he was bound to these men, to protect those he could not kill. Tunguk was not sure if this was a final curse, the course meant to bring him home. Or if it was a blessing, disguised as they always are as painful curses. He knew only that he was tired.

"It is good you are alive," Ostuk smiled.

"Good for some," they watched Foster. "You and I are not among them." Ostuk gave a breathy laugh. Tunguk took in the swell, barely twice the gunwales now. The clouds hung higher and a shade lighter than before. "We have prayed for storm," he admitted. "You have prayed better."

"It's better that we're afloat." Ostuk looked to the steering oar lock, at last refitted after a great battle with Arwoset and his nephew—fine carpenters.

"We will be met before Galliput." It was more of a statement than a question.

Ostuk nodded. "We're weeks out, and they need only stop." Tunguk raised a brow. "We came out of the storm behind them." He nodded ahead. Tunguk searched the horizon. "I haven't seen it. The woman reports it at perhaps two miles, and toward the coast."

"Then they have not see us. They still sail." Ostuk did not respond. He knew where it led. "If we run to sea…"

"It will delay them, but it will not help. They will circle, and we are too slow to slip them."

"There are ways."

"Ways I cannot try. I would like nothing better than to avoid being boarded. By my auspices, I could be fined, have my ship confiscated, imprisoned, or killed outright for treason, and your lot would do me no better. I'd prefer they sank, but I can't offend them by running. We'll be caught. As I understand it, they only want the two fugitives. You'd be wise to stay on with the rest of your friends for Drummoc."

Tunguk nodded. "It would be wise."

"Hateful cunt of a storm, weren't she, lads?" Gionn's voice boomed from the corner of the hold. "Thank the gods we'd a fine captain to see us through. Move over, you smelly bastards, I've come to make small talk." He swatted a man and took a seat on the bench where three Mattaka rowers sat as featureless shadows in the near-dark. "I noticed you bow cunts weren't trusted as I was to help steer in the storm. Fair shame. Those starboard wankers were stabbin' oars the way a boy pokes around for anythin' wet. No sense of touch. Could've used you." They let out a soft laugh, knowing as well as anyone that they were in the bow because they were fresh, and it was a fresh man's pride to find fault in the big, experienced men in the middle. Here was one of them—a halot, no less—speaking to them for the first time.

"Aye, I've been at the blunt end of a few storms and that was almost as fine a captain job as I've seen. There was one finer. Cunt named Fermis. But not so many of us lived to tell of that one, so it's a great ethical dilemma for me, whether to tell it at all, seein' as he died in the process and failed the bulk of his men despite heroics that would make Dannan blush. Though I do owe me life to the man. Me inclination til now has been to let the bastard wallow in obscurity. Anyway, Ostuk. There's a name for you to remember." He leaned in and lowered his voice to a less-public tone. "Which one of you is Agwik?"

"I am Agwik," one of the shadows replied.

"Luck-loved cunt. Can I trust you men with a foul rumor that should not be repeated under any circumstances? If you're noddin', I can't see your flat, ugly faces in the dark."

"You can trust us," another voice relied.

"The woman. The dog woman." He let the words hang a while. "I understand she has said things about one called Agwik."

"What things?"

"None that I would repeat. The kind of things a woman says about a man when she's stuck on a ship with idle hands and time to think."

"Will you bring her a word for me?" Agwik said.

"I'm not your fuckin' handmaiden, cunt. I'll bring you the hoof of me boot. Besides, you don't want to get on the good captain's bad side."

"What do you mean?"

"That's the foul rumor I was talkin' about. Word around the ship has it that old Ostuk is an unmarried man. Lonesome on long sea voyages. Not too many nice young girls stow aboard his dog ship. Of course, she's no eyes for him, but she'd be a fool not to consider a husband with a good income and a bit of the proper blood for her sons if she got the offer."

Parks waddled toward the rear of the ship, where he'd been assured a receptive audience. On the way he passed by Gionn, already moving bench by bench through the rowing deck, speaking in hushed tones: "They say the boy he lost was secretly his bastard son by the wife of one of the crew. Do you happen to know which one?"

He snickered to himself, and found a man sitting alone in the rear. "Hey Tunguk," he whispered. "You'll never guess which one of the crew I just saw fucking a dog topside." He paused. "Tunguk?" He felt the man's face. "Shit, sorry bro. I thought you were someone else."

"What did you see?" The man asked.

"Nothing. Sorry dude. Forget I was here."

By the time he passed back by Gionn, he'd moved again. "—said we only survived because he made offerin' to *Uinab* for our safety." Parks had no idea what that meant, but the listener muttered a string of Reverse-Eskimo under his breath at the reference.

They reconvened at their bench, where Tunguk and Kjartke waited. "I think I overdid it with that last one," Gionn sat. "Oh, and Kjartke. I'll need you to smile once at the one called Agwik. No questions, just the once."

"If the woman must smile for your plan," Tunguk said, "it would be easier to stand for mutiny." It took Parks a moment to pick up on Tunguk's sense of humor again, and he wondered if half the things the man said weren't just old man jokes that he'd taken seriously.

"Aye, it's a long shot to ask charm of the woman, I agree, but this cunt's too popular for mutiny. Even I can't bring meself to stand against him, and I'm the only beneficiary of it, along with the Blubber Seal here."

"How will we know if we've convinced him?"

"We don't have to convince him, just got to get enough eyes starin' and whispers circlin' that he suspects the chance of it if he stops. The Navy scares him because the crew don't. But the crew's the bigger danger.

"Gather, me sons, and the oracle of Gionn shall tell you what you'll see, better than any poye or priest of Hadalis, for I have seen it not in signs or omens, or the flight of birds, or scattered bones, or entrails. I have seen it in loads of salted cunts who cut the captain's throat or didn't. Small ship or great, it's no matter. The numbers are different, the way it moves, but it's the same foul daimon who calls for blood. As I speak, a man climbs the ladder for fresh air. Some of that air will reach the crew with news of how two handsome cunts were up and down the benches, whisperin' about nothin' the men will discuss.

"Within the hour, you'll see a sailor below. One of the older bastards. He'll be makin' talk with the rowers he thinks loyal, and askin' of who they measure on what side. On a smaller ship, they might move the benches. Sit 'em in a mix. But that tips the captain's fear, and don't work when the belly's this big and no one's rowin' much anyway. No, they'll go after the knots. Now before Parks nods along and pretends he knows what I'm on about, I shall explain. In a mutiny, you got your ones who's set. They want the captain, or not, and they'll be stabbed to bits before they change their minds. Ones like us. Normally, I prefer to remain pliable in me opinions, but it appears I've signed on with the only cunts this side of the Orin more cursed than meself.

"Opposite us, there's the seabirds, blowin' this side or that in the wind. Between the two are the knots. They tie the birds to the boards and make your party go one way or the other. You loosen a knot, you loose the birds he's bound as well, and soon enough you get the stubborn cunts all alone. That's when it's safe to have a stab. You'll see the crew, and some of the rowers who's knots for 'em workin' the benches. Problem is, everyone they talk to denies anythin' about a mutiny. They was just makin' talk. Gossip and bucket brags. That worries 'em, cause they seen the men lookin' at the captain sideways and talkin' hushed, but they'll do nothin' but praise the man when confronted.

"If you're a smart little pilot boy, that tells you the captain is well-fucked. Nothin' you do can shake loose a single knot, and your fears are thick enough to make shadows across the deck. You see, a mutiny's about nothin' more than confidence. Can't know how many men stand with who until it's too late. You might have the numbers, but if you don't have the confidence, you don't stand up. You squeeze your legs tight around your bollocks and pray the other man stays shrunk as well.

"Now he knows his sailors are solid, and we can't reach Drummoc without the sailors, and we can ill-afford to lose oars. There'll be no risk of a fight. These aren't good mutiny waters. He'll treat with us in private. We'll demand only safe passage, and promise his own safety in return, as well as his ship and cargo. That leaves only the one problem."

"Sweet," Parks nodded and smiled.

"Thick cunt," Gionn continued. "The fuckin' Navy ship will attack us. Let's imagine this captain has spent his career ferryin' dogs up and down the coast, and has never maneuvered in battle or led men to defend a boardin' party. If somethin' like that were the case, if all the men were shit rowers and worse fighters, there might still be a bit of trouble."

It was three days before the trouble came. For three days, she threw food at dogs leaping against leads, and noted which rowers liked to "take air" on the deck, despite the winds that still carried on in lesser fury. A chance for them to talk to the crew, and to advertise strength to the ones they cornered below in hushed tones. There were four or five of them, and they worked hard for Ostuk, but it had begun to stir resentment in the rest of the rowers and the passengers. She did not know what they said, but their voices sharpened as the men first brushed them off, then took offense. Ostuk was a popular captain now. They must have sworn many oaths that no mutiny brewed among the benches. The day before, a fight had erupted. Two men, tired of whispers, had offered fists. One of them was Agwik, the one Gionn asked her to smile at on a single occasion. Kjartke had still not done it. She lied to the men after they pestered her, and the fight brought truth to her words, so that she would never have to. It was true now that once, when he appeared above deck to hang himself over the side when the seas were calmer, she raised her mouth as he walked back to the hold, right in front of Ostuk.

The captain approached her as she tied up the stores of meat. Too much had been lost, she thought. The dogs or the people would be hungry when they arrived.

"It is bad news for your mates," he didn't waste time on greetings the way a Mattaka man would. "The ship was seen this morning, heading to sea. First time in days." She finished her knot and met his gaze, but offered him nothing. "That means they know they passed us, and they are circling against the sun. The next time they approach the from the land, they will see us." Kjartke shrugged. "Then we will be rid of them," she said.

Ostuk nodded. "I don't think they will want you or Tunguk. Unless they ask for your mate by name," he looked over to where Foster and the boys followed behind Kjarkte's path, untangling leashes and holding the dish of fresh water for the dogs, "I will perhaps forget that he is on board." She saw it for what it was. An offer: let them go, you can stay. A man without fear makes no offer, she recalled the saying. Let him have his fear, then.

"The men say you are a fine captain. Do not ask a woman to choose for you." Kjartke headed for the hold.

It had not gone as he hoped. Ostuk took a gamble, telling them of the Navy ship well before they would have seen it. Better for it to swoop down on them before they had a chance to organize against him. He thought if he cut it out at the heart—offered safety and divided the group—they would turn on one another. There was no reason two Mattaka should help them at all. Yet somehow, she managed to give nothing away and insult him at the same time. Ostuk didn't understand who these foreigners were, but they had captured those around them, and made them distrust a dog captain.

Arwoset joined him, gray and heavy with lack of sleep. "The men still say there is no mutiny."

"You believe it?"

"There is a kaim that moves through them, and I do not yet know what it wants."

"What are our numbers now?"

"Hard to say. No better than before."

Ostuk puffed air out from his cheeks. "I will not ask my crew to spill their blood for me."

"Good!" Arwoset laughed. "We will not fight for you. But they know if they harm the crew, we all drown. We will stand before you, and they will think we fight." He chuckled and clapped Ostuk on the shoulder as he peeled back to his duties, slower by the day under constant watchfulness. The captain made a mental note to relieve Arwoset later so he could get an hour or two of rest. He wouldn't ask for it.

It was a ship of fill-ins. Being only a man down meant that another needed to rotate over. If few hands were needed and some could rest, it was well, but in a storm, all hands were needed often. That meant a man would rotate over to help. And another to fill his place if that was needed. The crew should have been more than nine to begin with, but with eight, there would always be an empty station. When something went wrong—as when one of the reefs came loose and Hagalut and Amarkuk had to wrestle it, there began a madness in which each man had to decide whether his station or the one abandoned by the man before him was more important, and rotate over if it was the latter. Within moments, Rewet and Anset were screaming at one another about who should move where, and Hagalut had to hurry to Anset's station at the boom, Ostuk pulled Jutvik to the steering oar so he could break up the argument, and when it was done, Foster was doing his best to help Amarkuk get the reef under control. When he'd sorted the crew, Ostuk walked halfway across the deck to the wrong steering oar before he realized his mistake.

The stowaway filled in for Tunguk, too. The old man tried to return to his duties, but he was taken by dizziness each time, and had to be helped below after spilling a dish of fresh water—the most valuable cargo they carried at any time. Fresh boys, a lashed man, and a woman—none of whom had ever tended dogs at sea before—kept his valued cargo alive. Most of the experienced rowers who would have signed on had gone into Jartse with the dog ship earlier in the season, and these new ones were full of whispers.

There may be a fill-in captain soon, too, he thought. The woman knew—he might as well try the stowaway. Ostuk glanced around to be sure those of his men who were not stealing dreams had the ship in hand, then he found Foster watering the pregnant bitch. He always cared for her first and last, and slept against her for warmth, or her against him—Ostuk was unsure. She looked as dire as ever. Not once had he made Galliput without losing a dog, and here, in some of the worst sailing he'd had, with the sails and the mast and the very boards of the ship plotting his overthrow, he had every animal. The men were happy for any opportunity to place a bet, and each had his dog he thought would be first. As the senior crew, Arwoset chose before the others, and chose her. Filikut, only half joking, bet on Foster when he was a wet, huddled lump of torn flesh.

"The dogs like you." Foster looked up from where he knelt.

"I can't tell if that's some kinda insult comin' from your people, or if you're givin' me a compliment because you're worried I'm gonna mutiny your ass."

Ostuk laughed. "I meant it as both, but I hoped you wouldn't catch either."

"I know about the ship. I seen it when they seen it. I'll tell you, brother, I wouldn't wanna be in them captain boots right now."

"I can offer you the same as the woman. Same as Tunguk. Only two will leave my ship. You are not on the manifest."

"What if we just give 'em the redhead, and a map that marks where they can take him?"

Ostuk shook his head. "You know as well as I they will take both, and I will be lucky to keep my ship and my life."

"I wish I could sit here and lie to you that I'd turn over Parks."

"Then you will join your friends in what it is they plan."

"Sir, I don't even know if they got a plan, and if they do, I guarantee you it's fuckin' stupid. But yeah. If they fight, I fight for them. Not because I got somethin' against you. I just got more for them."

"You openly declare you favor mutiny?"

"I never said anybody favors it. I think we all favor cruisin' to wherever we're goin' without incident. I just think you're smart enough, and I respect you enough, that there's no point pretendin' I'm gonna turn on my crew like that. You got yours, and I got mine." Ostuk studied him. He was within his rights to have the man killed. Foster scratched behind the ears of the dog and stood to meet the captain.

"But if you decide to fight them boys out there," he motioned to the shapeless waves and the ship they knew drew circles through their path, "I'll fight for you, too."

Foster's heart leapt when he saw it was Parks' turn for prayers. The pregnant dog raised her head from his lap, sensing the change, and he felt bad as he set her gently on the wet deck. When he spoke to Ostuk, he was half-sure he would be arrested or worse, but for two days they ran in the waning storm without change, until that morning. The Navy ship appeared heading seaward a few miles back, and this time she didn't fail to notice the big outrigger. Her prow turned on them, and Ostuk's hand was forced. Foster had no idea what his friends were planning. Even prior to that, every effort of Parks' to visit him earned them a crew member in shadow, so their talks were limited to dogs, health, the weather. The big man was too upbeat for there to be nothing, but he hadn't a hint of what it was, or of his role in it.

Once the ship appeared, Ostuk stationed an armed crew member at the top of the only open hatch, and confined the rowers and passengers below deck. That of itself nearly caused a mutiny, until he agreed to allow one person at a time to come topside for air and prayers. All morning he'd suffered the parade of Mattaka, who did anything from stand at the rail for a few minutes, to sing and thump and wail for the better part of an hour. Foster wasn't even sure his people would get a turn, but now that stupid grin peeked over the ladder, Filikut stepped aside, and Parks lumbered to mid-deck, as close as he dared approach his friend without drawing attention. Foster was surprised at first that he had a privileged position up top, if wind and spray were any kind of reward, but he figured they were happy to keep him separate from his companions.

Parks hoisted his hands skyward and began to intone dramatically, his words lost to the wind. A stir drew Foster's attention back to the hold, where Filikut shook his spear at Tunguk's head, and the men argued in Mattakatan. Two others rushed over to aid in the quarrel—they didn't want two men of the mutinous sort on deck at once, he was pretty sure—and the rest watched closely to see if this was the start of the rush they had feared.

"*Psst!*" Parks crawled through the dogs, feet away. "Sup, homey!"

"We got ten seconds," Foster watched as three crew members hurried their direction. "What's the plan? Can't fight. My back catches fire if I even lift my arms overhead."

"Uh—" Parks hesitated. The crew were upon them with shouts. "Fuck."

"Below deck!" Arwoset yanked Parks to his feet, Rewet and Anset close behind. "No talking. You pray, or below deck."

"I'm praying, bro!"

"You talk."

"Nuh-uh. This is how we do religion in America, and frankly, I find your ignorance and intolerance of our sacred spiritual practices insulting."

"Come," Arwoset pulled.

"Hold up, dude. I don't think it's fair that you and all of your Reverse-Eskimo buddies, which is one hundred percent of this boat besides me and my bud, get to rattle off dozens of the same prayer to the same gods. How do you expect ours to have a chance? You guys are outpraying the shit out of us. The least you can do is let us raise our voices on high in unison, that our prayers might be heard over the loud tongues of your people. What's the point of pretending to let people pray if you're going to tie our hands behind our backs so they're ineffective? Your boys get to boil whale fat. We're just trying to talk. To God," he added.

Ostuk arrived by then. He spoke to Arwoset in Mattakatan, and Arwoset released Parks. "Pray together," Ostuk said. "Arwoset will join you."

Foster rose, and they strode tentatively to the false deck, which he scaled after Parks. Arwoset settled like a hawk, mere feet behind.

Parks looked around, and Foster recognized instantly the subtle movements the man took on when he was neck deep in bullshit and confidently plowing forward. He lowered himself to his knees, and Foster mirrored him.

"If you're going to stay, you need to kneel," Parks said. Arwoset frowned, but joined them. "We will now speak in our sacred language." Parks raised his hands and eyes skyward. "Ionn-Gay ays-say, en-whay e-hay omes-cay …up-way…"

"You speak in the farri's tongue, or mine," Arwoset interrupted.

"Our God doesn't understand your foul tongues." Arwoset glared. "But we will use it anyway. Oh, Father, uh…when the red sun, dawns upon the deck…bring us luck. Bless my friend Foster, for when he see-eth the red sun, he shall sing the immortal song, 'Who? Who let the dogs out? Who. Who, Who, Who.' And it shall be done." He turned to Arwoset. "This is kind of a call and response thing, so he's going to say his part now."

"My turn? Um. Oh, Lord…I pray that you make clear your meaning to us, for we know not the red sun. But let the goddess Beyonce bring thy message, or Geronimo who chases the naked men, that we may be delivered from this voyage safely home, because like I said, I am weak from the whip, and the signs and omens you send are unclear, and need to be rephrased. But if your intentions are…like a special ed crayon drawing, save us also from yourself, for it is better to wing it than to John Bobbitt ourselves, oh God, so make sure you have thought this through."

"The Lord is wise in his plans, and he smiles upon us, his children. When Ron Howard is seen to pray with us, we will be delivered, if Jed Clampett shall set his children upon the raccoons."

"Enough," Arwoset stood. Parks hurried out a last prayer: "Thy works be done. Let there be a Katrina, that we reach Galliput, for Tunguk says by then, those who chase us will not have enough shit to get them back to Nunoc, and will have to go to Drummoc either way," Arwoset yanked him up. "So let the crew come to their senses, and may the sea crush our enemies but be chill with our friends, so help me God, amen."

Arwoset prodded them off the deck and back to Ostuk. "Thank you for letting us join in prayer, Captain Hook," Parks gave a salute.

Ostuk turned to Arwoset. "Do not let the redhead on the deck," Arwoset said. Foster saw Parks' face pale.

It was the last of his friends he saw topside. Even Kjartke and the boys were not allowed up to tend the dogs. Foster made the food round, and when he knelt before the one he named Winnie. When Kjartke showered the pack with chunks, he would scramble for a handful and see to it that she ate first. Now there was nothing to distract the others, who crowded their noses under his arms. He elbowed the team out of the way, so that she could sniff his offering and meet his gaze with a question that knew something was wrong. Reluctantly, she nibbled a piece, then took down her abbreviated portion. The others were not so bothered by the change of roles, so long as they were pelted with meat. He couldn't stand the way Kjartke threw it haphazard, letting them fight over who gets to eat at all. Foster aimed his volleys, and when a swarm fell on the landing site, he quickly aimed another at the ones crowded out by the first, even to the point of noting which dogs couldn't compete at all, and delivering an extra helping by hand, as he reckoned they didn't eat half as often.

When he looked up from the dwindling rations, he saw the white sail in full for the first time, near enough that it never quite disappeared below the crests. She shot over the tops like a dolphin, leaning hard on her keel. The oars weren't in the water, yet she stalked like a predator on a wounded animal—fast, patient. Favored no side over the other, nor did she turn in confusion, where bow was stern and left was right. It had been at most six hours since she appeared, and now half that distance was gone. So long as the weather continued to improve, there would always be men to spare, standing over the hold where even if the benches cleared in their favor, the men had to climb the ladder one at a time, and not a one would get a foot on the deck.

No matter. Ostuk moved first, and whatever Parks had planned was mercifully put down. He ran through last-ditch scenarios in his head. The storm could pick up, and when all hands were needed, they'd come up. Maybe he could shoulder one into the hold and buy Gionn enough time to climb the ladder, which could get Tunguk up, and the rest. Or Gionn's knife—he'd been using it to trim frayed leads, and they hadn't taken it from him. He could hold it to Ostuk himself and demand the crew surrender. Or cut the dogs loose, and get someone up in the frenzy. And if his friends below hadn't managed to raise the mutiny that Ostuk feared, all of those gestures would be futile.

Foster reminded himself that these men didn't want to kill Parks. They wanted him for a ransom that didn't exist. He could continue on to Drummoc. Raise a ship and a crew. Or wait until Lenet arrived, first thing in Spring, and ask him to turn his ships against Nunoc, assuming his assault worked at all. Assuming the warship wouldn't just get back in plenty of time to sail north well before winter arrived.

As dire as things had been in the past—times when he didn't think they would live at all—nothing made him as sick to his stomach as the feeling he now had: that Parks would be ripped away from him for good. Tunguk would have to honor his bond somehow. Would he get himself killed in the process, leaving Foster adrift at the mercy of Ostuk, Kjartke, and the currents?

He looked up at the tip of the mast, now crisp in full against the light gray clouds, where the man had gone up to keep them afloat, and stayed. For a long while, a pull like a thread of inevitability ran through his chest. Led him through with the sense that no force of nature was strong enough to harm him or his friend, though men and women suffered and died all around them. In that moment, it snapped like the halyard and he felt himself quiver in the dread that he and all around him might slip without a word beneath the tides of those same forces that for the briefest time had failed to notice two small men who tumbled across vast waters.

Ostuk ran as long as he could. The fair turn of weather that allowed him to stave off mutiny brought the Navy vessel to bear. It was one of the smaller abiamas—twelve oars a side, with a second set of benches that seated another twelve total, staggered and brought up on an outrigger deck that hung over to either side, giving them thirty-six oars and probably a crew of four more. He shuddered at the idea of them having come through the same storm on so small an open boat, bailing the entire time and swallowing waves. At least he could keep to the mid-deck, where the waves rarely reached.

The water washed around the prow, where he knew the heavy ram waited just beneath the surface to punch a fatal hole in a ship several times its size. A dwarf by warship measures, she was a fury in her element—running alone, unsupported in coastal waters, where she outpaced and smashed the smaller longships and darraigs, held steadier in weather with her deep water keel, and delivered messages and impatient dignitaries between fleets and ports. There were enough men to win a boarding fight with anything less than a docogon, and depending on her roster, she had a thrower's chance at that. A shield wall on either side kept the rowers from peltasts, and on her bow stretched bare-breasted Piolla, Amposi mother of war, of siege, plague, and strife of cities.

They still did not row. The wind was all she needed to close, and they saved their arms for maneuvers should Ostuk run, or if they lost their heads and decided to ram. He ignored their signal as long as he could—the red banner that called for halts and surrenders. Though it would only be moments before they'd be close enough that he could no longer pretend he didn't see it, Ostuk held a small hope that the swell, a man's height at worst now, would find a way to do what the monsters of the past week had not, and turn her for the bottom.

The air dropped cold, and behind it a gust rattled across the deck, strummed the sails and sheets, and hopped across the waves to do the same to the abiama. Arwoset helped by making a show of pointing her out, and Ostuk held a hand over his eyes and studied her with the kind of shock he thought a man might show to have a mate appear out of nowhere to port. He ordered the crew to hoist their own red banner, which they pulled from a pile of others—to match the signal was to confirm. He reduced sail, but barely. They still needed to carry speed, and the wind was coming more from starboard now, edging them toward the abiama. It was a long dance to bring the pair together. The Navy men had to first tack behind them and well across, then come back to the original side in order to get close without wasting their arms. Ostuk gave Arwoset command of the steering and climbed the false deck. They were close enough for hand signals now, and the captain ordered him to haul in the sail, a motion that brought his two hands together in a peak before his face, then swooped them down and out along a flat line. Ostuk held both palms high overhead, a simple refusal. He gave the signal he would have given to his men in a storm, carry speed. If they wanted to talk, they'd have to come to him. He wouldn't bob at the mercy of the waves, and what he didn't signal is that he couldn't trust his rowers, either.

The abiama reduced her own sail, and let the wind take them closer together. She gave the sign for a boarding. Ostuk signaled a collision warning. Overstated in this case, it conveyed that he wanted them to keep distance, that he feared they would be swept together. Once again, she signaled for boarding, and again, Ostuk refused. It was well within his right. The seas were far too wild to keep the hulls from bashing on a good crosswind, and just high enough that he had to keep his angle into the coming sets. They caught him, and he must pace them, but they had no authority to turn him back, or to make him risk his vessel. The abiama would have to wait for calmer seas, and if they didn't come, she would follow them to Drummoc.

The oars came out, and she maneuvered dangerously close—not more than fifty yards away. He could see the men's faces now. They were wet and miserable as his dogs. She signaled that she had a message—not different in effect than to call for boarding. Ostuk fired back for them to keep distance. The captain responded by pointing to the red banner.

He sighed, and motioned to lower the sail. Rewet and Anset helped him carry a heavy coil of rope, and fastened one end to the false deck. The wind nearly ripped the skin boat from their hands when they untied it, but Ostuk flopped in to weigh it down. He wouldn't fuss with the heavy wooden daille—it would encourage too many men to return with him. Rewet and Anset still had to cling to the gunwales to keep the craft from skidding across the deck. But they secured a knot to the stern, and between them carried it to the swirling waters. Ostuk was handed a paddle. Now the wind favored them: they only needed to lift it slightly, and it shot free of the deck and plopped into the freezing sea without scraping or crashing on the way down. Ostuk felt the bottom roll and shift to the shape of the water. It felt like a leaf, the blue-green sea lapping right up the sides. The wind kept full tension on the rope, frothing at the mouth for the two men on deck to feed it faster.

He closed the distance in no time, then raised his hand for his crew to stop him just outside of the oars' reach. The spray made his skin and his leather tunic shine. One of their side lifted his oar, and Ostuk took it in his hands and wedged it under his bench to keep him a fixed distance from the abiama. The rowers squinted back at him. It was difficult to tell what they thought of the man who drug them across the Attavaik in Autumn, their fates now connected like their ships.

"Why do you not return to port?" The captain shouted.

"I carry dogs to Drummoc."

"You carry prisoners of the Viceroy."

Ostuk shrugged. "I did not know. These men come to my boat. I need rowers. I put them to work."

"You will turn them over."

"As soon as it is safe to join our ships."

The captain laughed. "Any longer, and we will not have the provisions to return. We will take them now. You send them in your boat," he indicated the skin boat. Ostuk nodded. "All three," the captain continued. Ostuk's chest grew heavy. "Three?" Did they know about Foster?

"The two prisoners, and the woman."

"What woman?"

"The dog woman. She helped them escape."

"I need her to tend my dogs. If you want her, you can have her in Drummoc."

"You are fortunate to keep your ship. We will take all three."

Ostuk felt his face heat up despite the freezing water that swept it. "This is my ship. I will send your prisoners, but the woman is my crew. Who will feed my dogs?"

"Anyone can feed a fucking dog."

"It is not true. The people are afraid of the dogs, and they will only take food from a trusted hand," he lied. "She is very kind. They think of her as their own mother," he recalled how Kjartke refused to even approach the animals, preferring to pelt them with food from a distance.

"Send them, or we will board and take them."

"You cannot board in this weather."

"Then we will ram."

"Are you mad? You will ram passengers who have done nothing? These dogs bring the Viceroy's coal. What is a prisoner worth? You ram my ship, he will have you executed."

"I will not chase you any longer. Send, or be sunk."

Ostuk measured the bluff. Most of these men had probably just turned blue coat, and their concerns for the Viceroy didn't extend past a winter job. If they sunk him, they'd report him lost to the storm, and get paid the same as they would if they brought the prisoners home without harming the king's dogs. What mattered most to them was avoiding a winter in Drummoc. He could not blame them. He'd never spent a winter of his life anywhere else, and even he looked upon his home with dread. It was his father's blood, his family told him. It drew him north every spring, where it craved the sun. But his mother's carried him south in Autumn.

The captain was right. He was lucky to have a ship, and would be luckier still to keep it. There were kings who started with less. Barduk started with less, twice. All the years crewing it took to raise the money, all the help he had—it made him sick to think these men, foreigners in the service of a foreigner, could confiscate it and install a captain on a whim. The thought of a ram sending them to the bottom warmed him with fury. He hadn't even bothered to ask why the fugitives were so valuable. He didn't ask the fugitives, and he didn't ask the sailors now. It was not his trade, nor his choice to have them.

They came from Yurutpa. Mattaka spoke of two great currents that fed the waters of the world. Yurupta was the warm current, fed by fate. It spanned the wide sea and brought the things that came and could not be stopped. Ralte was the cold, swift current that welled up from the deep, from Man himself, made of his choices amid the turbid waters of Yurutpa. They were obsessed with it, Ostuk thought. To the point that he felt they resigned themselves to the world. Yurutpa became a dumping ground for their fears, their laziness. The Mattaka could stand on the shore and see it close from all the folds of the world. It lapped Ajatse with such determination that few dreamed to sail against it, and it's tide line darkened the knees of the people. But they had a habit he admired: when faced with a problem, a Mattaka man would name the choices he made that led him here, and the choices that lay before him. If it were few and few, he could endure the unspeakable with dignity, knowing it was no more than fate. But Ostuk had met too many who could look back at their own choices and assign them to Yurutpa, then do the same to the ones he was faced with. It was a favored man who lived in Ralte, and could stay there.

The icy spray streamed off the tips of his hair, down his cheeks. It was true. It was everywhere, and tireless. He felt it turn him from the Orin even before his first voyage to Nunoc as a dog hand. Then it was behind him, pressing him on to his trade. The wise man steered within it, he thought. Did not waste his strength to slip beneath the surface for a final breath. Even now, he felt it was so. And if the two currents ran together, all the better. They would carry a man far. Here he was, a captain of a ship. It was so common to him now he often forgot how few could say the same. This man opposite him, he supposed. And what waters did he come here on? It was difficult to tell them apart at times. That is what the Mattaka said. That is what Ostuk himself said, when his eyes searched across the glimmering sea for the cold ripples that cut a channel through the swell, always watching, always waiting. The fugitives, the Navy, the storm. Maybe they really were swept in from Yurutpa. If he put himself at ease, these waters would gently press his bow in their direction. What else was there? No good choice surfaced. Yet here he was, as he had been all along, with choices, nonetheless.

"I will send them," Ostuk said. "In this boat. Too rough to board." The captain set his jaw in frustration, and Ostuk knew that as much as the man would have loved to walk the deck of the *Juhketappat* for one reason or another, he understood the peril of the weather.

"Three of my men will come with you. To escort the prisoners." The captain did not wait for an answer. Right away he called names. When the men were aboard, Ostuk waved to his crew, and they drew in the rope that connected the vessels. Soon Ostuk could see the faces of Rewet and Anset, though whatever they felt about their captain bringing foreign officers on board, they hid behind stone. He waited while they helped the sailors off first, then scrambled onto the false deck, and stowed the boat. The crew looked to him for a word of what was going on, but Ostuk led the sailors past them onto the main deck. They tensed at the sight of the dogs, and stayed well clear of them. Wherever Foster was, he was hidden well. Someone must have warned him. Every man paused at his station to hang on the words of the captain. Arwoset signaled Filikut to replace him at the steering oar, and came to meet them.

Ostuk turned to Rewet. "These men are here for the prisoners—the two stowaways," he held to his story, "and the woman." They did well to hide their surprise to hear her mentioned. "Go below. They will resist. Have them brought up by loyal men: Agwik, and his cousins. Tunguk. The Vjarku boys." Rewet frowned, but did not question the order.

"Anset, take our guests away from these beasts and prepare food and fresh water for them," he indicated a patch at the stern, one of the few areas free of dogs. As the men followed, he turned to Arwoset and lowered his voice. "Bring the boom to center and prepare to raise sail." A glimmer of confusion was replaced by fright.

"Captain." The word hung like a question.

"Foster. Is he among the dogs?"

"Aye, where he always is."

Ostuk still couldn't pick him out. "Tell him I accept his offer."

His own words made him lightheaded. There was a shift. It all stood as before—the rocking deck, the dark waves and the storm clouds, the crew at their work. But Ostuk saw it all as though a river of silver water washed over his world and left it clear, immediate. He had floated in the silt and debris of Yurutpa, or convinced himself he did. Now he felt the churn of the white current spin him into a different channel, and the shock of the cold water gave him his senses. He did not think it would take him far, but he felt the crisp rush of Ralte raise eddies around him as it swept him away from any land he might call familiar or hope to return to.

A procession slunk up the ladder, Rewet and Tunguk in the lead. The guards looked more bewildered and miserable than the prisoners, who came in the middle with Agwik and his three cousins. The dog boys huddled together at the end of the line. None but Tunguk had even thought to bring a weapon, Ostuk laughed to himself. He waved to Anset to bring over the sailors, though they hadn't been fed yet.

"Are these the three you wish you take?" Two of them looked to the third, who grinned with familiarity at Gionn. "Aye."

"The *Juhketappat* is a private vessel, under contract to the King of Ampos. These are my crew. Boarding a vessel to kidnap crew against a captain's wishes is piracy. Surrender your weapons to them, and we will give you quarter to Drummoc."

Foster joined his side in time to see Gionn's face turn from morose to a fit of laughter. Parks squeezed Gionn, giddy with joy.

"Not much quarter if we get rammed," the leader protested.

"Perhaps your mates will be kind enough for a rescue." The expression on the men's faces did not share the confidence. They drew their knives and spears and lay them on the deck in turn. Ostuk climbed atop the false deck to get a view of the abiama. It bobbed parallel, fighting the efforts of the wind to drive the *Juhketapppat* into her. He looked back at the boom, positioned just port of center, his crew at the ready. The wind still carried across the deck in the direction of the abiama.

"He who is king of these waters," Ostuk raised his hands. "Fill my sail."

A nod to Arwoset was all it took. The crew hauled the sail up in a fury. It wasn't even secure before the wind pressed it into a seamless bulging triangle. The *Juhketappat* pitched hard into the amu and shot sideways. Ostuk alone stood on the tall vantage of the false deck. It took the abiama only moments to notice, but they were moments lost. He'd arranged the boom just off-center so the wind would also carry them forward into the swell—the easiest direction for the abiama to evade. They saw it, and the rowers hurried to switch sides of the bench. They backpaddled with impressive timing. Ostuk saw the ship slip away from the flank of the charging amu, and he wished he had time to order a correction. In the short distance, there was none. It was one thrust, and suicide to miss. He held his breath, and it felt as though his heart paused to watch as well. With one good stroke, the sturdy arm bore down and smashed into the front quarter of the ship. Four oars were ripped from their rowers and splintered. The abiama lurched over until her gunwales nearly drank of the sea, then spun free and settled sideways to the waves.

It was a good hard blow, but they hurried to right her with oars, as hands scrambled to raise sail. He'd bet everything on surprise, and none was more shocked than Ostuk. He'd gone over with every intention of giving them their prisoners and going about his job, but the Ostuk that returned was not the one who left. The thrill of the maneuver and the decision to make it at all sunk as he saw his one chance to destroy her outright had failed, and he'd forfeited any hope he had of treaty or mercy.

Ostuk leapt onto the main deck. "Go!" He could not even think clearly enough to give a direction, but it was understood. They swung the boom again to set themselves back on course.

"Captain, rowers to oars?" Arwoset asked. Ostuk shook his head. "Hold." There was no point, with a much heavier ship and near as many oars on their pursuer, nothing they could do would outrun them. Many of his rowers were unsalted, and their coordination was poor. He needed them as fresh as possible for the inevitable evasive maneuver when the abiama showed her ram. It would be hard to line them up in such seas, and if they could dodge contact for a few days, they could force the Navy to decide whether to turn back and report them, or pursue to Drummoc. Even as he said it to himself, it rang hollow.

He raced to the stern, were Hagalut oversaw the steering. Oars that previously moved like a single animal grasped in desperation for the water, while the sail struggled to come up. The abiama was still broadside to the waves and reeling when the *Juhketappat* went up and over a solid rise that shielded the enemy from his view. Ostuk prayed that when it passed he would see only a keel peeking above the dark green wake. It seemed ages before the wave made its assault.

It was not his fortune. The abiama limped over the top, halfway righted, the sail raised but collapsed and in need of the angle that she would surely find before it mattered. Already the oars were coming together, and he knew they would be stowed the moment she had steering, to save their strength for the same dance.

Ostuk jogged to where his patchwork guard held their captives. "You!" He indicated Foster, Parks, and Gionn. "You have made much trouble for me. Now you will make it for our enemies. Arm yourselves, and guard these men. Do not kill them if you can help it. We may need to ransom the prisoners."

"Aye, aye, Cap'n!" Parks sounded off.

Ostuk faced Agwik. "To your benches! Await my orders to row. And if you feel the ram, do not wait to take the deck with anything sharp or hard you can swing." Ostuk turned to Kjartke and the boys. "If we look to be boarded, cut loose every dog on the ship. We will see how they fight with 'evil spirits' howling at their legs.

"Tunguk!" The old man was the only one left. Ostuk spoke low in Mattakatan. "You have experience at sea. What kind?"

The false deck swarmed with women, children, passengers who could not row or fight. They lay skins across the boards, and pressed them in so that the ends had a slight overlap. The spray plastered them to the wood— every blanket, tunic, spare yard of scrap leather that wasn't secured to someone's back nearly covered the outermost half, beyond the cargo stores. Tunguk left them after he was content they understood. Along the gunwale of the starboard side, he arranged a passenger and a knife at intervals, and gave them instructions one at a time.

Foster had no idea what they were doing or why, but the activity comforted him. He wondered if the old man hadn't simply come up with busy work to calm the fears that washed over the ship. Something told him there was less madness than method at work.

Spray danced overhead as the peaks of the waves crept skyward and the clouds darkened. The terror of the recent storm returned to him, huddled in the sopping cold, the air thick with the smell of vomit and wet dog. Now it was balanced against the safety that the terror afforded them—the fine line between too rough to fight, not rough enough to capsize. Some storm, but not too much. He'd grave doubts whether the rising breeze gave a drowned rat's ass about his particular fancies.

The wind still ran across their intended direction of travel, almost perpendicular to the thin dark line of coast he could no longer see now the waves were picking up. New waves caught on and formed with the wind, while older sets followed the prevailing direction, so that they crossed each other, the younger ones still small, but already causing concern among the crew. If they grew at all, there would be no way to avoid getting hit broadside and head-on at once, while being driven ever-closer to hidden rocks near the coast. And they had no option of changing to a slower direction. The Navy ship was already overtaking them.

All he had was Gionn's knife, which he gripped like a handle that could steady him against the lurching deck. It was enough to deal with the three prisoners at their feet. They'd made no effort to move, or even bargain. Their expressions looked more like men led to the gallows than given safe quarter to land, which told him enough about how those who knew the ships and the weather far better than himself weighed the odds. If dozens of men stormed over the deck, they may have had decent numbers, but a single small blade wouldn't even get him close enough to use it. Gionn at least had a good short sword, but he was in the middle of berating Parks about the harpoon he carried.

"—should call yourself terrible things on me behalf, cunt. I shouldn't be required to profane meself with the kind of earfuckin' you deserve. It's a shit weapon if you're not a squain defendin' yourself against a seal. Do you not recall what happened the last time you used one?"

"I do recall, but this is all they had for me, bro. I had to leave that last place in a hurry and I didn't have time to stop by the local armory."

"One stab. We got one good stab, then it became a fuckin' stick."

"Yeah, well, turns out everyone on this ship who owns a spear agrees with you, and decided to keep it to themselves. Maybe I kill one guy and take whatever he's got."

"Please fight alongside me. That way I can get me cracks in while they're distracted cuttin' you to bits."

"Why am I getting all the flak? Foster has a little bitty knife!"

"It's a fine knife. And he's no good in a fight no matter what he's got. It's me great fortune to add however long it takes them to kill the both of you to me days."

"Foster!" Ostuk called him over. He gladly stutter-stepped over and let the bickering dissolve in the wind. "If they sink the hooks in, kill those three first."

"Aye, sir." He didn't know if he had it in him to execute an unarmed man with a knife, but he knew who did.

"I do not want you in the thick of it."

"Sir?"

"If the fighting turns bad, get your mate. Leave the other. Go to the place where the false deck meets the stern. You will find Tunguk and the crew. Do as they say while the others hold the fight."

"What's the plan?"

Ostum grinned. "I speak the truth when I say I don't know."

"We have a rule where I'm from. I wonder if you have the same." Ostuk waited for him to continue. "Captain always goes down with the ship. Last man off."

"Do your captains follow this rule?"

"I had me one that did."

Ostuk nodded. "I will consider it. My mother's people have something like it. They call them 'sea ropes' in your language. They are how Mattaka must live when they are with the water. But Mattaka do not go far from shore. Sometimes, it is hard to know what ropes to carry where they have not yet been."

"The Code of the Sea."

"Is this what you call it?"

Foster nodded. "The rules of what a man ought to do and ought not to do. With the water, like you say. Only problem as I understand it, every man's got one, and everyone's is different."

They fell silent as they watched the Navy ship struggle into the wind behind them, gaining nonetheless. "Tell me what you see," Foster said. Ostuk looked at him. "With your cap'n's eyes."

Ostuk pointed at the ship with a nod. "He takes the weather-gage. When he is between us and the wind, he will turn. The one with the weather-gage chooses the attack. When to attack. If to attack. Then the wind will be at his back when he rams. A good fighting captain in a good warship would maneuver first for the weather-gage, because to lose it means the battle is half lost. This ship? We have no chance to take it from him, so I surrender it."

"What do we do when he gets it?"

"We pray the seas darken until he has no hope of lining up a thrust, or boarding."

Tunguk finished positioning the last of the passengers and joined them. "Is it well?" Ostuk said. The old man looked at the Navy ship on an intercept to the wind.

"We will see if we give a fight," he answered.

"You will tell me if I must change position when they ram."

Tunguk nodded, then a shadow passed over his face.

"What?" Foster asked.

"They row." Sure enough, he thought. The long oars bit the water like insect legs to help the sails get them in position to turn again with the wind at their backs.

"It will not be long," Ostuk guessed.

Tunguk shook his head. "Too soon." He looked at his companion. "They row too soon." It was all the explanation he offered. The task of getting every oar in and pulling at the same pressure when the water was so steep and changing angle by the second seemed miserable. Some of the rowers barely got in at all on certain strokes, scraping the top off the waves and fouling their rhythm, like someone trying to scramble up a gravel slope. But they gained more than they lost, and the sail shifted position to turn the attention of the terrible carved woman onto her prey. He couldn't see it, but Foster knew somewhere beneath that white wake was a big chunk of metal that could break the outrigger loose, or punch a hole big enough for a dog to squeeze through in their hull, right at the water line. Now she was racing toward them with the wind. The rowers steadied themselves against an easier stroke and gave her a few extra knots behind the bullet that had zeroed in on the *Juhketappat.*

At the moment, the exposed starboard side was turned to the ram, while the outrigger plowed the sea away from the enemy. Tunguk said a string of something to the captain in Mattakatan. Ostuk acknowledged it, then said to Foster: "Remember what I said."

"Aye, sir," Foster took the hint and headed back to his position over the prisoners.

Ostuk called over the men responsible for the boom. He explained the order, and sent them back to await his command. It was simple, but simple was not easy. The abiama closed fast, and if he acted too late, she would be upon him. Too soon, and she would have the chance to adjust. The hole she made need not be fatal. As soon as the ship was fixed, she would not back-paddle for another attempt. They would set their hooks and come over the sides to test the merchants in battle.

"You will tell me when?"

Tunguk looked surprised. "How should I know? You are the captain." He laughed that understated chuckle that had come to fray Ostuk whenever he heard it. Oh well, he thought. At least it would be his choice. A hundred yards. Less. It was clear they aimed for his forward quarter. That would put them dead center if they were too slow, and if he dropped sail to slip behind them, it would be easier to turn on a slowing ship than one that went by too fast. The men on the boom were tense. They were guessing their own distances, and they wanted the order now. He'd seen them shunt 600 times, though. He knew how fast they were better than they did. As long as they didn't fumble with the ropes. It occurred to him they'd never pulled the maneuver—or any maneuver—under attack.

The abiama was faster on a line and more agile under oar. Many who did not know the Mattaka songs thought the amu was stolen from Ampos. That the people hugged the coasts in their skin boats. Ostuk knew as well as any seafaring Mattaka that it was the Amposi who stole from the Mattaka. That their ancestors came to Ajatse on the back of the amu. When big ships with square sails arrived, they did not adopt the deep water keel, but they were happy to use the strong tree trunks of the northerners to make bigger amus, and fix them to ships that could compete as cargo carriers with most of what ran the far side of the Orin. They could carry as many or more soldiers when it was called for. But they made for terrible warships. A boarding fight was their only option, and they lacked the ability to evade the rams. Their decks were ideal for a large number of Marines to defend, if they had any, but even then the Navy would just back out and ram them again until they sunk without drawing blood.

He had but one advantage. The *Juhketappat* did not have a bow or a stern. The abiama broke inside fifty yards, and he was certain he had waited too long when he yelled the order. His crew loosed the ropes that held the boom in place and let it spin until it crossed the deck, then held fast. The wind caught the exposed part of the sail and turned her with the sun by a quarter turn, the amu slipping in between the abiama and the ship. She now doubled back across the swell, and her speed slowed, giving the *Juhketappat* more of a sideways drift. The abiama cut as well, but they had anticipated a sudden halt, not such a dancer's pivot.

The ram swept by so close, some of the rowers had to raise their oar to avoid having them torn from their grips by a collision with the amu. A pair of men in the rear hurled grappling hooks onto the false deck, but the sharp claws skittered off the wet leather and back into the Attavaik.

The passengers erupted in cheers. Some of them embraced, and a few fell to the deck to thank whoever had assured their safety.

"Looks like yall get to live a few more minutes!" Foster grinned at the prisoners, who couldn't hide a bit of relief. Only Ostuk was unconsoled. It was a miss, but they would not allow the same maneuver twice. He prayed Tunguk was right, and they had rowed too soon, in weather not fit for fighting. He interrupted the crew's celebration to give another order. The boom came loose again. They crossed back and turned on the abiama to take the weather-gage. The abiama still ran with the wind and had not yet made a move to turn. Ostuk crossed their wake, then shunted again so that he lay in directly at their stern and kept his sail wide open to stay as close as he could. When they turned, he aimed to shoot right by them and get as much lead as he could before they retook the weather-gage. He could not prevent it. They would catch him anyway. But with good fortune, the storm would continue to worsen. It was already beyond the point that a sound man would issue a fight, Tunguk assured him. His only hope was to stay away from the ram until a fight went from unwise to impossible.

They headed directly for the coast now. "Look how slow they run," Ostuk said to Tunguk. "They are tired." As soon as he said it he knew it was to convince himself more than anything else.

"It is strange," Tunguk said. "They do not turn."

"It is strange," Ostuk agreed, "but as long as she points that way, I am happy."

"They still row, as if to flee." Tunguk was troubled by the behavior, and it bothered Ostuk in turn because he didn't understand why.

"Maybe they realize they can't take us in the storm. They make for the coast to ride it out."

"That is the look they give."

Ostuk frowned. "You think it's a ruse?"

"They are damaged, or afraid, or wish us to think it."

"Should I leave them? Keep to sea?"

"How should I know?" Tunguk reminded him: "You are the captain."

The possibilities ran through Ostuk's world. They showed weakness to let him run, then they would turn after him and take the wind. Or they avoided the storm. Perhaps to turn back for Nunoc, where they would declare him a criminal, and place a bounty on his ship and his head. Or they had taken more damage than he thought when the amu struck them, and could not maneuver to fight. The safe choice was to avoid the fight altogether. To run, not risk an ambush. It was safe for now, but if they returned home, all would be lost in a long Ajatse night, or in two. It did not matter. He would not run a dog ship again.

Whatever they planned, Ostuk knew it depended on him taking the only course a merchant captain in a slow ship without a real fighting contingent could do: head south. They could not dream of anything else. Maybe he was drunk on Ralte. His words to Foster returned: he who owns the weather-gage chooses if to attack, and when.

"Run them down," he called to Arwoset. The crew stared blankly at him for a moment. "I will not be stabbed full of holes and left to drown."

"Ostuk," Arwoset called him by his name. "We do not have a ram."

"We bring the amu to bear on her. Force them to board on our terms, and we cut them down as they do." He looked to Tunguk, as if for permission.

The old man shrugged. "I will be on the false deck to see their faces when a dog ship attacks."

The younger members of the crew laughed and gave a shout of approval. The others went about their tasks with less spirit. Ostuk headed to the bow, where he could see the abiama grow near as their sails overpowered hers. "Steer to her right," he called. On his boat, port and starboard were directions relative to the amu, not the bow, and he didn't want to confuse the crew. It was important to keep the amu between them and their enemies.

Long years on the sea had taught him that a ship talks with her body the same as a man. She stands proud, slumps, staggers, runs with grace or temper, grasps, and hesitates, though not a board will move the way a face or an arm does. Something about her was not right. She lumbered like one tired from a fight, panting to the shade for a rest. The oars were well-pulled, but they too told of a plan that he could only guess at. The fact that they rowed at all but failed to seek the advantage for another thrust was wrong, even to one who had never seen a warship in action. One did not waste his men until he needed the speed and the agility, and here they were in open sea heading for a coast that was yet miles away.

"Banners up!" Amarkuk warned, though Ostuk saw them at the same time as everyone. There were six alternating: red, white, red. To "raise all flags," keeping the colors apart to catch the eye, was a sign of distress—of surrender. A merchant like him carried many colors, but a small warship only needed the two. They were asking him to come their aid.

"Tunguk!" The old man was nowhere to be found, already below deck telling the rowers to prepare for the attack. The crew were busy. Ostuk motioned for Foster.

"Do you know this signal?"

"No, sir."

"It means they call for help."

Foster nodded. "You believe 'em?"

"I did. Until I saw the flags."

"Well. We were gonna attack either way, right?"

"That was before I knew they wanted me to." Foster started to answer, but Ostuk interrupted. "And don't say, 'you're the captain.'"

"Well, I'm tickled that you want the opinion of a dog feeder. Wish I knew what to tell you. But I stand by my statement: you done us a favor. I was willin' to fight before they missed us, and I'm willin' if not able now. What's changed?"

Ostuk gave the question some thought. "It was they who held the advantage. Then us. Now I wonder."

"If they plan to fight us, it's gonna happen one way or another. If not, we still got 'em."

"Captain!" Amarkuk called his attention back to the ship. The sail collapsed to a thin line as the sailors hauled it down. The oars raised out of the water and stopped. They were waiting for him.

"Hold course," he confirmed to the crew. If they were planning to turn on him for a sudden attack as he approached, they would only have oars to do it. It was so obvious a display of weakness that he could not shake the feeling he was being lured. Yet it was decided. The men and women on the *Juhketappat* would live or die by the decision he already made.

The wind seemed to encourage them forward, skipping the ship over the tops of short rollers with a confidence that came from speed. Even as the sea came between them and full view of the abiama, the flags held their eyes above the swell. Ostuk searched for Tunguk, and found him perched atop the hold.

"You old fool! Will you fall twice before you learn?"

"It will not be the second time," Tunguk quipped.

"I want you topside. Find the coxswain for the ladder. And tell him 'oars at the ready.'" When he had a man to call down, Ostuk returned to the bow. The once-spry abiama seemed to heave for breath, inert on the surface, unable even to turn and gaze upon her enemy as he approached. Within fifty yards he saw why. She did not rise and fall as much as he would expect, and his eyes knew it all along, though his head took its time. Her gunwales ran low, as though over-burdened with a cargo he knew was not there. The spray that slapped the sides separated itself from another spray—one flinging itself back at the sea. Every man with two hands to cup together threw water over the sides.

"Trim sail," he called to the crew. "Keep her to our port and hold as best you can. Let us look before we ram."

They didn't even need to draw even before he could see the problem. Her bow dipped below the stern. Even from this distance he caught glimpses of the sea as it snaked inside the ship at the men's knees. Provisions floated the length of the boat, colliding with legs, benches, and one another. Ostuk grinned ear-to-ear.

"Not bad for my first ram thrust," he said as Tunguk and Arwoset joined for a look. They could not see it, but the amu must have cracked her hull where it spun her. They were taking on water the entire time. Suddenly their haste to oars in foul weather, their flight for the coast after a narrow miss—it all wove together. The abiama knew she had one chance to nail herself to the boat and board. She probably didn't even mean to hit with the ram, only intending to get close enough to use the hooks. Failing that, she sprinted for land in a race with the sea that was clearly lost. They had no movement left. A large swell raised both ships, but snuck over the lip of the abiama with an onslaught of more water than they could have bailed in hours. It nestled them lower, where it would be all too soon before the next wave big enough to crest the top did it again, and then again, until it was the Attavaik herself who swam across her mast.

Everyone on deck stopped what they were doing to line up on the false deck and watch. Even the prisoners came. It should have felt like victory. An army driven before them, a blood-painted field. Not one somber mouth broke to raise a word. It was not long ago that they feared the same for their own ship. First from the storm, then from the ones they watched foundering before them. It felt to Ostuk as though the same waters welled up in his chest to bring his heart beneath them.

The captain climbed to the quarter deck from thigh-deep water, a sad figure drenched to the bone. He waved at Ostuk and pointed to the flags. No mistaking the surrender. This was what he came to do: send every man who could speak his ruin on his way to Urkuk. It was done.

He met eyes with the prisoners, and expected them to make a plea for their mates. They could not watch. Instead, they turned for the main deck. The men all stopped bailing. They stood, too proud for desperation, awaiting a response, a move of any kind. They would waste no more effort either way.

"Captain." It was Foster who spoke first. "Permission to take the prisoners aboard."

"Permission to fuck off, cunt," Gionn responded. "They'll kill us all and sail merrily back to Nunoc."

"What if we make them promise not to kill us?"

"They will speak of this in Drummoc," Anset said. "It will be the same."

"And they have to promise never to speak of the fight," Parks added.

Ostuk shook his head. "The Mattaka do not bind a man to a promise made under threat of death."

"Sir," Foster went on. "The Code of the Sea says you don't let a man drown if you can help him. Friend, enemy, total stranger, it don't matter. If I were over there, I'd wanna be over here. And I'd be happy to come under whatever conditions you had in mind."

"Forgive me, I lack your vast experience in maritime operations," Gionn said to Foster, "but the Code of the Sea as I understand it demands only that any survivors left floatin' on bits of wood must be speared to death with merciful vigor, that they are spared the unpleasantness of drownin'."

"I do not know of this code," Anset spoke up, bold beyond his experience. Ostuk could see Arwoset's displeasure before the boy could give his opinion. "But if one of these men speaks to the Navy in Drummoc, it will be bad for us. They won't care that we pulled them from a sinking ship if we are the reason it sank." The older men held their tongues, but if they disagreed, they would have lashed into him for speaking out of turn.

The Mattaka "ropes" had nothing to say. Their people were coast-huggers, and wars were fought on land. Ostuk supposed if a hunting boat saw another full of hated men slipping beneath the waves, they would no more help than they would bring food to a starving rival clan who contested their hunting grounds. Perhaps there was nothing to say because they could not dream any other way.

"Captain, I ask you," Gionn pleaded, "would these cunts have spared us if their ram had found its mark?"

"These men? They would not give us the courtesy of a spear. Tunguk," he called to find the man already at his side. "Arm all hands and bring them to the false deck." The old man left. "We will need their provisions, too, if we're to make Drummoc. Bring them over first. Then Gionn collects their weapons as they board." He felt the mood of those around him plummet like the drop down the backside of a steep wave. Ostuk knew it was likely that not a soul but Foster and Parks stood with him. If ever there was a time and a reason for mutiny, this was it. But he had a head start. He was willing to choose first, and he did not know if anyone had the courage to catch him now.

"Throw over your hooks!" He shouted to the other captain. The men scrambled into action, and soon three ropes with sharp grappling points bounced across the deck. They waited atop the leather skins for someone to fix them to the wood. For a moment no one moved. Again it was Foster who broke rank. He bent gingerly, lifted a hook, and cut it free of the rope. Then he drug it past the rest of the crew and tied the end to one of the cargo lashings. Parks followed suit, and soon the rest of the crew lumbered into action, man by man, as it became obvious that this would be the way. Even Gionn, swearing under his breath, moved to the edge of the deck to oversee the boarding, probably eager for someone to initiate a fight so he could have his stabbing, after all.

Rowers jogged over in a great mass, and the initial hesitation erupted into a flurry of action. The men of the abiama pulled the ropes until the amu kissed the edge of their ship, now well-below the level of the false deck.

"Provisions first!" Arwoset called. It wasn't what they wanted to hear, but the sailors did their best to harness the floating barrels of fresh water, the dried meat, the jars of fat and all of the trappings of a long voyage. The sinking ship now pulled heavily on the *Juhketapppat*, sending her weight onto the amu and sloping the false deck toward the abiama. The first man to scramble aboard was their captain. Ostuk met Foster's gaze with a laugh at the corner of his mouth, and Foster returned the grin as he shook his head. Before even half of the men had boarded, a swell lifted up the conjoined ships, and when it set them down, the far side of the abiama dipped entirely beneath the surface. A surge of water filled the deck and sent every minor supply they'd decided to abandon swirling among them. The men lost their footing and splashed back to their feet, now waist deep in freezing water. Rowers rushed forward. The many hands of the *Juhketappat* extended to meet those of the Navy ship, and men were yanked coughing and squirming aboard.

"We have to cut her loose!" Arwoset warned, and he was right. The weight of the water-laden ship was in danger of rollin their own vessel. A dozen men remained on the boat, struggling to get into position to catch a hand. He saw Foster slap Parks and disappear into the throng behind him. One of the ropes tying them together snapped, sending them spinning apart at that end.

"A little longer!" A Navy man who'd made it aboard begged. They shouted at their crewmates to move to the one part of the ship that was still attached. A few more made it aboard, but the others had to wait behind them to get to the only section that could reach between the ships. Over his shoulder, bodies cleared a lane. Foster and Parks ran up, carrying the little skin boat between them. At once he saw their plan.

"Get me a rope on that boat!" Ostuk ordered. Parks alone sat inside. No shortage of men hurried to lift him into the water, just as the second rope snapped. The remaining one did nothing to hold them together. Anset cut it loose before it could threaten them any more, and the entire false deck leapt up out of the water, sending many people against the cargo as the weight suddenly resettled.

But Parks was already being fed out. Within moments, he was at the ship, more water than wood. It had flopped to the other side, the gunwale completely under and never to come up. The tall mast tilted toward the coast while the remaining men swam up onto the near side—the only part of the abiama out of the water. Parks held out an end of his paddle, and a man pulled him to the edge. The last eight men crowded down into the skin boat.

As they pulled them back, Ostuk looked at their captain.

"I ask nothing of you. We will carry you to Drummoc as prisoners. Then you will be free. What you say of us to others—"

He interrupted. "What you don't ask, you shall receive. The men of my crew will harm you as much as they would if you had left us to the sea." He glared over his companions as he said it. They were a combination of gratitude and shock. Not a man hesitated to turn over whatever he had at his waist.

"We can't spare the rope to bind our prisoners, and we have no walls," Ostuk spoke to Kajrtke and the dog boys in Mattakatan. "They will sit on the deck, behind a wall of dogs." The boys grinned.

"Nice call on the lifeboat," Parks joined Foster with a high-five.

"Thank Tunguk," Foster said. "He's the one had it ready to go. When I seen that boat settin' right where Ostuk told me to get my people and meet Tunguk when they boarded, I had a feelin' I knew what was up. Ol' boy would much rather board than be boarded. You were aimin' to take their ship even while they took ours, weren't you?"

Tunguk guarded whatever expression crept into the corners of his furrowed face. "Do not speak loud of intentions. The sea gods will hear, and they will be foiled when they are needed."

They were already under sail before they could even think of stowing the new provisions and hemming in the prisoners. No one on board was much of a quartermaster, Foster realized. He had no idea how he should ration the dog food that was also theirs. The new supplies were welcome, especially with another forty mouths to feed and water, but whether they would be enough gnawed at him. He supposed no one knew, or maybe the gods to whom the passengers made their thanks did, but they weren't saying. The clouds turned to coal and the wind swept its fingers across the water as though strumming to warm up for whatever brewed in the distance. It had been a brief respite, and only enough for a quick battle. He knew they approached Galliput—the point of no return in the autumn blast. From there, whether they made it without starving or dying of thirst depended on how fast and often their sails were filled. And on staying above water.

He lingered a while on the false deck with a smattering of passengers. All stayed to watch the Navy ship turn the water green and disappear for good. If he was safe from a storm, it was a warship, and from that, back to a storm. Before it, the whip, the boat thieves, and he was too tired to recall what else. Something told him if there wasn't one more looming, it was because the last one ended him. Was anyone as exhausted as he was? Even Parks? His friend was on another end of the false deck, waving dramatically at the sky. Foster wondered if he hadn't become half-serious about it. He passed close enough to hear the prayer.

"Riders on the storm," Parks sang to he-knew-not-who, outlined against the lashing seas. "Into this house we're born, into world we're thrown, like a dog without a bone, uh…" he paused for the line, but it wasn't forthcoming. "Lawd, bring my homeys home. Riders on the storm."

Foster shook his head and hopped down onto the main deck. The adrenaline of battle left without a proper release. His limbs barely responded to the commands he gave them to carry him back to his place among the dogs. A wet tail thumped the deck to betray an otherwise motionless animal. He settled in, and she put her chin on his leg, her swollen belly heaving with whimpers. Foster stroked her head. "Best take it easy, girl," he jerked his head up to the clouds. "Gonna be another good one." It was then he noticed one of the groups of prisoners, half the contingent, cowering in a pile around which a minefield of dogs had been tied. The animals took no interest in them, but they climbed over one another to stay as far away from the teams as possible. Every pair of eyes was fixed on him in horror. Foster winked at them and grinned.

14

Well of the Dead

Foster joined the crowd that gathered at the lip of the false deck two and three deep. There was no room left at the edge. Prisoners and passengers locked shoulders to anticipate the first land underfoot for near two months. He leaned between heads to get a look. The island grew before them all morning, but the carriers had taught him how to be patient before disembarking. After taking hours to dock, there were times they sat on the boat for days and left without ever setting foot on a gangplank. But an aircraft carrier was a kinder ride. Now the white giant that stood guard over the expanse of rock and ice loomed closer as though to take a look at the sad souls arriving at his doorstep. Even the sea-hardiest had lost a few shades. It wasn't the weather. The storm that spun them every which way but down left a day after they took on the Navy men, and seemed little more than a bad dream by the time their destination welled up off the horizon. The sailors swore it was a fair journey for early Autumn. But the eastern passage was always into the long swell that circled the Southern Ocean like a merry-go-round. Not a following sea to be had. They beat their way through on a chilly breeze that seemed to pity them their early struggles the way Foster felt for the poor bastards confined to deck.

He was never instructed to care for them, but it became his default every time he made the rounds among the dogs. Warm as it was by Antarctic measures, it was goddamn freezing at times. And wet. Always wet. At least he had a wet sleeping bag. Few of the men managed to salvage theirs from the sinking warship, and they weren't as keen on cuddling with dogs as he was. He had no help feeding or watering them. It was not for the boys, or Kjartke. Dogs always ate first. But the quarters were too tight to watch them waste away. Every foot of the deck was covered by man or beast or gear. They maintained a strict observance of their roles for the first couple of weeks. But Foster was too polite, and his own upbringing forbid him from ever believing another person was of lower status than himself. Soon, he teased them as he worked, and they teased back. "Does it feel just like a woman?" One asked of the dog pile he slept in. Then he arranged for supervised walks of the false deck to get the men a little exercise. When one took sick, Foster brought him below to be nursed by Parks in the relative comfort of the hold.

By the end of the journey, they moved about the deck however they liked. At times, their sailors helped the crew of the *Juhketappat* under the direction of Ostuk. The rest of the rowers and passengers kept their distance, but Foster learned the names of his favorites, and addressed them whenever he was sure the crew couldn't hear. Twice, they stopped for days at a time so the water barrels could be refilled in turn by the little wooden boat—the daille, they called it. It was a rotation of prisoners who went ashore with Ar-woset and Anset to manhandle the heavy barrels up and down the glacier. No one would dream of using the dogs. Still, the men fought over the right to set foot on barren, icy land, even for a few hours. It was the Mattaka rowers who crewed the boats when they raided a seal colony, though. The meat they took was nearly enough.

No one had eaten in over a day, and the portions dwindled before them for weeks prior. The water held out, but neither man nor beast had anything in his stomach. Foster stood accused of overfeeding both dog and prisoner alike. It was probably true. But no amount of provisions, or supplementary hunting, could stand up to such an addition to the passenger list. The real proof of his incompetence was the fact that nearly every single dog on the ship had survived—apparently, unheard of. Excluding puppies, all but six would arrive safely in the next few minutes. The standard practice was to let the weaker dogs starve, and feed them to the stronger ones, thus sparing more meat for the people. He didn't know it, nor would he have done it. With Tunguk at limited action, the decision fell to him, and there wasn't anyone on the ship who hadn't cursed his name. Now everyone craved the firm rock beneath their feet, but none more than he. Even the dogs and prisoners seemed to begrudge him, though they would have starved much sooner if he hadn't been so heavy-handed.

The port before him was no more impressive than the one at Nunoc. A little harbor that could load three of four ships at once, and a rocky plain with rollers for pulling unused ships out of the water. There was no good way for them to remain afloat for long with the kind of winds he imagined raked the place. Only one waited near the water, and he could tell it had been dry-docked recently. Of the ships left uncovered, she was the only one without a thin dusting of frost that bloomed in the seams along their sides. All vessels pointed the same direction, into prevailing wind, he reckoned.

"Drummoc. Drummoc. Drummoc." Foster'd expected something of a town, as many times as he heard the name. A few buildings of timber and stone that paled to Nunoc's main street sat exposed on the plain behind the dock. Behind them, a small army of Mattaka dwellings dotted the landscape, packed as tight and irregular as ever.

No Navy boat escorted them in this time. The hungry rowers set her to drift sideways, the false deck leading toward the dock, where men with long poles waited to receive her ropes. Behind them, what seemed like hundreds of people had congregated. Far more than could be attributed to the families of passengers, though he couldn't imagine anyone had anything better to do than watch a ship coast in.

All of the rowers were still below deck, and the prisoners rearmed. It was necessary if they were going to pass off their story, but it still worried him. So far, they seemed as happy as everyone else to make land.

No one said a word. No shouting as they neared the dock, no waving. It was more than manners. Never in his career had he set out on a boat without knowing beyond a shadow of a doubt it would reach its destination. The last weeks of his life had taught him that that was how every voyage began in Antarctica. Even with yards to drift and long poles stretched like friendly hands, no one took anything for granted.

They caught the edge of the false deck and eased her toward the logs that hung from ropes to keep the amu from crashing into rock. It had been badly damaged when they rammed the Navy ship, they learned a day later when it nearly broke free, and only a heroic effort by Arwoset and Anset, dangling over the edge with rope and adze while waves tried to peel them free, managed to save the ship. The things he saw men do to survive here made him feel like he was a lesser man than Kjartke and the dog boys. Foster no longer cared to prove himself, to find his place. He had abandoned his own self-respect like a map that no longer led him where it claimed, and settled into the feeling of being a child in a strange land where nothing made sense or cooperated, and every small concession was the gift of life.

The gap narrowed and people leapt off in a cascade as she nestled in to port. Passengers and onlookers alike erupted with cheer and greeting. Foster had planned to disembark calmly but the jubilation swept him up and he launched himself onto land, stumbled, and decided to go to his knees as he was going to fall, anyway. He crawled onto the cold rock and pressed his lips to the rock. Everyone embraced everyone. He was sure most had never met. A smile worked its way up, followed by a fit of laughter. People swarmed around all sides of him to get to someone else. He would have been content to enjoy it as an onlooker, but one of the prisoners, unknown as he, caught his eyes. They hugged like free men, and as soon as they let go, others reached for them, turn after turn. An old Mattaka woman kissed him on the mouth. Whether she'd come from ship or shore, he couldn't say.

It was more of a homecoming than he'd ever gotten after a deployment. It seemed like the spectacle would abate, but the mill of the crowd and the shouts of family and grateful sailors refused to diminish. He stuck out a hand for another of the men he'd fed, and was met with a confused look. Foster realized there were no handshakes here. Instead of wrapping his arms in a more familiar embrace, he grabbed the man's wrist, showed him how to grip the palm, and shook his hand up and down. He spun to a friend and showed him the move as well, while Foster laughed at the sight of them yanking one another's shoulders from the sockets.

Tunguk watched it all from the edge of the false deck. A pair of albatrosses soared overhead, and they brought the spirit world. He saw whalers unloading their wares to sell in the city, and coal ships anchored in the harbor awaiting their turn. He wrapped his fingers over the collar of his tunic to hang across the top of his sapak before he realized it. These spirits were old. Hard to hear over the wave-roar of the people. Behind them, he sensed ones who were older still. Ones whose faces had turned to whispers until those left them, too. Only faint tracks remained where many traveled, and tugged gently at his feet to come this way or that.

They were thickest here. He watched as a boy stood on the quay and studied the ship. Wondered if the boy had seen him, too. There was great pain in his face, and he must have followed the tracks here many times to do as he did now. Of all the joyful celebrants, he alone was grim. He could know nothing of the world across the seas, but he seemed certain there was a place he was meant to go, along the heavy tracks, away from the black tukits glazed with ice, where the tracks narrowed and few men could find them. Perhaps farther, away from these spirits who walked in circles to the underworld, having lost their stories in the wake of the 600 ships that churned these waters.

The boy's lips did not move, but Tunguk heard the oath he swore: "away." Drummoc was the last and the least place in the world for him, and he knew once he found his ship, he would not return. The pain behind his eyes beat with his heart, and he was dizzy. His chest joined his head. The worlds changed places until he was not sure which he was in. An arm wrapped around his waist. Only then did he realize he was close to falling.

"Whoa, brother! Let me help you." Foster led him off the deck and onto the rock. He felt the permanence of the place close around him. It was unsettling, after the sway of the sea and the spinning vision. The shapes ceased their dancing. Faces were made clear, familiar and unfamiliar. Farther off, the low buildings, things that could not be blown away. His feet would not move. He did not trust them, anyway. Slaves of habit. Tunguk let Foster lead him into the crowd.

"We gotta get you fed, old man. You had a long trip. And some asshole gave all the food away."

"Foster!" Ostuk's voice stopped him from the deck. "You forget my dogs."

It was several more hours before he could leave the ship for good. Every team had to be taken off the boat and mustered at the harbor with the help of the local families who seemed to be the counterparts of the Nunoc people who raised the animals, if not kin somehow. Kjartke was no help. He sent her to take care of Tunguk. He and the boys fought them as they leapt against leashes and yipped for the shore. The swelling mass drove the rest of the crowd clear to one side. Many lingered to point and grin—to admire the state of the dogs, and that they survived at all, he imagined. Then he settled beside the three boys, none of them as high as his modest shoulder, and watched from shore as the rowers pulled the ship on rollers with help from the Navy. Ostuk's boat was done for the season. It looked like a miserable job. It would be a while before he saw Parks and Gionn again.

The last dog to slink away from the harbor needed no leash. She followed him on weak legs, anxiously fixed on what he held. Try as she might, she couldn't hold off giving birth well before they arrived. Six pups were born before the *Juhketappat* limped into town. Three of them died in the first 48 hours. Foster held the end of his leather tunic folded over his belly. He peeked in at the other three, and they looked back with glittering eyes that only just slipped open, squirming against each other and testing the seams of his shirt. The boys walked ahead with their last teams. They veered on a path that lead to the right of town. It seemed like a path to nowhere. Another sea across the narrow peninsula. Then it swung around the farthest of the buildings to slope inland, toward nothing else he could make out.

It did kind of seem like a shithole. A chill ran down his spine. It was already cold here. Much colder than Nunoc. But it was the thought of a winter of darkness in ball-freezing wind, huddled in a rock igloo, that stung him. Still, he could use a break from near-death experiences, and terrible as the weather must get, people lived through winters here all the time. It wasn't the cold that worried him. It was the mental strain. The boredom. The sameness. What did people do to pass the time when leaving wasn't an option? Or even striking a light? He looked up at the hulking mountain, snow-capped and clouded at the peak. Did Mattaka go for hikes? Maybe he could get in a quick climb before the weather got too rough. Nothing about it sounded appealing, but he'd come so far south. As south as he'd ever go. For some reason, much as he longed for a boat home, it seemed a waste to come so close and not stand atop the bottom of the world.

That was it. Parks doubled over with exhaustion. The sun set earlier by the day, giving the impression they'd wrangled the ship well into the night. A bright crown over the mountains across the channel—the thin strip of peaks that he knew must tower over the mainland—was all that remained of the light. Every rower, every crew member, and as many of their Navy guests had pushed and pulled the *Juhketappat* over log rollers, one heave at a time. Every log they cleared had to be carried to the front and set before to extend the track, and the ship held in balance with rope and pole the entire time to avoid it slamming down hard on the outrigger, or even worse—the other side. They snailed their way right past an array of slender ships that must have belonged to the Navy. Other than a fleet of Mattaka skin boats, they were the closest thing to the water. Ready to launch at a moment's notice, if a moment was a day long.

The *Yookie*, as he'd come to call her, was destined farther inland by a hundred yards, where the merchant fleet spent the winter. They nested her beside a jumble of others. There was one just like her—the only one with an outrigger—and the rest had little in common other than looking like a bitch to ride on. Three were fatties, more rounded and having the look of a deck up top and a hold below, though he couldn't see that high. There were several longships with shallow drafts, about the size of the one they sunk with Klimut and the gang, and something or other with a deeper keel. A bigger sister that reminded him of the one set to sail from Nunoc. Most conspicuous was an outrigger model a little slighter than their dog ship, its fresh pitch chipped and gleaming, its edges still close to square.

He'd imagined a fleet of coal ships like Lenet's. There were none. Just beyond them, a graveyard of gutted hulks dotted the rock. Most weren't even secured. Huge sections of timber lay missing. Not one of them had a mast left. He imagined this is how Foster's people collected fleets of cars: up on blocks in a field, rusted out and gutted to keep the next one turning over. Wasn't what he expected of a booming trade, but then again, three were missing, and there could be a lot more spending winter somewhere more hospitable.

As soon as she was in position, the local Navy took over setting braces and securing her against the wind. It was a miracle these things were seaworthy in the spring, exposed to the Antarctic elements that froze and cracked wood, buffeted the hull with ice and gravel, and generally tried to kick her off her feet.

Parks rose too fast and the world spun for a second before he could fix his gaze on the pale reflection coming off the snow-covered mountain in the distance. It seemed closer than he knew it was, and the contrast lit up the tight sprawl of Drummoc.

"Makes you regret every decision you've ever made, dunnit?" Gionn said. Parks thought about making a smart quip, but his lungs burned cold and he nodded instead.

"Where is Foster?" Ostuk joined them.

Parks gave a shrug. "Dogsitting?"

"The admiral asks to see both captains, and the three halots."

"Me and Foster actually prefer the term 'honkies.'"

"You have done well to secure the ship," he went on. "I am sure you know it's the only thing secure." Ostuk headed off toward a small party of men on approach.

"This is where we can't say stupid things, cunt. You and I. No stupid things."

"Maybe we should go find Foster."

"Do you recall our story?"

"I think so."

"Good. Remind me."

Ostuk turned and beckoned them forward before Parks could respond. They joined just behind the captain of the Navy ship—Amachar was his name. Before them was a white man in his forties, short and sturdy with a small gut that Parks knew insulated a barrel-thick torso. Cropped brown hair drew back along either side of a middle peninsula as gray flecks crept in everywhere but the top. His face looked haggard beyond his age, though his round cheeks wore a deep rose from the wind, and his chin bristled from an infrequent shave. Thick sideburns plunged to his jawline and swept back over his lip in a big, knife-trimmed mustache that framed a face of sleepless crescents beneath blue-gray eyes. He was dressed in simple leathers, shabbier than the men on either side, both Amposi like Barzos, both short and thin and near as old. They look pretty official to Parks, but he doubted they were accountants.

The man awaited them with crossed arms that seemed positioned to hold himself up more than to challenge anyone. The two groups took each other in for a moment before Ostuk spoke.

"You will want my cargo manifest."

"Dogs?"

Ostuk nodded, and the man did as well. He held out his hand.

"Admiralty letter?" Ostuk handed it over, and he passed it to his companion without looking.

"Are you the admiral?" Gionn blurted out.

The man sighed. "I guess I fuckin' am."

"Got to work on your presence a bit, then?"

"Gionn," Ostuk pleaded.

"No offense, of course. I also lack the presence of an officer, or any kind of worthwhile cunt for that matter. You and me both."

Parks backhanded Gionn's belly. A shot of air forced its way out of his lungs.

"Aye. You and me both," the admiral said, undisturbed. "I'll hear how forty men of the Amposi Navy ended up on a dog ship." Amachar opened his mouth, but the admiral held up his hand to silence him. He considered them, then pointed to Gionn. "From you."

"Who, these cunts?" He thumbed toward Amachar. "Dunno. I was at me oar."

"Did someone not explain the circumstances, perhaps later in the voyage? Would you have been curious about the forty extra passengers? Wonder how they came upon your ship?"

"Of course. I'm always suspicious of new cunts who join mid-voyage like that. It's like you said. I asked about it. And someone explained it." He thought for a second, and pointed at Parks. "Him. How was it you put it, mate?"

"A letter."

"Right. Letters. Someone on the ship had a message, for us."

"For the Assistant Viceroy."

"Right, that cunt. Oh! There was an urgent message, of grave importance for the Assistant Vicecunt. Amposi bein' lazy filth, they preferred not to bring it themselves, but hurried after us that we might carry the message for them. But their seamanship was…Amposi. And as they drew near to flag us, the storm laid 'em arse-over-barrel and had a good toss. To the credit of their luck, our able captain plucked 'em from Uinab's foul corpse before they went over boatless to Manhas."

"Message?" He extended his hand.

"Lost in the wreck, Admiral," Amachar answered.

"Do you recall the contents?"

"Sealed, sir."

"'Course."

"Sir, we have excellent seamanship. It is difficult to position two boats for a message. We were caught abeam the set—"

"I'll not second-guess a man makes the southern passage and still breathes, however he manages it. Me numbers are low, and I've reason to want them otherwise. We're grateful to the gods who spared you. And to you, for the sparin'," he addressed Ostuk. "I've already heard kind words of you from some of the men. I'll see that you're reimbursed for forty passages at top fare, soon as the Assistant Viceroy returns."

"Thank you, Admiral." Ostuk met eyes with Amachar, and the Navy man nodded. One of the Amposi made a polite gesture to Amachar. He returned it and parted their company without acknowledgment from the admiral. He stared at Ostuk until he, too, made the gesture and went off in the direction of his ship.

"As for you two," the admiral turned to Parks and Gionn. "And your unaccounted mate. Do you require work?"

"Consider us signed," Parks said. He got a strange look from the admiral.

"Would any or all of you be willin' to make a return trip north into the teeth of Omera, before the winter bites?"

Their faces lit up. "Your majesty, I think I can speak for all of us when I say, hell-to-the-yeah. I'm down. Foster, that's all he can think about. Gionn, you down, bro?"

"Happy to sail in good company, Admiral. Eh. May we have a word in private?"

"The meetin' place of liars. If it's worth sayin', these men'll hear it," he said of the two in his entourage.

Gionn wrinkled his nose and thought it over. "It pains me, sir. These are me mates. But I cannot live with meself if I'm not honest. T'would be a great disrespect to yourself and the others in the crew. That's a rough passage, rougher than this one knows. It'll takes the best of men, workin' as a single man, each knowin' his part and havin' the hair to pull it. These two, Parks and Foster, they're good lads. But they aren't worth a free sniff on the boats. I wager they've less experience as sailors than most do as passengers." Parks face plummeted. "Ask 'em anythin' a green bucket would know, and you'll hear 'em stutter nonsense. I love the lads. Been with me through thick and thicker. We've fought and sailed together, and they're useless cunts at both."

"Gionn, you little red slut," Parks muttered.

The admiral nodded. "I was afraid of that."

"Aye, it's too bad. Fine conversation, this one, at least." He indicated Parks.

"I meant that you all want to go north. I've no shortage of those. Can't afford another. And men who can't sail, or fight, or lie on behalf their mates are no good in the reserves, either. We'll find you somethin' to feed you. And I thank you for bringin' me forty good men and a pile of dogs."

The admiral turned for town. Parks glared a hole in Gionn's cheek as he stared at his feet.

The old fool still would not come inside. It was a good tukit. Stone covered in skin, near the middle of the town, with many tukits and lanes woven around it to confuse the wind spirits. It even had windows on the front and the back, in the northern style. She had heard the Kammatuk Mattaka were fond of these holes in their homes, which they sealed with wood and skin and ice when it grew cold. Kjartke could not understand the purpose of a hole in the wall. Not in the north, and not in a place like this. It was like Ostuk the Dog to make his home as his person, a mix of two peoples that fell short of both. He said it was theirs for the winter, and did not mention where he would go.

She rolled and tied the flap of fur seal that hung within, and put her hand through the opening into the fading light. Testing the sill, she leaned her forearms on it and craned her head outside. Tunguk still sat against the wall beside the door. He ate little. Now his eyes moved through the lanes as though he watched people walk, as though he listened to their conversations, where the lanes were empty. Kjarkte thought he would not see Spring. She'd known old men, strong and capable, who suffered a small wound, or a brief illness. The people assumed they would be strong again soon, but they always seemed to need a little more rest, a little more time. They spent less and less time in this world. Needed more and more help when they did. There would be another small thing. It was always small. Then it would grow worse, no medicine or song would take. Or they would smile and recover their spirit, perhaps for some time, until the family woke and they did not.

The others did not see it. They leaned heavy on the old man, and he could no longer bear it.

"Tunguk!" She called. He ignored her. Kjartke shrugged. Maybe this window would be good for her. She could have the tukit while the men saw to their own unraveling, and she could check on the old man while he waited outside.

Voices interrupted her dreaming, an accent she knew well. Foster rounded one of the tukits with Anset. When he caught sight of her, he said his thanks and the sailor departed. Tunguk's eyes fixed on him like a bird's. At least he knew his bond.

"Man, I'm gonna need to tie me a string to this place if I'm gonna keep comin' home," he looked it up and down. "Not too shabby. I guess. I don't fuckin' know."

"It is a good house," Tunguk said.

Foster grinned. "Then it's a good house. We just need to get us some street signs. How do yall even find shit?"

"Two places." Foster had heard this one. A few times. But he knew by now to let him elaborate. "You know one place, you are lost. You must know two places."

He looked around. "I see lots of places, I just can't tell 'em apart." His gaze turned upward to the tip of the white peak rising over all the buildings. He knew it was inland, and suddenly knew the harbor and the main strip were the opposite direction. "What's that mountain called?"

"That is no mountain," Tunguk said. "It is Urkuk."

"Urkuk. Any good hikin' trails?" Neither offered him anything. "Alright. Well I'm gonna go try out my navigational skills. Rustle up some food, maybe whatever passes for a drink. Anybody care to join?"

"I care to sit," Tunguk said. "But it is not a place for one like you to walk alone."

"What good will you do?" Kjartke snorted. "Rest. There is food inside." She disappeared, then stepped through the door flap and tied her knife sheath to her belt. Tunguk stood in protest.

"You are bound to no one, and no one to you. Now that we have arrived, you can make your trade. We will not ask you to care for old men and fools."

"There is time for work in winter. I choose."

The Tunguk he met not long ago would never have been sat down so easily by a woman, but this one braced his hands against the wall and slid back into his place. She waved her hand for him to lead. Foster gave her a look of surprise.

"If I show you, how will you learn?"

He glanced up at his mountain, and down at his newest home. Then he turned and followed the narrow zigzag arcs through the maze of wigwams, stacked of flat, uncut stone. Drummoc must have been grittier than he imagined, if he needed an armed woman to escort him. There wasn't much she could do if a bunch of Navy men gave them trouble, other than let him know they needed to run before he would have caught it himself. Maybe it was like walking through the ghettos back home: you needed someone of the local color to pass more-or-less unmolested.

Voices echoed over and around the wigwams and shattered like glass on the jagged rock, but the source rarely materialized. Children's shouts, or women in conversation. Tools scraping and tapping. He expected to see street-walkers and porch-setters. Instead, they passed only one boy the entire way. Every few turns he would look back for his peak. Even when he lost it momentarily, it reappeared in the curved "V" between roofs.

Kjartke still wasn't much of a conversationalist, so he kept his focus on his direction, knowing full-well his route was far from ideal. By the time he found the backbone of structures that lined the way in front of the harbor, the sun had gone entirely and taken his mountain with it, except for a ghostly glow fading in the twilight. He recognized the tall hulk that was Parks before the details came into view. Foster let out a whistle, and his friend headed their way. As he approached, Foster turned to say something to Kjartke just in time to see her disappear back into the town.

"I was wondering if someone was coming to get me," Parks said. He lowered his tone. "There've been developments." He explained the encounter with the local admiral, and Gionn's betrayal. Foster nodded along with a slight smile.

"It's almost a relief," he said. "I knew he'd fuck us eventually. Of all the times and ways he could've done it, I'd say we got off pretty easy."

"Easier than good old Oduy," Parks pursed his lips.

"Soon enough, we'll be down to three." He noticed Parks take a hard swallow. "She got where she wanted to go, and we can't say she didn't earn her way."

"Just as well. Easier to travel. Easier to piss when you don't have to hide your wiener."

"Speakin' of wieners."

Parks followed his gaze to a muscular shape as it disappeared into a long, low building that glowed with light.

"That's the only pub in town if you aren't Navy," Parks explained. "I've been standing outside for a few hours now so he'd have to face me if he wanted to eat." Parks spat and pulled a wad of something from his lip.

"You dippin'?"

"Brown man medicine," he took a strip of cloth from his belt, placed the chewed herbs on his shin gash, and tied it off. "Not bad once you get used to it."

"I'll take seven more lashes before I put that shit in my mouth again."

Parks patted him on the back. "How's that doing, anyway?"

Foster grimaced. "So good, I didn't even have to punch you just now."

"Come on, bud. I'll buy you a plate of dried fish and and a glass of bathtub hooch. We can make some new friends."

"Can't afford anymore of those."

"Eskimo Joe didn't turn out so bad."

"He's a fuckin' angel of goodness and mercy compared to everyone else I've met. But the way he looked when I left him, I don't know, brother. Might be you and me."

"I'll be your Lone Ranger if you'll be my Squanto. North-ho!" He struck a pose, one arm square on his hip, the other extended in a direction that Foster wasn't sure of, but was sure it was not north. "But first, the bar. And probably five or six months of spooning for warmth."

Gionn ducked through the door flap into the dancing orange light and slid along the wall until he felt he was a safe distance from the entryway. He waited with the corner of his eye fixed on the opening for the men. They were definitely following him. Maybe to the bar. Maybe for other reasons. The four young squains had picked him up when he left the shitter, where he'd spent a few hours dodging Parks and attempting to strike up friendly conversation with whoever happened through. He'd made many an ally in the shitter in his day, but none to be found here.

Why he didn't just walk right by the man was beyond him. You don't have to talk to him, he told himself. What's he gonna do, bash you? The cunt's unarmed, and he couldn't fight if he was. Nothing he could say would console himself. He wasn't afraid of them, Foster and Parks. Old Squain-o and the mean woman. He could kill them all if he had to. But he felt something he'd not felt in some time. Something like an open wound, where the flesh was gouged out. He'd known better and lost more, and long grown accustomed to it as it scabbed over, but this was fresh.

He'd nearly ditched them at Nunoc, and felt nary a thing. It would have been a good ditch here, too, if that admiral hadn't tricked him. What kind of high-ranking Navy cunt demanded integrity from his men? He'd be routed in his first real battle, which would not be with the enemy, Gionn suspected. If he could even find a man to follow him. He thought about trying to get in his good graces, become his mate, so he could be the one to draw the knife. The possibility of crawling back to be kicked away was too sickening to bear.

"Where's your pride, cunt?" He whispered aloud to himself, to his own surprise. That's the one always gets you, he added quietly. That's the one you should dodge, or cut. "Gionn. Gionn. Gionn." He whispered aloud again. He'd find a crew and a boat, and be back out of here. None to remember him, or for him to remember. It always worked out, no matter how hard he tried to the contrary. As he pressed into a rough wall in the public house, though, he felt as though he'd lopped off his hand to escape a frayed binding, and he was bleeding out.

It always works out, he repeated to himself. A cruel joke, that. Who are you, where are you, who's trying to kill you? The three questions he knew would sort him, give him his feet on a pitching deck. Some cunt named Gionn. Drummoc. Never been to Drummoc. Worse'n I imagined. Four squains.

He refocused on the door. No one entered. Far too much time if they'd indeed been heading for the bar. Definitely trying to kill him, then. Or did they know him from the boat? Maybe they were rowers. He couldn't see much in the hold, and couldn't tell squains apart when he did. Just four youths on a walk. Not everyone who follows you is trying to kill you, he reminded himself. Most of 'em are. But not all. He felt himself relax a bit. Besides, he carried a good sword to their stone rubbish. They knew that. If they really wanted him dead, they'd let him drink himself arseways and get him on the way out.

Who's tryin to kill you? Not soon, but now? Right now? No one.

He butt-pushed himself off the wall and scanned the room for the first time. It was crowded with familiar faces from the ship. Half of them Navy, they chose to drink in the common house, and though he didn't specifically recognize many of them, he could tell the more ragged squains had starved with him on the ship. The bulk of the crowd was local. Nothing else to do here. There were no proper tables or chairs, either. One long bar on the wall held the rot pots that the cooks guarded with more severity than the Navy cunts did Drummoc. Most ate standing from a bowl in hand. Only a few squains sat on the floor. They didn't seem to mind people stepping over and around them.

Oil lamps flicked shadows across the crowd like rippling water. They were thick, but nowhere near as boisterous at the Nunoc pub. It was still too loud to be heard without giving half a shout. This was the kind of room he liked to walk into. Easy to go unnoticed, but you could still shoulder your way out in a hurry if needed. He realized he'd failed to make his customary scan. Little point in Drummoc. Even the winter Navy here was the fleet of lost souls, the stuck and the exiled and the trembling spear. He noticed his chest regain some of its swell.

Gionn stuck both hands into the room like diving into water, and spread the bodies to plunge through. He'd have to swim near the back to get fed. It would be unwise to drink, but unlikely he'd resist. On tiptoes, he could get a look for the servers. He'd enjoy the new arrivals' bounty for the next day or two: free food, on the admiral. Charging a tired ship on arrival was an unspoken crime. The drinks would go to a tab, though. Even the food, after. He'd heard cruel things about Drummoc tabs. It would have to be paid at some point, but there'd be days or weeks to find work. His hands pressed down on shoulders to loft him higher, until he spotted one: an old squain woman with a pitcher. Not what he wanted, but she'd point him to the boy.

He pushed through, and spotted a group of four men with full bowls—a mixed lot from well-north, clustered tight to keep out the locals. These were more his people.

The nearest had his back to him, and he elbowed in that direction, making them sharper when it was a small squain in his way. When he was close enough to distinguish the group's laughter if not their words, a fair-brown head began a slow turn to profile, then all the way around. Gionn froze, and dropped to the floor behind the body of the crowd a moment before the man would have faced him. His pale skin turned whiter and his cheeks flushed. He crawled backwards at first, then spun and scrambled on all fours. Feet stumbled over him and stomped his fingers while his heart urged him onward. It recalled to him that time he ran through the heavy brush in Guaracan, vines and thorns and thick shoots tearing at him all the way, though he dared not slow. He didn't know where he was going or what a mess he'd arrive in, only that he must arrive in any state, anywhere but here.

A wide hand reached down and palmed his head to a stop. A cold, shooting pain from within surged down his spine. His eyes remained fixed on the fur seal boots in front of him. It was too crowded to pull his sword here, and Foster still had his knife. He thought about ripping the ankles out and clambering over the top, but something held him—something other than the strong hand.

"Is that an 'I'm trying to avoid you' crawl, or more of a 'groveling at your feet for forgiveness?'"

The voice was unmistakable. His face flared with hope like a lit torch as he looked up at Parks and Foster.

"Mates! Shield me to the exit. You'll have your grovelin' until you grovel for me to stop."

"What friend did you vouch for now?"

"Get me to the fuckin' door, cunt!"

Foster laughed and tried to spot who he hid from, but no one was obviously interested. Gionn squirmed between their legs to the far side.

"Fine. Crawl." They walked in a human shield behind him as he scuttled around knees and slipped under the flap.

The dark wrapped around them like a shroud as a brisk stride carried them down the main row of buildings. Only then did Gionn pause to look back. No one followed.

"You were only in there a couple minutes," Foster said. "How'd you manage to piss somebody off that fast?"

"Ah, he's been pissed a while. Some cunts find me disposition hard to get on with. Are you still sore about the whole Navy thing?"

"You mean the thing earlier today where you betrayed our friendship and made sure there was no hope of us leaving the island, then ran away and refused to so much as look at us?" Parks scowled.

"Aye, that one." He brushed himself off. "You've took it wrong."

"Can't wait," Foster said.

"I just saved your lives, ungrateful cunts. You saw how bad goin' south was with a deck overhead. Neither of you could survive a northbound passage into the autumn gales at an oar, which is what it'd be. Admit it: you're shit sailors. Did I lie? You'd spend it prayin' you weren't called upon to do anythin' heroic, much less row, because it you were, everyone's dead. Do you know what ice is?"

"Are you fuckin' kiddin?"

"Well I don't know! Most cunts go their lives and never see it. Some of 'em think it's a sailors' tale. You seen it on mountains, but did you know it floats upon the waves in winter? Crowds around your ship and crushes the hull between it's cold fingers?" He made a twisting motion between his palms.

"Yes, we know what fucking ice is and we've seen every kind you can imagine. A couple you can't. Where we're from, we put that shit in our drinks," Parks said. Gionn recoiled in horror.

"If you don't believe me, I don't blame you. Everyone thinks he can do everythin' til he tries. And I've been dishonest at times."

"Ha!" Foster's laugh rose an octave.

"But you can believe me on this: I done you the best favor I can do a man of any standin' in me heart. I spared you me mateship. You've known me only a short while, but you know me well-enough. You throw your fates in with mine, you'll not get 'em untangled. I'm a shit mate. I don't want to betray you, but I will. Soon as I see a shred of gain in it. Better I let you down now than when it gets you killed."

"I believe it. But let's not pretend you were tryin' to do us a favor."

"Speakin' of favors. I don't *think* the cunt saw me, but I'd hate to spend the night in the poorman's quarters. It'd be the first place he looks. If there were a private hut you had at your disposal—"

"No," Parks said.

"Alright, then." He slunk off a few steps. "Wouldn't be askin' your loyalty. Just a safe place for a night, a week, whatever you thought was fair." They didn't respond. Gionn resumed his walk, then turned again. "Just that it'll be hard for me to get food and drink for a whole winter without bein' seen. If I didn't have a mate to help me. That bein' the only spot for it, and him bein' likely to also want food and drink throughout the winter. Would be hard not to run into the cunt without someone to help me." Gionn waited a moment for a response, then hung his head and shuffled off down the lane.

He soon disappeared into the Antarctic black, a cold black that hung absolute and reminded that it would gather more of the day for itself until day was a memory. Now even the mountain was gone. Foster wasn't sure why he expected otherwise. Maybe he thought Kjartke would stick around to lead him back. There was no hope of finding the wigwam in the dark. They headed back to the flickering pub, where whoever's enemies may lurk, they were enemies not yet shared.

Dried fish and water restored them. Whatever the liquor was, it smelled foul, nor was it free according to Ostuk, so they let it walk past with ease. Neither spoke until they were full.

"You think ol' girl's comin' back for us?"

Parks looked around. The crowd had thinned, and a handful of drunks and travelers who couldn't stumble home, or hadn't a home to stumble to, begun to claim spots on the floor.

"We've slept worse places than this."

"I wonder if that poor man's hotel he mentioned is any better."

"It isn't, because Gionn's there."

"Don't say his name too loud," Foster lowered his voice. "His 'mate' might still be here."

"Gionn Gionn, Gionn," Parks belted. "Fuck him."

"'Fuck him' is fine. I been advocatin' for 'fuck him' a lot longer than you have. But that's different than fuckin' him. I prefer to part ways in peace."

"Not a courtesy I can imagine he's ever shown anyone."

Foster grinned. "Don't be so butt-hurt. Your problem was you liked him. You thought he was your buddy. Me? I'm lookin' at the only person in the world I'd expect to not cut my throat."

"I didn't trust him. I just thought he might possibly be a little more grateful, all things considered."

"Butt-hurt. Come on. Let's bring him a bowl of fish so he don't come after us out of spite."

Parks lowered himself against a wall and closed his eyes. "Don't take too long. I need a body-heat-buddy."

Foster had no idea where the poor folk slept, but it made sense that even the penniless needed to be out of the elements here. And it would be conspicuous. Lit, or loud, or smelling of farts. He walked in the direction Gionn had gone until a small flame appeared. He turned back and noted the oil lamp outside the pub still visible in the distance. Two places. Made sense that there would be some way for a visitor to find a meal and a place to sleep.

The poorman's quarters, he'd called it. It was flat-walled with a steep vaulted roof, though barely more than six feet to the top of the wall. Even where the Mattaka outnumbered everyone else, it was interesting that all of the public buildings fought tooth and nail against their architecture whenever they could stand it. It still made use of the same rock, probably the only abundant material, but there was plenty of timber framing, and even the stacking struck him as different. It was not important enough to have a real door, though. A pair of heavy skins hung inside and out, and he wondered if some other arrangement would be made once the winter started to howl. He slipped in, and was relieved to find a pair of lamps burning, one on either end. The floor was a sprawl of bodies in various stages of sleep, not a lane to walk nor a rhyme or reason to it. Most of the faces were obscure, buried in their own arms, or a blanket, or the dark of the middle. The majority he could make out were Mattaka, and something told him Gionn would not enjoy being surrounded by many of them. One hand on the wall, he tiptoed over people with more consideration than they likely expected of one another until he made out the silhouette of a small concave nose, delicately sloped except for a sharp drop below the bridge where it had broken and healed long ago. Not the straight, flat profile of the Mattaka people, it was both foreign to the place and very familiar to him.

"Fish," he kicked the leg where Gionn sat upright and awake against the wall. A hand came up to accept it, but Gionn set it on the rock floor and resumed his distant stare.

Foster retraced his steps, turned left out the door, and held course until he could make out the form of the pub, though the light had blown out. Only then did he realize the moon had returned from behind the clouds to lay a silver sheen across his path. Over the line of the town, the mountain face glowed against a backdrop of stars daring to peek out here and there. He collected Parks, and they snaked their way through wigwams—backtracked once all the way to the main drag to reorient themselves, then another half hour of canvassing until at last they happened across one with a window, just to the right of the mountain behind it. No mountain, actually: Urkuk. Tunguk reclined in the same position as before. Their footsteps woke him.

"You are back. It is good. I am too old to sleep outside."

The crowd that gathered at the harbor upon first light dwarfed the one that welcomed the *Juhketappat.* Navy men pushed forward through Mattaka, who hung back with a removed curiosity. One and all faced the ship that had been pulled out nearby the day before. It was a long, open build with short quarter decks and a single mast dead center. There was little else to her but benches all the way through, and space along the middle that served as a hold, though no provisions had yet been stored, nor was the sail even on the yard. The sparse vessel loitered alone in the water. She pitched gently against the cleats in a cold morning breeze that snaked its way down from the mountain heights to join the sea. A light gray blanket of distant clouds over the mainland across the channel suggested their sun may not last, but for the time, Drummoc basked in a mild Autumn day that stirred every part of it to life.

A mahogany-skinned Amposi entered late and marched with purpose before the ship. He wore thin slippers and a pair of leather trousers that seemed ready to rot away from his legs. It was a sharp contrast to the pale brown tunic, beaded along every edge with a wide collar of more beads that dipped down over his sternum. On his head sat a simple round cap, half a sphere, and more beads on the edge. The upper half of his articles looked like a set—one that remained tucked away from common use. A simple choker necklace wrapped around his throat. Every spot of skin above it was painted red and black and white.

The crowd stirred at his arrival, a ripple of whispers and a few jeers. A mix of anxiety and amusement. He raised his hands for silence, and a fair portion obeyed. The man began to sing in his tongue, which brought more impatient outbursts from the Navy at the edges. It failed to deter him, and he finished his verse before reaching his hand into a leather bag strung from his belt. A roar went up as he produced a single white albatross feather.

A second man used the applause to slip before the crowd. A few noticed him, and changed their calls. He was a full-head taller than any man around him, lighter-skinned, with a wide face scrunched tightly from brow to lip. A sparse beard grew better on his neck than his chin, and he wore a wide-brimmed leather hat that curled under its own weight at every opportunity it got.

Painted Face sung a few more lines, then touched the feather to the man's head. He turned to the side, and held it aloft between the crowd and the ship. A chorus from the center immediately began to scream and curse. "Closer!" They blistered him with abuse. He crept nearer the ship, but not close enough to satisfy the crowd.

"Closer!"

He negotiated the distance with a begrudged step and a glance back, fearful of the reaction he'd get if he failed to listen. When his original distance was halved, he stood firm, maybe twenty feet from the moored vessel. A number of the men who'd cursed him gave a cheer. It was enough. Painted Face tested the breeze blowing offshore, and adjusted his angle that it his body no longer stood between the wind and the feather. Hundreds of lips fell silent.

The feather danced and jumped between his finger and thumb as though it knew what was coming. He lowered his hand at first, then crouched to bring it even lower until it was only a few feet above the ground.

"*Wapat!*" The man screamed. The plume shot from his grip. It swirled once, and bounced off the ground. The crowd gasped. Then it tumbled twice more, found a current, and lifted clear over the side, gaining height as it sailed out to sea.

The men in the center erupted in furious threats as Painted Face made a quick retreat. One man had to be restrained by his friends as spit flew from his red-veined face. The cohort at the center earned the taunts of some of the Navy men, and shouted a few kind words in return. All around, others laughed hysterically, or shrugged and turned for their business.

"The fuck did we just see?" Foster frowned.

"I have a feeling it's going to be a long winter," Parks said flatly.

Kjartke was waiting outside for them when they found the hut. It was getting easier, especially in the daylight, but they still passed it by several "blocks" and had to double back when that became obvious.

She held out a scrap of soft brown leather. Parks snatched it up.

"What is that?"

"Uh-uh!" Parks twisted away. "It's addressed to me."

"It come in the window," Kjartke explained.

"Where's Tunguk?" Foster couldn't hide his impatience as Parks read to himself.

"Wandering."

"Did you read this?" Parks looked up at her. She glared back, and he realized she thought he was insulting her.

"What's it say, brother? Come on, ain't no 'addressed' to nobody here."

"It's top secret. I can't read it aloud," he handed it to Foster. "But it concerns you."

PORKS
MEET WITH FAWSTER GION
INGPUTKA DARK
MATE
CAR TO LET NON SEE
BURN LETERES

"And you didn't see no one drop it off?" Kjartke shook her head. "Not even a hand? Man? Woman?" She repeated her answer.

"You mind givin' us a minute in private?"

They closed the flaps of the wigwam behind them and lowered their voices.

"Kind of fun, right? I never thought I'd get a letter."

"Gionn knows how to write, don't he?"

"So he was fond of saying. I don't know. I feel like he would have better spelling than this."

"That's the sense you get just from talkin' to him, is it?"

Parks pulled back the window flap to let enough light in for a second look. "You think it's an illiterate trap."

"It's illiterate, alright. What the fuck is 'ingputka' supposed to be?"

"Maybe it's another person we're supposed to bring. Or the person we're meeting, and he's got dark skin."

"I'm pretty sure it means after dark. Maybe a place? Don't look like just a misspelled word. Though I'm sure it's misspelled."

"'Mate'. Could be a chick. Who wants to mate with us?"

"All of us?"

"Don't even act like you can't name a few girls who would've written this."

"It's how they say 'friend.' Meet me after dark, I'm a friend. Care to let none see."

"None of that eliminates the possibility that some old girl's hungry for a slice of white meat."

"I don't think the literacy rate's very high, *Porks*. And someone knew you could read this."

"It's my air of intelligence. They heard your drawl and knew they'd have a better shot writing to me." Foster opened his mouth to speak, but Parks interrupted. "Yeah, yeah. Someone wants to kill us, probably Gionn."

"So you're not gonna go."

"Go where? I don't even know if this is a place, and if it is, I have a hard-enough time finding a wall to piss on after dark."

"Good. Cause there's better ways to make friends than meetin' someone off of the Drummoc Craigslist because both of yall share an interest in writin' love letters with the caps-lock on."

"I just wish I could reply and say we're not going to make it. Feels rude to leave someone waiting out all night in the cold."

"Even if it's Gionn?"

"Fuck Gionn. I'm just fucking bored. It's gotta be, like, what? Nine a.m.? And I don't have shit to do until spring."

"I could use some help."

"With what?"

"I plan to make the most powerful friend a man can have, and get myself some gainful employment doin' somethin' cushy, probably indoors, if not a fast ship outta here."

Parks laughed. "Really, Mister Fawster? And how do you plan to go about that?"

"Barzos." Foster quickened his step to keep pace with the admiral, who marched spear drawn away from the settlement toward the long, low building that housed the latrine.

"Never heard of him," the admiral growled. The two Amposi men Parks recognized from the landing followed at a distance far enough to be polite, but not so far they couldn't hear every word.

"Yes, sir, I realize that. He's an official somethin'-or-other on Nunoc. Asked me to bring word to the Assistant Viceroy for him."

The admiral stopped. "Is this a different message from the one went down with the ship?"

"Yes, sir."

"One you'll not share with an admiral?"

"It ain't a secret or nothin'. It's just a job reference. Barzos said to give his regards to the man, let him know how he's been, and maybe he'd look out for us."

The admiral resumed his march. Foster hurried after. "I know there's protocols and procedures for meetin' with a man of standin'. That's why I'm goin' through you."

"And who did you go through to get to me?" Foster stuttered something, but the admiral cut him off. "Relax, me son. You want the protocol for visitin' the assistant viceroy?" He stopped again and pointed over the roof of the latrine, across the channel to the foot of an immense range, dressed in the white of ice, black rock at the hems. It hid its face in low clouds and stood off against the island, as though willing to ignore its presence if it kept its distance.

"There he is. Go with me blessin'."

"The mountains?"

"Camne Drumlag. Where he's been for weeks." They arrived at the door to the latrine. "You can come with me if you like. If you can take care of yourself."

"Is it dangerous there?"

"I was speakin' of the shitter."

Foster blushed. "Sorry, sir. I didn't mean to interrupt your business."

"Then you'll not lend me a strong arm?." Foster and Parks looked at one another. "I've word that someone's been lurkin' in there. Hidin' his face, sayin' odd things. Shitter's a popular place for an ambush. Bound to run into your man, eventually."

He pushed through the flaps. Foster shot his arm through to catch them, and followed with Parks on his tail. It took a few seconds for their eyes to adjust. The room was nothing but four walls and a roof over a natural crevasse. Large rocks sat near the trench. At the far end, a man squatted with his trousers down, holding onto a rock for balance as he hung his ass over the opening. He looked at them with surprise, then carried on. There were no inner walls, no privacy. Little piles of small, sea-rounded rocks were scattered the length of the crevasse. It dawned on him that they were the local equivalent of toilet paper. Either this was the only shitter on the island, or the only obvious one. The Mattaka probably had other ways. The whole scene felt like a desperate northern attempt to insulate themselves in one more way from a hostile continent.

"Have you seen a strange man lurkin' about?" The admiral called.

"Fuck you!"

"*Hoy!*" One of the Amposi shouted. "That's the admiral!"

"Still?"

"Aye."

The man returned to his business. "Looks like the crapper is once again safe for the law-abiding citizens of Antarctica," Parks proclaimed. The admiral thrust his spear into Foster's hand, then dropped his trousers and peed into the opening.

"If you do decide to cross, can you do me a kindness?"

"Happy to."

"Inquire about me boys. He's still got twenty-six of 'em. Ask him when they, and he, can be expected to return."

"Why's he got twenty-six of your boys?"

"He's supposed to have near 200. Sent the rest back early, no explanation on offer." He shook himself dry. "Not safe for him and his family with so few beside him. And none of the local boys are back, either."

"Is that normal?" Parks asked.

"Normal? I've never heard of an assistant viceroy. I guess anything this one does is normal. And I'll be askin' the next one to explain himself." He took the spear back from Foster.

Many boats arrived at the harbor. Every time he passed, there was another. A tall mast, an amu. A warship, thick with oars. Runners and rammers. Mattaka in their skin boats paddled alone. All day long, they came with passengers who had never been here. Who did not know where to go. So many ships coming, and few that left. It troubled him. He watched for Lenet and the men, and was glad he did not see them. There was the *Juhketappat*, clear and brimming. Others he could hardly make out. It made him wonder if it had always been so busy.

His head throbbed, and he had to shut his eyes against it. When he opened them, they were at his side. His heart fluttered and relaxed, like a taut rope that suddenly gained slack, and it took a tremendous effort not to smile. Foster and Parks followed his gaze out over the water. The empty water. The whaler had already been pulled ashore, where it waited among its crew—he suspected for some time to come.

"Whatcha lookin' at?" Foster asked.

"The sea."

"What's it tellin' you?"

"It is time for certain people to come home."

"I can think of one of them, eh buddy?" Parks said. "An old man who wanders off and stares into space. You don't rest up that ticker and that noggin', you're not going to remember your name, much less be able to keep up with us."

"You have been talking to the woman. She thinks I am dead."

"You do kind of look like a corpse that got stuck on the heel of a ghost like a piece of toilet paper. But that's not why we're here."

"More adventure."

"More adventure," Foster confirmed.

"Do you hate us?" Parks asked.

"Yes."

"But you'll protect us."

"If I can. It is dangerous."

"Always."

"More now. I talk to people. It is a strange time here. The spirits are restless. The people are restless. You must not go alone."

"What are we talkin'? Are there people who wanna mess with us?"

"Maybe. Already there is word of tricksters stealing food, stealing tools and objects even at twilight. It is not until Winter we would expect them."

"Hood rats, we call 'em," Parks added.

"Then you know. Do not believe what these 'hood rats' say. They are lies. Keep your things close."

"Speakin' of tricksters," Foster nodded to Parks, who produced the strip of leather cloth from his pocket and held it in front of Tunguk. The old man regarded it from a distance.

"It is letters."

"Sorry, bro. Forgot about the whole literacy rate issue your people have. We want to know if you've ever heard this word. *Ingputka.*"

"I know this place. What are the other letters?"

"Then it's a place. Here?" Tunguk nodded.

"Someone wants to meet us." Foster explained.

"Who?"

"Probably Gionn," Foster said. "But we don't know."

"It is not Gionn. If we go, best to leave now. We will be back by dark."

"They want to meet after dark." Tunguk's eyes slipped back out to the sea. "What does it mean? Ingputka?"

"It is a well."

"Like for water?"

"The well of the dead. Those who live here know it, but they will not go at night. At night is when the spirits come out. I wonder who writes you. Your people do not know this place. Mine will not meet you."

"You sayin' it's haunted?"

"It is a bad place for good things, but a good place for bad things. Whoever sends for you is clever. Only the dead will hear you."

Even in the daylight the poorman's quarters took his sight the moment the flaps swished shut behind him. It wasn't even clear if the room was bare, or brimming as it had been after dark. Foster pressed his shoulder to the wall and brushed in the same direction he had before. Now he could make out a few shapes shifting on the floor, a lighter gray than the surroundings. The lamps were not lit. No sense wasting oil when anyone who wanted to see could just go outside. Within moments, he felt the emptiness of the room, and didn't know how. Maybe the tiny footfalls echoed a little more, or his eyes had grown accustomed to picking out movement.

"Gionn." He said quietly, and heard the words roll across the rock. "Gionn!" He said louder, sure that the man would silence him for fear his name would be overheard. No response. Maybe he was out, but if he didn't want to be seen, there weren't many places he could go, and this would be as good as any to escape an ambush. Foster walked to the spot where he'd found him before. It was empty.

"Is that food you've got?" The voice came from the opposite side.

"Fish. And water."

"Brother Foster. I knew we were mates!" Foster followed the sound and handed over a bowl of dried white fish and a bladder of water. Gionn didn't waste time with thanks. He downed what must have been half the water in a single gulp, and shoved a filet into his mouth before he bothered to speak. "Where's Parks?"

"Butt-hurt."

"I feel fuckin' terrible, the way things played out. Mostly because I'm stuck between sleepin' in squain piles and bidin' me time in the shitter."

"Yeah, I wouldn't do that anymore. People are startin' to notice."

"Fuck me arse-side."

"At least your ol' boy hasn't found you yet."

"Aye, thanks to you. And Parks. I swear, cunt. Swear an oath. Get me to him and I'll have us new as old in no time. I been up thinkin' of the things I'll say. Do you know how many conversations I've had with the two of you since I last saw you?"

"Is this one goin' as good as you planned?"

"It's nothin' like me plan, and I'll kindly remind you to stick to your verses. Here, let me try one: I know we're not mates. Can't be. Never were. But by the gods who gave me nothin', we're brothers. Born from the same filthy cunt, into the same filthy world. We don't have to trust each other. We don't even have to like each other. But let us see it through—together."

Foster nodded. "That was pretty good."

"If I say so meself."

"We ain't gettin' back together, though. Me and Parks and Tunguk had a talk. We like you here. You can't hurt nobody. I feed you, or you starve. And any little bite I give you, you gotta take."

"I don't like the way this is headin'. You'll need to save your copper for Kjartke if that's your aim."

"Ingputka." There was a confused silence. He repeated himself.

"Stop spittin' on me, cunt. I heard you. And I'll hear no more of your nonsense squain talk."

"Do you know it?"

"I don't care to."

"How much privacy do we have here?" He lowered his tone.

"As much as I'll get."

"We got a letter."

"A letter."

"You know. Writin', on a page. A message."

"Letters. More than one, I assume."

"No it was one—what? I mean, yeah. I guess. It was one letter, one page, with multiple letters written on it."

"From who?"

"We thought it was you. But Tunguk says otherwise."

"Wasn't me. Who could possibly have his letters, know you got yours, and want to tell you somethin' to your own benefit that he can't say to your face?"

"That's what we're afraid of. They wanna meet us."

"Nice knowin' you."

"And the letter—or *letters*—asked that you come, too."

The proud square head hung. "Mentioned me by name, did they?"

"Yup."

"Do you recall how the name was spelled?"

"Why?"

"I'd like it to be spelled right, cunt!"

"G-I-O-N. One "N".

"Close enough."

"What does it mean?"

"Means we're back together. Mates for all the ages."

"You know who wrote it."

"Maybe. The man who begrudges me, he's got his letters. I wouldn't expect him to misspell me name, but there it is. He likely seen us together. You're marked now, same as me."

"Who is he? What's his name?"

"No man of particular import. I've always called him Shitstain."

Foster chuckled. "And you say he doesn't like you?"

"All that stuff I said. How you was useless, can't fight. I didn't mean that. You're fair cunts. I was just tryin' to protect meself. Mates are never kind to me in the end. I travel alone. I scrap alone. Wank alone. Served me well, so far. But you know what occurred to me? Sittin' here, alone, as I would have it? I'm never that kind to me, either. It'll be an ambush. That, I can tell you. For once, though, I'm not squirmin' or fleein'. And don't take this as a compliment, cunt. The difference—I think, the only difference—is now I got someone to face it with. Maybe not a mate, but someone like a brother who don't really like you, but he looks out for you anyway, cause your mum's made him feel bad enough about everything you do. If this has to be it, I'm glad to draw me last sword and last breath with the likes of you."

"That was one of those lines you practiced, wasn't it? You just want us to go with you because you'll have four instead of one. And if we get cut down, it might give you a chance to run away."

"I tweaked the bit on the end just now. Did you like it?"

"Honestly? It was solid. Didn't need it, though. We're bringin' you for the same reason."

A clouded moon shone like a silver bulb through a veil and spoiled their perfect darkness. It was still plenty dark that Parks could not see the faces of his companions. Their rough shapes shifted side to side, fidgeted with whatever weapons they held. All but the Eskimo Joe-shape. He held so still, the eyesight that turned men to blurs in the daytime lost him entirely. But he felt the reassuring presence.

Perfect darkness would have been better for slipping away from an ambush. This would at least give them a chance to see one coming. There was nowhere to hide. This was Ingputka, and Ingputka was a small crevasse on an open plain of rock. He couldn't see the hole, but Joe had told them it was to their left. Whatever happened, they must run right of the moon. Right was Drummoc, a little under two miles by his reckoning. If it had proper city lights, they'd be able to see it. Left was a plunge into the well of the dead. Look at the moon, he reminded himself. If you have to take a few swings first, or get knocked down, look at the moon before you run. Right.

A cold shiver reverberated down his spine. "This place is seriously fucking creepy," he whispered. Foster shushed him. Parks had never seen a ghost, nor did he care to start now. He didn't even believe in them, though the fact gave him no consolation. Every outline, every wind-scattered pebble was fodder for his imagination. He prayed it was only humans who wanted to kill him. His spear would solve that well-enough. Hands clawed over the top of the crevasse and pulled themselves up, an army of red eyes in rank against them. The breeze came over them from inland, now. They could hear it gain momentum, down from the cold heights. Specters walked between them, sized them up, tickled the back of his neck and dared him to flinch.

"Guys, I feel like we're not alone. Am I the only one not having a good time?"

"Piss yourself," Gionn suggested from a dozen feet ahead. "Calmed *me* down a bit."

"We gotta stop talkin', yall. Keep your eyes peeled for movement. We got here first. They'll be comin' from Drummoc."

"Fuck Drummoc. I'm watchin' the arsehole of the dead."

"I can't even see you fuckers."

"Yeah, me neither. Tunguk? You got a visual?"

"I can see what is coming."

"What does that mean?" Parks sounded flustered. "Like, in general? Or something's coming, and you can see what it is, but for some reason you're not sharing any details?"

"I watch for those who come."

"*Not* a clarification."

"Warn me if you see the ghost of an old squain woman," a fifth voice rumbled through the dark from the direction of Ingputka. Parks felt a hot surge of electricity shoot through his face, and he clinched too late to prevent a squirt of liquid from shaking loose down his thigh. Their feet scuffled over rock as they spun to level their weapons at the sound.

"Had to put her in the hole back when I was sergeant-at-arms." They all froze in confusion. A silhouette emerged walking in their direction. The sheer terror of the initial noise settled into a tug-of-war between fear and memory. It was familiar, though Parks couldn't place the almost-Irish accent he'd come to know from Gionn. "She was carvin' curse stones for everyone she thought had it in for her sons. Throwin' 'em down the well, so the dead would torment 'em."

"Admiral?" Foster guessed.

"Costig," the silhouette came forward and removed the hood of his cloak, so that the outline looked more like a man than a ghoul.

"Where the hell'd you come from?"

"Joe, you're supposed to be watching for interlopers!" Parks caught his gasping breath.

"I don't recall askin' to meet a Joe."

"He's our local Injun guide," Parks explained.

"Then you'll forgive him. I was wedged in the crack."

"In the crack that leads to the land of the dead. I'd have shat myself."

"Aye. Good lot it's the same that runs under the latrine."

"Are you alone?" Foster asked.

"My business requires it. I'll not ask who you are that you suspected an ambush. Do you trust this Joe?"

"More than fuckin' Gionn," Parks said.

"Gionn, where you at, brother?"

"You will have to shout," Joe said.

Parks and Foster raised their voices in alternation. "Gionn! *Gionn!*" Off in the distance, from the direction of Drummoc, came a faint cry: "*Hoy!*"

"Where you at, dude?"

"Who's there?" The voice reached them.

"Get over here, you fuckin' pussy!" They heard footsteps jogging back in their direction.

"Me letters were good, then?" There was a hopeful lilt of pride to Costig's voice. "You understood them?"

"Oh. Uh, yup," Parks said. "Super clear."

"Two 'N's in me name, cunt," Gionn panted up.

"I trust you'll survive the offense."

"How'd you know I could read?" Parks relaxed his spear for the first time.

"I knew you were a learned man when I saw you were useless, and far from home."

"And you figured our Mattaka friends would know the place," Foster ventured.

"Aye. Plain to see why the squains won't come 'round after dark."

"I don't get why they'd go here at all."

"It is a sacred place," Joe said. "Children come to prove they are brave. Lovers hide from sight. The people come to ask questions of the dead, to answer in dreams."

"Do they do it?"

"Yes. But the dead are as the living. Most are liars, or fools. It is hard to know who speaks the truth."

"The question is why an admiral must bring us here to terrify us when we could meet at the hall over a nice drink," Gionn retorted.

"It's the Navy we're hidin' from. Apologies for givin' you the rough tongue when you landed. Had to make a show of it. I don't know how much you know of the situation here, but there's work for you if you'll have it. The pay's handsome, and it'll get two of you north before the winter."

"None of your cunts'll do it, and you're throwin' coin at strangers. Nothin' about this sounds appealin'. Well, except goin' north. And the coin. What was the job, then?"

"Tolba has declared himself Farri."

"*Ha!*" Gionn snorted.

"Who the fuck is Tolba?" Parks said.

"King of Ampos," Gionn explained. "Thus, of Hiade."

"OK, what the fuck is Farri?" Foster added.

"Is this one light?" Costig asked.

"I told you these cunts were worthless."

"You'll have to get a history of the kingdom from your mate another time. If you've got no ties, though, you'll be perfect. The farri dispatched a ship to bring us word before Winter fell, so we could make our preparations. They tried to time it so news would arrive after the traffic had left for the season. But there was one delayed."

"The whaler in the harbor."

"Aye. She's the only ship in a position to sail who knows what traffic's to come in Spring. We got men quit for the whalers every year. But this time… I'd say that the enthusiasm is runnin' higher than usual."

"I'm lost," Parks confessed.

"You're sayin' men are defectin'. Because that news is somehow valuable?"

"If they reach Taclann, it is not valuable. It is *in*valuable, and quite harmful to the interests of Ampos. And they'll sail any day—soon as they get the auspices."

"How many men under your command?" Foster probed.

"Currently? A louse over 400."

"And you can't stop a boat with what—sixty oars—from sailin'?"

"Ask me how many were under me command when the news arrived."

"OK."

"Fifty marines."

"Still lost," Parks said.

"The whaler lost most of her crew to other ships earlier in the season. Once we learned the farri was sendin' reinforcements, the admiral at the time and forty of his closest mates promptly quit and signed aboard. Two days later, the new admiral had all of 'em arrested. Then *he* quit and filled their seats with his own. I went from sergeant-at-arms to admiral in under a week, and only because I got me letters and enough men who'll stand for me.

"Executed the first admiral for treason, and I yanked his mates from prison and re-enlisted 'em, mostly because I need the men, though it's done well to make the former admiral and his boys sweat, knowin' the men whose seats they stole are, at least for now, carryin' blades for Farri Tolba."

"You can't just arrest everyone on the ship?" Foster was confused.

"I can order me men to slaughter every single one of 'em, and they'll do it. Then the next day, sixty of 'em will gladly take their places, right after they kill me."

"Fuck. Sounds like you got a bit of a discipline issue in your Navy," Foster said.

"Aye, a bit. There's good loyal lads, praise Tamar-Atxl, but if I send an Amposi—especially one they well know—I send him to his death."

"You want us to infiltrate the ship? As *spies*? And do what, exactly?" Gionn huffed.

"Stop it from reachin' Taclann. Redirect it to Nunoc. Somehow. I don't care, there's a thousand ways."

"Will our gold-laden purses not be a giveaway? I suspect we can't be paid in advance."

"You cannot. But the Viceroy will reward you handsomely. You'll also be deliverin' a message on me behalf, concernin' his new assistant."

"Two of us," Foster clarified.

"That's right."

"What about the third?"

"I need one to keep an eye on the Assistant Viceroy. You said you had a reference from his man. Perhaps you'd be right for it."

"No can do, brother. Me and him are a package deal," he indicated Parks before realizing the admiral couldn't see his thumb. "Me and Parks."

"I'll not be stayin' here all winter. No deal," Gionn said.

"Think about it, Gionn: it's perfect. You claim Barzos sent you. The dude's over there on camp-whatever—"

"Camne Drumlag."

` "That one. You could avoid your old buddy *and* make some coin."

"He'll not be there all Winter will be?"

"He'd be mad." Costig thought for a moment. "So it's possible."

"No deal. Whaler, or nothin'."

"By nothin', you mean you'll spend the winter here with nothin'. Have you got a lad doesn't like you?"

"No. Foster's a bit of a mongrel. Doesn't have a head for complex social relationships."

"Uh-huh," Foster said.

"You know them mates you always have a foul word for. Always jabbin' and makin' like you don't get on. In his mongrel world, there's good people and bad people. Virgins and whores, and none between. Must have grew up in a great hall or somethin'. Besides, I'm the only competent sailor of the bunch. I'll be on the whaler."

"I don't care who does what. You get the whaler to Nunoc, you'll all be reunited in the spring, with purse to get you anywhere you please."

"Look, we appreciate your offer. We're just gonna have to work out a few details. Can we think on it?"

"That ship could get pinned as early as tomorrow mornin'."

"Foster's the least-charmin' of the two. He'll come with me. Your lesser viceroy will enjoy Parks' company."

"Me and Parks don't split."

They went on arguing, but their words melted into meaningless echoes, clapping off of one another. Parks wobbled, then went very still. He looked at the sound, and felt as if he stood behind himself, watching them all from above. The air bubbled with noises that meant nothing. Not just his friends. The land itself seemed to whisper in hushed tones. The sky and the rock, the mountain and the unseen fissure. The things he feared who slept within. A square sail against a blue sky flashed in his mind and he blinked hard to settle himself. There was a feeling of dizziness. He tilted over and crashed into the ground with a thud.

Thin hands grabbed his elbow to help him up. Eskimo Joe looked frail, but his bones felt like steel claws, fire-tempered from years of use. Another pair of short, meaty hooks took his other arm. Costig provided most of the heft that brought him back to his feet.

"Are you well, lad?"

"Aye," Parks answered, and wasn't sure why he answered as the admiral would have. "Yeah. I'm good. It's so dark, just lost my footing."

"Admiral, sir," Foster went right back to it. "Is there any way you can get all three of us on the whalin' ship? Actually, make that four. Tunguk comes with us."

"By tomorrow? No chance. Two'll be desperate enough."

"The ship will not sail tomorrow." Tunguk spoke for the first time. There was a pause while they processed it.

"How do you know, old man?"

"I do not know. We will see."

"For fuck's sake," Gionn protested. "You're all a batch of warts I can't pick loose!" He muttered a string of curses under his breath as he started off.

"Where you goin', fool?" Foster called.

"I despise intrigues. Sailin' and impalin', them's me trades."

"He'll come around. I'm sure I can… incentivize it," Foster assured the admiral.

"No time. Sorry we couldn't come to terms." The admiral started away. "It goes without sayin'—"

"Never happened," Foster said.

Parks startled awake again. He sat up against the wall and looked over his shoulder at the only light in the wigwam—the sliver of moon that peered under the flap of the back window. It must have been well after midnight, and he'd gotten no more than ten or twenty minutes sleep at a time, if you could call it that. Even in the twilight between dreams and waking, awful voices called to him, or a terrible old woman sat in the hut conspiring his murder with Foster. It would jolt him awake, to find Foster snoring beside him like a baby with sleep apnea. Nightmares of Drummoc, a natural disaster back home, a buzzard creature that ripped beakfuls of flesh from his neck and shoulders. None of them would give him a minute's peace.

It was an act of will to hold his heavy lids up. They were tired, beyond question. He focused on the slit of light, then on whatever sounds he could pick up. Drummoc was devoid of crickets. No birds called, no traffic buzzed. The sea was far enough to keep to itself. Only the wind had anything to say. It moaned down off the mountain and thumped over the tops of the huts. The flaps in the window were remarkably still. The Reverse-Eskimo layout always made him think one of their great spirits had emptied a sack of wig-wams on uneven ground and let them fall where they may, but he saw a glimmer of order to it, the way the wind eddied and rose over the tops, find-ing no easy lane of travel. A loose stone clacked against its neighbor. It felt as though a giant trapsed across, reaching down to shake a roof here or there in an attempt to scare a meal out of its burrow. He was glad they weren't still on the open rock, or worse: Ingputka.

A sudden tap against the outside wall scared him as a rock slapped off and rattled on its way. He began to hum to himself in a low tone. After a few bars he realized what it was: an old song his mom used to sing to him at bedtime. She would start, then his dad would pick up the same lyrics after her, and finally him. Three rounds of voices weaving and stumbling through one another until they lost it in laughter.

"Kookaburra sits in the old gum tree," he began, too soft, then picked up the volume as much as he dared without pissing off Kjartke. "Merry, merry king of the bush is he." Parks pointed his mouth at the window in hopes the sound of the wind would muffle some of it. "Laugh, kookaburra laugh, kookaburra how gay your life must be. Everybody now. Kookaburra sits in the old gum tree—kookaburra sits—merry, merry king of the—old gum tree—" He stopped in the middle of the round. The sliver of moon was almost gone. A small nick remained. It must have moved behind a cloud, or the roof of a hut, but he stayed dead silent for half a minute before resuming.

"Laugh, kookaburra—king of the—gay your life—" There was a sudden rustle and he turned back to the window. The long silver line was back in full. Whatever had blocked it was gone. This heart thumped and he pressed his back to the wall, unable to make a sound. He felt around for the spear and clutched it to his chest with both hands.

"Foster." He got only snores in response. "Foster," another sharp whis-per. "I think there's someone outside." Parks turned the spear around and jabbed his friend with the butt. Foster shrugged it off without missing a la-bored breath. A shuffle came from the other side now, near the door. Then another. Feet sliding across rock. He tracked it and jabbed Foster harder. It earned him a grunt. The shuffle moved in line with the entryway.

"I'm losing my shit," Parks told himself aloud. "There is no one here. They made me go to the ghost place at night, and I'm just having bad dreams. Why would anyone—"

The flap swung open and a figure darted inside before it swished closed to blackness.

"*Fuuuuck!* Intruder! Fuck! Wake up, *intruder! Intruder!*"

Foster sat bolt up in a panic. He heard Kjartke scramble for something across the room. "Intruder! There's someone in here!" His chest seized up and he thought he would die of a heart attack before the man could cross the room to kill him.

Foster wriggled closer to him and pressed against the wall. "Fuck, where at? Where's he at?"

"Over there!"

They heard Kjartke lunge. She let out a a little cry of distress, followed by a thud. *She's dead,* Parks told himself. "Joe!" He pleaded for the old man to strike.

"Quiet," Joe replied. He heard another rustle as Kjartke got to her feet.

"It is Tunguk." She pulled aside the front window flap enough to reveal the old man standing in the doorway where she had tried to attack him. He held her spear.

"Motherfucker. Parks. What the fuck is wrong with you?" Foster demanded. "You damn near gave me a coronary. We could've killed Tunguk."

Tunguk chuckled. "There are few who you could kill." Everyone settled back down to their position. He didn't need to see her or hear her—Parks could feel Kjartke's venom from across the room. He hoped the old man hadn't roughed her up too bad.

"Bro. What were you doing lurking around outside?"

"No lurking. Out for a walk."

"Go to sleep, bitch," Foster muttered.

"How can I sleep when I've got people creeping on my window, barging in in the middle of the night?"

"You wander with the spirits. I was not at your window."

"Well if it wasn't you, that's even more fucked, because *somebody* was out there."

"No more Ingputka for you," Foster said.

"Last time I checked, spirits of the dead are see-through. They don't block light from coming in one second—" A hand pressed over his mouth, slender, gentle, but adamant. He had not heard Kjartke cross the room.

"Lie down." She barely had to touch his shoulder and he sank into a ball. "You like songs. You cry like a child. We sing to children, better than you." She began in a string of low, monotone syllables that soon rose and fell along a simple range. Her fingers settled on the top of his head. It was all in the Reverse-Eskimo language, but that didn't matter. The melody reminded him of his own lullabies, moving in a predictable rhythm, always returning home where it started. The last thing he remembered was wondering why, and being grateful, she was nice to him. Within seconds, he sank into a dreamless sleep.

Foster hadn't intended to visit the harbor, but when he found the public tavern near-deserted the next morning, he took a bowl of the daily special—cured seal meat—and followed the flurry of activity to the launch. A few hundred people milled about like a festival crowd that just didn't want to go home after the event. The whaling ship was already pulled out and braced on rollers. Had he slept that long? At least they hadn't left. In theory, one more chance to get out of here, though in practice even his unflagging determination had begun to sag.

Whatever flurry of activity would have invested itself in the ship had exploded in every direction. Groups of three, four, five Mattaka scrambled to free their boats from the upside-down flotilla. The ones trying to get to the middle cursed the ones on the outside to work faster, and still others already had theirs in the water. Bows and arrows and spears graced every hand that wasn't hauling a hunting boat down to the water. It looked as though they were preparing for war with an army of rowboats, but their bright enthusiasm told him otherwise. It was a scramble of excitement, not fear or anger.

Several dozen Marines stood in units of sixes, in full leather armor and caps. They watched the crowd intently, though they made no move to interfere just yet. Beside the beached whaler, dozens more men gathered in arms. There was no uniform that he could spot, no way to know if these, too, were Navy, but he suspected they might be those who'd booked their seats. The scrunch-faced captain was the only one he recognized. One of every few stood with their eyes on the rest of the crowd. Most lounged and joked, or retold stories that involved lots of swinging and shouting. All had weapons at hand.

Someone slammed through his left shoulder in a run. A Mattaka youth didn't even bother to turn as he bounced off Foster and continued on his course. A flame shot across the lash marks on his back. The constant intensity had gone down quite a bit, but any touch, anywhere close, still lit him up, and now that it was well on its way to healing over, any movement, sharp or stretching, cause the skin to tear free of thick scabs at the perforations.

"Fuckin' cunt," he muttered, and immediately chastised himself for sounding like Gionn. No sooner had he thought the name than a hunchback in a cloak pulled over the top like a shawl, shortened to cover only the mid thighs, caught his attention. A tuft of black hair peeked out the front. He couldn't see any part of the man's face, but by now he could recognize that frame if it was in a line-up of burlap sacks filled with vulgar murderers.

"Gionn!" He gave a sharp whisper. The shape froze and turned away. "Yo! I see you, faggot." The cloaked figure backed up toward him but remained turned.

"Stay in the thick of the crowd, cunt." They moved, more or less together, toward the border between a group of off-duty regulars and another group of Mattaka.

"You almost didn't recognize me, didn't you?"

"I immediately recognized you. Literally, the second I saw you."

"I colored me hair black," he pulled back the cloak just long enough for Foster to get a look. "It's coal dust."

"Oh, I can tell."

"Ah, fuck it." He lowered the hood. "Shitstain and his lads left already."

"You don't think they saw you?"

"I slept on the *Fuck-a-tappat*. Couldn't take another night of squain farts."

"It was one night."

"Was it? Seemed like weeks. Anyway, had me the best view in the crowd when it got underway. Perched up there all by meself. Got to watch the show and wait for the coast to clear."

"Why the hell are you even out here now?"

"I intend to apply for work as soon as it opens up. Me and most of these cunts."

"Foster considered the crowd of Navy men who didn't seem to be on the job. "The whalin' ship? Somethin' happened."

"Whaler. Stop sayin' 'whalin' ship,' you sound like an arse. And aye. It would appear there is one more seat. I was hopin' for a bit of a melee, increase me chances, but alas."

"If the admiral can get us two, and there's another, we just need one more. All four of us can get the fuck off this island—it's an island, right?"

"Most of the year."

"Get off this island, and get paid to do it."

"Just the same, I'll be on that ship whether you are or not. And cunt: believe me when I say, from the bottom of me shallow well, I hope you are."

"Because…is there an insult to follow?"

"Because I'd hate to be the biggest bucket on the ship." He cackled. "No other reason."

"Well I came here thinkin' I could convince you to stay, so me and Parks can go."

"It's not that I'm unkind. Breakin' apart mates and all. I am, but the bigger reason is that I will be killed by cold or cutthroat before Winter's end." They slid aside as two bony Mattaka boys spun by, throwing haymakers at one another. "You'll still bring me fish, right?"

"Did I miss somethin? Why is everyone jumpin' in boats?"

"Albatross season."

"Didn't know people hunted those."

"They do when the first to bring one back gets upward of a year's wages in the mines." Foster furrowed his brow. "The pinnin' went tits-up. Oh, come on. You'd have seen it yesterday. Everyone gathered around the ship and all."

"The feather blowin' thing?"

"Aye. Tits-up."

"Is that good or bad?"

"Good for us, bad for them," he jerked his head at the crew gathered around the whaler. "It's an Amposi thing. Not surprised you've never seen it, bein' ignorant of as many things as you are."

"Is it like a blessin'?"

"It's an augur. Albatross like to travel long distances. They won't go with a ship that's bound to sink. If the feather pins to the hull, means a safe voyage. One of the crew of that whaler apparently fancies himself a reader of signs and an idiot who likes to dress up and have people look at him.

"This mornin', he tried to pass off a petrel feather. Nearly got himself killed. Then he accused the admiral of stealin' his bag of albatross feathers. Navy squared off with the whalers. They were cursin' and shovin' and swingin'. A fight damn near broke out. Someone got stabbed. I was hopin' for a general slaughter to clear up some of those benches—but me luck wouldn't have it. Just the one dead."

"A man gets stabbed to death, and that's your idea of a fight 'nearly' breakin' out?"

"It is. Was one of the other whalers who got him. The captain and the admiral wanted no part, neither one, and they got between it. Captain declared a bounty for the first and only the first man to bring him a bagful of albatross plumes."

"And you think you're gonna get that seat. Out of all these men here?"

"Near all these men are Navy. The captain already thinks they got designs on him: to stop him, or infiltrate his crew. I hope no one spreads rumors of the sort. It would make it unfair to the Navy lads tryin' to get aboard. He'd be inclined to choose from the unaffiliated riff raff and dock rats."

"Is that what you been doin' in the shithouse?"

"None of your cunt affairs what I do in shithouses, mate."

"As a person who at one point considered the possibility that you might become a friend, I have to warn you that the admiral's hot on the trail of the potty lurker and his spear's longer than yours." "As a person who at one point thought he'd have to kill you, and at another thought the same as you describe, and then rocked back and forth a few times, I appreciate it. And if I get the seat, I'll be glad to do all in me power to open up a few more. Provided you keep me in fish and water until then."

"It's seal today. And I have no reason to believe you'll follow through on your word."

"You'll do it, then?" Foster nodded. "Ah, you're a madman," Gionn clapped him on the back. Foster winced. "Don't ever change. Now fuck off, before you call attention to me."

Tunguk sat outside the tukit with his back against the rough stone wall, what was wearing into his usual spot. Already his spine knew the grooves and sharp outcrops. It settled like a stream into the spaces it could fit. His view was limited. Before him, the back of another tukit. The path curved around it to either side, and split in both directions, so that he could only see parts of three tukits and the odd curves that disappeared around them. It was no busy street. He'd been in the spot all morning, and seen only traces of people as they flashed across one corner of the eye or another. There were so many ways around Drummoc, it was said you could visit the same relative every day of your life and never travel the same path twice. That is not what people did. Once their routes were set, only a strange obstacle could turn them, and even then, they would regain the path as soon as possible. An obstacle, or a great fear or passion. The Kammatuk had heavy feet. Where they walked, the ground wore low.

When he looked up, a boy stood before him. His days were thirteen or fourteen. He stared down at Tunguk with the sun behind him, from a shadowed brow.

"Why are you here?" He asked in Mattakatan.

"It is a long story."

A rustle from within turned his attention to the doorway. Parks stumbled out squinting against the gray light and stretched his arms in a gaping yawn. Tunguk looked back and the boy was gone.

"Fuck. How long was I asleep?"

"I have something to show you."

They walked clear of the town, across the rock plain that spread between the sea and the mountain.

"We going on a hike?" Parks' gaze wandered to the white slopes.

"A hike. Foster asked me of this, too."

"It means like a nature walk. Just going on a mountain, or a trail or something to look at rocks and birds, usually plants, too, but I haven't seen too many of those. Catch some good views and shit."

"Mattaka do not go there."

"How come?"

"It is a place of tricksters, and the dead."

"Kind of like the place we went last night?"

"No." Tunguk stopped and pointed. "Do you see this? It is called the west face by your people."

Parks looked at the gleaming white blur in the distance. "Cool."

"Urkuk has many faces. It is hard to know which one you see. They call the people to hike. You must not listen. If you meet him, you must ask questions. Test him. If you can make him say his true name, he will do as you ask. But you cannot. So do not listen."

"Okey doke. Is this what you wanted to show me?"

"No."

Joe led him across the featureless expanse until they came to a thin crevasse, about four feet across, that widened and veered off toward the mountain in one direction and tapered toward the sea in the other. He stopped and faced Parks.

"Is *this* the place?"

"Yes."

Parks looked the crevasse up and down. "What is it?"

"You forget so soon?"

"Forget what?"

"Ingputka."

A chill went down Parks' spine remembering the creepy nightmares their late night meeting had given him. "Well how should I know? It was so dark I couldn't see my dick in my hand." Seeing it laid bare in the daylight, he felt a little ashamed. It was a crack. There was nothing to imagine waiting for him just beyond sight. None of the terrors he was so sure crouched in the shadows.

"Kjartke cannot sing to you all of your days."

"No? I'd be OK with that." Parks stepped up to the edge and peered down into the black abyss. "I guess you brought me here to show me I'm being a little bitch. Overcome my fears?"

"No." Joe joined him. "You returned by the way you come. The spirits follow you home."

"We all went back the same way."

"Yes. You are sensitive."

"Me? *I'm* sensitive. Have you met Foster?"

"You must jump."

Parks looked at him in horror. "Down there?"

"Over." Parks sighed in relief. "Then you go toward the sea, beyond the latrine. Return home by a different path. Then the spirits will not be able to follow."

"How come they can't follow me just because I jump and walk on the other side?" Joe seemed bewildered by the question. "I don't see how that makes me any harder to follow."

"It is the way it is done."

Parks studied the gap. "Can I go down a ways and jump it where it narrows?"

"That is not Ingputka."

"I thought Ingputka was the crevasse."

"No. You jump here."

Parks muttered to himself. He couldn't believe he was about to do some Indian crack-jumping shit to bring an end to his nightmares, possibly his life if he overestimated his athletic ability. When was the last time he jumped? His leap onto the deck of Ostuk's ship with Gionn came to mind, but it was pretty close to the dock. Before that? Probably high school. Anybody can jump four feet, though, he thought—and doubted it as soon as it came out.

"Fuck it." Parks backed up, then second-guessed his distance. He didn't want to get tired just running up to it. Joe offered no help of any kind. A few steps forward, and he bent his knees into his stance. Parks chugged his thick legs and pumped his arms. He was shocked at how slow he was as he lumbered past Joe, then planted and launched himself. Both feet landed on the other side at the same time, sending a sting all the way up his legs to his ears. He tumbled to the ground, rolled, and panted back to his feet. The bandage on his shin fell down, and the wound burned in protest when he replaced it.

"You coming?" He called to Joe.

Joe laughed. "I am old." He pulled a small sack from his tunic and turned it upside down, shaking its white contents loose into the crevasse. He threw the bag itself down after them.

"What the heck was all that?"

"Feathers."

The young sailor paused a moment to consider the big man in the distance walking alone in his direction before entering the toilet. He had not seen someone come from inland before. It was one of the halots from the dog ship, he was sure. There were already strange rumors about them. That they were cursed, that they practiced bone work; agents of the farri—the old farri, he supposed—or fugitives seeking the refuge of impenetrable winter. Whatever they were, none of their acts could surprise him. The men had not been ordered to stay clear, but the way the officers spoke it was clear enough. He shook his head before pushing through the curtain into the shitter.

He was already inching back against a grip on one of the steadying stones when his eyes took enough light to notice the man easing down right beside him. Poqoba was unsure where he came from—certainly he'd been inside the whole time. A quick glance up and down the length of the crack showed him that not a soul was in relief, yet the man gave him less than two feet of space. He was quite ready to go, but the sudden closeness made him hesitate. The other had no such qualms. Poqoba kept his eyes forward as his neighbor grunted and shimmied into a comfortable position.

"Hoy, cunt! Pass a few of those arse-rocks me way."

Poqoba let go with one hand to shove a few his direction, though he seemed to have plenty already.

"Good man. Navy, then?"

On the ships, he was accustomed to conversations amid whatever business a man had, but ashore, most gave the respect of distance and silence, unless they knew you.

"Aye." He gave a curt answer, hoping the man would take the message.

"You lot near got marked up by those whalers, today, eh? Wouldn't be tryin' 'em if I was you. Whalers are tougher'n sailors."

"You are mad. We had the numbers and the men. The whalers were the ones who backed down as soon as their captain blinked." He immediately regretted engaging. "Besides, most of them were sailors two weeks ago."

"Aye, that's me point. Who gets the benches? The best of the cunts who want 'em. Which means any one of them's worth two of you."

"I do not want to be a whaler," Poqoba was indignant. "It is a low trade."

"As opposed to playin' nanny to squains? Anyway, don't make much difference. I hear the boat'll never make land." He gave a foul grunt.

"The feathers were stolen."

"Not what I mean, simple cunt."

Poqoba knew he should not ask. He gave a squeeze to speed up his exit, and waited to see if the man would offer on his own. "What, then?"

"Rumor is the admiral's got designs on 'em. They think he'll attack the ship, but he's not that daft. He's got agents in there, or will soon enough."

"Ha! Where did you hear this?"

"I got me sources. Amposi Navy's wormed-through with some of the most despicable cunts who float. But there's a few loyal ones, yet."

"I am a loyal man."

"Then why didn't they tell you what everyone else seems to know?" He moaned with satisfaction as he smeared a rock over his bum. Then he lifted it to his nose and gave it a sniff. Poqoba leaned away in horror. The man extended the rock toward his face.

"Have a go at that."

Poqoba squirmed away. The man stood, and Poqoba let out a sigh of relief. He was too tense to finish up, anyway. Before he could rise, the man turned to face the crack. The sailor knew better than to look when he saw the elbow begin to jerk back and forth in rhythm.

"Lend a mate a hand?"

Poqoba leapt to his feet and fled the latrine.

Gionn was nervous about who might arrive in the meantime, but he did not have to wait long. The admiral entered with his short spear, the two Amposi officers behind him.

"I know you. Ostuk's boy."

"You must be the commanding officer of the shithole."

"I'll need no help with this one, lads." Costig nodded his men off to their work. He gave them a moment, then peeked out the flap to ensure they were well on their way.

"Is there somethin' different about your hair?"

"Is there? Went down on a squain whore last night." He felt his head.

"You've got your audience. It'll be quick."

"Quick. Will your offer stand if I go it alone?"

"No."

"Why not? I'm the only sailor of the lot. I'll have her put in at Nunoc, or Manhas. The lads'll only slow me down."

"Because I don't trust you. And you'll not take the ship by storm. You need men who'll stand with you. Men who others like."

"Are you callin' me unlikable?"

"Entirely. Besides, you hate intrigues."

"I do. Fuckin' loathe 'em. But not as much as I loathe Drummoc."

"The offer stands, on the terms I set." The admiral started out.

"Wait. I owe you an apology, mate."

"Accepted."

"Don't you want to know what for?"

"I assumed wastin' me time last night, and again as we speak."

"The whaler didn't get pinned today, but you almost did."

"How was that your fault?"

Gionn smiled and crossed the room to meet him. "I understand why you think it takes two men to redirect a ship. Lots of plottin' involved. Rumor-mongerin'. Standin' counts. Seems like a job for twenty, never mind two, and one bein' an honest man. And though I've no love of intrigues, I did stop a whaler from sailin' by meself and without resources, made it look like your fault, and all with only a few drops of blood spilled."

"Have you got a feather for me?"

"Aye. You're welcome to rummage around for 'em." He waved his hand at the crack that ran the length of the room.

"Well done, lad. I wonder if you'll be able to stop her long enough for me to change me mind." Costig started out.

"I've applied for the open seat!" Gionn called after him.

"I know," he said as he disappeared.

Gionn swore to himself and checked the coast before stepping out. He watched the admiral walk the walk of a tired man back toward the town. Another figure caught his eye, approaching Drummoc on a different angle and a meandering line. He recognized Parks though he couldn't make out any detail, and it made sense how he'd stood out to Foster at the harbor.

A flash of white called him back. Something tumbled along the length of the crevasse in his direction. He watched the single feather skip across the ground, unwavering, as though it walked with one hand on the edge to feel its way along. The breeze lifted it and fixed it firm to his crotch. Gionn considered it for a few moments, then plucked it and held it before his eyes, framed against the white face of the mountain.

"Funny, cunt." He tossed it over his shoulder and along on its way.

When Kjartke returned with provisions, Tunguk and Brother were gone, but from afar she saw Foster sitting outside the tukit in Tunguk's place. She hesitated and ducked back out of his vision. These men—Foster and Brother—they or their people had strange habits. If a person arrived, or left a place, they must always speak to that person. Often, they would talk of nothing out of hatred for silence. It was difficult to know how to respond, and if she did not, he would demand to know why, or complain of her to others and make jokes. They called it, "making conversation." If she came now, and no one else was there, she had no doubt that Foster would make conversation. Demand to know what she was doing, or will do soon. Or ask questions that would be considered rude even for a sibling or a husband. She had learned the trick to ask him a rude question in return, that he would talk and she could ignore him. It worked even better with Brother.

She did not know why it was so vital for these men to always say something. Few people had demanded it of her until now, and she would be grateful if it was that way again. Yet there was nowhere to hide, and many things to do. A deep breath passed from her chest, and she forced herself to walk to the door of the tukit.

"Afternoon, Darlin'." He was fond of announcing the part of the day. "What you been gettin' up to?" She raised the water bladder and the basket of dried meat a little higher, that he might see. "Well, thank you. You didn't have to do that." He knew it was for her and Tunguk, yet he acted as though she had done it for him. Or that it did not need to be done.

"You seen Parks or Tunguk?" She shook her head. "I've just been settin' here, tryin' to figure out what ol' boy sees in it." She felt now that she was well-trapped. "Where I'm from, we do somethin' similar, but it's on porches. Raised platforms in front of the house, with a roof so it don't rain on you while you're settin'. I guess it's the same. But I think I'm realizin' that I just like the light. Never been in total darkness for months at a time." Foster shrugged. "Might as well soak it up while I can."

Kjartke set down her load. "You will stay for winter?"

"Not if I can help it. So, yeah. Probably."

She went into the tukit and reappeared with a bowl and a handful of long, thin leather strips. Kjartke poured a little water into the container, then set the leather into soak.

"What's that for? You makin' rope?"

She nodded. In the meantime, she produced a piece of good flint, and a second stone of a different kind. He watched her with a smile, in a way that told her he would say more soon. She lined up the stones, and delivered a quick blow—once, twice. A smaller piece sheared off. The larger one was set aside. Kjartke took a long time to turn it over in her hand, study the lines that ran through the blank, before she pressed the tip of her stone against the edge, pulled back, and tapped off another chunk to shape it.

"Damn, girl. I knew you could do fifty-thousand other things, but I didn't know you could do that, too. You gonna make us some arrowheads or somethin'?"

"What is it like?" She blurted out. Foster was taken aback.

"What is what like?"

"The place you come from. You have light, always?"

"I mean, more or less, yeah. Not at night, but all day, every day."

It wasn't quite the speech she was hoping for. "Is there a story of it that you tell to children? How it came to be? I am a child to your people. I know so little. Maybe it would be good to hear as your children hear."

"Fuck." He took a moment to collect himself. "I mean, shit. I'm sorry. It's just, you ain't never asked me about where I'm from before. I don't even know what to—is there a story? Hell, I don't know. I got lots of stories, not many of them are for kids."

"It is fine if you do not wish to talk."

"No, no. I don't mean to be like that. I'll talk." She clenched her jaw. "Let me see. You wanna hear about…me growin' up in North Carolina? Or how I met Parks?"

"The first one."

"Well, that's a story within a story, within a story. But what would I say to a kid who just got dropped off in the Appalachians, and couldn't make no sense of it? I guess I gotta start with what the Appalachians are." His voice faded as she honed in on her work, roughing out the shape, turning it over again and again before choosing her mark. She alternated sides, and little by little the stone yielded its edge. The pieces flew off smaller and smaller, crescent moons inside of crescent moons. Moon after moon, until the sun began to ride the tops of the tukits, and a long shadow fell across her hands.

Foster broke off his story. "What's up, brother? You limpin'?"

Parks nodded. "Re-aggravated it long jumping a portal to Hell. You know. Tuesday shit. Need a fresh wad of 'baccy."

"Where's Tunguk?"

"Don't know. He said he was gonna jump right after me, but when I turned around, he was gone." Foster tensed and pressed his hands against the tukit in preparation to rise. The smile that spread across Parks face eased him back down.

"Don't be playin' with me like that."

"What's she doing? Making weapons?"

"Ask her."

"I'm just going by her general body language here, but I don't think she wants me to."

"That's just her restin' bitch face. She's actually been in a pretty chatty mood. We were just talkin' about Appalachia."

"The Drummoc of the north."

"If California's the Ingputka."

"If he pulls out his banjo, you just let me know," Parks addressed her.

"I do not know 'banjo,'" she raised her head, "but if he pulls it out, I will not need your help."

"Anyway, good talk." Foster climbed to his feet. "I think I forgot to bring Gionn some seal jerky or somethin'." He and Parks laughed together at something she did not understand.

"Thank you, by the way. You were already gone when I woke up." Kjartke pursed her lips and gave him a single nod. He slid down roughly and extended his bandaged leg in front, the other knee bent between them. "I guess we got so caught in trying to get back to our spot, me and Foster. I felt like we've been going backwards this whole time, scrambling here and there, always trying to worm our way into one more boat. It feels like we have so far left go, I kinda forgot that you're here. I mean, I know you're *here*, here. But you're *there*. This is *your spot*. This is where you were going all along. We didn't even have a little party and cake for you. Just started plotting our next move. How soon can we bail on Kjartke? Leave her all to herself with nothing, where she doesn't know anybody.

"I guess we never really stopped to consider how rude that might be. Hell, we knew what the deal was. We're just your ride. You don't owe us shit, and we—we probably do owe you." He paused. "Comments, so far? No? OK. Well. I just want to make it clear that we aren't trying to leave you for any personal reasons. You are a bit…prickly, at times, but it's got its charm. I just wanted to make sure, before we go, if we go—I don't know what the hell's going to happen—I just want to make sure you're going to be cool."

Kjartke did not look up from her knapping. "I am cool."

"Have you thought about how you're going to make ends meet? Pay your bills? Put a roof over your head? You know: work."

"Aye."

"And?" She gave him a puzzled look. "Care to share your plans?"

"I have talked to the woman."

"What woman?"

"Nante."

"Nante. Is that—she work at the…house of the evening?"

"Poye. She is mother of the girls."

Parks swallowed hard and nodded. "Mother. Right. Where even *is* the brothel? I feel like I haven't seen any signs or any literature about it."

"Anyone can show you."

He gave her a moment of silence that felt like a mercy. But without his voice, it soon became heavy. He was not one for silence. It became more like pity. Brother was at peace when he spoke, when he moved, and his stillness was restless. A fire lifted in her chest and throat, and she hoped he would speak again without her going first.

"You know you can stay with us, right?"

"I will stay. In Winter, I will go."

"Even longer than that. You're always welcome here. Winter, Summer—"

"This place belongs to Ostuk. It is not yours to give."

"True. True. But I feel like he would agree, if we asked him."

"What if I stay? You will be gone. I help Tunguk die, then I must work."

"Yeah, but you're good at a lot of shit. Oh!" He waved his hand at her flint. "You could sell arrowheads. Is that what that is? You could make shit and sell it." Kjarkte chuckled. "Is that not a thing?" She shook her head. "Well I don't know. What else do women do?"

"If she is married, she will care for her family. Make 'shit,' as you say. For her family."

"What if she's single and not looking to mingle?"

"You say I do not talk." Kjartke set down her piece carefully, but in frustration. "I do not speak your language. You say these things I do not know, and you are angry when I cannot answer. Single to mingle. What is this? You make me rude, but I am not rude. It is rude to speak when there is nothing to say. It is rude to use speech that conceals from others, or to force speech from one who would conceal."

"Whoa, hey! Sorry." He put up his hands. "Sorry. I didn't mean to be rude. I don't speak your language, either. This is how I speak mine. I'm what my people call 'colorful.' Charming. But if you would have me use the simple tongues, I can do this. I should. It would be rude not to." She squinted her response. "I'm just asking what a young unmarried woman can do to feed herself and keep a wigwam—or whatever this house of rocks is called—here in Drummoc."

Kjartke hung her head, and Parks did not press her.

"What if, like, someone sponsored you?" A flash of frustration crossed her face, but he caught it. "Sponsored. You don't know this word." She shook her head. "It means when someone doesn't quite have the means, no money or food or house, someone else who has these things provides them, because they are good people, and we take care of our people."

"Ostuk sponsors us?"

"Uh, yeah. Yeah, I guess. But I meant a little more permanent. So you wouldn't have to work."

"I do not know if he will do that. He acted boldly," she said it like an insult. "It may be that he does not keep what he has."

"I don't mean Ostuk."

"Who, then?"

"Uh," he pointed his thumbs at his chest. "This guy. Me. Maybe Foster can chip in, too."

"Two sponsors?"

"If we have to. But I would be willing to be your, sole sponsor."

Kjarkte laughed. "What do you provide? I bring food and water. I trim your tunic. I make you sleep. When have you brought a kill? Does a child provide for his mother?"

"Damn, girl. Burn. That means you have made a good insult against my people, which is me and Foster. To which I reply, yes. These things are mostly, if not one hundred percent, true up until now. I know it seems like two guys with no jobs or income, who are leaving first chance they get, might not be very good sponsors. But actually, we kind of have something in the works. I can't talk about it. Super secret. But if this thing hits—and it's looking pretty solid—we're going to get paid like…kings of a fat tribe. And where we're going, we won't need it. Either we'll make it home, or if home isn't there, we'll die like gentlemen. What if I arranged that the top secret guy who's looking to pay us many gold coins—you know this? Gold coins?" She nodded. "Or whatever denomination, he didn't really specify. Anyway, what if we arranged that he just gave the money to you, instead?"

"Gold coins."

"Many. Probably. Again, didn't really catch an exact figure. I'm guessing they go a long way out here. Much purchasing power."

"When I give a gold coin for my food, and all have seen it. Who will see that no one comes to take them from me?"

"Maybe we can hire bodyguards. Armed mercenaries to protect you."

Kjartke polished the last few flakes off of her arrowhead and held it up to one eye. She handed it to Parks, who took it with a look of surprise. "When the light returns, I will make the rest of the 'shit'." She gave a wry smile. "Who did you think it was for?"

He fumbled for words. "Thank you."

"You cannot be sponsor."

The plan was to lie on the rock plain until sundown. In the distance, the rounded tops of Drummoc and the square line of harborside buildings were the only features that rose above a knee. He could make out people milling, and when they came to the shitter they seemed near enough to spot him, but Gionn reclined on the cold ground, and no one stared into the nothing beyond the settlement long enough to pick out a lump and recognize it as a man. That, or they didn't care.

At the start he told himself he'd stay no matter the wind or the cold—his life could have depended on it. But then the wind and the cold came, and he began to consider just how many fingers and toes and bollocks he'd forfeit in the name of ensuring his safety. Either he'd been spotted already, or he hadn't, and if he had, it was madness to freeze to death and save Shitstain the trouble. Not that it would be much trouble. He'd arrived at the port that morning for the debacle with a good fifteen impolite mates. But if Gionn been seen, he might as well cause what inconvenience he could in the process.

If he hadn't—and he was quite sure he hadn't—then letting the rock suck the warm blood right out of his corpse did not seem like a clever plan. With no one looking for idiots on the plain, or anywhere in general, it would be quite easy to slip into the rear of town and snake through the huts—wigwams, Parks called them. It would neither be safe nor prudent for any of the men he'd seen to wander the bowels of the squain town near dark. The chance of rounding a corner to an unfriendly face—at least a pale one—was low, and it would be easy enough to run this way and that and shake them. The chances got better and better the colder he grew.

Gionn soon found himself among the wigwams. The first people he crossed—two boys—gave him a look that would have sent him to flight if it had come from a grown man, but they passed without a word. He was reminded of the stories he'd heard of the place, especially near the winter when the men are home and there's little to do. You need not know a man to earn his knife in Drummoc. A man in Oxba told them he served in the Navy a season, and they wouldn't dare lose sight of the roofs of the main street unless they went in force. There's nothing a drunk could have that was worth so little, he wouldn't be killed for it as he stumbled home. Gionn wondered how the fuck Foster and Parks had managed to prance in and out for multiple days with no sign of trouble.

He quickened his step and let the glow of the sky steer him toward the harbor. At first, he popped out too soon, several buildings down from the poorman's quarters, and had to slip back to cover ground. There were plenty of men on their way to and from the taverns, Navy and public. The second time he found his mark and slipped into the building within moments.

It was mercifully empty. Squains did not like the indoors except in the foulest weather. He liked wherever they didn't. The oil lamps already burned along the periphery, where a few hopeless souls had retired to the wall, well apart, to stare into the dark for he supposed the rest of their miserable lives.

"Good evenin', stranger." The voice plunged under his solar plexus like a sword before he even turned to find the face. It was far enough, and opposite the door. His blood screamed out of the veins and begged him to run for it. He wasn't sure why he didn't. His legs felt like trees, rooted deep to the soil, and his hand trembled like branches. Run where? There was no point.

Gionn looked to him out of the corner of his eye, and scanned the dark for the others he was sure would appear—and did not. "Don't believe we've met. You can call me Polc." The man crossed the room to stand before him. "And what can I call you in return?" An arm extended for a seaman's greeting. He looked to the other hand. It hung empty at Polc's side.

"Gionn." He left the embrace to hang in the air.

"Came in on the dog ship, did you? Honest trade, that." Gionn again looked behind him to the door, and around the room. "Will you be winterin' with us?"

"Not if I can help it," his voice came out hoarse and he had to clear a gritty lump from his throat.

"The whaler, then?" Gionn nodded. "Ah. You and every lad on this island. Be a shame for the new farri if she sails. But sail, she will. May your luck be with you for a seat. I mean that in all sincerity." Polc's attention fell on Gionn's right hand, pressed firm against the front of his thigh, the handle of his short sword dangling just opposite. "Will your mates be joinin'?"

"Which ones? I've got a more'n a few here."

"Do you?"

"Aye. Came in on the dog ship, like you say." His voice cracked, soft and high. "Good mates with all the rowers. Then there's the cunts we rescued. Thing like that, it bonds you. They'd die for me, and I the same." He managed a burst of volume for the last line.

Polc nodded and paced, offering Gionn one side, then the other. "A good mate is a fine thing. Worth forty enemies, they say."

"I mark 'em for one or two."

"Aye, I never quite understood it, either. In my experience, a good enemy will cause you pain that forty mates'll not soothe. As the fates have the spun it, I've none here. Enemies, that is. And none to count me the same. Well, I won't keep you. Just thought I'd make introduction. You'll hear no more from old Polc, unless you find me in the tavern and care to share a cup. I do not cultivate enemies, but I could always use forty more mates." Gionn frowned and pursed his lips. "Quiet type, then. Well, pleasure to know your name, Gionn. If I don't cross your path before you leave, have a blessed voyage, me son."

Polc clapped him on the shoulder and sidestepped to pass. Gionn felt hot sulfur rise in his veins until his face burned. His nose cleared, and his eyes brimmed. He moved to block the exit.

"Once more, please."

"Beg your pardon?"

His mouth quivered, and his eyes finally raised to meet the other's. "'Me son.' Please call me that just once more."

A nervous laugh slipped out. "Mate, if I've misspoken, forgive me. I find it a common term in every port."

Gionn glared hot steel. He felt the skies cease their spin and turn in the other direction. "And what might your trade be? Polc. What brings a man like yourself to Drummoc? Come to enjoy the mild climes and notorious squain hospitality?"

Polc forced a laugh. "I understand they don't like to be called that." Gionn stood his ground. "Apologies. I was so eager to learn who this strappin' block of a man was that I forgot me manners."

"I'll wait while you remember 'em."

"Me lads and I escort merchants through rough waters. Mostly Amposi. Never lost a charge, I'm proud to say."

"What merchant hires an escort to come so far south in Autumn?"

"Ah, none. Actually, we were hired to deliver a message. Very important stuff. The investor needed a fast ship, and an honest crew, and important messages pay more than escort contracts."

"What's the message?"

Polc gave a weak grin. "Well, it weren't for you."

"Shall I ask around?"

He let out a desperate little laugh. "Mate! I'm doin' all in me power to share a kind word with a stranger."

"You're doin' a fine job. Keep it up."

Polc shook his head and sighed. "I suppose the whole island's heard by now, anyway. When Farri Tolba declared, he hired us to bring the word to Drummoc and reinforce the garrison until the proper Navy arrives with the thaw. You know. 'Forewarned,' and all that."

"Forewarned." Gionn stepped aside. Polc nodded, and hurried toward the door. "Shitstain." He paused for a half a moment without turning, then pushed out.

If it wasn't nightmares, it was wind. Another round of the ones that started right at sundown, rushing from the interior to meet the sea. It sounded more like an avalanche over the rooftops than passing air. By Parks' reckoning, it was midnight before the thundering hooves calmed to a whistle through narrow pockets where the tops of wigwams bent apart just right. By then, his leg was an inferno.

It hadn't been great before, but something about that jump and having to truck it home the long way had sent a fiery tingling sensation coursing through his lower extremity. The entire shin was tender to the touch. The witch lady had said the medicine would burn. Could she have meant this? After hours trying to sleep on a skin of fur seal atop bare rock, the inflammation had crossed his knee and stiffened it, making it painful to either bend or extend all the way.

At least Foster's sleep apnea seemed to be doing well with the cold air and hard beds. Back on the ship—the real ship, with hot running water and lights and doors that clicked shut—he was a miserable bunk mate. More than once, he'd weighed the benefits of smothering him with a pillow. Now, it wasn't more than an intermittent whistle, like the wind.

Parks' eyes watered as he chewed a change of herb for his wound and packed it. He was solid against infection, but there was nothing any dry leaves could do for a 200-plus pound man landing hard on a limb that had been locked up in the hold of a ship for ages. At least Joe had been right: he wasn't having nightmares anymore. Somewhere across the bare floor, Kjartke slept without a sound. It was only last night, but already he'd lost most of the memory of his head at her leg, her hand in his hair, the voice that folded him into rest. He'd fake a bad dream every night for that, if he thought for a second she'd let him get away with it.

Instead, he sat up and rolled his sleeping bag into a cylinder, placed it under the back of his knee, and leaned against the wall beneath the rear window. The breeze filled the cover like a sail, and though the ends were tied, the moon slipped in under the curved edge and across his face. It was almost painfully bright in the virgin dark, and he had to squint to look at it. Parks pressed the back of his head against the awkward slope of the rock. It reminded him of shitting in an airplane bathroom. There didn't seem to be any Reverse-Eskimos who were 6'4, or who enjoyed things like being comfortable when they sat or slept. He closed his eyes and tensed, wondering if his imagination would leap at the opportunity to assault him again. He felt the air with his skin, felt the beat of his heart. Still, and even. He might well be able to get some sleep, if his leg would shut up for half an hour. He dared not complain. She already thought he was enough of a pussy that asking for medical advice for an "owie" on top of a bedtime song would kill whatever chance clung to this world from its deathbed. Even the chance felt good. There didn't seem to be many of those around these parts, at least not for anything that mattered to him. Certainty felt like paralysis. He had an inkling of an understanding why Foster was obsessed with ships that, in his hillbilly fantasy, could sail him right back to the top of the Blue Ridge mountains.

That was the last thing he remembered until he snapped awake, what must have been about fifteen minutes later. He was already forgetting a dream. Foster on a ship shaped like an ancient helmet that he must've seen in *Gladiator*. It turned into a snowmobile, and they drove deep into the frozen the continent. Eskimo Joe showed up at some point holding a sign like Wile E. Coyote that Parks couldn't read, but he knew said "TURNN ARROWND," misspelled—he wasn't sure of the exact letters. The rest was gone.

His leg had quieted enough that he thought he might have a shot of passing right back out. The moonlight played across his extended foot, the same boots the old tribe of Reverse-Eskimos had given him when they landed. They'd seen better days, but it felt like no small miracle that they were still intact. Kjartke had stolen them a half-dozen times now to restore them to life.

Real shoes: add that to the list of things he was going to invent if they were stuck here as long as he suspected. Once he became the first Antarctic billionaire, Kjartke might have a different opinion of his ability to take care of people. He wondered if the girls in other places were any hotter than the talent he'd seen since arriving. Maybe he'd buy her a wigwam mansion as a big "fuck you," and wave sayonora from the deck of his coal-powered steamship, with a couple of imported South American girls on each hip. "It's cool. Yeah, no hard feelings about the sponsor thing. No, keep it. Keep it. We'll call it a gift. I'll let you know if I need any more arrowheads." He grinned, and the moonlight disappeared from his foot.

Parks froze. It took his face tingling to realize he wasn't breathing. He let out air as slowly and quietly as possible. His heart lurched against his collarbone. *Tap, tap, tap, tap, tap.* Five quick pings against the sill outside—it sounded like stone on stone. Eskimo Joe had definitely been inside when he fell asleep. Could he have left? Was Gionn fucking with him? He didn't dare sound alarm again, out of sheer embarrassment.

"Joe." He whispered, hoping the response came from outside. "Joe." This time he vocalized it.

"Parks?" The voice came from outside. His face flushed and his leg screamed. He felt he should know it, but he didn't.

"We're armed." He answered.

"Outside the window. Tomorrow night. Dress for a long walk. Bring Foster." The moon appeared again on his foot. He quivered with something between fear and excitement. The voice nagged at his memory, but that wasn't the thing that chilled him. It sounded for all the world like the man spoke in God-blessed, unaccented American English.

15

THE PRISONER

"You fuck!" The whaler captain screamed at Costig as he walked back to his men. "Face me!" He pushed through a handful of his own who braced at the admiral's heels, sweeping back and forth to bellow and spit in the unconcerned ear. "Face me, you jumper. You spineless cunt! Stop and unhand me man!"

Costig halted, and when he did, the four men at his side followed suit. They dropped the man they carried, each to a limb, face first onto the ground where he curled his arms around his ribs and continued to drip a puddle from his nose. To one side of them, better than a hundred Amposi Navy drew up in leather and arms, with the Marines front and center of the mob, clad in armor, many with helmet and shield of thick hide. Behind the captain, his entire crew—about fifty whalers—white-knuckled their weapons and stalked the admiral cautiously. A loose cloud of Mattaka and the unaffiliated hovered at the edges to take in the unfolding fracas.

He turned to face the man without a hint of a care on his face. "Aye, Cormdran?" Costig was a head shorter, and thick as he was, fell entirely within the shadow of the big captain. Cormdran's nostrils flared on his red face as he leaned as close as he could over the man without touching.

"What fuckin' authority have you got, you short fuckin' sergeant?"

"I'm told I'm an admiral now, and me authority is that of Farri Tolba, and the Viceroy of Hiade. So I'm also told."

"You miserable cunt. You've no right to interfere with honest trade. You're title-drunk, paradin' your small cock around hopin' for a compliment!" The whalers laughed.

"I've not stopped your trade, only arrested a murderer."

"What murder?"

"You saw as well as I. He stabbed a man to death yesterday in this very spot."

"Aye, me own man! None of your concern."

"A murder on me rock is me concern."

"I'll discipline me own men, you worry about yours. Kindly return him before I become unkind." The whalers swelled at their captain's words.

Behind the admiral, the Marine sergeants turned their backs to the fray in order to hold their own men off. They lunged into their commanders like dogs at a lead.

"If you can't keep your man from stabbin' his mates, how'll you keep him from stabbin' mine? You may have noticed a bit of tension on the docks. He pricks one of me lads, and I won't be able to stop them from slaughterin' your crew to a man. And it's a good crew. I know—most of 'em was mine. Our side'll lose as many as yours. For what?"

"For the respect of the crews. Who'll sail your provisions if you arrest every rough cunt? By Euskus, I swear! Is this a port, or a fuckin' temple?"

"You don't have to like it, Comrdran. But you do have to count. Look behind me. I've a sight more than you, and more than that in reserve. What'll it be? One man lost? A man who wasn't even one of yours until two weeks ago? Or you and me are the first two dead, and you can ask Euskus who gets your boat once all the bodies go over to the gulls."

"You're a short cunt hidin' behind a large body, Costig," he nodded at the force behind the admiral. "And your mustache is vulgar. Is there enough of a man there to decide this? You and me. Single combat. Mine'll stay put if yours will. When I kill you, I get me man, and I sail unmolested."

"Gut him, Costig!" One of the Marines shouted, and both sides erupted in cheers and taunts for their champion. They pushed so hard that Costig and Cormdran had to turn and lean into their forces to hold them from a clash.

"I've already got what I came for." Costig shouted over his shoulder..

"Jumper!" Cormdran tossed one and returned to the center. The whalers followed suit and lit into the admiral with their tongues, while the Navy shouted encouragement. "Are the pants too big for you? Go and count your men, arse-cunt. That's what you're good for! I may not count as high as you, but come near my ship or my crew again and I'll cut down your lads until they number with mine, and one less!"

"I'll fight you if he don't!" One of the Marines lumbered forward toward the captain. Costig shot in and wrapped his meaty forearms around the man's waist, then lifted and slung him to the ground and pinned him there. A pair of whalers came forward from the other way. "Back with you! It's my fight, mine and Costig's." One of them hung back. Comrdran grabbed the other by the shirt. He landed a heavy fist across the man's jaw and crumpled him. "Back with you!" He looked up to where Costig was escorting his Marine back to the ranks. The four guards again had the prisoner airborne between them as they retreated into the crowd.

"Fuck you, Costig! I'll be sure to give your regards to the boys in Taclann!"

Gionn watched the two sides hem and haw in an ebbing retreat that started off, lunged back, and made off again. The men of each cursed to their mates and threw jabs in the air to show how they would have handled themselves if it had come to the melee they claimed to want. The crowd of neutrals, mostly squainfolk, dispersed with the hopes of a bloody show. A good forty to sixty extra seats would've helped his prospects, but one was better than none. He slipped through the scattering body and knelt at the edge of the sea. With the bowl emptied of his breakfast, he dipped an icy bath and poured it over his head. His scalp tingled and a shiver ran the length of his body and back as he tousled what he could of the black coal from his hair. It took another bowl, and another, but the proud red began to peek through. The water and his hand went from thick black to lighter and light grays until nothing ran down his face but a clear freezing brine. His white skin huddled up into bumps and he buzzed with a clarity that was almost worth the discomfort of the bath. It would probably be a while before all of it worked its way out, but he couldn't see it, and he imagined a crimson mane dripping unblemished in the first sun.

With it, he felt an old fear leave in a familiar feeling. He was ashamed of his shame, why he hid at all. Every time things went poor, the panic took him, then the resignation. When he was in the grip of it, there was nothing he could do, even though he knew better. The lucks always had him. His was a strange one. It had become almost laughable, the way he knew that no matter how close he came to annihilation, something would turn it away even as the blade pressed against his throat. There was no need to worry or fear, though he always did. He knew the brink of misery well, and the path back was just as familiar. Just as some men were dragged away from victory by their feet every time they fought within reach, he was drawn apart from ruin no matter how vigorous his efforts.

He reminded himself again not to fret himself the next time. Not to make deals or apologies with Fosters, or slink in shitters and squain camps. That after the resignation came regret, the bowl of cold water, the resolve never to come to this place again. And soon, the light, brilliant red breaking through the black of coal. The feeling when a ship noses into the trough and starts up the wall of the next wave.

"Gionn," he said aloud. A squain girl rolled her head around to look at him. "The arsehole of the world." He smiled at her. "No one."

Tunguk's stomach crackled like a low flame beneath his heart. He walked through the spinning lanes of the tukits as the din of the harbor died down. He first noticed the feeling as something *more*—a weight he was not accustomed to, or a new object left out in a familiar place that he could not point to. The feeling itself was strange, as an old friend he did not recognize after many days of age had warped the statue of memory, but it was familiar. Soon he knew it was not Tunguk, but another thing added on, tied and dragging behind. It was not Brother, or Foster, and akmanuak. That thing had now become part of him, too, and he felt it always. This one loomed out of sight and begged to be named. He glanced to the side lane as he passed, and saw no one. It was clear behind him and ahead.

He continued on, but the pressure remained. Another lane went by, and he stopped even with the entryway of the home to his right. After two breaths, he stepped backwards and looked down the path, but Drummoc paths did not extend far before they bent out of sight, and no one was there. Again, he went on. Where he came to a fork that called him right, he went left, and when he thought he should turn, he went straight. It was as though gentle hands tugged at him, begging him one direction, and he had to pull to go anywhere else, which was the way he liked to wander. Those hands, he also knew, and it was not them he felt, either.

Tunguk listened to the path behind him, but it was easy to walk quiet with skin boots on hard rock when there was not yet ice to crunch underfoot. A flurry of wings ahead caught his attention as a gull landed atop one of the tukits. He veered toward it. When he was still several tukits away, the bird crouched and sprung into flight in his direction, and jerked hard to the side when he noticed the man. Tunguk came to the spot it left, and instead of going on, he made a slow circle around the building, his eyes turning the corner before his feet. When he had nearly come to the place he started, he paused to wait.

A figure flashed between the buildings along his original route. Tunguk completed his circle and found himself behind the boy. He shuffled his feet to announce his presence, and drew alongside. The boy hesitated, but continued to walk, a scowl etched deep in his face, twin lines sinking between the eyebrows, just as there was ever the beginning of a grin on his own mouth. They walked for several turns before he spoke.

"You are following me," Tunguk said in Mattakatan.

"You are the one who comes to me. I have my own places to be."

"I have traveled. Maybe I know them."

The boy shook his head. "From the looks of you, they are not places you would know."

"I think you are right." They walked for another stretch of silence, and it was clear who remained with who.

"Is it steel?" The boy asked.

Tunguk lifted the sheath that hung from his belt and let it fall again. "Good steel."

"Is it wet?"

"Since before I was born." Tunguk felt his rounded answers prod at the boy, and he smiled to himself.

"You say you have traveled far."

"I did not say."

"Well? Have you?"

"It seemed so to me."

"What is the best thing you have seen?"

"If I tell you, you will not want to travel far." Tunguk laughed at his own joke, to the boy's annoyance.

"Tell me! Or you hang your head in shame. What great deeds have you done?" He demanded.

"I think the answers are many, but when I try to recall, they do not volunteer."

"Try harder."

"I crossed a sea that could not be crossed. I tied a knot that cannot be untied. I killed a man who was my better, and I took a great fortune. I could tell you where it lies. I met a king—I met two kings. One of them knows my name. I bedded a woman no one could bed. Her gown floats on the waves. I fell in battle. And I learned a song that no man knows." The boy's eyes lit up. "That is what you wanted to hear?"

He frowned. "Is it true?"

"Well. I may have crossed the order. But if you had sailed with me, you would think so."

"*Pssh!*" The boy rolled his eyes. "You would not be here."

"I am sure you will have the choice to do better."

"I will."

"Now, what can I do to make you stop following me?"

"I told you," the boy veered down the next side lane. "You are the one following me!" He waved his palm overhead in an obscene gesture, and vanished into the town.

Parks snorted himself awake as the first light teased around the edge of the window. He scrambled to his feet the way he hadn't managed since his Navy days, and before that, Christmas, or the first day of a family vacation as a child. Terror or a lust for adventure, those were the only things that could rouse a man like that, especially after a night of terrible sleep. It had taken him another three hours to fall asleep once his visitor departed. He'd spent the time running through feverish scenarios in which he broke the shocking news to Foster in a dozen ways, all met with extreme delight. Had he misheard the man in his delirium? Maybe the whisper garbled the accent he thought he knew, or maybe he dreamt it entirely. It didn't feel like a dream, not the least because he spent the next several hours feeling like he had done too much coke before bedtime.

Someone knew their names, and wanted them to go somewhere. What was it he said? A long walk, dress for a long walk. Or hike. Did that mean camping? Parks wasn't sure, and wished there'd been a few more instructions. But all these secret nocturnal rendezvouses had him beaming. They were the belles of the Eskimo Ball. Everybody wanted a piece of them. The Foster in his head had grilled him on every possibility—a mistake, a trap, a stupid idea, a hallucination—and he shot them all down and won over the stubborn seaman every time. It took a lot more convincing to throttle his own enthusiasm enough to nod off.

Now that he paced the dark, scraping together his map and his bladder and spear, it began to well up again. How many people did he know who spoke like an American? One. And even then, none. Foster's drawl was a far cry from the President's English. But here he was, a California boy, somewhere like Antarctica, yet so unimaginably far away. If he was here, could someone else be, too?

It was a man's voice. Two men got off the boat before them, if he counted that bitch Carabiner, and he was the only one of them who had a survival suit. But they were in a raft, motorless, though with more emergency supplies than he had possessions in the childhood room that he rented from his parents the past six months. That wasn't here, though. They put into an entirely different sea—*that*, he was sure of. And the rest of the crew. As bad as he wanted to tell himself one of them got into a suit and came out the same way they did, he recalled the rest of the things they had to do to come this far. Even if someone made land, the chances were nil. Someone from the rescue team, then? Sucked through the same interdimensional time warp? Or maybe this sort of thing happened more often than he realized. It's not as though he could call the news and report it. Lost at sea. Was there an American ex-pat slinking around the wigwams of Drummoc, praying for someone to arrive who could tell him what happened in the last ten Superbowls?

Parks squinted in anticipation as he ducked out of the door into the low sun, still contemplating a rise into view over the wigwams. His eyes adjusted to find Kjartke sitting outside the hut doing her arts and crafts.

"Give me your arrowhead." She held out her hand.

"How come? Are you Indian-giving it?"

"You know how to tie?" She showed him a short, narrow bone shaft, notched at one end, brownish-gray feathers tied to the other. He felt his tunic, which did not have pockets, and went back to retrieve it. It took longer than he expected to find a tiny black arrowhead in the dark, and he was glad to see she hadn't just abandoned him while he swept the floor with his hands. Parks passed it to her. She began to wrap wet strips of tendon around the base where it fit into the bone.

"Do I get a bow, too?"

"I will make you bow. And arrows to shoot. This one, you do not shoot."

"Looks kind of small. Is it more like a decoration? Just for looks?"

"Same as other arrows. It is not looks. It is a place for the kaim to live. Luck, your people say."

"One day I'll convince someone that these people aren't my people. Racial stereotype."

"You know this word, then?"

"Luck?" She nodded. "Yes. My people also have that. Some of them, anyway. So it's like a good luck charm? Good things happen?"

"This? This is arrow. You must catch your own luck." She held the tip near her face, closed her eyes, and muttered a low song. Then pressed her lips to it in a kiss, and handed it to Parks.

"Thank you. That's the nicest thing anyone's ever given me. Here, at least. Even if it isn't lucky."

"You know how to catch?"

"In general?"

"Luck."

"Maybe you can tell me."

"The first arrow a woman make for a man, it is for the kaim."

"These women. Are they making them for, would you say, friends, brothers, random passers-by—what?"

"It is the husband. But I see you need it." Her look quieted his interruptions. "You must be careful who you choose. There are many lucks. A bad one will be happy to make home, much as a good one. You must dip the arrowhead in seawater each night until you find your luck, so it is not inviting to bad ones. When you see one you would carry with you, you sing him in."

"And then I'll have good luck?"

"You will have *that* luck. If you find luck in a hunt, you choose to sing him in, and you will have him when you hunt. If you escape your enemies, and you choose him, you will escape your enemies. If your voyage is good, even though the weather would wreck many ships, you can choose him, and that is your luck."

"I think I get it. But only one? Or can I get, like, a whole quiver of that shit?"

"One. There are many other places they live. It is better to go to them if you can."

"Sick. I mean—it is favored among my people, what you say. I'm actually a quarter Irish, on my mom's side, so I know all about that luck."

Kjartke nodded and picked up a new flint blank.

"Hey." Parks said. She looked back up. "I was being a sarcastic douche earlier when I said that's the nicest thing anyone's given me. But for real. I think it is."

"Sick."

Parks laughed, but quickly pulled it together when a look of frustrated confusion swept over her face. "Sorry. No, we're cool. That was a laugh of endearment. Ah, fuck it. If you see Foster, can you tell him to speak to me ASAP? As soon as he can find me. Tell him I bring news of great luck."

Gionn twisted off a sip of water from the bladder. "Not a fuckin' chance."

"You haven't even heard the proposal."

"If it don't involve me on a whaler sailin' north, you can pull your pants back up." He passed it to Foster, who took a swig. They sat in the poorman's quarters, two bowls of fish between them, and nearly everyone gone to take in the dawn.

"A second seat opened up this mornin'."

"Aye, I heard. Will you be tryin' for it?"

"Me and Parks. Will be tryin' for both."

Gionn snorted. "Maroonin' the squain cunt on Drummoc. That'll be a fine way to thank him."

"It'll be the best way to thank him. We're a chore, and he's too old for it. Ain't fair to drag him halfway around the world for our sake."

"Or convenient for you. Seein' there's but two seats."

"I'd take him if it made sense. And he'll say he doesn't like it. But he'll be glad. When we're out of his hair once and for all, he'll watch us disappearin', and he'll know he did what he could, and be glad that it's done."

"If you're gonna leave him here, you should at least have the decency to cut his throat. Don't be a shore-putter."

Foster narrowed his eyes. "Speakin' of shore-puttin'. My proposal."

"That. I thought you might find a way to tack back."

"I came up with two options that take into account all of our needs. We can all be happy with either one. I'm gonna let you pick."

"And what are me needs, cunt?"

"You need to survive. Gettin' on that boat and far away from your old buddy seems like the best way to do that, but there's an easier way."

"I won't spy on the bureaucrat."

"That was option one. You go to the admiral, agree to let me and Parks get on the boat. You pal up to the assistant viceroy, and leave with a chunk of change in Spring."

"Next idiotic plan."

"Hang on. One last chance. Are you sure you don't want option one? Because that's my favorite, and I think it'll be yours, too, but once you turn it down, there's no goin' back."

"Good riddance."

"Alright. I didn't want it to come to this, just so you know. The next best thing that I can think of, is you do the exact same thing I just said. Or your buddy Shitstain might end up realizin' you're here before you ever get a chance to sail off."

Gionn smiled and nodded as he chewed. Then he hung his head and shook it side to side. "I was wonderin' if that would ever occur to you."

"It occurred to me half a second after I realized *you* were shittin' *your* drawers over him. I just ain't the kind of guy who likes to fuck people if he don't have to. Way I see it, you've had every other option. I've fed you and watered you so you wouldn't have to choose between starvin' and stabbin'. If you can't do a favor for two guys who saved your ass, I won't feel bad doin' one for myself."

"It pains me to hear it, mate. I was very glad to believe there was a man as honest as yourself in the world, and I had known him briefly. This is well-beneath you. And I must say, you'll be careful from here on, because once you start on that course, it wont be long until you'll count yourself among the Gionns of the world."

"I got plenty of room to maneuver. Besides, you seem to get what you want often enough."

"I have never in me life gotten what I want. Only what I need."

"What I need is a ship home."

"Nah. That's what you want. Do you think I was born a cunt?"

"That was my assumption."

"No, mate. I was made."

"You're a self-made man, alright."

"Aye, we'll agree on that. Unfortunately, I'll have to pass on the second plan, as well."

"You think I'm bluffin'."

"I think it's possible, but I know it don't matter. Normally, I would pretend to squirm and let you think I was afraid and ready to give you your way. Then fuck you good and hard when you realized your predicament. But seein' as you did save me arse, and have fed me well—despite just threatenin' me life—and judgin' how tired I am of keepin' me stories straight…and considerin' me tendency to get meself a bit tangled up and make embarrassin' errors that are quite funny when I look back, very far back…

"All that counted, I'll be grateful to inform you that it was all a big mixup. Had a long chat with the man I saw. Turns out he is not Shitstain, but a fellow that looks exactly like him, right down to his tiny rat teeth and odor of an infant who's fouled himself. His name is Polc now, and we are well aware of one another. You might say we've called a truce, except we have never met before, so that wouldn't make sense, would it?" Gionn winked.

Foster studied him. "I can't tell if you think I'm retarded, or you're tryin' to tell me in your smart ass way that you and him had a chat and decided to call it square, which don't make sense, even though I have no idea what you did to him, based on—like I said—the smell of shit in your drawers."

"Bit of both. Of course it's fuckin' Shitstain," he whispered. "He wants me to keep that in hushed tones. Shitstain!" He yelled. "Wake up, cunts!" He shouted to the few Mattaka, too old and infirmed to be out moving. "Shitstain's here!" His voice evened out. "As it were, we patched things over."

"Patched things over?"

Gionn grinned ear to ear. "So much for your schemes, cunt."

"When in your *life* have you ever patched things over?"

"Eh, just the once, far as I can tell. But I've recently had a lot of practice tryin', what with you sops, gettin' your arseholes inside out every time someone temporarily changes loyalties and all."

"And you expect me to believe it now."

"Believe what you want, mate. Walk right over and tell him about old Gionn. You'll notice me gorgeous garnet is restored," he stroked his hair. "Nothin' to hide here. I'll have a drink with you at the tavern if you like. Raise a cup to no one bein' able to fuck me at the moment."

"How'd he find you?"

"Seen me from the start. Never had a chance, but it appears dear Shitstain is ready to have another go at bein' mates, or at least ignorin' one another."

"That strikes me as odd."

"Aye, so it struck me, too. I won't complain."

"What if he's just lullin' you into a false sense of security, so he can ambush your ass when you stop takin' precautions."

"He could have had me at any time. He prefers to be called Polc, which was not what I called him even before I found a more fittin' name. And to that, he prefers I call him nothin' at all. No, old 'Stain's got bigger troubles than me, it would seem. Wouldn't be good for him if a certain charmin' character went around tellin' old stories."

Foster nodded. "He can't be callin' attention to himself by murderin' people, especially ones who would make life hard if they got away."

"Sharp cunt. Took me a night of turnin' to get it all sorted. Goes without sayin', keep it stowed."

"You don't think he'd just kill you to make sure? You don't strike me as a secret-keeper."

"I do think it, and that's why I'm talkin' to you. If somethin' happens to me, do me a dead man's service: find Costig and sing the story I'll be tellin' you over our drink at the tavern." Gionn groaned to his feet. "Now come on. I'm sick of water."

Foster shook his head. "Find someone else stupid enough to do you a favor. As much as I'd like to try whatever the fuck passes for booze around these parts, I ain't out of moves, yet."

Parks leaned heavy on the spear as he limped into the wigwam maze. His leg had swollen below the knee overnight and an electric sensation zapped across the bottom of his foot with each steep, while the old wound throbbed with his pulse. He looked both ways. Every few doors, Reverse-Eskimo youths hung in groups with no particular purpose, looking bored or tormenting one another. Even the Navy didn't seem to have much to do. Four boys, all drunk, wandered by laughing among themselves. One of them glared as he passed. They didn't look like much—the oldest couldn't have been more than in his late teens. None of them swinging near his own weight class. He straightened up and took his weight off the butt of his spear. His size comforted his doubts a little, but he wondered if there was anything he could hope to do if a small group of armed and malnourished midgets decided to drain him.

It seemed simple enough to use the thing in his hand, but he imagined there were techniques that would allow people like Bruce Lee to take on entire cohorts of the clueless, and he didn't know any of them. Was there a spear-poking class these dudes attended at some point? Or were they thrusting just as blind as he was?

Pretend you're walking home at night in Brazil, he told himself. He might could take a few punks if he had to, but it was best not to look like a victim. The first step shot a pain all the way up to his hip, but he rolled through it to the next, and after a few his limp melted most of the way into his stride while the spear swung freely in his hand. After a few yards it actually started to hurt less than when he favored the leg, which told him his body was healing fine, if only he would pull out his tampon and trust it. Parks gave the spear a ninja twirl the way he'd done a thousand times with some broom he was supposed to use to sweep the shop.

A young and unsupervised Eskimo girl looked at him, and he gave her a tip of an imaginary cap. An awkward step send a jolt of pain into his knee, and he played it off by putting a little pimp swagger into his walk to hide the rest of his limp, the spear dancing in his hand like a decorative cane. Where the fuck was Foster?

Every time he thought about it, it made him giddy. For all his friend's obsession—the scheming and scrambling and stubborn insistence that home was still where they left it, and there had to be a way back—how funny would it be if he, Parks, was the one who found it while Foster ran around like a chicken with his head cut off?

At last, he broke into open ground. In the distance, the harbor was already a flurry of activity, even without a boat in the water. Foster might be among it, but he'd check the main drag first. He fluttered with anticipation. Just as he'd resigned himself to this world, all of this might end up in his rearview, after all. At most, a winter away. Then he wouldn't need to know or care what anything was about. The politics, the delicate cultural relations. They could bustle on without him. Maybe if he could just find his way to one of his people, home would be a shorter stroll than he realized. All he needed was Foster.

Three men appeared from a building down the strip. He recognized the squat frame of Costig, flanked by two officers the way men of rank always had a few brown noses angling for a sniff. Maybe *he* knew. At any rate, the deal had been spinning in his head ever since the night at the creepy crack. Gionn wanted on the boat, and so did Foster. It was blasphemous to bring it up, but Parks still couldn't see what the rush was. A winter here might suck, but sailing in that weather as the winter descended on them sounded exponentially worse, especially if they had to say goodbye so soon to their native friends.

They'd be dead on the beach where they landed if it weren't for Tunguk and Kjartke. Neither one would say it, but they didn't have to. For some reason, he thought they would bring him and Foster to a bustling port, put them on a big steamer, and wave farewell from the dock. Now he thought about what they would do—an old man who spent his days aimlessly wandering the streets and a woman whose top job prospect was banging whatever disgusting creature wandered in with pay and nothing better to buy. The sailors he knew from his years of service weren't fit to turn loose on a hated ex, much less a half-decent girl. And these, in this distant pool of wastewater struck him as some combination of gangbanger and homeless vagabond. A shudder ran down his spine.

Going all-in on a handful of seats on a boat full of gutter punks while the only two people who'd offered them an ounce of help wallowed away their lives in this shithole they'd have never come to had it not been for their sudden inconvenient presence couldn't be their only option, much less the best one. Foster's world was non-negotiable. In his, there was always a place for a spring in his step, a song in his heart, and a spin of the spear in fortune's direction.

"I was walkin' with the ghost, yeah," he sang. "Those are the only words I know. I was walkin' with the—I was walkin' with the—I was—I was—I was—break it down," he beatboxed a bridge as he approached Costig's bunch. "I was walkin' with the ghost. Take me to the one that I love most. Put some butter on my melba toast. My crew, we be chillin' on the coast."

Their eyes met, and he gave a sly nod. He saw Costig look at the man to his right, then nod back in his direction and he settled his walk into something more respectable. The melody sank into a low hum, and he was grateful he didn't have to freestyle anything else. Quit while you're ahead, that's what his old man always told him. The two officers walked out to meet him while Costig stayed put.

"How are you gents this fine morning?" One of them lunged at his spear, catching it with both hands, while the other wrapped him up and slung him to the ground. His shoulder crunched onto the rock and he felt it slip out of joint and roll back in as both men pinned him hard, each to a half. He heard yelling nearby, and he lifted his head to see others running in his direction right as the fist drove through his jaw.

Ostuk sat cross-legged on the floor of the tavern polishing off the last morsels of meat from a bowl that rested in the crook of his ankles. Before him sat an untouched cup of reddish-brown liquid. There were many familiar faces around the room, but he dined alone, as was his custom these last few days. The thunder of the storm and of ships colliding in the rough sea had already lost most of its force, the outlines fading already, details smoothed over, pain and fear smoothed over, only a few flashes here and there in the lowering gloom. Men leaping aboard a boat. The halyard fluttering. The climbing belt. He struggled to call up the way his ship felt against the abiama, but every bob of the hunting boat as he faced down the crew was unforgettable. Nor did he remember half of the orders he gave as the ram closed on them—he could probably rebuild them if he tried—but the things floating back and forth in the warship as it filled tossed and rolled in his eyes as clear as if it were that morning.

Not a man had breathed of it, as far as he could tell. When they landed he was so sure he would never see the deck of the *Juhketappat* again that he placed all of his possessions with family and mates, and insisted that the crew tell their relatives they would not return to his service next season due to a dispute over the loss of Ijak. This, he felt should have been true. But no man blamed him, and he had to compel their distance for their own safety, so sure was he that it would be his last run, and there would be grave consequences for his choices. Ostuk could not bear that other men be arrested with him when they had no more say than anyone else on the ship. Yet there were no signs of such a thing. It was early, and Winter's shadow long, but he had steeled himself for ruin, and now wondered what he might do if the season returned without a word of his crime, and the dogs must be brought north, and south again. It was his trade, his only one, and it had not been easy to make it. The decision to act as he had, to surrender all of it on a single order, felt like a knife plunged into his stomach. That dog captain had bled out on the deck of a dog ship. He was ready for the soldiers, for a flight, a fight, a new land, to beg a path from the six hundred ways before him. To be killed, or exiled, or sent to the mines, or to take a new name and make of it what he could from the whirling waters of Ralte.

Now, the possibility he feared most was that his fears never came to be. That all he risked, all he lost, go unnoticed, and in the spring, the same Ostuk he had known for many years would board the same boat. North in Spring. South in Autumn.

"I'd offer to buy you a drink, Brother," Foster lowered himself to join the captain. "But so far, everything's still free."

Ostuk smiled. "Nothing is free. The landing hospitality has ended."

"Ain't nobody charged me yet."

"You are going nowhere for Winter. And be sure, nowhere until you pay your tab."

"Fuck. *Fuck.* I bet Gionn fuckin' knew that, and he just let me buy him meals like I'm his sugar daddy." Ostuk laughed. "So all these people are payin', too?"

He nodded. "Still want to buy my drink?"

"What the hell is that, anyway?"

"It is hasqa. Export, they call this one. The water is taken off, so it can make the voyage."

"Is that some kind of traditional Mattaka alcohol? What do you call a drink that gets you drunk?"

"Hasqa. Mattaka have no drink. Nothing in Ajatse will turn like this. But they will spend much of their pay for it. Many of the men, they no longer earn, but work their debt. If a man tells you the farri bound the people here, it is not true." He raised the cup. "The people bind themselves. Amposi make the export too strong. They are smart, and the Kammatuk are thirsty."

"What's it taste like?"

Ostuk shrugged. "It's good you came. You can tell me." He handed the cup to Foster. He buried his nose in it, and pulled back blinking. "Smells like somebody mixed up rum and brandy…and egg nog." He took a timid sip, and his face crunched up in disgust, then softened. He tried it again. "That is a…new flavor. Man. I don't know if I like that." Foster took another swig. "I'm no connoisseur. Weaker than moonshine, stronger than wine. Got some, what is that? Fruit? Rye? Fuck, I don't know. Tastes like it'll get you fucked up."

Ostuk waved his hand to keep it. "How are your wounds?"

Foster shrugged. "Ain't got time to care. Got places to be."

"There is only one boat going places. Forgive me, but I do not think you belong on it."

"That's fair," he nodded. "But I would add that I don't belong anywhere around here. And if I gotta be out of place, I might as well do it on a boat gettin' closer to where I ought to be."

"I cannot."

"Cannot what?"

"Take you."

"Shit," Foster laughed. "Did you think I was here to buy you drinks and make polite conservation so you could ferry my ass home in exchange for a firm handshake? No, brother, I'm some kind of dumb, but not that one. Nah. I'm here to buy you drinks and make polite conservation so you can ferry my ass across the way to talk to the assistant viceroy."

"I heard about your last talk with a viceroy." Ostuk smiled.

"Rumor has it this one's a lot nicer. Besides, I got a good reference."

"And you think he will arrange your passage?"

"I don't think, I just gotta try."

Ostuk nodded. "Boats cannot just come and go to Camne Drumlag. It is very easy to go, but the admiral must clear the passage."

"Already taken care of."

"Then we can use one of the Navy's darraigs. My ship is trouble once it is stowed."

"You'll do it?"

"Aye, if you find the rowers."

"What about your crew?"

Ostuk shook his head. "None of them work for me. And if they did, they would want to be paid. The money I made from the voyage, it is lost. My family had many debts to settle. If a man were to accuse me of wrongdoing, and demand compensation, it would be found that I have nothing to pay him with." He grinned.

"How many do I need to round up?"

"A full crew is twenty-four. The trip is short, but it is always best to have a full crew."

"You think I could do that by…today?"

"If you have money, it is easy."

Foster frowned and nodded. "You know anyone who'll do it for free?"

"The people I know, it is best they do not know me."

A pair of boots squared to face them. They looked up at a man with light brown hair who smiled through small teeth that failed to meet at their sides.

"Apologies, sirs, I don't make a practice of rammin' me way into others' affairs, but am I mistaken that you're in need of a crew who'll work for free on short notice?"

They looked at one another and back up at the man, who squatted to the floor. "Nothing is free," Ostuk said.

"Ah, you're right, Captain, but what you've got for me won't cost you a thing. I, too, have business to attend with the assistant viceroy, but it was me own luck that had me arrive a single day after he'd set out to inspect the minin' camp, and he's not returned since."

"You're the boat from Tolba."

"Farri Tolba, that's right, Captain. Well-paid to deliver word to the commander of the garrison at Drummoc. Which I thought would be an admiral, but we've been through a few of those since I landed, and this assistant viceroy lad seems to be the man in charge. Problem is, I can't get an admiralty letter for Camne Drumlag. First one was too busy throwin' off the blue to give it. The second gave it, and the one now took it back. Think he's sore at me over the whole whaler thing. As though I could help it. Only local captains allowed, he says. Only cleared affairs. Seems like I'm lookin' at one of each. And if their crew happens to disembark and stumble into a word with the official, I see no harm in it."

"You got twenty-four men'll work for free? Today?" Foster asked.

"You can pick 'em from the forty-eight I got."

Foster and Ostuk looked to one another, and the captain gave a curt nod. "Welcome aboard, brother," Foster said.

"Call me Polc."

Shrill, indistinct voices rambled over one another, closer, farther. A grotesque rock formation loomed gray in front, and someone stooped near the base. It was Foster. One by one, he opened three taps that looked like garden hose hookups. Water cascaded onto the rock. He turned. "We're just gonna leave it runnin'." Something like longing or regret, or a sense of something important forgotten and drifting farther from ever getting done welled up in his chest. There was another flurry of sharp-tongues, and it felt like something gnawed at his neck. Parks slapped, and then scrambled to scratch the spot. He awoke on the floor in blackness. When he brought his fingers to the flesh, it was dry and unblemished.

A sigh of relief moaned out, and he could tell by the way it echoed that he was indoors. Indoors, where? Parks flailed his limbs in a brief panic for any beacon of touch. He scooted and jerked until his foot slammed into flat vertical stone. The leg cried in protest, and as soon as he calmed his movement he felt the deep ache in his right shoulder. Deliberately now, he crawled toward the contact until his hands found a wall. They weren't smooth, but these stones were large and cut with care, not the small jagged piling of a wigwam. His back straightened against the surface and it rose flat all the way to his head and beyond. A quick pat of his belt, and it was all gone—the map, the arrow, for sure his spear. Even his water bladder was gone. The memory of tonight's meeting flashed before him, and his heart raced.

"Fuck. Hello?" He shouted. "Anyone in here?" He had to lean against the wall and straighten his inflamed leg to one side to work his way up, and he did so slowly, knowing well that not many places these parts were made for men of his stature. But stand, he did, and raise his good arm overhead. His fingertips made contact long before his elbow could lock. Timber— about eight feet, and flat, not domed like the huts.

Iron hinges creaked as a heavy wooden door swung open directly to the outside. It filled the room just long enough for him to pick up the squared corners. A silhouette entered with a little yellow light and the latch found home. Parks retreated until his butt hit the wall as the light followed. It touched off against something, and flickered up in a bowl shape and illuminated the place well enough to see that he was alone in a bare cell, except for a mustache that curled down to the jawline to betray a grin from the mouth it hid.

"Dumb bastard," Costig said.

"The fuck? I thought we were buds." His jaw throbbed as he spoke, and he wormed it around in circles to find some slack.

"Buds."

"Mates?"

"Lad. You're useless to me as a mate. If but one man—mine or anyone's—sees you swaggerin' up to me to have a tale, you'll not be on any whaler. What by Dreyfus was so important that you'll have that and a poorman's winter when I'm tryin' to get you north with a heavy purse?"

Parks hesitated in the flickering light. "I was just going to ask if you had seen Foster around." Costig stared back in disbelief. "Also," he continued. "I had an idea. For our deal."

"There'd be no deal if I hadn't had you arrested, and there still might not."

"Hear me out. What's the big sticking point? Everyone wants on the boat. Foster, Gionn, me, Eskimo Joe—you got two seats and too many butts. I was thinking. What if I just volunteer to stay?" Costig again remained silent. "You need a dude to spy on your little assistant viceroy, right? I'm your dude."

"You'd part with your mates like that?"

"I've got a lot of mates. Not all of them are leaving. Look, you don't want me and Foster together on that boat, anyway. Gionn's a turd, but he's right. We couldn't sail a bass boat through a whale's asshole. You want that boat stopped, Gionn's your man. Even if you didn't want it stopped, and he didn't either, he'd still probably find a way to sink it. Correct me if I'm wrong, but you're sending it to Nunoc?"

"Aye."

"That's like, the next train station over. Foster can wait for me there, and I'll meet him first thing in Spring. Right after I get you whatever dirt it is you want."

Costig nodded. "I recall sayin' the exact thing to you, but I'm glad it sounds more appealin' when it's your idea."

"Just out of curiosity, what's the pay?"

Costig let out a breath heavy with regret. "I should be able to get each of you an argot."

"Is there any way you could just set aside whatever I'll need for a boat in the spring—nothing too fancy, but not super shitty either—and give the rest to my friends Eskimo Joe and Kjartke?"

"You want to work all Winter with your eye on the assistant viceroy—an act of treason, punishable by execution if you slip up one share as bad as you did today—and you want me to give most of an argot to a couple of squains?"

"Is that a lot?"

"Ha!" Costig erupted.

"Cause I wanna make sure they'll be pretty set by the time I peace out."

"Mate. You're the dumbest cunt alive, I'm sure of it. Aye. It'll be easier to get it to them than you, anyhow."

Parks extended his hand. "This is how we seal a deal where I'm from. You grab it," he guided Costig's palm into his, "and squeeze." Parks cried in pain and nearly went to a knee. "OK, OK! Let go!"

"Did I win?"

"Fuck," he shook his crushed hand at the end of an already-throbbing arm. "One of those, huh? Alrighty. Call it done."

"We've just the one problem. I can't let you walk out of here. It'll look bad."

"Do what you gotta do, I just need to be home before midnight."

"Oh? And why's that?"

"Gotta meet a man."

"Who?"

"Gionn," he lied. "And Foster. We have to work out the details of our little arrangement."

"Ingputka?"

"Hell, no," Parks shuddered. "Somewhere a little less terrifying."

"It's like I said. If I open this door for you, your reputation and that of your mates is done. There has to be a consequence."

"Well I'm pretty beat the fuck up if that helps."

"It don't."

"What've they got me on?"

"Your charge? Approachin' an admiral, weapon drawn."

"Can I just go on bail? Do my trial later? You can take it out of my pay."

"Bail? You mean a bribe?"

"No, just a friendly payment that says I'll probably be back to meet the judge."

"Who do you think the fuckin' judge is, me son? I saw you do it with me own eyes, and I'm the one passed the sentence. You think this is a ship? You think there's men'll stand to forget your crime?"

"What if we smear some fake blood—oh! Some seal blood! Smear some seal blood all over me, and you throw me out the door, and you go, 'And *stay* out, laddie, cause if you bring that big spear of yours anywhere near me again…' I don't know, make some shit up."

"You want me to let you go with a talkin'-to."

"And fake blood. Like you roughed me up. You don't think people will buy it?"

"I'm sorry, son. It's a bit more of a price, what you did."

"How long am I supposed to be in for?"

"Til tomorrow afternoon."

"Fuck! I mean, that's not that bad, but I really, for real, super serious, I need to go to my meeting. That boat could leave any day now, and me and Foster and Gionn need to get our acts together. I can't afford to get out tomorrow."

"You won't. You're set to be executed."

Tunguk passed her without speaking and disappeared into the tukit. It was as fast as she had seen him move since they landed at Drummoc. The window flap behind her fell shut from where she had tied it, and she knew the back one was down, too. His voice rose, and seeped out the edges, flat and rhythmic. Kjartke shook her head and returned to her arrow work. It did not matter to her what the old fool did, as long as he did it for himself. This, she repeated to herself, but she wandered again and again to the sound. Maybe if she stopped for a moment, she could hear the song, and would know something of what moved him. The blank she worked settled on her lap and she raised an ear, but could not catch enough to make it. Finally the voice stopped, and soon after he appeared. She hurried back to her knapping.

The old man stood in the door and closed his eyes, letting the dim light pour through his lids before he opened them.

"What do you sing?"

"Did you hear?"

She shook her head. "If I did, I would cover my ears."

He gave a satisfied smile. "It was first and last a song of akmanuak."

Kjartke let out a laugh of contempt. Of course it was them again. What else would wake the old man from his death dreams? They could not be still. One who moves will move against trouble soon, and often, she remembered the first half of the saying. It would be them who killed him. She knew it, and he must have known it, too. But now, Tunguk standing tall before her, motionless yet bristling with energy, she thought that they were also the thing that kept him alive.

She was sure these men could not help her. If this thing did not kill them, the next would. Was it Foster, or Brother? Both, maybe. Both useless boys, daring in the way that children are, to poke a thing until it stirs, and run when it does. They would not leave the tukit if they were wise, so they were never in the tukit. Great troubles passed before her, ones that Tunguk could not stop. Stabbed or drowned or pursued again, forever running. Her stomach tightened, and she felt anger slip over her. Just as boys, they cared for no one, and all was done for their ends. They deserved what came to them, and she hoped it came quick, so she could be rid of them.

"It is a war song, then," she said with disgust.

"I do not know if I recall a war song," Tunguk said.

"What, then? You will have to learn one. If they are not already dead."

"It is one that I took as a boy. I have never sung it. We will see how it goes." He laughed. Tunguk smiled at her, daring her to keep asking questions as if she cared. She knew his tricks.

"If trouble will come here, you must tell me."

"Will you help?"

"There is nothing I can do for them."

"Then sit. Do nothing. No man is your husband." He looked at the arrow she was making. At the others by her side. Her face grew hot. Kjartke wanted to pick up everything and march to the sea. To throw them so none would benefit from her hand. When these men died, she would throw them there, too, without a tear, that at least the gulls would find good in them.

"What is it? The song?"

"It is a song for the clever man." He laughed, a slow roll at first, rising and taking his breath. She could not help but join at how foolish he looked, and soon they were both lost to it.

"It would be better," she barely choked out the words between fits. "Better, if you had sung this, when you learned it. Old fool."

Tunguk caught his breath. "Only a young man may do a thing for the first time. It is good I kept it."

"A young fool, today." Kjartke let her mouth settle into a distant smile. She paused as long as she could stand. "What, then?"

"Brother is taken prisoner. He will be killed tomorrow."

"And Foster?"

"I must find him. We will need help. Maybe then the song will sing to me."

Tunguk left in the direction of the harbor. Kjartke tried to return to her work, but her blood ran too sharp. Instead, she rolled her things into a piece of leather and tied it. A few more arrows would not help. For the first time, she wondered if they even knew how to aim a bow. It seemed to her so obvious that she had not stopped to ask, but now it passed before her, the way they rowed and tied rope, ran from fights, held a spear with clumsy hands, the way they spoke and gathered water and argued over scraps of letters. Now she wondered if she was not wasting her time. The only thing she had seen them do with any skill was lie, and talk to dogs. Maybe they did not need weapons. Or a boat. The only thing of use to them was an old fool.

Something struck the wall of the tukit and bounced to the ground. She turned in time to see Norwet, one of the boys from Nunoc who tended dogs with them on the *Juhketappat*, grin over his shoulder and run away. Kjartke stooped and lifted a much smaller piece of rolled leather than the one that held her arrows.

Foster leaned on the oar, shoved backwards in the oarlock, and waited for the command. "*Ho!*" They shoved in unison, and the darraig creaked across the rollers several feet. It was surprisingly light for its size, but he was grateful it sat very near the water and not yet stowed for Winter. After they grunted the ship into the water they still had to have something left to row it. He felt the pressure of the eyes upon them, and though they hustled, none of them did so under the illusion that they would be able to launch. The harbormaster had seen them straight away, and now there were several more men gathered round him, half a hundred yards away, watching them wear themselves out. If the Amposi Navy was anything like the American one, they'd let them get the boat all the way into the water before descending on them with a barrage of profanity, then make them haul it all the way back to where it started.

"*Ho!*"

They were halfway home before the man approached. He wore flecks of gray around a bowl of straight-chopped black hair, a wide flat nose, and stringy muscles that held together long, thin limbs. His leather was pridefully hemmed with beadwork, and around it he wore a cloak that was once stained something like blue, fading to gray faster than his hair. These seemed to be a status symbol, maybe a uniform of rank, because Foster had only seen them on a handful of the men, mostly preening officers.

The harbormaster looked them over, unsure of who to approach. He settled on Polc.

"Admiralty letter." He spoke in a well-polished Amposi accent that Foster thought sounded like a cross between Filipino and South American Indian.

"You'll want to speak to the captain about that," Polc motioned to Ostuk. The officer repeated his demand.

"I would ask you the same. When you issue it, I will have it."

"Camne Drumlag?"

"Aye."

"You need clearance."

"This is the man who is cleared. We are hired to take him," Ostuk indicated Foster.

"What is your purpose?"

"I have a message for the assistant viceroy from Barzos, his man on Nunoc. The admiral already said I could go, so long as I got my own crew."

"I was not told of any ships to Camne Drumlag today."

"He's been kinda busy. I'm sure if you went and asked him, he'd tell you. It's Foster, with a message from Nunoc."

"You take a Navy ship, you cannot go without a pilot."

"You are new to Hiade?" Ostuk asked. The man hesitated. "How many seasons?"

"It is my first at Drummoc, but I have many seasons."

"First at Drummoc. Then it is understandable you do not know Ostuk. I am the captain of the dog ship *Juhketappat*. I have hauled in at Camne Drumlag twice a season since I was a boy. Bigger ships than a darraig. I am a pilot for these, and all waters between here and Nunoc. You can see that we have respected your laws. Will you speak to Costig while we haul down? Or you can push my oar and I will return with the letter."

"I do not have time to find Costig. You must have the letter before you launch."

"Sir," Polc broke from his oar and joined the growing circle. The men who the harbormaster had left behind now began to walk slowly toward them. "Is it not your duty to issue the letters yourself?"

"Aye, if I'm told of your passage and your clearance beforehand."

"Who is it tells you?"

"The admiral, or one of the other officers whose rank can clear a ship."

"Then who's to blame that you've not been told? It seems the error lies between the two of you. You've met our pilot. What concern could you have of lettin' us pass?"

"All traffic is the concern of the harbormaster, and Farri Tolba has sent word to secure the ports. Only official passage in the trade and security of the land. We cannot have everyone with a skin boat floating wherever they like."

"I'll allow you to look for skin on this darraig. And you can have a go at me face, as well. Have you seen me abouts?"

The man frowned, then nodded.

"And who might I be?"

"You're the hire with the word from the farri."

"Aye. I'm the cunt who told *you* to secure the ports on behalf of your king, and he has paid us—meself and all these men you see here—to reinforce the garrison as well. That means we're all arms of Farri Tolba. You have before you a man, cleared by the admiral with important word for the commander of this outpost, another man with more years of pilotin' these very waters than any other we'll find, and a crew consistin' solely of your own fightin' men, trusted to defend these ports against any threat a sea king could wash our way. Now if you want to find Costig, run along. We're already sailin' against the light. But if we're not cleared to row for Camne Drumlag, I ask you cunt, who the fuck is?"

The midday sun made a piss-poor showing when Gionn meandered out of the tavern, a bellyful of hasqa giving a warm glow to the edges. It wasn't much, but his pale skin took in every ray, and it made him feel a man again. A level drink and a walk, no more ducking the daylight. Besides, Shitstain was off fondling Foster at the dock, and half his men with him. It made his innards churn when he thought of it. What could those two possibly have going between them? The only thing Foster knew that could hurt him was exactly how many mates he had on the island—a very round number that might get old Polcy thinking his bollocks smelled right for a change of tactic. Surely the cunt wouldn't hang him alone to the wind, if he was clever enough to sort out the situation. Gionn shuddered. Even if Foster was good for it, it wouldn't be much for a few prying words to dig up what was needed.

There should be no truce. Gionn cursed himself for not seeing it right away. He could have saved a bit of pant-pissing, but now he was sure of it. No truce unless this "Polc" felt his own fuck-line ran a fair bit farther. There was worse in it for the bastard, at least with Gionn knowing what he knew. But if he had no mates and failed to tell them, the only trouble rested on his breath, and there'd be no sense letting him breathe it.

Faerkus or Euskus or fat Gilda, one of you thriftless cunts give me mate the gift of shuttin' the fuck up, he thought. *Mate.* The word felt like a rib shot. Was it that he knew he didn't mean it, or that he did?

Gionn lowered his eyes and tried to veer around whatever begging squain emerged across his path. She stepped to block him, and he half-cocked his fist before realizing it was Kjartke.

"Out of the way, cunt. You've frightened me, and I hate you for it."

"Walk." She indicated a path into the thick of the huts. The word was soft and undemanding. He could flatten her, or brush her aside, but something told him that walk is what he would do.

"Will you be the one protectin' me when a gang of these brown rascals decides to have me fair pelt for a cape?" He asked even as he followed her into the town.

"Kammatuk are not my people."

"Glad that's settled, then. Have you worked up cramps for me? I can't yet fathom why you'd want to keep me company, but you should know it's not yet bleak and hopeless and wintery-enough for me to go down—" Her hand thumped against his chest, and when she removed it, he caught a small scrap of leather before it fell to the ground.

"What is it?"

Gionn turned it over. "Looks like the hand of a child. Do you mean to tell me you haven't got your letters?" He chuckled at his own joke. Her glare made him clear his throat. "'GION,'" he began. Kjartke's patience cracked behind her dark eyes. "What? I swear, that's what it says. Misspelled me name, but it's right fuckin' there." She stopped walking and looked at where he pointed. He wasn't sure why, it wasn't as though she could verify it, but she must have decided it was enough, because she continued on without him. He jogged a few steps to catch up.

"'GION. USE KEY TONAT.' Tonat? What the fuck is that? Is he callin' me a 'tonat'? 'Use key tonat?' I don't get it. 'HAFF TO MID. HARM NO MAN?' Tonight! Tonat means tonight. 'Use key tonight, half to mid. Harm no man. ONNAR DEAL, LOOCK UPON YAR PASSAGE?' Honor deal. Look? Or luck? Luck upon your passage. Look upon your passage? Fuck it, makes sense either way." He beamed at Kjartke. "How'd that cunt know you'd bring it to me?" Kjartke shrugged. "And more important, what the fuck is he talkin' about?"

"Brother is prisoner. He will die tomorrow."

"Brother? You mean Brother Parks?" She nodded. "Ha! I knew I'd out-live that cunt." He pinched the sheet between two fingers and flapped it up and down. "When you opened this, did a small metal object fall out and clink upon the ground?"

"Are there more words?"

"No. I think he used all the ones he knew."

"Thank you." She quickened her step.

"Hang on, woman!" Gionn hurried to catch up. "So what's doin'? Does the old fella know?"

"It is good you read for us. We will help Brother."

"Not so fast. This was clearly addressed to me. It stands that old—" He glanced around to be sure they were alone, and whispered the name anyway. "*Old Costig,* intended for yours truly to pull weight in whatever you got goin'."

"You say we harm no man. Keep secret. This, you will find difficult."

"*Ha!* I mean, aye, a bit. But I'm afraid you don't understand all the man-plans goin' by just beneath the surface. We all have our little arrangements.

Parks, Foster, Fumble-Fingers here," he waved the scrap. "Ask yourself: why did he not address it to Foster?"

"How do I know he did not?"

"For fuck's sake! Give me a sliver of your faith. Did we not work well together before? Did your name once cross me lips?" The way she hesitated told him he had not immediately met with dismissal. He was getting quite good at reading the differences between her silences of favor and of impending murder. "There's a rhyme to it. Could be he means to catch me with the key and rid himself of two problems at once, but I don't reckon him as that sort of cunt. There'll be a reason he calls for me."

"Brother tells me of your man-plans. I do not care."

"Since when do you care for 'Brother'"? He caught her by the forearm and held her. Immediately, he regretted it, and watched her free hand for the knife he expected to untie them. Kjartke looked at his grip and back to his eyes. It was not rage he saw, or even defiance. Something moved across her eyes like a bird shadow between the sun and the glinting sea, then it was gone. She used every effort she could muster to make her face a rock. But he had already seen it. Before him stood not the terrible squain bitch he'd come to love to fear, but a helpless girl, begging him to see what he'd expected.

Gionn let his hand melt free of her arm, and made no move to restrain her. He held still as though he stood before a frozen tern that might fly at the first twitch.

"I know you don't need me help. I need yours. Yours, and Parks' and Foster's and Costig's, and whatever else I can get. Do you know I've been slinkin' from a ropy cunt and his crew of wankers ever since we landed? Worried he'll kill me, a little, though when I think of all the wonderful things I'll do if I live it starts to sound like a decent favor. I came here on a ship of forty oars, plus crew and passengers. I participated with some degree of enthusiasm in the rescue of forty more—plucked 'em from a sure and miserable death. How many of them hundred or so cunts do you think counts me a mate? If half of 'em would scrap for me, no man here could touch me. Polcy would be messin' his trousers. And he is, just a little. Just a brown dab or so. I got good slander on him, but soon as he realizes it dies with me, and there'll be no loud mouth cunts to bury him or even pour out a cup, good Gionn…" He trailed off.

"You can turn a key as well as I. Just pretend I'll be of great use and tow me along. It'll be good to see the bastard again."

"Half to mid. You know this meaning?"

"In normal places, with normal days and nights, it means half the time between when the sun goes down and the middle of the night. Here, I've fuck-all notion. Does it mean the usual time that it would be, or the time on your sun? Couldn't tell you."

"We are here."

"Aye?"

"Why do you speak of places, of times that are gone? This is where the sun will set. We count from here."

"Fair enough."

"Half to mid." She started away.

"Kjartke." The name stopped her. Gionn wasn't sure he ever used it on her before, now that he said it. "I once came to you for a favor. Said I'd owe you. Well, if you can take somethin' to your grave, or mine, whichever comes first, I'll owe you twice." He knew the way she said nothing was her kind of nod. "Can I tell you about me mate Shitstain?"

Costig sighed. He sat on the raised wooden cot covered in mats in the admiral's quarters—a room scarcely longer than the bed. A small writing table held blank leather and an inkwell and quill beneath a single dim window that opened onto the alley of the next building over. A large trunk next to it took up most of the remaining floor space. He was lucky to have it. No other man on the island could lock himself behind a door when he needed.

His hands supported his cheekbones on the pillars of his elbows, dug into wide knees. A blink, and his lids refused to return for a moment. He listed, then jerked up to clear his vision. At last, it came, when he couldn't have it. Costig could sleep in a loud mess, the lee of a rock, or across the thwarts nipped by spray. This place was the worst of them. He merely garrisoned it. Held it against attack for whoever pranced down next from the shores of Ampos. His leather armor stood stiff in the corner like half a prisoner, slumped into the wall. That quill had seen more exercise than his spear these last weeks. Good for his letters, at least, he snorted.

He always wondered what the admirals did behind this door when he waited long hours, sometimes days for word to proceed. As soon as it closed behind him, it felt as though someone patched a leak that had poured in around his calves. There was quiet, and outside, the sea. A low thumping presence against the wood. Within, the damp that never dried, always at his feet. He lived among every conversation, every request and every order. It was cursed, in a manner. Nothing new would come to him as long as he remained in these quarters. He'd never before enjoyed the privilege of removing himself. A Marine sergeant-at-arms was the rock upon which the waves broke. Now that he could erect a fortress, he found himself staying longer and longer. The wind and the cold were always worse to those who could warm themselves. His innards knotted at the thought of the men beyond. The things to read, to sign, the petty rivalries, the proud officials, the work-shirkers and the arse-ticklers. No sergeant need care for farris, or assistant viceroys. Only in here was there any respite, and only for him. Outside, there would always be the sea.

Three quick knocks broke his peace. "Admiral." He stared at the door as long as he could. A second set of knocks followed—respectfully persistent. He willed himself to his feet and shoved a small rolled bit of leather in his trousers. Was it a couple of weeks, or was he older by a year? He closed his eyes, drew a deep breath, then burst through the door.

The crowd in the Navy hall swarmed him, and he took an immediate left out the room. Gerachay and Wayranapan closed on either side like human shields. A barrage of voices called his name, begged a word or just shouted their questions. Somehow, a couple of the bureaucrats had gained admittance. Costig shouldered past them. Outside, a larger contingent of civilians and the odd sailor added themselves to the mix. The three men blew past the wagging fingers with such haste the crowd paused its pursuit. Costig turned.

"Well? Keep up!" He resumed his march toward the harbor. The swarm nipped at his heels.

"Willakuy!" Gerachay both announced him to the admiral and invited the man forward.

"Sir!" The official trotted along. "Regarding the assistant viceroy's order for a door-to-door squain count. Shall I carry through?"

"Aye, if you want to die before you get the second figure."

"Aye, sir. So, do it?"

"No, you idiot. Do not count the fuckin' squains."

"Very good, sir. And another. Then shall I also not count the treasury?"

"I'm the one ordered you to do that."

"Aye, sir." He furrowed his brow.

"So count it. I need to know how much he took."

"Thank you, sir!" Willakuy fell back. Costig stopped and called after him.

"Hang on! Do you think he wants a low number, or a high number?"

"Sir?" Willakuy came scurrying back.

"The squain count. You think he wants it low, or high?"

"Eh…" Willakuy drew his lips back in constipation. "Low?"

"I think he wants it high. Give him a low number."

"So, you do want me to count them?"

"I want you to make it up! Is that within your ken?"

"I think so."

"Next!" Costig and the flock left him to mull it over. A flurry of bodies at the ships caught his attention. Men he didn't immediately recognize were hauling down a darraig. He strained to see who might think they had clearance, when a familiar face popped up. Foster.

"Fuck!" He muttered to himself. Costig thought about having them stopped, but maybe some good would come of it. There surfaced a vague recollection of his granting consent. He carried on his course.

"Wendell!" Gerachay shouted. A man in a faded blue overcoat came up grinning from the harbor. He intercepted the throng.

"Costig! You're the fuckin' admiral!"

"Good to see you, Wendell. Where've you been off?"

"Huntin' camp, mate. Sir. Orders of Admiral Turrha."

"'Mate.' Good for you."

"Understand you had him executed. Will I report to you, then?"

"Is it long?"

"I suppose."

"Are we still gettin' meat?"

"A bit."

"Then it'll wait. Find me in a day or two."

"Good to see you Costig!" He peeled off. His voice rang faintly as he remarked to someone, "Costig's the fuckin' admiral!"

They came to an abiama surrounded by Navy men, the only other vessel in the water. A young Mattaka man waited impatiently. He lowered his gaze as the admiral approached. "Sir. I thank you for an admiralty letter that I may bring back the supplies."

"Got everything you need on there?"

"No, sir. We have sent for four teams of dogs. And sir. I apologize. Wiser men have counted. It is not enough—the oil, the hunting weapons, and the coin."

"It is not what you asked for, but it is what I can spare. You got your food and your furs, and your dogs and sleds are comin'."

"Aye, sir. We are very grateful. It is only that I wish not to anger the Assistant Viceroy. I was expected many days ago, and to come back without his wish—"

"Lad, it's the Navy. If he's not learned of delays and shortage, he'll have to make their acquaintance. What I want to know is who told you to take an abiama?"

The young man looked perplexed. "It is these men who loaded the abiama. They say you tell them to."

"These men are fools, and I said no such thing. We can't spare a warship for a supply run. You'll have a darraig."

"Admiral, sir. It was in a darraig for two days. We tried to sail, and the harbormaster said the darraig was needed, and we must take abiama. He said we need new admiralty letter. This ship was loaded."

"Well I outrank the harbormaster, and I say it's a fuck-up. Unload her, lads!" He called to the sailors. "Get yourselves a darraig."

"Sir. With respect. The dogs are on the way. If we unload, we will not be ready until tomorrow."

"Then tomorrow, it is. Captain!" Costig called to a Navy man. "Send the dogs back when they arrive. They can't overnight in the town proper."

He could see the frustration boil in the young man's face as he bit hard to keep his tongue. He stuttered, and managed to gather himself. "Admiral, sir. The assistant viceroy demands—"

"Lad, I don't give a fuck what he demands. He'll get his supplies when you get your shit together. I won't have a warship doin' supply runs when we've got two farris and only one sea." The miner seethed and barely managed to walk off at a respectful pace without further word. Costig called the captain back.

"When you load the darraig, count the cargo again. Make sure it's all there."

"Sir, it's the same cargo. Off one and on the other. If we count it again, that'll take another day of itself." Costig's eyes gleamed. "Oh. You heard him, lads!"

"I thought certainly today would be the day he hit you," Wayranapan chuckled.

"Won't be long, now," Costig smiled. "You might say, any day." They laughed. "I'll have all the main harbor fuck-ups before I fuck off to the calm harbor."

"Speakin' of, sir," Gerachay motioned to a Navy man. "The timber for the calm harbor is ready."

"Ready? Why the fuck isn't it underway?"

"No admiralty letter."

"Hear me, lad," Costig barked at the captain who approached him. "You were to launch yesterday. If you're Navy, and local traffic, you don't need a fuckin' admiralty letter."

"Aye, sir. Is the harbormaster aware?"

"He is now. Because you'll tell him right before you launch that if he holds me boats for a letter again I'll make parchment of his flesh. I got builder's sittin' on their thumbs. You'd best hope you get there before I. Wayranapan!"

"Sir!"

"Why are all me warships in dry dock?"

"Did you want them out, sir?"

"What by Dreyfus has turned me Navy into welps beggin' for me tit? Is there any man left among you capable of actin' on his own industry?" He addressed the hangers-on: "How many of you need a letter so's you can take a shit? We're starin' at a siege in Spring and the only oar any of you is strokin' is the short one. I want these fuckin' waters churnin' by the time I rise in the mornin'. Everything between a twenty-four and a forty-eight is drillin' close-quarter maneuvers in rotation. Make sure they're seaworthy, and when you got 'em all done, start again. Anyone not assigned otherwise rows one day out of four, and thanks the gods I don't have more ships to put you in or it'd be three of four. Any man found unfit through lack of skill or effort shall lose his commission and his board. Have Rixtan to oversee the drills, and see that he knows I'll hold him to the merit of the crews."

"Aye, sir."

"And where's Wendell? Is he near?"

"I do not know, sir."

"Remind me to see him about that huntin' camp. Until we know otherwise, I assume somethin' is fucked. Put word to the squains: small vessel restrictions are lifted until further notice." He felt the silent gasp cross the military men in earshot. "For huntin' only. And they may not congregate in groups exceedin' four."

"They are not likely to obey, sir."

"I know that. Tell 'em, anyway. I want as much food piled up as possible. Nine of ten from every catch goes to the farri's stores. That's the price of defendin' 'em. Am I done here?"

"Sir." Costig hid a smile when on of his old Marines stepped forward uninvited.

"Purpose."

"Squains dumpin' buckets on the harbor side."

"Post a squad. Arrest who you catch."

"Aye!" He disappeared.

"Lamaqar," Gerachay announced. The Viceroy's coal minister came forward, obviously annoyed to be seen after so many ordinary military men. It was no small pleasure of Costig's the way his jaw clenched while he waited his turn."

"Admiral. We still await word on the coal. It is not known if the assistant viceroy will send it."

"I want dogs in those mountains soon as the ice reaches Camne Drumlag. Take every lump of it, and do so until the mines close for the season."

"Aye, sir. Eh. I must also point out that we lack the coal ships—"

"Any ship big enough to carry a bushel is a fuckin' coal ship. You'll blacken this shore before Winter. I won't have a navy pass us right by to rob us blind at Camne Drumlag. They'll have to kill more than a few squains with stone points." He didn't bother to mention that it would also piss off the Assistant Viceroy, but for once, a gleam came over Lamaqar's eye as they shared a common purpose.

"Any more stupid questions concernin' the main harbor? Main harbor, only." None of the remaining audience spoke up. "Come on, then!" Costig marched toward the town. As soon as the group drew near the buildings, two Mattaka boys appeared on the street. They looked square at the admiral and waved their hands overhead, jumping up and down. This time, his men needed no command. A squad broke off and ran after them, but they fled into the stone huts. The men came to the border and turned to Costig in hesitation. He waved them back with a grunt, not least because he knew Tur-rha would have organized a manhunt into the town, led by Costig and the Marines, that turned up nothing if no one got knifed in the process.

The admiral quickened his pace, deciding that the next man to molest him would have to do it panting. It was another of his Marines who drew even. "Admiral! Inventoried the steel as you bid."

"And?"

"It'll make good ballast. Wouldn't count on much of it in a fight. I've put in with the forge, but they say you've ordered nails, and they haven't time for steel."

"The nails'll be done and on their way to the calm harbor. I'll see to it personally you get your steel. What spirits have the men got?"

"Glad to see a Marine make Admiral, sir. Eager to fight if they have the points."

"I'm keen to see how many of these blues feel the same. Have our lads take them up Urkuk for exercise."

"Take who, sir?"

"Every last one of 'em, in turn. March 'em hard. Mark who quits. I need to know who I've got if it comes to it. Every week until Winter, and again soon as the sun returns. I'd rather a few dozen barrels and a few hundred dead than to wonder who'll turn the third day of a siege."

The Marine looked troubled by the order. "Our lads'll be square. Don't know about the Navy."

"No, but you will."

"Aye."

Costig pushed through the door of the Navy tavern and locked a beefy grip on the shoulder of a man sleeping on a table beside an empty cup. "Wake up, lad!" The teen startled to his feet. "You're to guard the prison tonight?"

He looked around Costig at the daylight streaming through the open door. "Sir. It is day?"

"Aye, it's fuckin' day. You're posted tonight?"

"Aye sir, first dark to first light."

"Good. I need you to fill-in near the harbor. We got bucket dumpers. I'll have a man relieve you, half to mid. If he's late, go anyway. There's but one prisoner, and he'll be fine without you, but I aim to add to their number tonight. What time did I say?"

"Half to mid?"

"Your cloaks a tatter."

"Sorry, sir."

"Mind if I have a square?"

"Sir?" He looked confused. Costig pulled his knife, lifted the tail of the leather, and cut half a foot before rolling it and stuffing it in his beltline.

He rejoined the dwindling crew outside. The quartermaster stood between Gerachay and Wayranapan like a scolded dog with his cap in his hands before his crotch. "Tell him!" Gerachay said. The man muttered an apology.

"I haven't got time for foreplay," Costig said.

"Sir, Turrha had made arrangements to secure buildin' materials for the new quarters to house the officers and visitin' dignitaries—"

"*Gerachay!*"

"The nails never got on the boat for the calm harbor."

Costig's forehead vein flared. "Have you been there the whole time, in the pack with your mouth shut as I sent the ship off? What fuckin' good is timber if they haven't got the nails? Why do you think I had the forges firin' nails and only that for weeks now?"

"Aye, sir, but Turrha had ordered all nails secured for the new quarters—"

"And all the timber, which I told you to free up for the calm harbor, right after I executed Turrha for treason. Did you think the dead man still wanted his nails?"

"Sir, had I known you wanted the nails, too, I would have sent them with all haste."

"You'll take off runnin' with all haste and stop that ship before I finish me sentence, or I'll drive them nails through your fuckin'—" The quartermaster burst into a sprint. "Ah, I'll decide later."

He stormed down the street to the long, low rectangle spouting black smoke from every chimney. The naval forge rang out its presence far in advance of his arrival. Costig couldn't recall the last time the air was so full of noise and soot, and a small fire of pride ignited in his chest. He barged through the door and took in the groups of squains hunched over anvils, or quenching metal in hissing fresh water that they had to haul in non-stop to keep the hammers swinging.

"Forgemaster!" He called.

"He is out," an older man lay down his tongs.

"Out where?"

"Two of the new apprentices did not arrive for work today."

"Where are me fuckin' nails?"

The old man smiled, and waved his hand at a line of baskets covered in leather sheets. "We make them as fast as we can swing. It is good for the boys to learn on."

"Poke your head out that door and holler to every Mattaka you see that Costig is payin' every strong young bastard willin' to run the whole lot down to the harbor. And stop makin' nails. Spearheads and arrowheads, none but that til I tell you otherwise." The old man smiled. "And you wouldn't happen to have ink an quill, would you? Somethin' to write with?"

"I am sorry," the man said. He looked around over the work tables and came back with a stick of charcoal. "This will mark."

"Much obliged," Costig stowed it away. "Runner!" He shouted as he came back into the daylight. The force of his voice against the soot in his lungs sent him into an immediate coughing fit. He couldn't reckon how the squains stood it all day. It was a cruel god who cursed them with the capacity to breathe black. "Runner!" By the time he got it out the second time, a Navy man appeared before the group. "The nails are comin'. Tell the ship to leave for the Calm Harbor soon as they're loaded. If it's already left, arrest the quartermaster."

"Aye!"

"Who've I got left?" There were only seven more behind his officers, two Navy, one bureaucrat, two Mattaka boys, and two Mattaka girls bulging at center, none of them over fourteen. One of the Navy buckled under his stare, thought better of his question, and left without a word. He loathed to hear what Tuilapoy had to bother him with. The Chief of Colony was a fine title for another Amposi crawler who administered the basic needs of the Mattaka, and he well-knew that he always had to go last.

"You," Costig beckoned to the Navy man. "Purpose."

"I don't know, sir," the man said. He had the deep brown of one of the colonies inland of Ampos, starved of the sea. "You told me to see you."

"Did I?"

"Aye. I was loading the abiama for the supply run to Camne Drumlag."

Costig tapped the side of his head. "You'll be last. Tuilapoy! What nonsense have I got to fuck with today?"

"Very few, sir! I have but three concerns to raise. These young lovers request for their marriage to be granted by the Kingdom of Ampos."

"Married. Married." He pointed at each couple. "Next?"

"It is my duty to bring to your attention a hasqa shortage that threatens the public tavern."

"How short?"

"It may not pass through Winter."

"They could use a break from it," Wayranapan joked.

"Aye, but if they run out, they'll riot," Costig grunted. "Fine. Move one of each ten from the Navy stores to the public stores. Ration the sales to two quarter-casks a week."

"Admiral, it is common to sell six or eight."

"Small wonder they're short. Three quarter-casks a week. They won't like it, but if they're half-drunk, we can handle it."

"Very good sir, we are very quick today!"

"Talk or lose your turn."

"The last of my affairs is but to remind you that tonight is the weekly public meeting for the airing of concerns and grievances of the Mattaka people," Costig rolled his eyes, "to be heard and dutifully addressed in all earnest sincerity and with forthright expedience by all officers and officials in whose power it is to remedy—"

"Are you still on that?"

"Would you have me cancel it again?"

Costig sighed and shook his head. "Postpone it. Tomorrow night." He motioned the last remaining man over. "A moment, lads." Gerachay and Wayranapan allowed the admiral to lead the sailor well away from walls and ears.

He'd probably never spoken to an admiral before he was summoned, and now he looked back at the officers as if he were shoving off from his home port for a perilous journey that he didn't expect to survive.

"What's your name, me son?"

"Atxlchar."

"That's the one. Heard a good many things of Atxlchar. Trustworthy man, they say. Has the respect of all the men." Atxlchar touched his chest with his finger as surprise swept over his face. "It's true. Which is why I need your help. You know the lads better'n I do. And you know the situation with the whaler." He nodded along. "What I need are a couple of good, loyal lads.

Keep this to yourself," Costig lowered his tone despite being far from anyone else. "But I want to put a few agents on that ship. Let 'em pose as defectors, while they do me work. I won't stop it leavin', but I can see that it don't arrive. Problem is, I haven't a notion who to ask."

"Are you…askin me, sir?"

"You? Ha! No, you're too valuable here. I need to know who you stand for. Take the rest of the day off your duties to think. And don't breathe a word. Just seat yourself in the tavern and observe the men with a keen eye to givin' me a pair of names. I'll need you to report to guard the prison at half to mid. If you're a bit late, it's fine. I won't meet you til some time past mid. That's when you'll give me the names." Costig winked.

"Aye, sir!"

"Off with you." The sailor could hardly contain himself from breaking into a sprint of delight. "That man has a dangerous task," Costig said as he rejoined the officers. "See to it he isn't tabbed for his drinks, today alone. And see that he knows it."

"That one?" Gerachay said in disbelief. "He's a fuckin' grassbender."

"Exactly. Better him than you." They laughed. "That'll be all, lads. I've me shit to take, and then off to the dog camp, and the calm harbor."

"We will accompany you," Wayranapan said.

"Not necessary. I can wipe me own arse."

"At least let us assign a squad of Marines. It is not safe for an admiral to go to the hinters alone."

"I'll let you fetch me spear. Then I need the both of you at the harbor. Cormdran's tryin' the seats today. Make sure we've got a full complement of ships on rowin' maneuvers, cock-to-arse in the harbor. He'll have to have a dockside knot-tyin' competition to decide it." They grinned.

Costig swept into the latrine with his spear. Four of his sailors were having pants-up chat, and they jumped to make like they were on their way out.

"Good luck at the whaler," he said.

"Ah, we wouldn't go for that, Costig!" They laughed as they strode casually out to give the admiral his privacy.

His shits were as close as he came to a rest. There were days when he was sergeant-at-arms that he forgot the last time he slept, and his body prayed for death as he whipped and cursed it forward. No one punched an admiral if he didn't like an order, and if the squains got worked up, there were other men to put them down. No more ships across the channel, or up and back to

Nunoc. No more Camne Drumlag. Nothing heavier than a quill. Costig despised it. Before, the only idiot he had to suffer was an admiral. As admiral, he suffered them all.

Now even his shit was ruined. He pulled the square of leather and the charcoal marking stick and lay them on the flattest spot he could find. Next to them, he unfurled the little leather roll, and moved the key aside so he could see the writing.

"FAWSTER," it read. On the new sheet, he wrote, "GION," and copied the rest of the letter.

It was a brisk three miles to the dog camp, inland along the arm that jutted out into the channel, Drummoc its shining fist. Urkuk loomed closer, and he felt for the men he'd force to march it in the coming weeks. Costig would not be going that far, today. His boots crunched across the border of the ice at the foothills—a border that would soon creep down to the sea itself. He leaned to crest the low ridge that ringed the dog camp.

The squealing wretches were kept well-enough away from the proper folk for more than just the noise. There was something about the creatures that unsettled him to his soul. The grinning fangs and almost-human eyes that raised to meet his approach from their leads. The Amposi thought them malign spirits, and as unappealing at the dogs were to him, he took great joy in watching the browner of the lads squirm any time they came within sight. If the gentle-faced seals had a murderous cousin, it was these. Still, they were the best and only way to get the coal down from the mountains. Twice a season they'd appear in Camne Drumlag—once before the melt, with tools and provisions, and again after a good freeze to carry ton after ton to be stowed until the ships could sail down from Ampos. First and last. To the miners, they marked the start of their labors and the relief and return to their wives and children. Sacred companions who toiled together for one another's fortune. But even to the Mattaka, those who worked the dogs were the lowest of men. Like the Mattaka themselves, they were a necessary nuisance in Costig's fate.

For some reason, they never barked at him. He knew men who they'd try to ravage, launching at their leads for someone they had never seen in their lives. Others passed without so much as a glance. It was said one who they ignored was either a great man, favored by the bright gods and thus a conqueror to the foul, crawling daimons, or he was marked by them to die soon. A hero, or a ghost. Either way, Costig was glad not to garner much of a look as he passed into the main of several huts that housed the families who bred and drove the animals generation after generation.

Sawi, they called the man passed out on the floor around an empty jar of Hasqa. It was short for something long. He was the only one in the the place, which smelled of fur and bile. "Hoy!" He shouted. It wasn't long before a boy appeared.

"Uncle." He tried to rouse the sleeping man with his foot. "Uncle, the man is here for you." His voice broke with the turning of manhood.

Costig shook his head. "One more for you, lad. Same place." He pulled a small leather bladder and lay it on the floor beside Sawi. "That's for your uncle, when he wakes. Payment. That I used his nephew for a small favor, and he kept shut about it."

The boy nodded.

"Suppose I should remember your name."

"Norwet."

Foster sat sideways on the little quarter deck, his arms draped over the gunwale as he leaned around to watch the black ram skip through the choppy water of the channel. It had been a brisk hour hour on the oars—for the crew, anyway—with Polc calling the strokes in the back while Ostuk piloted them from the huddled sanctuary of Drummoc. It felt so much bigger when he was lost among the wigwams, but seeing it go reminded him just what a precarious handhold human beings had on this remote crag of the world. He was the only idle one aboard until an easterly picked up and the men could raise sail and rest their arms. They weren't much faster under sail than oar. The same wind raised chop and blew off the haze to reveal their destination: a line of black mountains that stood like a wall to fend off invaders who charged south the penetrate a land that had never known men, except as petty raiders who came now and then to make off with seal or fish—the ones who survived. Ajatse, the Mattaka called her. It struck him that he was just an island hopper until now.

The darraig bounced along, spraying him with freezing water that seemed to wash away both his worries and his hopes. The warship that had pursued them to Drummoc and sunk for their troubles wasn't much bigger than this, and it would have felt like a pathetic layer of insulation had he not spent weeks in a skin boat. The prospect of riding a storm in this thing made him almost suicidal with despair, which he let run off his face with the next blast of water. There was no room for anything but rowing. He huddled as far as he could from the others while they rigged the sail, and still found himself leaning this way and that to clear a path to a sheet.

Now he had his peace again. The rowers had no interest in him. Most of them looked like children, despite what he thought was his own youth.

They were a mixed lot, but not one of them had the look that he'd come to think of as Amposi. Though they all spoke English to one another, he couldn't follow a goddamn thing they said, between the sailors' jargon and inside jokes. Now their work silence exploded into shit-talk as they secured oars and enjoyed the breeze. If American Navy recruits were borderline-retarded, he realized, at least they could read and form sentences when they had to. He'd only ever been near Mattaka rowers, who spoke their own language, and so apparently got the benefit of the doubt—the wise natives. He wondered if they were just as idiotic. Either way, he felt like an alien, and didn't know if he could relate to anyone here, even if he wanted to.

So he turned back to the peaks, and prayed the wind would hurry them along.

"Farther than they look," Polc squeezed between the rows and sat across from him on the quarterdeck.

"I'd swear we're almost there. Is it really a whole day?" Foster faced him politely.

"Aye, and we should have left sooner. Ostuk's worried we won't make it before dark. I'll row these cunts to their graves before that happens."

"Appreciate it, brother. I'd be fucked without you."

"And I, without you."

"And both of us without him," he nodded to Ostuk.

"I've always believed that the gods only introduce us to the people we need to meet."

"I've had a few I could do without."

Polc gave him a courteous laugh. "The squain seems like a good dog. That's what they call it when they're a half, I understand."

"He's a better one than I am."

"Maybe I should be at the other end of the boat, then. Here, I thought you were the one worth chattin'." Foster looked out over the bow. Polc went on: "I don't know how you took that passage with a whole ship of 'em. Ostuk seems square enough, but I have to admit, they're not the easiest folk to get on with."

"Guess I'm just used to 'em."

"Can't say that I've spent much time in Hiade. Or want to again. But pay's pay." He shrugged.

"Whereabouts you from originally?"

Polc grinned and leaned back. "Ah!" He pointed an accusing finger as he chuckled. "You've broken the Sailor's Silence, me son! Don't you know not to ask a man far from home of his home? There's like to be good reason he's where he is, as there is for all of us. And you'll keep yours, and I'll keep mine. That right, Teague?" He asked the nearest rower.

"Who asks me affairs?" Teague erupted. "You fuck yourself, you fuckin' cunt!" He laughed hysterically, reminding Foster of nothing as much as a schizophrenic homeless man stammering to himself, complete with spindly beard and and enough missing teeth that he couldn't count without staring.

"You'd best find your manners, Teague. Foster here is an unlikely fellow. Them's the ones you least inquire. Or cross."

"Shoot, you can cross me all you like. I couldn't whoop your worst man. My only defense is you'd get exactly what you earned off me—not a damn thing."

Polc sized him up. "What do you say, lads? I'll take the false on that."

Teague locked onto him and snarled. "True."

"True," the next-nearest rower chimed in.

"Tenpenny on it," Polc said. "I'll match every man aboard."

"I'll take," a third said, and the first two signaled their agreement.

"Conditional that no man here be the one to test him."

"Fuck off," Teague said.

"Are you out?"

"In. Nine to who cuts his throat!" He called. The others roared with laughter.

"You can see why we put him in the front," Polc thumbed at Teague. "As far from the captain as he can get."

"Give yourself plenty time to jump when you see Teague stand!" He laughed himself into a fit, and no one else.

Polc lowered his tone so the waves took most of his voice. "I don't know nothin' about the bastard. If he's a murderer or a prince. Although I can guess which is the likelier. But on me boat, we don't care what you done. Only what you do. And since we got him in Gharnadil, all he's done is row, drool on himself, and bark his way into the dog seat. He can't see that there's no such thing as a soft man this far south." Foster wanted to believe it, but every throbbing bone in his body told him otherwise. "Fuck, if you want his seat, say it and I'll throw him over now."

"Only seat I'm after is goin' the other way."

"And you think the Assistant Viceroy'll grant it?"

"Don't hurt to ask." As soon as it came out, he felt the sting of the healing lashes on his back.

"I'll cut the shit, because you're too hard to flatter and I've no taste for it, anyhow. The man's a sniffer by reputation. You know..." he raised his nose high and and took a haughty pull. "Though I've come far and to his great benefit, I've had no luck to see him. I realize it's no favor to carry you here when I've just as much to gain, namely, me pay for the deed done. But when you get before him, if it wouldn't be too much to ask…"

"Brother, I take care of those who take care of me. He'll get your message if I have to deliver it myself."

Polc clapped him on the shoulder. "I knew I'd measured you well, me son. I'll take that and thirty penny." He grinned.

The dogs alerted when they saw Tunguk. Most of them wagged to their feet out of habit, for many times they had seen him on the ship, and he came with food. Their noses reached for him, and they tripped over their leads and untangled themselves in turn, settling only when he held his empty hand for the teams to sniff with a whimper. He saw no one around the little group of tukits, so he walked among the pack until he came to her—the one who nursed Foster. She raised her head with recognition as he knelt, but was unmoved. Her eyes returned to her pups, nursin from another mother the next team over.

"The young ones look strong," he said in Mattakatan. "Will you trust me to them?" Her lips closed nervously as he reached his hand, but she did not rise as he placed it on the back of the nearest one and picked him up by the scruff. The pup whimpered for having been ripped from his milk. Tunguk looked him over, then replaced him. He eagerly sank back into the nurse's teat.

Tunguk stood and stepped over tails and taut leads to the main tukit. Before the door, he paused and lifted his tunic, then his sapak, to check the marks on the dry skin of his belly. The ink was smudged, but the lines stood firm—a bar, with two smaller rectangles rising off the end at a right angle to different heights. Satisfied, he brushed aside the flap to find Sawi snoring on the floor, an empty jug turned over at his side, and a full bladder sitting before him plugged tight. Ferrakut and Ulwet glanced up at him from where they idled on the floor. Across the room, three other boys of a similar age passed the rocks between them, stacks of three, single ones—a game called *hama*.

"Where is Norwet?" He asked the two brothers from the *Juhketappat*. Ferrakut shrugged. "He would not say."

"The admiral brought hasqa for our uncle," Ulwet pointed out the round bladder. "He spoke only to our brother."

Tunguk bent and picked up the skin, then gave Sawi a poke in the ribs with his foot. The man only shifted position. Tunguk kicked harder.

"Ah-yi!" Sawi grimaced and sat up. "Tunguk! You are back so soon."

"I bring work for your boys." He held up the hasqa. Sawi lit up.

"They will do fine work. What is it you ask?"

Tunguk walked to the doorway, pulled aside the flap, and set the bladder down outside. Sawi dragged himself to his feet, lowered his gaze, and walked out after it.

"We will go to your forge," he spoke to the boys he did not know—sons of Sawi, he thought. They tensed.

"We do not keep a forge," a boy of twelve answered.

"It is good that you say that."

The boy thought it over, then surrendered a nod.

"The thing I ask you is different. I have paid your father, and he will hear good of you, even if you choose not to help."

"What do we get?" The youngest one, maybe eight, said. The brother who had spoken first slapped his stomach.

"It is fair to ask," Tunguk replied. "Do you know of Vitjukvattajuk?" They all nodded. "Tell me what they sing of him."

"He is stronger than four men. He made a fool of the admiral many times, and when he was caught, he broke the prison as only Barduk had before him, and killed many men who came for him. Then he sailed far, and won many victories."

"Always when our people were harmed, it was he who avenged them," the youngest added.

"I do not know if Barduk was the only one to break the prison. Or if no man has done it."

"He did. And Vitjuk, too," the middle boy swore.

Tunguk nodded. "That is what they sing. I think it is young men who want their name in song. They hear of the great battles, but not of the suffering. Tired men, hunted wherever they go. There is no song of a man who dies old, who dies with a smile among his family."

"I would be sung and die on a blade," the oldest brother boasted.

"Do you think a man sails a ship without a crew? Fights a battle without an army? How many men are Barduk? You will not hear their names. And Vitjuk? Many died because of their folly. Many beside them in battle. Others, later. They lived much between the verses. How can you sing of one? If you do, you sing them all. These are the songs of our people—many people. Who is the man who trimmed their sails? Who is the man who was first to die when they fought? Who was the man who kept his tongue when his word would betray them? Or lied when the truth would be their end? Do you know what smith hammered their blades? I assure you it was done. Do you know the woman who held him that he could sleep? What sons they left? Who was the man who made the song, that you could remember? I know the names we call them. They are Barduk. They are Vitjukvattajuk. The two men in six hundred days and nights who broke the prison. Alone, with the strength of many men, as you say.

"You ask what I offer you. Nothing. There is no pay. You may not speak of it, though you will wish to be known. If you fail, you will die, your family will die. If you are victorious, you will sit here in this tukit by dawn, play hama, wait to bring the dogs to Camne Drumlag, or across the sea to Nunoc. And when you hear the people sing of the one called Leopard Seal, they will say he had the strength of many men. If you can trust an old man, I swear an oath that there will come a time it brings you a smile."

The boys sat speechless. None of them could meet Tunguk's eyes. The air within the tukit seemed to echo off the stone walls with a sound so faint it could not be heard, only felt on the edge of the skin where the small hairs stood. The oldest of Sawi's boys stood. That was all he could do. Tunguk turned a gentle eye to him.

"Do your uncles have many sons?"

Parks lurched awake feverish from a dream, as though he was trying to stand. The second he put weight on his left leg, the pain that shot through his knee and up the inside of his thigh put him back against the wall. He whined and caught himself, and hoped he hadn't woken Kjartke. It took him moments more to remember he was not in the dark of the wigwam, but the flat-walled jail. The air was dead and stifling. In his fitful sleep he'd wedged himself into a corner where the big, smooth blocks of the outer wall met the jagged incongruity of the one that separated him from the next cell over. Somehow, it was the inner one that gave him comfort. He scooched his throbbing shoulder into it, and let the little corners and edges press dots and dashes into his skin. It reminded him of the safety of the wigwam.

Again he forgot his dream, but it was as unsettling as the others. The dark was not absolute. Now little square edges of gray light showed that all along the front wall, there were smaller blocks that were not sealed in, at regular sizes and intervals. Small enough that he would get a forearm through and not much more, eight feet off the ground. The air was thick and dead. Every breath felt like he took it from and returned it to a small paper bag, and it made him shorten his breathing even more until he wheezed and blinked away silver from his vision. Parks jerked in a panic. Clam down, bro, he told himself. You're hyperventilating. There's air. There's plenty of air. Just chill the fuck out and breathe it.

With force of will, he halted his gasps and held them in until his chest screamed, then let out one long, slow exhale that emptied his lungs. The air returned on its own, a gentle rise of the low back, and before he knew it, he had taken three, four breaths that he didn't even notice. Now he wondered how long he'd been asleep. The sun was out, he knew it by the cracks of light, but not whether it was setting or rising. He didn't even know which cardinal direction the jail faced. He'd fallen asleep and jerked awake half a dozen times already, for a minute or a few hours—he couldn't tell. At least with something to look at for the first time since Costig slammed the bolt, he felt like time had returned. The dark was forever, or no time at all, but the thinnest slice of light gave him back his seconds and minutes somehow, and he had one more thing that placed him in his world.

"You shouldn't have come," Eskimo Joe's voice swirled amid others that he neither recognized nor understood, and he shook the delirium free. Fucking solitary confinement, that's what it was. They'd locked him up to go nuts. What had he and Costig agreed to, anyway? Execution, he knew that much, but somehow Parks thought he was supposed to come away safe. Some kind of deal had been struck, but he couldn't remember what, only that he had felt like it was good. He racked his memory for their conversation. All that was left were fragments, like a chunk of ice that had been smashed on the rocky ground. Was there a deal?

"Foster!" He screamed, and remembered that his jaw was in agony. That made more sense. He was concussed, too. Strangely, his head didn't hurt. It felt light, liable to drift away if he didn't keep a grip on the string. "Joe! Foster!" He thought about yelling for Kjartke as well, but he was afraid of feeling like a little bitch, especially since he wasn't sure if he could pronounce her name as such a high volume. Kuh-yart-key. Kee-yart…kuh-jarta-keh…he shook his head. "Hey, can we get some air flow in here? Open this bitch up a little? Know what I'm sayin'?"

He tried once more to work to his feet, but he didn't even get to weight his bum leg. A cramp snaked around his stomach like a half-filled water balloon, doubling him over in pain. It shot down from his navel to his scrotum with a punch to the balls. Parks threw himself into the fetal position and squeezed his thighs around his forearms while his hands cupped his junk. It felt as though he'd gone on the worst bender of his life, and followed it up by taking the worst ass-whooping, to awake in some alley in South America where white men did not tread. Except if that were the case, he could vomit and stumble away. Nothing came up, and he would die in the morning if the walls didn't come tumbling miraculously down. He knew with all his heart that he should use his last energy, if it were his dying breath, to drag himself mightily to his feet, probe those blocks for a weakness, come up with a plan, bust out, and limp home to curl up on Kjartke's lap for a bedtime song. There was nothing to lose. No pain worse than what awaited. But nothing in him would cooperate with his flawless logic. He did not want to quit, yet as he lie panting and squeezing himself for any kind of relief, he knew that he could not go forward, either.

"White boy dyin' on the cold-ass floor," he moaned as much as he sang. There was a long pause while he waited for anything else to come to him. "Don't wanna feel this pain no more. / Won't somebody come, somebody open that door? / white boy cryin' on the cold-ass floor." *Clink.* He heard a sound like there was someone in the room with him. Like the tap of rock he'd heard in the wigwam, the night the voice had told him of their meeting. Shit! Their meeting was tonight.

"Hello?" Parks listened. Seconds passed. The sound did not return.

"Left my Ma in Cali for the blue ice floe," he resumed. Somehow it made the ball cramps a little more bearable. "wrappin' bonds with Foster and Eskimo Joe." *Clink.* He heard it clear that time. It was faint, but there was another right after it. His head turned toward the inner wall. *Clink.* It was coming not from the same room, but from the other side. "Niggas always try, but they can't..." he paused to think. "Break my flow." *Clink,* it came like an accompaniment. Someone was tapping a rock on the wall of their cell to his song. "White boy dyin' on the cold-ass...flo'". He cringed that he couldn't come up another rhyme. Technically, it was three different words. He shrimped his whole body over to the wall, and looked up at the little glowing lines near the ceiling. "The admiral got a look at my big ol' spear." The clinking sound started up in earnest, off-rhythm but constant—the sweetest melody he could imagine. "Po-lice whooped my ass and they locked me up here." *Clink, clink, clink,* the reply. He had a sight, he had a sound. His head spun with nausea, but he didn't mind, as he counted time and waited until he could speak again. He had a friend.

The darraig carried a dying momentum as the men hauled in the sail. At the stern, Polc and Ostuk's words were drowned by the flurry midship. Foster tried to read their body language—both smiling politely, a shrug here, or a spread of the hands. Camne Drumlag towered before them, not more than two miles off. He still saw no sign of civilization. Was it the name of the mountain range? The peak before him? The port? The sun had already retired behind the wall, but there was plenty of light bleeding around on the shores of the mainland. As with most places he'd seen here, it looked as though some ancient god had built a fortress right up against the sea, so steep was the rise from the water's edge. There was no beach or harbor apparent, though much of it was still indistinct. No such welcome mats graced the Antarctic coast, though he was grateful for the absence of most of the ice cliffs that he knew from his work on the research vessel, and the charter. The glacial freeze seemed to have retreated to elevation in most places to reveal that the rock was no more hospitable. It was as though the land demanded they huddle at the edges at all times, quarantined to a handful of livable zones and prepared to leave the moment the weather turned, or the food migrated, or any conditions other than ideal ones prevailed.

Teague was turned around on the bench, and his eyes were fixed the same way, but they were glazed over. Foster knew he wasn't looking at anything farther than the hairs on his nose. The rest of the men were busy fiddling with ropes, locking oars. This one had been idle since the order came. His left cheek twitched, and now and then his fingers would jump in reply. All of this Foster watched from a careful corner of his vision, lest he do anything to catch the man's attention. A body moved down the line of the boat, over benches and provisions and men. Without looking, he thought Polc had returned, but it was the captain's voice that found him.

"We will anchor here for the night. There is a good place for the line to make the bottom."

"We're not goin' to Camne Drumlag?"

Ostuk looked over the ridge line at the creeping twilight. "It looks as though there is light enough, does it not? I thought we might make it, but the surface was rough. It is a difficult landing in daylight. To ask rowers who have not done it to try as they go blind…safer to stay here."

"I reckon that's why you're the captain."

"Wait until you see it in the light," Ostuk nodded to the mountains.

"Must be beautiful."

"It is terrible," he laughed. "Your people call it the Last Place. None is more south than here. The first time I saw it, I was a boy. There was a cloud there," he pointed to the peak, "hanging over the tops so that you could not see them. I felt that only a great hero would be brave enough to go there. I was sure that some cruel spirit dwelt beneath it. That the world stopped at the edge of a storm. Of course, I know now that many common men go every season, to take the treasures of Tannawauk while he is hunting. I have been as far south as any man who has lived, and as far north as Nunoc. For me, it is the first place."

"Is that by choice, or by law?" Ostuk seemed puzzled. "That you've never been farther. I heard somethin' about not crossin' somethin' or other, but I got to admit, I have no idea what that means."

The captain nodded. "Both. We are forbidden to cross the Orin. It is the sea that separates this land from the others."

"But you're only part Mattaka, right?"

"It is enough. I am grateful to own a ship."

"I'm already plottin' out my ass-kissin', for me and Polc. You can bet I'll put in a good word for you, too. Who knows? Maybe he'll grant you a—I don't know. Some kind of a pardon, or exemption. Hell, if we're lucky, he might even clear us to go on your ship. No fuckin' with that whaler, needed. You could be the first of your people to go north."

Ostuk laughed. "My people have always gone north. By choice, if not by law. The songs tell of three lands that they came to before this one, each worse than the last. Each time, they were driven by Gotak, and each time, they escaped. When they saw this place, they tried to return the way they had come, but he blocked their way."

"Who's Gotak?"

"Do you know this creature—the angotak? It is a whale with teeth like a dog, black as night and white as snow."

"'Course. We call him Shamu. The killer whale."

"They are his children. Gotak is the great one who drives all the things that breathe air or water before him. He swallows those who are slow. You cannot retreat, or turn aside. The only way to escape him is onward. The Mattaka are slow, but they are still here." He grinned. "Eventually, they will have to go again, though some say not for many days yet. I think it is sooner."

"That's a cool story, brother. Who knows? Maybe you'll be the one to take 'em."

"With respect, I ask that you don't mention me to the assistant viceroy."

"You don't want a good reference?"

Ostuk shook his head. "It's better if men like that don't know your name." He swatted Foster on the back, and laughed when he cringed in pain. "Besides, if he finds favor in me, I'll never get the fuck out of here."

"Far as I'm concerned, your name's Dog Cap'n, Cap'n."

"Get some rest. We row at first light." Ostuk started to the stern.

"Hey!" Foster stopped him. He made tilted his head at Teague, still lost in space, possibly even asleep with his eyes open. "Any way I can sleep back there with yall?"

Kjartke crouched in a triangle of shadow two buildings down from the prison. It was a good moon for the deed, just past full, but too bright for her liking. A thin cloud hung before it, casting a hazy silver stream over the land, enough for a building or a man to cast a shadow. It was good, too, that it was behind the prison, so that its shadows darkened the ground by the three doors that faced open rock and the sea. Each had a lamp of whale oil that burned beside it for the lone guard.

She turned the heavy iron key in her hand, new enough to still hold its black. Her fingers pressed over the points—one, two, three. Kjartke knew of locks, as she knew many things of the Kammatuk Mattaka and the halots, through stories that came to her people with the traders. But she had never seen a key. And though she passed many doors since she arrived, none had this thing on them. An iron that held fast an entry to all except its master. What could it look like? How did this thing in her hand tell it that she would pass? From the shape she tried to see the way it fit. Long and thin, three horns of different heights. It made little sense. Gionn would know how to use it, but she had watched the sun go down, and she knew the midnight. It was half the time, as he said, and now it was past that, and she was alone.

When they spoke before, she let herself be fooled. She had resolved to do it alone before they met. Tunguk would know a lock, but he did not appear and she did not seek him. When Gionn offered, and he made himself weak to her, she thought it better to have him—if nothing else, he could make the key work. It could not be difficult, though. She'd watched the guard for hours, hoping he would open a door so she could see his way of doing it, but it was clear he was not trusted with keys. A lookout. One to scream for help. That is all it would take. The Navy hall was the next building over, and there the officers slept, and many of the best men, with a thin alley between.

She pressed herself into the wall as a figure moved past her: a tired man rubbed his eyes and walked clumsily.

"*Gionn!*" She whispered as loud as she could. The man startled, and she repeated herself. He jogged over and sat on the wall beside her.

"You are late."

"Eh. I thought about bein' prompt, but it didn't appeal to me." He looked up at the moon. "Bit bright, isn't it? What'd I miss?"

"This man paces."

The guard walked the length of the facade toward the hall, craned his neck into the dark, and reluctantly came back the other way.

"You wanna kill him, or shall I?"

"Harm no man. The letters said."

Gionn groaned his annoyance. "Well he also said half to mid. I thought Costig would at least bend one over for us."

The guard paced to the far end again, this time venturing out of the lamp light in a wide circle, pausing to scan the moonlight field beyond the quarters, toward the harbor, before he doubled back. Gionn nodded to himself.

"He's off watch. Waitin' for his relief."

They looked the opposite way down the street at the next-closest lights, the public tavern, as a pair of Mattaka boys stumbled out laughing and headed into the town. The only ones awake now would be in one tavern, or the other. With some luck, none would have to cross the prison to go home, and it was too early for most to go home.

Now the guard walked straight out from his post to look into the place where the boats slept for winter, where the whalers slept at all times, fearful of sabotage. His frustration grew as he returned to the prison, and again he looked off to the harbor and shook his hand around his spear.

"Ah, come on!" Gionn moaned. "Dutiful cunt!" He turned to Kjartke. "Do we know which door is Parksy?" She shook her head. He pondered it. "The far one—with all the space before the next—that'll be the main lockup. The other two have less wall. Smaller cells, so's you can separate the really interestin' ones from the drunk sq—your people."

"They are not—"

"Not your people," he interrupted. "Right. Apologies, I forget. That aside, our mate won't do well in the big one. Not if he's got company. He'll be in one of the wee ones. I suggest we listen for sounds of wankin', or sobbin'—like to be both. Can't waste our time tryin' wrong doors. If Costig means to rid us of this cuntsbreath guard, it won't be for long."

They fell silent. Nothing came across the rock, except the steps of the guard and the gasps of the sea. The man shook his head in frustration and started out in a march, as though he intended to head right into the hall, then stopped himself and did a long semicircle back to the near side of the prison, looking all the way for any sign of someone coming to set him free.

Gionn pulled his short sword halfway from the scabbard. "Are you sure?"

"I am sure." He stuffed it back in.

A stream of curses they could not hear came from the mouth of the guard. He made one more round, edge to edge and back, then he clenched his fists, swore again, and burst off in the direction of the harbor.

"That'll be us, love." She was past him before he could finish his sentence.

Gionn sprang after her. No sooner were they up than a breeze swirled in off the water, flickering the flames of the three fires. The farthest one went out. "Fuck." He caught up to Kjartke and darted ahead to the lamp by the nearest door. With a mighty gust, he blew it out so that only the middle one was lit. They took each an end of the plank that barred it from being broken from within, and tossed it aside.

The key clanged as Kjartke fumbled it against the mechanism. Whether the wind or the noise, or a sense well-honed, the guard picked that moment to turn. Gionn froze, then realized they were in the shadow of the prison, and all he could see was one burning lamp and a single door. He was a hundred yards out by then, but a sense of duty, or being a ripe cunt, spun him back to his post.

"Hurry the fuck up! What are you doin'?" He looked at her jamming the thing violently against the hole. "Have you never been with woman?" Kjartke said something in Mattakatan that he was sure was a curse to have his bollocks rot off over a long period, followed by a gruesome death.

The guard was heading to the middle one. He'd not gathered anything was wrong, other than a need to relight the lamps, but he'd have it done several times at the pace they were pulling. Gionn hustled to intercept him.

"Hoy, cunt!" The man startled at the arrival of another from the dark. "You shouldn't be out here alone. Have you not heard about the gangs of squains who go round stabbin' folks?" The man wrinkled his brow in confusion right as Gionn's fist crossed his temple.

He delivered another firm stomp to stop his wriggling, then sprinted back to the door.

"It's the wrong one! Try the other," he said. There was a firm click, and Kjartke glared defiantly as she shook the bolt to see which way it gave, then slid it back.

"Keep watch," he told her, and went inside. It was black as pitch in the cell, and smelled of piss. "Cunt! Parks! Get up, mate!" He felt along the wall. "Hey, gimme a light!" He called to Kjartke.

"You blew it out."

"Fuckin' get the other one!" He turned the corner of the outer wall, then the back, within moments. It was tiny, little more than a sleeping closet. It had to be the wrong one. There was no one here. He came to the rough stone of the inner partition. Gionn stopped cold. He shot out just as Kjartke came with the lamp.

"Where is he?" She asked. He huffed out the light. At the end nearest the Navy hall, there was a sharp clang of metal ramming home. It was impossible to see, but something moved through the darkness—a great body, larger than any man—away from them and into the alley between the prison and the hall.

Kjartke bolted after the movement. Gionn swore and ran after her. She disappeared down the alley, and he saw a flash of shoulder take a right turn just as he rounded the corner. He overshot the turn and had to place his left foot on the wall of a hut to push him back into the lane without losing speed. Again in the moonlight he saw her vanish in the maze of squain homes. It was all zig-zags now, and he took them as fast as he could without tripping over the edges of stone walls, in some cases so close that only a single person could pass between them. Finally, a straighter bit gave him the chance to dash ahead and grab onto the fur seal tunic.

She tried to swat free the hand that slowed her. "Stop it, cunt!" He protested. "I'll be lost." Kjartke said nothing, but she no longer tried to separate as her black hair tossed silver-blue in front of him. He heard voices to their right, high and panicked. They went wide around another hut and tried to head off the sound, but it came again from behind them. Whoever it was, they were going slow, making many turns. The heavy shuffle of Gionn's boots seemed to drive them wherever they could squirt free. Kjartke lead them in an S-shape and shot around just in time to catch sight of something. They picked up speed, scraping legs and banging toes at every corner until the mass lumbered before them. Gionn could now see it was not one but many—a writhing body of heads falling over itself.

"Tunguk!" Kjartke braved a shout, and their quarry stopped. Gionn panted up to a group of children who struggled to hold a large figure on his feet. The old man appeared from the head of the column. Gionn counted six—no, eight—faces no higher than his chest. Parks tossed between them like a ship on the waves.

"Hoy, cunt!" Gionn greeted him. The party took a grateful breath as they realized their pursuers were on their side.

"We must move," Tunguk warned them.

"No," Parks managed through labored breath. "My arrow."

"What's he on about?"

"We gotta go back."

"We're not goin' back, thick cunt. You get caught again, it'll be the last time."

"I gotta get my arrow."

"He's off his senses. Let's go." Gionn reached to help support him, but Parks fought away.

"His *kaimatjuk*," Kjartke explained to Tunguk.

"Where is it?" The old man asked.

"Admiral," Parks said.

"It's gone, mate," Gionn insisted.

"I need it. Let me go. I gotta get my arrow," he swayed deliriously. A sudden strength took him, and Gionn and the boys had to clasp his limbs to hold him from bolting.

"I will get it," Kjartke said. "I know the look." Gionn caught her elbow as she started off. She glared impatiently at him, and he muttered a curse under his breath.

"Tell it to me."

It was easy enough to wind his way back along the shadows opposite the moon, though he had no idea how he was going to find the group again. Gionn listened for a minute at the edge of a parallel alley down from the prison, and after a silence braved a peek around. The lights were still out, the door wide open, and the man he'd cracked still strewn across the ground. Had no one even heard them? He tiptoed over to the edge of the building and gently closed the door so that it wouldn't arouse immediate suspicion standing agape. The hinges creaked the last few inches, and he cringed with them.

The man was bloodied but breathing, and Gionn passed quickly to the edge of the Navy hall. There he hesitated, and wondered how he was going to find a contraband arrow in a building full of men who would cut him down for the very act. They still laughed and shouted within, no doubt a few casks of hasqa in play. He'd no right to enter as a civilian. No chance of going unseen. If the admiral had Parks' stupid arrow, he'd have in there, where he kept his quarters.

A flicker caught his eye, and he spotted a man emerge from the hall with a stumble, his spear in hand, at a half trot as though late for something. Gionn looked to the unconscious guard. He may not even spot the man, but his line was clear and straight for the prison. The relief shift. It had to be. Why was he even bothering with the arrow at all, he asked himself? Parks had made off with the others. He could steal any arrow he liked, or none at all, and the idiot wouldn't know the difference. He probably wouldn't even remember asking for it the next morning, such was his state. And it now occurred to Gionn it may not even be among his confiscated possessions. It was probably beside his mat back in his little squain hut, if anywhere.

He hadn't wanted Kjartke to try the Navy hall. Now Gionn wasn't sure why, but he knew it had been accomplished, and all he needed to do was leave, say he couldn't find it, if anyone even asked him of the matter. But he was just as certain he wouldn't. Like so many things wise and in his interest, it stood before him as some condescending prince, a lecture on what was best, how to comport himself, perfectly argued and certain of itself beyond any apprehension that he even had another choice, let alone would be dumb enough to take it. He saw a glimmer of himself fighting beside Parks and Oduy. A senseless gesture of pride. Now he felt all the other possibilities slip beneath the surface and bubble away, as they often had when his luck lead him to the one he had no cause to take or hope to gain from.

"Fuck!" He said, and started out from the shadows to intercept the watchman. "Help! Come quick!" He waved the man down. "Are you the relief?"

Atxlchar's vision swayed as he tried to make sense of what appeared in his path. "Aye," he replied.

"Well, you're fucked. Someone broke the prison." Gionn pointed to the guard splayed across the ground. Atxlchar's eyes swelled in terror. "Best rouse the men. All of 'em. If you make a good show of it, the admiral might not flog you to death."

He trembled in stunned confusion.

"Go, lad!" Gionn turned his shoulders back toward the hall. "This is all your fault, you late cunt! I'm tryin' to save your arse, but you gotta listen. Sound the alarm! *Now!*"

Atxlchar slipped and sprinted back to the door of the hall. Gionn jogged after and positioned himself on the far side from the prison. He caught the handle as it closed behind Atxlchar, and held the door open with his body. There was shouting within, and in moments they poured out, throwing on cloaks and raising spear or sword.

"Hurry lads, that way!" Gionn waved them on and pointed at the prison. "All hands to arms! All hands to arms! To the prison!" They came by the dozen, first the drunk revelers, then the sleepy officers, like bees from a broken hive. Torches came to life and the quiet was shattered by shouts of confusion. Costig walked out rubbing his eyes, and blinked hard when he noticed Gionn. "All hands to arms! The prison's broke!" He continued. Costig glared, and repeated his cry: "All hands to arms! Every man to the prison!" The hesitant sprung to action at the admiral's command, emptying the hall. He leaned close to Gionn.

"Whatever you're doin', do it fast." Costig grabbed a few stragglers and hurled them along, waving the hall empty. The alarm of voices rang off the buildings, and more men headed their direction from the enlisted quarters.

There was a long pause after a man left, and Gionn peeked in. One more nearly ran him over, hopping into his boots. He slipped in. The Navy hall was one long room with two rows of proper tables, bedstuffs strewn over the tops, the benches, and the floor between them. At the end nearest the entry were the doors—four of heavy wood, the last wider than the others. It gave to his push, and swung inward against the wall. The room was small and sparse. A single wooden cot frame, covered in furs. A writing desk, and an officer's trunk. The only things that gave it away as belonging to an admiral were the fact that it was a room at all, and that there were three hooks on the wall to his left, two of them with keys, and the last bare.

He considered closing the door behind him and bolting it, but the window was too small for his shoulders, and if someone came banging, he'd have to open it eventually, with a much better story to tell than if he let it hang open. Just looking for the admiral.

In the corner near the desk, a stiffened leather cuirass and a rounded helmet supported vambraces and greaves in a neat pile. He kicked them aside, but it wasn't there. Gionn found the modest trunk latched but unlocked. A quick toss, and its contents decorated the floor. A change of clothes and a dirk, a bladder for water and another for booze. A small purse of coin, a rolled bag, a long watch cloak, a whetstone. The new admiral hadn't the time to embezzle anything worthwhile, yet. He shook it and stared inside, then threw it against the opposite wall and swept the leaves of parchment from the desk.

Arrow, arrow, arrow. Where's the fuckin' arrow? Gionn ripped back the furs from the bed, then upset the entire frame. He looked around in disbelief. There was nowhere else it could be. "Fuck!" He threw aside the armor again and scattered the clothes. It was all bare stone and threadbare cloth. There was nothing of value, and nowhere to keep it. He dumped the purse—a few coppers. "It's not fuckin' here!" There had to be something he wasn't seeing. He stomped the legs of the bed frame until they came off. Unless one of the others kept the contraband. "Fuck!" He snatched the keys from the wall and flung them, then punched the writing desk again and again. When it hurt his fist more than it gave, he coiled it back and smashed it against the wall. Nothing! He'd have to search the other rooms, and by then some cunt would be back to nick him. He grabbed the door in both hands and slammed it open and closed in his fury, once, twice—something fell. Behind the door, a long leather roll slid to the ground. He stared agape at it for a moment, then loosed the tie and tossed it open to find a spear, a map, a water bladder. An arrow of knapped stone.

Parks hobbled, dragged, stumbled, and at times, floated on a raft of bodies that bore him through the winding river of streets. Half a dozen times the whole thing splintered, and they had to pry themselves from beneath him and hoist him back up with as much help as he could muster. Every step was pounding agony for his left leg. The cramps that had seized him had only retreated enough that he might stand and move, but never did they admit to an intention to leave. His stomach welled up in his throat, he belched like a deep-voiced bird the whole way, "*Braaak!*" Nothing in the world would have felt better than a nice round of vomit, but his stomach was empty, and it refused to come.

When he did try to move his feet to take the load off his helpers, his head spun and he tottered beneath a moon that seemed to swing like a pocketwatch from a chain. What time was it? What time was he supposed to meet that dude? And where the fuck was Foster? He'd asked for him several times, but the only tongues he heard were Reverse-Eskimo, occasionally commanding him in broken English. The cell seemed to send him into rot, from the inside out. He wasn't sure if he could even stay upright were they to let go, but no thought of abandoning the rendezvous crossed his mind. He intended to crawl alone, if he had to. Joe would come if he asked, but something told him not to.

A woman's voice—she was still with him—barked at the old man in Native. He thought he'd heard Gionn, too, which didn't make sense, but it was so many long ages ago that he could have dreamed it. Maybe this was a dream, too, and he'd wake up in the black cell.

A thick sheet of leather raked painfully over his face and head as he was hurled through the flap of the wigwam, chest-first onto the floor. The little army of faceless midgets poured in and helped him to a sitting position, which he immediately abandoned for a fetal one as his stomach lurched again. His taint had released its death grip on his balls, but they still throbbed with the memory. Most of the pain flickered in a line running down his shin, from knee to ankle. Or kneaded his guts like play-doh squeezing out either side of a clenched fist. He had a mild moment of panic when he realized his eyes were open and it was still completely dark. The wigwam's interior was terrifyingly like the cell. Parks scooted back until he hit a wall, sloped and jagged.

"Light," he begged.

"It is bad to be seen," Joe said. Parks didn't have the strength to beg. The high, tense voices of the midgets who had been his saving grace leaped over one another like a pack of barking dogs. Kjartke silenced them, then another string of Native, cool and slow from Joe, sent them out into the night. A hand touched his shoulder, and he swore he could smell his mother's perfume.

"You must take water," Joe said.

"No."

"Try."

"Medicine."

"It is in your head. You drink, you sleep. You will forget it."

"I need my medicine." After a pause, the bag of herbs pressed against his hand. He felt the thin, smooth fingers that held it, and it made his entire hand tingle, like he'd accidentally brushed against his crush in junior high. The idea of chewing this shit now was revolting, but it was the only thing that cooled the fire that had been building in his leg. Besides, if it just made him vomit, he'd be overjoyed. The lump he pulled was too big, and most of it fell from around his lips onto the ground. The bitter taste stung his throat and seemed to radiate directly to his stomach. But as he chewed, his leg calmed in anticipation. Parks realized he couldn't even tie it up.

"Can you help?" He wasn't sure who he was talking to, but it was Kjartke's hands who felt the wet lump between his fingers, and knew what he wanted. She packed it into his shin gash and wrapped the binding a little too tight, causing him to wince. The leg tingled with relief, but his nausea grew, and he prayed he would heave soon.

"Rest," Eskimo Joe said. "They will not look for you tonight. But we must move before first light."

Another midget called through the flaps, and Joe answered. In the brief frame of moonlight, Parks saw three little heads duck in, followed by what could have been an ogre by comparison.

"Here's your shit, shit cunt." He didn't even have the energy to care one way or another that Gionn was involved. "How you feelin', mate? You looked like a gutted seal." Parks moaned in response. "'Thank you for freein' me from prison and certain death,' some might say. 'You're welcome, cunt!' I might reply." Another groan. "Well, at least give me a proper 'fuck off.'" Groan. "Alright, then. Mind if I fuck your girlfriend?" The last one was more of a whimper. Gionn let out a low whistle. "Day in the brig and and he turns to mush," he said to someone else.

"Norwet. Take this man where he will not be found." Tunguk said to one of the boys.

"Am I to be murdered? I thought I'd stay here with you crab-pickers."

"You were seen," Kjartke said.

"Go with Norwet and his brothers. It is safer for all."

"Fine. Hate to leave me best mate Parksy to die alone in such shit company, but that's the north and south of it. Ha! Kiddin', you rotten cunts. You can always count on your pal Gionn. Remember that. Even when it seems not to be true. Especially then. Same boat, same crew, that's us. Sweet dreams, sweet prince!" the voice faded as Joe ushered him out.

He felt Kjartke tugging as his belt, and followed with his hands. "My arrow," he ran his finger over the fine jagged edge where it hung by its head from a noose in a strand of leather.

"You must not forget to wash it in the sea before light." Parks jerked in anxiety, but she put her hand on his elbow. "Not now. Too many men look for you. We will take you when we move. What things here tell of you?" He didn't understand the question.

"We have prepared your bag. What else is yours in this tukit? It must all go."

His possessions. "Arrow." He thought hard. "Spear?"

"It will stay," Joe said. "Too big. It is a Mattaka weapon."

"Water."

"Here." Kjartke was tying something else to his belt—the sealskin bladder.

"Map." She shoved it under his belt.

"Is there more?"

"No," he said with a bit of surprise. Other than clothes, he had three things in all the world—two of them, useless.

"If you have hidden a thing, you must say. We will be searched. It is too dark to look now."

Parks thought it over. His glasses? No. He saw himself floating in the water in that survival suit, pelted by rain and wave. It was gone, too. A parade of things flashed before him, swept in the current. All belonged to his former world. His surfboard swept past. Old outfits, things he would wear if he were going out, and a Navy uniform. A wallet with soaked bills, keys on a bob. His phone rang and flashed just beneath the surface. A necklace of pearl and gold that he had never seen before. The hat of a court jester. The XBOX from the *Qarapara* with the shitty second controller he and Foster fought not to use. There were other objects, more than he could catalog, faint and fading in the swell.

"That's everything." He suddenly felt like he had when he pulled out of his parents' driveway to report to San Diego for the very first time. Beforehand, he was sure it would be momentous, full of tears, or a sense of daring independence, like a conquistador with his foot up on the bow of a ship. Yet he was not sad, he was not hopeful. He did not feel regret, or a sense of accomplishment, or even anxiety for what lie ahead. He knew they were waving, but he didn't look in the mirror—just swished the back of his hand between the seats of the cab of his truck. There was not relief, and though he did feel gratitude—deep gratitude—he was sure whatever debts he may have had were settled, maybe even before they could be incurred. Parks would have loved to feel any of those things. Instead, he only felt the magnetic pull that sunk his foot on a pedal and drew him forward. It was not escape, either, but it was inevitable. Santa Cruz shrunk and was swallowed as fast as the horizon rose up ahead. One thing replaced by another. At the time, he had no idea that the acne-faced kid would have his turn, as well, but now he was glad that he did. There was nothing left of the boy but a name, and the man he'd become had been barely sufficient, himself.

"Where you takin' me, brother?" He looked at Foster as he knew him now, sitting beside him in the pickup. It had never happened—they'd meet much later, but it didn't strike him as odd to see him here in the memory. Was it that, or was he dreaming now?

He jerked awake, and had a sense that much time had passed. Across the wigwam, he heard the soft whistle of Eskimo Joe's snoring. Nothing moved within. Kjartke was probably still there, but he couldn't be sure. His stomach lurched and twisted as if an alien baby was preparing to rip through his belly button and devour the rest of him as its first meal. Bile bubbled into his throat. His head throbbed above his rising heart, every beat tightening around him while his skin sought to crush his skull. His right ear began to pop in a painful roll like a snare drum. Parks threw himself to all fours, and as soon as he did, his stomach sent mustard gas up his throat into his brain. He was overcome with a nausea he hadn't felt in as many benders as deployment pay could buy him, and the room spun even though he couldn't make out a single feature.

Again his stomach jolted, and now he could feel everything racing up his chest into his throat as if a dam had burst. Old instincts that wouldn't allow him to puke in a friend's room took over, and he crawled as fast as he could in a direction—he wasn't sure which. The rock on his left leg send a column of pain down to his foot and up to his left ear, but he bore through it and by some miracle, the crown of his head struck the soft flap and delivered him into the moonlight. He lifted to his feet—almost. It just sent him staggering forward, slapping the ground a few times in a futile attempt to haul himself up before he landed hard on his chest. Another old instinct had kept him alive for many years, and he set himself on his side, tilted just forward, so that if he lost consciousness he wouldn't drown in his own vomit.

The pain in his head reached migraine crescendo, and he hoped he would die soon if it didn't stop. Someone finding him was the least of his worries. Parks forced himself to open his mouth and gag against the pain. Nothing came out. He tried again, and felt movement. Now he gagged uncontrollably. A little bitter fluid tickled the back of his tongue and swallowed itself. A cold shiver rippled through his body, but it didn't stop. He just kept shaking, so hard that it turned warm. *I'm legit dying*, he thought. "Kuh." He tried to yell Kjartke's name. "Fuh. Fuh." Fuck it, he thought, and rammed a thick finger down his throat so hard he thought he cut his windpipe with his fingernail. He barely got it out in time before the most vile liquid erupted out of his mouth and splattered the ground. It was the consistency of water, and there wasn't much of it, but it just kept coming—a convulsion violent enough to plow through an offensive tackle, followed by a few thimbles of liquid, one after the other. He screamed them out, and saw stars bounce off of one another even with his eyes clamped shut. Parks wretched so hard his insides cramped, and he thought his stomach would come up, too. He was sure the whole town could hear him. Just as the percussion in his head reached a crescendo and he thought he'd rip his lungs apart, everything faded like a vacuum tube turned off and sank into a click.

The gut-ripping nausea was gone. His head still beat, but it felt light. He got to his feet with remarkably little effort, and looked around. The wigwams were silent. No one had come to his aid if they heard him. More importantly, no one had come to stab him, or drag him back to jail. Beyond the roofs, the snow-covered mountain was navy blue against a black sky. He suddenly remembered his meeting. Could he still make it? Everything in him told him to walk. Just walk and see what happens. Compared to how he'd felt moments ago, he felt like a feather wobbling in the night air. The leg still tingled, and his vision rocked back and forth. He was overcome with a lightness, as if the few ounces of liquid were all that weighed him down. Yet it was gone. He felt too weak to move. Where was he supposed to go, anyway? Foster should be here. He couldn't go without Foster. As the anxiety flooded him, so the pain returned like blood rushing to his head. *I gotta go get Foster.* He swung his head back and forth, trying to find the wigwam with Joe and Kjartke in it. It was lost among the haystack, and his stomach flooded with a panic that he would not see it again. He would walk away from the wigwam, and it would never reappear. His leg singed as if nearing a campfire, and his head beat harder. Parks threw himself back on the ground as though his life depended on it before he had a chance to collapse.

He writhed in pain, having flown too close to the sun by trying to stand. The heavy feeling came back first to his legs, his torso, his arms, then his head. Once again he was a leaden weight, sweating bullets in his furs. He hocked a loogie and spat bile until his throat was dry. It smelled terrible. For minutes he lay sprawled on his stomach, held up by his forearms, until it occurred to him that as bad as it still hurt, he was human again. A human in agony, but no longer on the verge of being torn apart on the rack. He lifted to all fours and forced himself to take slow, deep breaths through the nose, out through the mouth, with a spit for good measure.

"*Ptooh!* Fuuuuck," he bellowed.

"You look like shit," a voice came from above him, with an American accent. "Where's Foster?"

Parks looked up in disbelief at the man who stood over him. The whole scene spun, and he blinked his blurry vision into order.

"You and me, compadre." He willed himself to his feet. "You say something about a walk?"

16

SONG OF THE LEOPARD SEAL

Dots of flame swarmed over the main street and harbor in chaos, gathering, dispersing, flaring up, touching here and going round in a way that reminded Costig of nothing as much as a stamped ant mound. He snatched one of them as he scurried past.

"You! Staunch the fuckin' lights. One torch per detail, and only the ones I call. Spread the order. I want half of these out or I'll light you cunts to find me way." They hadn't the oil for such waste, much less the fiber or anything else worth a burn. None of it would be coming until well into Spring, either. Even if he had the desire to find the man, at night, there was no prayer of it worth lighting a candle for.

Wayranapan lit his way to where the Marines had gathered the occupants of the public tavern and the poorman's quarters—the only public buildings filled at this hour. It was a sad lot of sleepy, confused squains and a fair number of Polc's men, well-greased. They mustered at spearpoint, while every man in the garrison raced about in a panic. Costig stepped through the men, one at a time, as Wayranapan held a light under each face. Only a fool would have fled to one of these buildings, but given the circumstances of his arrest, he half-expected to see Parks towering above the lamp.

"Red," Wayranapan announced. It was the wrong red and Costig knew it, but he motioned for the man to be taken aside. There was one more—probably brown, but close enough—before they cleared the gathering to head home.

"I'll speak to 'em later. Meantime, have Atxlchar take a look." He motioned to a fidgeting shape still hunched where Costig planted him. "And ask the guard if he remembers yet who cracked him."

"Shall we roust the whalers?" A sergeant asked.

"They'll have shit themselves well enough by now. If they see a force comin' at 'em with torches, we'll be in a fight we don't need. Search 'em with due warnin' in the light. If he's hidin' among the ships, let him sleep one more. But post watches round the shore to listen for boats launchin'."

"Aye, Costig."

A man broke from his returning squad to approach. "Latrine is clear, sir."

"Did you look in the crack?"

There was a pause. "We did not see anyone—"

"Look in the crack. Pass a torch down there. Not too close. Last I need is a shithouse fire." He turned to his officers. "Gerachay! Send these men to quarters. He's a sop, but he's got enough sense to know we'll not be stormin' the squain shop tonight. I want them rested and reportin' before dawn."

Gerachay split off to chase the men home. Most of them barely looked busy. A winter navy wasn't supposed to do much more than mend ships and keep the peace until the good winds returned. He'd always thought that Drummoc was undermanned, especially once the regulars were reassigned and the seasonals slipped away to more lucrative climes. Scarce more than 400 bodies. If they were all good men, it was enough to hold down the na-tives, assuming they didn't try anything. The kind of men who served in the winter force at Drummoc were not good men. Those were the ones brought home to Ampos, or deserting as soon as some captain offered them work. One in ten, he figured. That's how many he'd mark for a fight on land, at least. Most of them were his Marines, and he'd spent years carving that force so that of the 80 or so he had, he could count on nearly half. The rest were spear-eaters. Even fewer were proper sailors. If a man had no place at home, and could earn none on a ship, his place was Drummoc. That was true of the greenest bucket straight through to the admirals. It was probably true of him, as far as the others reckoned. Here were the criminals who would be caught elsewhere, the knot-fumblers and oar-draggers, the last-born sons, arse-cunts, those who were exiled then exiled from exile. The type who forgot an order on the way there, and got lost on the way back to ask again. They had to think it over when you asked their names to make sure they didn't say the one that was wanted here for murder, or the one wanted there for debt. If they didn't already drink themselves into a stupor, they would after the first winter. It was a place for the cursed man and his hateful wake. The cruel man, lord to none but a helpless squain. The crazed man, whose daimons whipped him along. If he were none of these, he was an idiot, well-meaning and unfit to do such things as stand in front of a prison door for a while.

The colony amazed him. How it could exist in such a place. How it sent many thousands of tons of coal a year to Nunoc and beyond. And it couldn't be more than a dozen men who bound the massive thing together, if he was generous. It was a miracle from the gods that it held so long under the very best of circumstances. Now these were the men who would have to go door to door in force. Prepare for a siege. And may the gods forbid, he thought, fight it.

Wendell beckoned to him from the prison where he stood at the open door with Tuilapoy and a squad of Marines. Costig knew he had better take over before they were able to look too deeply. He acted for Ampos, but he knew it would not be seen that way.

"Hoy, Costig. Missin' somethin'?" He held up but two keys—one of two prongs, and one of three.

"How the fuck did someone get to me quarters?"

"How the fuck they get there twice?" Costig frowned in confusion. "I found these among your things. You may care to check what else is gone. Someone tossed it while we was about here." He did not have to pretend to fume. Fucking Gionn!

"Sir, we found an old squain in the hall yesterday. But we searched him. He did not have anything," an Amposi Marine explained.

"Would you have me believe the prisoner walked through the door like a ghost? Or did he unlock it from the inside and shut it up again?"

"They got the key alright," Wendell said. "But that's not me favorite bit." He led Costig into the middle door by torchlight. The floor of the room clicked with loose stones that skipped against one another as they walked. The admiral swept a path for himself to either side with his boots. The torch fell on the wall to his right—the one that bordered Parks' cell. A massive hole stretched from waist to ceiling, and the wall that had filled it lay underfoot. Wendell swung the torch to the other side. Costig poked his head through an equal hole in the left wall that led into the general lockup, larger than both of the other two cells combined.

"He burst the wall!" One of the Marines' jaw hung open.

"Who else was in here?"

"Just a few boys. Fighting in a public way," Wayranapan explained.

"Eight, sir. I was there when we took them," the same Marine added. "We threw four in main. Four in here. Just like we are supposed to."

"I don't suppose you know their names? Or the look of 'em?" The Marine shook his head. Costig stepped a foot on the bottom of the hole and lifted himself to the ceiling. He pinched the edge of one of the flat, jagged stones that pressed into the roof beam, gave it a shake, and ripped it free. It clattered to the floor. Then he pushed out another, and another.

"He didn't have to burst the wall. No mortar, I knew that. But it bears no load! You chip out one stone, the rest'll follow."

"The inner walls were late, Admiral," Tuilapoy said. "They were added only after the riot, but the brig is older than the records."

"Prison riot?"

"It started here, aye. Some of the old ones still recall. It was but one great room. There was a fight, dozens of men of two rival families. It took over a hundred Marines to suppress them. They were all thrown in here together, where they finished the fight. By the time they opened it up, it was blood. Blood everywhere. Men torn to pieces. The only ones alive were those who could no longer stand to kill the others. The people were so angry, they attacked the garrison. Half the roof of the prison was fired. That is why we build walls inside the prison. That is why we have the rule to put those who fight in separate cells."

"I'll grant you most men prefer to break out of prisons, not into the next cell over. Wayranapan! When we write the Spring lists for Nunoc, remind me to send for proper timber and stone, and masons to work it."

"What do you think he was after? Freein' a few squain boys like that?" Wendell asked.

"It makes no sense, but it does make a good story. And a popular man will he harder to find." He clenched his teeth in dread of the morning's work. "I'd just as soon talk to the man who opened the door for 'em."

"When these men arrived, we spoke to them. They came with a man of red hair," Wayranapan reminded him. "And it was a red man who sounded the alarm to Atxlchar."

"Aye, me memory has not escaped me. Spread word that we want to offer a reward to the man who alerted us of the escape, and to get his testimony. I don't think he's an imbecile, but it won't cost us to find out. Then have the men bring in every man or woman on this island who's head or bush might pass for red in a rare light. Tomorrow," he added. "Call off the search. Everyone to quarters."

"Shall we post men between the harbor and town? In case he hides among the ships and would slip away?" Wayranapan asked.

"No. I don't want to inflame the whalers any more than I have. He broke with eight squains. Do you think they ran for the harbor when they could take one turn and be among their own, where we dare not pursue?"

"Aye, sir."

"Wendell, I know you just got back from a voyage. You'll be tired."

"I'll be mustered before the dawn tickles your toes, Costig. You want me to lead the party into the town?"

"Fuck you, I'm leadin' it. But there'll be fun enough for the both of us."

"You remember me, right?"

Parks blinked his vision still. The salt-and-pepper whiskers had grown into a respectable beard, and black hair curled down over his ears by now, littered with glinting grays. He was leaner, and though the fur seal tunic and leggings had a way of filling out anyone who put them on, he was as robust as ever—one of those annoying types who probably did triathlons and played in a rugby league despite creeping up on fifty. He'd left the deck in a white t-shirt, so at least he'd managed to upgrade his wardrobe since their last meeting. Parks remembered him, alright. Just not his name, and he'd asked at least twice already.

"*Qarapara,*" he replied with false bravado. "You're alive."

"Yeah, well. For the most part."

"Thanks for that, by the way. So glad we got that gig." With a groan and a grin, he straightened himself and locked eyes on the blessed figure before him. His smile brimmed over. When the man looked bewildered, Parks spread his long arms into an open harbor.

"Rain check. You smell like vomit." The arms fell to his sides in mild defeat. "Wasn't expecting to find you half-dead. You sure you can make it?"

"Well, I wasn't expecting to find you any percent alive. And yeah, I'll make it. We're not going far, right?"

The man laughed. "Depends on your definition."

"Soooo many questions," Parks' felt his spirits lifting with the shock.

"There'll be time. Right now, you're gonna need your strength."

As soon as he moved his feet to follow, Parks was grateful for the silence. They were already mile-weary though he'd gone but a few streets. Every step felt like he sunk a little deeper into mud, his tall frame shrinking to meet his guide, despite a few inches' head start at the outset.

They kept deep within the wigwams, heading inland along the little peninsula. He'd never been this far into town before. The wind blew everywhere but upon them, giving the place an otherworldly feel. He glanced back as if he would be able to see the home he shared with Joe and Kjartke, but the round tops clumped together indistinguishably like goosebumps on the flesh of a cold arm reaching for the sea. At first, he hadn't given much thought to where they were heading, but it became obvious it was nowhere in Drummoc, and he was embarrassed that that hadn't occurred to him before. The rich dude from the ship was not so much an expert navigator of the impenetrable maze, as he was just holding a direction until at last they emerged behind the town, the same direction Joe had taken them to go to the Buttcrack of the Dead, although they'd traced the perimeter then—a much shorter trip than bouncing through in little arcs like a pair of pinballs. The shitter was somewhere to his right, he knew, filled with feces and ghosts. They remained centered, and the peninsula expanded to both sides until they stood on the main body of land, unshielded from the merciful breeze that nevertheless found a way to rattle his bones.

"Hold up!" He huffed. The man, impatient in his stride, stopped ahead.

"We have to keep moving."

Parks looked back to the left, where he knew no bottomless abyss waited to snap at his feet. Where he could hear the waves lolling against the rock. He started toward the coast.

"Where are you going?"

"I have to dip my tip."

"Whatever that means, we don't have time for it."

It didn't stop Parks. "You coming?" He called back.

"We don't have time!" The man held his position, but Parks leaned himself forward, leaving his friend to be swallowed by grays.

The air grew saltier and thickened as the sound of the waves led him to the shore. Not far up the peninsula, he could make out little lights towards the harbor. The moon was enough of a lantern that he found a steep little draw, sat on his butt, and crab-walked to where the water licked the rock. He fumbled for the leather cord on his belt, and realized how cold and swollen his fingers were. They shook as he loosed the little noose Kjartke cinched around the arrow. Gripping it tight at the end of the shaft, because he didn't trust himself to hang on, he fixed all of his concentration on the point as he guided it to where the sea sloshed up. Finally, one of the little waves was enough to lap over the end of it, all the way to his hand. He yanked it back, and shook it dry before replacing it on his belt.

Was that enough? Maybe he was supposed to scrub it clean. The Reverse-Eskimo definition of "wash" was probably something other than his. But if so, he hadn't been too impressed by their standards of hygiene, so anything he did was sure to exceed the requirements. Somehow, it made his entire body feel refreshed, as if he'd been the one to bathe rather than the flint arrow.

With painstaking care, he picked his way back up on all fours until he could once again stand. Now terror pulled around him like a shroud. Had he been an idiot to take the detour? The man was clearly shy, given the nighttime maneuvers. Parks didn't blame him. For the most part, meeting new people had not exactly gone his way. Here was his chance to connect with something really, truly familiar. To get some answers. And—was it too much to hope?—to get home? The excitement of someone from his own world was matched in equal parts by the panic that he had lost his shot. It was hard to even tell where he left from. He scoured the field, limping as fast as he dared.

"Hello?" He spoke. It didn't seem right to raise his voice. "Hello?" Fuck, he thought. He'd fucked himself. "*Qarapara* guy! Where'd you go, dude?"

"You don't remember my name, do you?" The sound frightened him to the pit of his stomach, then sent a wave of relief surging through him. The man was there, right in front of his blind ass, crouching on the rock expanse. He rose as Parks approached.

"Course I do. Wisconsin Johnson. That's what we called you. Cause you act like a poor man's Indiana Jones."

"But you don't know my real name."

"I do, I'm just more of an alias kind of guy. You know. Nom de plumes. Street names, and shit. People call me the Leopard Seal."

"Do they."

"Yessiree, Bob."

"Well if you're done with your field trip, Mister Seal, I think there are some people who might be relieved to see you."

Parks' stomach fluttered. "Who else?" The man grinned. "Your wife and daughter?" He nodded. "Who else? Not Carabiner."

"Carabiner."

"Fuck! You know what? Screw it. I'll take anything. And the Old Man? Hapgood? Gardner?"

The man's face went solemn and dipped toward the ground. Parks nodded, unsurprised. "Bastards. I wish *we* had a life raft." He could hardly name the swirling emotions that filled him. The bodily misery was lost in a storm of grief and jubilation, jealousy and butt-clenching excitement. So many weeks—months, by now—of loneliness and torment and nobody but Foster. It could have been any halfway memorable asshole from his grade school days and he'd have felt the same thrill. None of them were anyone he cared to see. Those ones were gone. It did nothing to quell his spirits. Faces, familiar faces. People who would understand when he made a joke, or mourned a roll of toilet paper. Or wanted to go home.

And home. If they could come one way, so many of them, how could there not be hope? The kind that only Foster could have fooled himself into. Parks felt it rise in his chest and suddenly knew how his friend could chase it with such vigor, whiplashed and hellbent on the only thing that made any sense to them, day after day, in the face of storms and sharp points. Now he admired Foster's downhill attitude, and felt ashamed of his own resignation. Could things be different if he put half the heart into it as the hillbilly? If he did anything other than try to survive in some semblance of comfort until the next morning? He felt indescribable guilt, as though he'd abandoned his only friend, as though he'd given up on searching for these people. An image of Joe and Kjartke flashed before his mind. Would he see them again? He had to. They would meet, his new friends and his old ones, and he would be the one to bring everyone together.

The gate swung open and all roads lay before him.

"I wish we had time to play catch up. It's farther than you think, and there are people looking for you."

Parks glanced back at Drummoc, dotted with handheld fire at the harbor's edge. Then ahead. The brooding mountain, like a ramp to the moon.

"After you, Wisconsin."

Kjartke scolded herself for closing her eyes. It was only for a short time. She heard him leave, heard him vomit in the street, and thought it was good that he went there to do it. If he could rid the bad spirit that moved in him he would feel much better, and she would not have to smell it all night. Now that she opened them again, she knew instantly he was still gone. There was no moaning or shuffling. How long had she slept? Tunguk still traded the thin breaths of the old. She considered waking him, but he would blame her.

The air was cold and still. High above a breeze avoided the streets. It was weather for the moon dogs to be out, lit for them who could not see in day or blackness. She held her ear for the sounds from the harbor, but nothing came to her. The search was done for now. Kjartke remembered where she heard his cries. Just as Ostuk's tukit left her sight she came to the spot where he vomited. It was not smeared, nor had a foot passed through it. So he did not continue that direction—he was too clumsy to have avoided it. Back toward the tukit, then. Or a turn inland, deeper into the town. At least he was not dead. Not here. But he would be lost if he was alone, and alone was better than what cause any man may have for taking him. It was not too cold, but he had a weak constitution. Both of them did. They were not born for places like this. She had seen them shiver when she was grateful for warmth. There was nothing wrong with him. Tunguk agreed. What made him ill was in his spirit world, safe from spear. But even a mild night like this would be bad for him. Men could find a way to die when a way was hidden. Just as no winter could take a man who cared to live. All Brother must do was give up. All he must do was continue.

Tunguk was slow to wake to her kicks. He had beaten her to the prison, but it took the strength from his old bones. There would not be many more deeds like this left in him. When she showed him the vomit, he turned inland to look over the tops of the tukits. She braved for him to cut into her, but it never came.

"He cannot go far, as he was."

"That one does not need to go far to find trouble."

"Then we must find him first."

She snorted. "Is this how you hold akmanuak? With the help of a woman? And children?" He faced her, perhaps surprised at her directness, though he gave but a slow blink. "If you had been one breath slower, I would have opened the door before you, and I am bound to no one. Then a sick man wanders from your home. Where is the other one? It is too long since he has left. There can be no good from it. They do not even want your protection. Why do they run to their death when you look away?" Kjartke narrowed her brow. She could not recall being so bold with him, and it lifted her breast. "If a ship turns north, they will leave you here, may the cold preserve you. It was a cruel kaim who brought you together. You have turned on your people for these men. What do they give you but trouble? What do you give them? You do not turn away what comes for them. You call these things to bear. Take them where they cannot live, to people who would harm them. Tunguk of the many tricks. What man is glad to know you?"

"It is harder than it looks." He offered a weak smile.

"That is how you answer?"

"Camne Drumlag."

She scowled in confusion.

"Foster sails to Camne Drumlag. Brother, he is lost." Tunguk pointed beyond the dwellings. "I think there. Kjartke," he turned to her. "Is here."

"You are not responsible for me."

"It is true. You can go as you please. There will be less trouble for you with less troublesome men. And it is true. I hold akmanuak with many other hands. Mine do not grip like they once did," he opened and closed his palms for her. "Good that you have a choice to let go. I think when you make it, I will slip. It would be dawn before I knew Brother was gone, if you did not say. Now, I can search for him before the men come."

She glared at him with suspicion.

"They are very brave," he again looked up the mountain. "Or they think much of my skill." He laughed under his breath. "Akmanuak does not require that I succeed. Only that I try." She could tell he was no longer looking at anything in front of him. "I did not ask for your help to break the prison. If we were killed, and Brother and with us, who would care for Foster when he returns? Or if I were killed, and Brother escaped, who will tend to both?"

"I am not bound to them."

"No. It is fortunate for women, you cannot take akmanuak. But it is unfortunate, that no one must keep you the way he keeps a bond. I must try to find them now." Tunguk started off, then looked over his shoulder. "It will be a good effort if we try together."

He disappeared into the tukits that ran inland. Kjartke pressed her teeth, then hurried after.

Four torches still glowed far off in a half-perimeter where the ships rested. That would be the whaler, and those would let the poor bastards who drew night watch know if the Navy launched a sortie against them. For all the trouble it was, at least there was some amusement in their paranoia. It was a clever man who might stage a prison break, or use one to rig an attack. None would have suspected such a thing from Turrha.

Somewhere inland, the yips of dogs carried across the plain, and much nearer, the sound of foot shuffles announced a large presence. The man stopped and turned about a few times.

"I know you've beat me again."

Costig scrambled up over the lip of Ingputka from where he'd wedged himself on an outcrop a few feet below the surface.

"It's a fine skill, to know when you're bested," he replied. "Underrated."

Cormdran laughed. "Arseful of a mess you had, there. Thought we were off for a while."

"I thought you'd forgot yourself this morning. You're a scary fuck, Corm, when you're spittin' in me face."

"Were your lads satisfied?"

"Aye, yours?"

"Aye, but we might need another over your drills. Is that necessary?"

"To prepare for a siege?"

"How am I to try the seats with you splashin' about from dawn to dusk?"

"Are you mad? I've done your work for you. Have a look at who splashes the least. You needn't even wet your hull."

"It won't be enough, you know."

Costig smiled to himself in the comfort of the dark veil. "The admiralty's an embarrassment. This navy is one or two punches away from toothless. You and I both know the lay of it. All I ask is that you curse me name like you mean it."

"I've been thinkin' up some good ones."

"You won't get to use 'em tomorrow."

"Broke the prison, did he? How'd he manage that?"

Costig grunted.

"Squain boy?"

"Halot, this one. Styles himself the Leopard Seal. Rumor is he and his mates left Nunoc in a hurry. Would you believe he took down the inner walls to loose the whole lockup? You'll hear he burst through them with a single blow. Don't believe it. He took the time to lay every stone on the opposite floor to give it the look, but he's one of those big wet cunts who sops over you with his size and hopes you don't test him. Like yourself." Corm laughed. "If you listen further, they'll say he walked through the door and we found it locked tight. The first is true. He had a mate open it with a key from the outside. Guard caught a look—you wouldn't happen to have any red-topped fellas on the list?"

"A few. None dumb enough to risk his seat like that."

"I'm sure you'd turn him in if you did."

"Course, mate." Corm clapped him playfully on the shoulder. "What's he in for?"

Costig scoffed. "Approachin' an admiral, spear drawn."

"Spear drawn? How do you carry a spear undrawn? Did he strike at you?"

"No, but he caught me on a shit day. I figure he wouldn't be in Drummoc if he didn't deserve it for somethin'. Anyhow, it isn't as though he can sail off. Pale boy hidin' among the coal fingers. He may live another day, if his luck is with him. It's the look of it that bothers me."

"I understand a man's got to keep up dignity. Just don't try to take it at me expense."

"You're a leech on me bollocks, while a snake bites me foot. You know what's comin' as well as I. Suppose I'll be short two more men before it's over. But I can't just bow aside for you. There'll be no sea trials. No permission to even launch the boat tomorrow for a pinnin'." Corm started to protest but Costig cut him off. "All the 'candidates' are needed for a search in the town. You can claim it was your decision to stay dry, seein' as all the good men would be occupied."

"Fair point."

"After that, I won't stop you. Can't. But I've a siege to prepare for, and it can't be done when every man doin' it is tryin' for your ship. Pick, and leave. I'm tired of watchin' feathers."

Parks hobbled side to side as much as he traveled forward. His feet crunched in the first ice he'd encountered since landing on the island. The first hint of elevation. What was it, Cooper? Cartwright? Something with a "C," he was sure. Almost definitely a "C". Every forty or fifty yards, just as he began to lose the dim shape that held his line, Wisconsin Johnson would stop in irritation and wait for him to slink up, then he'd start again without a word. At first, he'd felt elation when he realized there were people—real live people who knew the place he came from as well as him, who could swear that it had happened, that he'd lived there, and that everyone and everything here was ridiculous. But already something hollow grew in his stomach. Wisconsin didn't seem half as stoked as he was. And the more he thought about meeting people unlike the ones he came to know, the more anxious he grew. Had they fared any better? Who would be helping who? Then there was the nagging voice that reminded him that he didn't even like any of them when they were on his ship. They always asked for things. Can you get me this? Can you bring me here? Throw this away for me. Why can't we launch the zodiacs today?

Carabiner was the worst of them. One of those people who read books and listened to podcasts on leadership and persuasion so he could strut around and delegate things, delegate delegation. Run power moves on people and give unsolicited advice, so he could tell you, and himself, that him jerking off his own ego was really just him teaching you valuable life lessons, and you're welcome. Already, he missed Foster. Maybe he was just annoyed that Wisconsin didn't want to chat much, and that he had to go on a forced march minutes after vomiting up his soul.

This time when he drew even, Wisconsin didn't take off right away, almost as if he sensed Parks' ass-dragging was a form of protest.

"We need to go up on the far side of this spur," he pointed left. "There's a bunch of dogs over here. They'll give us away if they see us."

"Is that uphill?"

"It's all uphill from here."

"I'm kinda down to stay…down. I don't know if you noticed, I'm not the hottest shit in the pot right now," he gasped for breath. "If we could just, take it gradual. Maybe go a little slower. That could be a thing."

Wisconsin shook his head. "We can't risk being spotted. There are people there. And we don't know if we're being followed. Do you want to lead everyone who's chasing you right up to our camp?"

"Those dogs are my dogs, dog. I sailed here with them. They love me. I know all those fools. Let's just keep off the steep stuff as long as we can."

"You'll be fine. Come on."

"How far?"

"Less than a marathon."

"A *marathon?*"

"Less. You're a military guy, aren't you? You probably run marathons for breakfast."

"Yeah, but never on a weeknight."

"This isn't my first trip. You're going to have to trust me."

"Totally. I do. That's the best way. But here's the deal, dude. The second best way is the only way my ass is going. It might be quiet, shorter, whatever. If I fall down dead halfway there, it won't do us much good. You take the high road, I'll take the low road. We can meet…I don't know, up there somewhere."

Wisconsin Johnson's brooding silence told Parks he'd won.

"Alright. We stick together. See those buildings?" He pointed ahead and off to the right.

"Yeah," Parks lied.

"We stay as far left as we can."

"Roger that."

"Radio silence, until I say otherwise."

"Totes."

Within minutes, every one of the little huskies was blaring like sirens racing to a midnight fire from their tethers a few hundred yards away. They hadn't spoken a word, and even Parks could barely hear their squeaking steps in the fresh blown snow. He couldn't see the dogs. Somehow, they knew. They didn't bark so much as raise an inhuman wail that sent chills to his bones. He could hear them tumbling over one another against their leashes, crying out as legs got tied up, howling like he'd never heard on the ship. They might as well have walked through a sonic spotlight. He was sure the entire town could hear them miles away, and if the guards were near, they'd know exactly where to head. The only relief was that their vow of silence meant Wisconsin didn't get to say, "I told you so."

It wasn't until they were well-past that the yipping wound down, and he could feel his partner's ire in their quickened pace, even now as the ground took on a noticeable uphill grade. He stopped for a pull of water, hoping Wisconsin would come back to gather him, but he just paused ahead and waited, minute after minute, until Parks started up again. Now the muscle on the front of his shin cramped, shooting needles into the top of his foot and under his knee. His forward hunch became more pronounced. Thick legs turned to oatmeal and gave out for a split second like some kind of muscular hiccups that he just couldn't shake.

"Is there any way we can stop for the night? Pick this up first thing in the A.M.?" Parks crumpled to a seat on the snow as soon as he came to Wisconsin Johnson.

"We can't be exposed like this." As if to support the case, a wind threaded itself through the hems of his furs, chilling the sweat that had gathered on his clammy skin. It was so much colder than he realized when he was moving. His teeth chattered in response and he folded his arms over his chest. "You'll lose more heat sitting on the ground. Best if we keep going."

"Can't."

"There are no good stopping points from here. No cover. You have to keep moving or you'll freeze."

He shook his head like an obstinate toddler. "Tired."

"You have to be tired. There's no easy way."

"How bad do you want to drag a corpse up there?"

"I'm debating that right now."

Parks chuckled through a shiver. His eyes stung from the growing whip of the wind. Tears gathered between his eyelashes and blurred his vision so that Wisconsin Johnson split into three spectral figures that danced apart and back together. Snot ran down over his scraggly mustache into his lips, and it tasted salty. He tried to think of a harder thing. Every time he had to do some miserable PT, he would get through it by remembering a wave that blasted him off his board and held him under so long, his face burned and he felt like capillaries were bursting in his sinuses. No matter how much he gasped, at least he could breathe. Now he sought the one that took him from the deck of the *Qarapara*. The whole thing was barely a memory. It had felt like years on a single breath. The freezing water, the fury of the storm. Surely if he could float ashore from that, he could rise and walk wherever he needed to go. A half a dozen clips of a few seconds each—that's all he had left of it. The rogue towering over the ship, and Foster oblivious. The resignation and peace he felt right before it hit. A moment of panic under the water. Of all things, his line crossing ceremony, then the beautiful salty oxygen of the surface. The rest of it was a mix of intense pain and what might as well have been stock footage of waves, probably confused now with ones he'd seen in surf videos, or on the way to Drummoc, or dreamed up entirely. Body surfing ashore. Banging his leg. The lift he felt when he came upon a back crouched over a small fire. There had to be something of it that could pull him from the ground now. And if he could pass here—if these people could pass, too—could he not return?

Parks creaked to his feet with the uncertain rumbling of an old motor trying to turn over, sparking and stuttering, finally churning to a kind of life that he could at least pray would last. Wisconsin smiled, bigger than he had even when they first met. Over his shoulder, a glow rose in a narrow line across the sky with a slight bow at the center, flickering like a crack of light under a massive door. It took him a moment to realize he was really seeing it—that it was really there, and not just an ornament of his sleep-deprived mind.

"What the fuck?"

Wisconsin gave it a casual glance, and laughed. "Happens now and then. It's not as bad it looks."

"What?" Parks got a look that said, *come on.* "Is this a fucking *volcano?*"

"Are you serious? It's been venting for weeks. Did you not happen to look up at any point?"

"I thought it was like, fog. Is it *active?*"

Wisconsin waved his hand at it and laughed. "Don't worry. It's a mild one."

"A mild one. Some mild lava is about to mildly incinerate our asses?"

"It's what volcanologists call a Fermboli system."

"I think I saw a documentary about that once. When I was high."

"It means it's extremely active, but since it constantly vents gas and spews off pressure in little eruptions, you don't get the big ones that would do things like bury the town below."

"Are you for real camping on a volcano?"

"Safest place. The locals are terrified of it. They think it's full of evil spirits or something."

"There's a lot of those places here."

"It means they don't like to snoop around very much. Our camp is on the lee-side. Even if the lava does make it over the rim, it only ever runs down the one slope. We've got a little cave out of the wind that's constantly toasty from geothermal heating. Plenty of fresh ice to melt for water. Only thing we have to do is sneak down to the town now and then to steal a little food."

Parks perked up. "My pal Eskimo Joe told me there've been reports of 'tricksters' jackin'. people's shit lately."

"I've been called worse. Look, it's not a good idea to sleep exposed, but I guess walking up the side where the lava flows during a venting isn't any better. Can you make it another mile? There's a few rocks that'll keep the wind off us. And the eyeballs."

Parks extended his hand for a shake, but his guide had already turned back upon the trail. He paused a moment under the thin flame that pulsed above him like a finish line. At least he knew how far it was now. His torso swayed and tilted. He stumbled forward, and caught himself in stride.

The rowers gave one last thrust and the prow of the darraig skidded up the natural stone ramp that served as the only landing at Camne Drumlag. Landing, because to call it a port would violate even the tall Southern standard for exaggeration. Nearby, a more vertical shelf had been worked to line up more or less flat and flush with any ship that would care to dock for loading. It, too, was natural. The only wood in sight was the logs tethered by thick rope that could be deployed to keep hulls from bashing into the rocks, and two wooden boom cranes butt-up to the edge of the natural quay. "Big" may have been a flat-out lie, but Foster saw it more as an allowance. These people probably thought they were towering machines. He didn't put them at much more than a decent backhoe.

There were only two men visible—both Mattaka. The sound of the boat, the men leaping over to push her ashore, froze them in their tracks. One dropped the wicker basket he carried, earning him a sharp word from the other, who shouted a single syllable. Four more Mattaka appeared from the little cluster of wigwams near the shore, equally baffled.

Polc hopped the gunwale to help his men shove against the oars, now reversed in the locks. "Spare a hand, you cunts!" He hollered at the gawking natives. They seemed to have a low and spirited conversation among themselves, which ended conveniently right as the crew brought the darraig to rest where the ground leveled off. This part had been choreographed: Foster nodded to Ostuk, who disembarked, then offered him a hand of help, which he refused. It was all the Mattaka needed to know who was in charge of the expedition.

Foster hadn't expected much more than a hole to shit in, and he wasn't even sure he could find that. Two dozen huts, none larger than Ostuk's back on Drummoc, were huddled together to take advantage of the only ground that was nearly flat. Most of the place was a steep slope that narrowed and disappeared into the wall of mountains that surrounded them on all sides, capped white even after the heat of midsummer. Near the harbor was a dutiful army of baskets brimming with raw coal. They were shorter than a man's waist and two-handled—perfect for carrying between a pair, though he shuddered to think how much they must weigh. Sliding and tilting was more likely. The majority of them gaped with holes, frayed at every part that touched something else, and some looked poised to collapse entirely if anyone attempted to move them. There was as much coal on the ground as in storage.

The Mattaka who had barked at the other when the darraig arrived separated himself from the group and slouched up to Foster. The air set thick with a tension he couldn't place. Nothing about Camne Drumlag would have upset him. There could have been a walled palace and a bustling city, or a single hermit camping on the shore to direct visitors. All of it would have made sense to Foster. It was Ostuk. Even Polc. He didn't understand what was happening, but he knew them well enough to know something was off. And he was the one expected to speak.

"You speak English?"

"Sorry?"

Already, Foster felt like a fool. "You understand what I'm sayin'?"

"Aye."

"Aye, *sir*," Polc corrected him firmly.

"Aye, sir."

"What'sa matter, me son? Are you not excited to see us?"

The man nodded. "We were expecting a supply ship. Have you any word of it?"

"You'll be answerin' the questions, cunt. Where's the Navy?"

Polc was either oblivious to his condescending manner, or unconcerned. Foster held up a hand, and saw a split-second of irritation from him before he nodded and stepped back. "Thank you, Polc. We don't know anything about your supply ship. Is it comin' from Drummoc?"

"Supposed to. Sir."

"When we get back, I'd be happy to speak with the admiral to see that it gets goin'."

The man nodded. "Thank you." He looked over the twenty-four armed rowers who waited behind them.

"I'd like to speak to the assistant viceroy as soon as possible."

"It is not possible."

"We have clearance from the admiral. I think if you just bring him a message for me—"

"He has gone to the mine."

Foster sunk a little at the news, and Ostuk must have felt it. "What need does such a man have to visit the mine?" It hadn't even occurred to Foster that it was strange.

"There was a cave-in. You see," he swept his hand. "All the men are there. He is occupied with the rescue of those who are trapped. We are sent to gather what supplies are not already there, then we will return to help."

"How many trapped?" Foster asked.

"Twelve."

"You know any of 'em?"

"I know all of them."

"I grew up in minin' country. I'm sorry to hear about your boys. Maybe if you take us there, we can pitch in."

The man shook his head. "We have people. It is the supplies we need. Tools, and oil. Food for the men who dig."

"How long they been trapped?"

"Four days. We have a way to get them water. But they do not eat. It is hard to breathe."

"You sent for supplies four days ago?" Ostuk asked.

"Weeks ago. They were much needed then. Now, we must have them."

"Look, we wanna help yall out, but we came all this way. We gotta talk to the assistant viceroy."

"Alexicus will not receive visitors. He is occupied."

"We haven't come all this way to be fucked off," Polc barked. "Our employer here has important word from a mate of your Alexicus. And I've quite an urgent message to deliver meself—from Farri Tolba. Unless you or your employer care to challenge the farri's claim, I'd say you lack the authority to refuse our quite simple request, and you'll take us at once."

The man sunk before the tirade. "Apologies, sir. You are welcome to our hospitality." He motioned to two of the men who waited behind him. "Anjisuk and Simet will show your men to food and fresh water. I will take you now, or we may wait for your men."

"'Scuse us," Foster called for Ostuk and Polc to join him to the side.

"I don't like the cunt. Tryin' to separate us from the arms," Polc said.

"What reason would he have?" They looked to Ostuk.

"These are simple people. They will not harm us. Even if they wished, the price would be too great."

"How far is it to the mine?" Foster asked.

"Depends on the mine. All are difficult. Most half a day, or a day. Some, much more."

"You know the way?"

"I have never left the port here."

"Then I say we stay together."

"I would remain with the ship," Ostuk stated in a way that asked permission.

"Agreed," Polc chimed in. "I don't like this cave-in. I'll post eight men with Ostuk, ready to heave off at a sign of trouble. The rest march with us." Foster stung, having forgotten that he was not in charge, and knew nothing about what was going on or what ought to be done.

"It is strange," Ostuk admitted.

"Yall don't get a lot of cave-ins?"

"There are cave-ins almost every season. It is strange that they try to rescue them."

They broke the huddle and Foster stepped to the front. "Our men'll eat and drink. Once they're rested, we'll follow you to the mine. If we can help, we'll help. If not, we'll only take a few minutes of Alexicus's time."

The crew was dismissed to the wigwams where the provisions were kept. Polc accompanied his men, but Foster took Ostuk strolling toward the tattered field of coal baskets. "That's quite a bit of coal."

Ostuk chuckled. "If you are here in Spring, you will not think so. This is but the remainder of last season. The dogs will return soon, and there will be no place to stand from here to the pass."

"Not always this dead, huh?"

"Even in the middle of winter, when all the miners have gone home to Drummoc, there are a dozen Navy who keep the camp. Even in the busiest part of the season, those who are sick or hurt, those who rest between one mine and another, those who tend the dock and the provisions will all be here."

"How many miners?"

"Six hundred."

"Six hundred did all that?" Foster swept his hands over the baskets.

"Apologies. When Mattaka say six hundred, it is different. Barduk sailed with six hundred ships. The sea is six hundred days old. There are six hundred miners, and six hundred ports on the shores of the Atlantic."

"The what?"

"The sea between the lands, from north of the Orin to the place the waters freeze again. What do your people call it?"

"We call it the same thing."

"All people call it so, but the Mattaka. There are six hundred names for the waters of the world. When a Mattaka is tired of counting, it is six hundred. If one like you were to see the mines, you would say perhaps a thousand."

"Plus twenty-six navy, one pompous bureaucrat, and his wife."

Ostuk's face twisted in horror. "What man would bring his wife to such a place." It was not a question.

Foster shook his head in disgust. Polc and the men were crowded around a wigwam where two of the men piled portions of cured meat into bowls with their bare hands. The other two ferried water—one ladling it from a barrel, the other collecting it in cups and walking them six at a time to the crew, who had not worked very hard that morning to earn it. It was a short row, though once he saw the narrow landing and the sheer rock all around, it was clear why they had slept at sea instead of trying the thing in a lowering curtain of darkness.

The man who greeted them berated the other four for their slow pace and clumsiness, all in English to the great amusement of the rowers. Or whatever they called it—he would have to make a point to ask someone the name of the language he spoke, as humiliating as it might be.

"You spill more than you serve!" The man cried, and kicked the cup bearer in the ass, which made him spill the rest. The crew roared with delight. "I would make you the camp whore if you weren't so ugly!"

"You would not put your family out of work," the man fired back to a chorus of "Ohhhhhhhs" from the crowd. Foster and Ostuk grinned at one another. They watched them posture as if it might come to blows while everyone egged them on in fits of laughter. It reminded him of the way he and Parks would agree before entering some dive in whatever port they were in, to slowly trade insults, make up, escalate, and jostle one another until they were screaming over the other sailors who knew their schtick and were pretending equally well to hold them back. When they were right on the verge of blowing a stitch, one would smash a bottle, or kick over a table to begin the melee, and with any luck the whole group would be hustled out of the place swinging at the air, without paying and before the cops could arrive.

The memory warmed him, and he smiled up into the mountains at nothing in particular. Only then did he notice the sixth Mattaka, a vague shape most of the way up the trail, walking as fast as a man could without breaking into a run.

Foster jogged toward the party, confused but certain of the significance, and he heard Ostuk not far behind.

"Polc! Polc!" He could hardly capture anyone's attention over the two Mattaka preening and throwing everything but punches at one another. When he finally got half a glance from his shipmate, he pointed up just in time for Polc to see the man vanish into the pass.

"Mother*fucker*." He marched up to their host, took him by the collar, and slung him on the ground. "Where the fuck is your man goin'?"

"Who?" He looked around.

"Play dumb and I'll ask the next cunt," He stepped on the man's chest and placed the tip of a bronze spear on his throat.

"He brings word of our guests to Alexicus."

"Up! If we don't catch him, you're done, and your men, too."

The Mattaka took his time standing. "Come on!" Polc yanked him. "Caxsen, Brodus, Neal! Mentewat, Rasden, Webo! Foster! Rest of you hold these here with Ostuk. We'll be visitin' the assistant viceroy. Shove off if any but us comes down that pass."

Foster assembled with the men named, but the Mattaka man didn't flinch. "On with you," Polc prodded with the spear.

"I have decided to stay."

"Then I've decided to kill you."

"So it is. No man here will show you the way. You have our hospitality as long as you choose, and if Alexicus wills it, he will send for you. He has made many requests of the admiral. Few are honored, but many are made of him. It is him who is man of this place, by authority of the viceroy, who acts for King Tolba. The Navy serves at his pleasure, and it is him who pays their wages. And ours."

"Whose throat do I cut?"

"You cut the throat of Sagalak."

"Polc!" Foster stepped in, but Polc did not immediately yield. "We ain't here to fight nobody. Not over a message. Which is all we got." He turned to Sagalak. "I understand your boss got a big dick, and so does the admiral. We ain't here to measure one or the other. Like the man said earlier, he's a paid messenger from Tuba or Teabag or whatever the fuck his name is." Sagalak smirked. "And I have word for Alexicus from his good buddy Barzos, on Nunoc. Neither of us work for Costig. We're in the same boat as you: just doin' our fuckin' job, while some other assholes make it hard on us."

The tension slipped loose from its knot. Polc took a step back and brought his weapon to his side. Sagalak studied them for what seemed like minutes. Then he nodded.

"Alexicus tends to important matters. But I think he will like to hear what you say. If you tell me, I will go myself. Once your boat has sailed for Drummoc. And when the supply ship returns, we will send for you, if he wishes an audience. Or we will send word, if he does not."

"How do we know you'll do it?" Polc challenged. "That you won't just craft some shit into a doll and make it dance for us?"

"Do you have your letters?"

Polc paused, dipped his head, and shook it.

"I do," Foster said. The crew looked on him with guarded surprise.

"You will write what to say. No man at Camne Drumlag can read it. No man can reply, but Alexicus. His word will sail to you, as soon as we have a ship to sail it."

Foster looked to Polc. He didn't even try to hide his annoyance, but he nodded in agreement.

Tunguk removed the sheath from his belt and produced a length of thin braided line. He passed it several times in a cross pattern over the leather that held all but the pommel. A tug to be sure the blade remained in it's cover, then he knotted it and unfurled the rest of the line.

"What are you doing?" It was the pest again, frowning with disapproval.

He fed the line through his left hand to create a pile of slack between the part he held and the knife. Then he studied the rear wall of the prison building, its roof sloped the opposite direction toward the street. His right hand dipped to the side, then cast the weapon up as he kept a grip with the other. It arced over the edge, but caught the last of slack and jerked back down.

"My mate is inside," Tunguk picked it up for another try.

"So you throw your knife on the roof?" The boy crossed his arms.

"Aye." Another try and it held. Tunguk arrested it's slide, then coiled the line and stood on his toes to set it atop one of the room beams that extended out of the stone wall, so that a few feet of braid running from a beam to a rooftop was all anyone could see, if anyone cared to look.

"You are an old fool. Do you mean to get him out?" Tunguk surveyed his work from various angles, and was satisfied. The boy went on. "Only one has escaped."

"Some say two. But I think you are right."

"Will you do it alone?"

"If I can."

The boy snorted. "You will be caught."

"Aye."

Again, he frowned in confusion. "You wish to be caught?"

"I expect it."

"Hm." he mulled it over. "What will you give me?"

"Give you?"

"To help. You are too slow and weak. Tell me what you plan, and what you pay."

"No."

"Then you will be caught."

"Aye, but you will not."

Tunguk pulled off his tunic and set it on the ground, followed by his story shirt of beads arranged in rows on a web of knotted leather. Then he replaced his tunic and draped the sapak over his forearm. The boy gave him a defiant look, proceeded past without a word, and turned away onto the street. The old man filled his chest with a deep breath, and as it passed out again he let his spine curve forward and his knees bend. His feet shuffled over the ground at half his normal pace, and his eyes fell just in front of his toes. Once he cleared the alley, he turned the opposite way from the boy—right, along the face of the Navy hall, massive against the squat stature of the rest of Drummoc. A Marine came out the door heading in his direction. Tunguk cut his path.

"I carve bead," he held up the sapak for the man to see.

"Fuck off," the man shoved past in stride.

A group of three bluecoats chatted out front, and they were next. "I carve bead." They interrupted their laughter to scowl in disgust.

"Mattaka bead is no good," one replied with the thick tongue of Ampos. "You sell to Mattaka." They did not wait for him to leave before resuming their conversation. He hung his head and shuffled on. Another man swerved to avoid him. "I carve bead," Tunguk said meekly after him. He pretended not to hear. The next one saw him sooner, and was able to avoid his solicitations altogether. The handful of people moving in front of the hall now either didn't notice him, or made every effort to give the impression.

"I carve bead," he called to no one in particular. Even the three men who he'd spoken to now took their leave. The heavy wood door of the hall stood before him at the top of a single stone step. Tunguk waited. He said it one more time, barely louder than before. He watched it like a hunter watches the breathing hole of a seal on the winter pack. Soon it swung open and two officers stumbled out, already most of the way drunk.

"I carve bead." They startled in surprise to find someone in their path, and split around to either side without acknowledging him. His shuffling gave way to a quick leap forward and four fingers around the edge of the door. Then his feet slid over the step and into the building.

It was mostly empty this time of day. A dozen men sat scattered at their hasqa, duty-givers, duty-shirkers, or those relieved at odd shifts. Tunguk shuffled over to the nearest one and repeated his pitch.

"Get the fuck out of here, old man," the sailor hardly looked up from his cup as Tunguk slunk off to the next group. A young Amposi with the hasqa fire in his voice spoke to two other men.

"I was thinking of Turu and Iluchar. Iluchar is the better man, but he is vain, and I am worried he will have to speak of things. Perhaps Rederich, instead."

"Aye, Rederich's good, but you can't stand for Turu," one of the others said. "Turu's a try-hard. What about Rixtan?"

"No one will believe that," the first said.

"Erak," the third offered. "Erak is a cunt, but he sets on a matter like a dog."

"Aye, but not always the matter needed," The first answered. "Now I see why he asks my help. It is no easy choice."

"I carve bead," Tunguk said.

"You're not allowed in here, you old squain," the second man said.

"So get us a fresh jug from the stores, and get the fuck out," the third said to the others' laughter. Tunguk hung his head and shuffled toward the middle door where he knew the hasqa would be. A quick glance back showed him that he had vanished from the eyes of all present though he stood in plain sight. He veered left, to the last of the doors, and found it closed but not locked. In one fluid movement he spun inside the admiral's quarters and pulled the door behind him.

His hand reached to the wall, and paused beneath an empty hook on the far right. Left of it there were two more keys—one two-horned, black with age on the left-most side, and a new one with three horns in the center. His fingers curled in consideration then snatched the oldest key. He hurried to lay it on the desk, then took the lid from the tiny ceramic pot of ink, dipped the writing quill delicately in the black paste, gave it a stir to thin it, and scraped the edges clean. With his left hand he draped his sapak over the chair back and lifted his tunic until he could hold it up with his chin. The key was cold against the bare flesh of his belly. The ink, too, as he traced the outline of the head, then went over it a second time to darken it. Tunguk replaced the writing instruments as he found them, and blew on his stomach to dry what he could. His chin released the tunic tail, he gathered his sapak, replaced the key, and sagged again into a shuffle as he exited the room.

His path met that of a Marine crossing the hall—one who had not been inside before. The young man stopped in his tracks. His jaw hung at the sight of Tunguk in the doorway.

"*Hoy!*" He shouted angrily. Everyone else in the hall looked up. "The fuck are you doing?" His hands clamped down on Tunguk's arms and slung him to the ground. Three more rushed over to help. The Marine knelt on his back and pressed his head into the floor. "He was in the admiral's quarters!"

"Dead man, how stupid are you?" One of the sailors from earlier laughed. By now another four Marines had arrived.

"Show me your hands," the first said. He rolled Tunguk over to look upon the bare palms. "Pull him up." They yanked him back to his feet.

"I carve bead," he managed.

"Shut up."

"You steal from admiral," one of the Marines mocked him. They tore off his tunic and felt in his waistline, around the seams of his thighs. Then pulled down his pants, exposing his nude body. Two men lifted him, and two more ripped off his boots and felt inside them.

"Nothing." He caught the eyes of one of the Marines squinting on confusion at the black smear on his stomach. "Maybe he put somethin' in his arse," another suggested, and they all laughed.

"You want to search his arse?"

"Fuck no."

"Old man, is there anything in your arse?"

"I carve bead," he repeated.

"He was trying to sell us beads," one of the sailors confirmed.

"Did you think the admiral would want your shit?" The man who held the sapak slung it across the floor toward the entryway. "Open your mouth." Tunguk complied. They looked inside. "Check those clothes for pockets." Now the hands had all let him go to stand under his own will as they tortured his garments for anything but leather and thread.

"Fucking idiot," the Marine who spotted him pronounced. "No squains in the hall. Admiral does not want your beads. If he wants beads, there are many men of Ampos who will carve them better than you. Get the fuck out of here before we crack you open. You come in here again, you await your death in prison."

Tunguk stooped to pull his pants on. The man kicked him over. He did not land hard, but the thud reminded his head of the pain when it hit the ladder on the *Juhketappat*, and he spun with illness.

"You dress outside. Fuck off!"

They drove him along as he scooped up his things, then the door slammed behind him. A few Mattaka women passing before the hall stared at this naked old man. He let everything fall. Tunguk worked his pants back on, hopping for balance. The drawing on his stomach was deeply smudged, but the lines he made were set much darker than the feathered smear. The pain behind his eyes beat with his heart. He smiled to himself as he pulled on his sapak.

A line of Mattaka boys came into view, pairs carrying a basket between them. Tunguk watched them pass. Six baskets in all, each of six hundred nails. When the last went by, he reached in and grabbed three. One of the boys carrying it grinned at him, and went on his way.

He slipped into the alley, and was soon behind the prison, where he rose on his toes again and gathered the end of the line that he left coiled atop the beam. With a quick tug, his knife clattered at his feet.

The question of how to botch the search well-enough for Parks to escape without making himself a fool, or worse—a traitor—left Costig bleary by the time he mustered 250 men behind the town as the sky began to change hue. Drummoc lay on a peninsula that widened to the main body of the island, and the buildings widened from harbor to base like a long, thin spearhead, with it's flat, broken tip the main street of taverns and smithies and halls and warehouses, bending around the edges to shield the quarters and Mattaka huts from the harbor.

From where he stood, the widest part, only Urkuk and his two wives lay behind them, barren and snow-blown all of the year. There was the dog camp, of course, a few miles on. And somewhere on the far side of the island, the hunting village that provided most of the fresh meat and fish for the colony. But there was nothing in between to sustain a fugitive. The winds that fell from those heights could reach gale force. Peel the skin off a man's face with the driven ice, and take his fingers and toes even in early Autumn. Then there was the mountain itself, a firebreather, restless and fuming by the time they woke, daring someone to brave its passage. Even if he had a boat and a crew to pick him up at the calm harbor—the only decent landing that could be reached on foot—Nunoc was the next station, a mere couple thousand miles, and a couple more to the continent. To flee in Drummoc was but to delay the sword, though it was a fine delay.

Costig had to remind himself that those forces that held the place in order now rallied against his own man, his thin hope of holding the place together against those enemies, without or within, whose sails clipped the horizon. There are other men, he thought. Other ways. But they grew desperate by leaps. There'd be blood to spill, and the price of failure would close in like ice in winter waters. Three men. These were the ones he needed to give a fighting chance. If Parks and his mates couldn't find their way through, then he could always resort to more direct measures. There would be a search of every building in the colony, hundreds of them. If it turned up the man, Costig would have no choice but to execute him, consoled by the knowledge that he gave them every chance, and chance is not always favorable.

There was a way to do it—to comb the town in force. At least some of the men were practiced to a degree. Every few years it was his Marines who led the way, though not for less than the stabbing of a member of the Amposi Navy. Once, he had done it for a squain boy who killed his bride, only after weeks of unrest in which the admiral at the time had feared the population would rear up if he did not appease them. Even then, not a man, woman, or child gave them any aid, though they hated the boy and were glad when he was found. Four Marines were assaulted, one died, and seven Mattaka with no stake in the matter other than the offense of the trespass had to be executed before all was settled.

He looked upon the faces mustered, coming visible now in the earliest dawn. A morning fog slipped its fingers between them, obscuring the flanks from view. There were not enough Marines for the job, and the ranks were full of Navy. They were somber, shivering, anxious. Few, like himself, had hardened leather cuirasses with a high stiff collar, vambraces and greaves to cover the lower limbs, and many, a round cap of a leather helmet strapped to the chin. He carried a small rounded shield of locust wood, as well. These were expenses most of the men could not confront. All but the helmet, he had been awarded piecemeal from dead companions for outstanding service. The helmet cost him his first year's wages, in place of the vaunted blue coat that most would have chosen. None of these but the shield would stop a direct blow from even a flint point.

The bulk of the force carried nothing but the short spear, favored for the confines of town and ship, maybe a knife as a second. It would be stone for the poorer among them, and bronze, or even steel for a good corpse-nick.

Their collective breath rose above them like the sulfur smoke of Urkuk in the distance. They would not enter according to the procedure of the previous admirals. In part, it was because Costig had never thought much of their tactics. It was also because he knew Parks would not escape unless they made a mistake. The best of his men were fond of mistakes and he assumed them even on the simplest maneuvers. Now, faced with an operation of such intricacy, carried out by men of such idiocy, for some reason, his stomach churned with the thought that they may not make one.

Wendell was not fond of it. He could see that much. The two of them would command a body of forty each, entering the town from opposite sides, whereupon they would search each hut, four at a time and ten men to a team, moving down by four huts when all teams had finished, until they met in the middle, when they would advance by a row and head for the outside again. Two more bodies of forty would hold each of the open lanes between the town and the sea to watch for anyone fleeing to the interior along the sides, and to reinforce those in the town if they raised the alarm. Thus they would sweep toward the harbor. Sixty more would remain exactly where they stood, guarding against a flight to the interior out the back of the town. The last thirty were those selected for today's training march to the rim of Urkuk. Their hopes of being relieved of that torture were dashed when Costig ordered them to swing by the dog camp for a quick look, then to complete the march as instructed, searching for prints in the snow. He gave the Marine in charge of the detail the mercy of allowing him to shorten the march if there was too much activity from the crater.

"Form up!" He called for the officers and sergeants to separate their men as assigned, and nodded to Wendell for an aside.

"Have you ever been permitted to tell an admiral his order is fuckin' stupid?"

"Admirals don't make stupid orders," Wendell grinned.

"Aye, you're right. What have I bollocks'ed up?"

"Was the usual way not always effective?"

"Not always. I found it a fair method for confusin' who was to search what, and what had been done or not. A clusterfuck of bodies climbin' across one another, gettin' congealed or separated as it were, stabbed here, then rushin' there in too great a force to do much but hump the arse in front of him."

"I'll admit to that much. Not much more order than a swarm. But the swarm has the advantage that no lane is unclogged, and none may slip behind the force. We shall have excellent order, and the cunt need only slip behind us as we move together and apart, four at a time."

"Behind to where? He's not a squain. He'll not find a hundred welcome homes."

"You're like to be right, but he has been seen consortin' with a few of 'em, and there may be some public favor granted for the fact that he freed eight boys from the cells."

"Who would have been freed the next day for squabblin'. He did them no great favor, makin' them fugitives."

"I agree with you, Costig. But you know that's not how the squain thinks. They'll praise the choice and damn the consequence."

"I'd rather miss him in a pass than have one of me lads lost and cut."

"Pardon me insolence, I'm but a sergeant as you once were. I think it a fine plan, if only the sixty who guard the rear fan out in a line and sweep along behind us. Then he couldn't pass, with all the lanes blocked, advancin' at us, one row at a time."

"Advancin' how? There's no lines in a squain town. Most of the ways are wide enough for a single man. We'll know the ones we searched and didn't, and move in file. File's the only way to move. When a man moves in line abreast, and before him stands a hut, does he go left or right for the next alley?"

"There'll be at least two to a lane, even here at the widest part. They can split up."

"And what at the next one? Split again? Converge?"

"I think the men can sort that out. We just make sure every lane is marked. It gets easier as we cover ground. Only for the first third or so will we be thin."

"It'll be three movements before they miss one. You know as well as I that even our forces are manned by idiots. We haven't the heads for it. You're askin' too many lads to make decisions."

"Only the heroes ever get stabbed. It'll be a tough job no matter how we do it. I'd just hate to do it twice."

"If this fog holds, won't matter much how we do it. There'll be plenty chance to slip us. I'll take good lads, in good order. If we miss him, we'll offer a reward they can't afford to pass. And if they do, we'll run through when the folk go to greet the boats returnin' from Camne Drumlag. Besides, I think they're expectin' what they always seen: a big, loud swarm bumpin' into each other. They're as like to move him for the sides, thinkin' it's comin' up, and run right into a line ahead, which if it turns front to back, becomes a line abreast blockin' all alleys in a moment."

"Huh. Never thought of that." Costig hadn't either, and it was an excellent idea he wished he hadn't had. "Alright then, Boss. Off we go."

Costig lead his forty to the flank on the latrine side of town. When they were gathered, he nodded for a man to blow the horn to signal Wendell's bunch to enter at the same time. It would come as no surprise to any squain who had a reason to fear it. There was no way to muster 250 men behind the town without someone hearing it, and most would have suspected it from the night's events. He feared finding Parks, but there were any number of other rackets to which a general search would prove unkind, and he had no idea what, where, or how many were prepared to fall on his spear for it.

They grouped ten to a hut behind the outermost four. Each to a lane, they rounded their mark to the flap-covered openings. Already, he had lost sight of the farthest two squads, having taken the most interior position. The huts were always offset, and never to the same proportion.

His deep voice boomed through the fog: "Hoy! Mattaka! You are subject to search. Remain in your homes until you are called out. If you leave before you are called, you will be struck down." The order echoed thrice to his right from the other squads. When he stuck his hand inside the flap of his mark to throw it aside he felt his heart abandon all sense of pace in his chest. "This hut! Out!" One of his Marines held it open as he stepped back and raised his weapon with the other three who had any purchase to deal a blow. The rest of the party watched the lanes that led to their position for runners or blind-side attack. He heard no movement from within. Beside them, he could see the next squad doing to same, and none had emerged from theirs either. Sometimes, the huts were empty, or the ones in them were very old or young, and very frightened. Either way, that meant he had to go in. Any of the Marines would do it if he gave the command, but Costig had ordered the search. He had freed the fucking prisoner, at that. It was his flesh to bare, and the day would go as he did.

"On me!" One Marine came behind and pressed his off-hand to Costig's shoulder. More than two men in, and they would end up piercing one another in confusion. He turned the corner in a crouch and went right along wall, swishing his weapon back and forth before him with the tip pointed at the ground, hoping to make harmless contact but ready to do harm if needed. The light from the door barely spilled over the center of the room. His shoulder brushed the side with the corner of his left eye on the exit that he hoped to reach. It took only a three-count to arrive again and praise the open sky. There was not a soul, not an empty basket within. Mattaka did not leave things behind if they could help it. They had few things, and many thieves about. A glance to the side saw the next squad over come out as well.

"Empty!" Costig called. He was answered by three more cries of the word from the other squads. "Line ahead!" They formed a single file behind him. Not a bad result for the first clearance of the day, and a good omen if it was one. He marched down the lane, keeping always to his right. It was only the first movement, and already it was unclear which huts were next. They were nearly identical, and once there were several levels behind them, it would be up to he and Wendell to determine if the one he saw were a back-set member of the current bunch, or a fore-set member of one they'd already done. He and Wendell were at least up to it. Under previous admirals, Costig was quite sure his men had searched the same ones three, four times each on occasion.

He passed three and settled on the fourth.

"This hut! Out!" Again, there was no response. With the men at the mines, their families would often stay with relatives, preferring to pack like barreled fish than to take their privacy, especially the outer levels where they bore the brunt of the wind. "On me!" The same hand found his shoulder. "New man," he ordered a switch. Everyone would clear huts today.

A boy of three bare as rock toddled out to the point of Costig's spear and stopped. An old woman came behind him, holding an infant of less than a year. She scolded the boy in her tongue and ushered him aside.

"Is that all?" She said something sharp and dismissive in Mattakatan. "On me," he repeated. Costing turned the corner the same way, and immediately flew forward through the air. By fear alone he managed to turn his point so that it would not break his fall, or break on the ground.

"Man inside!" His companion called to their squad. "On the ground!" He challenged whoever had thrown his admiral.

"Fuck off," Costig groaned to his feet. He kicked a pile of pelts and leatherwork into the lighted middle and waved the men who poked their heads in back to their posts. His heart was near eruption from the shock. "On me, lad, and raise your bollocks." They completed the circuit at a slower pace, brushing aside a few more things. He exited, and cried, "Empty! Fuck, I mean, three! *Three!*"

"Empty!"

"Empty!"

"Empty!" Came the replies. That luck would not remain with them all day, he knew. He confronted the old woman. "We seek a fugitive. Have you seen a halot, tall and pale, bit soft-bodied with a funny accent."

She grinned through two missing front teeth. "No catch Leopard Seal!" Then laughed as she led the children back inside.

They held their praise the first few hours of sail so as not to prick the ears of the fates. A gentle breeze rolled off the high mountains behind and eased them off toward Drummoc. Every inch of the sail stretched to collect the good fortune, and Ostuk pressed the oars even though he'd let them rest on the way over when the winds were fair. The quiet urgency to make headway finally came clear to Foster just after noon, when their friendly tail was driven off by a thundering beast out of the northeast.

The squall intercepted their course and kicked up knee-high rollers right away. Sailing was still a mystery to him, but one that unraveled one painful experience at a time. With the gusts appearing ahead of port, they got the order to haul close, which meant they had to angle a little to starboard and stow the oars. The tall gray column overhead that marked the clouds of Drummoc indicated that Ostuk had taken an angle out to sea as much as possible when he could. Now he was forced back to the other side of Drummoc, unable to run any farther into the wind. Foster realized that had they tried to take a straight shot home, their present course would put them well inland without a lot of tacking to and fro and going nowhere. It was a brilliant bit of seamanship on the captain's part that they would not have to tack back across until nearly upon the island, and even then missing by just a few miles. That, or he'd made the trip more times than he cared to remember. The men huddled as the prow dipped over the waves at an angle. Each one shaved off frigid spray over the sides. The water in the ship sloshed out of the shallow bilge and soaked their feet every time the vessel tilted, which was constantly. Four buckets went around in shifts. He had already finished his first shift— about a half hour—and already the next one was creeping his way. None of the bailers seemed concerned, though. This was light water. There were many more things a man could use to throw it overboard, but there was no sense tiring themselves out until there was a need for it.

Already it was clear that they would spend the night at sea again. When Foster asked, Ostuk said it was an early start and good fortune that allowed the trip in a day—or a reckless captain. A stout crew could row it in shifts if it was calm. The good ones took their time.

As mild as it was compared to their trip down on the dog ship, he was already feeling the early pangs of seasickness, and he tried to find a line on the heaving horizon for his eyes to hold. Foster had relocated midship since no one was rowing. He intended to share with the man, but out of deference to the one who "hired" the crew the guy gave up the bench entirely and sat with someone else. Or maybe out of disgust for one who was obviously deep in status and shallow in experience. None of the rowers spoke to him any more than they had to. That was more than fine by Foster. He didn't feel like speaking much to anyone at that moment. Which was probably why Polc joined him from aft.

"Still favor a trip north into Omera's bite?" Polc chuckled. "If this sea greens you, you might reconsider a few thousand miles of swell as low as the mast on a good day." He was not wrong. Every bone in Foster's body wanted out of Antarctica before Winter clenched around him, but those were the opinions of bones on dry land. Here, miserable in the modest seas, he wondered how bad it could possibly be to sit in a hut while the wind and ice blew through the endless night, as opposed to the same on the open deck of a pitching ship—one that didn't even have a proper deck like the dog ship. The only reason he even considered it was that other men, more knowledgeable, aimed to do the same. But those were a different breed than someone who slept deep inside carriers. If the trip down was hell, he had no word for what he expected.

All of that survivable misfortune was dependent on him being able to stop the ship at Nunoc as Costig requested. If not, it was Taclann. He had no idea what or where Taclann was, but if it was beyond the peninsula, it was across Drake's Passage—the most miserable stretch of water in the world, even in the relative comfort of the vessels he'd worked on. The shitstorms of the coast were bathtub typhoons by comparison. Here he sat with twenty-four crew, plus Polc and Ostuk, who held him in at least some regard, even if it was forced. If someone put a gun to his head and said he had to find a way to stop this ship against the wishes of all aboard, in his queasy state, he had no idea how he would even begin, or if he cared enough to try. There would be far more to contend with on the whaler. Worse seas. A more urgent sense of destination. And not a friend aboard except Parks.

He managed a weak smile for Polc. "I never been round to these parts before. Gettin' here was the worst trip of my life. But I can tell you, beyond a shadow of a doubt. I'm willin' to do it again or worse if it means I never have to see this fuckin' place again."

"Well, you'll be in good company. I'd join you meself if it weren't for me duties here. But you'll still have your mates you came in with."

"Mate, anyway. I don't think my Mattaka pals are goin' anywhere."

"Ah, I thought there was two of 'em."

Foster felt himself knot up. He wasn't sure what Polc was probing for, only that what he said now had more than a little bearing on Gionn's position. All he knew is that these two were familiar, and they didn't take much of a shine to one another. If Polc had beef and numbers, why hadn't he moved on his enemy? Was it bygones, or did he hope to find out exactly where the man stood and who stood with him first? If someone had asked him ahead of time, Foster might have said he'd be happy to let Polc eliminate a man who had never shown him an ounce of loyalty. Who was in direct competition with he and Parks for a seat on the only bench out. Now that he had the chance, he could feel deep down that there was no chance of him betraying the son of a bitch. It wasn't even a choice. It was just so remote, so foreign that he couldn't even hold the idea in his mind. His first thought was to praise Gionn and their friendship, and talk up all their other friends from the dog ship. Make them sound like a merry crew too massive to contend with. Something about it felt off, though.

"Two. That's right. Tunguk and Kjartke."

"I meant the halots, not the squains."

"One," he tried to hide a hard, phlegmy swallow. "Parks."

"Parks. Is that the big oafy lad?"

"That's how I would describe him, yeah."

"What about the red man?" Foster didn't answer right away. "Did I not see you disembark with such a fellow?"

He pretended to give it some thought, more than anyone should have to. "Um. Yeah. Yeah, there was a redhead on the ship with us. Gionn, I think it was. Like you say, it ain't polite to ask too many questions of your fellow passengers. So I couldn't tell you much about him. Seemed like a decent-enough guy." It was out of his mouth before he realized what he'd done. No one who had exchanged so much as a word with Gionn—let alone been stuck on a ship with him—could think him decent, or have any less than a feverishly strong opinion of the man. He had not painted him an enemy, and he had not claimed any allegiance. It was far better than any scheme Foster could have come up with had he gave it his most diligent consideration. Polc would wonder what he was hiding. Here was a man who did not hate his rival, the relationship of whom was uncertain. Was Gionn without support or not? Someone was hiding something on his behalf, and Polc could fuck himself sideways trying to figure out what. At the same time, there was no obvious reason to include Foster and Parks among the people they would cut down if they did decide to go after the bastard. And if Polc was wondering if and what Gionn had betrayed of him to others, he was still utterly clueless, trending toward worried.

"Well, if you and your mate Parks find you'd rather not drown on a whaler, I'm sure I could find work for you. Least through Winter. It'll pay enough for a passage to your faraway and unspoken shore in the spring—if you don't drink it all, that is."

"'Preciate it, brother. But I don't think we'll need it."

"Fair enough, me son. It stands, if you change your bearin'. And you can pass it to your shipmates, as well. Pay enough to go around."

Foster nodded. "Sorry we couldn't get you to the assistant viceroy."

Polc gave a good-natured shrug. "He'll have to come round, eventually."

"'Scuse me." Foster leaned over the gunwale and hurled.

The sons of Sawi looked like they had slept as little as Norwet. Milak, Ravitak, and Arnake blinked hard along the perimeter of the pack. It was fortunate the five of them were outside when the Navy arrived. The dogs had gone mad, scrambling over each other and hurling themselves into fights over tangled leads. The boys set upon them, cracking jaws loose from necks and keeping the lines from strangling them. Saunlauk and Siguvik, the cousins of Sawi's sons, and so of Norwet and his brothers, trotted back with the one that had broken free and run for Urkuk. By that time the men with spears had managed to conduct their search at a distance the dogs found only irritating, but not infuriating. Most of the Navy seemed more concerned that leads might break than with finding their quarry.

Norwet knew the father and the two adult cousins of Saunlauk and Siguvik, who also helped them contain the pack. They traveled on the ships between Nunoc and Drummoc, as none of the boys had before this season. And though they knew much of the others, this was the first opportunity they had to meet Sawi and his wife, his sisters, cousins and their families. Many more he knew were on the ship that did not reach Drummoc earlier in the season. All those here were family in some way—fifteen besides the boys— and all of them were gathered in a tight group in the wet snow while the men probed their huts and their storage for a man who had escaped the prison, or his red-haired accomplice. Sawi was furious. He had no chance yet to speak with the boys, but the way his face boiled when he shot a look their way now and then told Norwet that he did not put all the blame on the admiral. There were many things in a dog camp that the Navy must not see. The busted lips and eyes that swelled on some of the boys, and most of all himself, were first among them. His left was half closed and the tender cheekbone pulsed with pressure. Worse, he had failed to give Ferrakut anything in return. The shirker was the cleanest of them all.

They had put Ulwet the runt to bed before spending a good portion of the night running two teams quietly through what tracks they left from the first snow to the camp. Dog tracks were to be expected. Better than fresh prints. But he was not sure how they would explain why sleds were drawn right up to the rock-line if anyone thought to ask.

His cousins came back panting and tied the loose dog next to Norwet.

"It is good you return when all the work is done," he teased. They didn't look any fresher than he did.

"We let her run. She found tracks, leading up to Urkuk."

"Do you think they brought him up there?"

Saunlauk shrugged. "But we were sure to run through them for a good ways, and back over the same."

The dogs twitched and whinnied. They sensed a change in the men. The searchers gathered near Sawi, groups of men trailing in to join the main body. Some looked like they had never walked in snow before. They were already shivering and miserable. Three Marines cursed them and slapped them along into more of a huddle than a formation. One of them spoke to Sawi, who responded with waving hands and sharp words Norwet could not hear. The group turned to leave, and Sawi kept up his driving, as though they were an incorrigible team on the trail. None of that fire was to be found when they arrived. Only their departure gave him over to a display of cheap courage.

To Norwet's surprise, the platoon of men turned not for town, but for the mountain. He had seen another group the day before pass the camp in the same manner: a few men driving the others as one drives young dogs to teach them and make them strong. As long as it had taken, their search had been hurried. They knew they had ground yet to cover, and preferred to be done. If they had uncovered anything Sawi did not wish them to, they said nothing of it. He did not bother to speak to the boys yet. There would be hasqa to take before that, even after such a short visit. The rest of the adults followed off to their tukits, and it was a while after that before they calmed the dogs. The adults who helped them turned over the task and went to join Sawi.

Norwet stalked after them. He made sure all were in the warmth of the tukits, and listened at the door for voices that swore at the Navy in between hot pulls of drink. Then he returned to his sleepless brothers and cousins. He found them waiting anxiously. It was not necessary to give an order, though he was the oldest. Every one of them hurried to the far side of the teams, where the dogs had piled little mounds of snow against the rolling winds of Urkuk so that they could shelter in the lee. It was here that they had worked furiously as soon as Norwet ran back to camp with the news that men were coming up the trail in force. Now it was difficult to remember exactly where.

They pored over the windbreaks until they found the one with fresh, sharp ice pack on the leeward side in a way that dogs do not build.

"They are gone," he bellowed at the mound.

"Help. Cunts." The mound replied.

They threw themselves on their knees and shoveled snow behind with their hands as fast as they could go. Ferrakut uncovered the pelt that they lay over him to make an air pocket. They grasped it and tore it free in a shower of snow.

Gionn gasped and did not stop gasping. His pale skin was purple and blue as he rolled himself out and did his best to kick the ice from his limbs. The boys brushed him vigorously and wrapped the fur seal pelt around his shivering shoulders.

"We must hurry. Someone will see you."

"I'm not goin' back to the meat hole." Gionn shuddered at the thought of the pile of frozen seal flesh and blubber, crammed into a narrow crawlspace made of stone and buried but for the entrance under a drift.

"They will give a reward," Milak said. "When they think one is hiding with the people."

"Would your cunts sell me out like that?"

Milak nodded enthusiastically.

"You can stay with the stores for now," Norwet said. "These men have gone up. When they come back, they may pass again to search. We will keep watch, and make you another dog mound."

"I'd rather rot with the meat. Fuck this. You, oldest boy."

"Norwet."

"That one. Take me to the home of Tunguk."

"Tunguk has no home."

"Then take me wherever we were last night. Much as I appreciate your hospitality, I shall hide with me mate Parks."

"If they search here, they search Drummoc," Milak warned.

"Tunguk says to keep you here."

"Ah, right. It's a good plan. But maybe he didn't know that here is quite uncomfortable. And quite far from the harbor, where me ship prepares to sail." He stood and dropped the pelt to the ground. "Which if I miss, I will be hidin' in meat holes or newly built prison cells all Winter, provided I'm not killed on the spot. Now that I think—and thinkin' has never done me well—it's hard to recall what I thought I'd gain from breakin' a cunt out of prison. Is it just me, lads? Or do you feel we may have been a bit taken-advantage-of?" He pinched a small gap between his thumb and forefinger. "'We must save Parks!' Who the fuck is Parks? Did you know Parks? Or you?" They shook their heads. "What is it we need him for? Last I saw him, he was so ill and out of sorts it was all I could do to keep from endin' his misery. Sick people are disgustin' aren't they? Cripples, too. It's not right how they make us feel all out of sorts, bein' round 'em. I would prefer to cut 'em down as a passin' kindness if it weren't that they often have things like families and mates prepared to avenge 'em. I can tell you that if you're ever on the edge about killin' a man who you think no one will miss, I'd advise against it. Three out of four times, someone will miss him quite a bit, indeed.

"Anyway, Parks…Not sure how we got tangled up in that line. The old man and the dark woman certainly have their guile, for a couple of squains— no offense. Now we are all stuck on their eternal side, or compelled to flee thousands of miles over the forgetful seas." He grumbled to himself under his breath. "I thank you for your help. I've got nothin' to pay you back, and don't come askin' me for favors. But I did give you that free advice about killin' men none will miss. That's a good one, hard to learn the hard way. And I'll offer one more: if a man asks you to help break a prison, or some other scheme that will land you thick among enemies, do as your fathers and uncles would. Turn in him for a reward."

As Gionn stomped off through the snow huddling around himself for warmth, Norwet and Milak met eyes.

Sleep never found him. Not entirely. There was no way to lie down in the snow without losing what body heat remained. Parks had to sit against the gnarled black boulder salted with windblown snow. The first time he managed to drift off he was awakened by a searing pain in his balls, only to realize they were becoming frostbitten pressed against the ice. He had to chip out a trench that ran from behind his tailbone clear past his gooch and cup himself in his trousers with his slightly-less-freezing hands until he once again felt the blood pulse in his nether regions.

The seal skin clothing had the initial advantage of being quite warm, but completely unbreathable. Minutes into the march he began to sweat from head to toe, and that sweat froze in a thin layer that crunched and pulled at his arm hairs whenever he rubbed himself briskly for warmth. No one had thought to give him any mittens, if such a thing had been invented. He noted to check, add it to his list. His hands mostly hid in his sleeves or his crotch.

Soon after he managed to drift off again the wind changed direction and swept across them in an icy blast that had to be hurricane force. The rest of the night was a game of whack-a-mole, with Parks and Wisconsin Johnson scooting one way or the other to keep the boulder between them and the howling current of air, with Parks using his lucky arrow to scrape out a new gooch trench each time, or feeling around for his old one. If Wisconsin was phased, he didn't bemoan it publicly. Like the man said, it wasn't his first trip. But he would have killed Parks for sure if they'd tried to take the high way in this weather and his current condition. For that, at least, he felt vindicated.

If it wasn't wind or frostbite, it was fitful sleep. The kind of light, strobing dreams of creepy images and sounds, people saying shit he couldn't make out but he knew from the tone was not anything he'd care to hear. It was sleep that tormented as much as it rested, with cameos from the wind and the snow in his dreams, or uncanny flashes of dream when he was mostly awake. He was so exhausted that his eyelids hurt and waves of nausea teased his stomach though there was nothing in him. Once, he tried to quench the thirst that cracked his lips and dried his throat by sucking on ice. It just gave him a brain freeze. The water bladder was long-since empty. Wisconsin had told him to come prepared for a long walk. Details would have helped.

At one point, he literally prayed for the dawn, to no one in particular and without a hint of his usual sarcasm and bluster. As awful as it was to move, rest was worse.

So it was from a surprisingly long bout of semi-stable unconsciousness that he awoke to the sound of voices very close by. Before his vision fully gathered he could see Wisconsin Johnson wide awake issuing a finger across the lips for silence. His first reaction was relief that other humans were near. That he could find rescue and company, maybe water. Maybe mittens. It took him a moment to realize that he was a fugitive, and no man would come up a mountain to help him. Even Joe would insist that he return home. He didn't understand lifeboats, or Americans, or interdimensional travel.

As the column passed, they braved a peek around. It was a few dozen men, definitely military. Parks couldn't make out details, but the sound and shape led him to believe they weren't having a much better time than he was.

"That makes things interesting," Wisconsin whispered.

"Doesn't look like they saw us."

"No, but what goes up must come down. The easiest way is the one they went. We're going to have to shade around to a steeper face."

"I don't know if I can do it."

"You have to. It's not much different. We've got to make it around the back at some point anyway."

"I meant I'm not sure if I can stand up. I can barely feel my feet."

"Then you don't have frostbite yet. Better get up while that's the case."

"And then what? I get up, we make it to your crew, hiding in some cave. Then what? We steal food for the rest of our lives? Come back down and make friends with the locals? I'm not following."

"Then we go home."

The word filled his chest with bitter remorse. "Home." Parks tried to imagine it, but he could not call a single image to mind in the white wasteland. "Where the hell are we?"

"Not nearly halfway up the volcano."

"Yeah, but *where?*"

"Antarctica."

"But Antarctica, *where?*"

"Oh, you mean why isn't it covered in miles of ice and devoid of human life." He grinned. "I guess you could say it's a pretty fortunate Antarctica, as far as we're concerned. We're in the last place on Earth where we can still be at least temporarily alive."

"Aren't you supposed to be some kind of a scientist?" He could tell the questions were starting to irk Wisconsin.

"Was. Yeah."

"Then what's the hypothesis? Did you guys see any wormholes on your way here?"

"No hypothesis, no wormholes. We came the same way as you."

"Which is what?"

"A white hole inversion effect in the fabric of quantum space-time that rearranged our molecular structure and that of our surroundings to a mode that was harmonic-enough to allow the subatomic rebonding that renders the universe as we experience it."

Parks scrunched his nose. "Really?"

"No, moron. I'm not a fucking physicist. But I am going to get us home."

"You sound like Foster. How?"

"For starters, I have to get all of us back together, way up there," he pointed.

"And then what?" Parks thought he saw Wisconsin twitch with frustration and a warm feeling spread inside him.

"Anything that can go one way can go back the other."

"Not true. You ever seen a baby slide out a pussy? Or a volcano erupt?"

"I've seen both, and if I believe it's not true, then we might as well sit here until we freeze into members of the landscape. You got anymore questions, I'll be happy to answer them. Once we're safe and warm in the cave."

Parks extended a hand for help up. Wisconsin Johnson didn't see it. He was already snaking wide to avoid the trail the Navy platoon left. It felt as though the ground begged him to stay a little longer. Instead, Parks flopped over to an almost-all-four position, hovering his miserable left knee off the ground. He scooted his legs out to either side as far as he could, then pushed himself back with his hands until his hamstrings cramped, and climbed his own thighs until he was more or less upright.

The frozen tear-froth in his eyes turned the whole place a blurry white streaked in blues and pinks and black. The men, his guide, even his own feet were indistinguishable. His shoulders, neck, and face burned with a light feeling that he had not experienced before. One that could have meant his body was fighting off what ailed him. Or preparing to give up entirely. His feet took him in the direction he remembered seeing Wisconsin head, knowing he'd probably be waiting up there somewhere. Low, under his breath, he felt a tune bubble out from the murky deep in the style of a pirate shanty.

"The ship is caught, she cannot sail. The water's ice, I cannot bail. Me body's frail, the winds, they chill me bones. A maiden there! A maiden where? I spy a rope of wet black hair. She calls me, walk the water white for home."

An offshore wind appeared first as a breeze that spared them fog, then began to squall and snap over the tops of the homes, like waves of a charging enemy reaching out to slash at the men. It drummed in their ears, ripped under helmets and around the seams of armor then darted off as if to avoid retaliation. Costig and his squad folded forward to walk. Just a few feet below head-level the force was nothing like that which whipped a taller man. Even a short one like Costig sought the refuge of the lower altitudes. This, he knew, was merciful by Autumn standards, and nothing to compare to the winter blizzards. Yet it felt like the winds were taking the search personally. They always sided with the Mattaka.

"This hut! Out!" He yelled over the howl. Heads filed through the door cloth and didn't stop filing. Seven women, eight children, and a very old couple braced themselves against the weather. "Anyone else?" One of the women shook her head, and he sent two of his squad in to confirm. They returned in moments. Costig beckoned the woman closer. He leaned beside her ear and screamed in slow syllables.

"Have you seen the one called Leopard Seal?"

"What is reward?" She hollered back.

"I've not set one." The woman shook her head. Costig studied her. He ticked off family members on his fingers, then shouted "Seventeen!" He waved her family back inside. One of his men trotted off to get the numbers from the other squads—they hadn't heard one another in some time. Half a day and they were near half-through, having turned up no traces or rumors, though no incidents in his half. Wendell had already arrested three boys on separate occasions, all for trying to slip off before the search got to their huts. With a key missing and the walls punctured, Costig couldn't very well keep them in the prison, but he hadn't yet decided what to do in the meantime.

"Line ahead!" Costig waited for his man to vanish around the bend to deliver the news. When the head reappeared, he led them past the next hut, turned a blind curve, and stopped in his tracks. Nestled against the outer wall of his home was the old man. He flicked a long knife delicately about what looked a small pebble, but must have been a bead.

"You!" Costig pointed his spear. "Do not run!"

Tunguk looked at him bewildered, and continued his carving. The squad came up to surround him. The men behind them jammed up as they stopped short of their four-building rotation. "Next two squads, around!" He waved them by. "This is mine." He and his men had to lean their bodies into the curvature of the hut to allow twenty men to step over their feet and fit to the next two dwellings, mostly around another corner.

"You were to remain inside until called. I can arrest you for bein' in the streets durin' a search."

"Oh."

"Who else is within?"

Tunguk cupped his hand around his ear against the wails of the wind. Costig gave up, poked his spear through the rare window. His hoarse voice cracked as he bellowed, "This hut! Out!"

A young woman of perhaps twenty emerged to face him. "The old man is not allowed in the street!" He admonished her.

She looked down at him, then back at Costig without speaking a word.

"Is there another inside?" This time she shook her head. "On me!" Costig felt the hand on the back on his shoulder. His heart struggled to keep up with itself. The old man was outside for a reason. Was he marking it? Trying to deliver a message of warning? For a moment he scrambled to come up with an excuse not to search it. Something his men could believe. But nothing pitied him the plan. If Parks was in there, it would bring no pleasure to have him killed. Yet Costig had given him his chances. He would not feel sorry for one so inept, and if the man couldn't avoid a cumbersome search with a head start, he would have made a lousy spy.

Costig threw himself inside and ringed the hut with care. He felt a few spears underfoot, but relief flooded him when it came up empty. "Have you seen the one called Leopard Seal?" He asked the woman. Costig was not sure who she was, why these squains had anything to do with the lads from the dog ship, but they would suffer as much if they were not careful.

"Aye."

"Come again?"

"Aye."

"Where?"

"I see him on the *Juhketappat*. We sail from Nunoc."

"And since?"

"Aye." Costig waved his hand to implore her on. "I see him always near the tavern. Near the harbor. I think he stays with one there."

"And since last night?" She shook her head. "You said you just arrived. From Nunoc?"

"By way of," Tunguk spoke up. The squad turned to him. "We are not Kammatuk. I am of the Kapadak, and she of the Haqawa." He grinned.

"Jargadak," she corrected him.

"In whose home do you stay?"

"It is kind of the captain to give us walls until the woman begins work." Costig read what crossed her face and knew what kind of work he meant. "He is called Ostuk. He stays with family."

"Has the Leopard Seal been by to visit either of you, or Ostuk?"

"He keeps close to the harbor. Mattaka weave medicine into their streets. Your kind get lost, Tunguk said. Costig sent two men back into the hut to retrieve any objects left inside, and had them set at his feet to examine in the light. There were spears and harpoons, a stone knife, bits of leather and stone, the kind of crafts every family kept. Two bowls of soapstone. No sign of another resident. Relief took him. They wanted to be questioned, to be searched thoroughly to dispel doubt. If they spoke of Parks near the harbor, that meant that wherever he was hidden, their pattern that narrowed toward the main street would turn up empty.

"Back inside until the search concludes."

"Will it be long?" Tunguk asked, shaving a few flecks from his bone bead.

"Aye. It will be. Your carvin' can wait." He ushered them back inside. "Two! And have them hold position ahead. I've got the lead." He cried into the wind, and a pair of men relayed it to each side.

Kjartke watched through the window as the line filed by and out of sight. "I thought he went inland, but they have searched. He is not in the tukits."

"It is difficult to search Drummoc. Because he is not found, does not mean he is not there. And there is much more inland than tukits. It means only that he has found help."

"So we trust him to strangers."

"No. We find who helps him."

"It will be dark before we can leave."

"We will leave soon. I must sing, while my memory is good." Tunguk pinched the new bead between his right thumb and held it against his chest. He chanted in low, hoarse Mattakatan, a repetitive phrase, three times, before he continued.

"'Song of the Leopard Seal?'" Kjartke asked. Tunguk's chant paused, then picked up again without an answer.

Seven boys walked the street in front of the public buildings, three ahead, and four back, well to the side. Ferrakut cupped his hands and called to Milak and his brothers. "Get behind us, squain!" Milak turned and gave them an obscene gesture. Ferrakut laughed, Ulwet, Saunlauk, and Siguvik at his flank. There were plenty of Navy earning their wage, as the men said of those who loafed and skirted the officers who put them to a task. The people also traveled the street—smiths carrying loads of coal, or iron, or the products of their work. Men young and old returning from the hunt. Now that the boat laws had been suspended, there were also men young and old returning from fishing and hunting, grandfathers and their grandsons hauling a fresh kill. It was as busy as the street would be until the miners returned. Groups passed in between them and the other boys, but they kept pace.

"I said 'get behind!'" He repeated. Milak stopped. He and his brothers marched up to the group.

"Fuck you, orphan boy."

"You are the orphan boy," he said too loudly for their distance, and just enough to catch the stares of those passing. "My father will be back from the mine soon with pay. It is too bad he will spend it on your mother."

"You have many words when your mates are behind you. When you are on the street, where you know you cannot be harmed."

"You have the same, and yet you are the one trembling."

"Orphan boy," Milak repeated.

"Fuck you!" Little Ulwet leapt forward. He was convincing, or Milak had angered him. "You are a pup of a bitch dog!" Ferrakut saw Milak's face ignite. Now he was not so sure if they were still following the words of Tunguk.

"I will bring you to her, and you will swear apology at her feet."

"Ha!"

"I will kill you." Milak was almost Norwet's age, well-older than them, and a full head higher than Ulwet. Ferrakut knew this was the way, but he instinctively pulled Ulwet back. "Rein your dog," Milak spat.

"You are the only dog I see."

Milak stepped forward and shoved him. Ferrakut knew the response, but something prevented him from returning it. Then Milak shoved again. "See? You are afraid?"

"There is no fighting in the street."

"You are fortunate I do not see you in town."

"If you do, you will see nothing after me."

"We will see." The boys postured.

"What the fuck are you doing?" Ulwet whispered to them. "Fuck you!"

He shouted at Milak. Milak gave him a shove as well. Ferrakut stepped up to him, but Ulwet flashed by and landed a quick series of punches on Milak's body. Milak threw back, and before Ferrakut knew what was going on, he was swinging at anything that moved in a blind flurry. Little hands like rocks fell all about him, but it hardly hurt. He hit Milak again and again, then lost him, and realized he was wailing on Siguvik at the same time that Siguvik saw it. They stopped and doubled on Arnake, the youngest of Milak's brothers. Voices shouted behind them, but they paid no mind. Someone slung Ferrakut to the ground and got on his chest. It was Milak. He braced for the blows, but what rained down here hardly slaps. He caught the older boy's grin, and realized he still had his wits.

A huge body flung Milak off of him, and in moments they were swarmed by six Marines who boxed them about the ears and whipped them around until they settled, panting.

"Stand down, you fucks!" The Amposi man yelled in his face.

Norwet had done as Costig bid him. He did not care to rush back to the dogs when there were plenty of hands to tend them, and no real work until it was time to bring the firestone down. He'd peeked inside the message enough to know it was a key he threw to Kjartke, then spent the next few hours watching the men run maneuvers in the harbor. It had become the instant pastime of every Mattaka, and especially the boys. Even the elders here had never seen such a flurry, and the lack of practice showed in the rowers' clumsy timing and quick fatigue. In that time alone he twice saw men lose oars into the sea when their boat passed too near another and the rowers collided strokes. The rumor was that a siege would greet them in Spring. Far from concerned, he and the other boys were excited for any break in their dull routine. The navies of the kingdom were not more than song and legend, and here two might clash as near as he watched these very ships. It did not look good for the men of Ampos.

It was on his way back he noticed the scuffle on the street. The Marines were already peeling them apart when he stopped to watch. It was an unusual amount of entertainment for a single day. Norwet was beginning to quite like Drummoc. Until he noticed Ferrakut, and Ulwet, and the other faces that came into focus with them. He walked as close as he dared, and heard the Marine berating them for fighting in public, how he should cut them down. He braced to watch a good portion of his family led off to the cells for who knows how long, and at what price their freedom would be gained. But just as he thought the rant would end in arrest, the Marines straightened up and started off, keeping a keen glare on the boys. It was fortunate for them most Amposi were lazy.

Norwet trotted over. "Ferrakut!" His brother startled at his presence. "You fool! Are you trying to get arrested?" Ferrakut sized up the Marines, then his brother. He cocked his arm behind his head and cracked Norwet on the eye with everything he had.

The line of men appeared first as a gray streak over the bare plain. The gaps etched themselves into the body until it became many, and well before he was close enough to make out who they were, Gionn knew his path to Drummoc was blocked. There was nothing to obscure him, even now a half mile off, and it was his luck that every face was turned to the town. He lay down on the rock, grateful to have left the snow. He wasn't actually sure if he was headed to look for Parks and the shit hut, impossible to tell from any of the other shit huts, or if he meant to find the harbor and secure his seat. They weren't just searching for Parks, he had to remind himself. That meant he had allies if he could make it to them. But allies who would struggle to hide him until nightfall, let alone Spring. Polc was now the least of his worries—a hated man who must pretend to like him. It was Costig—a mate who pretended to hate him—who he feared. He was sure if it came to it, Costig would pretend his spear right through Gionn's neck and lay a feast for the gulls. It was some consolation that if he were to be executed, he would use his last words to secure a similar fate for Shitstain, and they'd have to kill him to stop his laughter.

"There is another way." Gionn startled and jerked around. The sight of the oldest squain boy's bruised face did little to calm his heart, but he followed Norwet back to the snow, then coastward, on the opposite side of the island. He'd seen a chart of it, of all places rolled into Parks' belt. The big fuck-about was the last man he would expect to carry such a fine map, and it gave him a sense of relief when he realized the man had no idea how to read it. Gionn had spent many a dull moment in a tossing ship, pointing out the features of interest between the peninsula and Drummoc, of which there were perhaps four or five. He explained the winds and the currents, even though he knew only rumors of them. His guide to the island of Drummoc was based on even less, though Parks hadn't a notion of it. It was their first time as fugitives, Gionn realized, and this, their second. Becoming a bad habit, but it gave him a warm spot for the wet loafer. Drummoc, as he recalled having seen it drawn for the first time there in an open skin boat, would have been on the point that aimed at the mainland and the mines of Camne Drumlag. The harbor was just around the side that opened to the bay, a small but critical protection from the open seas. Norwet now led him much deeper along that side, to the calms of the bay in the shadow of land. It was a steeper coast, rocky, no points to beach a ship that he could see. Anything that ventured here would do so under its own power, for the winds were light.

They came over a slope to find two dozen men beneath them at the shore. Norwet pressed ahead with confidence, and Gionn shaded after him. There was no apparent reason for the congregation at first. No structures, no harbor, no good beach. But Gionn saw four squain boats piled off to one side while their owners gutted and cleaned a mound of penguin carcasses. A few hundred yards away, a trio toiled lazily on a long frame of timber, between which they fixed rounded logs. Navy men—hardly concerned with their job, and not sparing so much as a glance for these two arrivals who veered toward the hunters.

"Ramp?" Gionn asked.

Norwet nodded. "It is where the people launch their boats in secret to hunt when they are not permitted. Now, the admiral has opened the sea. They hunt without fear."

Gionn could see the reason. What were steep rocky bluffs to either side suddenly sank across a narrow stretch until the rim was no more than a few feet above the waterline. The edge still would have prevented anything from landing, but it was clear the load of timber and tools came from a ship that pulled alongside the natural quay to unload. And if they got that ramp done, anything light enough could run right up it, haul ashore, and launch again. The ramp itself looked light enough for a dozen men, probably less. It was a siege-breaker. Costig was happy to let the squainfolk stock up on food, while he prepared a place for his own ships to sneak out and in with supplies and messages if someone blockaded the harbor. Nothing from sea or land would call attention to this place if the ramp were stored behind the foot of the the outcrop a quarter-mile from shore. He couldn't tell from his vantage, but Gionn had a feeling there would be enough room there for an entire ship or more.

As they drew near, it became apparent that none of the hunters were under sixty, though they carried themselves well from a distance. They looked at their guests but didn't pause their work. Norwet greeted them in Matta-katan. One of the old men answered in the kings' tongue.

"Is there a reward for him yet?" Gionn and Norwet gave each other a nervous look. The man went on: "The men were by to look for you."

"Those cunts couldn't find a lump of coal in their arses with a two-finger headstart."

"You can settle it for us. Some say you helped the Leopard Seal break the prison. But some say that you are his enemy. That you raised the alarm."

"Parks, I call him. Or Cunt, or Cockskin, or Maid o' the Mast, but above all, I call him Mate. Never Leopard Seal. Is that a real type of seal? I'm from less-blubbery climes, but I've not encountered it."

"Nor I."

"The man busted out on his own. I am innocent of doin' a kindness, and I did raise the bloody alarm. So that I could steal things from that cunt Costig while he was distracted."

The men grinned. "I like Costig," the same one said. "He lets us hunt."

"If you're takin' the birds back the sea-way, I would be indebted for a ride to the harbor. Well, not indebted, because I won't pay you back, but in keepin' with the figure of speech, anyway."

"It is a busy place to hide."

"I'll be reportin' direct to me whaler."

"You will go with us."

Norwet stepped forward with concern on his face. "Please. There are many people who help this man and the Leopard Seal. If he is taken, many will suffer." The older men seemed to have a discussion without a word exchanged between them.

"Under the penguins," he said to Gionn.

When Tunguk's song faded, they stepped out into the teeth of the wind that devoured the sound of the searchers toward the harbor. Tunguk turned left and came upon the spot where they found Brother's vomit the night before. It was gone with the boots that came through it. A faint, dry dark spot was all that remained for one who knew it should be there. Kjartke kept herself to their surroundings as Tunguk took it in. She listened for the voices and the heavy steps of men scraping the sides of tukits. To be caught on the street now would be their end. When she took one of the stone spears, Tunguk had only regarded it, but he did not make her return it. There could be no capture, even without Brother.

"I see him." The old man stood and stared down the lane. Kjartke followed his gaze before she realized it led nowhere. "He leaves the tukit in the night. There is one way he knows. When he does not have a guide, he knows to find the coast, and then along the side of the town. This is the way his feet remember. He does not think, so his feet take him here." Tunguk indicated the spot they stood on. "Here, he is sick. He is clumsy, but it is not smeared when he finds his stomach. When he stood again, he went this way," Tunguk pointed deeper into the tukits, inland toward the mountain. "If he is sick, and he starts the worn way, why does he turn to the place he has never been? Would he not continue? Or follow his feet home?"

"He is sick. He stumbles blind," Kjartke said.

"Maybe."

It was as though he waited for her to find his thought. "Or he meets one who knows the way."

The dark blur came into sight fifty yards ahead. A Thousand Journeys to Wisconsin, he had named it a dozen or so ago. The volcano, whatever distance remained, Parks let them dissolve in his mind. There was the snow between him and Wisconsin Johnson. He would walk it, and be done. Every time he arrived, his new buddy would rush ahead again, usually without a word, and if so, not a kind one. Their pace seemed to agitate him despite the detour. "Ain't no stopwatches, man," Parks had puffed once when he came even, but he was abandoned just the same. First out of sight. That was the beginning of a journey to Wisconsin. Then he would lift one of his feet. The snow sank maybe four, six inches with every step, but his boots were not made for it. His legs were heavy, and his stride that of a man perpetually stooping under a low doorway. As optimistic as he was of making the cave, he was certain that his knees and back would never straighten again. From his tilt, he would lift out of his own footprint straight up until he cleared the wall, then drop forward and repeat the process. Every time he did it without tripping felt like a monumental victory—he just drove the lane on LeBron and laid one up before the buzzer.

In theory, boots made from the thick skin of a seal should have been waterproof. His feet were soaked the moment they hit the snow. Each lift came with a wet suction feeling as the bottom remained in the print a little longer than the rest of the material. It felt like he walked on a thousand tiny needles, and the cold had spread to make his knee caps feel as though they were frozen underneath. Every four steps, he allowed himself a rest of three deep breaths. The wind that whipped across the face filled his lungs with the same needles each time he inhaled. The warm out-breath was precious, and every one of them went straight down a sleeve onto his throbbing fingers. The path they cut had the elevation and the wind on the left, constantly driving him downhill. He prayed for a switchback to at least give that cheek a break, but they held course, one frozen foot after another until he saw Wisconsin. Then he told himself that it was all he had to do: just make it there, then the journey was over. Just 50 more yards, 40 more yards. The punctuation was the only thing that kept him from giving up entirely, and he suspected his guide knew that and measured his intervals.

Despite the pain of wind and frost and a leg that he would rather lop off than take another step on, he still struggled to stay awake. His consciousness cut out in flashes, like a video skipping forward, and he'd be a few steps beyond where he last remembered. It would take a heavy blink, and ice crunching free of his lashes, to get him back to his current state of misery. Thirty yards.

The next thing he knew, he was belly-down in the snow. There was a feeling of ease, as though his feet finally decided to cooperate and carry him forward, which he realized was the ease of toppling over. His left leg screamed furiously, and he curled into a seated position to get the knee bent and off the snow. Parks cradled his kneecap in his sleeved hands, and the fractional boost of warmth felt spectacular, but only served to defrost some of the pain. It felt like the bone itself was eroding. Or burning up like a slow cinder from within. Parks did a quick inventory to see if anything else was damaged. Everything he turned his attention to admitted a pain of its own, quieted only by the uproar of his lower extremities. He realized his head hurt—had never stopped hurting. His stomach twisted in nausea. Both of his shoulders ached, even though he carried no pack. His lip was numb because his snot had frozen into an icicle from the tip of his nose to the top of his chin. Flesh tore as he tried to open his mouth, and he had to gingerly peel it free with his fingers. The brief minute of exposure blistered his fingers, and peeled even more flesh off his nose. There was a second of warmth as blood welled to the surface, then froze in the blast.

Parks caught a glimpse of the state of his footwear, and understood why his feet refused to cooperate. Both boots were torn completely through, and the right one, bearing most of his weight, much more so. He could see the exposed flesh through the seams that flapped like a mouth with each step, connected only at the heels. They were purple-blue, with round patches of ashy white. He leaned forward as much as he could and massaged them in agony until he felt the smallest amount of warmth trickle back in. By now, he was shivering—mild, but constant and beyond control. Sitting still in the snow had been a respite for his feet, while the rest of him sank into frigid slush. The fine, icy snow crunched as he rolled over to teepee himself to his feet, but his left leg collapsed beneath him in searing pain. Parks managed to roll up the cuff as far as his shin.

The entire leg was pale white, swollen to twice its normal girth and snaked with ribbon of green and purple capillaries. He peeked under the other for comparison and found it similar, but more purple than white, and less distended. It was too much. He was taking a break. Parks pulled the little pouch of medicine Kjartke had tied to his belt and fumbled for a pinch.

"Let me see that." Wisconsin had doubled back to him, his warm pink hand now extended. Parks placed the pouch in his palm, and he sniffed the dried herbs, then nodded. "I know this one. Grows in the mountains in Chile and Argentina."

"Is it good? The witch doctor wrote me a 'scrip for my leg."

"It's a natural antiseptic. You'll want to chew it to moisten it before you pack it into that wound," he pointed at the divot in his shin.

"I know," Parks stuffed way too much in his mouth and let half of it dribble down his chest and onto the ground. He packed a wad under the rank leather strip—made a note to eventually acquire a less-disgusting bandage—and reached for a hand up, only to realize that Wisconsin was already walking the other direction.

It took him some minutes to find a way to his feet that met his pain tolerance, and he immediately noticed that the bastard had extended the journey anew instead of stopping thirty yards out and giving him the thrill of a finish line. As soon as he got going, a pleasant rush of warmth filled his leg under the herb. The pain was cut in half. Soon it swept up to his stomach, and his head. There was a mild feeling of nausea that he'd gotten used to— the taste was bad but the aftertaste had grown to the brink of intolerable. Yet somehow, it worked. A light head-rush gave him a little clarity, or at least eased his awareness of how uncomfortable he felt. This was not a thing that human men should endure, he thought. Even if Wisconsin Johnson offered to tell him how much farther it was, he would have refused the answer. The smallest discouragement would drop him in his tracks, and somehow he knew that onward and upward was now a lot closer than backward and down.

The arrow slapped against his leg awkwardly, and he had to adjust it like a long, ungainly manhood bunched in his trousers. His breath now refused to go any deeper than the shallowest part of his lungs. His ribs cried in protest if he tried to expand them. It was little gasps, four steps, and another series of little gasps before starting up again. His feet had hurt less before he saw their condition. Now, probably out of fear and disgust more than reality, they dreaded every footfall. Little icy crystals snuck through the sole and tore at the soft white skin. Three times he made it to his guide, and three times he was left again. Now he felt the only thing carrying him forward was his bent torso and the pull of gravity. His feet struggled to replace one another to the cadence of his fall. A violent shiver ripped through him, stopping him in his tracks until he realized it wasn't one of cold. In fact, it was a feeling of incredible warmth that set every nerve in his body tingling. His skin felt almost hot for a brief second before the wind raked across it with in a stampeding squall, stinging him with snow. He could not see below his waist or a yard ahead. Parks' head throbbed on cue like a bass drum, and he remembered hearing something somewhere about early Polar explorers who stopped to rest out of exhaustion, and felt a sense of comfort, a place that invited them to sleep a while, despite the protests of dogs and companions. Those that did never continued. There was no easy feeling here. It was forge ahead in misery, and if misery numbed, he had lost. Parks cursed Wisconsin Johnson. He lifted his foot to step in the direction of his tormentor. The next thing he was conscious of was his face buried in the snow.

By now the people were poking their heads out. Kjartke and Tunguk crossed the path of a restless pair of brothers, an old person, testing the streets. The searchers had moved on toward the harbor long ago, and there was no time to come through again. They stood outside doorways, tilted their heads up and down lanes for a sign on the wind. These were the brave ones, the fools, the ones who the family could spare. Most huddled inside away from the howl and the threat of spears. To be on the street now gave her the feeling of clan with them, even though they were Kammatuk. All had little to lose, or something worth the risk. There were still many men behind the town, on the sides. None could leave the shield of tukits, and if those men came through, their steps would be hidden by the gusts. The others moved aside politely for her and Tunguk. None of them ventured far from their home, and it was clear these two were on the move. These strangers.

They traveled as far as they dared to the edges of the town and back, weaving the opposite way of the searchers. Brother was too sick to go far. The Mattaka were observant of those they did not know. Any with eyes would have seen them with Brother, on the ship or in the town. She still refused to call him what these people did, just as they were ignorant of his other name. It was almost certain he had found refuge with one of these who knew him only by reputation. Perhaps if they saw her and Tunguk, they would reveal their guest. Or he would have the fire to stand outside himself, waiting to be seen. Every tukit had been searched, and it made her stomach empty. He had not been discovered. So the one who hid him was clever, or he was gone beyond the town, which was death in his condition. In her short time in Drummoc she knew that the only thing that lie beyond the last row was the dog camp, miles inland and too far for him to walk. If he tried, they were too late.

They had been through most of the lanes, and no one spoke to them. There seemed too many to explore, but Tunguk claimed to know the paths men take. That the tukits guide people along certain curves, and only with great effort can one think to take another. Her clan was too small to know this. All ways were traveled. But she felt the beginnings of it on Yunoc, crowded among the people who fled this very place. Now Tunguk's ways were exhausted, too. They returned to the place where he changed course.

"The poye you spoke to about work," Tunguk started. A knot tied itself in her chest. "She can ask the bones where he is. But we must wait. The women's house will be searched near the end." It annoyed her that he called it by the name of respect, as only the ones close to it would. Kjartke preferred he scorn the place. It felt like pity that he did not. She refused to ask the poye, but she could not say it. He would want to know why.

"We have waited long enough." She looked inland. "This is the path you say he took?"

Tunguk considered her before responding. "It is the first. There are many branches of the tree beyond it. But this is the root." Kjartke handed him her spear. She walked to the tukit on the left side of the lane, pulled the flap open, and said, "I wish to speak to the woman of the home."

"Fuck off! Close that, you let the wind in!" An old man barked. Her nose curled, but she let the skin fall over the opening.

"I wish to speak to the woman of the home," she repeated in the doorway of the one to the right. No one answered, but she heard the stir of movement. A woman slightly older than herself appeared.

"Who are you?" She refused to speak in Mattakatan.

"We search for one we lost."

The woman thought for a moment, then ducked back inside. Tunguk gave her a look that told her what he thought of her efforts. These people could see she was not theirs as easily as they could see it in Foster, or Brother, or Gionn. He expected her to retreat. Instead, she started down the lane where Brother fled.

"Where are you going?" A different voice called to her in her own language. A much older woman than the first had made her way out of the tukit, and wrapped herself tightly in a fur to shield the wind. Kjartke came as close as she dared without giving offense, and raised her voice over the rushing air.

"We search for one we lost. He was here at dark," she pointed to the ground. "He was sick, then he passed your home. Did you hear?"

"You search for the Leopard Seal."

She gave a reluctant nod.

"I told the men, I did not see him."

"I am not with the men."

"You will make much of the reward, though. One like you."

"I am not with the men. I despise them. I have uttered man curses to the moon. It is because of them I am here, far from my people. What they have taken is worth more to me than a fleet of ships, and all it carries." The woman tightened her attention on Kjartke. "I have come with my grandfather," she indicated Tunguk, who struggled to hide his surprise. "To find my husband. It is he who keeps us with home, with food. He who protects us from the Navy of Ampos," she spat. "If we do not find him before they do, I will be forced to the women's house," she swallowed hard. "Please. Did you hear?"

The old woman hesitated for what seemed the length of day and a night. Then she beckoned Kjartke inside, and sent three young children out to stand in the wind with Tunguk and their mother, against the protests of the younger woman.

"I heard one who was sick outside my family's door in the night."

"He passed here."

"Aye."

"Which direction?"

"Inland. Many pass that way. The path between my tukit and my neighbor's is wider than others."

"Thank you." Kjartke smiled to herself. Tunguk knew where the ways split. She need only ask along each to find his path, and again at the next divide. One as clumsy as Brother would have been heard the length of his passage. No Mattaka walked like him. Now she had only to find other women who would do the same.

"There was another."

Kjartke paused. "Tell me."

"It is all I know. He spoke to one. I could not hear the other, and the words of the Leopard Seal were soft. One with quiet feet took him on."

She rejoined Tunguk, and they proceeded until he signaled that the common path went two ways, to either side of a hut. He smiled at her. "Let us see if you will fool this one, Granddaughter."

The morning fog had long fled before the wind that gasped it's last heavy breaths between steady breezes. Beyond the last line of tukits, they could see the men who kept the rear of the town. The line was loose, in poor order. Many clumped together in conversation. Some sat. But there was no path beyond them without being seen, no cover for some distance. The confinement was still on, as the search wound down silently at the opposite end of Drummoc. If they were seen, even now, they would be arrested or killed.

It was Kjartke's tongue that lead them here. Many refused to speak to her, but there were enough that they could trace the paths Brother took on his way out. His breathing and his steps were heard by all. It troubled Tunguk. The turns were countless, but the ways the Mattaka traveled, few. Brother would never have come through the thick part of town on his own, and whoever led him did not always steer the Mattaka ways. It was a hidden route. A broken route. One of dark and crouching, chosen with care. By the tukits who heard, Tunguk knew where they took the wide and easy lanes, where they slid over the outside walls with their feet upon the neighbor, where they turned sharply to avoid someone in the street. It brought them here. The people in the last few tukits would not admit of hearing things. It was plain enough, anyway. The one who took him brought him beyond the town. They could follow no farther. Only the dog camp lie across the plain, then the wilderness.

"Is he with the boys?" Kjartke asked.

"We will see."

"But you think not."

Tunguk took in the body of Navy ahead. They were up early, had spent all day unprotected from the gusts through the bowl of land. The few who watched kept their eyes on the tukits. It would be possible for a brave man to walk right between the line if certain men did not move their heads from where they started. It had been many years since Tunguk felt brave. The flank stretched near the highlands to their right. The headland of the peninsula was a short mount they called Tannavin. The coast on that, the lee side of the island, was steep bluffs that with the rise toward Urkuk made a bowl of Drummoc. But between Tannavin and the bluffs was a narrow passage, and an easy walk to the far side of the bluffs, where it was steep put passable for a ways. The men did not bother to post one on the bluffs to watch this way. There were reinforcements on the flanks of the town to catch any who left to the sides.

But those had moved along with the search party. They now stood well beyond the part of town that was across from with the low passage to the far side of the bluffs. It was here he led Kjartke, after they doubled back through town until they drew even. They could clearly see the flank of the rear guard as they walked the short distance between the cover of the tukits and the passage, but the guards could not see them—or did not care. Soon they had the heights between them and the main force as they picked along the slope toward the dog camp. Beneath them, several hunting boats full of penguins hugged the coast, passing from the thieves' harbor to the main now that such a thing was wise. Kjartke paused to watch them for some reason. He was not certain she knew. The ground on all sides rose so that all land followed a ridge in the center of the little arm—the ridge to Urkuk. It was on the lee of this that they came to the dog camp. All of it was slope, covered in snow.

The dogs spotted them from afar, and their alert passed through the ranks until most bristled and tugged at their leads. Tunguk noted the deep wash of tracks from those who marched up the mountain each morning of late. The freshest of these only went up. They had not yet returned. A few more, still fresher, passed through the main current. Late travelers who hid their feet in others'.

One of the boys came around a tukit with a cut of meat from the stores, and stopped in his tracks—Saunlauk, he recalled. Tunguk acknowledged him. The boy dropped the meat to return the gesture, then hurried off. He came back soon with his brother Siguvik, and with Ulwet and Ferrakut. It was the first time Tunguk had seen them in the light. They bore the marks of a good row on their grins.

"He is not here," the old man read their faces. Ulwet shook his head. Tunguk examined the anxious pack.

"These are strong dogs. They will turn to fighting if they have to sit. I will work one of the teams if you will harness the sled." They got the message. The cousins gathered the dogs, while the boys from Nunoc prepared the short sled. It was thin hide slung between bone, not one of the heavier coal sleds of good wood brought in from the north. This was a hunting sled, good only for a few hundred pounds of game. It was so light that the dogs would not even feel it behind them if the driver fell off. They chose a six dog team, hitched in a single line with a proud old female in the lead. There were three more females, and two spirited young male pups barely old enough to pull. Tunguk knew this meant they feared for his ability to control a strong team. He looked at the steep face of Urkuk in the distance, and sensed they were right.

Sawi and one of his brothers appeared heading toward them. His three sons shadowed close behind. The boys stopped their work, but Tunguk urged them on. "I will deal with Sawi."

"Tunguk!" The man called cheerfully. "Are you hunting? There is a search on. I am afraid these men will see you."

"They will see an old man hunting. It is too far for these legs to walk."

"I think so, aye. Can you wait until it is done? Come back at first light. The sun will be gone soon. You do not know this mountain. It is bad for strangers."

"I tell him this often. He is a fool. You will sooner teach manners to your dogs," Kjartke blurted.

"You are probably right. But these men, they came to my family's camp earlier. Very rough with our things as they searched for one they called Leopard Seal."

"I have heard of him."

"That is what my boys tell me. He was on your ship. But you are not known to him except as fellow passengers."

"A father knows when his sons lie."

Sawi gave a mischievous smile that warmed over. "You are a clever one. But I do not think you will find him out there. You understand. I do not loan my dogs to others. If these men see you doing things they do not like, they will ask me why this man, friend of the Leopard Seal, uses my dogs freely. I am afraid I have no answer."

"Aye, you are right about this. If they see me, you will call me a thief. I will not deny it."

"I am sorry, Tunguk. You are a good driver. When it is time to take the firestone, you will have your pick of teams." Sawi waved a hand, and the boys reluctantly began unhitching the dogs, who whined at the prospect of going back to leads after being teased with the trail.

"Your family is known for your fine dogs," Tunguk said. "But many people own sleds. It is hard to say who it belongs to, unless it is known to the one who made it."

Sawi nodded. "You are right." He headed back, herding his sons along before him.

"Where is Norwet?" The boys turned up their hands. "Then you two will be our dogs," he tossed the end of the empty line to Ulwet.

"Sawi is a drunk," Saunlauk said. "After we returned, someone passed late. Every dog was furious."

"Sawi did not even wake," Ferrakut confirmed.

"It is just the tricksters, he says," Siguvik added. "The dogs bark almost every night now."

"You said you found tracks," Ulwet pointed out.

Saunlauk nodded. "Follow the Navy tracks, then where you see our feet turn, and the paws of the dog, follow these. We doubled them so the men would not take interest, but where our feet stop, they go much farther."

Tunguk yanked on the steering handle of the sled, sliding it in front of Kjartke. "Best to practice driving with dogs who listen." He lowered himself to the edge, then swung his legs out along the taut skin deck and leaned against the back brace. Ulwet and Ferrakut each slung one of the leads branching from the main line over a shoulder, the older boy in front, and leaned into the tension. The sled skidded away, and Kjartke lunged to catch the handles.

The heat of his breath melted a small divot in the snow. Cold air ran into the humid chamber and seized Parks' lungs, then returned warm and melted the finest outer film of the icy drift. The one eye that was above snow level watched the process. He did not feel pain, only absolute inertia. No order that came through his brain reached his limbs. They lay as responsive as a log on the slope, the wind now dying around him, whistling through thin channels it carved and piling up a bank on his left side. There was no sense or urgency or panic. He felt nothing, and it was the best he'd felt since they started.

Slowly, the tingling sensation returned to the outer layer of skin, more electric than cold. Superficial. Again he willed himself to push up on his elbows, and nothing moved a millimeter. Parks watched a few more breaths fog against the ice. This was as far as he would go. He could not see Wisconsin Johnson, or anything else more than a few inches away. There was no noise of boots crunching. It was possible his friend was standing two feet away, and he would have no way of confirming. No voice to raise. But it felt as though he were alone. The blood came to his head in a sudden rush, and there was a dizzying feeling like his body was peeling up the side of a wall before he blinked himself back to his senses.

Parks knew if he remained here, he would die. Now he was just trying to decide whether or not that interested him. The rotten egg smell of sulfur carried past him on the breeze. He tried again to shift, even a little, but it felt like he was speaking to someone who couldn't hear a word he said. "Welp, that's a problem," he thought. On the other hand, if this was what it felt like to die, he'd felt worse—every single day since he set foot on the continent. Every minute since he lost the deck of the *Qarapara*. That would be just his luck if all of that struggle led him to this. Hours in the freezing water, near-evisceration by Joe and his tribe, the kayak and the one-armed man and the battle, the seasick days, the dry mouth and constant cold, all the no-good sons of bitches and their lust for moving ships, the raging storms and the walk here, surviving ten minutes at a time. It felt like too much to end on an unremarkable snow bank. After all that, he had earned better. But neither nature nor the people he met seemed to care.

One by one, he tried to call to mind things that would move him. Foster, Eskimo Joe, the woman whose name he hated to pronounce. He could hold none of them in his thoughts for long. Foster led him to the bars of South America, of Asia. The Reverse-Eskimos vanished into the icebergs and oblivion they had sprung from, glacial Antarctica, modern ships and squawking radios. "May Day, May Day," he heard in garbled static as the border of world and dream oscillated like the surface of the sea. Even Foster's drawl became impossible to remember. The image of the man himself twisted into a vapor he couldn't reassemble. Things he almost remembered but never happened spun before him like a merry-go-round: the carrier deck crowded with strangers, strange civilians in revelry, ports he'd never visited in Ireland and the North of Spain. He saw his home in the Midwest, then moved it to California where it belonged. Someone sat at a desk with his back turned, writing of his exploits—maybe it was him. He'd have quite the story to tell if he ever got back. He called up electric lights, so many that they obliterated the darkness and radiated warmth through every smooth-paved street. The lighted ways left no mystery. A bar, a bar on every corner and something to eat. He looked through his half-reflection into the window and saw the crew of the *Qarapara* laughing hysterically and sloshing beverages between them. Behind him, though he couldn't turn, he felt the eyes of his friend, freezing on a wet ship in the ice pack across the street. He still could not make out the figure, even in his imagination, but there he was, huddled in a shroud, Antarctica behind him, a desert swallowed by ice and gray cloud as it should be. He was a lunatic to try to summit a mountain in the snow. Now he knew why. Every gust and breaker and blade told him the same story. He thought he'd been learning to accept it, but he was now more sure than ever: this was no place for Parks. Not among the ice with Foster and the Eskimos. He sought a warm cavern and civilized faces. The freeways were his currents, and the blistering sun his refuge. America the beautiful, a blue-eyed girl awaiting his long return. No one he ever knew. He would take a new name, a new lover, fresh friends somewhere he'd never been, untouched by the oceans and yet as familiar as everywhere else he'd lived. He came here to go home.

It was the smallest effort that moved him, as though lifted by strings. He pushed the ice away and straightened his back for the first time in a single, smooth motion. Parks stared down at where his feet disappeared in snowy prints. The sudden lightning bolt of pain, the groaning resistance he'd come to expect was gone. Flakes of ice congregated in his scraggly beard as the breeze crossed him from upslope. Cold as it was, he felt grateful for it. When he shifted his weight to step, his left leg cooperated for once. And when he weighted it to move the other, he felt a stiffness that came from the habit of agony, but a new life surged through his veins. The witch pimp lady had been right: it was as miserable as possible, right up until it healed. As though the slimy herb pasted beneath his pants had pulsed him awake. Parks felt immense distance and altitude behind him. He dared not look back.

Now that he stood a solid six feet and four inches above ground, the rotten egg smell hit him twice as hard. It took a moment for his eyes to acclimate, but when they did, there was a clarity unlike any he'd known at sea level. Whatever ailed him—infection, he figured—had spent weeks breaking down his vision from squinty to snow blind. Here above the island, in the rarefied air, he could see for miles. And twenty yards away sat Wisconsin Johnson.

He leaned against a curved cone, narrowing halfway up into a tilted gnome hat—a rough chimney made of billowing ice. The top fumed with smoke twelve feet above the surface. Every time the breeze curled it vaguely in his direction the sulfur smell doubled down. The vapor melted and rearranged the opening, then froze as soon as it was inches away from the spout, packing extra snow around it to extend the structure.

Parks wasn't hurting like before, but as soon as he moved the dizziness reminded him he was not in the clear entirely. It took half the distance to gain his bearings and his balance.

"Looks like you got your second wind," Wisconsin called.

"Didn't wanna give a brother a hand, eh?"

"Can't."

"So you're just gonna bring me up here to watch me die?"

"You've got forty, fifty pounds on me. What am I supposed to do, carry you up a mountain? I'm here to point you in the right direction. You have to walk it. Of your own volition. Or you can lie down and see how that goes for you. Even if I wanted to help—and believe me, I do—this is your hike, buddy."

There was a cruel logic to it that Parks couldn't deny. He squinted up at the slope, which became dramatically steeper. "How much farther?"

"Worst is over." The peak sent a steady current of thick smoke into the clear gray sky. Wisconsin saw Parks' concern and grinned. "Don't worry, it'll be fine once we're around the back side." He stood. "Meantime, if you see any molten rocks falling from the sky…move."

Where before every fifty yards was a desert and an act of survival, they walked nonstop for hundreds at a time. There was no trail here. They carved their own switchbacks. The snow thinned as the grade grew, until it was packed ice that refused to yield and slid them half a foot downslope every few paces when a foot failed to find a shelf. The volcano bellowed and hissed from the crater above them like a chained dog trying to ward off pedestrians from its yard. Wisconsin Johnson still kept a sadistic pace, and the only time he was ever close enough to chat is when he turned a switchback and crossed paths a few feet up the slope.

"Are we there yet?" Parks taunted.

"No."

He had to wait until the next switch to keep up his pestering, but it lifted his spirits and gave him a burst of energy every time he saw Wisconsin cut back. The bastard hadn't exactly done him any favors. At the very least, Parks was going to annoy the piss out of him.

"Hey, how'd you find this cave, anyway? You just decided to trot up a volcano hoping there'd be a natural dwelling at the top?"

"If you knew your geology, you'd have realized there would be plenty of opportunity for shelter on an active volcano. Especially when all the people you're sheltering from are terrified of it." They parted, then crossed again minutes later.

"Hey, what kind of rock is this thing made out of?"

"Igneous."

"No shit, I could've told you that!" He shouted as they parted earshot temporarily.

"Remember how you contracted me to take you and your family to Antarctica?"

"Yes."

"Am I still on the clock?"

"No," the fading voice replied. Parks realized if he planned it out in advance, he could annoy Wisconsin John twice, one coming in and once going away.

"Do you like answering my questions?"

"Love it."

"Have you ever shit your pants?"

"No."

"'Look at me,'" Parks mocked in a fake French accent. "'I am Wisconsin Johnson, and I have total control over my bowels.'"

The next time: "What's your favorite Greek food?"

"Pita."

"Favorite baseball team?" He exclaimed as Wisconsin tried to power past their brief overlaps as quickly as possible.

"Padres."

"*What?*"

"Padres!"

"Oh, I heard you. Fucking *Padres!*" All he got was a middle finger response.

The switchbacks grew shorter and more frequent. Their route carried them twice as far forward as back, and steadily up the face. Parks scanned for anything that looked like it might be a dark opening in the rock. A rest stop. It had to be soon. Much farther, and they'd need climbing gear to ascend.

"I was a little out of it when we first met. Who all did you say is up there?"

"My family, and Carabiner."

"Your old lady's single, right?"

"All yours."

"Why didn't you just throw Carabiner overboard? You were on a raft in the middle of Antarctica. Nobody would have known."

Wisconsin Johnson laughed. "I'd be lying if I said I didn't consider it. Less talk, more walk."

"It's never too late. I mean, we're on a volcano slope." His guide ignored him until the next switch.

"How did you get all the way down here, anyway? To Drummoc?"

"Sailed. Same as you."

"Not in a twelve foot life raft." Parks had become so used to a frustrated response that it threw him off a bit when Wisconsin passed without a word. "Right?" He shouted.

"No!" Wisconsin shouted back.

"Then who brung ya?"

"We got picked up by a merchant vessel."

"Bet they were impressed by your inflatable hull and full fucking kit of survival gear." Again, the silence. "Right?" He added.

"The boat threw them off, but we abandoned it soon as we were aboard. We'd ditched the suits and the gear that would give us away."

Parks sensed an opening. The switchbacks had become steeper, and Wisconsin made the mistake of sending a trail not terribly far above the one Parks was one. The big man fell to all fours and scrambled straight up the slope to cut the corner, joining the other from behind. There would be no escape from the torment now as long as he kept pace. The frustration in Wisconsin's body language when he realized his error was tantalizing.

"Why?'

The man's face contorted. "Just to make you ask questions."

"But why would you abandon the gear?"

"I told you. So we wouldn't strike them as completely out of place, and be killed for sorcery or some kind of nonsense."

"But if it was the first people you saw, how'd you know where you were? How'd you know you'd be out of place?"

"The ancient fucking sailing vessel gave us a clue."

"That's weird. Me and Foster PTFO'd and woke up in skins." Wisconsin tied to create some space between himself and the buzzing mosquito, but Parks refused to back down. "Do you still have your maps?" He recalled the orange PVC cylinders he'd last seen the man wrangling into the boat—two of which ended up with him and Foster. Wisconsin tensed in hesitation.

"No. Wave took them."

"Well, you'll be thrilled to know that it took them right to us. We got two of them, anyway. Hell, here's one right here!" He pulled the folded leather out of a cinch sack on his belt and brushed off the ice and wet that had snuck in. Wisconsin didn't even bother to turn.

"Are we there yet?"

"You're the one with the map."

"Why do you keep answering me if it annoys you?"

"Call it the bad habit of civility. We don't have a lot of choice who we survive with."

"True dat." The slope rumbled under their feet like a tiny earthquake. "Whoa, boy!" Parks slid to the ground and struggled to right himself. "Is that normal?"

"It's normal on an exposed face when it's about to erupt. All the more reason to walk faster."

"So when you landed here, if people on the boat knew you, why'd you come up here?"

"It's not safe down there. Known and welcomed are different things."

"I found it pretty hospitable, at least until I was sentenced to execution. There's even a poorman's quarters for shitty people like my former bud who have no money and no friends. They seem to have a policy of not letting people die of exposure. You saw all that, and decided to live in a volcano?"

"I have other people to take care of."

"I do, too."

"Yeah well, you took your chances and now you're in the same place as me."

"Touche. So how did you even find me?"

"You sing too loud. Can we hold off the interrogation until we get there? It's a little hard to breathe at altitude when you have to yap incessantly."

"Thanks, I'm managing. You can always just stop answering." Parks waited for a reply. "Right?"

"Right."

"You can, can't you?"

"Yes. I can, if you push your luck."

"So if you heard me singing, you didn't see us land. How'd you know we sailed here?"

"Call it a logical leap."

"So you must have spied on us. The first time I heard you. You said Foster."

Wisconsin nodded. "I'm down there often enough."

"And Gionn?"

"I don't know a Gionn."

"He came down with us. I thought we were done, but I vaguely remember him busting me out of jail. Him and a bunch of kids. He'll be on the run, too. Can you bring him up when you bring Foster?"

"None of them are my responsibility."

"I'm just flattered I made the cut."

Wisconsin sighed. "Won't be long, now. Look, I know I'm being a hard-ass. I'm not trying to make friends with you. The way I see it, you're one of mine, like it or not. My one and only goal is to get you back where you belong. You, and everyone else."

"Nice, stepping up to the leadership role. I dig it, but you're not gonna like Foster."

"He's at least quiet. And won't shit on my Padres."

"You can't shit on the Padres, Padres *are* shit. It's like rain on the sea."

"Who's your team, then?"

"Bro. Come on. Giants."

"Like I'm supposed to guess that based on how soft and entitled you are?"

"Shots fired! I told you I'm from Santa Cruz."

He nodded. "That's right, you did. Back on the ship."

"Seems like that was a few thousand back at this point. Or forward."

"Have you ever been to any games?"

Something irked Parks about the question and it took him a second to place it. Wisconsin was trying to change the subject. He'd lost the advantage of annoyance.

"So what was it like being too dumb to bring your survival suit and getting pelted by freezing ice water for days?"

"I've mostly blocked it out."

"How long was it before you got picked up?"

"I don't know. Few days."

"So you must have hauled ass here to beat us. We pretty much came straight down. Few minor detours." The brooding silence returned. "How long would you guess you got to Drummoc before us?"

"Couple weeks, maybe."

"Spend any time in the town?"

"Just long enough to know it wasn't for us."

"I don't know, dude, I'm kind of partial to the Reverse-Eskimos. Never can remember their real name, but I know it ain't squain. You didn't happen to catch it, did you?"

"Mattaka, I think."

"Shit. That's what it was. I knew I'd know it if someone reminded me. I have the worst time with names. People I've known forever, ethnic groups, it's like a pair of invisible fingers shoves into my ears whenever they say it, and one second later I realize I didn't even forget—I never heard it to begin with. Like my boy Eskimo Joe. What's his name? Tunguk. That, I do know. But I refuse to say it, because it makes me feel like I'm talking with peanut butter in my mouth. I've christened him. Like I do with most people. My philosophy is the shitty name your parents give you is probably as good as all the other ideas your parents have. We should all get our names from our various escapades. For example, Eskimo Joe reminds me of an Eskimo, and Joe rhymes. It's pretty cool and laid back, just like Joe. And when I give people a name, it tends to stick. Even Foster got called Fucker by everyone in Antarctica for weeks because I said it once. He had to steal three big-ass ships and ransom them for a name change. I've even got people calling me the Leopard Seal. You know what that means, right?"

"It means you're a blubbery predator who's awkward traveling on land."

"Ha. Close, but I meant the other thing. It means, sir, that before long, no one will call you anything but Wisconsin Johnson."

Parks looked up in surprise as the rim of the crater snaked closer than he imagined possible. The wind lifted the column of smoke clear of them, but the smell was still suffocating. They were well around the leeward side of the mountain now. Very little lay between them and the open vent, and a million tons of magma. There was no sign of the cave on this face, and he could see all of it now. Wisconsin was leading them around to the back side, the steepest, where he claimed the lava would not spill. The safety of it all was beginning to gnaw at him. This far from the summit, the amount of rock in a cave wall between them and the inner chamber had to be pretty meager. The idea of huddling safely inside while fire rained down above, only to have the wall blow out from pressure, or vent poisonous gases into the shelter, seemed idiotic even by his standards. Parks' survival experience was limited to shows on the Discovery Channel and a few weeks in the tumult of life on the polar coast. And he couldn't remember what Wisconsin's degree was in, but it wasn't volcanology. As many things as he forgot, he remembered what they weren't.

"You sure this is safe?"

"It isn't a question of safety. It's the only way."

"But you haven't been here during an eruption yet."

"This type of volcano is extremely stable. Lots of small eruptions, all the time. You let off pressure that often, you don't have to worry about the catastrophic releases."

"Right. It's that certain type. What was it called again?"

Wisconsin Johnson gave it careful consideration. "Fermboli."

"Yeah, that's it. Named after some volcano in Italy, I think. I saw that in a documentary."

"You mentioned it. Anyway, we're almost there now. You might as well check out the digs before you pooh-pooh them."

Parks stopped. "Except I'm pretty sure it wasn't Fermboli. That sounds like a word that I would make up in a wrong guess on Jeopardy." His guide's shoulders raised in agitation, but he kept his pace. "Are you sure that was it?"

"Maybe I'm mistaken. I'm no volcanologist."

"Don't be so hard on yourself, bro. You're probably the current leading expert on the continent." Parks was a little bummed that didn't earn the laugh he hoped for. "But yeah, I do remember when I was researching Antarctica before we started working down here that there's a volcano here that erupts like that one in Italy. I just don't remember the name." He squinted into the low sunlight washing around the face, yellowed in the sulfur haze. "Do you?"

"No."

"Shit. You knew all the names of every boring-ass island and inlet between the Falklands and the South Pole. I figured you'd at least remember the most prominent volcano."

"Like I said."

"Not a volcano guy. I remember your ex-wife told me you were some type of scientist. What was it?"

"If you heard it from her, it was probably sarcasm."

"Pseudo! Ha! I remember that one. Pseudo-scientist. Can't believe you guys split up. How excited do you think they're gonna be to see my ugly mug? Did you tell them, or is it a surprise?"

"Of course I told them. I think they'll be thrilled if we ever get there."

Something wafted up from the deep recesses of his attention. It was the awareness of something missing. Something lost, or left behind. It took him a few more steps to place it. The clockwork tap of the swaying arrow against his thigh that had matched his pace like a metronome ever since they left camp was gone. His hands snapped down to an empty loop on his belt as his heart lurched into his chest.

"Stop!" Parks screamed. He turned back, and a sense of relief buckled his knees with joy. The arrow had managed to land tip-down in the snow, not more than fifteen yards back. It easily could have slid down the icy slope and lost itself under a lip of ice, a rock, anything at all would have obscured the small black stone blade and bone shaft from view. He hustled back and drew it triumphantly like it was Excalibur, then brought his lips to the flat of the head in a tender kiss, and cradled the missile to his breast with his eyes closed.

Immediately, it made him wobbly and disoriented. He saw a dreamlike flash of an arrow fired from the top of the mountain. It arced through the dimming sky and settled somewhere far below near the base. Beneath him, the volcano shuddered to life like a big diesel engine trying to turn over. The smoke from the crater became more intense, and he felt woozy—detached. With a quick shake of his head, he staggered back toward Wisconsin Johnson, all but the vague outline of the man lost in the glaring sunset. He clutched the arrow tight in his fist instead of replacing it, his heart still reeling from the fear that he had lost his gift. What before felt like a short walk to the end now made him uneasy. Maybe it was the fumes, but he felt his stomach twist for the first time since he'd found his second wind. His leg began to protest, at first gently, and worse with each stride. Even his vision fogged over again. The clear skies of the lower face disappeared in the nauseating mist.

For the briefest second, he could not remember how he got there. The whole journey, their long interrogation, it all blurred and bled in his memory. He thought back to a second ago, retrieving the arrow. Then talking volcanoes. Degrees, pseudo-degrees. Each dim memory brightened as he rested on it, and led to the one before it like a trail in loose dust. He rewatched their walk up the volcano, his dramatic escape from execution, jail, the sentence, singing to himself in the hut. Beyond that he imagined Wisconsin and the crew, hiding in a cave as he and Foster ran around town, dark meetings at the haunted crevasse, the latrine, the bar. He imagined what it must have been like for them to get here first and head to the forbidding mountain out of fear. The ship journey: his, and Wisconsin's. Back to the peninsula, the rough sea doing it's all to hold him under in a stupid orange outfit. The boat.

Parks frowned.

"Can we go now?" Wisconsin Johnson's impatience carved furrows in his face. Parks blinked and steadied his gaze into the blue-gray eyes, set above the beard flecked with gray. The lean, muscular frame loomed over him, a few feet of altitude up the mountain.

"Yeah," he muttered, adrift in thought and not sure where. Though he had his arrow now, the feeling that he had left something behind only intensified. Like the absence of a hum he'd grown so accustomed to, he'd forgotten it until it was gone for some time. Everything he left the town with was still there: his water. His map. His arrow. The salt-soaked skins. It felt older. Almost ancient. As if he was naked, without something of great importance that he couldn't recall, abandoned too long ago, as in his chronic dream in which he realizes he forgot to take a single class in high school, and had to re-enroll in his senior year despite being in his thirties. It was always finals, and he suddenly remembers he's once again forgotten to attend the class or do any of the work. That dream panic that he at once knew couldn't be real nor reasoned away gripped him. The boat. Maybe whatever it was, he'd forgotten it on the boat. Like Wisconsin Johnson forgot his survival suit when he bailed. Like he'd nearly forgotten his maps. It was them that caused him to scramble onto the lifeboat late. Parks could still see the white t-shirt and the armful of tubes, hunched like Golem over his Preciouses. He remembered thinking that dude wouldn't live the night even if the raft stayed on the right side of the surface.

"Geographer!" He called out. "Right? You studied geography. And old cartography and shit like that."

Wisconsin snorted. "Once upon a time."

"Quick: What's the capital of Wisconsin?"

There was a moment's hesitation. "Madison."

"Very good. I don't actually know if that's right, but the only two cities I know of are Madison and Green Bay. Oh, and Milwaukee. The sports ones."

"And what was *your* major? In the Navy, I mean?"

"No changing the topic. I'm going somewhere with this, I just haven't quite figured it out yet."

"I'd prefer you held your verbal diarrhea until we get there."

"How did your maps end up overboard?"

"There are these things called waves. If the contents of your impractically-small boat aren't lashed down, they tend to help themselves."

"And the third one. Did you keep it, or did you lose it, too?"

"I lost all of them."

"Dang! I was working up this theory that maybe, *maybe* the reason we ended up here, was that the maps opened a portal to an alternate reality."

"Maps don't do that."

"Right. Normally."

"Ever."

"So you didn't have a map, or a suit. You just got plucked from the water by an old sailing ship. Why didn't they keep your boat?"

"It wasn't exactly the *Queen Mary*. We're talking about a deckless merchant ship, packed so full that we didn't even have a place to stretch out when we slept."

"Did you take any of the cool survival gear? Those life rafts have more shit than I do in my apartment back home."

"Again, it would have been a little tough to explain vacuum-packed rations and flares and first aid kits."

"I probably would have tried. What'd you do, just climb over but-ass naked so they wouldn't ask about your L.L. Bean?"

Wisconsin shook his head. "Clothes are clothes. I don't get the interrogation. Carabiner can explain everything to you. I'm done."

"Are you?"

"Yes."

"But *are* you?"

"One-hundred percent."

Parks scrunched his brow in frustration. It was hanging at the back of his mind, like a name he almost recalled. "So did you guys stop at Nunoc or what?"

Wisconsin sighed. "For a couple of days. Just to resupply."

"What do *we* call it?"

"I don't understand."

"Nunoc. Or Drummoc. What's the American-English names? My map's all in Latin and shit."

"I don't exactly have a way of calculating our latitude and longitude and comparing it to a chart."

"Yeah, but if you had to guess?"

"There are literally thousands of islands in this God-forsaken place."

"Livingston? Remember that one? Maybe it was Nunoc."

"No. Too far north."

"I want to say Deception maybe, but mainly because that's the only other one I remember."

"Same problem. You're going North, we're moving South."

"I just thought since you and Carabiner were constantly bro-ing out over obscure Antarctica shit you might have a better guess than I do." Wisconsin held a straight line now, intent on the back side of the volcano. They were less than 400 yards vertically from the rim. Another rumble sent Parks momentarily to his hands and knees. "Why won't you bore me with your knowledge?"

"Because climbing a snow-capped volcano while it decides when it's going to erupt is a little bit distracting."

"Huh. Tell me something I don't know." He leaned into his stride to keep pace, but it was all pressure now. His concentration danced, and it felt like the thin air swirled around him and pressed on his skull from all sides. Don't stop now, he heard himself in his head. But the closer he got, the less he wanted to arrive.

"Name an island I've never heard of." Wisconsin ignored him. "Can you?"

"I can, but what would be the point?"

He noticed now a faint tremble in his legs. Parks came to a halt, and it became more pronounced. There had been a few major jolts, but he realized what he'd been feeling most of the last third was a steady quaver of seismic activity, like the engine of an aircraft carrier resonating through the walls. It unsettled him, and he wondered of his guide also felt it. Was he simply trying to ignore it, to keep Parks from objecting? Letting the danger hide behind its constancy? His knuckles were bone white around the shaft of his arrow. It felt like a line to the things he remembered. If he lost it again he may as well lose himself. Parks held it inches before his face. The feeling of panic when he lost it had not vanished, it had split into many and lodged into everything he could think of. His vision focused intently on the serrated stone until his eyes hurt. Then it blurred, the arrow almost vanishing as he refocused on the glare of the sun setting in a putrid haze, spilling around the sharp flint.

Suddenly, the feeling of loss reversed. What nagged him was not something absent. It was something that was always present—a tap against a thigh, the flow of magma through an underground chamber, threatening to surface.

"What's your favorite color?"

Wisconsin Johnson had managed to gain a fair lead while Parks distracted himself with geological events, but he stopped cold, barely within earshot, and turned to shout his answer. "Blue! Now hurry the fuck up! We have to make it before we lose the light."

"I don't think I want to go."

"Are you crazy?"

"Maybe."

Johnson stormed back toward him. "You can't spend the night exposed. Not again. And there's no way in hell you're making it back down."

"If you had to pick one and only one Red Hot Chili Peppers song that you think is most indicative of the bass talent of Flea, irrespective of all other factors like vocals, guitar, popularity—if you were on a volcano about to erupt, and I was annoying you the piss out of you and endangering our lives with the delay, but for some reason you decided to answer a completely irrelevant and asinine question anyway, what song would it be?"

Parks found himself blinking and struggling to hold eye contact with the glare he earned himself. A vein swelled on Wisconsin's forehead, and he clenched his jaw. Only then did it occur to Parks that being in a weakened state on the side of a volcano with someone much healthier, then giving that person some reason to murder you, was not the best plan he had ever concocted.

"Suck My Kiss. Now I'm going to offer one more time. You can walk with me, in total, blissful silence, until we get where we belong, or I can leave you here to go wherever you prefer to die, because there's nowhere—I repeat, *nowhere*—else for you in all this miserable world. Do you understand?"

"I think so. I'm actually not super knowledgeable about bass, or any of the deep cuts from the early Chili Peppers days. I'm mostly about the radio stuff. But given my very limited knowledge, I would agree with that, or maybe Around the World."

Wisconsin Johnson spun on his heel and started up the trail.

"What's your name, by the way?" Parks refused to budge.

Without turning, he replied, "Apparently, it's Wisconsin Johnson from now on."

"I meant your real name."

"I thought you said you remembered."

"I did, but I was lying because I was embarrassed that I spent weeks on a boat with you and still forgot. Couldn't think of any way to explain that without admitting that I'm a huge turd, so I gave you a nickname. We never called you that, but I thought of it back on the boat and I was meaning to tell Foster so we could start. Anyway, what's your name?"

"Richard."

"And your last name?"

"Spigot."

"That's funny. Ol' Dick Spigot! That's definitely wrong, though. I had a dream about a spigot recently. I was just thinking about it earlier."

"You can't stand there and tell me my name is wrong when you don't even know it."

"I don't know it, but I'll know it when I hear it. I'm really good at that. Muh. Muh, Kuh. Muh, Kuh. Muh, Kuh."

"What the fuck is wrong with you?"

"Those are the sounds. It's something with a Muh and a Kuh. Maybe initials M.C.? Go ahead and tell me, I'll know it when I hear it."

Wisconsin rolled his eyes and laughed. "Last chance. Let's go."

Parks dug in his heels and crossed his arms. "What's your real name?"

He turned away and curled his shoulders forward in a brooding posture. Parks felt a kind of excitement. Beneath his feet, he felt the low tremor stretch its wavelength until the mountain rolled. There was a jagged crack, so loud and close he nearly fainted from fear. Above his companion, smoke whipped out like a bedsheet unfurling, followed by a booming explosion. Streamers of lava arced through the sky like fireworks. He cringed and looked for cover, but there was none. Most of the debris was blasted down the main slope, but he saw a shotgun spread pass over them. Just above, a molten hailstorm hissed where it met the snow in a wave that rolled downhill. Parks threw his hands over his eyes, the arrow shaft pressed against his right orbital. He let out an involuntary scream as the sounds of impact raced all around and past along the slope. When he opened his eyes, little snow craters smoked all around them. It felt like a minor miracle that none of the fiery rock had landed on them, but the volcano had already belched a secondary burst, this one just powerful enough to lap over the rim on one side. It continued to puke, the lava now rising up like the streams of a fountain and falling within itself.

"Hey, Brother," he heard a familiar drawl from Wisconsin Johnson. A few yards ahead, the fur-seal back wheeled around to face him, and he felt his heart stop in terror as he saw Foster grinning ear-to-ear. "Come get warm."

Parks tried to scream again but his voice seized up. He threw himself downhill in a wild slide over their patient switchbacks, every bone in his body smashing against hard-packed ice as he careened out of control. All he could see was a tumbling world of white, striped with black flashes. His body went limp, and he remembered thinking he was surprised that he was both still rolling and still alive to remark on it. Something hard hit his foot and shot him over onto his stomach, spinning sideways like a fallen penguin until he finally came to rest. Parks was running almost before he could get to his feet, nowhere but down, down the way he came. He was dizzy from the fall, and the spinning world evaporated around him. Now he was on the deck of the *Qarapara*, sinking persistently among the bergs. Out of the cabin stepped Wisconsin Johnson. Parks backed up as the man approached.

"Wrong way," he grinned.

"Wrong way," a voice came in his left ear. He saw the woman and her daughter. The girl echoed her mother, "Wrong way!" He tried to moved right but bumped into Carabiner, smug, patronizing concern plastered on his face. "Bro, what are you doing? You're going the way." There was a swarm of bodies around him: the Old Man, Hapgood, Gardner. They all reached for him as he backpedaled. "Wrong way! You're going the wrong way!" He was running out of deck. Parks risked a desperate glance over the rail. There, floating in the tossing water wrapped in an orange survival suit, was Foster. He waved both his hands, and said something Parks couldn't hear. When he turned back around, the crew and passengers stalked toward him, repeating their chorus and begging him to remain. He took and another step, and another. There was nowhere left to go. Parks got a running start and threw himself into the rail at the waist. He flipped over the side and into the frozen sea.

17

ONIK

Rock rang against rock in a steady rhythm. Between strikes, a song hummed through the hundreds of tiny pores where rough edges shied away from each other. It had been words, but now it was a trembling rattle, lower and with pause for breath. Little more than a moan. Norwet swayed and had to catch himself on the wall. He cursed Milak, whose shoulders held him aloft, and felt around in the utter darkness for the jagged edge he'd damaged. One hand touched the point of aim, and the other swung over, stone clenched as he hurried to remove the first before the second landed. Most of the effort did nothing. Shards of rock peppered his face. Behind him, he could hear a fainter rhythm on the other side of the wall, but he paid it no sight.

"Let me try!" Someone beneath him said.

"No. I am getting it."

"You are doing nothing, bitch."

Norwet ignored the taunts but began to feel that the others were right. The rocks were loose, as promised, but not loose enough to pull free. Each of the boys but him had smuggled in the best hammer stone he could find, but as the biggest it was his right to wield it.

"Hand me a different one," he let it clatter down.

"I can do it," Milak said. "Trade with me."

"Ten more hits. Hand me a new one." Another found its way into his palm. He turned it over so the dull nub pointed out the side of his fist. It rolled off without harm once, twice, three times. Milak made sure to count them aloud. The blood boiled in Norwet's cheeks. He ran his hands over the gnawed edge of the spot he had worked for so long, the loosest of the stones between the ceiling and the rest of the wall. Then he passed it to his right, over several more. All of them gave a little to the touch. It rested on a thicker protrusion, flat and chunky, not as loose as the rest. He curled his lips under and smashed it. "Step to your right," he barked at Milak to get a better angle.

"Six. Seven," Came the reply. Norwet adjusted his aim for the seam where this rock met its neighbor.

"Eight."

He gave it a hard shake, and measured the spot for another blow. This time the arm obeyed without his effort. It coiled and sprung to its target in a quick motion. There was a satisfying snap, and a large piece fell. One hit to spare. He threw down his tool. There was a rough angle where his strike chipped an entire section away. Norwet pinched the lip of its neighbor with both hands and shook it free, flinging it across the room in triumph. There was a gap big enough for him to fit his hand through, and the next rock came without effort. He tossed each one behind him as instructed, and soon the opening was low enough that all four boys could rake the stones away. There was a shout of joy from his brothers in the next cell, and by the sound he knew they, too, were peeling a gap in their wall. As soon as the opening was chest high, Norwet scrambled through, stepping on a body that groaned in protest.

"Get up!" He and Milak took the big man by the hands and tried to lift him, but he was dead weight, barely able to sit upright. They went back to the wall and lowered the gap. Soon, all eight surrounded him, and between them they just managed to hoist him into the middle cell. Stones skipped and clanked everywhere as they drug this corpse to the next wall. He did not seem to know or care who moved him. Siguvik tripped stepping over the next gap, and they dropped their cargo across the hard border. He grunted in pain. Those at the feet tumbled him through without ceremony, then they all dragged him across the spacious floor of the main lockup.

"Where are we?" The one who called himself Leopard Seal asked.

"You have broken the prison with no man's help. We wait at the door, and pray the next one to open it is Tunguk."

The harbormaster peered around the cluster of old Mattaka at the skin boats they dragged ashore. He carefully selected a bead from his satchel and strung it over a strip of leather while the men, unaccustomed to customs, shot one another impatient glances.

"The admiral say there is open traffic," one of them spoke up. "No harbor price."

"No, but you still have to declare your cargo and roster. Have you never used a proper harbor?" Again they could only look at one another. "You won't be allowed to sell these at the harbor, you know. Every last one of them must be removed to the market." The old man nodded. "Anything besides penguin?"

"Aye."

The harbormaster paused tying off the bead in mild surprise.

"We capture the man who it is the admiral seek."

His eyes went wide. "Leopard Seal?"

"No. It is the red one."

The excitement dropped off considerably, but the harbormaster shrugged and nodded to a pair of nearby Marines. "These men will take him."

Behind them, the penguin pile in one of the ships began to rock and bubble.

"No. We keep. You pay reward."

"I am not aware of a reward."

"We keep. We talk. The admiral will pay."

The topmost birds tumbled off, and an arm flung itself out. Gionn pressed as many as he could off himself and wriggled out an opening. Guano streaked him hair to boot and blotches of dried viscera clung to his skin. One of the Mattaka saw him roll over the side of the boat, and they rushed away from the official to surround him with their spears.

"Bastard squains!" He cried, and spat a wad of something foul from his lip. "Is there not a shred of honor among the lot of you? No coin too low to stoop for? Betrayin' a mate in good faith for personal gain! After all I've done for your people. Brought your filthy dogs so you filthy dogs can choke on coal." He lifted a penguin carcass from the ground and flung it into the sea in a rage. "May you drown boatless, and Euskus take your daughters, and the mine your sons!"

They recoiled and fired back in Mattakatan while making protective gestures.

"Go ahead and curse me!" Gionn taunted. "If you cunts had an arsehole-full of power, you'd not be in a place like this."

A small crowd drew around the commotion. "We will take him. The admiral will pay you, I am sure," the harbormaster said.

"No. You get the admiral. We wait."

Gionn noticed a familiar figure towering among the onlookers. "Well, neither of you can have me. I am betrothed to this handsome cunt! Cormdran, is it? I have pledged me service to the crew of the whaler, and you'll need a fair stroke more than two Marines to arrest one of theirs. I'd wager they're tired of bein' taken in and may well draw a bit of blood if you try again."

They all looked at Cormdran. He laughed to himself and approached the group. The Mattaka and the Navy held their tongues while he studied Gionn up and down.

"Half share."

"What?" Gionn said.

"Half share."

"The fuck do I look like? Some squain pilot boy, never stood on a stout board or buried his steel? You'll find no better sailor south of Ampos, let alone on this wart on a frostbit flap."

"You look like a man covered in penguin shit about to be arrested."

"I'm doin' you a favor, cunt. Do you really want a half-share man of me ilk ridin' the westerlies for more weeks than you got cargo? Every time a cold wave slaps one of your lads he'll gladly blame you for it, which is fine as long as the water holds. Have you seen what men do when they don't drink a few days? If we're down to wet wood and ridin' low in ballast, the half-share man's the last one to lighten the load, and the first to call for it. If you were clever, you'd make me a two-share man."

Cormdran and a few members of the whaler crew burst into laughter.

"I'm as serious as cockrot. You want a loyal man, make sure everyone on the crew hates him for his contract, and his preferred seat in the middle that you've also awarded him. See to it that after every wave that washes aboard, they pray to wipe their eyes to his vacant seat. That he never sleeps for fear of takin' ill with a case of the stab-holes. That man will stand for you no matter the odds, because you're the only one who's any good for him."

"Are you really prepared to negotiate from your position? Do you care to pass on a half-share, knowin' well that if I don't like the next words out of your mouth, I walk to me ship with an extra half-share for me troubles, and you with these men to the prison that I doubt will be broken twice in as many nights?"

"There's no extra half share. It'll go to a lesser cunt, if not meself."

Cormdran grinned his concession, and started off. Gionn looked over the official, the two Marines, the stone spears leveled at his face. In the distance he could see more Marines coming their way, drawn by the sudden cluster of bodies.

"Fine! I'll give up the seat in the middle. Two shares, and a starboard bench."

Corm roared with laughter. "One share, and you'll sit on me lap if I say."

"One share. Not the lap thing. And I am assigned a mate-at-arms of me choice from among the grassbenders."

"It's a fuckin' whaler. Even I don't have a mate-at-arms."

"If I get one to agree to it?"

"You can make one your wife if he'll agree to it."

"Done."

"Do you know a whaler's oath?"

"Several."

"Pick one and swear by Euskus."

"By the swift sea and the man beside, these boards me law. By Euskus, and the captain, too, me blade, me oar, me rope that binds, to each his due, to each his due."

"Never heard that one before. Are you certain there's no slipknot in there?"

Gionn fidgeted as eight more Marines neared. "Always served me fine."

"Rather like it. Simple."

"Oath sworn. Now intervene, cunt!"

Cormdran nodded to his men, fifteen or so gathered among the crowd. "Release my crewman, squains, or we'll release your bowels."

"He is ours," the vocal of the Mattaka protested.

"Lots of things are lots of people's until they're taken. Fuck off!" The whalers casually clustered around the old men, their weapons at hand but not yet threatening. The hunters saw the closing Marines, the exhausted crew itching for release. They reluctantly broke off and returned to unloading their carcasses.

The harbormaster spoke a quiet word to the leader of the arriving squad. "You!" The man beckoned at Gionn. "You will come with us."

"Are you tryin' to arrest another of me crew?" Cormdran challenged.

"Admiral's orders to bring him in."

The whalers mustered between Gionn and the Marines. Already, more of each side hustled over to the standoff.

"Me crew was not involved in the prison affair. Were you?"

"Not involved," Gionn echoed.

"What grounds do you have to interfere with private vessels conductin' lawful trade?"

"If he was not involved," The Amposi officer said, "he will be released once he speaks to the admiral."

"The admiral wants to speak to a man of the *Gairhle*, he can discuss the matter with me."

Gionn grinned. He crossed to the group of Mattaka, snatched a penguin from the arms of one of the men, and flung it into the sea.

It returned with a murmur of voices, in and out, quiet and nonsense. A scraping sound from beneath worked its way into flesh as a small vibration, punctuated with shudders and quick jolts. Parks was aware of movement. It was not his, but he moved. The first attempt to open his eyes was met with a blinding glare. His eyelids clenched in pain. Again he shook. Something held him fast. Dug into his chest. When he tried to raise up, he felt a pressure close around his ribs that sent him back in a panic for breath. His leg was in agony, but when he tried to adjust it, the foot was stuck. Both of them were held in place. The realization hit him that he was strapped down, and he had no idea where. The loll of his head side to side with each bump told him he was on his back. Another attempt to open his eyes met with the same brilliant light, a few shades grayer, no features of distinction. He felt he was outside. The memory of the one who lead him up the volcano came flooding back, and fear flooded his chest. He began to flail violently against the restraints. The excruciating pain in his leg barely registered above the certainty that something was happening to him somewhere and he had no power to know what, much less stop it. The voices picked up at his thrashing and he felt all movement but the race of his heart scrape to a halt.

This time, he managed to keep his eyes open. His lashes were crusted with ice, and all he saw was a blurry canvas. All he felt was the cold sting of crystals melting into his eyeball, and the needles of agony that coursed the veins of his left leg. A black figure appeared over him from the left, then another from the right. He moaned and flailed against his straps again. A hand pressed against his chest without force.

"Be still. You will hurt yourself." It took him a moment to recognize Kjartke's beautiful broken English. More figures appeared at his feet. "I make it loose." Her fingers slid between the knotted ends and the breath rushed back into his lungs in a big heave, followed by grateful panting. The one to his right slowly transitioned from black silhouette to gray-white hair and and gray-brown skin.

"Joe."

"I am here, Brother. You did well to lose me, but the rope is tight."

"Where are we?"

"Urkuk."

For a brief moment, the panic of the crater returned. "It's erupting."

"Soon. A week, maybe less," he assured.

As Kjartke cinched the strap again, the boys came into shifting focus. He knew that he knew them, but not from where. Grom, he thought, but could not remember the other's name. First it was Gionn and Barzos, then the gang of oompa-loompas who pulled him from his fever in the cell. Now he opened his eyes to these. Parks was astonished into a little bubble of laughter that ended in watery eyes that he could not help but be saved by someone. He wanted to thank them, but it felt inadequate, and even less necessary.

"Can you loosen my legs? I gotta bend my fucking knee. My whole fucking leg is asleep." Kjartke moved to the straps that held his lower body. She pushed the entire platform a few inches to give herself an angle. Only then did he recognize that he was on a sled. Halfway through untying it, she stopped. Though he couldn't feel it, Parks saw her finger probe between the sole of his boot and the upper. It was too far, and his eyes too dim to see what happened next. His foot flicked with movement that only registered farther up his leg. Kjartke braced her hand across his shin, and he screamed.

"Tunguk." She pulled back. The old man knelt on the other side and peered across. His tunic hung off of him like a wet curtain.

"Did you lose weight? Or did you get a discount at Big and Tall?"

Tunguk pinched the leather and grinned. "It is nice. Maybe I will keep it."

He noticed that the one he wore was unusually tight. Parks squinted. "Hey, is that mine? Bro, how'd you get my threads?"

"You do not remember?" Parks shook his head. "You cursed many years from our lives."

"It is hard to change a man who fights it," Kjartke licked her bottom lip. He noticed a fresh split, swollen and caked with blood. His shoulders curled in shame.

"Are these your pants, too?"

"It was enough to give you a warm shirt. You are too big for our trousers and boots."

"We cut your boots off," one of the boys chimed in enthusiastically.

"One is ruined! But we will fix the other and bring it to you," the younger said. It struck him as strange. He was positive that he was still wearing them. Kjartke tried to roll his pant leg back, but as soon as she got to the calf he writhed away. Joe nodded to let him take over. Metal sung against a sheath as his blade appeared. Carelessly, or with expert care, he zipped it under the pant leg and split it from cuff to knee in a smooth draw.

Kjartke side-waddled to his shoulder. "The snow ends miles before town. When we arrive, we must wait for night to enter. The sled will not pass. The boys will remove it. Then you must lean on Tunguk, or on me. I do not think your leg will stand. You must use the other."

He saw Joe lean his face to the leg just below the knee and sniff deeply through his nose. Kjartke followed his attention. Her face did not change, but it felt as though a shadow passed between the low sun and the sled party.

"It is worse," Eskimo Joe said. "He will not walk." Parks could not see what they examined, but when the boys leaned in for a curious peek, their twisted expressions sent a cold tremor up his torso and out the top of his head.

"Will we carry him?" The older boy asked.

"He is too big. Eight strong men would be troubled."

"He can stay with us."

"Sawi will not allow it."

"Sawi will not know. We have hid a man before."

Joe shook his head and stood. "There is a place before we reach the dogs, little-traveled. We will take him there." His expression flattened into the distance. "But not tonight. It is too far. You must go ahead. Return with the sled, and find a trail tukit and a team. Bring it to us. We will not survive the night without it." He looked at Kjartke. "The poye knows you. Can she be trusted?"

Parks felt her hand tense against his arm. "Perhaps."

"Once we reach where we hide, you must bring her."

"Is everything OK?" Parks asked.

Joe smiled. "It is your luck that we found you when we did. Now, it is possible that things will continue."

His face scrunched at the phrasing.

"You are a fool," Kjartke scolded him. "You wander to Urkuk alone."

"I wasn't alone. You'll never believe who took me."

"I know," Joe replied.

"See what you have done?" She went on. "You must listen to people who help you. Now many are in danger, and for what? So you die with others?"

"Kjartke." Joe's voice was quiet and firm. Her dark eyes loomed over his, cutting through the icy droplets.

"The next time you find trouble, maybe none will find you." She rose and went ahead, out of his line of sight. There was a pause, then Joe went around behind him. The boys started off after Kjartke, and moments later, there was a yank as a line went taut and the sled scraped to life. The pain of holding himself rigid against looser bonds radiated throughout his body in an instant. Even sitting up was unfathomable. Parks knew they were there, though all had vanished, but the hint of loss unearthed an ancient fear in his gut—as when a mother steps away from her ailing son for a moment to return soon with medicine. He was alive because these four climbed a mountain for him. If at any point they left, he knew beyond an inkling of a hope that he would lie with his back on a sled until the frost brushed his eyelids closed. Joe was right. It was no virtue of his that held him in this world, but sheer, dumb luck—a luck beyond reasonable expectation, that every time he looked up, he found a hand extended. And Kjartke was right, too. If we was careless, he would one day find what hung above him now: open sky, and the light failing fast.

Though his shoulders were pinned, he wrapped his right hand around the arrow she made him, and curled it to his chest. The tip hovered inches below his chin, which he tucked to examine the weapon. Parks closed his eyes, and became aware of the subtleties of the pull from the front, the confident hands that steered from behind. Though the jerking sled gave him the constant sense that he was about to go over, he realized that they knew what they were doing, and he let his body roll with the terrain. The pain fell by a small, precious margin, and his breath flowed more freely into his ribs. In his mind, he again saw the black silhouettes above him, here in a place no man should be. His lips cracked and a smile crossed his face. In a dry, quavering drone, he sung.

"Naaaaah. Nah-nah, nah-nuh-nah-naaaaaah. Nah-nuh-nah-naaaaaah. Naaah-naaaaaaaaaah." His eyes opened. The air steamed, and he looked down at the black point aimed at his throat like a microphone. "Naaaaah. Nah-nah, nah-nuh-nah-naaaaaah. Nah-nuh-nah-naaaaaah. Heeeeey, Juuude."

The sun ran low across the sky for the headland beyond the channel, the jutting upper jaw of Hiade. The two sides were back: the overwhelming force of Marines and Navy, exhausted from a long days search of the town; the whalers, armed most of all with pride and obscenities, defiant for the belief that these men wouldn't dare test their patience again, though they'd already taken most of the crew once, and a mate the day before without resistance. Costig stalked off twenty paces to meet Cormdran midway between the crew of the whaler, backs against her hull, and his own force, more than 200 mustered. All of them had to be sick of puffing their chests and rattling their spears by now, but even those who'd half-heartedly gone through their paces in the streets now found the fire to look like a real bunch of barrels, ready for the melee. In a cruel way, the whalers were a blessing. Their presence gave his men some sense of the life they'd need to carry through Winter for the guests of Spring. It was almost a shame they'd have to go.

"Costig! If you've come with a notion to take one of me lads," Corm twisted the side of his mouth back toward his crew to make sure he was heard, "You'll have to take every last one of us!"

"You'd have a better pull if you left the traitors and criminals on me island where they belong!" Costig growled back, then lowered his voice so that Corm alone could hear. "I thought you said you hadn't me reddie."

"Recent acquisition." Corm kept his voice below the shouts of the crowd.

"Ah, then you'll admit you've harbored a fugitive."

"I'll not admit it til you tell me the reward."

Costig laughed. "I've not announced a reward. Not for him, or the prisoner."

"In that case, I've signed an able seaman. You should be thankin' me it weren't one of yours."

"Did you think I would just let him sail off? Of all the ports where a man can slip like a shade, Drummoc is not among 'em."

"Aye, but I may as well call for a mutiny on meself if I let another man go."

"Keep him. I haven't a place to put him anyway. I'll have a few questions for the lad, and if he satisfies me curiosity, I'll gladly send him to his death on the Orin."

"Yours is a stout curiosity, Costig. I aim to sail day after, auspices willin'. I'll hang on to him. You can ask your fill right here, in front of everyone."

"No man of any respect would betray his mates in front of his crew and his enemy, alike."

"Then it ought to be a short interrogation."

Costig shook his head. "I've got a better plan."

Costig held on to the quay to steady the little skin boat as Gionn stepped aboard. The extra weight caused it to jerk hard against his grip until the big body was settled on the other bench across the deck, bulging and sinking with the ripples of the harbor. Two of the whalers fixed a rope to the end of the vessel while all parties pushed to the edge to have a closer look, their tempers resolved for the time being so that whalers and Marines mixed shoulder to shoulder, all attention on the boat that Costig lazily rowed into the slapping waters of the evening.

The rope caught with a violent jerk about a hundred feet out, more than enough to hide a quiet word on the northeast breeze.

"I figure you're gonna ask me if I had anything to do with the escape, or if I know where the prisoner is hidin'. Save your breath. The answer to both is, 'aye.' Now in the remainin' time before suspicions arise within our respective cohorts, I propose we work out exactly the terms of our arrangement, as this is like to be the last conversation we have before I take an arseful from the Westerlies on your behalf, if the crew don't find me out and chop me into bait."

"One argot. Each. I want a two-man team. You've got no chance alone."

"Have I got to be your press gang, as well? What's the pay for that? You're not makin' it easy, you know."

"I'd recommend the fugitive. That'll be another problem done if he's nowhere to be found."

"Ehh," Gionn grimaced. "Didn't like the look of him last I saw. If me companion dies in the service of the farri, do I get his argot?"

"You get one, and no more help from me. I ought to haul you in for the way you done me quarters and let them two sort it out. But it's up to you. Get yourself a second man, and a single coin."

"The terms bein' I prevent the whaler from reachin' Taclann by a means of me own choice."

"The means'll be to force her in at Nunoc, if you want your pay. That's the only stop you've got, and that's where you'll claim your wage."

Gionn shook his head with a wry little smile. "So many things wrong with it. Where to begin? I know I got an honest face, but what if, by some miracle, they don't believe that they owe an argot to some cunt who just rowed in on his word?"

"I've been thinkin' about that. It'll come with a message."

"That says?"

"Whatever I entrust to your mate." Costig beamed. Gionn squinted his displeasure. "You'll do well to see him through, and he, you. He'll carry the word to convince the Viceroy, but yours will get you before the man. You'll need to find a lad named Tasua. He'll be a Marine, sergeant-at-arms or better. Tell him the followin' and he'll know who sent you: 'Nimaket lies faultless for the mutiny on the *Kawal-Atxl*. Costig knows the hand that held the rope.'"

"Which brings me to the other problem. I'm more than happy to divert your ship north, south, or down, but the last time I was in Nunoc…Hm. Let's see. I suppose you'd say it was recent-enough that some cunts would remember."

"Uh-huh. The rosters of Nunoc are no better than ours—worse in some regards. If you do this, there's little that can't be forgiven. So long as you didn't murder an Amposi citizen or somethin' of the sort." Gionn puffed his cheeks and held his response. "Alright, well, you could always lay low, come back here in Spring and get it from me."

"I'll never come here again if it's for me fuckin' coronation, much less when it's under siege."

"Then you'll have to wait til I can send word."

"Siege. You'll be under fuckin' siege. No ship of yours will make it north, no matter how many feathers you stick to it."

"That's your choices. Nothin' else to be done. Nunoc's the only stop, and that's where gold coin sits about."

"You could pay me in advance."

Costig let out a slow roll of breathe that turned into modest laughter. "You do have an honest face. But I'd worry to carry an argot on board a whaler, never mind how you come of it."

"I'll risk it."

"You won't. Where's your reason to raise a finger if you're already paid?"

"Me honor. And me generally cunty disposition. Believe me, I'd do it for a copper, and maybe out of spite alone, if you hadn't already promised gold. Pay me now, and I'll see that ship to Manhas if need be—just not Nunoc."

Costig thought it over. "What about Foster? Parks? Are they on any better terms than yourself?" Gionn's smirk was his answer. "Tell you what I'll do. You get one of them lads aboard, and I'll have him hold your argot."

"Do I get to hold his?"

"I think not."

"And what's to stop him from handin' it over just the same?"

"I've been a sergeant for years, and a day as an admiral is enough to know which man'll do what you ask of him."

"And what kind of man do you reckon me for?"

"The kind I'll gladly send to ruin a ship full of poor, unuspectin' cunts who just saved his arse from arrest and execution."

Gionn mulled it over. "If anyone's found with it, I'd rather it be him."

"Done. You see one of 'em on the ship, and I'll see he travels heavy."

"Why?"

Costig was taken aback. "Because that's what we just agreed to."

"No. Why do you give a fuck? I've never seen a man carry so much draft for his king. Did you know you're not Amposi? Not even a squirt. From your ice-white arse to your shiny red cheeks, cunt, you're a square fuckin' halot. You're not a mongrel, or a blaggard, or a jumper. If it were me in your boots, I'd rob these cunts blind, load a few of these ships with everything that's not a rock, and head for Mabhan. Let whoever shows up in the spring fight it out for the privilege of freezin' his bollocks off watchin' squains dig holes. Why the fuck are you so loyal to Ampos?"

"The Navy gave me an opportunity when I had none."

"The Navy'll take anyone with at least three limbs, one eye, and a month of free time. Half of these cunts were fightin' the Navy a season ago!"

Costig nodded over a grin. His eyes dipped to the shifting skin beneath their feet before returning to meet Gionn.

"I like things a certain way. Sergeant or admiral, me job's the same: I get shit men like you together to do things that shit men otherwise wouldn't be fucked to do. Row ships. Build ports, colonies. Protect shit people from one another. Because whether or not they realize it, they like things the same way as I do. They just don't have the sense to see a good thing, and hold it together. Or to see a bad one, and make it good.

"Most fellows would look at a cunt like yourself—involved in all manner of murder, thievery, intrigues—and if they didn't give you good steel, they'd run you as far as the wind. Me, I know you're good for almost nothin'. But you do have your uses. There's somethin' you can do to make things the way I like 'em, even if it's standin' half a watch before fallin' asleep. And in your particular case, your calamitous nature may even tip the balance of a battle. Maybe a war. There aren't enough decent lads in the world that I can be choosy about who I get to put things the way I like 'em."

"Aye, but why for Ampos?"

Costig coiled his finger three times in the air overhead. The boat jerked as men on the dock reeled her in.

The sky was the color of the last gray before pitch when Ferrakut and Ulwet collapsed atop the ridge above the dog camp, and the little cluster of tukits that belonged to the family of Sawi. Their legs seized the moment they stopped moving, and it was some time before their panting could rough out a word. They had run, or as near to it as one could manage, with the sled in tow from where they left the others huddled in the wind shadow of a short black wall that peeked from the snow, less than the height of a man. It was the only cover the three of them would have until the boys could return with a trail tukit, and already the night winds were rumbling down the slope, whipping the edges of their clothing and the hair that fell out of their hoods. It had been a speedy descent, with the wind following, yet even the next few hundred yards to the camp seemed an impossible distance.

The moonlight rippled in a wide pool below that they knew were the restless dogs, shifting and digging to set themselves to the weather. Nothing else was clear from this distance.

"Will we ask Sawi for a tukit?" Little Ulwet said in gasps. It was plain to Ferrakut what he meant.

"I think we let Sawi rest. He will understand."

"Do you think he waits for us?"

The notion had not occurred to Ferrakut. Now he strained over the bowl of the camp for the lines of a man, sitting up to tear into the boys for their involvement. For risking the family. There was no way to know. "He will not be out in this wind. Will he?" The brothers exchanged their doubts in a look. "Then what?" Ferrakut continued. "Leopard Seal will die tonight if we do not return."

"If we tell Sawi, he will not let a man die. He will send a tukit." Ulwet ventured.

"No. Sawi would not let him die. And the others, too." Again there was a bargain of wordless expression. "Maybe we will go around the far side to see," Ferrakut said.

"Aye, I think that is good," Ulwet jumped to agree.

They dropped into the bowl just far enough that the gusts passed overhead, then circled as wide as possible to the back side of the camp. A stranger would have thought there many more people living there. Half of the buildings held sledding material: leather harnesses and straps, raw leather in various stages of processing, wood scraps, tools and provisions for trail work—the sleds, themselves. It was a great expense to build a tukit of stone. The songs were fond of reminding them that once all tukits were trail tukits, bone and flesh. It was only with the mines and the northern builders that Mattaka learned to frame a more permanent dwelling, and most families had but one. Though dog work was among the lowest jobs for the people, Sawi's family had four for living and sleeping, and four more overflowing with broken equipment awaiting the mends that must occur before they could make the firestone run.

It was the wealth of a dog man that one always owed him a favor. The viceroys of Ampos had learned long ago that it was easy to lose firestone between Drummoc and Nunoc. Ampos owned no firestone. It was the king's mine, the king's harbor, the king's ships. Every black lump belonged to the men who chipped it free. As it stood waiting for the sleds, every man among them was rich. But from the season's load was deducted the rent of the king's mine, the king's harbor, the king's ships. It was the miners who paid the dog teams, and the ships like the one that had carried Ferrakut and Ulwet. They paid the wages of the Navy who guarded the colony, and the passage. Only once the ships made it to port were their wages issued, and if the ship carrying their firestone or their pay should not make it, it was the miners who lost, and the miners who must repay the ship's expense from the next season's load.

Of the many hands outstretched, the least was Sawi's, and he was the last paid, if at all. But men who had nothing left when it came his turn had instead raised these buildings, or worked dogs in the sledding season. Brought meat for his family, or good pelts. Even good hasqa.

Yet the tukits overflowed, and many of the lesser sleds and scraps were simply covered in worn-out hides where the snow buried them. These would be dug out soon to see what had survived. It was among these lumps and outbuildings that Ferrakut and Ulwet drew their sled. By now, their eyes had adjusted to the dark of the camp and they could pick out the shadows of each tukit in the moonlight. All of the boys in the family were working age, and they had worked endlessly since the ship arrived, as their cousins would in Nunoc when they returned the other way. Both knew exactly what was where, and neither had seen a trail tukit. They would be among the faceless mounds, with or without the opening still exposed. Their legs buckled beneath them as they picked the nearest one. Without tools, they had to wedge their bare hands into the icy mix and scrape it aside as would a dog. Right away, their fingers froze stiff, and for every few swipes that took a thin crust of snow, they had to rewarm them in their armpits, their crotches, anywhere that still held heat. Ferrakut worried at how badly Ulwet was shaking, even when he rested. As he reached for his brother to silently get his attention, he noticed his own hand trembling just as bad. They dug for what seemed like a great age, but only a couple of feet of snow changed places. It was unclear if they were anywhere near the covering, or if this one even had what they needed.

"We have to ask," the older boy said. Ulwet just nodded through chattering teeth. They clasped hands and pulled each other to their feet, but the younger one sank immediately to his knees again, too exhausted now to stand. Without hesitation he began to fight for his feet, but his brother stayed him. Ferrakut started out on his own. He had resolved to plead their case and save themselves the effort of a distressed search, but out of instinct he still crept as quietly as possible to the edge of the supply tukits. Every round corner was taken with a lean and a step, a lean and a step. The wind blew across the ground between himself and the tukits where the family lived, taking any sound with it that might have warned him someone was awake and about. It was madness, he thought. Why do I not just walk over there? His head nodded in sleep for a moment though he stood shivering. When he shook it free, he knew there was no other choice. Ferrakut straightened up and walked unconcealed from the cover of the outbuildings.

He neither saw nor heard the one who took him. A hand slapped around his mouth, and he tasted iron where his cut from the fist fight reopened against his tooth. His legs didn't even fight as he was dragged right back to where he started and set on his bottom. It was Norwet who held a finger before his lips, then leaned in to whisper.

"Sawi waits up for you. It will be bad."

In hushed excitement, Ferrakut frantically relayed the situation while Norwet plead with him to keep his voice down. "We have to get it to them. Leopard Seal is dying. Maybe the others, too."

"Stay here." Norwet returned shortly with a troop of shadows, and Ferrakut need not count to know that every boy in camp was among them. They led him back to the spot where Ulwet sat, arms hugging his knees, shivering uncontrollably.

"It is the wrong one," Milak confirmed of their dig site.

"Can you dig for us?" Ferrakut plead. "We will steal a team and take it back."

Norwet snorted. "You will go nowhere. Look at you. I will take it."

"You do not know where they are."

"Then tell me."

"I will go, too," Milak said. "I know the land better. The dogs will be afraid to drive in the dark."

All of the boys but Ferrakut and Ulwet plunged into the snowbank that held the trail tukits, two of them with proper shovels. The wind held their clinking away from the rest of the camp, and it was not long before their hands peeled back leather. The tukit they were after was no more than stitched hides and bones for frame, and leather straps to secure the two. They were visible now in the moonlight, but still wedged beneath a pile of snow and one another, and there would be no way to see if they were any good or not. They would simply have to pick one and pray that its seams were not in a pitiful state of repair.

"He watches the dogs," pointed out Ravitak, the middle son of Sawi.

"He expects you back tonight. You left without supplies," Norwet explained. "We will not be able to steal a team without him seeing us."

"Maybe if we all pull, we can go on foot," Arnake suggested.

"It is the only way," Saunlauk confirmed.

"Dogs will be faster. You did not see the state of him," Ferrakut said.

"I told you, Sawi watches the dogs," Ravitak repeated.

Ferrakut looked at his little brother. "Can you walk?" Ulwet gave a brave nod, though the rest of him disagreed. "Then we will give Sawi what he watches for."

The first dog sounded before they came into sight, their presence betrayed by heavy steps. Ulwet leaned as little as possible on his brother's shoulder, but he was too exhausted to hold his own weight entirely. A ripple of bays and yelps rose from the pack, and as they rounded the tukit to emerge as if they'd come from the trail, they saw the entire ground teem with indistinct shapes leaping over one another, yanked back by leads.

"Quiet, you bastards! You will wake Sawi!" Ferrakut shouted. Most of the dogs lost interest entirely at a familiar, though some still barked and pulled the slack out of their tethers to smell the new arrivals. No one neared them but to feed them, water them, or work them. Any visit by a man was cause for excitement, at least for the younger pups. The knot in Ferrakut's stomach tangled its way up his chest as he waited for Sawi to fall upon them, but only dogs appeared in the moonlight as they worked their way around the rim of the pack. They stopped to let Ulwet rest a moment and Ferrakut strained into the night for his uncle. Terrified as he was of the price for their trip, all he wanted was for the man to spring out and shout at them, to crack them as he might and be done with it. The anticipation was far more cruel.

"Come on," he said louder than he needed. "We must go before the dogs wake our uncle. He let us go with Tunguk. We will allow him his rest." With fortune, Sawi would soften his blows to their respect. The dogs' activity rose and fell like a wave beside them—swelling as they drew near and circling back into their furrows as they passed. Soon they were beyond, and still no Sawi. Maybe the old fool had decided to be angry in the morning, when the light returned and the winds had calmed.

"Do you see him?" Ulwet whispered. Ferakut shook his head. Now his path to the tukit where they would sleep was clear. All of the children—the boys and the two daughters of their auntie Ianate—stayed there, along with Ianate and her cousin Iniasep. The two women would scold them if they woke at all. Likely the other boys had left unnoticed.

The quiet of the dogs behind them told them that no one approached. Ulwet started for the safety of the doorway. Ferrakut caught the tail of his tunic.

"He is gone!" The younger said. "Sleeping."

"They said he waits." He decided to try a ploy. "Uncle, is that you?" Ferrakut asked the night as if he had heard movement. There was no response. His sight adjusted now to see the silver reflection off the dome of the large tukit where Sawi slept, farthest from the chaos of the dogs. With measured steps, he lead Ulwet to their own doorway. He felt the pull of the interior, the quiet, and easy sleep. Instead, they circled the outside in its entirety, and saw no one.

"I think it is safe," Ulwet practically begged. He had been so brave, so eager for action when the boys brawled beside the harbor earlier. The trail had sapped his enthusiasm with his strength. The sharp cold returned to Ferrakut's toes every time they paused. He pulled his brother on, toward the other dwellings. The next two were paired very near their own, so that they formed a wedge into the prevailing wind that shielded the fourth, where he thought their uncle may rest. Even though it was farther from the dogs, there was nowhere for a mile they couldn't be heard when someone approached them. But they had left without dogs, and if Sawi could think he would know they need not pass them on their return. They slipped behind their own tukit into the narrow passage between the next two. Ferrakut's eyes held to the far tukit like an archer sighting his enemy. They crept down the channel, mercifully out of the wind now. The air clapped around them as it bounced over the roofs and echoed through the hollow. Ferrakut's heart stopped altogether when he saw a figure slumped against the backside of the left tukit, mere feet away as they passed.

They froze in terror, waiting for the man wrapped in a fur seal blanket to speak to them. For too long, he neither moved nor spoke. Ferrakut shook off his brother and knelt before the shroud. The smell of hasqa struck him, and a light snore emanated from the folds of the pelt. There was no way to make out the face.

"Uncle?" The man did not answer. Ferrakut scooted closer, and noticed a jug pinched between the thighs—no doubt empty. With as much care as possible, he tried to pull back the covering. The man startled, and he and Ulwet screamed at the same time.

Sawi rubbed his eyes and threw aside the blanket. It took him a moment to understand what stood before him, then he rose with great effort and chattering curses. Even out of the wind, he should have been freezing, were it not for the warmth of hasqa coursing his veins. Sawi supported himself by leaning on the tukit.

"Where is my sled?"

"It is with the others. Tunguk sends his thanks."

"Tunguk!" He scoffed. "You are sick of dogs, then? You will give up your father's trade to wander with that one?" They shook their heads fervently. "He has lived long, with what to show? He begs me for work! He has no family, so he takes mine. Runs with condemned men to the spear." Sawi bent to pick up a thin rod of flexible wood—a crop they used to break up dog fights and discipline stubborn teams. "I would let you! It is what you want, you will see how it goes. But you bring these people to my camp. You take my tools, you harness my family to criminals. 'What a fool, Sawi must be! He drinks in a stupor!' You think I do not see when my forge is sooted? You think I do not hear what goes on? Who is jailed with the Leopard Seal? I tell you for love of my brother. You think it is a shame to work dogs? Men will turn away from you. They will scorn you when you are far away, asleep in your camp. No miner thanks you for your price. No sailor dreams to work the dog boat. Have you split rock? Breathed the black air? Have you pulled rope in a storm sea? These same men sleep great ages under a mountain, or a wave. You have a tukit with few to share. You have always food. Always family. Tunguk sleeps nowhere. Earns nothing. Tunguk is not mourned. What you see when you wander is all in the spirit world. What is there, on your passage—it is misery. This is what you want for your family?"

"No, uncle."

"Take off your tunics."

"Please, it is cold."

"You knew it would be cold when you left."

"Please no!" Ulwet implored. Sawi flipped at the tail with his crop.

"Off!"

"It is not Ulwet. I made him go along."

"He makes his choice. Off or it will be worse!"

Faint, skimming over the rooftops, Ferrakut's sharp ears picked up the first excited yelp. It would rise soon, and even Sawi in his hasqa-sleep would not fail to hear them this time.

"You are a drunk! And rude to guests!" Ferrakut roared. Shock overtook Sawi's face, and it seemed for a moment he may lose his footing. Then he erupted in a wail as though he had been pierced with a volley of arrows. "You shit! Off, you bastard! You speak to your uncle this way?" Ferrakut threw his tunic in the snow beside him. He turned his back and threw his arms over his face and head as Sawi descended, crop flying this way and that in a torrent of profanity. The sting on his cold skin drove him to his knees, and he covered helplessly as the stick fell again and again, while his brother shouted pleas on his behalf. Sawi pulled Ulwet's tunic, too, and Ulwet gave in, helping him get it off. The younger boy got a few stray lashes, then it returned to Ferrakut in force. No dog boy was a stranger to it. He settled in his manner and let them fall until the stinging swipes faded into one another. In his vision, he sat feet away in the snow, watching his still, curled body beneath the crash of the rod, feeling nothing but the cold of the snow, hearing nothing but the distant voice of his uncle. Until the voice fell beneath a greater sound. The song of dogs filled the wind. The rhythmic blows died altogether, and he turned to see his uncle looking over the tops of the tukits in confusion. Two great voices made of many lesser ones swirled around them: the jealous cries of the pack, tremendous and mournful; and the little yelps of triumph—the excited few, bounding farther into the distance.

The Unniakattuk galloped down the slope and leaped over their heads in a race for the sea. These winds were the night sailors—gathering in the heights for fear of the sun, they hurried to their ships under cover of darkness. The loose upper layer of snow down the trail swirled under their pounding in a ghostly mist beneath an otherwise clear sky. Here and there, a muscle shivered, and Tunguk did his best to relax it. To let the shivers spread like raiders through a seaport was to be overrun by the cold. He gave his shoulder a jerk to pop Brother's head back into an upright position. There came a moan, almost awake, then he began to babble his song again. There were no words left of it. His voice rasped and cut out as though the same winds scoured his throat. But he spoke. Tunguk instructed him that he must keep singing, so the winds would carry their sound to the boys returning with the dogs. It was the only way they would be found. This was a lie. There was little chance they would be found. But Brother must not be allowed to sleep.

They leaned against a short black wall, too steep to take snow, bodies pressed into one another. There had been more between his bones and the air in the past, Tunguk recalled. He'd spent worse nights exposed many times, but never did a mild one chill him like this. Mild as it was, the water from his nose was a growing icicle. Despite the violence of the winds, there was a calm to this place. It did not feel hostile, only seemed to wonder why these people were here. The stars beamed from an unbroken sky. If the boys knew how to hang a weight and move it from each to each as they turned around the spot, it would not be difficult to find them. He did not think to mention it before they left. If they did not know how, or lost the line, they could pass within feet and miss them. The sound of anything approaching from below was shielded by their position upwind. The dogs could be past before they heard them. Tunguk could only see clear as far as Kjartke, kneeling at Brother's feet. She kneaded the toes of his right foot until her hands tired, then rested and started again. Never did she bother with the left.

They sat on bare snow, without as much as a skin beneath them and the ground. He had tried to send her away when they first found the tracks. They were unprepared. Little food and water, no cover. But neither of them thought Brother could have made it as far as he did, or guessed at the trouble of getting him down again. The song faded, and he gave a sharp elbow. Brother grunted, but did not resume. It took another, and a word of encouragement.

If the tukit did not arrive soon, there would be no more songs from this one. The cold was only his first enemy. Even with shelter, his leg would be enough to take him. Tunguk might make the dawn, he thought, but he would not be able to walk out if he did. Kjartke was strong. She may lose some to the frost, but she would leave here. They spoke of none of it. Tunguk did not even think of what they would do if they could keep Brother alive for a face or two of the moon. When things were difficult, he knew it was unwise to dream so far ahead. Until a star changed places. A step. A breath.

Kjartke did not say that she was cold, or needed a break. She moved to the far side of Brother and pressed her body into his. Tunguk looked down the long leg. It was but a short crawl, yet at the thought of it he could already feel the warmth leave the skin that was pressed against his companion. Though it was close enough to remain under the wind, he could feel the cold air that would bite him. The freezing skin against his palm and fingers, ice upon ice. For the briefest moment, he let himself wander to his obligation. It pulled taut against his heart, and he felt the beats stutter and jerk to catch up—shallow, gasping pulses. It brought him to his back after the long run, where Foster and

Brother stood above him discussing his fate. Tunguk wrestled himself once more to the foot of Urkuk, where his head felt swollen. It throbbed with pain that ran from one ear through to the other, but there was slack again. Here was one who would require great care. He would be helpless for some time if he lived, and perhaps always. A miracle would bring him safe to town, where he would be too weak to sail, and men would search for him, Navy and reward-seekers, alike. There was the other, he gazed to the stars of Teptawe, who taught the people how to find their way in ships when they came to Ajatse, twirling over Camne Drumlag. That was as much as he knew of Foster. It was too much. No dream could bring them all safely through. It was too far, as to paralyze one who knew nothing of the passage, or lure a fool to his death. He needed something closer. Tunguk returned to the feet of Brother.

The air between the folds of his clothes had warmed enough in his stillness that he dreaded the first shift that would force it out the ends, to be replaced with bitter chill. Even if he saved the toes, it would do little good, and the effort to make the effort seemed wasted. But that was too far, as well. Tunguk made a bargain he had offered himself many times. You do not have to go, he said. But you are sitting. Get to your knees. He thought he may not even do that, but as soon as his attention wavered, his body flung itself to all fours before he had a chance to object. His hands and knees burned from the snow. The threadbare warmth he had taken so long to raise left him at once. Can you crawl to his feet? He asked himself. Then you can remain there, or turn back. But to move will help with the cold. He raised a hand and a knee and shuffled forward, then again. The brief respite for the pair that was elevated was enough to drive him to the soles of the swollen limbs. They seemed the feet of a giant. Tunguk sat to shift the cold to his bottom. He noticed the song had stopped.

"He must sing." Kjartke scowled, then shook the giant. His head tilted from one side to the other. She pounded on his thigh, though it might as well have been a log for all it did. In her frustration, she leaned back and lay a sharp slap across his face. He moaned. One more, and turned his head. "Sing!" She threatened. Brother let out a long, low hum. He followed it with an uneven series of frail sounds through his nose. At the end of the leg, Tunguk could just make them out, but they held.

He looked down the mountain, where everything loose rose up to advance the line of snow ever closer to town, moon after moon, until it would collect against the walls of the tukits in drifts that before the sun returned in the Spring would threaten to come over the tops of the outermost homes. His hands stuck to themselves. Through his sleeves he massaged them until the fingers moved of their own. Then he wrapped a sleeve-covered grip over the toes of Brother's foot and held firm to release the outer layer of frost. There is little else to do, he told himself. Can you hold his foot for a moment? Then you can choose if you would continue, or return to the wall. Tunguk breathed a heavy cloud of frozen breath, and squeezed his palms against the bare toes.

Every joint rattled in and out against the lashings as Norwet held on to the straps that secured the parts of the trail tukit to the sled beneath him. They shot across the lee slope of the foot of Urkuk, cutting over icy snow that caused the runners to skip and tilt to their right with every dip and rise. He twisted his body left to weight the far end, and Milak stood behind him with most of his weight on the runner of the same side, shouting commands for the dogs to ignore.

It was something of a surprise to them to find themselves hitched after dark, and the boys were afraid they would not get them off before Sawi heard them. But once the dogs were running, they fell into their usual pace—with a light load of skin and bones, far too fast for the dark. Milak fought to slow them. They were trail drunk, though. Wild with the exuberance of an unexpected run. Yet each time the sled stuck fast, they had to be urged to move again against their nervous uncertainty. The dogs could probably see fine in the moonlight. That is what Norwet suspected. But it was not a dog's way to choose terrain for the sled. It was the driver's, and even Norwet could not see more than the bouncing outline of the animals fanned out from a single point before him. Six in the team, they clawed across a slope well-off the trail his brothers had taken. The Unniakattuk blistered that way with gusts of shimmering ice, and Milak was confident-enough that he understood where they were going to avoid the blasts as long as possible. Now it was no longer possible.

The open face stood before them. The wind grew to a roar as the first dog crossed the ridge, and he felt the sled drag to a near-stop. The runners lightened. Milak was on foot, pushing them over, where they were greeted by a sting that burned their eyes shut and caused every stray flap of material to snap back and forth like fish in a net. The dogs pulled sideways at their leads and averted their eyes, and the sled lurched to a stop. They wanted no part of it. Milak shouted and pushed. Norwet hopped off and grabbed the nearest dog, turning him so the wind was on his cheek, then crouched and yanked the others into the same orientation urging them on in a sort of a tack that kept the brunt of the blown snow off their center. With a few violent pulls, he got the chief dog to move again, much slower than before, the others followed at his threats. Suddenly, the sled was going, and Norwet had to dive onto it as it sailed past. It seemed as soon as they got moving the wind lulled like a sea between sets, and they could see the night sky above in utter clarity. Up the mountain, the moonlight caught twisting tails of snow with lighter flurries between, all of it blown loose from the slope. Norwet found if he squinted his left eye half-closed and kept his right mostly open, he could see the dogs picking their way forward, now out of the main current.

Milak settled them into a groove between two wavering bands on what must have been a higher strip. They whipped together and apart, at times meeting across the team in a shower that slowed them to a crawl until they separated again, and Milak drove them on. There was no way Ferrakut and Ulwet would have made it, he thought. It did not seem likely that they would, either. The directions he heard contained too many pauses and revisions, and the confidence of Milak only hardened Norwet's doubts. They had come too far around in order to keep speed beneath the winds, and now they proceeded only where the snow blew least. It seemed to him they needed to cut back across the worst of it to regain the trail taken by his brothers when the sun shone. His eyes strained for black patches in the dark blue snow. It was in the shelter of one that Tunguk rested, and it was black that meant they neared a collision with a wall, or a plunge over a rocky height.

Norwet pointed his finger over his head in the direction he thought they should take, right in Milak's face. Their course did not veer.

"This way!" He craned his neck back.

"Not yet!" Milak shouted back. "We will carry faster." To drive his point he yanked the team right, downslope and toward the sea. Norwet could not deny that the winds were lighter here, but the place that his brothers left Tunguk was one of heavy gusts. They had chosen the spot because it was the last to provide some cover before the "plain," they had called it. The flatter terrain, the fairer winds—this had to be what they meant. The most violent flurries disappeared down the steeper far side of the height that ran across the middle, while the rest fanned out and lost much of their force around the boys. The initial burst had been the choke point where they gathered again. Now they gained speed and rhythm, though it still blew across their flank and forced them to fight left at all times to avoid drifting too far. The line of sight was not much better, but out of the shadow of the ridge they could at least see beyond the dogs now.

It was a fine team they had taken, and the penalty would be proportional when they returned if the animals were harmed. For now, they drove with an excitement he was not accustomed to. A team was more energetic when they raced, but it was soon spent, and on long hauls the lazy ones would often rest on their leads. Every dog pulled with a quiet vigor, as though they sensed the determination of their drivers. Impatient as he was, Norwet relaxed his grip on the straps. His frozen fingers were blistered and torn. Now he was able to balance himself better, and it would be some time before they were upon the place. Ferrakut and Ulwet had seen Teptawe emerge from the sky straight ahead as soon after they began, and he neared Urkuk now. Given the time they arrived, he thought they had told stories of their speed. It was probably not as far as they said. But after several miles on this course, his stomach grew uneasy. It felt as though Milak would go by them before he turned toward the ridge.

Suddenly, the winds calmed and stray flakes danced through the air in the waning moon. The team seemed to take on an extra step at the improved conditions, and Milak urged them on. Norwet felt as though dropped from a height, the way his heart rose. He frantically signaled to stop the sled so they could speak. Milak ignored him at first, but when Norwet tried to grab at his hands, his cousin relented.

"It is too far. They were in the wind. We have passed onto the lee side."

"It will be back," Milak said. "It is just a shadow."

Nothing about it reassured the eldest boy. "I do not think Ferrakut and Ulwet traveled very far. They are big with their talk."

"The place they said is not far. Three miles from here, maybe."

"You cannot be sure."

"*You* cannot be sure. This is my home."

"What if we passed them already?"

"Then we will see them when we turn back. Do you want to turn too soon? Retrace our tracks if they are just ahead? By the time we see our mistake, they will freeze. Better to go too far."

"If we approach from upwind, we cannot hear them."

"If we approach from downwind, they cannot hear us."

The two boys scanned the interior for signs of the terrain, but the shadows told more tricks than truth. "There may be tracks. If we cut back and forth—"

"There will not be tracks after this blow. Not in the dark."

Norwet ground his teeth. He was sure they had come far enough. But Milak was right. It would be their death if they turned back too soon. He simply climbed back on the sled. When the others blamed them for killing the Leopard Seal, he would at least plead he had argued for the true path. The dogs jerked into action, and they proceeded in the haunting calm. Every shake of the timber and crunch of the snow beneath a runner taunted him. He did not have the courage to insist on his way. He feared being wrong more than he did failing to find them. Norwet wondered how long he would let Milak have his way before insisting once more. He saw them in the spirit world, huddled on the brink, the team arriving at his own direction.

His focus was blasted as the wind returned in full fury when they passed a low cut from the ridge to their left. He had to hang on with blood-iced fingers, but maybe Milak knew the way, after all. He credited his cousin: there were no shouts of gloating. They pressed on. The dogs now fought to the right to turn a greater angle to the blasts. Twice, they became tangled and the boys had to pull them apart. Norwet got off and whipped them on while Milak pushed until they ran as one again, and he could retake the sled. Their speed crumbled. The chief dog was insistent in his path, and it was the best they could do to make some forward movement while he dragged right along a slope. Just as quickly as the wind had come back, it vanished, and the dogs trotted to a stop. Again, Norwet got off to urge them on, but this time they were outside themselves with frenzy. They leapt over the leads and spun to be free of him. The two farthest upslope began to fight, and it took both boys to pry them apart. Norwet had to grab the biggest by the nape and drag him forward again and again before they were finally underway.

The rest was due to a small knob of rock, a hundred feet or so, that rose of its own, cutting the wind into two tracks around it. When they came to the far side, Norwet realized why the dogs had risen against them. An eddy of snow swirled around itself, sending a whirlwind plume shining skyward on the far side, higher than the rock itself. The dogs again yipped and refused to budge, but this time, the boys made no effort to force them on. It was a jodvig, a terrible wind spirit that he had long heard of but never seen. Though it roared, they had not noticed its voice among the other winds, and the dogs alone had fought them off. If the sled had come too close, it could have been torn apart.

There was no discussion needed. Norwet and Milak fought the dogs back around. Once they were aimed at the left side of the rock, they hauled with gratitude. The wind came back as they cut the interior side, a smaller pass between a ridge and the rock home of the jodvig. They had to block their eyes as the blasts now took them dead in the face again. Milak took the sled through the narrow pass with skill, but Norwet could hardly hear his shouts to the dogs, even a foot away. Again, the lead dog left his sight. His lips cracked, and he had to peel away the frozen crust so often to take a breath that he just held one hand above his nose, wrapped in his sleeve. Milak's head knocked against the back of his. The driver was trying to use him as a wind-break. He turned to swear in protest, and when he faced forward again, something slapped across his face and stuck hard. Norwet let go of the sled to rip it free in a panic, and fell over the side. Milak saw him go and immediately turned over the sled to stop the team. Both boys would be needed to right it. Norwet peeled himself off the snow and leaned forward until he reached the others.

He clutched the thing that unseated him. It felt like soft leather. In the pale light, he unfolded the small, square-cornered sheet before him. He could not see the detail, but it was no article of clothing. Though Norwet did not have his letters, he knew them when he saw them, even by their faint shapes in the dark. The boys nearly leapt as they took to the sled again. The dogs disappeared into a shadow ahead, beneath the shining stars, and the wind that leapt from the black rock. Suddenly, the team stopped. Norwet swung his legs off and hustled to the dogs, intending to urge them forward. The wagging tails pounded against his leg when he bent to secure the lead. Only then did he see a muzzle buried with joy in the hands of Tunguk.

By the time Ostuk ordered them to oars just before sun-up, Foster had been awake for hours praying for light. They had no sleeping bags, and the winds of the previous night had sent them cuddling in vain against the shivers. Their feet and asses sat in water too shallow to bother bailing. While there were no waves to speak of, anchored on a shoal on the leeward side of the island, there was a terrifying moment past midnight when the insistent winds snapped the anchor line and set them adrift. The rowers had to quickly get them to deeper water, where they improvised a sea anchor out of one poor son of a bitch's pants. After that, Foster was unable to do more than nod off and jerk awake as his muscles spasmed for heat.

As soon as they took to the benches, he begged an oar just to get warm. His once-broken hand felt tender at first, but it was only the cold, and the anticipation of familiar pain. Once he settled in, all but his fingers and toes came to life over the next few hours as they fought a gentle crossing breeze to round the peninsula to the harbor. All he could do was brush aside thoughts of nights to come on the whaler, in the violent seas he'd sailed through once. The memory of the drowned-rat look of the warship's crew before they rescued them. Their ship would be bigger, but would it be any more suitable to human life? The call of the stroke and the curse of the man behind him when he lagged were enough to keep his mind returning to the task.

To his surprise, the harbor was a flurry of activity in the early dawn. Already there were two ships—"darraigs," he supposed—cutting wake, at times within pistol shot of shore. One alternated between short sprints and tight turns to a second sprint and turn before switching maneuvers with the other boat, which rowed ahead at speed, executed a full stop, switched the direction of the benches, and backed water as furiously as possible. They couldn't have been at it for long, but the men looked like zombies. It was obvious they needed the practice. Even without a clear idea of what the maneuvers were supposed to look like, Foster knew slop when he saw it. Nor did they bother to yield to the approaching darraig. Ostuk had to lay off, and time a run through their pattern when they rotated stations to make the landing.

The quay, too, was alive. Men added to a growing row of barrels and odd supplies that had not been there when they left. No sooner was one thing delivered than they would head off somewhere for the next load, while a contingent stood watch with spear and sword. Without clear uniforms, it was impossible to tell who they were from the water, but their guarded behavior made him think it was the crew of the whaler, which loitered nearby in dry dock.

They ran her aground and pushed her in. Polc gave Foster a polite dismissal from the chore. He took in the scene with his arms crossed tightly around his chest against the damp breeze. A dozen or so of Polc's men—the bunch that stayed behind—were already dispersing into the distance. Probably none too eager for their boss to put them to work. The pile of goods grew around him as he lingered. There were barrels and barrels—from little casks to great hardwood monsters, browned with some kind of sealant, filthy and gleaming with whatever cold grease had been smeared on top for waterproofing. It made handling them a struggle, with two men required even for the lighter ones. Fresh water, Foster assumed, though hasqa wouldn't surprise him. There were seal skin sacks, stuffed full and tied off. Ceramic jars, sealed with wax. None of it made him very confident. The mildest seas fouled so much of the whale meat, and the memory of the soaked and half-rotten chunks he fed to the dogs, and eventually the men as well, told him that the brine would find a way in, eventually. Then there were the rocks. Twenty-, fifty-, hundred-pound rocks manhandled from God-knew-where. That would be their ballast, even more so as the provisions dwindled. Each one was a small prayer against the western swell's ceaseless effort to swamp them. He wondered where people were supposed to sleep, or even where their feet would go, and shuddered to avoid considering it in any more detail.

"Cuttin' it close, aren't you, cunt?" Foster glanced up as Gionn let the big, smooth monstrosity he carried thud into the pile.

"Yo, if I were you, I'd crawl my ass out of here. Polc's right over there with two dozen of his closest friends."

"Good, I've been meanin' to have a word with Polc-y. Meantime, you still keen on tryin' a seat?"

Now, presented with the choice, a sudden resistance welled up in his throat. With a hard swallow, he managed an answer. "Yeah. Parks around?"

"He wouldn't be, would he?"

"Sorry, brother, I'm gettin' me and him on that ship. We sure appreciate you and all these other try-hards carryin' them rocks for us, though."

Gionn smirked. "Rock-choosin' is important work, you worm-puller. Not trusted to the likes of you."

It took a second to sink in. "Wait. Are you on?"

"Full-share, mate. Offered me double, but I didn't care to mark meself above the other bastards."

"How the fuck did you pull that off?"

"Oh, I've got quite the tale for you when the waves are crashin' and there's fuck-else to do. Me luck has delivered me from the brink as always. And if you're a bit more polite than your usual cunt self, I should be glad to put in a word for you in the trials, which you will notice have begun without you."

"All these dudes are tryin'?" Foster despaired at the dozens of men arranging the gear. "For one seat?"

"These are the crew, me son. Do you see the two squain lads over there waitin' for their pubes to bloom while that big cunt gives 'em an earful?" Foster had to scan back and forth before he spotted who he recognized as the whaler's captain, towering over two Mattaka boys in their early teens.

"Is that it?"

"If you don't hurry, it is. Good thing Polc showed up, or there'd be twelve of his boys makin' a run for it, as well."

"How many seats left?"

"Two."

"Two?"

"More than one and one less than three."

"But you're on."

"True. There was one, but there's wild rumors aboundin' that Costig aims to plant spies among the ranks to run the ship afoul. Corm's banned all Navy from the trials, and just this mornin' he dismissed three former blues under suspicion. Turns out one of the crew—handsome red cunt—seen 'em gathered in a late-night meetin' of hushed tones," he lowered his voice.

"Wouldn't that leave four seats?"

"I would, and did, until two were filled by Polc's carpenters. Worth more than a good sailor, those. Hope he don't run into a need for repairs on his return. So that leaves two, and he'll be tellin' those boys it's one so he can see 'em hustle."

"Then I'm gonna grab Parks."

Gionn placed a hand on his chest. "As I see it, you've got a pair of advantages. One: you're not a squain. Two: like meself, you've managed to run afoul of Costig, which is a better endorsement than any the crew could bestow."

"For goin' to Camne Drumlag?"

"You'll be under suspicion for knowledge of the prison break."

"What prison break?"

"I can explain, if you'd like to miss the trials and winter in this shithole whilst tryin' to avoid arrest."

"I ain't goin' nowhere without Parks."

Gionn pursed his lips in frustration. "Last I saw him, he wasn't in sea-shape."

"We'll see about that." He tried to take off, but Gionn grabbed him again.

"Thick cunt: those Marines over there have been waitin' for you. If you make it a fair number of yards from the crew of the whaler, you'll be arrested and questioned. Even if they let you go, it'll be too late to try the seat."

"Since when do you give a fuck?"

"If you don't come, I don't get paid," he whispered sternly.

"If Parks don't come, I don't come."

"We'll never get him to the harbor. And if we do, he'll die aboard within the week."

"I think you're full of shit." Foster looked over to the Marines, who turned quickly to chat among themselves.

"Corm!" Gionn shouted. He took Foster by the arm and drug him toward the captain and his two candidates. "This is the cunt I told you about."

Foster straightened up. "Pleased to meet you, sir." Gionn burst into exaggerated laughter, and Cormdran followed.

"Got a wit, don't he? He'll have you goin', here to Taclann."

"You're the one, then? Mates with the Leopard Seal?"

"I don't mate with him, no. And he's the only one calls himself that."

"Not anymore," Gionn grinned.

"But he's like a brother to me," he continued.

Cormdran mulled it over. "Half share."

"We'll take it," Gionn said.

"You can *try* with these lads for a half share. That's generous of me, given your circumstances."

"And my friend?"

"What about him?"

"He'll be wantin' a seat, too."

Cormdran laughed in his face. "You think I'm puttin' that cunt on me ship? I may as well paint me arse for Costig and bend over the quarter deck. Bad enough I got his associates. But you were at Camne Drumlag, and this one's a good liar."

"Aye, and we had no part in the affair, and know nothin' of his whereabouts."

"What the hell are yall on about?"

"Have you not heard, lad?"

"Heard what?"

They both waited for the other to speak, with Gionn finally giving in. "You want the bad, first? That's how I like it. I can tell you the good, though. Maybe we should start there, as it's the current situation. Although it's also bad if you have any interest in things workin' out over the long term. More like a brief lull in a massive gale of terrible developments."

"Just fuckin' tell me."

"Eh. While you were toodlin' about with the mercenaries, your mate managed to get himself arrested, sentenced to execution, break the prison, and disappear like a shade into the night. That first part is the bad news, by the way. The second I would say is good, for the time, but now every man on the island is after him, and we can't well ask Corm here to have a roust with the Navy over the hirin' of a fugitive, so looks like we'll just have to pour one out for him and make the best of it, you and I."

Foster's jaw clenched tight. It felt as though an invisible hand wrapped around his Adam's apple and held his throat in a tightening vice, as he stared past the others into the oblivion of the town. He'd set out hoping to return with some kind of favor from the assistant viceroy that would get the both of them out of here for good. Now he stood empty-handed and without the only unquestionable ally he had when he left. Any chance he had of getting them both on that ship had been torn from under him in his absence and despite all efforts to the contrary. The last time he stepped off a ship onto this port, he thought it a miserable setback—a temporary pit stop that they'd put behind them after a piss and a bite to eat. Every minute he spent here, this place seemed to sink its teeth deeper, like a steel trap around his leg. All this way. All this way, and this may yet be the last place he ever saw.

"But he's alive?"

"Far as we know," Gionn said.

Foster turned to Corm. "I appreciate you offerin' me a tryout. Me and my friend—my mate—we're a package deal. If he's here, so am I."

"You say it as if you have a choice," Gionn interjected.

"I don't. There's no choice. Me and Parks are a team."

"That's very noble of you, me son. Would he say the same of you?" Corm asked.

"He would."

"Then I'm afraid our red mate here is right."

Foster frowned. "I don't follow."

"Costig wants the whaler gone," Gionn explained. "He won't hassle crew."

"You walk a few yards that way," Corm tossed his head toward town, "there's nothin' I can do for you. You won't even make the tavern before you're arrested."

"I ain't done nothin'."

"You said yourself you're mates with the prisoner. You think he'll let you roam about? At best, you'll turn a blind eye to the Leopard Seal, and more likely aid him at every turn. Better to lock you up, try to bash loose a few rumors. Maybe get your lad to risk bustin' you out."

"I don't think the admiral would do that."

"He'd be a twat if he did anything else. It's your last days, me son. Spend 'em how you like. But if you're not tryin' the seat, you're not mine, and no one's but the fugitive's. You'll get a half share if you can beat these squains in a fair trial, and you'll thank me for it. Given your predicament, I ought to make you work for blubber." The boys looked at him pleadingly. He could feel them praying he would saunter off to jail in a fit of pride.

More than half of him thought Gionn was lying, and the captain in on it. What they described was a hostage situation, not a fair and honorable carriage of justice. But if it were true, he was stuck in the harbor either way. And he knew there was a second seat for Parks. The trick would be to convince Corm to take him. That, and how to even get word to his friend and smuggle him undetected to the ship. A pang rippled through him as the thought that they'd be leaving Tunguk and Kjartke for good once again surfaced and withdrew to the murky depths of his awareness, where he preferred it. It was going to be hard enough for him alone, much less both of them. Their Mattaka friends belonged here. He didn't like it, but he knew it.

"Alright."

Gionn lit up. "You'll have a go?"

"Like you said. Don't see as I have much choice."

"That's the spirit! Watch out for knives," he blurted out in front of the boys. "All these cunts are stabbers."

"I'll have no stabbin'," Corm growled. "Rixtan's got the harbor closed so's his men can slap oars together and call it rowin'. That means this will be an honest land trial. Right. None of you got the ropes, eh?" They all looked at each other, without reply. "I know you're smithies' boys," he addressed the Mattaka, then turned to Gionn. "Should have seen all the ones I sent off. None between eight and eighty, except the one old woman in the bunch!" He laughed. "What kind of work have you done, me son?" He asked Foster.

"I don't sail, but I do have experience—"

"Don't say it." Gionn cut him off.

"Say what?" Corm shot back.

"Ah, fuck. You've gone and made it worse." He held up a hand when Foster started to speak.

"What was he goin' to say?" Corm demanded.

Gionn sighed. "Dogs." Foster realized he was about to describe his dubious naval experience to someone who just banned all applicants with any such association from his ship. He hadn't made the connection that Corm might not distinguish between the Amposi Navy at Drummoc and the American carrier group. Gionn had.

"He worked the dogs down from Nunoc."

Cormdran grinned. "Is that it? That might be the one job lower than smith's apprentice." He shook his head in disbelief. "Well, whatever you done before, one of you son of a bitches is gonna be the richest metal-poundin' dog boy who ever took an oar, if you can hang on to Taclann—and survive a few things here and there. I don't think I need to explain what's at stake. None of you's fit for my crew, but I'll need a full complement if we're to make it. We *will* lose men. Probably you. If not, there's shares to be earned if you can take the slack. As for your trial, I don't care who you been or who you know. Only what you can do. What's the one thing every ship needs to sail? Ah!" He cut them off before they could open their mouths. "Don't guess. That's the first rule of me ship. If you don't know, and *know* you don't know, you'd better fist your mouth and finger your arse so I don't hear a fuckin' word out of either." Corm waited, but none of them dared a try.

"He among you who returns with the finest bucket I've ever laid eyes on will call himself crew by day's end." Corm glowered over them. "What the fuck are you starin' at me for? Do I look like a fuckin' bucket?" The two boys staggered back and sprinted off together toward the town. Foster weighed his options.

"If I go over thataway in the act of tryin' out for your ship, would they still arrest me?"

"Probably." Corm shrugged and stalked off toward his men.

"So I gotta find a *bucket*, that don't already belong to yall, just lyin' around the immediate area?"

"Not the worst thing I've ever done to get on board," Gionn said.

"Yeah, well, you've already noticed a few differences between me and you. For one, I don't like to abandon my friends high and dry. This is fuckin' stupid. I want to get home. If I gotta leave Parks to the wolves to do it, I'd just as well take my chances here."

"Have you already forgot the bit where you're arrested if you take ten paces from the harbor?"

"Maybe that's what I need. One way or the other, I gotta talk to Costig."

Gionn wrapped his arm around Foster in a squeeze that shielded them from the idle ears of the rest of the crew. "Mate, *who* has kept you alive this long, and will they be round to get you soon? I cannot fathom you've survived on your own wits. Costig has no use for you, or any of us, except on that whaler. We are quite the source of grief as it is, and the only reason he tolerates it is because he thinks we might still carry out his nefarious deeds. Do you really think he couldn't find an idiot like Parks on an island of shacks? He's makin' an enemy, and a very public one, because Costig has already decided who he wants to snuggle up to the assistant vicecunt. The blessin' is either way, we won't have to winter here, because if we stay to care for your sweetheart, all three of us'll be makin' the slow slide down a spear, and your squain mates, as well."

"Then you're gonna have to help me figure out a way to get him on the boat."

"No I won't. We'll meet him in the spring."

"You wanna sail all the way back down here?"

"Thick cunt. He can sail to us. Write the name of a town on something—somewhere far north of the Orin—and send it off with any of these mongrels. I assure you, one or all of them knows where he is."

Foster grinned and set a patronizing palm on Gionn's shoulder. "Son, you ain't learned a damn thing about me if you don't think I'ma have his ass on that whaler. Now if you'll excuse me, I gotta find a bucket."

"Good. Find yourself the finest bucket in Hiade. Then you'll have one thing you're good at, and whatever you're good at, you get to do for the rest of your life. Every time it's too stormy to hang an arse over the side, someone's gonna call for a bucket. Every time the bucket's full, someone's gotta empty it into the wind and the swell. Before long, your name'll be 'Bucket.' I'm already forgettin' what we used to call you."

He left Foster anchored alone, the men flowing around him on their way to drop off rocks and barrels, and head back empty-handed. It felt like a fair chance the cunt would do something stupid and he'd come back to find this, the latest bid for an extension of his breath, ruined upon some shallow pride. It didn't matter, though. His luck was with him. From crew, to mutineer, stranded, prisoner, fugitive, rower, spy, now crew again—and that, the most recent of them. Gionn didn't know if Foster was cut out for it, and he was certain Parks was not. But with them or without, and near or far beyond, his own fate was clear: he would not be long for the last place in the world.

"Polc, was it?" Gionn waited behind the keel of the forty-eight that had carried these men from some loyal harbor of Ampos to the Attavaik. He gave a pleasant wave and a nod. They'd finished stowing the darraig from the Camne Drumlag run, and the ones at his side lingered at first.

"Don't keep your thirst on my account," he shooed them off. "I'll find you at the tavern." Nearly the entire crew scrutinized him on the way by, though he refused to give them the courtesy of a look. At the least, they were aware of his face, and its place on the island would have found its way back to their captain at intervals.

"Gionn."

"I know you've had a long row in the service of the fellow with the droolin' accent, so I don't want to keep you. Just came to apologize, if I got off a bit rude when we first met. I was surprised to see you—given that we've never seen one another before, and all. Took me manners right out, and I hope you'll forgive me on account of the valuable information I've come to share." Now it was Polc's turn to forget his pleasantries. He waited with his hands cupped before him.

"I'm afraid you'll sail a few short in the spring. We just signed on both of your carpenters." Polc smiled and shook his head without a hint of surprise. "Further, it pains me to report that you've a number of disloyal cunts among your ranks. A good half the ones you left were in the pool this mornin', until they saw your sail."

"If they want to leave before they get paid, all the better for the rest of us."

"That's a good humor for it! Can't keep a man down who thinks that way. I just figured you'd like to hear, since me crew already outnumbered yours. Could ill-afford to lose more to me ranks. Already got fifty of the most seaworthy lads in the south."

"Do you count your Foster among them?"

"Aye, he don't look much, but I'd caution you not to short him."

"Short him? I'm terrified of the cunt. A man of letters with no apparent purpose to be in Hiade, keepin' with the likes of yourself? There's no way any good can come of that—least not my sort. You'll have all the berth you care from me."

"You're a fuck of a lot easier to talk to than I thought. I like the way you just give up. Here I was, pissin' meself the other night. Didn't even realize how pathetic your position was. If you'd have cut me down the moment you saw me, I'll admit I'd have been tossed."

"Figured as much. Would you believe the squain cunts I paid to stab you took me money and fucked off? Then I thought it was me luck when I seen you crawl out of the tavern with actual mates. Hadn't accounted for that. How'd you come by 'em? Anyhow, you're a chatty cunt. Chatty cunts chat."

"I did, eventually. Once I realized you'd only have a yarn with me if you thought an honest murder would come back on you."

"Call me a fool, but I'm glad it worked out that way. Isn't this much more pleasant for the both of us?"

"You are a fool, and a liar. If I cup your bollocks, will me palm come back wet?" Gionn reached a hand for his crotch. Polc slapped it away, and Gionn howled with delight. "Mate, do you know how good it feels to not be afraid? To have absolute power over your own fate, even for the briefest spell? That's when you really find out what a man's made of, when he can do whatever the fuck he wants without any personal consequence. I could say the word, and you'd be dead before you could say 'Hadalis!' If you pulled your sword, fifty of me newest brothers would be upon you, and if somehow you got to me, rest assured I have made accounts for that." Polc grinned, but Gionn saw through the threadbare courage. A real Polc smile would have bore those tiny little rat teeth he so despised, with their stupid spaces.

"Are you wonderin' why I haven't?" He stepped in. "'Is Gionn just tormentin' me before he rams one home? What has come over this mad cunt?'" Gionn paced off and took his time making his way back. "Aye, there's truth to it, but not the one you think. I do understand why you would think I might act as such, given half a chance. But there's the knot: half a chance, I've never had. In all your years of knowin' me—since we met a few days ago in the poorman's quarters—when have I had you as I do now? Have you ever once found yourself at me mercy?"

"You've made no waste of your opportunities to be a cunt."

"Aye, and if the worst man you've met was a mean cunt who called you mean names and roughed you up a little bit when you needed it, I'd say that's a fine life. Might trade you if I was offered. Not because there's anything I like about you. You were always me favorite, but it was because I enjoyed how pathetic you were. Never really felt threatened by you. What are your cunt brothers up to? Surely, you're the favored son, so it must be somethin' a far sight worse than Drummoc. Though I admit me sight don't stretch that far."

"I won't beg."

"Good, I hate beggars. All I want is that you ask yourself a question. 'Why in the round world would Gionn let me go?' That's what I'm doin', by the way. Uncut and unfucked. Free as an albatross to cross the seas. Why?"

"I don't fuckin' know."

"Because you've mistaken me. Your Gionn is quite the scoundrel. He'll be upset, that's for certain. Just waitin' for his chance to seize the slightest openin' to send you and yours under. A vengeful cunt. Full of the pride that'll carry a man to the nine shores. Lie-weaver, who'd sour your name. Thief, bent to take all that is yours. One who would murder your young, foul your streams, send you to flight, and follow you all your days until at last, with no place else to go, your Gionn would boot you over the side, and with great patience, watch you as you sank boatless to Manhas.

"Yet here I stand, and here I leave you to your affairs. If you choose to come after me, so be it. Do it knowin' that I'm without quarrel. That had I any sense or ambition to live, I'd make this day your last. I'm tired, cunt. Go away! Go, and leave me be. I'm willin' to pass on a clean stroke in the dim hope that it finally occurs to you we have nothin' the other wants." Gionn leaned so close that his breath fell hot on Polc's cheek. "So if you live to see your cunt brothers, you make sure to tell them I had me tip in you," he grabbed a firm handful of Polc's backside. "And I sheathed me blade."

For the second time, Norwet's head bobbed back and struck her on the spot where Brother had split her lip. Kjartke winced, and tasted fresh blood, but she said nothing. Nor did he excuse himself. She did not care to renew the battle from before they left. The only way for both of them to fit on the sled was for one to sit between the legs of the other. Norwet insisted that a man does not lean on a woman. Kjartke agreed, and added that a woman does not lean on a boy. They fought with the tired spirit of two who had not slept, until Tunguk interrupted: "Norwet…" He did not need to say more. The boy let his protests slump with his shoulders. Now Milak drove them as fast as the dogs could carry, from the new site toward the edge of the drift. It was only a few short miles from the dog camp, but they could afford no delay in getting the poye.

Brother, for the time, was alive. The team nearly drove past them, but for the wind taking the map from Tunguk's feeble grip as he tried to bind it over Brother's toes to replace the missing right boot, a gesture against the cold. It horrified her the way the animals crowded around her and Parks, tails slapping, brushing, tongues pulsing between their vile teeth. Their arrival brought him to life, and he managed more words for the dogs than he had since they found him. Kjartke tolerated it when he scooped one onto his chest and held it for warmth while the others sniffed them and lifted their paws onto her back to peer over.

It took the boys what seemed half the night to erect the tukit. They complained the bones were not familiar. The structure collapsed twice after much time spent binding the frozen straps with frozen fingers. They raised it right over the sled where Brother lay, and after a fight with the wind, the seal skins were secured over the ribs of whale, and they all piled inside. Even the favored dog was allowed to stay. With no time to make a good effort of it, the air drafted under the tails all night, and there was no room to turn, but they had come with blankets to place on top the snow. With water and seal meat, seal fat. She put globs of it on her finger and wiped them off in his mouth, forced him to swallow, and rubbed more in the wound.

By the time the sun returned, their bodies had warmed the tukit so that none desired to leave. It was Tunguk who urged them to their feet. The place they stayed was too far. Too cold. They could not remain. He gave Milak exact directions, and the sled carried her and Brother to a place well-off the trail, nestled in tall rock out of the wind, a few miles from the dog camp. Meanwhile Tunguk and Norwet disassembled the tukit, and Milak went back for the shelter and the others. Again, it rose over Brother, who slept a fevered rest, mumbling, snoring, rippling with chills. The boys had done well, though it was not their place to remain. They left Tunguk along with Brother. He would not move again unless under his own power. At least he was near enough to town that she might get the poye and return without the help of the kaim.

At first, the boy's shoulders had been stiff as he gripped the sides to hold himself steady over the trail. Now, they settled heavy on her breast. His head bobbed in and out of sleep. She did not know how he could drift off. The speed of the sled, the power of the team that courses through every joint of the sled so that it came alive. The trail, turning to slush on the top and splattering them with every bump. As much as she despised the dogs, the way they bore her along like some spirit who rode on the back of its beast made her come alive. It was told among her clan—long before she lay eyes on one—that the best dogs would return as Kammatuk, and the worst Kammatuk as dogs. She wondered which of these six had walked these trails on two feet, too thick to learn their own limits while they cinched tighter and tighter, until they became a hide of fur, a sharp mouth, and a lead that carried its burden. Would these soon stand where Milak held the reins? In their first pass, they would likely be those who worked with dogs, and dogs would be a better friend to them than men.

Norwet's head just missed her, and she cradled it to her shoulder until he succumbed. These two—their brothers—would be in the greatest danger of rejoining the teams, here from their narrow foothold among the people. They were doing well. But it was wrong of Tunguk to involve them. To work a sled, haul firestone, it was safe enough. The dog families were too poor to get in much trouble. Here, she saw they had a fine chance to travel well beyond the others, perhaps beyond the Kammatuk altogether. Alongside it was a great danger, though. There were many ways for them to venture beyond their strength as men, among the Tunguks. The Leopard Seals. They walked astride a steep ridge. She asked Tawaket that their footing be true.

When the sled scraped to a halt, she woke Norwet by pushing him into the snow. Ahead, the powder became ice, and the ice too thin for the runners. By midwinter it would extend to the coast, but for now, she had maybe two miles on foot to reach Drummoc.

"Will you wait for me to come with the Poye?" She asked Milak. His eyes lowered. "It will be fast on the sled. She will not want to come so far."

"My father waits for the dogs." He did not need to say more. She knew the sled would be gone, now and for good. Kjartke turned to town without acknowledgment and parted from the dog boys. Her feet tingled on the hard rock. It was a feeling she had known before. The frost had not taken them, but it would be some time before the warmth returned, and every step until then would be as on shards.

There was a sentry near the foot of Tannavin, a few hundred yards away from her approach. They made no secret of staring at one another as she passed into the back row of tukits. It would be common to see Mattaka returning as the sun dipped, but not so early. The feeling of unease hit her with delay, like a sound that arrives from a distance after one sees the thing that sent it. The admiral would have posted him to see if anyone traveled to the interior in a suspicious way. There was no way to avoid being seen, either then or when she returned with the poye.

Kjartke did not understand the story, but she knew it was the admiral who helped them get Brother. There was an agreement among the men they did not share with her, and it made her angry. It seemed that she was part of a dance in which she was not allowed to know the steps as the others did, yet expected to perform as well. She knew only that they danced for the Navy and the Kammatuk alike, and the price of a mistake was clear. Was the man who saw her a trusted friend who would let her come and go according to the admiral's wishes? Or would there be others waiting when she returned? Her spear was back with Tunguk, so it would be difficult to kill him, and it would bring a passion to their search that they could ill afford. This was the very thin thread that must hold if they were to come with help, and with food when the gifts of the boys ran out. A single armed guard could keep them to the wilderness until they all died. She was no hunter, and though Tunguk had killed plenty of game, that was not the Tunguk who waited for her.

Within the tight curves of the tukits, she felt a security wrap around her. All clans put their tukits close, but only the Kammatuk had so many, and made of stone, at that. It was a people anchored to this place. They had forgotten how to move. Beyond the walls on all sides—the harbor, the coast, the island itself—even these places were not their home. The King of Ampos held all but this island of stone lumps, and here even he feared to tread except in force. She ducked into the home of Ostuk. There was nothing there she needed, but she listened in the dark for a moment until she was certain that Foster had not returned.

The brothels of Drummoc huddled just behind the buildings of the main street, close enough that any man with a little hasqa would brave a walk. Here, the lanes were safer than anywhere else, she was told. The Mattaka did not tolerate crime against the patrons, and it was the only place beyond the warehouses and the quarters that the Navy would protect. There was no central building. The tukits looked like any other, except that all bore the mark somewhere low on the outside wall.

A halot appeared from the door in front of her, and they blocked one another's path. She stepped back and leaned against a wall. He smiled as he passed. She averted her eyes to the ground. There was no way to tell which one the poye kept, so she stood outside the one the man had left and called in Mattakatan. After a polite pause, a woman emerged, the age of her mother. She took in Kjartke's wind-burnt face, the wet and the matte of travel on her clothes and hair.

"Can you tell me where to find the poye?"

The woman led without a word. They rounded three more tukits and veered hard toward the street and back around in a hook. She listened for a time, then raised her voice through the skin that covered the door. "Nante! A girl to see you."

Kjartke did not like being called a girl, but she thanked the woman, who wandered off before an answer came. The cover brushed aside and a head of black hair stooped out, and seemed to not stand up all the way. Her tired eyes blinked before she realized it was a girl of ten or twelve, before her womanhood. A shudder washed through her as she wondered what one so young was doing here. Then it occurred to her, in the way that she had expected to see someone else.

"Are you…the poye?"

A hearty cackle rolled out just before an older woman joined them. Her hair was ash gray, tied back in a single tight braid streaked with silver strands, that fell to the back of her legs. The top row of bead and oblong bone peered out over her tunic, what must have been a sapak, but the poyes of her people did not ornament themselves in this way, and she thought that not even the Kammatuk would do so.

"Does your clan have poye so young?" The older woman asked.

Kjartke shook her head. "Maybe Kammatuk do." After she spoke, Kjartke realized it would seem an insult, but the woman just snorted.

"My granddaughter will be a poye. It is much to learn." The girl leaned toward her leg.

"Apologies, Nante."

The woman waved a hand. "You have come a long way, Jargadakne. Will you work for me, or I for you?"

Kjartke gathered her wits and scrambled for the story she repeated to herself during the long walk. "My husband is hurt. Hunting. He is hurt hunting."

The poye waited, expecting her to finish. "You may bring him to me."

She shook her head. "It is far. He cannot walk. My grandfather. I left him with my grandfather." Kjartke began to find her step. "He said I must hurry."

"What is his wound?"

"He is cut on his leg."

"Far from here?" Nante looked at the state of her clothing. Kjartke nodded. "He should tie it and walk."

"He cannot walk.

"I do not like to go far. You can have some men help him."

"It is bad. Grandfather said to tell you the wound stinks."

"When was he hurt?"

"Before the night."

"The wound should not stink so soon."

"It was a spear. Foul from seal."

"Even so, it will not stink so soon."

"Please. He had to sleep exposed before we found him. Now the frost has bitten him."

The poye looked at her apprentice. "What do you say, Hastate?"

The little girl wrinkled her nose at Kjartke. "If it is fresh, it would not stink. We could give him a poultice."

"Aye, I agree. There is a man who keeps dogs beyond the town. Sawipelagannapuk. You must go to him and ask for a sled. He will help you."

Kjartke opened her mouth in frustration then clamped it and composed herself. "Please! He is in fever. And he is a big man. We cannot move him over rock. He will die if you do not come."

The poye sighed. "What can you pay?" Kjartke froze. "If you cannot, you can work." She bit her lip, and shook her head. "You will not work for your husband?"

"He will not allow it."

"If he dies, as you say, you will have to, regardless."

"I will find a new one," she said too eagerly.

"Where will you live while you look? Who will feed you?"

"How much do you ask?"

"It depends on how you work. Could be a few weeks—"

"If we pay."

The poye gave it some thought. "A silver. Or a silver's worth of trade." One silver did not sound like much to Kjartke, but her people did not deal in coin. She knew there was copper, silver, gold. She had never held any of them in her hand. The poye took her delay for hesitance. "It is for my cost, and the surgeon."

"Surgeon?" It must have been more than she expected, if it paid two.

"If the wound is as you say—if it is beyond my medicine—we will have to send for him. It will be too long. He will come with us."

She nodded. "We will pay the silver."

"Before we go."

Her chin lifted and her eyebrows raised in a pout before she caught herself and folded it into a stern scowl.

"I did not think you had it. It is well. We will not go until dark. It is time enough if you must gather it."

"Dark? He cannot wait until dark."

"Then he will die," she shrugged. Kjartke started to speak but the old woman raised her hand. "You think I cheat you. Make you pay a great sum. It is a lie, though you would cheat me. I ask a small price. It is you who asks too much. Great danger! The town is watched, and there are many here who need me," she stroked Hastate's straight black hair. "A silver is nothing if we do not return. You bring it, I will help you. Not because it is fair. Because you have a rude courage. That, I like. You may work for me yet," she wagged her finger. "Bring me my silver, daughter." The poye turned and ushered her grandchild into the tukit. She started in after her, then raised her head. "I am curious to meet the Leopard Seal."

Milak emerged first from the tukit, his chin sunk in his chest as he shuffled through the fresh snow blown in the night before. The other boys slowed their work to steal glances. They expected to see a broken mess. As the oldest boy of Sawipelagannapuk, he was most to blame, even more than Norwet, and Norwet had already taken his due like the proud Vjarku that his father, his older brothers would have expected. Sawi was proud of him in their place, though he did not show the boy. Now Milak joined the others, and Sawi could see they were surprised to see him again so soon. In part, it was that the sled and the team returned intact. In part, the work before them. But he worried he may have set a light example. Norwet in particular watched him closely, no doubt weighing whether Milak had received less than he.

The younger boys had been digging since first light, clearing the snow from the stockpiles of sleds and tukits. When he woke, he found one that held the trail tukits excavated. They claimed they were searching for a better sled, and did not know which held what, but Sawi suspected a tukit was missing. He did not even know how many he had, but it seemed a fine punishment to have them dig out all of the material he would soon need for the firestone run. To count it, check it, mend it, put it all in order. Normally he would not start so early, but this season much had changed. The *Kurrhatetgiuk* was many months late from Nunoc. Even the word "late" sat like a stubborn lump in his throat. It was a hopeful word, for he knew there was nowhere to stop in between, and few places a wreck could even find shore. And if it had, starvation and exposure were as like to have finished what drowning could not. Many old stories protested, though. In his father's time, there was a merchant thought lost for a year and a half, until a Navy ship desperate to find fresh water stumbled upon the survivors—more than half the crew. And much earlier, it was told that a whaler was missing three years before they rowed into port at Nunoc, having been trapped by the ice for two winters and sheltering under the overturned hull, dancing floe to floe ahead of Alutjake's grip.

Most did not share his hope. It was a thin thread between two fingers by which they might return. One that vanished into the cloud-crowned swell. Yet he held it and would not relinquish it so easily. Whatever the fate of those aboard the *Kurrhatetgiuk*, it was certain that the season's work would be done with far fewer dogs, and with the death of the Vjarku boys' father on Nunoc, the family reins would be held by much smaller hands—Seleku and Vjarku, alike.

The routine of seasons past was replaced by a tension that hung about the entire camp, and he had not felt such urgency, such weight since his first run after his father departed for Urkuk. There were men left, of course, but today belonged to the boys and their tired feet, their bruised fists and faces. It did not sit well that they thought him a fool. All in Drummoc knew that the Leopard Seal freed a number of children, though if they knew who, they had the courtesy not to say. Now they stole from him. They questioned if it was too early to prepare the equipment when he set them to it. What nagged at him was that it should always be done so soon, with such vigor, but none expected Sawipelagannapuk to stir from his slumber until the opportune time had passed. It was as though he walked in his sleep, and at last blinked and found himself in a place he remembered through a thin fog, his movement clumsy, his bark unsure of itself. The morning's hasqa coursed through his veins and made them tingle warm. His sight was light and disconnected. Everything took an extra moment. It was not his way, and had not been for some time. In the crisp air, there was an immediacy that frightened him. Where his memory failed him, left him hesitant, he could not help but wonder if he ever knew at all, or if he must now learn for the first time.

His foot tapped the lip of ice into the track of the runners that stretched up the bowl toward town, one beside the other. If he walked them soon, he would find the place the boys' stories turned their own way, for these were the only tracks they agreed upon—that they returned after bringing their passengers as far as the snow would take them. Norwet's tracks left the foot of Urkuk at first light, and carried three: himself, Tunguk, and Kjartke under Milak's rein, from where they found them the night before. The prisoner was missing. Norwet thought him clever, but Milak thought him dead—those were the words of Norwet. Sawi knew it was his story that Milak repeated. If they argued on what to tell him, the oldest boy chose. His own son knew the terrain almost as well as he did.

Sawi squinted up at the bright spot in the clouds. It took them some time if they left at first light and did not stop. The dogs would make good ground, from deep in the island if they ran as first claimed. The tale did not last long when it was Milak's turn in the tukit. He knew there was too much light to account for. His tracks did not start as far away, and after they brought Kjartke and Norwet to the rock, they doubled back for Tunguk and the Leopard Seal. He would be well-hidden by now in the tukits of Drummoc, wagering the Navy would not search again so easily. This, Sawi accepted. At least until Milak had taken up a shovel with the others. Both of them worked hard for ones who had spent the night exposed, huddled among dogs. And the dogs were not so tired as Sawi would expect. The light and the land would tell how far a team could travel, but the wag of tongue and tail how much they did.

He watched his son—his oldest son, if no word came of the *Kurrhatet-giuk*—pull broken sleds with his brothers. They were not men, yet. Not like Gilak and Eurak. None could remember when the Seleku took up their trade. It was said within the family that they came from Matjese with the dogs themselves, the ancestral keepers. The miners whispered it was the dogs who birthed them. Gilak and Eurak would not have harnessed their dogs to the ruin-bringer, nor would his daughter, Tailesepne. From miners' sons, he would expect this. They had little to do while their fathers toiled but to wield their knives and dream of a swift death across the seas. Sawi did not blame them. Any fate was better than a life in the mine. He could not grasp why it was the dog keepers who were held so low. They at least worked beside their fathers, where foolish spirits could not get to them. It was the open air for them, two short seasons of work. They were the veins through which the black blood of Drummoc flowed, and without them, the heart of this place would cease to beat. There was no mine without dogs, though none would thank them for it.

Arnake and Ravitak tossed another sled into the pile beyond repair. It stood to his chest beside a small row of good haulers. The last run had not been any harder than usual, but now he regretted his customary rush to throw them in stores as they returned, to be repaired later. There were parts enough here to build a few new sleds, and because he pulled them unusually early, there was also time. Sawi shuddered to think what would have happened if he had delayed. Regardless, he would need plenty of good sled wood from Ampos in the spring. Even if a siege did not hold it up, he was not sure he could afford it. The firestone would have to make it out through the same, and without the dogs he expected from the *Kurrhatetgiuk*, he was at least 100 short, before the problem of good drivers was even considered. These same boys who brought the Navy to his camp would have to work the sleds he could piece together with the dogs he could muster. It was hard to see how they could move enough to earn what they needed to even pay the extra drivers both now and for the spring load, much less have the profit for sled wood. And there would not be as many dogs to spare the Vjarku in Nunoc, either—again, if the two dog ships that remained were not besieged.

Some of it was simply handled rough by the Navy when they shook things loose from his storage tukits, looking for the prisoner. There was so much, packed so tight, they gave up. It was not possible for a man to hide behind such a tangle of wood and leather. At least, Sawi thought not. He remembered the visit from Tunguk—he let them alone without a care as to why. Now he cursed himself for his stupidity, though he could not have expected these children would have some part in such a thing. He scrutinized the way they acted when they pulled something. Did they hesitate? Did they linger, or take extra care? Now he was not so sure. The morning the Navy searched, they all behaved so strange. He could feel their unease, see the looks they stole one another, hear the sharp whispers. It was not the fear the rest of the family felt. There were things here the Navy should not see. A dog man could not live by dogs, alone.

Beyond the camp, there was no place a man could live. If the Leopard Seal fled to the wilderness, he was dead, or he would have to return. Milak would have him believe it was so. Sawi scanned his tukits as a bird scans the sea for a meal just beneath the surface. If he could not come back to Drummoc, this was the only place he could shelter. If he was found beyond, it would be assumed that he had support from the Seleku. How else would he receive food and supplies? It was good the equipment would be ready early, even if it meant facing the stark inadequacy of it. At some point, the Navy may return for a more thorough search, and Sawi wanted to know before then what, and who, he called his own.

He thought again of the light, and the way a team runs when it knows it's coming home. His vision raced with the possibilities of what they might carry, how far, how fast, and he followed the runner tracks as they crossed in the spirit world. There were Norwet's, there were Milak's. Then the others that disagreed with both, woven through the snow like a basket. All of them lies but one.

Sawi returned dizzied to the place he stood. He widened his stance, placing a foot in each of the sled tracks. They pointed his chest to the western side of the bowl, to Drummoc. He switched his feet, and now he looked over his camp again. The women at their work, the boys at their work, the men waiting somewhere for the worst to be done, a warm jug between them. How he craved to join them. It was difficult to think of the season ahead. It was like a lie no story could explain away, no matter how bad he wanted to believe it: a family that made it through. A good haul, new sleds, new children, and children's children. The Seleku, as always, behind the dogs and the pulse of the Mattaka.

He stepped out of the shallow ruts and faced the mountain, obscure behind the top of the ridge. Sawi wondered again if he was not missing a trail tukit.

Husband. Kjartke was ashamed to call him that, even in a lie. Now it had hold of her, the way a lie hooks into the flesh and tears at it as one tries to pull free. She knew it was not her husband who would die if she did not return, but it gnawed at her as though it was, as many times as she brushed it aside. Her husband, the Leopard Seal. He now lived in the spirit world with the real Brother, because it was a good lie, and she told it with passion. Birthed him into being where he could cause her grief, like her other husbands. Parnakvanuk, who fought with honor when the people of Klimut came. Klimut, who she hoped suffered much before his end. Now this one, a false husband, no better fated than the others. It was becoming a respectable curse to marry Kjartke, daughter of Oljarbaruk.

She closed her eyes, though it made no difference in the pristine dark of Ostuk's home, empty of all the men who carried her here. A flood of old voices competed for her attention. Foster with his doting, the senseless jokes of Brother. Deeper ones, farther down and pressing to the surface before rolling away again where she kept them. Her father had something to say, but she clenched in the way she had learned to silence what nagged her. He pushed back, though, and she gritted her teeth harder. The pressure rose in her ears until finally they all gave up at once to a ringing quiet.

Tunguk pulled back the flap, and her eyes adjusted. She knew he would not enter a dwelling when a woman was alone. He hoped she would come outside to speak, so she let him wait without acknowledgment. He had the patience of an old man. It was a very long time before he tired of her, and said through the door, "Klimut will die soon."

It should have been a relief. What was the use of it, though? She looked at her son, asleep on a hide beside her. It was a husband who provided for his wife, and it would be some time before the boy could do the same for his mother. If no one came in search of wives, or food, or the few things the clan could carry.

"I will not tell if you smile." It was all she could do to keep her mouth from twisting at his joke. No man of the clan would say such a thing. She despised him, because he was here when she arrived, and so was one of them, but without the honor of the people. And she was still upset with the way he disarmed her so easily. But now Kjartke had to admit she enjoyed the trouble he made for these people. The blood he spilled. It annoyed her that he overtook her when they tried to flee, but she had to admit he should have killed her, and did not. It was too much to like the man. Though now she knew him to be just as outside as herself, and there was a strange kinship to it.

Tunguk followed her gaze to the child. "He is Kapadak. These people will see to you. You can live as a widow. There are none who need a wife, but if it happens, you will be a good choice."

It was true. A good choice for someone else. This clan was now as weak as her own was. Mostly old men, except Kullunuk and Rumit. Either would be kinder than Klimut, but though their wives hated her, she did not care to spend her years praying for the women's deaths. What fight could these people give if others came, as they had to her camp? Klimut's son was not her own. She carried him, but he could be torn from her arms just the same. If he was not, he would need a wife himself one day, and it was likely he should have to do as his father to find one. It was less than two days that she had lived with them, yet for all the talk of the other Kapadak clans, Kjartke had not seen one. And that, only if he planned to stay with his kin, raise his family in the ways. Many young men now chose the wooden wife, a more vile fate even than to take up with the Kammatuk. If she held him long enough, would this boy of no father remain to help his old mother, of no standing? Or would he be gone as soon as he could steady his feet upon a deck?

"Why have you come?"

"To bring you these words."

"Any could have done it."

"But then you would have to mourn for them." When she did not answer, he said, "Listen to the voice of an old man, child. This is the last time you will have to hear it."

"Good."

Tunguk started to close the flap. "Where will you go?" He paused.

"I will take them to Nunoc. When I have found them passage north, they will be beyond my help. It is not required of akmanuak that I hold them prisoner."

"Ingut will give you a boat?"

"I may choose my boat."

"It is far. I think you will not make it."

"Make it or not, I have not-far to go."

"Hm!" She made eye contact for the first time. "Will you ask?"

"Ask what?"

"For someone to clean your kills. Stitch your clothing. Grease your hull. Repair your weapons."

"I know all of these things."

"Then you are here to be kind?"

"That one, I am still learning." Kjartke nodded. "Nunoc is no place for you, and I could not ask a mother to leave her son. Besides, I think you would find these men a nuisance."

"I find many men a nuisance. In Nunoc, at least I would pick the nuisance."

"You think there is a husband for you there?"

"Maybe. Or work."

Tunguk chuckled. "You have not been to Nunoc, then."

"I have heard enough."

"No. I care nothing for you, Kjartkene. I would still never let you work at Nunoc."

"It cannot be worse than to live among my enemy."

"You are a girl of the arm, and what stories you hear beyond its islands call you to the rocks."

"If you know these things better than I, how can you be so noble to steer me from them?"

"Noble?" Tunguk laughed. "I say only there are better brothels than Nunoc." She blushed at the outward mention of the word. "If that is your wish, Drummoc is a better place for you."

"Drummoc?" She was in disbelief that he could even mention the place. For the Jargadak, it was no less than a descent to the underworld, and none would make it any sooner than they had to. "Is Nunoc not the finer port?"

"Much finer. It is ruled by a fine viceroy, and a fine Navy, and they have a fine power over the people there. There is much traffic for a brothel girl to earn a living. Maybe that is why women do not last so long. The poyes of Drummoc take more care with their own. There are no fine officials. You have heard the difficulty of the people there. You have not heard that their homes are their own. Their town is still sacred. What the Navy dares in Nunoc, they do not in Drummoc. It is very far. Too few in the winter. They cannot be as cruel as they would like. In Nunoc, a woman lies with sailors who will never show their face again. In Drummoc, it is those, but it is Mattaka, too. They are treated differently."

Kjartke's face burned hot with embarrassment. In her two days in this place she had not said so many words to this man as now, and his courage to speak so insulted her. "What does it matter? You are going to Nunoc. And I do not care to come."

"It is true, Nunoc is much easier to find a ship north. If I tell them this, they will want to go to Nunoc." He paused and let it sink in.

"Why would you help me?" Kjartke blurted.

Tunguk smiled. "I promise that you will not thank me."

She opened her eyes to the rustle of the door flap in the breeze, pulsing between dark and the thin slit of light that tried to nose in underneath. There was a strange peace to it. It had been so long since the men were gone. There were moments to herself, of course. But always with their needs hanging like a shadow. Brother's face flitted across her vision like a bird, reminding her it was still the case. This was different, though. Tunguk said himself her obligation was paid. Drummoc. The name brought her disbelief. It was a foreign word to her when she set out. An impossible place. Now here she was, and sooner than expected. It was these walls, and beyond the walls, all around her. She had arrived, and there was nothing her father could ask of her. Nothing Parnakvanuk could ask of her. Or Klimut. Foster. Brother. Tunguk. When she left her second son with the women and stepped aboard the boat, she realized that no part of her thought she would one day sit here. It was Urkuk she fled to, not Drummoc.

There was no grief for the boy. No time for it. Someone always needed meat trimmed, or a tunic mended. They needed her to paddle, to hold a spear as though she would save their lives. They needed her to be quiet while they schemed, because they needed to believe the things they said. It was hard enough to hope to reach this place without a woman making questions of the matter. There was no moment she could spare to think of Refetkut—his name only just earned before she left, according to the tradition whereby they waited for his character to reveal what he would be called. Though she had little to say, in the spirit world there was no quiet.

Now, she heard once more the splash for her first son, who had no name, and she looked up again at Klimut, whose eyes bore into her. She knew he waited for her to wail, to tear at him, to run toward the water so he could take her in his one hateful arm and carry her away. Her lips tightened with Jargadak strength, as she determined that nothing he wanted would ever come from them. Kjartke held his eyes. She did not run. What moved over his face was the finest blow anyone dealt to the Kapadak that day. Then she followed him when he turned for the boats.

It was a blessing there was no time then, either. A wife had much to do, and she did it all as well as she could, so that none could say she was bitter, or derelict in her work. Never did she fight over it, or criticize, because he expected it of her. Yet never did she give more than was necessary, or give it with love. She only stayed busy, so that again there was no quiet. It was almost worse with Brother and Foster. Too often, they spoke at her, and expected to hear in return. Her sharp tongue slipped a few times, and with it her strength, which she gathered behind her setu—the marks a Jargadak girl received around her mouth when she reached womanhood. But she found herself, and held it until it returned.

This was why. A wise woman did not waste herself in futile battles the way a man does. When all was lost, and lost again, she held it. There was no hope of anything when her father was slain. No hope of anything when she left Refetkut. Still, she held it, and let six hundred waves rise and fall. Let the men slash at one another, flail for ropes, and pull against their bonds. Without a word, she remained, until all of it passed—gale to the west, mighty spear to death or wilderness. This was why. She sat alone in a stone tukit, one with a window. Beyond it was Drummoc, where a man could ask, but Kjartke, daughter of Oljarbaruk, need not give. There was nothing else to do. For the first time she could remember, maybe the first time, her world fell quiet.

Her chin grew hot. She realized she was holding her breath, and drank deep of the cold must. There was the sound of water, the feeling of a slow rise, as with a swelling wave born across the deep when after a lifetime driven before the wind, it feels the seabed beneath it and rears in anticipation. Her blood churned and foamed. All at once, they began to speak to her so their voices mingled like roaring surf. Her lips quivered, and the salt burn washed her eyes. She thought to press it back, and immediately felt ill. She knew she had lost, and she did not care.

Kjartke snatched a fur seal blanket and clamped it over her face. A scream that she did not know she could make issued forth in a blast that felt it would never end. Tiny and muffled to her ears, her body reverberated like a cliff pounded by a storm. She ran out of breath and drew the blanket back just enough to gasp, then followed with another. By the time it faded, silver light danced before her across the walls and her throat throbbed raw. Her chest heaved for air. She squeezed her eyelids shut to force the rest of the water out and over her cheeks and tried to blink it away. As she struggled to breathe, she forgot first her people and their stories. The place she came from. The place she sat. Her own name vanished, and she became the rise and fall of her body, the wet and the cold on her skin. They wrapped around her and gave her comfort. For a while, the bare senses remained with her, and it pleased her. But before long, there came a voice so small it was felt rather than heard. "*Kjartkene.*" It felt as though it was addressed to another. Then she knew the other as herself. It did not repeat, but in the spirit world she said it back, and slowly became aware that she carried this sound as she carried her setu for all to see. She remembered the tukit of Ostuk, and it rose up around her, followed by the homes of Drummoc and the ships drying in the Autumn breeze. Ajatse took her to her breast, and did no more for her. One by one, people came to pay their respects. First was Oljarbaruk, in front of whom she felt shame. If he was unhappy with her, he did not let on. Then her first husband, and her second. The people of their clans. Two boys. At last she could look upon them, and only now realized it had been some time before she dared to see their faces. None of them had a word for her, nor did she feel she held a word away from them. Their presence was good. It was short, and neither was upset to see it pass in turn to the next. A dog came to her and licked her outstretched hand, and it did not bother her. She recognized the mother from Nunoc, her chest fur stained pink. Then a tukit of skin rippled on the snow plain. Tunguk and Brother waited. They did not know if she would return, and they were neither hopeful nor angry. Beside her he stood, a giant of a pink-fleshed man in full health: the Leopard Seal.

"You know your husband's there."

Kjartke smirked. "He is not my husband."

"Then he won't mind if you put in a little work for the poye. Little this for a little that."

"I cannot."

"Who forbids it?"

"It is not the way of my people."

The Leopard Seal scanned the empty plain blown by white dust. "What people?"

Kjartke straightened up. "I am of the Jargadak Mattaka."

He repeated himself. "What people?" The two of them watched the tukit roll across the ribs that held it together. "Those women at the whale? You could have gone with them. You came here with us."

"Not with you. With them," she nodded to where Tunguk and Brother sheltered. "He is not you."

"He might be."

"No. You are a spirit. Not of our world. They think you are Leopard Seal. I know he is Brother. They think you freed yourself from the prison and escaped the admiral."

"Didn't I?"

"I opened the door. Tunguk—" she corrected herself, "opened the door. We carried a weak man, who the admiral never sought, and now he dies."

"Then why'd you help him?" She did not know how to respond. "You came all the way to Drummoc to be a whore. You risked your life to save a criminal. Now you won't do either." When she opened her mouth to protest, the Leopard Seal vanished. His voice rang across the plain in one of his terrible songs: "Kjartke, Kjartke, all alone. Where have all her people gone?"

Her eyes snapped open in Ostuk's tukit. She flung the blanket aside and crawled for the door, desperate for a breath of fresh air and the sting of light. It greeted her with the intensity she remembered as one emerges after a long winter storm in the short hours of sun, where the senses return with such force they take a woman's feet from her. Kjartke leaned against the wall in front of her while her eyes adjusted and her breath slowed to the cool, clean air.

She picked her way through the lanes without knowing where she intended to go. Every bend and every jagged stone came alive for her, and where it met sky, it glimmered. The whole town bore the dry crack of lips after a cold wind as they begged again for moisture. A feeling of disorientation hung about her. She was not lost. It was only here that she could think of. Everything before her was crisp. Familiar, and confiding new detail she had not seen before. At the same time, she could summon no thought that was not apparent. They hung out of sight, and she knew they were there, but Kjartke could not find the faces, the names. The place she was going. Only that which was before her. It was a light feeling, as though her feet barely touched the ground, her fingers barely brushed the walls. Nor did she fear she had forgotten. She knew she had not. For once, the spirits had left her to herself, and Drummoc did not seem a distant, terrible place. The stark gray lit up—there were six hundred grays, and in each little dashes of color—all the colors the gods had given. There was no danger that pressed her on, or hope that pulled her forward. Only the momentum of the lanes themselves, now widening and drawing in people from the tributaries. Old women, groups of boys. A man of Ampos passed, like a sea bird before the shore is sighted. The first flutter of recognition. She found herself standing before a tukit. Then she knew it was the poye's tukit—the old woman and her granddaughter inside. The tall, square buildings of the harbor rose ahead, and she could recall their faces, too. One by one, they returned to her. Tunguk, the others. She wondered if she had the courage to leave them there. The men who carried her to Drummoc. The Kapadak. The Jargadak. To live here, among the Kammatuk.

The words of the Leopard Seal returned to her. A woman did not live alone. She was supported by her family. Or she could lie with strangers. There was Ostuk, at least. He had lent them his tukit. How long would his kindness last? Why did he not take a wife? It was not possible to bring up the matter, and by the time it was answered, Brother would be gone, and his friends with him. She wondered if she could even help. The poye might not do enough. Or if she did, they could all be found and executed anyway. What was the best hope? What if he lived? Kjartke saw no good from it. As soon as she thought it, she knew she had done more for them with less to gain. It was selfishness that held her outside the poye's door. She did not want to. She did not want to.

Kjartke stepped forward. Her mouth fell open as if to call, but no words came. Instead, her feet carried her swiftly through the buildings to emerge at the harbor. He is not my husband, she repeated to herself. He is not my husband. That is a lie. The guilt softened, and she remembered that they could not leave until dark. The poye would let her work, but she would also take silver. If she returned at dark with silver, then it was settled. If not, then she could work. This, too, was a lie. She knew it had only now occurred to her in her own defense. But it was also true. She need only find silver. Kjartke did not even know what it looked like, yet it ignited her breast. She would find it. Or she would stand before the door once more, and choose.

Her eyes rose to the bustle of the harbor. Men gathering things for a voyage. These were the kind of men who cared for such things. Maybe it was there. A strange token of the halots and the Kammatuk. A story to her people, of no worth. Again, she remembered there was one Jargadak on the island. All of these before her were people of wood and metals. Of black firestone. For all the crowd, she may as well have stood once more on the snow plain. "Kjartke, Kjartke," the Leopard Seal taunted.

A movement caught her eye. It was too far to see faces, but the walk, the posture, lit up for her the same as though he stood feet away and greeted her in that slurred voice.

Foster felt the weight of an invisible line at his toes. It ebbed and flowed with the busy crew, coming and going, and he tested the edge of it to the limit of his courage. The Marines were making a good show of ignoring him, but he had a sneaking suspicion if he strayed too far, he'd be jumped as sure as though he'd crossed a street into a rival gang's block. There were no buckets here. He'd made a search of every ship-side, every pile of junk. These people didn't just leave valuables lying around for the taking, and to them, anything was valuable. A stick or a stone carved into a certain shape was a precious commodity. His only consolation was that the two boys who ran off into town hadn't reappeared. Maybe it was no easier there to do what at first sounded like trivial bitch-work concocted to humiliate more than to challenge. Not in Drummoc. Stuff. Stuff was treasure. It was the difference between comfort and misery. Life and death. All here belonged to the elements. Rocks, water, flesh. Whatever man could wrestle away, he guarded jealously, and Foster didn't exactly see any bucket-making materials around these parts.

He raised his attention to the town again, and the line that wrapped around the Navy hall—Mattaka mostly, and a handful of whalers. The growing pit in his stomach flared again. He'd been gone for barely more than a day and a half, and Parks had managed to tip everything ass-over-teacup. Beneath it all was the sense that everything would work out. They would figure a way around it and sail home, somehow. His own history seem to bear it out. Things turn to shit, you get through it, so they can turn to shit again. Foster could hardly remember a pleasant period of life, even before he washed up on this God-forsaken version of Antarctica. What was good always floated atop an undercurrent of dread that it would soon be ruined. And in the ruins, he took it for granted he'd claw his way out. Now he wondered. He remembered Oduy, dead before his expression could change. There was a son of a bitch who probably thought he was out of the woods one more time. All Foster had to do was get to Parks—a condemned man, whereabouts unknown—through a town full of people who made Gionn look refined, smuggle his ass to the ship, convince the captain to somehow sail without the Navy getting wind of the extra passenger, then travel a few thousand miles in an open boat through the worst seas in the world, during the harshest season. Redirect the boat away from a place he'd never heard of, to where, he did not know. Then somehow get that same boat or another and look for a rip in space-time or whatever Parks' latest theory was in order to bob up in the Southern Ocean and hopefully be rescued, as opposed to say, crushed by pack ice, or starved. Oh, and he had to find a bucket without leaving the harbor.

He hated to even entertain the thought of abandoning a friend, even if it was one who sowed his own misery. That would pull a couple teeth from the jaws of defeat before they used the rest to devour him. Then he could die slightly later, and without pride. Foster wondered what Parks would do for him. It didn't matter. Parks' standards were for Parks. He couldn't for the life of him understand why church folk called pride a sin. That was all that moved him some days. The fear of humiliation, not to others but before himself, and all that he had got into his head that one called "Foster" ought to be. Maybe that was it. A Foster would starve before beg. Die on the principle. Meanwhile, someone like Gionn would whistle right along to whatever tune the winning side was singing.

The fact that these lines existed told him Parks was still on the lam. The one around the Navy hall, and the one before his feet. If they showed him the body, or killed him before he made the town, he would go. To leave now would be to bet everything on an imagined shot at his own world. As long as Parks was out there, there was at least one small piece of it right here. Wild notions swirled through his head. If he can hide, I can hide, too. Foster knew nothing of geopolitics back where he was from, let alone here. There was a siege coming, though. Gionn was right: Costig might turn on him if he didn't board the ship, but he would have other things to worry about come Spring. Maybe he could return the favor when the enemy was at the gates, presumably with grateful ships of their own. All he knew for sure was he had to get to Parks, and hiding behind the leg of Corm wouldn't do it.

He looked at the Marines he figured were figuring him. Ten, fifteen scattered into casual groups. It was hard to say how many were actually keying on him. There was the town. A few hundred yards sprint. None of the military here would touch it. A few wigwams' distance, and they would give up chase. He knew it. And he didn't know where their wigwam was, even now, but he had a rough idea. That was enough. It was a start, and a new shitty situation to claw his way out of.

He measured his opponents the way he did in high school track on the 4x400m relay. They had a good one-fifty head start. He might get fifty of it back before they noticed. Foster checked the foot traffic. There were plenty of people about, especially by the hall. If he could time it so they got in the way—he stopped cold at the starting line. There in front of the warehouses was a cold glare affixed on him, as welcome as it had ever felt. He waved his hand in a "get your ass over here," motion, then remembered quickly retracted it to his side, open palm. Kjartke tossed her head for him to cross the rock to her. He shook it, and gave her the same toss with more insistence. She was clearly annoyed, but she came anyway, vigilant of the Marines around her but unafraid to be seen.

She looked like a cat that had just been forced to take a bath, and never had he felt a stronger urge to take her in his arms and squeeze the daylights out of her. He waited for a sign—any sign—that he might. Under the Antarctic frost of her demeanor, he sensed it was the same. They stood without a word, four feet apart. She glanced down at his feet and the space between them, then side to side at the crew scurrying past.

"You are stuck?" He smiled and nodded. Foster could feel the gears turning in her head as she took in the activity. "You are a whaler." The subtle way her voice dropped off in disappointment on the last note broke him, and he knew there would be no joyful embrace.

"I'm what I have to be. But I'm still me." She averted her eyes, subjecting him to one of her unreadable silences. "Parks is a fuckin' idiot." It almost earned him a laugh, and her eyes returned. "I need you to take me to him. Tonight. We leave tomorrow."

"You wish to say goodbye."

"We'll both have to say goodbye. I wish to take him with me." Her hesitation made him fill the air. "It was always the plan. You knew that. We get you here—"

"He cannot go."

"It's not your call."

"It is not yours."

"Then take me to him and we'll let him decide."

"Do you have silver?"

"Silver?" She didn't bother to elaborate. "What do you mean? Like, money? You want me to *pay* you to take me to my friend?"

"For the poye. For medicine. Or I take you to bury him."

Foster did his best to hide his reaction. "That bad?" What did she mean? Did he have the flu, or was he mortally wounded? He knew he wasn't likely to get a descriptive diagnosis out of her. "Fuck. *Fuck!*"

"Do you know the look of it?"

It took him a second. "Silver?" She nodded. "Yeah."

"Do you know where I can find it?"

His face pulled back in a shrug. "You could always line up with them fuckers and turn him in," he pointed to the disordered stream of people extending from the entrance to the Navy hall. "Admiral just announced the reward. Three gold for alive, three silver for dead."

"What good will it be if he is caught?" She snapped.

"It was a joke. That's why it's funny." Kjartke seemed even more agitated by the explanation. "Do you have reason to believe anybody you see over there might actually know where Parks is at?" She shook her head without bothering to look. "Well, that's somethin'. Soon as they announced it, every-one who heard either ran off to look, or lined up to guess. I was worried one of 'em might actually know somethin'."

"You do not have silver."

"No."

"You do not know where to find it?"

"I don't know. Maybe. Hell, I can't leave the harbor, and I couldn't even find a goddamn bucket around here."

"Bucket?"

"It's a thing…a sort of bowl that can hold water, feces, whatever you put in it."

"I know bucket. Why do you search for it?"

"I need one to get a seat on the ship." Something that might have been amusement shimmered across her face. "Tell you what. Let me see what I can do. We'll meet behind the poorman's quarters after sundown. Maybe I'll trade you silver for a decent bucket and a trip to see Parks."

"What are you two conspirators on about?" Gionn clapped Foster on the shoulder. Kjartke ignored him, and addressed Foster.

"Silver. Or I will not take you."

"You'd prevent me from seein' my own friend?"

"You are no help to him."

"Hell, I was gone! How was I supposed to know?"

"I would sooner take him." She nodded to Gionn.

"Flattered, cunt. I'll have no part in any of it."

"I'll be there if you will," Foster assured her. Kjartke looked them over, then headed off. "Was that a yes?" He asked Gionn.

"I'm chafed of your 'yeses,' but aye, it be an 'aye.' I'll have to teach you about women if we ever meet another. Now what's this about silver?"

"I need some."

"And I, as well. You could always turn in Parks."

"I already made that joke. Kinda surprised you haven't tried."

"Won't say it didn't stir me loins, but somethin' tells me I'm not eligible. Three argots for a fugitive! If you had a hope of gettin' him aboard, the old man has sunk his ram. Good excuse to liberate our pay from the treasury without resort to thievin', though. Not as thick as he looks, that Costig."

"Kjartke's gettin' me my bucket. We need to get her a piece of silver."

"For a *bucket*? I told you not be fucked over it."

"Don't worry about what me and her got goin'. What are our chances of gettin' it by sundown?"

"Our? Me son, I've got all I need to float."

"If you don't want to help, that's fine. But I don't even know what kind of silver she means, and I couldn't tell you if it's a nickel or a fortune."

"Don't know the first, and it's the latter to a squain. Enough you'll get the spear if a man catches you takin' it."

"Can you point me to where I might find it?"

"I cannot, as me pay depends on your presence on that ship. I'm a short nothin' away from an argot and passage out, for which I would gladly *pay* an argot. If I do nothin', and you do nothin', we sail tomorrow, and only somethin' can stop us. You stay where Costig can find you, but not so close he can get you. You're the one he trusts to carry me gold."

"I can't imagine why."

"He'll tell you to hold it on your honor until we divert the ship. You'll actually be handin' it over right away, as I can be a distressful mate when I'm unhappy. All that requires you to be here. The only cunts likely to have a silver within your reach are our cunts, and those cunts need to be on our side. If you rob one and cavort about the town with Kjartke under a foul moon, I'll be distressed."

"That's a tough perdicament. For you. Because if you do anything to fuck me, you'll fuck yourself. And if I fuck up on my own, well, that's no good, either. Sounds to me like your best bet is to make sure that whatever dumb shit I do, I end up on that bench in spite of it."

"I'm already on at a full share, cunt. I can sail without the gold. Make me coin the honest way."

"You could." Foster grinned. "I wonder if that's what you'll do."

The whaler looked even less substantial bobbing against the log buoys on the harbor side than it did in the dry dock. The crew busied themselves heaping a hill of goods over the side—rock ballast and cask after cask. It struck Foster as more of a museum replica for kids to scamper across while their grandparents took photos than a seaworthy vessel. He felt seasick just looking at it. Beyond it, the same two "warships" from earlier splashed around another in clumsy maneuvers, having traded crews but without improvement. He imagined what it would look like if there was an actual enemy sitting off the coast, blocking any hope of supply or escape. Would it be dozens of them? Hundreds? It wouldn't take much to render what he saw useless. If all went well, he and Parks would be long gone before that happened. But if it didn't, he didn't see how Costig could spare any fucks to give over a couple of spies who never showed up for work. That wasn't even to consider the trouble he'd seen firsthand at Camne Drumlag. He still hadn't decided how or if he should pass along word to the admiral. Mine cave-in, or something else: it would be one more headache that helped the two of them fade into distant memory.

Foster pressed two fingers into his mouth and gave a shrill whistle that caught the ears of all at work.

"Yall listen up! Those who don't know me, the name's Foster." He caught Gionn out of the corner of his eye fuming in tense silence, probably considering whether to clock him before he got too many words loose. "I'm tryin' out for a seat on your ship, and Captain Corm here has generously promised me a half-share if I make it. Fair as that sounds, I reckon I'm worth at least as much as any one of yall, and if you doubt my word, I'd invite you to put your money where your mouth is. I'm puttin' up my entire half-a-share against any man who thinks he can box with me." They looked confused, and he wondered if they even had the sport. "You know. Throw hands. First man to drop loses his half-share—assumin' I make the boat." They roared with interest, and everyone stopped what they were doing to elbow their neighbor, or laugh at the prospect. Even Cormdran smiled at the gall.

"There'll be no throwin' among me crew!" He said to a chorus of protests and curses. "I'll have no broken hands shirkin' oar. You think you're worth an extra half, lad?"

"Aye, sir, I do."

"I'll let you wrestle for it." The men let out a cheer. "Amposi rules! If you can find a taker." They shouted their approval and hustled around, each looking to the next for the man who was game. Gionn hissed in his ear: "What're you on about, dumb cunt? That won't get you silver, even if you had a chance." Foster shrugged him off.

"*Moipa! Moipa!*" Everyone began to chant and clap their hands together. It took a little more urging before he realized that was the name of a man, and none of those he expected to see step forward to screams of delight. Moipa was mahogany-skinned, not a hair above 5'6 and a buck-forty by his reckoning. He could've been thirty, he could've been fifty—these native folk didn't age the way he was used to. Moipa waved off the crowd in half-ass humility.

"Bet on the fight," Foster whispered to Gionn.

"I'm not bettin' on you cunt."

"Then bet on him."

"I got nothin' to bet!"

"Half-share?" Moipa smiled.

"If I make the boat, your half share's mine. Otherwise, you get to keep it." The crowd "ooh"ed with laughter. Moipa held up a bent arm, his fist closed. Foster didn't know what to make of it, but he imitated the gesture, and Moipa linked his elbow through Foster's and pulled them chest-to-chest. For a brief second, he panicked that the fight had begun without his realizing, but when Moipa let go and retreated, Foster realized they had just shook on the deal.

"Tenpenny on Moipa!" Someone cried, then another. Half a dozen crew were flapping a hand in the air looking for takers. Foster turned close to Gionn.

"How many tenpennies make a piece of silver?"

"Ten. Start comin' up with your next scheme, cunt."

"Not enough. Help me get some action goin'."

Gionn stepped back. "Not a man fool-enough to wager on you, cunt," he proclaimed for everyone to hear. "Can't blame 'em, I wouldn't put tenpenny to a decair. Not even against this shirker."

"Shirker?" Moipa objected. "I fight. What you do? You will give your shares next?"

"Shirker. Look around you, timid cunt. Every coin is on yourself. No man will take your opponent at any odds, and you offer him a straight bet? Have you less faith in yourself than everyone here? A man of any piss would put his full share against the half, and a fair sum as well. Make an honest contest of it."

"He bet half. I bet half."

"I only see it makes a difference if you plan to lose." A moan of delight rolled through the crowd and tinted Moipa's face. He waved off Gionn, and cursed to himself in own tongue, unswayed. A man in his forties with a little pot belly called to Gionn in near-unaccented English: "Your boy any good?"

"Him? He'll be on his back faster than a squain wife in coal season." The crowd laughed, but the man's face drew tight in a painful conundrum. He stared at Gionn, then Foster, and back to Gionn as though hoping to find something in particular. Then he gave a contemptuous smile and wagged his finger knowingly. "Four tenpenny!" He called and threw the large copper coins before his feet, then rummaged in his trouser. "And four antu," three smaller coppers fell, "and three pennies of the farri, and one of Choreto. Against the lot!"

All of the waving hands fell, and the men offering bets on Moipa convened privately. They rose again, and one spoke. "Ten."

"Twelve," the first bettor countered. They convened again, and came up nodding. The rest of the men cheered the wager. Gionn leaned in to Foster. "You're welcome, cunt. I just moved a silver's worth into a single hand—*if* you can win. What you wanted, isn't it?"

"Knowin' where to find it's half the battle."

"And this Moipa cunt's the other. Somethin' tells me this'll be ugly."

Cormdran stepped forward. "If the wagers are in, I'll call it. Amposi rules. For those of you so blessed as to not be Amposi," he let the laughter die down, "that means no strikin' with the hands or kickin' with the legs allowed. First arse to touch the ground loses."

Foster loosed his belt and stripped his tunic. Moipa kept his on. He began to shimmy and stamp his feet, changing level, swinging his arms in a choreographed dance that betrayed countless repetitions. It wasn't as though Foster hadn't been here before, either. His high school didn't offer wrestling, but he did play football. By the time he graduated, he'd lost count of how may times he'd come to blows over anything that could be twisted into a point of pride. How many times he'd be jumped by a group, or been the one who did the jumping. Even among friends, there couldn't be alcohol shared in a country yard without the boxing gloves coming out, or a wrestling match with unclear rules that could only end by submission. His Navy years didn't exactly pacify him, either.

All in all, it was enough experience to know that when a crowd of people sends an unremarkable man as their champion, this was not a fuck-around kind of dude. Then again, neither was he. There were as many defeats on his record a wins, but it was rarely a fair fight, and the fact that he was used to all things unexpected meant that there wasn't much a single man could do in a refereed bout that would surprise him. Best of all, there was no one on his side, except the lone bettor. Not even Gionn. Nothing in the world filled him with more fire than knowing everyone expected him to fail.

He folded his arms across his chest and patiently waited out the histri- onics. Moipa's movements became more and more frenetic. It seemed like a warm-up gone wrong, and Foster was happy to let it. The more energy he wasted, the more his own weight advantage would come to bear on the smaller man—at least twenty-five pounds. Moipa waved his hands to the sky, then slapped his left forearm, and repeated the sequence with his right, his two knees, then three tremendous claps of his own head that seemed as though they knocked him halfway out. He shook the cobwebs clear, and fi- nally approached the center of the space ringed by the crew of the whaler.

Corm joined them. Foster thought he would explain the rules, or have a few last words to formalize it. Instead, he raised his spear and paused. The silence that fell was all the explanation he needed to square off and settle into his stance. The butt of the weapon clacked down onto the rock, and Amoipa exploded into him much faster than he anticipated. All Foster could do was shuck and circle out of the way to separate. As soon as they were free, he shot in again trying to control the upper body. This time, Foster caught him by the bicep on one arm, and the wrist of the other. Moipa instantly freed his wrist and snaked his arm for an underhook, but Foster used his strength to clamp down on the forearm before it could pass all the way around, pinning the arm to his side. Moipa yanked to free the arm, and their other hands jockeyed for position in a stalemate.

Foster was surprised at how well he was neutralizing. If he could continue to lean on the smaller man and sap his cardio—that was as far as he thought before Moipa's head slammed into his nose hard enough that his vision flashed black. It returned in time to see the knee coming up as Moipa yanked his head down with both hands, now freed.

He couldn't have been out for more than a few seconds when Gionn came into a hazy focus. The crowd was still cheering. Foster felt blood dripping into his sinuses. He hurried to roll over and gasp for a breath through his mouth. It was pride again that thrust him to his feet to see the whalers near death from laughter, clapping Moipa on the back.

"He headbutted me."

"You noticed as well?" Gionn said.

"Is that allowed? I thought it was wrestlin'."

"Aye, the Amposi are a soft lot. They only let blows with the head, the elbows, and the knees. Their little hands and feet are too tender for a proper go of it."

"Fuck." He snorted a miserable amount of blood into the back of his throat and spat a bloody loogey. The metallic taste welled up again right away from the bottom left of his gums. He pressed his tongue to the spot, and a tooth popped the final thread and floated across his tongue. Another pull and spit, and it fell a pinkish-yellow between his feet. "Fuck."

The glare of the one man who bet on him caught his attention. The winners scooped up his coin and distributed it among themselves while he tried his best to finish Foster with a look.

"Well done, cunt. You've managed to lose in a gamble what you could have sold for more, and still chewed your food thoroughly."

"Mother*fucker!* You didn't tell me I could have just sold my half-share for a silver."

"To be fair, I've never seen a man do somethin' so idiotic, but aye, it was probably possible. This way is better, though. Now you don't have a chance to get yourself killed runnin' coin with the squain woman, and I can have a pleasant laugh at the memory of this event every time you smile."

"I don't exactly understand the exchange rates around here. Is a half-share worth more than a silver?"

"Normally, quite a bit more, but this ship is particularly auspicious. Given the trade we can expect out of Taclann, there's truly no way to estimate the value of an arse that survives to claim his prize."

"Son of a bitch."

"Not so harsh, cunt! I'm keepin' you safe."

"You're keepin' yourself safe."

"Aye, the both of us! We're stuck as mates, now. It's like that blood bond you got with the old squain bastard. Except I don't see meself honorin' it with quite the same enthusiasm, or for as long. But it's there just the same."

"Moipa!" Foster spun.

"Cunt! What're you doin'?" Gionn called nervously. Foster squared off with the winner, and the crowd again fell quiet in anticipation. He clasped his hands before his face and gave a little bow. Gestures these parts were a minefield of ignorance for him, but Moipa seemed to take his meaning, and imitated it in return.

"Thank you for honorin' me with that ass-whoopin'."

Moipa smiled. "Very good. You strong."

"I'm just sorry that half-share you fought so hard for won't be comin' your way."

The man's demeanor changed entirely, and he said something in Amposi, then, "What you say?"

"Well, I don't much see the point of continuin' to tryout for the seat if it don't pay."

"Don't be a limp loser," Cormdran bellowed. "You know well there'll be plenty corpse shares to go around."

"It's not that. I didn't even want a full share. Half is enough. I was gonna sell the other half for one, single, solitary piece of silver. See, I got a debt I owe to someone here on Drummoc, and a Foster don't run on his obligations. If I can't pay it, I guess I'll have to stay and work it off."

Cormdran's face collapsed into horror, as though he just remembered that his car was parked in a tow zone. "Fuck!" He screamed. "Hall tabs!" The rest of the men turned sour as soon as they heard it. "We forgot to reckon the hall tabs! Gewar!" An Amposi man scurried up. "Run! Get the fella to bring the counts. Fuck! Why did you not remind me?" He kicked Gewar off in a sprint toward the tavern. "Any of you bastards who owe and can't pay, you're off! We sail without you."

There was a general scramble of the crew through their belongings, as each tried to recall how much he'd eaten and drank during his stay. The man who just lost what seemed like every penny trembled in a stupor.

"Shit. That's a serious bar tab," Foster said.

"Aye, you're more like to sail free if you murder a man at port than desert a Drummoc tab," Gionn explained.

"How'd you run up a decair? Did you not just land?" Corm asked Foster.

"I have no idea what I owe for my bar tab. That ain't who I owe."

"You are on this ship!" Moipa angrily declared. "You come!"

"I'd love to, brother. Just gimme a piece of silver in the standard denomination, and I'm right there with you, and your extra half-share."

"No silver. You come! It is just."

"Would that I could."

Moipa turned to his belongings and came up with a spear of weathered bronze. Foster jumped and started to back away, but Cormdran got between them. "Here." He held out a coin to Moipa. "One decair, advanced against your first pay. You'll owe me five penny interest. *If* this swindler makes the roster." Corm looked at Foster. "He still owes me a bucket."

Moipa snarled as he took the coin and smashed it into Foster's palm. "I'm also gonna need you to pick up my tab." Moipa's eyes bulged, and he screamed in a short burst before storming off.

"Was that a yes?"

"A spear would have been 'no,'" Gionn says. "Don't forget this." He took Foster's palm and lay something in it. The tooth.

"I doubt it's goin' back in."

"You've already made a name for yourself, cunt. Don't leave things lyin' about that can be used to curse you."

Costig sat on one side of a long table in the main room of the otherwise empty Navy hall. Even with the door and all the high windows open it already dimmed to the early afternoon sun. His light darkened as Wayranapan led an older man in and showed him to the seat across from Costig. Smith, likely. He still wore a sooted apron, and it would take a special fool to keep a private forge and declare it to the admiral, though a few weeks into the job, nothing of the sort would surprise him. The old pounder seemed more interested in admiring the architectural detail than taking his chair. Earlier, he'd had a formal greeting all worked out for everyone, but after the first twenty or so, he no longer bothered. Costig realized that though this man had spent his entire life on Drummoc, he had probably not once set foot inside the imposing hall from which the officials of Ampos held sway over his people. Compared to what he lived in, it must have seemed a fortress of the gods. He turned side to side, jaw open, then lost himself somewhere far away, eyes glazed in dream. Costig and Wayranapan shot a sideways look to one another.

The latter cleared his throat, snapping the man back to the place he stood. As though suddenly remembering his purpose, he settled into the chair.

"I have seen the Leopard Seal. I come for the reward."

"Where?" Wayranapan demanded.

The man paused, as if he didn't expect the question and wasn't sure how to answer it. After some careful thought, he perked up. "In the latrine!"

"Name?"

"Sewadkut."

"'Latrine,'" Costig repeated. "Right, then. We'll search it a tenth time, and if he's there, you'll share the reward with the other fifteen people who said the same before you got here."

Wayranapan escorted the man back out. A shadowed figure excused himself by the pair, and Wendell appeared in the hall. "Hold the next one!" Costig called to Wayranapan. Bald on top and cropped round the sides, his head was the same pink as his face and the flap of skin that swung on the front of his neck when he walked despite his thin frame. It was not possible to recall the last time his face was without the half-grin that made the man welcome company to the bluest blue coat and the lowest oar-scraper, alike. Wendell had looked much the same when they first crossed paths more than a decade prior, and held the same rank: a fellow sergeant-at-arms of the King's Marines, though it was rare enough to catch him on a deck, these days. He no longer had his own platoon, either. In fact, Costig was not aware if he had any particular post, anymore. Admirals asked him to do things when it didn't make sense to ask anyone else, or anyone at all. When he needed men, he took them, and brought them back in good repair. He was not an officer, or a spymaster, a rough hewer of souls; not a counter, and as far as Costig knew, no man of letters. Wendell was of an unnameable ilk, but he was kin to Costig in that he was loyal to the enterprise by which things that needed doing were done.

"Wendell! Sorry mate, I know I still owe you a chat about the huntin' camp."

"Oh, come off it!" He waved his hand. "I don't envy you, tryin' to fall asleep of late." The brief reminder made Costig blink hard and shake his head. "I'll return you to your squawkers shortly enough, me son. Come only to tell you that we held the supply boat to Camne Drumlag on grounds that no ship shall leave when there might be a fugitive aboard."

"How'd he take it?"

"The squain lad? Oh! He's a model of temperament. Plain to see why they sent him. If any man had given me the excuses I gave him for why we couldn't just search the thing, I'd have threaded me needle a few stitches." They laughed. "Aye. But I do wonder about the whole affair. Heard this assistant viceroy sent home most of the lads. And now squains are runnin' his requests. Suppose I should call 'em 'orders.'"

"Orders belong to me."

"Suspected you might feel that way."

"You're in your way where you dance merrily about your concerns."

"Ah, no. Concerns are strong things. You might say those belong to you, as well! Mine, mine are smells."

"Smells?"

"You know when you smell a thing. Maybe it's a bit familiar, but you can't place it, and you wonder if it's this or that, or one you never had."

"Aye, and what things are waftin' by you?"

"Oh, so many! So many, Costig! I'll just say, I was gone a fair spell, and when I come back and smelled all the things that had come in off the breeze— that whaler, and that official, a possible siege! Desertion, mutiny, and all the strange goin's-on I'm yet to pick out," he tapped his nostril. "Let me just say I was overjoyed to find that you were admiral. I cannot imagine dealin' with a third of it with Turrha at the helm, may his soul hear no ill."

"That's one of us, then."

"I mean it, lad! You know this place as well as I." Costig also knew that Wendell knew that statement was a kind lie. "So many frayed ropes to the wind, whippin' slack. It's a gift of the gods, this land, and sometimes I think it's only them doin' anything to keep it. You don't need a siege to break the back of Drummoc, and I certainly hope Donnab doesn't know it."

"Aye, Drummoc. But it'll take more than a siege to break the likes of us."

"It will. It will. Course, you and I know the battles the men see are not the ones to be won or lost. You and I, we fight the hidden battles. Every lad here knows there's a siege closin' and a Leopard Seal on the loose, and we need them for those fights, to be sure. What they don't see is the whaler preparin' to sail, or the fella settlin' in at Camne Drumlag. I tell you, I don't envy you."

"I trust if you thought I've mistaken the situation, you'd have the courage to say as much."

"Oh, certainly! I know you got your cause for your doin's, and an admiral need not seek the counsel of a lowly Marine. As I said, we men fight the hidden battles. Me only hope is if you need a spear at your side, you as well would say the same." Wendell pushed his chair back and stood. "Did I mention enough times that I'm glad it's you sittin' there? Fear not, me son!" He touched his nostril again. "I'll keep me nose open for you."

Costig's cheeks stung. He wondered if Wendell might feel differently if he laid it out for him. Such an act could only serve to bolster his pride, though. There was no secret that gained in the telling. Nor could he be sure anymore how well he'd kept them. The conversation played back in his head as he tried other ways to ease his mate's concerns without seeming to plead for permission. In truth, he still didn't feel like an admiral, and there was something about turning away an old barrel like Wendell that felt almost treasonous. He couldn't shake the feeling he had as a young Marine in his first command—being of certain faith that he had learned well and was leading with ability, and at the same time, longing for a nod of assurance that he had not, in fact, missed something terribly important, though to ask would break the ranks of confidence.

The sound of the chair gathered him. He blinked heavy again before he recognized the woman. She sat bold, near defiant. The fringes of her clothing and the moons of her eyes reminded him that he was not the only one working quite hard under peril. She held onto her silence like a stout shield, so eventually he returned to his preamble: "Do you know the whereabouts of the one who calls himself the Leopard Seal, or those who aid him?" She looked scornfully at Wayranapan, then back to the admiral. "Don't worry, lass. Wayranapan is a good cunt. We'll assure the one who turns in the fugitive is never known beyond these walls—provided you don't spend the reward like an idiot." She didn't budge. Costig sighed and tossed his head to dismiss the officer.

"I don't suppose you've come to turn him in."

"I don't know where he is."

"Right. Then what brings you to to me hall?"

"Bucket."

Gionn raised an eyelid and caught Foster's forearm when he felt him stir. They leaned against the remnants of the personal gear—the last to be loaded come the following morning—along the quayside. Men slept, others tried. A good half were too full of anticipation to do anything but pace around, or play the bead game of Ampos that he despised. It wasn't even necessary to post sentries, with as many men about, though it was now too dark to see the line of buildings. The ship afforded no real safety when it was on land, but they felt naked without their backs to the boards, and every man kept his weapon near, and wore armor if he had it.

"Hold, cunt," he whispered. "How will Costig find you with our pay if you're about?"

"He ain't gonna stroll into this bunch. I'm sure he's got a plan."

"Aye, and it involves the things he knows, which is where you are."

"If he don't, he don't."

"Is there no way I can talk you out of it?" Foster shook his head. Gionn sank a little. There was a chance he'd return with two argots, and a smaller one that he'd have Parks with him. But it hardly mattered. Sad as he was to lose the coin, it would have been a massive fucking undertaking to play wet nurse to those ones and knock the *Gairhle* off course. Much easier to make an honest wage. Nonetheless, it was a letdown. It took but a moment for him to let the whole affair go, and the lads with it. They had served their purpose, and in truth, were terrible influences. It was important to keep the proper company, he thought. And too long in the same would shape a man to fit, no matter his disposition: cunt to cunt, and kind to kind. It would course his blood, and he would lose himself. Gionn removed his hand from the arm, and already struggled to recognize the one who had led a man from a prison cell, not once but twice. So accustomed to peril and narrow escape was he, that he failed to notice that this time, and every one since he came into their company, none of it was his doing. He wondered how they'd manage without Costig's oversight. There, again, not a thing that he should concern himself with. It was apparent just how far he had drifted—not just to Drummoc. The pit in his stomach, the worry in his bones did not belong to him. He became clear as the night air. Sure as he knew their skin boat was the one to take him from his marooning, he knew this one would return him to himself.

"You can come if you like," Foster offered. "I could use your help sneakin' him back. If that's what we do."

"Sorry, cunt. Me brave and helpful side needs a rest if he's to show up again soon."

"Yeah, well, everything in moderation, I reckon." Foster rose, and walked into the darkness. He didn't bother with a farewell, and Gionn wondered if it was because he thought they'd meet again soon, or that he didn't have one to offer. It felt as though something had been severed in a stroke, and it was good to be rid of it. But there in its place, it's ghost throbbed, refusing yet to part or to be of the same use—a reminder of what he would have to get on without.

As he faded, another figure hurried out of camp. Gionn recognized the dumb cunt who had bet his all on the fight and come up short of his hall tab, trailing far enough behind and beating the same path.

As he approached the line of buildings, Foster realized they had set a time, if "dark" could be called that, but that it may be some wait. After months among the Mattaka, he still wasn't sure how they measured a day or a year, or found their way from featureless shore to shore. It lacked all Western precision. He aimed for the hole beside the poorman's quarters—the one he often used to enter and exit, and hoped he would be able to feel out a path to their wigwam, where he suspected she might be biding her time.

A hand caught his arm as he passed the back corner of the building, and his ghost nearly jumped out of his corpse. "Jesus, woman!" He gasped. "What's wrong with 'hello'?"

She raised her other hand and dangling in the moonlight, he made out the shape of a bucket. Foster took it as though it were some archaeological wonder. He turned the cylinder over, tight-joined wood, buckled within two iron rings and cool to the touch from the wax coating. A leather strap wove through two holes and held its surprising weight with confidence. A fucking bucket. That's what he was drooling over, like a golden ticket. It hadn't taken long for his standard of pleasure to collapse to the simplest layers between himself and murderous Nature.

"Do you have it?"

Foster dug the coin out of his boot, lamenting the lack of a pocket. Though most of the time, he didn't own anything to carry.

"Silver?" She held it up to glow pale blue under the rising moon. It was probably the first time she'd seen it, he thought. His tongue flicked over the empty slot in his lower jaw. He'd certainly paid fair price for it. The coin had her transfixed. Not in lust for its value. Hell, he couldn't read a thing that went on with that one. But it felt like a combination of bewilderment and awe. She snapped out and squeezed it in her fist.

"Come. We are followed."

Kjartke led him on, as parallel to the main drag as possible. In a few turns, they came upon a wigwam like any other. There, she bent to the door and called, "Hastate." A girl poked her head out, then back in. Within a minute, a woman in her early sixties, pulled the flap open and held it for a man of the same. She held a leather sack tied at the top, and he carried a straight package of the type Foster had seen the Mattaka use to wrap their weapons, but much shorter than the spears and harpoons he was used to. Neither looked excited to see him. Kjartke must have sensed their discomfort. She rattled off something in Mattakatan that seemed to ease their nerves a little.

"We will go separate through the streets," the old woman spoke low. "Behind the town we will meet." He realized she said it in English for his benefit.

"Yall the doctors?"

"She is the poye," Kjartke explained. "This man is the surgeon." Foster shuddered at the mention of the word. Poye. Like the woman on Nunoc with the whores and the disgusting herbs. He looked again at their gear, and hated to imagine what kind of crap passed for medicine with these folks. He felt a sharp pang of concern for Parks. Hopefully, whatever it was didn't require much help from these two. Kjartke handed the woman the coin. Whatever they were worth, it felt excessive.

"I don't suppose either of yall can put teeth back in?"

They parted along separate tracks. Right away, he understood what Kjartke meant. Several times, he caught a glimpse of at least two men who made no effort to conceal themselves, matching them now to the side, now a bit behind. "Who are they?"

"Kammatuk boys."

"They gonna try and rob us?"

"I do not think it is their aim."

"Then what are they after?" She didn't answer, so either she didn't know, or his question was stupid. Her silences were a single word with a dozen definitions. More like a hundred. It no longer offended him, or made him anxious. It felt like a reply in its own way. "You think those snake oil motherfuckers will be able to help Parks?" He changed the subject.

"Tunguk hopes it is so."

"And you?"

After a pause she said, "I hope, too."

"I ain't askin' about hope. Is he gonna be alright?"

"He will need much help. They will give it. But it is good you come. He will like it."

Foster weighed her words. "Good, because I might have to say good-bye?"

"You will. Your ship leaves. It is for Tunguk to keep him, now. And for me," she added with noticeable effort.

"There's really no way he can travel." It started as a question, but turned into a sinking admission. Another silence. "What'll happen to you?" This time, he knew she didn't respond because she needed him to clarify. "If I go. And if…he goes, too."

"You ask me often what you must ask the poye, and the bones."

"The bones? You mean the fortune-tellin' stuff, like that lady did on that island."

"Aye."

"You don't like me askin' you about the future."

"How can I answer?"

"Sorry, darlin'. In my culture, it's common to ask those things. We just guess. You say a few things you think might happen, or that you want to happen. It's not like I'm gonna force you to do anything. I just wanna know that you'll be alright."

"With my people, it is different. We call it *onik*. In your tongue, 'thread.' You make this place, and there is a thread between you. It pulls you, and you can use this to go there, or to knot it off, so that it never comes to be. But you do not know what lies along the thread. How far, or what things you will do. It may be that to follow takes you through mountain, rough seas, places where men wait to take from you. You may be required to do things you did not think, because your thread was too far, and much can happen in between. It is best to make the stitches short. To tighten before the next. If I say many futures, they will pull me all ways, and I will have to knot them, or cut them, or I will be tangled and become lost."

"Shit. My bad, then. I'll make it a point not to say the future from now on."

"You can say it. If you allow that you will travel the thread."

"Sounds too risky. I'll just shut up."

"We will see Brother tonight," she said. The image of a secret hideout flashed through his head, Parks huddled in a blanket around a campfire with Tunguk. "Huh." Foster felt a lift of excitement at the thought of surprising his friend, with first aid and good news. Would he think it was good news, about the ship? A little tug of anxiety nibbled at his ribs. He cleared the thought, and realized what she was getting at.

"We will see Parks tonight," he repeated.

Her palm touched his chest and stilled him. Kjartke ducked into the wigwam in front of him. The shock of her trespassing faded when he noticed the window and realized it was their hut. He didn't even know they were near it. Behind, he heard the chatter of voices bouncing off the walls. She soon emerged with a leather blanket, tied at the four corners around a substantial load. Foster knew they didn't own that many things—a good portion of it must have been food, and full water bladders. Maybe spare blankets. Under the knot, she jammed the end of a harpoon, tied the line tight, then hitched it to the shaft so that the point would not come free, or the load slide. Then she hoisted the bindle over her shoulder, and handed him the spear.

"Hang on, girl! You want me to carry that?" He said of the bindle.

"No."

Foster felt terrible swinging a little bucket and a spear while the woman bore the brunt. But she was a damn sight tougher than him, and he knew it. Kjartke led him around to the back of the hut, then shushed him and leaned against the wall. He followed her lead. It wasn't long before they heard the voices again, bickering among themselves. They were close now, ringing around the alleys from both sides. Then they faded, and he heard a tinny echo from inside their wigwam. She motioned him to follow her quickly.

"We must not be followed."

Kjartke slung the load to the ground and positioned herself on one side of the door. Foster took the other. He gripped the rope of his bucket in his left, planning to swing it like a jab before a spear thrust if need be. In his right, he tossed the weapon and caught it in an overhand grip, as if preparing for a throw.

"Like this," she shook her harpoon, and he realized she wanted him to change his grip back the way it was.

"Wait, what's the plan?" He whispered back. "We tryin' to kill these fools, or just scare 'em off?" Right away he wondered if he shouldn't have asked her to commit to another future. It was a moot point. Kjartke barked something in her language. Two boys slunk out of the wigwam and stopped at their points.

"Lookin' for this?" Foster shook the bucket. He recognized them as the two blacksmith boys trying for the whaler. They hung their heads. "Were yall about to rob this lady?"

They shook their heads. "No, no. We did not know it was yours."

"We would not rob," the other said. "We thought she set it down."

"So you *were* gonna steal it."

"Aye! Steal. We would not rob."

"Uh-huh. I fail to see the distinction." None of them seemed to make sense of his remark. Kjartke said something else, and one of them responded in the tone of a child whose older sister scolds him. Her harpoon relaxed and the butt came to rest on the ground. They looked as if someone had just cut them open and drained them of their reason to live. He lowered his weapon in turn.

"It's humiliatin', isn't it?" They looked up at him. He raised the bucket. "Makin' us run all over the creation after this. Fuck Corm. I'd like to take a steamin' hot shit in this thing and make him wear it on his fat head as a helmet." One of the boys let go of a weak grin. "I guess we're headin' opposite places by the same way. I'm tryin' to go home, and yall are dyin' to get the hell away from it. Trust me, sons, I been where you're at. There was a time a god-awful prison of a boat was the only thing that could get me out of where I was born, and I would've died if I hadn't joined up." They were hardly moved by his consolation. He went on: "Have yall ever heard of the—what's it, the 'onik'?" They nodded. "I just found out about it tonight. Apparently, I been makin' an onik straight back to where I came from this whole time. From what I understand, that means I'm bound there, one way or another."

Foster lobbed the bucket, and one of the boys caught it. "I don't need that to get there. It'll happen in its own time. Right now, I got to see about the guy who's goin' with me." Their faces lit up, and they started to scurry off. "Hey!" They paused. "When yall meet a red-headed cunt named Gionn, tell him everything I owe him's in there," he pointed. They peered over the rim and rattled it before the message sank in.

"Come on," Foster said as the boys disappeared. "Let's go find Parks." Maybe he expected her to show some sign of joy that he was staying—at least a sign of hiding it with great effort. This was a new silence to him. Her scorn was gone, the tight lips softened. In her eyes was something like frustration, and deeper, fading like the sandy bottom as he waded into the river, pity.

"You do not understand," Kjartke picked up her bindle.

"What's that?"

"Onik. It is too far."

"What do you mean? Parks?"

"Home."

No one spoke once they rendezvoused with the poye and the surgeon. Kjartke lead them deeper into the back country than Foster had been by far. The ground underfoot turned to slush, then snow. A mild, but steady wind whipped cold down the mountainside, chapping his already mutilated lips. Everyone had some kind of load, and he carried only a spear. Kjartke traded the bindle shoulder to shoulder now and then. His feet began to freeze right away. There must have been a hole in his left boot, because his foot was immediately wet. If it weren't there already, the icy ground was enough to rub one. He hoped Kjartke would have time to mend it when they stopped.

She took them along a ridge, where she cautioned him alone to be quiet. The dog camp was nearby. The others seemed to know exactly where they were. The moonlight came and went with thin clouds, but it was enough that he could see the mass only a few hundred yards down. Foster wondered if any of his buddies from the ship were there. Most of all, he wondered about the mother, and the three pups he helped nurse to port.

It was almost three solid hours of hiking, hemmed in by the dark. Twice, Kjartke stopped the party for ten or fifteen minutes to let a cloud formation pass so she could find whatever star she was using at the time. When they finally came upon it, they had nearly entered before Foster realized the black mass in front of them was not another boulder in the trail. Nestled in a nook of larger rock to protect from the wind—and casual eyes—there stood a wigwam like the ones he had seen on the island of the Mattaka people with the coal ships. The skin variety that made him suddenly grateful for the sharp walls of stone they enjoyed in Drummoc, even if you couldn't stand up in the thing.

Kjartke spoke in her language, and it lifted his shivering heart when he heard Tunguk answer. They stepped through in a line into absolute dark. There were awkward collisions as they tried to fan out to open floor space, the docs to one side and he and Kjartke to the other. Foster bumped into a foot, and there was a blood-curdling scream.

"Who's there?" Parks voice was frail and ragged.

"Hands up, motherfucker! It's the po-lice!"

"Foster? You son a bitch! Your face. Where's your ugly face?"

"It's right over here, behind my voice, brother. I don't guess anybody got a light?"

"We will make lamp," the old woman said from across the wigwam.

"She will make lamp," Parks droned, and cleared his throat. "Who the fuck is that?"

"The poye has come for your wound," Kjartke said.

"Kjartke's here? Fuck, it's a family reunion," his spirits were high, though Foster could sense the effort.

"All for you, brother. How you feelin', Antarctica's Most-Wanted? Man, I can't bring your ass nowhere!" There was a clack of stones and a shower of sparks flew.

"Oh. A lot better than yesterday. This is only the second-worst day of my life."

Another burst of sparks, and a little pile of kindling took. A hand touched what might have been a wick to it, and a single flame came away, then settled in a small soapstone saucer with a spout. It wasn't enough to even light every wall, but the poye bent over Parks' left leg and began peeling back the wraps.

"What the fuck happened to you? Can you walk?"

"Uh. Hard to say."

"He cannot," Kjartke answered.

"She says no. I haven't really tried. But I'm bound to need to piss eventually. You didn't happen to bring water, did you?" Kjartke opened her bindle and passed a pair of bladders to him and Tunguk. Parks wrapped his lips around it and sucked greedily. "You'll never believe who I saw," he gasped, and went back to drinking.

"Who you saw?"

"Who took me up the volcano."

"Is this a volcano? I thought it was just a cloudy-ass mountain."

"Volcano, dude."

Tunguk spoke to the poye in their language. "You have herb? Let me see." She said.

"I wish I had some herb. What is your primitive equivalent of ketamine? I would like some, please."

"He was using this," Tunguk tossed the little sack across to her. In the faint glow, Foster saw her smell it, then chew a pinch for taste before spitting. "Who give this?"

"Medicine woman. On Nunoc."

"Poye give you this?"

"The local madam, yes. Actually, she give to him, too," he imitated the accent.

"No more," she said. "Both. No more."

"Shit, I haven't touched that stuff since we left. It's fuckin' nauseatin'. I don't trust herbs that come from places where there's no vegetation."

"It is of Ampos. Healer's poison. It is luck you are alive."

"He did not take it on the ship," Kjartke said. "It made him seasick."

"It is luck. You would be dead on ship. This: this is given to those you wish to die only after you are gone. It feels better first, but it rots the blood. Wound will not close."

"Are you shitting me?" Parks was suddenly animated. "I'll fuckin' kill her. She better pray I never get back to Nunoc."

"Chill, brother. You're alive. Don't get yourself worked up."

"I'm not even pissed about me. Nobody tries to poison my boy Foster. You were laid up on her floor with your back torn off, and what does she do? Gives you poison! That's against the fucking Hippocratic oath. And she charged Barzos! Barzos should get a refund!"

Kjartke and Tunguk pushed him back down as he tried to crunch up. "Barzos needs a refund," he repeated.

"Well, at least now we know why you were actin' like somebody comin' down off of heroin the past few days. I'm shocked you made it up that mountain."

"He did not," Tunguk said. "We found him before we were halfway up."

"I did," Parks insisted. "That dude. You remember the one?"

"What dude?"

"You were alone. We tracked one set of footprints."

"From the ship. He took me up there, then, holy balls have I got a story for you, later. Anyway, I realized he was fucked, then I saw you, and I ran back down as fast as I could. That's probably where you found me."

"There were no prints but yours. Up, or down." Tunguk confirmed.

"It makes thin the door to the spirit world," the poye said.

"I swear, dude," Parks pleaded. "I was there."

Foster smiled and shook his head. "I think what she's tryin' to say is you were trippin' balls on some lethal shit. Somebody spiked you hard."

"I've tripped balls, before. Those weren't balls."

"Leopard Seal," the surgeon said. "Listen to me." Everyone fell quiet, but he didn't go on.

"I'm listening," Parks finally replied. Again, there was a long silence.

"Did you feel?" The surgeon asked.

"Feel what?"

He and the poye spoke quietly in their language.

"Man, I feel terrible. We never would have had to go to that witch woman if not for me," Foster said.

"Don't beat yourself up, dude. It was a learning experience. Now we know not to talk to viceroys."

"Or admirals."

"And don't put anything you get from a brothel in your mouth."

"Will he live?" Tunguk cut across their conversation to the poye, and his words stilled their breath.

"If we treat now, aye, perhaps."

"Treat now," Parks bellowed.

"The lower has the frostbite. It has gone black, but it is no concern. It is at the wound, here." Parks wailed as she apparently touched below his knee. "The leg is dying. If we leave, it spread. Two days, maybe three."

"Do you have anything you can give him? Any herbs to stop the infection?" Foster asked in a somber tone.

"No herbs. We take the leg."

18

SPEARS

The peace of being underwater was incredible. Even the cold enveloped him like a blanket. Only at the surface was it terrible, where sea met air, met land—whipping one another into a frenzy, all contending for a brief reign that none could hold, nor give up its yearning for. Only seconds ago, he sputtered against white foam reverberating off the bluffs and measured the rise of the incoming set. It was not his wave. Now he wondered if he had the energy to even attempt another. Or the breath to surface. It was curiosity, because Parks knew he had no say anymore. He thought otherwise on the *Qarapara*. Here, with the hiss of the surf pulsing over him, there was no mistaking it. The water would hold him under as long as it wanted, and do whatever else it pleased after that. His lungs burned, but it was only a sensation. The desire to rise, to swim, to live, had been replaced with an inhuman patience that awaited the verdict, and the next moment he might have a small window to move in some meaningful way with the sea. He felt absolutely that if it knew he was there, it had no ill will toward him, and no sympathy. It would carry on with or without him.

Parks broke the surface with a gasp. Bearing down on him—lurching and falling as the water that echoed back to sea collided with it—was the most promising wave of the set. Not that it mattered. It was the only one he would have a shot at. Any longer, and he'd be smashed against the rocky bluff. With the last of the life in him, he spun his legs toward it, turned and kicked. His arms were useless. His face plowed under. It lifted him forward, and by the grace of his weakness was not enough to carry him. He dropped short of the rock, while the wave pounded headlong, surged back and swept him sideways so fast he thought he would go airborne. The face of the rocky ramp stared at him, and he was sure he wouldn't clear it until he felt his stomach slide across it. The surge nearly took him to the top of the slant, but it wasn't enough to spill over like the one he'd seen earlier. It peaked, and his

728

heart sank as he felt it drag him back down the slope toward the sea. Parks flailed and clawed, but he couldn't have held onto anything if there had been anything to catch. His feet lost the edge, and his left shin banged with terrific force into the lip of the rock.

And suddenly, he was still. The water missed pulling his center of gravity back off to certain drowning by a foot or so. Before another one could come in, he squirmed the few feet to the top of the slope, rolled over onto the flat rock, and squinted into the low midday sun.

"Hell, no," Foster's voice brought him back to the wigwam, where a small flame glowed over his knee. He could barely make out the lines of a now-respectable beard to his right, though he could feel the others hovering around him—their shifting, their heat.

"Nobody's takin' no legs, no how."

"He will die," the local witch woman answered.

"Exactly. He'll die if we cut off his leg. What you're describin' sounds to me like somethin' our people call a basic infection. What we *need* to do is clean the shit out of that wound, and give him some kind of natural antibiotic to kill off all that nastiness. Surely, yall have somethin' you put in cuts that keep 'em from gettin' like that."

"It is too late. The poison does its work."

"Tunguk! You gotta tell these people. You're supposed to protect him."

"It is the only way," Tunguk replied.

"Goddammit! Parks! Parks, you gotta pull together, brother. Look, I know it's bad, but better to take our chances with fightin' it off than tryin' to chop a big-ass leg in a tent, in the snow, with no surgical equipment, no blood transfusion, no anes-fuckin'-thesia. I knew a dude from the Navy, had his leg done the same way. It took more than two dozen operations by specialists who cut shit off for a living, in a pristine goddamn palace of a hospital with plenty of funding and sanitation measures, and he was still a mess. Kjartke, help me out. Even if by some miracle he survives, what're we gonna do? Whittle him a prosthesis out of whale bone? He won't walk. Not ever. We gonna shuttle an amputee around this island without gettin' caught? *And!* And, we got no psychological counseling. I know yall know fuck-all about that, but losin' a limb is depressin'. People off themselves over it."

"It is common," Tunguk said flatly.

"He speaks the truth," the one they called the surgeon answered. "In the mines, hunting, many men are hurt. I cut many bones. My tools are sharp."

"How many of them survive?"

"As he say, it is common."

"How common?"

"If I cut two, one will live."

"So half."

"If I get before it sours."

"Is this one sour?"

"Aye. Fresh cut or crush, it is easier. When it is sour, it must be cut above the rot. Hard to know where it reaches."

"Tunguk, can I talk to you outside?" Kjartke had to lean over him so they could pass, and even the slight bump of Parks' opposite side sent a wave of agony up from his leg. It hardly even felt like his own. The lower part could have been gone except the light that fell on it. At the knee, it erupted. Even the nature of the pain changed in the seconds since the suggestion. For days, he saw it as his body's revolt against the torture he'd put it through—a sort of fever that shook his whole person and would pass in its entirety. Now, he felt every heartbeat like the charge of an invading army, beating back his own defenses. The rest of him was a sympathetic victim, under assault from foreign powers who gained ground by the minute. More than anything else, he felt the pain as betrayal. Parks had no idea where he was, beyond the confines of the wigwam. He didn't know the state of the world, or the world itself. These people gathered over him not by his own doing. They cleaned and dressed his wound, brought meat to his lips, brought water and warmth. They moved him. A sigh escaped, and he felt his dead weight sink into the wet blanket beneath him. His strength left, and the pain coursed over him to the crown of his head, yet it had lost the dread it once carried. He could feel all of it, and that was it. It was merely there. His hand lifted before he knew what he was doing. It wrapped around Kjartke's palm, and she did not draw away.

Foster's shoulders hunched and his hands retreated into his sleeves as he and Tunguk stared at the same stars back over Camne Drumlag. There were so many of them. It was like the pole kept men at bay so they could crowd together and shine as loud as they pleased. The thought of the miners at the camp, digging or giving up on their friends—of the people asleep in the town—the thought alone stirred a joy in him. It didn't matter that they might all be against him. There were clmen here, surviving just as he was, in a place as terrible as it was ungodly beautiful.

"I didn't wanna bring it up in front of the docs. You know that leg ain't even our biggest problem."

"Then you will stay."

Foster gritted is teeth and nodded. "Looks that way."

"It is good. A whaler is no place for one like you."

"I'm not even a little insulted by that."

"Kjartke will not tell you she is pleased."

"Ha! She won't be once she realizes what that means."

"Do you see that star?" Tunguk pointed.

"I see a million stars."

"There are two above it, to the port. They cling together."

"Maybe. Yeah. I think so."

"It is Aku. When it was time for the Mattaka to leave their lands, the elders prayed that they would be shown where they might live. Hawe heard this, and he sent his dog Aku to find a good place. He told the elders to sail until they saw him, and the lands he circled would belong to the people. Aku wanted to return then to Hawe, and Hawe thought much of his dog. But he ordered him to stay with the people, to watch over them, and to help them find this place again at the end of their travels. Do you see his nose, how it points?"

"Yeah, the little triangle?"

"Before the sun rises, if you hang a rope from his snout, you will climb down to the harbor. This is true now, but in other seasons when the sun comes late, or early, you will fall into the water."

"Good to know. You remember why we're here, right?"

"I remember."

"The only reason Parks is out of jail—the only reason 'Brother' is here—is that we have a deal with Costig. He expects me on that ship, and he expects Parks at Camne Drumlag. Soon as he finds out neither of those things is gonna happen, well, we better hope he has a kind heart. Cause there's no other reason for him to keep embarrassin' himself."

"If he seeks us, it will be hard," Tunguk allowed.

"Now imagine Parks hoppin' on one leg with an arm around you and me. *If* he lives. I don't have quite the same confidence in Mattaka medicine as you do." Tunguk held his gaze on the constellations. "Even harder, right?"

"Aye."

"So the leg stays. And we gotta cook somethin' up for the admiral."

"Will he be our guest?"

"I meant come up with a plan to deal with him."

"It is wise to cut the leg."

"And then what?"

"We will see."

"Exactly. Even if that works, it gets us to tomorrow, and a thousand other problems."

"It is the one before us."

"Yeah, well, you can start thinkin' about the next one, cause I'm about to put a boot on this one." He turned toward the wigwam. "They better not be sawin' when I get in there, or I swear to God," Foster left muttering threats. He flung the flap aside.

Tunguk again found Aku, sniffing across his range. It was a good night for walking. The clouds were thin and sparse, and they did not linger in any place. The wind blew in little gusts that lost their breath and spent much time panting. In the dog, he felt a sadness—confined to the territory of a people who were not his own, his lead buried in the black snow at the highest place in the sky. How he must long to return to Hawe. Perhaps one day the people will learn to find their lands without you, he thought.

The pain in his head returned, and he had to tuck his chin to his chest and close his eyes until it eased the tension in his neck from looking up. He opened them to drink in the moonlight off the snow, the brush of little flurries that stirred up and eddied back with the breeze. It was then that he saw the man, wrapped in a cloak, close and fast approaching.

By the time Foster made it back inside, the surgeon's roll lay unfurled on the ground beside a second lamp. He nicked a little bitty steel blade through thin strips of animal tendon and drew them in half as many times as he could. The tools made him shudder. The only thing that looked familiar was a flimsy sheepsfoot blade shorter than most kitchen knives stuck in a straight bone handle. Was that supposed to be a bone saw? It had to be. Other than the knife, it was the only steel, and only thing with teeth, though they seemed too fine, and a good many were already rounded off.

"Oh, hell no. Wrap that shit up."

"What's he doing?" Parks raised his head.

"His tool roll looks like a caveman torture kit. I'm talkin', I don't even know what half of that's for, but not a bit of it could pass for surgical equipment. Is that flint? I wouldn't even dress a deer with that."

"Tools are good. I do many cuts with them," the surgeon went on with his prep work.

"Yeah? Did you wash 'em in between? This man is awake and conscious, and he can make his own medical decisions. And if he loses consciousness, I'm the closest thing he's got to next of kin."

"If you were wise of healing, you would see we must," the poye said.

"Parks, you gotta help me here or you're gonna be in the next Saw movie. These people mean well, but they don't even know what a germ is. He's lookin' to sew you up with animal parts. If you think you're infected now…"

"Drink," the poye set a jug on Parks' stomach.

"What is this?"

"Hasqa. For pain."

"Booze. You can't even sit up, and they want you to get blackout drunk on a blood thinner before they start slicin' arteries." Kjartke wrapped her hand around his forearm. "Please," she said flatly. "You must let them cut." He pulled away.

"I know I'm outvoted here, but follow me for one second. I know these people came to help. I know they really, truly believe that's what they're doin'. But who are you gonna trust on this one? My nonexistent medical expertise that I learned from TV shows and mandatory CPR class makes me the leadin' fuckin' expert on the continent." He pursed his lips in frustration. "I had a seat. I forgot to tell you. I had a seat on a northbound ship just this afternoon, and I walked away, right into all the bullshit that's gonna bring us, because even if I *knew* I could get home, which I don't, I'll be damned if I'm gonna knock on your mama's door and tell her I left her boy to bleed out in a tent in Antarctica. You're not my friend, motherfucker. Half the time, I can't stand your ass. You're my brother. I came back to make sure you live."

The surgeon paused. Every flickering face turned to Parks. He lay motionless and silent so long that Foster thought he might have fallen asleep, until at last his voice cracked.

"Fuck it." He pulled the top off the jug. "Cut." Parks tried to bring it to his lips, but he sputtered in his position. Kjartke took him by the arm and tried to help him up. Foster stepped over in a crouch to the opposite side, and together they raised him to one elbow so that he could drink.

"Parks," Foster said.

"Ugh." He swallowed hard in disgust. "That's not even close to the worst thing I've had. How much of this do I have to down?"

"If you are strong to pain, none."

"Fine, I'll kill it."

"Parks," Foster repeated.

"Thanks for coming back, dude."

"Of course, brother."

"It's done," he said before Foster could object any further. "I'm done." Foster nodded. "Do me a favor, though?"

"Name it."

"Take a gander at those tools for me and make sure they're not caked in Reverse-Eskimo blood."

"Absolutely. I can't promise you sterile, but this ain't gonna be no Civil War hack job."

Tunguk reappeared in the dancing shadows at Parks' feet. He surveyed the wigwam—the surgeon's prep, the hasqa at hand—and while his face did not change, Foster knew there was no need to tell him what had transpired.

"You have a guest." The words froze them for a moment. He looked to the poye and the surgeon. They stopped their work.

"We will wait outside," she said. "It must be fast." Tunguk saw them out. Whoever waited beyond the skins had no desire to be connected to a fugitive, even by a pair who were themselves associated. For a second, Foster considered taking up the spear he brought, but it seemed futile. He racked his brain for a single face that he would be happy to see. None came.

The flap brushed aside, and a shapeless cloak swept in with the hood drawn up, Tunguk at his heels. It was a man, that alone was clear from the size.

"You're under arrest," a deep voice bellowed. Costig threw back the hood and swished his damp hair. His mustache heaved with laughter.

"That joke was almost funny when Foster made it." Parks grimaced through another swig. Foster didn't share their amusement, and if it was a joke, he wasn't sure how long that would remain the case. His initial relief at seeing one he was used to thinking of as a friend faded to a dull horror. Kjartke didn't know the whole story, and Parks couldn't be expected to realize the full implications in his half-fucked state. It was without a doubt the last person they should want in their company. He kicked himself for not grabbing the spear, which now sat across the wigwam and closer to the admiral. A hundred thoughts jostled for his attention. Were there more men waiting just outside? Down the trail a ways? Costig wouldn't be dumb enough to come alone with bad intentions, but if he knew exactly where they were, he also didn't need to advertise those intentions, or take them right away. It was possible he was still under the impression they were cooperating. If that was the case, no one would know he was here, and if Foster could reach a spear somehow before the truth hit the man, a few more problems might be solved. He wondered if Tunguk realized it, too. If they both moved on him, and quick, they stood a chance. But by his reckoning, Costig could whoop all of them, combined, with half a second's notice.

If he wasn't alone, none of it mattered.

"I'm impressed you found us," Foster offered.

"I'm rather dismayed. I posted a rotation of the biggest nitwits and fuck-offs I could find to watch the foot into town, and you still managed to be sighted. Have a seat, old fellow. I don't care much for men standin' over me." Tunguk settled into the place the surgeon had vacated, and Foster smiled inwardly. They were on the same page. It was possible that Costig was, too. He opened the front of his cloak and removed his short spear. Though he was clearly right-handed, he set it on his left, next to the two spears and the harpoon.

"Plannin' to stay a while? Which of you'll do the huntin'?" He chuckled at the prospect. Costig looked to the other side, at the spread of surgical tools. He leaned over Parks' leg to examine the wound, and recoiled. "Ooh! Tough cast, mate. Was that the saw man I seen out there?" He said rhetorically. Kjartke touched her fingertips to the bottom of the hasqa jug to remind Parks to keep at it. Costig let out the sigh of a man resigned. He met the gaze of each in turn, and Foster felt the silence like a scalding cup he could not yet put down. The admiral reached once more into his cloak, and lay a pair of gold coins on Parks' good shin. Each bore the same odd symbol, clearly stamped but weathered with age.

"Two of you have arranged for payment in advance. You," he looked at Parks, "upon satisfaction of duty." When no one volunteered a comment, he continued: "What is your intention?" Foster peeked at Tunguk, almost praying to see a flash of steel the way he had when they first met him—the impossible speed of a practiced hand. Either the old man thought it was a bad idea, or he left the choice to Foster.

"I think I speak for all of us—me, Parks, Gionn—when I say we want to help."

Costig nodded. "Will you?"

A quick lunge for the admiral's weapon would make him reach for Foster. If he could tangle for a few seconds, it might be enough for Tunguk to draw his knife. A hundred more thoughts. The men who may wait outside, a corpse to rid themselves of. Moving ahead of a navy, searches, battles, arrest, escape, they tangled in a mess in his head.

"No." And then were gone. Foster felt the full weight of the commitment. Suddenly, a thought occurred. "Not like we agreed, anyway."

"How?"

"I'll be your spy."

Costig's gears turned. "And the whaler?"

"I'll bring the coin to Gionn. Keep the third one. Parks helps me on my dime. Two for the price of one."

"No good, lad. I don't trust Gionn."

"And you trust me?"

"I do, now."

"Then let me try. Let me try to convince him."

"I'd have you on the ship, or at Camne Drumlag, but you can't do both. This one's no good," he jerked his thumb at Parks, "and the other's only good until gold graces his palm."

"At least I can do my half. Half a job's better than none."

"I don't do half jobs, me son. But if need be, I can handle the assistant viceroy meself. This post stands or falls on the whaler."

"You see what's happenin' here. I can't leave."

"Go," Parks coughed through a swallow of hasqa. "I'm in good hands, dude."

"No. Fuck, no."

"It's the only way. Right?" He squinted at Costig.

"For him, aye. Since you done me the honor of the truth, I'll return it. You, lad, are a sore on me arse. I could grin it if you were usin' your new name to keep me fed on that cunt over at Camne Drumlag. As you are, I don't know what to do with you. Least not what you'd find agreeable."

"It's just a little cut. I'll be good as new in no time."

"Oh? Have you had a leg off before, then?"

"I just got back from Camne Drumlag," Foster interjected. "You're gonna need him more than you realize."

"And why's that?" Costig sobered.

"I was asked to tell you that there's a cave-in at the mine. They got guys trapped. Alive. Waitin' on a boat from you."

He shrugged. "I'd be more surprised if you told me there *hadn't* been a cave-in. They'll get their boat when I get me twenty-six men. And none of it makes me need a cripple on his death bed."

"That's not why you need him. I only mention it because I promised to pass it along."

"Why, then?"

"You can ask Parks. Once he's recovered. Because he's the only one I'm gonna tell. Try to wring it out of me if you want—that's the only reason I can think of why you might keep him around, and I'll take it to my grave. All I'm gonna say is you ain't too popular in those parts right now. If you think a whaler headin' the other way is your biggest problem, you're gonna want a 'mate' across the water. I know how you're thinkin' you could handle the problem if you had to. Don't bet on it."

"That so?" Costig tried to laugh it off but Foster could feel the doubt germinating. The round face smiled inwardly as he glazed over, and after a moment's contemplation, gathered his weapon in his meaty palms.

"Spears," he said. "That's how I work. You point it at your man, and you get there first or you don't. I'm not the best—I've met terrible bastards. Terrible bastards who would have done me with a flick had they not been me own. But I'm handy enough to be here. And I know how to get such bastards to work together, to bring 'em to bear as one where I point. Not so fuckin' sure

I'm an admiral, though." He looked up at Foster. "Nothin' straight about it. No spears. I can't seem to find a problem that'll stand in front of me!" He laughed. "When I was sergeant-at-arms, I thought I had a hundred ways to do it better than those cunts in blue. What I found was another hundred things I hadn't considered. You put your finger in one leak only to find the next one. Had some clever notions, too, and thought as soon as I had 'em, it was good as done. Still quite proud of a few, and they still might prove such. But I'm man enough to admit it was me own mistake, when I saw a couple of lettered lads on the quay and mistook 'em for spears." He gathered the two gold coins from Parks' thigh and turned them over in his palm. "You two have gone as keel-up as you could without sinkin'. Wish there was another way." Costig shook the gold against one another, then tossed them into Foster's lap.

Foster went woozy with relief. It left as soon as it came. In his hand, he held the promise that he would abandon Parks. Abandon Kjartke, and Tunguk. Ride a bench into a kind of hell he was certain he still underestimated, and conspire with a murderous thief to somehow ruin the ship. How many ships had he weaseled his way onto by the skin of his teeth now? Three? Four? There would be another if he wanted to make it back. All that with the hope that Parks had lived, had done his part. Or he'd be sailing through a siege into his own execution. He didn't even have a fucking pocket. How was he going to carry this shit onto the whaler?

He flipped one of the coins back to Costig.

"What's this?"

"My share." The admiral stilled. "I'd give it to Tunguk and Kjartke to hold, but somethin' tells me it's gonna be hard to make change. I want you to see to these people. See that they're fed, that they have what they need for the winter. Is that enough?"

Costig rumbled into a chuckle. "Me son. That'll do more winters than a few."

"Good. Bribe who you gotta bribe. I don't want any of them to have to worry about coins while I'm gone," he glanced at Kjartke. "And when I get back from stoppin' that ship, I want to see them alive, and on the right side of the prison walls. You said you had faith in me. There's mine for you."

"No, I said I *trust* you. I've got no faith in you, at all. It's Gionn I have faith in, but no trust." Costig stashed the coin. "If that ship makes Taclann, don't bother comin' back." The admiral bundled his cloak, pulled his hood low, and stood with his spear. He took one more long look at Parks, nursing his hasqa. Tunguk rose to escort him, and Costig paused. He motioned Foster to join him just outside the door. The cold stung his face, and twenty yards away he could see two silhouettes waiting them out.

"I've a message for the viceroy at Nunoc." Foster trembled at the thought. Costig went on. "Gionn has the word to get you before him. Keep your part to yourself, and the gold as well if you're wise." Foster nodded. The thick mustache leaned close enough to brush his ear as he spoke it, only once. Then Costig turned to Tunguk.

"Move camp." He slipped into the night.

Parks took another swig and let out a wet belch that turned into a long moan. "I do *not* feel good."

"There has to be some other way."

"Stop. I can't deal right now."

"I'm not talkin' about your leg. I mean the ship. There has to be a way I can stay. Yall are gonna need all the help you can get." He lit up. "I have to stop it, but he didn't say I have to *leave* on it. What if I can stop it before it ever gets out of the harbor? Do it somehow that Costig don't get blamed? How much of that gold coin would it run me to pay Ostuk to bring a letter north for me?"

"Stop. *You* stop. No more schemes."

"I'm not schemin', I'm tryin' to help you. I'll do exactly what I promised. But I can't leave you like this."

"That's all you talk about," Parks slurred. "How you gotta go north. Go north. Look at me. I'm south. This is south. I jumped off the ship cause you told me to." Foster wrinkled his brow in confusion. The hasqa was coursing his veins now. Parks continued. "Now we're in this together, you and me, and I need you to go apart. You don't know how to walk with one leg, and you can't teach me. Fuck! They're gonna cut off my fuckin' leg. And you know what? Take it! I don't want it anymore. Of all my legs and arms, it's the one I hate most. Oh God, I think I'm tipsy." He moaned. "Um. I…your turn, now. To talk." He belched again and took another pull.

"I wish I knew what to say, brother."

"Say something, that makes me feel no pain."

Foster laughed. "What, like tell you a story?"

"Any story. No pain."

"I don't know if I have any like that."

"Think."

Foster mulled it over. "OK. I actually heard one just a few minutes ago. There was this guy, I assume one of the gods, and we wanted the Mattaka people to be able to find this place. So he made his dog come here and show them the way. And he put the dog up in the sky. Turned him into a constellation, so he guards over the people." He looked at Kjartke. "That right?" She shook her head no.

"That story blows," Parks bellowed.

"Alright, alright. I ever tell you about how I joined the Navy?"

"I probably wasn't listening."

"Pussy Holler?"

"Now you're talking."

Foster settled in at Parks' side, half-lit by the flickering lamp. "Usually when people ask, I tell 'em the recruiters were all over my nuts cause my grades were just bad enough, and I lettered three sports, and crushed the ASVAB. And that's true. But I almost didn't join. I was dodgin' this recruiter all summer after I graduated. Tryin' to get me to finish up my paperwork like I was blue-ballin' him. There was this girl, pretty girl, goin' into her senior year. That straight-A's, on-every-committee, daddy-was-a-sherriff's-deputy kinda chick. She was supposed to be workin' this summer camp for kids, but every Wednesday they had some outside group come in and do some shit with the kids, so the counselors got off at 2:30. I'd pick her up, and we'd go down to this creek in the back of this holler. People called it Pussy Holler, cause that's where you went if you couldn't be at home. I was done kicked out of my house for over a year by then, livin' at my uncle's, and she sure as fuck wasn't gonna let me in hers.

"So we'd hang out there. Man, not once could you ever get a minute of privacy, though. There was always someone just off in the bushes bangin', sometimes a few different ones. Drinkin', smokin' weed, just tryin' to stay cool. She wasn't as good and pure as she made out to be, either. That girl put on a good show for her parents and her teachers, but I got the real deal, son. Ooh! Let me tell you. The thought of leavin' that behind to go get my soul handed to me at Coronado was not all that appealin'.

"Well, one day I was playin' basketball with some of my friends, when her daddy pulled up in his car. He goes, 'Hey, boy! Hop in, I'll give you a ride home.' We knew each other and all—everybody knew everybody—but no part of me wanted in that cop car, much less with that dude. But he insisted, and it's kinda hard to just run away from a cop for no reason, so I went.

"He had heard I was tryin' for BUD/S, and he was all excited to hear about it. We talked the whole time. Talked about the Navy, the high school football team for next year, a bunch of other bullshit. I said somethin' when we passed up the road to my uncle and aunt's house, but he told me he had somethin' he wanted to show me. That son of a bitch took me all the way out to Pussy Holler. When everyone saw that car comin' up the road, they started bookin' it out. Had to pass right by us, but he just waved and let 'em go, even though he could've busted anyone he wanted for DUI or possession. He gets out the car, and makes me get out too, and we're standin' there lookin' at this creek. And her daddy tells me, 'I used to take my wife here back in the day, when we first started datin'.' He said, 'You know what I love about this place, son? This far out, you can do whatever you want. Nobody'll hear 'em screamin'.' Then he winks at me, gets in his car, and drives the fuck off. Left me to walk fourteen miles to get home.

"I never so much as looked that girl in the eye, ever again. Didn't return her calls, nothin'. The very next day, I hit up that recruiter. I didn't know where I was gonna end up, but I figured anywhere in the world is better than here."

"Will you take me there, when this is over?"

"To Pussy Holler?" Foster laughed. "Fuck you, I'll give you directions."

"Anywhere's better than here," Parks repeated.

Foster slumped as he exhaled. "I don't know, man. I realized somethin' while me and Kjartke were walkin' here, with my balls clinkin' like little ice cubes. I'm always lookin' for a ship. I thought it was the Navy. Then the *Qarapara.* Every other ship since then that I thought was gonna take me north. North, I kept thinkin'. North, to what? I might as well be sayin' 'Heaven.' That's what I think it is. The one place I've been meanin' to go, that'll save me from all my problems. It's a fuckin' delusion. That ship could've taken me as north as the pole, and I don't think I would have found it. I finally felt for a minute like I saw the last chance vanish, and I was stuck here, with you. It crushed me. Like watchin' everything you ever wanted sail off and disappear. But once it was gone, I can't even describe it. Light. That's the best I can do, and it don't even come close. I felt *light.* I'd given up everything I hoped for, and I could finally just be where I was at, and do what I needed to do. You're my brother, and I was goin' to help you through the rest of whatever short, miserable amount of life we had left, and then everything would just be easy."

He shook his head. "Now that I finally made peace with that, Costig shows up and puts me right back on a ship to nowhere. That's not even *supposed* to arrive. Worst of all, I'm abandonin' the only family I got left."

"You're helping me, dude." A sober clarity came over Parks' voice. "All of us." Foster hung his head, unconvinced. "I don't know if we can make it back, either. I didn't think so. But now you got me wondering."

"I don't have the heart to wonder, anymore."

"Hey!" Parks drew deeply from the jug. "Did Marty McFly just give up when there was no fuel for the flux capacitor? Did that guy from *Quantum*

Leap stop trying to jump to his dimension because he had to wear a dress? Hell, no! There's a way. There's got to be. And wherever it is, I can tell you one thing: it ain't here. As soon as you walk out that door, I can dream that you make it. If you want to help me, go. Get your ass on that ship. And if you find a way home, do your boy a solid and go to 5425 Guerrero in Santa Cruz, and tell my mom—something. Fuck, I don't know. Make something up. Tell her and my dad I love them."

Foster's head raised in a grin. "Brother, if I find a way home, I'm gonna prop the door and drag your cripple ass through by the leg you got left."

The poye and the surgeon returned to empty each a load of snow from their parka tails. "More," was all the man said, and they were back out with Foster and Kjartke at their side. Tunguk stood apart, lost in the distance. Foster wasn't sure whether he didn't feel like hauling snow. Or he was back to losing his mind. This whole mess with Parks at least seemed to sharpen him. There was a life once more flowing from those old lungs, turning to a cloud of vapor.

After another round, his curiosity was settled when the surgeon cut back the pant leg all the way and began to pack the snow tightly all around the knee. Parks' protest was met with, "Drink." It was a clever stroke he wouldn't have given them: numb the nerves above the cut site, and slow down the river of blood that would follow. The biggest danger was Parks bleeding out in front of them. That, and infection in the days after. Foster took in the little oil lamps, the jug of oil beside them. The fresh white snow.

"Do we have a bowl? A pot of some kind?" Their bewildered faces begged an explanation. "Water. We need to boil water, then we're gonna put every single knife, tool, and toothpick that touches his leg in there before we cut." The poye began sputtering something he probably didn't care to hear in Mattakatan.

"No bowl," Kjartke said. "It is a waste of whale oil." It was *not* a waste, he thought, and he paid silver for whatever the hell he pleased to use. But if there was nothing to boil it in, he decided not to fight it. "Then we scrub." He picked up two handfuls of snow and rubbed them furiously together, letting it fall away, then pressed it to the backs, all the way up the forearms. The snow was icy, and it felt like sandpaper, but he peeled himself as raw as he could stand. Foster gathered up the leather of Kjartke's bindle, piled snow in it, and put the bone saw in the middle. He folded it shut and rubbed that, as well, finishing by scraping at the teeth with a wet, snowy corner. The docs were baffled, but they went about their preparations as he repeated the process on every single tool. By now, the only thing keeping Parks awake was the shivering. He trembled as he brought the drink over and over to his lips, maybe from cold, or something else. The sound of the slosh grew hollow to tell the level of the hasqa.

He knew he would have to go soon if he was to make it back to the harbor before daylight, even with a late-rising sun. No one dared get rid of him, though. The surgeon reached for the small steel blade—the closest thing to a scalpel. Foster put out a hand to stop him. "You, too. Scrub," he made the motion with the snow. There was an exchange in their language. Tunguk said something, and everyone made a brisk pass over their hands and forearms.

When Foster put a little snow on Parks' lower leg, he cried out and jerked with the first motion. The snow castle over his knee blew apart. "Ho! Still! You no move!" The surgeon scolded him. "It is bad," he repacked the icy cast.

"Fuck, go gentle," Parks pleaded.

"That was the gentlest thing that's gonna happen, brother." Parks breathed like a pregnant woman, then nodded them on. Foster scrubbed the caked blood and dirt from around the wound, and Parks curled his lips in and groaned, even with nearly a fifth of booze to numb him. He could barely see what he was doing.

"Can we get some more light? Lamps? Anybody got more lamps?" No one answered him. "How are you gonna see what you're doin'?"

"I can see," the man assured him. "I can feel." The idea of performing an amputation by squint and touch curdled his stomach, on top of the utter lack of medical knowledge, technology, or sterility. Somehow, Parks managed to writhe every part of his body except the leg they were working on. When the skin around it began to well with blood from tiny scrapes, Foster knew there was nothing else he could do.

"You finish!" The surgeon called again. Parks made a show of taking down the last sip, then flung the bottle into the skin wall. "Bite this." He handed a thin piece of wood to Foster. As he brought it over the lamp, Foster frowned at a half-dozen sets of overlapping tooth marks, then passed it to his friend.

"Wait, are we going already? I kinda have to pee," he took the stick from Foster.

"Bite."

"Are there any instructions? I mean, like, what I should expect? Or like, a pep talk to get me motivated?"

"To move is bad."

"OK. Um. I feel like I need a little more ramp up. I'm not as drunk as I thought I would be." The surgeon ignored him. He nodded to the poye, who lay across Parks' good leg where she could use her hands to assist. "He is big," the man addressed the others. "Not enough to hold down. He must be still," he shot Parks a look. "You," to Foster, "hold this leg." Foster pressed his ribs into the thigh of the limb that would be cut, and wrapped his arms under it as though to take it in a choke hold. Tunguk and Kjartke did not need to be told. They scooped his arms and lay across his chest. Kjartke took the stick from him and tried to insert it into his teeth.

"Hang on! I need to say goodbye to Foster."

"No goodbyes, motherfucker. I'll be back before you know it. Come on, we're doin' this."

"Easy for you to say. You're not the one about to have an amputation."

"If it makes you feel any better, I just lost a tooth." Foster turned to him and hooked back his cheek to reveal the gap.

"Ha! Hang on. I gotta hear this. Tell me how. I could die on this table. It's not even a fucking table." Kjartke plugged him with the stick.

"Bite," she said in a tone so firm yet forceless that even Foster felt his jaw tense and his body relax. She sang in soft tones, as she did the night he woke them in the wigwam. Foster couldn't tell if it was the same song, but it didn't seem to have the same effect. The poye sang her own at Parks' feet, different and colliding with Kjartke's. Neither yielded to the other. One ran across Parks' cheek, the other fell on his leg.

"Oh-fuck-oh-fuck-oh-fuck-oh-fuck," Parks muttered through the clenched stick. The surgeon leaned forward, and Parks screamed so loud it stabbed Foster's eardrum. The big thigh muscle twitched against his ribs. He peeked over the snowcapped knee. The surgeon jerked his hands away to reveal the tiniest incision just above the rotten part of the wound—less than an inch, and only skin deep.

"You must keep him still," the man admonished.

"Bro! That was nothin'," Foster called over his shoulder. "Look, I have no idea what you're goin' through. I'm sure it's fuckin' terrifyin', and I've never felt pain like you're about to feel. In fact, I seem to remember I was the only one against it. But here we are, man. It's open. Ain't no goin' back. I need you to find your Stonewall Jackson. If there's a hard son of a bitch anywhere in there, I need you to go and get him, right now. Just for a while. You can be a pussy when this is over."

"Didn't he die?"

"What?"

"Stonewall."

"Everybody dies, eventually. I'll bet he took it like a man."

"He's gonna saw through my fuckin' bone. I'm not Stonewall."

"Then be Parks. Just hold still." Foster nodded to the surgeon, who scooped his hand under the calf and drew the blade across the shin and around the side as neat as a zipper. Parks let out an unholy wail and his big body spasmed under Kjartke and Tunguk, but he held the leg still. The sight of flesh parting, the deafening cries, made Foster feel as if his own insides were being torn apart. In one slick move, the surgeon passed the scalpel to his other hand, switched his hold on the calf, and brought the cut all the way around to circumscribe the calf just a couple of inches below the knee joint. Blood welled out, dark and hesitant. It wasn't a straight cut, but dipped several inches in the back before rising again to capture as much good flesh as possible. He'd assumed it would just be a saw across the leg all the way, but it made sense to Foster that the man took it a layer at a time. He knew exactly how he wanted to close it before he ever nicked in.

"Oh, God," Parks panted, sweat or tears streaming his face. "I feel everything," the stick muffled his words.

"It is good sign. Do not be strong. Strong men stay awake."

"How much more—" He screamed as the surgeon made a cut perpendicular to the first on the back side of the calf without even looking. The poye wobbled like a bull rider on the free leg, but Foster's limb remained in place. She slipped her bare fingers under the flesh and rolled it back like a pant cuff to expose a bloody mess of muscle and bone. Foster had to turn away and close his eyes to avoid passing out. Bile welled up in his throat, and he forced it back. She packed another layer of ice over the skin. When he finally found the stomach to look again, he saw that the muscle around the cut looked much darker than the neighboring tissue, like meat that had begun to spoil. There was already a long cut down the shin, and the skin had been peeled almost to the foot in the brief interval that he turned. Parks had not seemed to notice. Again, he looked away to avoid spewing on the open leg. The surgeon's complete lack of urgency alarmed him. The man took his time feeling all around the muscle, moving the flame around to see various spots. It was almost as though he was giving a massage, testing it for spring, for suppleness and tension. Parks moaned incessantly, loud enough that Foster could only hear Kjartke's song during the gasps. The poye's ended, her attention fixed on the operation.

The surgeon's eyes met Foster's.

"Hold," he said softly.

A scream to humiliate the previous attempts erupted from Parks' lungs, and just as quickly fell silent as his head lolled to the side. He'd passed out.

"Hold," the surgeon said again, louder. Parks whole body yanked as if from electric shock. Air howled out of his lungs like a wounded coyote. They wrestled him as he tossed like a sleeper fleeing some kind of monster. "Hold." He tensed again, and Parks' body went stiff. His arms raised, and Foster could see the small bodies of Tunguk and Kjartke struggle to stay on the ground against the the witless strength of a man whose body thought it was fighting for its life—and maybe was. It must have been nerves he was clipping.

By now the pain was too great for Parks to come out of his stupor, and too much to let him rest. None of his movements seemed voluntary. Foster's muscles cramped from the constant tension of his grip. All of his squeezing amounted to little when his friend moved, because it was impossible to get any traction on the snowy ground. The best he could do was to sprawl his hips flat toward the earth. "Hold." He had never stopped holding. What did the old man want him to do? Parks wrenched in pain. He no longer cried out. It was just a shifting stream of whines and whimpers, and the occasional nonsense string of words. His breathing seemed to rasp up to choking sounds before stopping altogether. After a tense few moments it would restart itself with a snort.

The knife went down on the leather sheet, and it irked Foster that it would probably be used again after touching a contaminated surface. Now the surgeon took the thin strips he'd made. With casual speed, he knotted one around a piece of tissue—probably an artery. They dug their fingers purposefully through the muscle, which didn't seem to aggravate Parks as much, and repeated the process until six knots had been tied altogether. The scalpel reappeared, and this time he brought it well below the wound and behind the calf at the top of the achilles.

The calf muscle jerked up the leg into a ball like an animal recoiling to safety. Each time he steeled himself for a look, there was more and more peeled away. Only his fascination allowed him to keep watching. The next cut was at the top of a deeper muscle, and Parks jerked awake again in a thrashing scream. For a second, Foster thought it was hopeless—he would throw them all aside like rag dolls. He was bigger, stronger, and amped on booze and adrenaline. The surgeon kept the blade moving though, and in another second he was still again. The quad muscles under Foster's ribs went completely tense and the knee pressed down against the rolled ball of leather that held the upper calf clear of the ground. It felt like a rock. Involuntary spasms shot through the upper leg beneath him, and he heard the torso shifting unconsciously over the snow. He could feel the pulse through the femoral artery, and it now plummeted and began to shake at irregular intervals.

"Fuck. I think he's goin' into shock." He realized that meant nothing to his companions. There was nothing to be done. He remembered a corpsman telling him that technically, all death is due to shock—that it only differs what brings it about. But he couldn't remember exactly what it was, or how to get someone out of it. From this point, the only thing keeping his friend alive was a matter of degree. Long enough or bad enough—Foster interrupted the thought. He saw the little knot on top of the exposed shin quiver, and remembered Kjartke's threads. He closed his eyes and pictured he and his friend on the prow of a ship slicing through low swell, far from this place.

The leg beneath him shook, but it came from the far end, where the surgeon tore at flesh and tilted it this way and that. He braved another glance, and a significant piece of muscle had been peeled down to join the skin. Now the pale yellow bone was near-bare in the lamp and Foster had to belch to keep his stomach down. As much shit as he'd given the man for his medical ignorance, he at least seemed deliberate about where he was cutting. None of it made any sense to Foster, nor could he look for long stretches. It was im-possible for him to make a connection between the bare, torn flesh to one side and the man to the other. It seemed a strange nightmare. The gravity of everything they were doing pinned him in place as surely as he held the leg. There were real consequences for fuck-ups. A piece of a man would not be going on. Things no longer happened to other people elsewhere, or even just to those around them. He could be next. They could both be flayed meat, and only a couple of "Reverse-Eskimos" had any inclination to prevent it. His heart rose a little at Parks' term. There was nothing sacred. No gallows immune to his humor. If there was anyone, in all his years in the service, anyone out of his family and friends back in North Carolina that he could choose to be stuck with in a bizarre and frozen land, he would take the man he held down at this moment over one more capable. Camne Drumlag was a bust. He should have been here to prevent this. His focus on the north dragged the both of them right through a bloody mess that would not be undone, ever, with the best of all possible luck from this day forth. Foster wondered if Parks would choose him, too.

"Hang in there brother, worst is over. Almost through." Foster didn't know if that was true, or if Parks could hear him. There was a gurgling sound from deep in the throat, and his chin heaved in little gulps. The first little wave of vomit sloshed out of his mouth onto his chest.

"Turn his head!" Foster yelled. "Turn his head so he don't swallow it!" Kjartke freed one of her hands to push his face toward Tunguk. Dark red bile spilled in bursts over his lap. The smell was putrid. The wigwam filled in seconds with the foul odor, and it was the end of his own resolve, as well. Foster leaned to the side and puked what little he had on the slushy snow by his arm. A headache started in. He knew he'd barely had enough water for days now. He was sick and exhausted, gasping through his mouth to spare himself the noxious air. The idea of the walk back to the harbor, the whaler—the image crushed him and he had to pull back. The only reason he was doing anything other than curling into a ball on the floor is that the man beneath him was in unimaginably worse shape.

A bloody hand touched his arm to get his attention. "Hold." The surgeon lifted the pitifully small bone saw. "Very important." Foster adjusted his grip and weighted his chest until it felt like his ribs would break. *Look*, he said to himself. *If he can lose a fucking leg, you can look.* The poye held back the muscle that dangled below the knee. The saw found the fibula a little higher than where the skin and muscle were severed, tilted at an angle. There was nothing for the first few strokes, but then Parks began to writhe. Kjartke lost control of her end altogether, and the right side of his body tried to flop over to the left. There was shouting in Mattakatan. The poye slid off the right leg but regained it, having to let go the calf muscle in the process. Someone's legs—it had to be Kjartke, kicked Foster in the back of the head. She was nearly thrown over on top of Tunguk. There were three sharp kicks on the free leg, then he fell still with a drag of the muscles that reminded Foster of a hose, tossing this way and that, snaking to a stop as the water pressure slowed. Through it all, he held his leg. He held his gaze. The saw resumed, and in a few more clean strokes, the skinny bone cleaved free at a bevel. Parks was now frighteningly unreactive. The strong thump of the femoral artery had disappeared.

"Check him for a pulse!" Foster called. "Heartbeat! Is he breathin'?" Kjartke gathered the arm that had thrown her and leaned her ear over his mouth.

"He breathes." Foster slackened his grip, and at last felt the weak throb of the inner leg, stuttering at intervals.

The surgeon was already on the tibia, again at a downward angle but less severe than the previous cut. He attacked the bone, and the man didn't stir. More than anything, it was the sound. It was similar to a coping saw through wood, but there was a wetness, a hollow tint that drew the teeth through every bone in Foster's body. He cringed, and swore he felt his shin ache, but he felt nothing for his friend. He couldn't dare try. Nothing about this place, or these people, lent itself to sympathy. There was a line, and what was beyond it was gone. All that was left was what could still get them through.

The leg jerked, and the surgeon gripped the bare rod of bone and flung it to the side of the tent like scrap. An incredible sinking sensation washed through Foster, and his skin tingled half numb. It was as though he had drowned in this place, and he could not call to his mind anything that the dim lamps could not reach. Not a thought, not a feeling, or a word. He watched in cold sobriety as the surgeon and the poye folded the muscles to-gether over the stump of bone, and sewed them into place. They stitched the ends of the tubes they'd tied off earlier, then worked the skin around it. A small hooked needle made of bone punctured it, and coarse thread joined the seams in a pucker. Inch by inch, the folds reunited, with the backside curving around to meet the shorter cuts of the front. At no point did Parks flinch. That concerned him more than any of the steer-wrestling they'd done earlier. It was almost like the poor bastard had given up on feeling altogether.

At last, they leaned back from their work. The surgeon arched and stretched the agonizing stoop out of his joints. The bottom of the wound was left open entirely for drainage. Every inch of the leg was covered in blood. The snow was a red slurry. They knelt in it. Their arms were caked, and it froze among the hair of their clothing. There was a hog's chance in a beauty pageant that it wouldn't become infected. The poye now packed some kind of dried plant into a strip of leather and bound the end of the stump loosely. Foster remembered the poison. What they give to people who they don't want to die while they're still around. He had no idea what this was, and there was no choice but to trust it.

The surgeon was already rolling up his tools. "Wake him. Like this," he referred to the numb torpor in which Parks lay, "no good." Foster's arms quivered when he pushed himself up to his knees. He crawled to the head to join Tunguk and Kjartke. Despite the freezing temperature, Parks was cov-ered in sweat. His own hands, near the wound for the duration, were filthy. It took a hell of a scrubbing with loose snow to get a respectable amount of blood off, and that was all he could hope for.

"Yo, brother," he shook his friend. "It's over. You made it big guy." Parks moaned and muttered unintelligibly. Tunguk must have feared the sweat freezing under his seal skins as well. He was already rolling the tunic up, and with Kjartke's help, they cleared it over his head in the back then dragged it down the front past stiff arms. It was hard to tell in the low light, but he seemed ghostly pale. As sweaty as he was his skin felt clammy and cool. It was tempting to let him remain blissfully unaware of the pain he should be feeling, but Foster now understood why the surgeon wanted him up. If he didn't wake to the brutal reality of it now, he never would.

"Water." Foster tilted the mouth of the bladder into his lips, the tiniest sip. When he heard choking, he turned Parks head and let it roll back out of his mouth. Kjartke gathered a handful of clean snow and pressed it into a wad that she held against his forehead. Again, Foster poured a little water, and again it ran back out. The poye, who had not bothered to clean her hands, massaged the thigh of the stump leg vigorously. That had to be a bad idea, but Foster had given up on reasoning with these folks. It seemed like everyone had their own idea of what might rouse him. Tunguk piled snow on his sternum and rubbed it in circles, which soon had him shivering. Foster kept talking.

"Parks. Parks, you gotta come back now." He slapped the sides of his face gently. "Come on. It's Foster." Now the poye rejoined her song from earlier, or one like it, as she rubbed the other leg starting from the foot and working up. His head jerked side to side, clearly an attempt to clear the ice. Kjartke brushed it free. Again, the bladder met his lips, and this time he coughed a little. Foster poured more generously, and he went into a fit. They turned him on his side as he seemed liable to hack out a lung. His face and neck turned bright red. Foster pounded enthusiastically on his back with an open palm until the coughing slowed and alternated with moans as he pressed his cheek into the ground. At last, Parks returned to his back under his own power. His lips moved. "Wuh. Wuh." On a wild guess, Foster touched the water to his mouth again. Parks sucked the tiniest bit, held it in his mouth, then spit it deliberately down his chest. They puckered for more, and he repeated the process, now almost swishing. Without ever opening his eyes, he took a bigger sip, turned, and dribbled all down his shoulder before loosing a few more coughs and settling back. The stump twisted, and pain immediately registered in his face.

"Hey, can you hear me?" Foster probed. "Moan once if you understand me." There came a moan that sounded more intentional than the rest. "You want some water?" He saw Parks try to move and sink back in agony. Tunguk and Kjartke helped raise his shoulders, and Foster brought the water to him one more. This time he gulped and swallowed. His eyes oscillated between half-open in a daze and clenched tight.

"Can you tell me your name?"

"Hmm."

"What's your name, brother?"

"Puh." He dribbled spit down his chin.

"What's your name?"

The eyes blinked open and rolled around the wigwam in a daze. "Water," he croaked. Foster gave him more, then repeated the question. "Leopard. Seal."

"Where are you?"

"Fuck," he closed his eyes and leaned back.

"Do you know what just happened?"

"Fuck."

There was a flurry of Mattakatan from the surgeon aimed at Tunguk. The poye added something, then both rose without ceremony and darted into the night. If they came by dark, they would want to return by it, too.

That meant Foster probably didn't have long, himself. A gloom fell over his imminent departure, and he noticed it wasn't entirely in his head. They had taken one of the lamps—given them a lamp, rather. He cupped it like one of the puppies he took from the mother dog on the ship and set it near Parks.

His fingers found the artery beneath the thumb. It was thin, surging to rapid then backing off, but a damn sight better than before. "You remember *my* name?" Foster interrupted him before he start: "And *don't* say it. Took me long enough to get people to stop callin' me that. I mean my *real* name."

"Tunguk."

"Holy shit, I think that's the first time you ever got that one right. Tunguk's here, brother. Who am *I*?"

"Foster. Did you cut off my leg?"

"Somebody did."

"Can I see it?" Parks lifted his head with great effort. Foster felt around in the shadows and cringed when his hand fell on mealy flesh covered with snow. He gingerly held it over the flame while Parks squinted. The second he put his head down, Foster threw it aside and shuffled his hand through the snow to clean it.

"Cold," he said. They lifted him and lay his tunic between his back and the snow. Kjartke covered his chest with a coat of seal. "You were…a good friend. Sorry."

"No apology necessary, brother."

"Not you. Leg," Parks pointed. Foster chuckled.

"You must go," Tunguk said. Foster nodded.

"Had a dream," Parks went on with great effort.

"You had a dream?"

"Not supposed to tell you."

"OK."

"You be careful…out there."

Foster looked over their faces: Parks', twisted in agony, eyes shut and fluttering, gulping shallow breaths through his mouth. And the others, unmoved as ever. If he thought he saw worry, or sadness, or anything else it was just as likely what he wanted as what was. Right now, he wanted to stay. He wanted them to want him to stay, and to be as torn as he was. There was much to do, and all of it would be done without him. Maybe he had taken it for granted in all his suffering and his pining for anything better than his current situation. For months, he was a part of them. They were a crew. At least two of them cared to see him live, and one without any obligation to do so. But they were all there, all in the same shit. Soon, he'd be in it alone. And they'd have to figure it out without his help, too. He prayed they would, and at the same time wanted it to be as difficult as it was survivable. This may be the last time he looked upon these faces. Kjartke. Tunguk. Parks. He let each one burn itself into his brain. Only his leaving, and his success, could secure them. Though success didn't guarantee his own return. Foster didn't recall feeling this raw when he left everyone he knew for the Navy. Now, he grasped for anything that would prolong it.

His fingers found the gold coin Costig had put in his trust.

"I showed you what silver looks like," he said to Kjartke, then held out the piece. "Maybe you should know gold, too." She hesitated, then leaned forward to examine it. "You can hold it." With a blend of suspicion and awe, she turned it over in her hand for a few brief seconds, then put it back. He held it towards Tunguk. "Ever seen one of these?" The old man made no effort to look. Foster stowed it.

Parks twisted restlessly. Low groans of pain rumbled up from this throat and out his nose. "Fuck!" Foster slapped his leg. Tunguk and Kjartke looked up at him. "I done gave away my bucket!" It was Tunguk's turn to laugh.

"Do not show skill for what you would not do."

"You're the second person to tell me that today." He scooted back past the end of the stump. The thick threads hurt to look at. He could already imagine the painful pull of scar tissue and tearing flesh, the tenderness of touch. Every inch he moved felt like one he would not regain, as though the slack were taken up on the other end. They already turned away from him to attend to Parks.

"Well. Reckon it's time for me to git." Kjartke passed him the shorter of the stone spears, almost an afterthought. He hadn't even considered that a whaler might need something to stick with. She returned to Parks, and he paused looking back. When he didn't immediately go, her head tilted his way. Either there was nothing on her face—or there in the dancing orange flame, glinting, indiscernible, the corner of a smile.

Foster backed out, and felt the flap close behind him like a door of heavy oak. His chest felt as though it would cave in, so hollow was he as he rose. The fresh air breathed through him, and within a few steps, he could not make out the wigwam at the end of his tracks. Above, there remained only Aku, dutiful in his rounds. A brief feeling of panic gripped him as he realized he'd been guided here, as he had everywhere on this island since he landed. Even if he could have seen a goddamn thing on the way out, he wouldn't have remembered it after that sleepless disaster of a night. The triangle head of the dog was the only thing he recognized—even the moon hid behind a thin cloud. At once, Tunguk's words returned to him. *Before the sun rises, if you hang a rope from his snout, you could climb down to the harbor.*

Son of a bitch. Foster oriented downhill and fixed his gaze on the tip of the triangle. *He knew I would leave.*

The whaler camp was a sleepy fuss of activity, even before the sun could muster its first ray. Sleeping bags of hide swallowed up handfuls of personal items, and in turn vanished into oilskin bound with leathers, each man's bundle wrapped tight-enough to stow beneath his bench. The eager ones reclined against their sack or chatted with mates. A few had yet to stir at all. It would be the last still sleep—the last dry sleep—and it was not something to squander on diligence. The Navy squad nearby were all sound asleep except the watch. Their presence was enough to keep the whalers on edge, and remind them of their suggested departure. Ten for now. There would be more with the morning. She was loaded except for arms and armloads. No rumor was needed of their intention. If anything, the distraction had been a gift. It would be a worry gone, but there seemed no shortage of worries to overshadow a sailor's tale. Now with a Leopard Seal eluding him and fleets sure to launch at distant ports, the admiral would perhaps be occupied long enough that it might even be possible to make an honest run to Camne Drumlag. It should have appealed to him. In fact, Ostuk had no plan, no want. He knew only that to load his dogs again would break a peace he was near to making at great pains.

He had walked the camp thrice. Foster was not among them. It was difficult to see what lump was who, but enough of them stirred, and this was a lump he knew well. Something beyond the security of the watch had taken him, and if it did not return him soon, it never would. In the faintest of first light, a flash of crimson broke in his vision.

"That for me?"

Ostuk looked at the square-folded oilskin under his arm. "No." Gionn sat as near as possible to a sleeping bag and oilskin without touching it. He nodded at the gear. "Is it not enough?"

"It will be, if the cunt who owns it don't show his ugly face before the captain gives the order."

"Foster?"

Gionn shook his head. "Some unlucky bastard who had to have a last night of the brothel, no doubt."

"Then you are not provisioned."

"I'm to find me bollocks retreatin' to me cunt in the moments before I am tossed over, aye."

"It is bound to be better than the other who fled with you."

"That one? May a fine luck find him, he was always gettin' me into trouble. Would you care for me to hold that for Foster?"

Ostuk's eyes narrowed. "Thank you. I will see it to him."

"We could call it the pay I never got for rowin' your ship."

"I do not have a ship. Or a crew. All that is mine would be at great risk. Even as Drummoc holds its tongue, Nunoc's ships will speak soon of my 'rowers'. I pray the debt is mine, alone."

"Aye, me as well."

Ostuk parted as a deep gray spilled across the sky. He passed a pair of Mattaka boys on the fringe of the group, huddled together inside a single blanket that was not long enough to cover both sides of them. A common sight in Autumn. The sons of the people had long preferred to die on what ship might sail than work among their own in honest trades. There would be new ones on the *Juhketappat* soon—if they could be found. It was not so easy to work the deck and the dogs as the oar of a whaler. He considered telling them to apply, warning them off their course. There was no wisdom for youth, though. A survivor's lesson, if that.

It was almost light enough to see detail on the row of buildings. The stretch between them and the harbor was clear but for the Navy squad, though he noticed a larger contingent mustering outside their hall. It would not surprise him if Foster had chosen his other mate over the one back there. Only one of them came to the deck daily to see him curled among the dogs, storm-be-damned. Many rumors turned the ears of the town as to why the big one had been jailed to begin with. An attempt on the admiral's life. A foreign agent. A man of the assistant viceroy, made an example. Ostuk knew one more. A wanted fugitive. How would Costig know? And if he did, how would he be able to avoid knowing the name of Ostuk, too?

Whatever the story of the matter, breaking the jail had made him quite the word among the people. Even if he was found dead this very morning, it would be a long time before they could stop telling of the Leopard Seal. Perhaps Foster had returned a kindness, and remained to help his mate. It was not the man who Ostuk saw so recently, dead on a line to the north. But neither knew of the arrest, then. Men could change faster, for less.

As he passed the posted squad, one of them rose to examine why a whaler would be heading the wrong way. The man recognized him before he could do the same—Amachar, the captain of the abiama he put to the bottom. Indeed, all of the men with him were guests among the dogs. Ostuk had not seen them since they disembarked. He paused. Amachar nodded, and he returned it before continuing on.

He made half the distance between the watch and the first warehouses when a flitting shape ducking in and out of the alleyway caught his attention. The sun now marched steadily up the mountains of the mainland. None would cross the open field unseen on this day, but there measuring his chances was Foster. He spotted Ostuk at the same time. The dog captain halted. Again he took note of the men mustering outside the Navy hall. There were enough that if a send-off turned to a battle, the gulls would be pleased. His instinct was to head for the buildings a way off, double back, and give him the oilskin and the sleeping bag. If he wore the hood up, the bag stuffed within, he would seem a fat man heading to see the ship. Maybe he could wait until the rest of the people gathered as they no doubt would.

But by then, there would be two hundred Navy instead of ten. With the company he kept, Foster might choose between whalers and the Leopard Seal. He could not live anywhere between. Instead, Ostuk tapped his chest in acknowledgment, then turned back to the men on watch.

"Captain," he addressed Amachar. The entire squad met him. "I have come to ask a favor."

Amachar looked off, polite but frustrated. "The favor I owe you, I have done."

"It is not me you owe."

Foster panted in a dog-tired haze. By the time he neared the town, the sky had begun to brighten. Costig's nitwits would be watching the approach, and anything to send the Navy sniffing the back country was disastrous. They told him of the fruitless search door-to-door, how it hardly assured anyone that Parks was not in town, or that he wouldn't be again, soon. Immense as it was beyond the tiny tip of the peninsula where Drummoc huddled, if they knew to turn their attentions outward, it would be the end. They needed to stay near-enough for food runs. There was nothing on the ice to hunt, and no one to support them. If fresh snow didn't cover their tracks, they'd stand for weeks. He could not be seen.

The second he saw a distant torch burning at what had to be the harbor, he broke into a jog. It was a slow race against the sight of whoever had watch, and the rising sun. He was reasonably sure he reached the wigwams in time, but he couldn't afford to wind through the maze of streets. He still needed to make the boat before it was light enough to see. Rather than cut through, Foster ran down the far perimeter, where he could hear the waves crash into rock and used the sound to keep himself from joining them.

Now he sucked wind at the edge of cover. It was light enough that he recognized Ostuk, and the squad of men he evaded the night before under darkness. Again, the only way to make it would be to run, and if a single man turned his way, he had no shot. Not even if he were fresh. Without sleep, without even food or drink, it was hopeless. His leg muscles squirmed in protest, and he was thankful that they were at least still attached. Now Ostuk waved him forward. Foster couldn't make sense of it. He seemed to be chatting the officer of the group, as if that would somehow distract him. Once more, the captain waved, and the rest of the men turned to stare right at him.

Fuck, he thought. They wouldn't recognize him yet, but there would be no element of surprise. No head start. To his left, a sizable force gathered outside the Navy Hall. No other way to do it. He let his chin hang, and walked straight at the squad in the middle of the open rock. Hell, he might be wanted, but not many of the Navy of Ampos knew what he looked like. They were probably stopping everyone coming and going. If he made like he wasn't trying to avoid them, maybe he could get close, catch them on their heels with an end-around at the last second. His pulse sped up faster than it had at any point during his run. He wondered if Costig would hold it against him if he had to spear someone to make the ship.

C'mon, c'mon, c'mon, he tried to cool his jitters and summon the energy for one more movement. It was more like football than anything. He'd approach the line of scrimmage nice and casual, and as soon as someone moved for him, find the sidelines. He only needed a hundred yards or so to make the whaler. The whaler was his endzone.

Ostuk split from the group and met him a few yards short. He pushed a bundle into Foster's chest.

"What's this?"

"For your trip."

Foster didn't understand it, but he hugged it under his free arm. "Thank you." He snuck a glance over Ostuk's shoulder. "I don't like the way they're lookin' at us."

"You will be let to pass."

"Are you sure?"

"No. But that is what they said." He clapped Foster on the arm and headed toward the town. Foster wanted to holler something—a word of gratitude, a goodbye—but he didn't have the energy to raise his voice. It felt pointless, anyway. Another person falling in his wake. Maybe never to surface. He turned to the squad. Did he have thousands of miles to go, or ten more yards? He kept his eyes low until he drew even with them, then at a glance, he stopped. It was the same faces that looked up at him, wet, cold, bitter, but alive, every time he fed the dogs. It was them he overfed, so that he thought the rest of the boat would cut him up next if they didn't reach Drummoc in time. Every one of them watched as he continued past. As soon as he was by, he felt almost guilty. It was obvious that his legs wouldn't have carried him on their own. He was still walking only because it was handed to him, as easily as the bundle under his arm. The clothes on his back. The spear in his hand.

Though he knew he was safe, he hurried his step, and not until he slipped among the crew of his ship did he remember to take a breath.

Gionn was waiting with a similar bundle and a grin hung wide between his ears.

"Ostuk found you, did he?"

Foster nodded. "He give you one, too?"

"What, this? Nah. Got me own."

Foster checked side to side and leaned in. "You stole it?"

"Course not, cunt! What kind of man do you take me for?" He didn't wait for Foster to answer. "That dumb bastard who thought you'd win an honest fight seems to have abandoned ship. Went into town last night, probably to pay his tab, and didn't want to face Corm when he realized your inadequacy cost him every penny he owned."

"Foster!" Cormdran bellowed. "Didn't think I'd see you back. Settled your debts, did you?"

"Aye, sir."

"Then where's me fuckin' bucket?" The crew laughed, half-listening as they rounded out their preparations. "Squains! Over here!" The two Mattaka boys hustled to join them. They shivered with a blanket around their shoulders. A chill ran down his own spine, and he suddenly realized just how cold he was— had been for hours. There wasn't a moment to think of it. Now he bristled with the fading adrenaline. His eyelids sank, and he shook them open again. "Whose blanket is that?" One of the boys, shorter by an inch, pointed at the other. "Then off with it!" He let it drop from his shoulder, and the second greedily snatched up the slack. "No lovers on me ship." His eyes went to the bucket sitting on the ground between them. A warm smile spread over his face. "Let me see that." Corm held it in front of his face. He ran his fingers on the seams of the staves, tested the rope handle, turned it over and knocked on the bottom.

"Aye, that's a damn fine bucket. Eckerd!" Corm got the attention of a seaman in a calf-length slicker. "Will you have a look at that?"

"One of the best I've seen, Corm."

"Fit for a farri. Is this Costig's night pail?" The crew laughed. "Did you pull it from his arse as it was steamin' one?" The boys were too timid to reply, but they grinned politely. The nearest one shot a look at Foster, that seemed both an apology and a plea at once. It did cross his mind, but no one would believe him.

"Which of you's bucket is this?" They looked at each other. The boy with the blanket replied.

"It is both." They nodded in agreement.

"Both! You share everything?" They shrugged and nodded. "Will you both pull the same oar? Which of you stands at the front of the spear, and which at the back? Euskus' sake, I don't even see a spear! Do you not know you're seekin' work on a *whaler?*"

"We work hard," the shorter one assured him.

"Whose bucket?" They clearly had not considered it. "Do you refuse your captain's question? Whose bucket?"

"Both," said the blanket boy at the same time the other said, "It is his."

"Both," the blanket repeated insistently. "We have little, but we work hard."

"Do you lads not recall I told you there is one fuckin' seat? One seat, and I see three shiverin' cunts before me with a single bucket."

"It is his," the short one repeated.

"We will go together. Or try next season." Corm's glare bore a hole in him. "And we have our bucket back," the blanket continued. There was a terrifying silence.

"Hoooooo!" Corm burst into laughter. "He'll have his bucket back!" The entire crew cackled with delight. "Apologies, me son!" Corm tossed it into his chest. "I believe it *is* your bucket. Don't let it our of your sight." Their shoulders sank. Slowly, the boys shuffled around and pointed themselves toward the town. "You're in charge of it, now." They stopped, confused. "As it would happen, one of me lads didn't muster this mornin'. You'll have your own oars at half-share, since you can't be bothered to properly equip yourselves." Their faces lit up, and they could barely avoid jumping. "No lovers, though!" They shook their heads in assurance. "Now be off! Stow your blanket and your bucket.

"And you," he settled on Foster. "You've no bucket, no shares, and I've no seats to give. Yet here you stand. I don't know whether to be impressed with your bollocks, or take you for a full idiot."

"I don't fetch buckets." Foster hoped he looked braver than he felt when he said it. The crew "ooh"ed and awaited Corm's move. "And I'll allow I'm a half-idiot, since I lost half a share. But as for why I stand before you, we both know if I stay, I'll be dead or rottin' long before the ol' Leopard Seal, and between you and me, his prospects are fuckin' dim. We also both know that you got three seats. You lied about there bein' one, I reckon because it's funny to watch idiots scramble around for buckets. But you had two, until yet another one of your boys bailed on you. That means you got three seats, and three prospects. Seein' as I don't cost you anything, and I promised Moipa here I would honor the tryout so that he could keep the half-share he won fair and square, and therefore he can repay you the silver you loaned him at interest, I would humbly request that you allow me to serve on your boat."

Cormdran grinned. "How 'bout that one, Eckerd? He talks like a tribute man."

"I have no idea what the hell that is."

"Knows exactly who got what and owes how much to who. You a smart cunt, then?"

"Not as smart as I used to be."

"Aye, nor will you be again when you speak to me. You've counted your seats well, but you forgot to count for the nature of the task. I ask me men to find a bucket, because there's nothin' simpler. If you got no sea legs, and you can't set cock aside long enough to fill a basic request from your captain, what good are you? Do you think one more oar makes fuck-all difference? Those squain boys? I don't know how they got theirs, but they didn't show up like heir to the fuckin' throne just because no one sits on it. I don't care if they stabbed an old woman to death. In fact, I hope it was their grandmother! They done it for me, because I said, and they worked together. And when I tried to cast them off, they didn't turn on each other at the first glimmer of gold. You don't have to know shit to be a whaler! Eight or ten good sailors, that's all I need. Any man can pull an oar given a few thousand miles to figure it out. Anyone can thrust a spear, though I see yours is a squain rock-poker. And we know well you can't fight.

"Me benches are full of backwash and grassbenders, halfwits and full-mongrels and more than a handful of filthy traitors!" He raised the volume on the last bit. The Navy defectors laughed. "But you'll not find among them a smart cunt who brushes off an order."

"My apologies, sir. I meant no disrespect to you or your crew. I had no intention of givin' the impression that I was entitled to seat just because it was there," Foster saw the lie as he told it. He set down the bundle, and the spear on top it. "None of these things were mine this morning. Those boys showed up with a bucket and a prayer. I settled my debts, and I came prepared. I've never been a sailor, but you want humble? I fed dogs to get here. I did right by my captain, and that was him who gave me this shit, as a gift. He didn't owe me nothin', he just wanted to see me do alright. And my crewmates? Ask this sorry son of a bitch," he nodded to Gionn. "After he gets done runnin' me up the mast, if he's honest, he'll admit I had his back even when I would have been just as happy to see him fall overboard."

"Aye, the cunt saved me arse. Though I do not intend to repay him, or forgive him for it."

"If that ain't enough to vouch for my character, I'm here with nothin' to gain but another day of breathin', and I'm willin' to work for free."

"Just yesterday I recall you loudly proclaimin' you were worth a full, and would take any man who thought less."

"Not my proudest moment."

"Are you that eager to work without pay?"

"I am, sir. Though my understandin' is that if I prove myself, I might earn it back." He couldn't have cared less about the shares. Foster worried he seemed too eager.

"Not from my half, you won't. If you've never served on a whaler, perhaps I'll forgive you don't know how the shares work."

"No, sir."

"What you are askin' is for one of your mates to die. His share bein' vacant, the rest shall sit or stand to award it among the remainin' crew. Is it out of pity you expect to get it?"

"No, sir."

"What say you lads? I put it to the crew. Will you stand for this man, Foster, to row without share, or shall we leave him to Costig?" Immediately, the entire crew sat, Gionn included. "We'll see the two-share men, first." A pair of men who seemed to be friends with Moipa rose to their feet. "Eckerd? Pitras? Ordacles? Irilo?" Three sitting men shook their heads. "On to the share and a half. Remember—" Moipa leapt up before he could finish. He scowled at the sitters. "You only count for one, as he's not yet crew, Moipa. And you two are half-shares," he said to the Mattaka boys. "You don't get to stand!"

"Hang on," Foster interrupted. "The two-share guys count for two?"

"A regular scribe, this one!" The crew laughed.

"And how many shares are on the boat? I'm just tryin' to figure how many I need."

Gionn spoke up. "Sixty seats, so a hundred and twenty."

"Aye, but I stand at sixty-two and a half-share. The crew holds fifty-eight, less a half," Corm explained. "You'll need more than half their number."

"So fifty-seven and a half. Means I need…twenty-nine votes." No one seemed eager to confirm his figure. Foster wrinkled his brow. "But with them boys, you got fifty-two guys signed up." He could see the wheels turning in Corm's head.

"So it is."

"Then you must have…" he ran the numbers in his head. "Six at two, that's twelve. So forty-five and a half shares with the other forty-six men. One guy at a half-share?"

"There's two squains at half-share." Corm was getting annoyed now.

"That's right," Foster corrected himself. "And the rest are just one? One full share?"

"Aye, and nine at one-and-a-half, not to figure Moipa. Now shut your arse and let them stand while I'm still considerin' you!"

"Sorry. Hang on. But if you got six guys at two shares, that's twelve. Then two guys at a half, that's one share, for thirteen. Then nine at one-point-five is…thirteen-point-five. So twenty-six and a half. Then you got thirty-five more men at a single share. Fifty-two, minus the six two-shares, and the two half-shares and nine at a share-and-a-half. Thirty-five and twenty-six-five is sixty-one and a half shares, if we count Moipa as one. Wouldn't that mean you have fifty-eight and a half out of one-twenty?"

"I'm at sixty-two shares, lad! Where do you get off with that?"

"So do I need thirty-two votes? Not tryin' to fuck myself, I just want to know where I stand. Twenty-nine is fine with me."

A murmur of concern rippled through the crew. "What's that, Corm? Are we cut square?" The one he called Pitras asked.

"Aye, hundred and twenty among us! I don't know what this cunt is on about. Numbers this, numbers that."

"Sounds to me ears as though he's suggestin," Gionn remarked, "the boat might be…*over-promised*." The last word set off a firecracker string of voices shoutin' over and around one another in every possible state of distress. Corm turned bright red and tried to bluster over all of them.

"Count!" Came a cry. "We need a count!" Several men were already on their feet, pointing at heads and going over the field. "Stop movin'!" Foster's cheeks grew hot, and he noticed Cormdran shooting arrows from his eyes directly at him. Gionn's shoulder rose up and his head ducked beneath the storm. If he couldn't fuck his way out of things, Foster knew by now he would try to vanish beneath them. Whatever he had started, it was not helping his case.

Several panicked minutes went by before men started announcing numbers. "Sixty-four!" The one called Eckerd said.

"I got fifty-nine!" Another man said.

"Sixty!"

"Fifty-nine!"

"Sixty-two!"

"Bead man!" Pitras demanded. He turned to Corm. "We need a bead man."

"We've shovin' off! We haven't time for a fuckin' bead man!"

"Bead man, or we don't sail!" Alongside Pitras, the other two-share men seemed the most irate. Gionn paled like a sheet at the mention of not sailing. He leapt to his feet and sounded a shrill whistle.

"Maybe we don't need a bead man. This one would seem to have his numbers." He jabbed Foster with a finger.

"How do we know that?" Pitras demanded.

"I've never over-promised a ship in me life!" Corm interrupted now that he had enough quiet.

"No one said you meant it," Gionn assured him. "The way Foster was talkin', me head was tossed. All the comin's and goin's these past weeks, any man could get mixed. What we need now is to sort it like honest cunts, so we can fuck off." He got a series of "ayes," and the distress on Cormdran's face dialed back a notch. "If Foster tells the truth of havin' his numbers, he can sort it for us."

"How do we know he isn't lyin'?" Pitras repeated.

"Each of us has had occasion to hear a number said from a man who knows it. A private number, that he alone remembers. I'll show you. Foster!" His name jolted him out of something between narcolepsy and a wild fear for his life. "I sold me father's boots at his passin'. The man who took the count offered me two penny each. How much did he pay me?"

"Four pennies."

"Too easy!" Someone said.

"All of us could have sorted that!" Pitras said.

"If a ship has a hundred and twenty shares," Corm challenged, "And the captain gives half his shares to his men, then half again, what has he left?"

"He started with half?"

"Aye, he did."

"He's got fifteen shares left."

Corm recoiled as if Foster has shown up in church with a hooker. The men were dead silent until he gathered himself. "He's right." There was another general clamor. "How the fuck did he do that so fast?"

A little crooked man that looked like he was made from twisted wire hangers bent around Foster's back and pulled at his hands. "He got no beads!"

"Get the fuck off me. What beads?"

"How did you do the count without beads?" Corm asked.

"I don't know shit about no beads. What, yall don't know how to do basic math?" Gionn inched away as if he was afraid to be associated. "I guess that's a dumb fuckin' question. Yeah, I can count. It ain't black magic." The mention of the last sent the entire crew into a new fuss.

"Fuck's sake, cunt," he heard Gionn mutter.

"Try him again!" Pitras said.

"How many pennies in a decair?" The coat hanger man asked.

"I have no fuckin' clue."

"Hunnerd! Ha! I got him!"

"Everyone knows that, you wanker." Pitras shoved him aside.

"Three docogons," Eckerd stepped forward, "landed their forces at Marahano. It was full benches, except one, two rowers had died at sea. Twenty-four sailors to the deck, and ten officers with two-hundred soldiers on each. Eight killed in the fightin', and the spoils were split among the men. How many were counted?"

"What kind of fucked-up word problem is that? I don't even know how many rowers are on a docogon, which I assume is a boat?"

"A hundred and twenty."

"Damn, yall sure do like that number. Let me see." He mumbled aloud: "So...Three-sixty minus two, three-fifty eight. Plus two-thirty-four each ship, that's...Seven-oh-two. One-thousand, three hundred-sixty—"

"Ha! Wrong!"

"*Minus eight*," Foster raised his voice. "Is one-thousand, three-hundred fifty-two." All Eckerd could do was nod and step back. Foster slapped at the coat hanger man, still probing him for the trick.

"Four brothers," Cormdran stepped forward. "Four brothers stand to divide a sum of silver. Forty coin, and they're too strong to fight over it. They decide to make shares accordin' to each man's years: twenty-and-one, nineteen, fifteen, and nine. How much did the third brother receive, once the bead man made his count and before his cut?"

Foster blinked hard. "Damn. we're gettin' real now." The fog of sleep hung over him at first, and he couldn't even think of how to begin. "I'm gonna have to talk this one out. So that's sixty-four shares total." He could tell by Corm's expression he was on the right track. "Problem is, you gotta make it out of forty. Divided by...I don't know, eight, is eight over five. No. Fuck. Each eight gets you five. Goddammit, this is fractions and algebra now. Each eight gets you five," he mumbled to himself. "OK. Fifteen over sixty-four. *X* over forty. So sixty-four-*x* into...six hunnerd. That's not an even number. He should have got nine silver coins, and three-eighths of another. If it's a hundred penny, that's still not even, but..." he whispered inaudibly. "Thirty...seven pennies, and half of another."

"'Fraid not, lad."

"I'm pretty sure that's right."

"I'm here tellin' you, it's not."

"Let me tell you what the others got." Foster felt his pits sweating despite the chill as he worked out the other figures. "Alright I don't know if there's half-pennies, but that's what's it comes to. Oldest boy got thirteen silvers and twelve and a half pennies. The next got eleven silvers, eighty-seven and a half pennies. The youngest got five, and sixty-two and a half pennies."

A wry smile crossed Cormdran's face. "Not a number right among 'em."

Foster frowned. The crew howled to one another. It seemed they were relieved that whatever he was doing wasn't going to work anymore.

"Who hired the bead man?" Corm looked up. "Don't answer that. I can tell you. Listen to the numbers again. Thirteen. Eleven. Nine. Five. Each with some pennies we won't fuss over. Which of those numbers I just said is lower than the number he got paid?"

"Son of a bitch."

"That's no way to talk about your brother. What was the pay?"

"Sixteen. Ten. Seven. Four. The pennies were as you said, and the bead man kept 'em."

"So he would have kept two silvers' worth of pennies. Except that only adds up to Sixty-three. One missin'. I'm guessin' the one guy who got paid more than he ought to at the expense of everyone else had to nudge the count somehow."

"What's the trick of it?"

"Of what?"

"How do you come by the numbers? It's a certain sort who knows 'em, and not one I care to have."

"I was forced to learn it by an evil woman. Locked up against my will until I did."

"A *woman*? Who has her *numbers*?"

"He's a spy of the farri!" Someone shouted.

"Which one?" Came another voice, a ripple of laughter.

"Aye, I thought so meself at first. But if you spend much time with him, you'll see he's not clever enough for that," Gionn volunteered. "The youngest son of a petty sea king. Cast out, or lost, or bored. That's what I think."

"Isn't he yours?" Corm asked.

"I just come by him at Nunoc. Took a likin' to him. Much to like about a cunt who's worse than you at everything, though he aren't as funny as the Leopard Seal. Still, he's honest. And I figured if I sour on him, I could always find his father for the reward—or the ransom, as it were." Corm bobbed with quiet laughter. Gionn continued. "Bead man at Taclann'll want three shares for a count, and more each time after."

"I was on a boat, got scraped for fifteen in Pogobas," Ordacles said. The crew groaned.

"I'd gut the man who suggested it!" Someone said.

"Fifteen from eighty," Ordacles clarified. Their fury burned red on their faces and Foster could see the violent fantasies running over the backs of their eyeballs.

"Fifteen's thievery!"

"A crime against a noble trade!" Gionn roused them, and they cheered their agreement.

Foster stood tall before Cormdran. "Captain. It sounds to me like yall are gonna need somebody to divvy up the pay when we dock." The men waited on his words without a breath. "I'll work for free. And count for…" he made a show of considering it, "one share." There were whoops of approval. Moipa led the celebration, then shouted to Corm: "We take him! He is good!" He wrapped an arm around Foster as though they were old friends. "Good barrel!"

Cormdran took in the crowd as though he surveyed the changing seas, the wind suddenly coming around to stern. He settled on Gionn. "Will you stand for his character?"

"Fuck, no! But I believe he can do the count. And if he's any trouble, we'll put Moipa on him." Moipa grinned and faked like he was going to throw Foster, who flinched in panic before Moipa steadied him to the crew's amusement.

"To your arses!" Corm shouted, and all but Foster hit the deck. "This man petitions work. He rows on prospect, and he has promised a count for one share. He has also promised that if I, in my ignorance of number and tempest of mood, suspect he skims a penny for the time it takes me to raise me blade, I shall have the captain's share of his hide." They didn't wait for him to pose the question. The entire crew stood, bouncing off of one another in anticipation.

"Stow your gear, lad." The whalers hooted and hollered their approval. Fatigue broke over Foster and he barely kept his feet. Slaps of congratulations rolled over him. There were brown faces and white ones. Matted or close-shorn, ripped, stained, ancient of days and flush with youth. They were hard. No doubt they were hard. None who weren't born on Drummoc was new to the gauntlet of the southern passage, and to be bred here was a trial of its own. These were men he would not stretch a limb without touching. Their breath would steam his neck, and their bodies twine in sleep. They would watch each other shit, and struggle together to keep keel-down. Tunguk, who knew the way; Kjartke, who knew his need before he did; Parks. Parks, who alone knew *him*. They hung back in memory, as though he left them weeks ago on a featureless white blanket, on a featureless black night. These were his companions now. He wouldn't trust a one of them with his worst enemy, who as luck would have it was also his only friend on the ship.

Despite their faults—they were nearly all faults—he couldn't help but be charmed. Their humor was sharp, if not their math. Like him, they were doing all in their power to get themselves to a better place. Unlike him, they were unrelenting badasses. He knew he was equal to none of them in the best five minutes of his life. Yet there was an unassuming humility to the crew. Even their boasting felt like a varnish that everyone was happy to have stripped. They were vastly more to his taste than the Navy men he'd met so far, though most weren't far-removed from a checkered service. But these were his for the time being. He would have to find his way among them, and if he ever wanted to see the others, he would have to ruin—and maybe kill— every last man who now welcomed him into their arms.

Costig stood at the head of two hundred winter men. As promised, they formed up off the harbor to make sure the whalers left. If he hadn't ordered them, most would have come anyway to watch and dream as those who beat them for the boat sailed away to whatever glory, while they made ready for ice and war. The wind itself seemed to hurry down, only to stop for a look once the boat was loaded. The *Gairhle* bobbed low and stiff—overdraft, in his own opinion, even for cold water and westerlies. A bit timid of Corm, but fine by him if he wanted to save Foster and Gionn the trouble. At least they were both on. If a luck ever served Costig, he did not count it among his men. He was equally at ease with those currents beyond his reach. He had done his bit.

Now they teetered like a feather on his fingertips, awaiting a wind. Whatever may happen, one less thing would whisper him awake. He knew well that you could not move men, only put them to where they might move themselves. Once the ropes were in, they were no longer his, and he would not likely try such a long throw again. It was all effort. He need not even help the other lad, though on his honor he likely would, if it weren't much trouble.

As the albatross man came out with his pomp, he got a pang in his gut. It would go off, he assured himself. With that, the long route to Taclann froze over, and even Nunoc fell behind a fog. The gift of winter. The world closed around him, and freed him from his wide concerns. Yet with it came the memory that he had scrapped all the work that had been done at the Calm Harbor—it was absolute shit. The whaler had given him one more excuse to hold the Camne Drumlag boat. The pain of the thought told him where his sleep would be lost now. Camne Drumlag. The coal had to be his next concern. At least there was plenty for his men to do. The work would whet their spirits, rather than store them to disrepair and surrender. Even if it was a half-hearted knock through the snow for a prisoner he hoped the squains would soon forget.

The townsfolk gathered, as well. It would be the last sendoff for months. They seemed not to mind what loomed. The excitement of the escape and the dream of a new farri—even if it was the one they already called King—appealed to them. It didn't matter if any of those benefited them, only that they were different.

"Wendell!" His old mate found his side. "As Admiral of the fleet at Drummoc, I order you to go over there, and blow with all your might."

Foster sat on his bench near the bow. The wood was no more than a thin plank atop a thwart, uncomfortably warped, but at least the last ass had worn it in the right couple of spots. It was a contrast to the ceremony he'd seen before—unloaded and unmanned. There was an inevitability about it. The witch doctor and Cormdran were the only men off the ship and the side presented a low target by typical standards. A white feather stood at attention between the man's fingers as he ran through his routine. When the final words were uttered, he knelt to accommodate the height of the gunwales. There wasn't a movement from ship or shore. Hundreds of souls fixed their eyes on the albatross, steady in his grasp. He glared at it with an intensity that seemed to command it to life, to a course ordained with the blessing of the gods and the elements.

Cormdran snatched it from him. He strode to the *Gairhle*, and slapped it against her wet side.

"Pinned!"

The crew's roar made his eardrums howl. The Navy and the Mattaka added their voices in jubilation. Foster felt a long tension uncoil with the ropes that held them to the quay. For all the near-battles between the sides, departure was the great forgiver. There was no grudge it could not mend. Those who left were grateful, and those who remained, sincere in their happiness for them. The act carried more than the men involved ever could. The butts of the spears drove them free and the water sloshed against their side until the oars found a grip. He looked back over the heads of his crewmates and set his blade into the Attavaik Sea for the first stroke of what—he had no notion. Before him, a voice trembled in song, and was joined.

"Carry! Carry!
Dance, the mast,
Turn, the oar,
through sea and air.
Carry! Carry!
Cross the back,
of ancient Uinab,
silver, fair.
Carry! Carry!
Broad the helm,
Gold the spear,
the fire of Hadalis
Carry! Carry!
Rise to break
Carry forth!
Atlantis! Atlantis!"

Visit www.ancientseakings.com

to sign up for the newsletter
and receive alerts about future installments in the series!